She has a
BROKEN THING
where
her HEART
should be

She has a
BROKEN THING
where her HEART
should be

J.D. BARKER

Published by:
Hampton Creek Press
P.O. Box 177
New Castle, NH 03854

Hampton Creek Press is a registered Trademark of Hampton Creek Publishing, LLC

Cover Design by Stuart Bache
Book design and formatting by Maureen Cutajar (gopublished.com)
Author photograph by Bill Peterson of Peterson Gallery

Hardcover ISBN-13: 978-1-7342104-1-5
eBook ISBN: 978-1-7342104-0-8
Paperback ISBN-13: 978-1-7342104-2-2

For my little girl.
The brightest spark.

Her name was Stella, and I loved her from the first moment I saw her. Even after watching her kill a man who looked a lot like me, I couldn't help but love her.

I didn't know she had killed him—not at that time, I couldn't possibly know. I only watched them kiss, but that moment spelled his end as surely as water runs downhill.

We would hide the body together, amid her apologies for what she had done.

Then she would be gone, disappearing into the night.

And I could do nothing else but follow, my heart filled with ache, her scent pulling me so.

—Jack Thatch | 22 Years Old

She has a
BROKEN THING
where
her HEART
should be

PART 1

"Think for a moment of the long chain of iron or gold, of thorns or flowers, that would never have bound you, but for the formation of the first link on one memorable day."
—Charles Dickens, *Great Expectations*

August 8, 1984

Eight Years Old

Log 08/08/1984—

Subject "D" within expected parameters.

—Charter Observation Team – 309

1

"Time."

"Hush, you little runt. I'm talking to my sister."

I watched as Auntie Jo plucked another cigarette, a Marlboro Red 100, from the pack sitting atop her checkered cloth bag and put it in her mouth, lighting it with a silver Zippo and sending a puff of gray smoke to the heavens.

"You said one hour. That was at five o'clock. It's six o'clock now. Time is up," I told her. She had no sense of time. Given the chance, she'd spend the entire day sitting here in the cemetery talking to the stones. Well, talking to Momma's stone. She didn't talk to Daddy. She didn't much like Daddy.

"*Knight Rider* is on in two hours."

"You won't miss *Knight Rider*."

"Last time I missed *Knight Rider*," I reminded her. "We left here at six-thirty, got home at seven, ate dinner, you *made me* take a bath, and by the time I sat down to watch, it was half over. You can't watch a show like *Knight Rider* from the middle. You gotta start from the beginning."

Auntie Jo puffed at her cigarette. "You have an uncanny memory for an eight-year-old, you know that?"

"Can we go?"

"Not yet."

I sighed and reached for the radio.

Auntie Jo had spread out a blanket over my parents' graves so we wouldn't have to sit on the wet grass. Rain fell most of the morning, and the sun in Pittsburgh, even in August, did little to dry things up. The ground was still all squishy.

"Four years, Katy," Auntie Jo said to Momma's stone. "Four years since that wretch of a man of yours took you from us—from me and your little baby boy, Jack."

"Daddy didn't kill Momma."

"He was driving, wasn't he?"

"It was an accident."

"He was drunk."

"Momma had two glasses of wine, and Daddy was drinking Coke. That's what the waiter said. It's in the police report."

Auntie Jo straightened the flowers in Momma's vase. Her fingernails were stained yellow. The flowers were daisies. I picked them out myself at Giant Eagle on the way here. There were no flowers in Daddy's vase. It was filled with stagnant rainwater and weeds. Auntie Jo wouldn't let me clean it out.

"He was drunk before he left."

I shook my head. "He was drinking iced tea at home before they dropped me off at your apartment. Momma, too."

"You can't know that."

"I have a canny memory, you said so."

"You were four."

"I was drinking chocolate milk. Momma put it in my sippy cup so I could take it with me. We watched *Magnum, P.I.* on your couch, then you put me to bed right after. I *did not* have to take a bath that night."

"Huh."

"The radio is broken." I had twisted the dial from one end to the other and got nothing but static.

"It's not broken, it's just hard to get a signal here."

"Then why did you bring it?"

"Because sometimes we do get a signal, and your mother liked music."

Bob FM was at 96.9. I turned the dial a little left of the mark for ninety-seven. Huey Lewis said something about a new drug, then faded back to static.

I dropped the radio back on the blanket near Auntie Jo's bag. "Maybe I'll skip the bath."

"You're not skipping your bath."

"If I skip my bath tonight, then we can stay until seven and I still won't miss *Knight Rider*," I explained.

Auntie Jo snuffed out her cigarette on the side of Daddy's stone, then placed it in a small tin she kept in the apron pocket of her faded pink waitress uniform. Normally she would toss the butt off into the grass somewhere, but not here, not at the cemetery, certainly not near Momma's grave. She found another, lit it up, and sucked in another puff. "Okay, no bath tonight, but you're getting one for sure tomorrow. Deal?"

"Deal."

"One more hour, then," she said. "What does this here say, Jack? Can you read it?"

"You know I can."

"Then what does it say?"

"You make me read it every year."

""What does it say, Jack?" She knocked at the side of Momma's gravestone with the hand holding the lighter. "Read."

I rolled my eyes. "Kaitlyn Gargery Thatch. February 16, 1958 to August 8, 1980. Loving wife, mother, and sister."

"My sweet baby sister. It should also say, 'killed by an evil man who drank himself into the grave next door and dragged her along kicking and screaming so he wouldn't have to be alone."

"Daddy didn't drink."

"He drank plenty."

Auntie Jo liked to drink, wine mostly. Auntie Jo assumed every-one drank. If Daddy drank, I never saw him. Momma did, not much, though, not like Auntie Jo.

Daddy's stone only had his name, birthdate, and the date of his death. Same day as Momma. If my Auntie Jo had her way, he might not have a stone at all. Luckily, it had not been up to Auntie Jo—the guys at the hardware store where Daddy worked all pitched in and paid for both, on account of Momma and Daddy not having put money aside for burials. Both stones were carved from the same slab of black granite. Momma's shone, having been polished meticulously by Auntie Jo when we arrived. Daddy's carried a layer of dust and dirt, the surface dull beneath. I'd come back later to clean it, make it shine like Momma's.

I was four when they died, and the rounded tops of both gravestones had towered over me. Now, though, I was more than a foot taller. I stood up now and smoothed my jeans over knobby knees.

"Where are you going?"

"I wanna go for a walk."

Auntie Jo frowned. "You should stay and talk to your mother. I'm sure she would like to hear everything that happened in the past year."

I rolled my eyes again and placed a hand on Momma's grave-stone. "Momma, I'm eight. I have no friends because most kids are dumb. Auntie Jo still won't let me eat chocolate chip cookies for breakfast, and school is boring. I'll report back in another year, maybe sooner if something changes with the cookies."

Auntie Jo waved the hand with the cigarette over her head. "Go. Just don't wander off too far."

I gave Daddy's stone a quick look. I'd come back and talk to him. I just couldn't do it with Auntie Jo listening in.

Snatching the radio off the blanket, I extended the antenna to full mast, increased the volume, and held the little box out before me as I started up the small hill toward the rest of the cemetery.

Momma and Daddy were buried on the south end of the cemetery under a red maple tree. This time of year, the leaves were fire engine red.

The static broke for a second and I thought I heard Elton John, but then he was gone again. I reached the top of the hill and made a sharp left, careful to stay on the stone pathway and not walk over the graves on either side.

I paused when I reached the mausoleums, all positioned in two neat rows with a stone pathway down the center.

Pittsburgh had a lot of cemeteries. This particular one, All Saints Hollow, was one of the largest.

The mausoleums.

I didn't much like the mausoleums.

When we drove by a cemetery, Auntie Jo said you're always supposed to hold your breath the to keep the spirits of the dead from finding you. I'm not sure why this rule didn't apply when you were actually in the cemetery, but if it applied anywhere, it would be at the mausoleums. The air was still here. I pictured the dead peeking out from the cracks in the stone, bony hands ready to reach out and snatch unsuspecting little boys, pulling us inside those squat structures, never to be seen again.

I drew in a deep breath, pulled the radio to my chest, and ran down the center of the mausoleums, nearly tripping when Steve Perry started to blare from the speaker.

I reached the far end of mausoleum row and blew out the air, the speaker again going back to static. I had no idea why the radio worked in the middle of those buildings, and I didn't really care. I could find another spot. I wasn't going back in there.

Looking out over two hundred and seventy acres of rolling hills, I could no longer see Auntie Jo or the red maple.

The cemetery came to an end at a thick tree line. A black metal bench sat beneath the trees, a willow sweeping over the top, a canopy of thin leaves and moss weighted in shadows. Upon that bench sat a girl. About a hundred feet from the girl, a woman in a long white coat stood beside a white SUV on one of the cemetery's access roads, her hands in her pockets.

It wasn't hot out, but it wasn't cold, either, too warm for such a coat. This didn't seem to bother her. She had it buttoned to her neck. As I came over the hill, the woman turned toward me, her eyes black, hawklike. Her hair, as white as her coat, fluttered in the light wind. She became rigid at the sight of me, her shoulders squaring off. Her hands balled into fists and disappeared beneath the folds of her coat. She held there a moment, eyes upon me, cautious and strange, then returned her gaze to the girl on the bench.

The girl wore a white ruffled blouse, also buttoned up, tucked neatly into a black skirt falling just past her knees. Her long brown hair, alive with waves and curls, dropped over her shoulders and down her back. One side partially covered her face, the other pinned back behind her ear. Her dark eyes were lost between the pages of a paperback book held in her lap with gloved hands.

I'm not sure how long I stood there.

I'm not sure *why* I stood there.

But I did, I stood there watching her, watching her turn the pages with a gentle determination, her lips slightly parted, mouthing the words silently to an enthralled audience of one.

"Jessie's Girl" blurted out from my radio and the girl's head jerked up, her eyes on me, one hand carefully marking her place in the book.

I fumbled with the radio's knobs and turned it down.

I didn't remember walking up to the bench, but somehow I had. I stood right beside it.

The girl's brow furrowed, and she tilted her head curiously. "My, you are an ugly little boy."

I wasn't sure what to say to that, so I said nothing at all. I knew I wasn't ugly. Auntie Jo said I was lucky that I took after Momma in the looks department rather than being cursed to look like Daddy. Although, I had a picture of Daddy, the only one I managed to hide from Auntie Jo. He looked like a movie star standing next to his rusty Ford, the same one he had been driving when—

"Your clothes are ratty, too." She had an odd accent, sounding something like James Bond but not quite.

A squeal came from the radio's speaker, drowning out Rick Springfield and all else. I switched it off, retracted the antenna, and found myself climbing onto the bench, sitting on the opposite end from her. Again, I didn't know why. My mind screamed for me to run away. This was a girl, after all. I had no business with girls, especially one like this, all prissy and proper and smelling of flowers. But I didn't run. I climbed right up on that bench and sat beside her, ignoring the strange flutter in my stomach.

I nodded up at the woman standing at the SUV. "Is that your momma?"

"No, not my mother."

"They why is she watching you?"

"That's what she does."

"It's kinda creepy."

The girl smiled at this, then forced it back as if she didn't want me to see her smile, as if it were something she didn't give away so freely. "What kind of boy wanders around a cemetery all alone? Where are your parents?"

"Dead."

"Really? Who killed them?"

Not what killed them or how did they die, but *who* killed them. As if death by another's hand was the most logical of things.

"What are you reading?" I asked, wanting to change the subject. I didn't want to talk about Momma and Daddy, not now. There had been enough of that today.

She held up the book so I could see the cover—*Great Expectations* by Charles Dickens. The paperback's spine was nearly white with creases, opened and closed so many times the color was gone, faded and cracked away. The cover wasn't much better. The book looked a thousand years old, some lost thing rescued from the bottom of a box in someone's basement.

"Is that the one with the boy and the raft?"

"Hmm. Ugly and uneducated, I see."

"What is that supposed to mean?"

"You're thinking about *The Adventures of Huckleberry Finn*. That book isn't even written by Dickens. Twain wrote it. Twain is a hack. Twain isn't even his real name. He was just a boat captain who managed to scribble out a few thoughts when he wasn't gambling and drinking."

I hadn't read anything by Twain or Dickens. My reading shelf consisted of half the titles from the Hardy Boys collection and a few dozen comics. I didn't know anyone who read Twain or Dickens, not even my parents or Auntie Jo. "What is *Great Expectations* about?"

The woman at the SUV had managed to draw closer. I hadn't seen her move, but she was only about ten feet from us now, watching from the corner of her eye, no doubt listening to every word.

The girl looked down at the book in her gloved hands. "It's about everything that really matters."

"I don't understand."

"You wouldn't."

"Can I see it?" I reached for the book and she shied away, moving toward her side of the bench. The woman edged closer, then stopped as the girl looked up at her.

The girl placed the book on the bench and slid it over to me with the tips of her fingers. This seemed to calm the older woman.

I picked up the book and read the description on the back.

"My name is Stella," the girl said. "I was named for the girl in that book, only her name is Estella."

I handed the book back to her. I half expected her to make me slide it back on the bench, but she didn't. She snatched it from the air and placed it back in her lap. "When a girl tells you her name, it's only polite to reciprocate."

"Reciprocate?"

She sighed. "Respond in kind, do the same."

"Oh, my name is Jack, Jack Thatch."

"A common name for a common boy. What is your real name? Nobody is really named 'Jack,' it's usually the informal of 'John' which never made sense to me—not like Mike and Michael, it's more like Bill and William, which is even stranger."

"My full name is John Edward Thatch," I told her. "Everyone always calls me 'Jack,' though."

"Of course they do. And who is Edward to you? Surely a family name."

"My dad's name was Edward. Everyone called him Eddie. How old are you? You talk funny."

Her eyes drifted to the older woman, then to the cover of her book. She fidgeted with the pages. "I'm eight."

"You don't sound like you're eight. I'm eight, too."

"Well, you don't sound like you're eight, either."

"Stella?" The woman said this in a low tone, almost a scolding tone, drawing out the name, then: "We need to go."

Stella sighed again and closed her eyes. She said something softly, too soft for me to hear, yet the older woman seemed to understand her words even though she was further away.

The woman shook her head and Stella frowned, slipping off the bench, one hand smoothing her skirt. She started across the grass toward the woman.

"Bye," I said, raising a hand.

She stopped then and turned back to me. "It was a pleasure to make your acquaintance, John Edward Jack Thatch."

With that, she started up the hill toward the awaiting SUV. The woman fell in behind her. As the older woman turned, as she spun around, the wind caught the edge of her coat and I saw something beneath it, an image that is still clear as day in my mind; the barrel of a shotgun resting against her leg.

I watched Stella climb into the back. The woman closed the door on her, then she was gone, lost behind dark tinted windows growing smaller as they drove away.

2

"I left ten dollars on the counter for the pizza man. I already ordered. When he gets here, give him the full ten—eight for the pizza, two for a tip, got it?"

"Got it," I replied. My eyes were glued to the television. Auntie Jo scored an Atari 2600 at a yard sale last year, and the game system had come with a box of game cartridges. Pac-Man was my current game of choice, and I was pretty good. I was even better at Ms. Pac-Man, but I had to go to the arcade to play that one. Pitfall was fun, too.

"Are you even listening to me?"

"Pizza, money, tip, got it," I muttered.

"Okay, and what don't you do while I'm gone?"

"Open the door."

"Except for the pizza guy."

"Except for the pizza guy."

Auntie Jo bent down and kissed the top of my head. Her uniform smelled like pancakes and burnt toast. "I'm closing tonight, but I should be home by midnight. Maybe a little earlier, if I'm lucky."

"What if the pizza guy is an axe wielding murderer and he wants to chop me up into little pieces?"

"Well, then don't tip him. I've got to go." She was out the door a moment later, fresh cigarette smoke trailing behind her.

Blinky the ghost caught me in the corner and I lost my third life, game over. "Dang."

When I was younger, Auntie Jo employed a series of babysitters when she went to work, that stopped last year when I turned seven. She couldn't afford it. She said it would be cheaper if she skipped work than going in and hiring someone to watch me. I didn't need a sitter, anyway. Most of them sat around and talked to their boyfriends on the phone (a few in person), and they all completely ignored me.

We came to an arrangement. No more sitter, and she would give me one dollar to stay out of trouble and the dinner of my choosing. I always picked pizza. There was nothing better than pizza. I used some of my newfound wealth to purchase comic books. The rest went into a mason jar hidden under my bed. At last count, I had thirty-two dollars saved.

Standing, I stretched and went to the window.

Auntie Jo was about a block down the road, across the street. I waited for her to duck through the door of Krendal's Diner, where she worked, counted to ten, then put on my shoes and slipped out of the apartment.

I crossed the hall and knocked on the door to apartment 304. When nobody answered, I knocked again, louder this time. I was about to knock a third time, when the door opened about three inches, held in place by the metal security chain.

A pair of beady eyes came around the side of the door. Those eyes were behind a thick pair of glasses taped at the center on a wrinkled old face topped with an unruly mop of gray hair. Ms. Leech. "What?"

"You've got books, right?"

"You've got books? Is that really a proper greeting for one of your elders?"

I knew Ms. Leech had books because she used to watch me for the brief period that fell between the babysitters and Auntie Jo letting me stay home alone last year. She had shelves of books, newspapers, too. Auntie Jo said she was a hoarder.

"I need to find a copy of *Great Expectations* by Charles Dickers."

"Charles Dickens?"

"Yeah, him. Do you have it?"

Ms. Leech looked past me to the open door of my apartment. "Where is your aunt?"

"Working."

"You're not supposed to leave your apartment when she's working."

"I didn't leave it. It's right there," I gestured toward the open door. "If you let me borrow the book, you can have some of my pizza."

Her eyes brightened at this. "You have pizza?"

"Not yet, but he'll be here soon."

Ms. Leech had a weak spot for pizza, particularly pepperoni. Sometimes she even put pineapple on her pizza. Auntie Jo said she might be going senile; I think I agreed. Pineapple had no business on pizza.

She closed the door, removed the chain, and ushered me inside. "Yes, I have books. I have lots of books. I think I have that one somewhere."

When she went to close the door, I reminded her we'd have to listen for the pizza guy. She left it open about an inch. She didn't want to. I caught her looking back at it twice. Ms. Leech had been robbed once, about ten years ago, from what Auntie Jo told me. They busted right through her door, came into the apartment, and did bad things. Nobody told me exactly what those bad things might have been, but she didn't go out much. She said they followed her home, and as long as she didn't go out anymore, nobody could follow her back again. Auntie Jo bought her groceries when she got ours. I don't think I ever saw Ms. Leech outside the building.

"I'll watch the door," I told her. "You go find the book."

This seemed to calm her.

She nodded and began her trek through the living room, careful not to knock any of the newspaper stacks over. "It's nice to see you take an interest in the classics, but don't you think you should start out with something like Hucleberry Finn? Mark Twain is so much better than that Brit ever was. Dickens gets all flowery and wordy. I sometimes think he checked the cover to remind himself what book he was writing, he gets so wrapped up in his own words. Twain is nice and direct, to the point, much more concise."

"This is for school," I lied.

"Has school started already?" her voice was muffled. I couldn't see her anymore, somewhere on the other side of the room.

"Not for two more weeks, but Mrs. Thomas told us to read it over the summer."

"Seems like advanced reading for third grade."

"I'm going into the fourth grade."

"Oh, well then…"

I had no idea what grade would normally read this book, if at all.

"Got it!" she said. This was followed by a crash.

"Are you okay?"

"Yes. Yes. Just my encyclopedias. They really should be on a shelf, but they take up so much room."

She came back into view, her hair even more disheveled than when she left, a paperback in her hand. "I do have rather fond memories of this book. I may have to read that one again when you're done. You will return it, won't you?"

I nodded and reached for the book.

"I suppose your aunt is raising you 'by the hand,' as it were," she thought about this for a second. "Many similarities between you and young Pip, I suppose."

"What does, 'by the hand' mean?"

She smiled. "I don't want to ruin the story for you. You'll see soon enough."

The cover had a picture of a young boy and girl, both dressed in strange clothes. The boy was smiling, the girl was not.

We waited for the pizza guy to arrive. He did not have an axe.

3

On August 17, our air conditioner broke.

We didn't have anything fancy, just a window unit in the living room, a big beige box of a thing that made gurgling noises when it ran and dripped water on the floor, but it kept the apartment cool on those few days out of the year when the sun reared its head in Pittsburgh.

August 17 was just such a day—93 degrees by noon and creeping up with each passing minute.

"I'm holding the rent back if Mr. Triano doesn't get his butt up here in the next hour," Auntie Jo said. She had pulled the tattered leather recliner across the room to the second window, the one without the broken air conditioner stuffed into the frame, and laid down with a wet cloth on her head. At some point in the past twenty minutes, she had removed her blouse and sat there in a pale bra and blue shorts, her bare feet dangling over the side of the footrest.

"That stupid thing always shits the bed when we need it," she said.

I considered telling her that the air conditioner was far less likely to break during the dead of winter, then thought better of it. "Do you want a glass of lemonade?"

"That would be lovely."

In the kitchen, I tugged a glass from the dirty dishes piled in the sink, washed it out, and poured lemonade from the pitcher I made earlier. When I handed it to her, she gave it a tentative sip, then gulped it down. "Maybe a little more sugar next time, but I think you're getting the hang of it."

I had yet to make the perfect pitcher of lemonade.

She closed her eyes and rolled the empty glass over her cheeks. "Why don't you go play outside? A kid your age shouldn't be cooped up all summer. You should be outside with your friends."

"I don't have any friends. There isn't a single kid my age in our building."

She waved a hand limply through the air. "Maybe we should move to a palace in the suburbs, then, get a giant castle with a swimming pool—maybe a sprawling estate where all the neighborhood kids can line up and fill out applications to be your friend. Then you can select the best of the best and send the others packing. That seems much easier than just going outside and taking a chance on maybe running into someone your own age, making a friend or two the old-fashioned way." Auntie Jo turned her head and squinted against the sun, painting a bright line across her face. "I love you, kiddo, but you really shouldn't spend the last two weeks of your school vacation in here with the likes of me. I can be a miserable bitch sometimes, and now is one of those times. I'm ordering you to go outside and have fun."

"But—"

"Now," she said. "And I don't want to see your face back here until six."

I knew better than to argue. I grabbed my comic book off the kitchen table and bolted out the door.

I found myself in the cemetery.

I hadn't made a conscious decision to go to the cemetery, but considering it was the only open space anywhere near our building and it was quiet, that's where I ended up. I stopped at my parents' graves just long enough to place the dandelions I had picked along Greenlee Road in their vases and wipe the dirt and grime from Daddy's gravestone away with my shirt. If Auntie Jo asked how I got so dirty, I would just tell her playing was a messy business.

When satisfied with my work, I made my way over the hill and past the mausoleums, careful to hold my breath as I ran the length of them.

I expected the girl to be sitting on the bench, but she wasn't. The bench was empty, save for a few red maple leaves caught in the metalwork. Clearing off a spot, I took a seat and opened my comic to the center, to the bulky paperback I hid within the pages, the book with the smiling boy and unsmiling girl on the cover. I turned to the first page and began to read.

Two days later, I returned to the cemetery. The day after that, too. The bench was always empty. I went back every day for the rest of that summer and long into the school year, but I wouldn't see the girl again for nearly another year.

I never noticed the man watching me from the trees, sometimes there, sometimes not.

August 8, 1985

Nine Years Old

Log 08/08/1985—

Subject "D" within expected parameters.

Audio/video recording.

"Is everything recorded?"

"Not everything. Almost, though. Pay attention. I'm only going to explain this once."

"Sorry."

"Fresh tapes are in those boxes under the desk. If someone is in there, you *always* record. If he's talking, even if he's alone in there, you *most definitely* record. That stuff is gold, that's what they really want. Be careful what you say here in the booth. The microphones pick that up, too, and it will be part of the record. If things get crazy, keep your mouth shut. Doesn't matter how crazy. Keep your mouth shut and do your job."

"Load fresh tapes."

"Yes."

"Can I ask you a question?"

"As long as it's not a stupid question."

"I was told not to listen to him. Not to let him talk to me."

"They solved that problem a few years ago. Pretty simple, really. Everything is on a delay. What you see and hear on these monitors actually happened thirty seconds earlier. It's safe that way."

"If that's the case, why's he wearing a mask?"

—Charter Observation Team – 309

1

"Help me clear this off," Auntie Jo said, peeling away a vine that somehow managed to snake up out of the ground and wrap around Momma's headstone in the two days since I had been out here.

I tugged at the base, and a clump of dirt came out with the plant.

I caught her studying Daddy's stone—the lack of dirt, no moss growing in the carved letters.

"How you can possibly have feelings for the man who killed your mother is beyond me."

I knew better than to say anything. Correcting her would only lead to an argument, and I wanted to check the bench.

Aside from a couple of days during the winter, I had walked out to the bench nearly every day, and every day I found it empty. I even took to trying different times of the day on the off chance I was just missing her, but still, she was never there.

I didn't see her in school, either. She said she was the same age as me, and all the kids in this neighborhood went to Lincoln Elementary. That meant she lived somewhere else, but if that was the case, then why was she in the cemetery that day? Who was she visiting? I couldn't help but think of the woman with her. Why the gun? Maybe the woman kidnapped her, brought her to the cemetery to—to what? That didn't make sense, either. Nothing about the encounter made sense, and I guess that's why I couldn't get her out of my head.

Auntie Jo spread the blanket over the graves and handed me a sandwich—ham and American cheese on white. About a week ago, I noticed she stopped buying Wonder Bread and instead brought home the store brand. Our peanut butter was no longer Jiffy, either. The jar just said *Peanut Butter* across the front on a plain label. When I asked, she said the diner wasn't doing as well as it used to and her hours got cut. If things didn't change soon, she might have to pick up a second job. I offered her my savings, now at one hundred twenty-three dollars, but she wouldn't take the money.

"Read," she said, nodding at Momma's gravestone.

"Seriously? Again?"

"Read."

"Kaitlyn Gargery Thatch. February 16, 1958 to August 8, 1980. Loving wife, mother, and sister." I didn't have to look at the stone. I had memorized the text of both long ago.

"Five years," Auntie Jo said softly. The smoke trailed up into the heavens from the cigarette pinched between her fingers. I couldn't remember a time when she didn't smoke, but lately she seemed to be smoking more. Sometimes she lit one cigarette from the stubby remains of the last one. She puffed, blew the smoke back out. Her teeth were yellow.

Ten minutes later, sandwich eaten, transistor radio and comic book in hand, I found myself heading up the hill toward the mausoleums.

The weather had turned cool early this year, and the wind kicked up, twisting and turning through the spaces surrounding the stone buildings.

The bench was empty.

She wasn't there.

Sighing, I took a seat and set my comic book down beside me—I slipped the corner under my leg so the wind wouldn't take it, and switched on the radio.

Static. A bit of Phil Collins. More static.

I tugged the antenna out to full length and slowly pointed it in various directions.

The wind kicked.

Static.

Then Phil Collins again, loud and clear, *Suss, suss, sudio.*

"You're on my bench."

I hadn't heard her walk up, yet there she was, standing about five feet in front of me in a long, black peacoat.

"Move."

I started to get up. My heart pounded so heavily in my chest, I couldn't think. My face flushed. Instead, I sat up straight and pursed my lips in the most defiant pose I could muster. "No."

She shrugged and sat at the opposite end, smoothing her skirt beneath her thick coat.

The SUV was parked at the far end of the access road, further away than last time. The woman in the long white coat with even whiter hair stood beside the vehicle. Another woman, also in a long white coat, stood beside her. Both were watching us, watching me.

"How have you been, John Edward Jack Thatch?"

"Okay, I guess."

"You're not sure whether or not you're okay? Seems to me your current state should be as easy to determine as the weather."

"I'm fine."

"And your parents? Both still dead, I presume?"

"I read it."

"Read what?"

I pulled my comic book out from under my leg and slid it across the bench to her.

She ran a gloved hand over the cover and frowned. "You read some rubbish called *Teenage Mutant Ninja Turtles*, and I'm supposed to be impressed? Issue number one, no less. To think there might be more."

When I reached over to open the comic, the girl pulled her hand away with such a quickness, the movement was a blur to me. I noticed a hint of embarrassment in her face, but it was gone in an instant. I opened the comic book to the center, revealing my copy of *Great Expectations*. The one I had yet to return to Ms. Leech.

Her eyes lit up at this.

The two women in white coats had edged closer and were moving closer still. They both stopped when I looked up at them. My eyes drifted to the edge of their coats, searching for a gun barrel like the one I had spotted the last time, but I saw nothing. Even as the wind kicked up and took hold, I saw nothing. Maybe I had imagined the gun.

"Did you understand it?" the girl said, still looking at my book.

"I read it twice," I admitted. "The first time, I had to look up a lot of the words and some of the dialogue was hard. It was easier the second time."

She leaned back and looked down at the book in her hand, also *Great Expectations*. "I've read it twelve times now. When I finish tomorrow, it will be thirteen."

"Why not read something else?"

"What's the point? There is nothing better."

"Oh, I don't know. I've read lots of books. I like some of them plenty better."

"Well, you're just a dumb boy."

"Are you mean to me because Estella was mean to Pip in the book?"

She chuckled at this. "You, Mr. John Edward Jack Thatch, are no Pip. I'm mean to you because you are just a dumb boy deserving of nothing more."

"Why haven't I ever seen you at school?"

"I don't go to school, my teachers come to me. Six in total, every subject you could possibly imagine. I've been told I am very smart, possibly gifted, and to go to a public school would be a disservice."

"Are you rich?"

"I live in a grand house, nearly a castle. We employ a staff of servants around the clock, and I want for nothing. I spend my free time traveling the world, visiting one exotic place after the next, studying people, and places, and culture. Is that what you want to hear?"

I shrugged. "If it's the truth."

"It is."

"Okay."

She fidgeted with the corner of one of her gloves, tugged at it.

"Why do you wear those?"

"It's cold."

"Not that cold. It wasn't cold last time, and you wore them then, too."

"Maybe I like them." She slipped a finger inside the one on the right and pulled it off. Her fingers were long and slender.

"Stella." The woman with the white hair glared, stepping closer.

Stella quickly put the glove back on. "I like them, is all." She slipped her hands under her thighs.

"Why today? Why this bench?"

"So many questions…"

"I've been here a bunch of times, and you weren't. Now today, you're back. One year from the last time. August 8. Why?"

A smile edged her lips. "Were you looking for me?"

"No. I was…I live close by. I visit my parents a lot. That's all."

"You sound nervous, Jack. Do I make you nervous?"

"No," I said, hoping the redness had left my face.

She looked up, her deep brown eyes meeting mine. "Your parents died on August 8?"

I nodded.

She leaned back into the bench, her eyes on the heavens. "Strange, the coincidences of the world."

"My Auntie Jo says there are no coincidences."

"Is she here with you, your Auntie Jo?"

Again, I nodded. "Back at my parents' graves. We come every year."

"Then maybe I'll see you again."

"You're leaving? But you just—"

"Stella." The woman with the white hair again.

Stella narrowed her eyes and settled deeper into the bench. "Not yet. I have one hour." I got the impression she said this not for my benefit but for the two women, because she said it much louder than necessary, if only speaking to me.

I saw something then, movement in the backseat of the SUV. A man. No, a boy. "Who's that?"

Stella followed my gaze, then frowned. "That is David Pickford."

"Who is he?"

"He's nobody."

"How old is he?"

"Why would that matter?"

"Just wondering."

She shrugged. "Nine or ten, I suppose. Our age."

"Is he wearing a mask?"

Her gloved hand went to my comic book, and she flipped the pages. "Forget him. Tell me about your turtles."

I smiled and did just that. This boy watching us from the SUV, the women in white, too.

I wouldn't see him again for thirteen years, and even that proved too soon.

2

"This is *not* an All-American Slam," I said, staring at the plate Mr. Krendal set in front of me. Thanksgiving was ten days away, and Auntie Jo had been picking up as many double shifts as possible, hoping to scrape enough money together for a full turkey dinner. That meant no pizza for a while. She suspended my allowance, too. I was okay with that. I had saved up one hundred forty-one dollars. Since Auntie Jo wouldn't take any of my money, I gave it to Mr. Triano, the building's super, to buy a turkey and surprise her.

Elden Krendal, the owner and sole cook at Krendal's Diner, had a policy. He allowed his employees to eat for free, provided they didn't order off the menu but instead ate whatever was in surplus before the food expired.

A few weeks back, when Auntie Jo asked if she could share her free meal with me, Krendal wiped his thick sausage hands on his once-white apron and knelt down in front of me. "This guy is little, too little for what did you say? Eight years old?"

He wasn't very tall, only about an inch taller than Auntie Jo, but Mr. Krendal was a big man. I imagined he nibbled away all day back in that kitchen just to maintain such a size. He probably weighed at least three hundred pounds and reminded me of a flabby Mr. Clean, the guy from those commercials, twenty years past his prime. The top of his head didn't contain a single hair. I once overheard him say he got tired of hairnets and shaved it all off. Auntie Jo said his hair got tired of him and left on its own accord. He had an infectious smile. I couldn't remember a time when he wasn't smiling. Even when he shouted out from back in the kitchen, he did so from behind a grin.

"Nine," I corrected him.

He shook his head. "You're skin and bones. You're not going to grow up to be a big strong man sharing plates with your aunt. You need a plate of your own."

"I can't afford—" Auntie Jo started.

Mr. Krendal waved a hand at her. "We will feed this boy until it's coming out his ears. Maybe someday he'll come work for me."

"I'm going to go to college and become an astronaut or maybe a reporter for the *Daily Planet*," I said.

"Or maybe a reporter in space? I imagine we need those, too," Krendal said. "Pick out a seat, I'll put something together for you."

Auntie Jo nodded toward the row of stools lining the counter, but I went to a booth instead, a small booth built for two people in the far corner near the bathrooms. Over the coming weeks, this became my booth. Mr. Krendal made a small paper sign that read RESERVED FOR JACK THATCH – ASTRONAUT REPORTER in large block letters and placed it out there every day before Auntie Jo's shift, knowing I'd probably be in, too.

Today, when he asked me what I wanted for dinner, I told him I'd like an All-American Slam like they have at Denny's, along with a chocolate shake. He brought me a chicken sandwich on rye bread with a side order of french fries and a glass of water.

"This is a Krendal's All-American Slam. It may vary slightly from the competition's meal of the same name," Mr. Krendal said. "When the kind people at Denny's stole the name from my menu, they did not take the time to read the description. I had a similar problem with the people from McDonald's. For nearly a year, I told them a Big Mac was supposed to be a bowl of pasta and cheese with bacon on top, but they completely ignored me. In my day, corporate theft of ideas meant something. People take no pride in their thievery anymore."

Krendal ruffled my hair and went back to the kitchen, leaving me to eat. I always asked for a chocolate shake. He never gave me one. He insisted people were not meant to ingest all that sugar, and water was better for me, particularly my teeth. At fifty-eight years old, he had no cavities. He was also quick to point out he'd never drank chocolate shakes.

I made quick work of the chicken sandwich and fries. The meal was delicious.

Auntie Jo fluttered around the diner as I ate. She smiled, too. I watched as she put on her best smile whenever she faced a customer. I also saw that same smile drop away the minute she turned her back on them. She didn't much want to be here.

I was about to pack up and go back to our apartment when she dropped four dollars on the corner of my table. "I turned three tables just to get enough for some cigs. Tips are horrible today. This better turn around fast. Can you be a dear and run next door and get me two packs of Red 100s? You can keep the change."

I wanted to say no. Auntie Jo smoked too much. This morning, she coughed for nearly five minutes straight before she even got out of bed.

If I didn't go, she'd just buy them on her break, then she'd blame me for any lost tips while she was gone.

Snatching up the money, I started for the door. "Be right back."

3

The sky churned with gray clouds tipped in white, and the air felt damp. It hadn't rained yet today, but I'd be willing to bet that it would. In November in Pittsburgh, that was a pretty safe bet, not one a local would take the other side of, that's for sure. Considering it was nearly noon, the sun should be high in the sky. Instead, I think it departed for Florida, leaving nothing but a dim bulb as replacement.

The Corner Mart grocery sat two doors down from Krendal's on the same side of the street, so I didn't have to cross traffic. The store took up the first floor of a wedge-shaped building, narrow at the front and widening further back, no doubt built to accommodate the odd angle of the street which had been built in such a way to accommodate the odd angle of the large hill upon which our entire block sat. Pittsburgh was not known for sprawling flatlands, only odd angles. Even the floors of our apartment dropped off at enough of an incline to propel my Matchbox cars from one end of the kitchen to the other without any help from me.

The door to the grocery triggered an electronic chime before swinging shut behind me. Although the front of the store had two large windows beside the door, every available inch of glass was covered with posters, signs, and advertisements for various items—everything from milk to beer to cigarettes and each line punctuated with an exclamation mark because a sign reading $1.25 CIGARETTES! was far better than one with only $1.25 CIGARETTES. There were corner groceries everywhere you turned in this city, and only the ones with the largest selection of exclamation marks survived.

I didn't recognize the man behind the counter with thinning black hair and a plaid shirt about two sizes too small. He greeted me with a nod and lowered his copy of the *Pittsburgh Post-Gazette*. The Steelers beat the Oilers yesterday, thirty to seven—the third win in a row. "What can I get for you, kid?"

The counter was a bit tall for me, but it felt a little shorter than the last time I was in here. I reached up and slid the four dollar bills as close to the man as I could. "Two packs of Marlboro Red 100s, please."

His brow furrowed, and he returned to the newspaper, shaking his head. "You know I can't sell them to you."

"Why not?"

He rolled his eyes toward the sign that said YOU MUST BE 18 YEARS OLD TO PURCHASE TOBACCO PRODUCTS. This sign had no exclamation mark.

"They're not for me, they're for my aunt."

"Who's your aunt?"

"Josephine Gargery. She's working and can't come down here right now."

"Jo...from Krendal's?"

I nodded.

"And they're not for you? You're not going to go around the corner and fire these up with your friends?"

"Smoking is disgusting. I'd never smoke. Mr. Cougin knows me. I come in here a lot."

"Mr. Cougin isn't working today."

"Isn't he the owner, though? If he is okay with selling cigarettes to me, then you should be able to sell them to me, too, right? If you don't, then Auntie Jo will have to leave work to come over here. If that happens, she's gonna be mad, probably Mr. Krendal, too. Then both of them are liable to complain to Mr. Cougin, and he's going to take it out on you. All of that can be avoided if you just sell them to me. I don't much like confrontation, and I imagine you don't, either. Besides, I'm not a narc. I'm one of the good guys."

He bit at the inside of his cheek, glanced down at the corner of his newspaper as if someone printed the answer directly under the Steeler win, then blew out a breath and pulled two packs of cigarettes down from the overhead rack. "Nobody likes confrontation."

"Nope," I agreed. "Nobody."

He handed back a dollar and thirty-eight cents with the cigarettes.

"Thank you." I took the change and the cigarettes and headed for the the comic rack at the back of the store. I already owned most of the good ones, but there was one in particular I had my eye on: *Superman* annual volume one, number eleven. I found it when I was in here on Tuesday, but I only had seventy-three cents with me, not enough to cover the steep dollar and twenty-five cent price tag on this particular book, so I hid it behind *Strawberry Shortcake* number four on the top shelf, someplace no self-respecting comic lover would go, and hoped it would be there when I came back. It was, and I snatched it down. I was flipping through the book, when the chime above the store's front door went off. I barely heard the muffled sounds of traffic and the shuffle of feet before the door closed again.

"Everything in the register, now!"

The voice was loud and gruff, coming from the front of the store at my back.

"Okay, sure, just calm down." This was the man behind the counter. "It's all yours, I don't—"

The explosion of a gunshot rattled the poster and sign-covered windows.

I dropped the cigarettes.

What happened next, happened fast.

I turned as the gunman did. I watched in slow motion as he spun around, long, greasy red hair swinging behind him catching in the hood of his filthy navy sweatshirt, his arm coming up, the gun pointing toward me, smoke still trailing from the barrel.

He squeezed the trigger not once but twice.

My heart burst with pain, a thud stronger than any I had ever felt.

A wetness bloomed on my leg, my thigh, a growing mass of warmth.

The gun clicked.

Two *empty* clicks.

No shot. No bullet. Some kind of misfire.

The gunman frowned at the weapon, nearly threw it at me, then turned back to the register and scooped out the cash, shoving the bills into his pockets. When he got the last of them, he took a step toward me, his eyes wild. "I know what you look like, kid. I never forget a face. You say a fucking word, and I'll hunt your ass down. I'll slice you open and hang you from a fucking streetlight."

A moment later, he was gone and I was alone.

I looked down at my leg. I had wet my pants. I didn't care.

I stood there. I don't know how long. I couldn't move.

Eventually, I found the strength to wander back to Krendal's and summon help.

August 8, 1986

Ten Years Old

Log 08/08/1986—

Interview with Dr. Helen Durgin. Subject "D" appears agitated.

Audio/video recording.

"I'd like to talk about your parents."

"I don't want to."

"You need to. It's best we all understand what happened."

"I don't remember. I was little then."

"You remember. I think you remember everything that happened that day."

Silence.

"It wasn't your fault, David. You were only two. You couldn't have known what would happen."

"I don't want to."

Dr. Durgin sighed. "What would *you* like to talk about?"

"How come nobody else ever comes to visit me?"

"You know why."

"But you're not afraid. You come."

"I'm deaf, David. I can't actually hear you. I read your lips."

"And that's why you're not afraid?"

"That's why I'm able to visit with you."

"So if you could hear, you wouldn't visit me anymore?"

"I would like to, but they probably wouldn't let me."

"You'd talk to me through the speakers, though? Like everyone else?"

"If they let me."

"Dr. Peavy used to come in and visit with me. He wasn't deaf."

"But he doesn't anymore, does he, David? Do you remember what happened to Dr. Peavy?"

"Yes. Dr. Peavy was mean to me. I made him stop."

"That was two weeks after your parents. If you remember what happened to Dr. Peavy, then you certainly remember what happened to them."

Silence.

"David?"

"I'm tired. Can we stop now?"

"Were your parents mean to you? Like Dr. Peavy?"

"My daddy was."

"And you made him stop?"

Silence.

"David, you have to speak aloud, for the record. You made your father stop?"

"Yes."

"How did you make your father stop?"

"I don't remember."

"I think you do."

"He wasn't supposed to hurt Mommy."

"That wasn't your fault."

David said nothing.

—Charter Observation Team – 309

1

"Read."

"Oh, come on."

Auntie Jo's gaze fixed on me, her lips pursed tight over the nub of a cigarette dangling from her mouth. "Read."

I rolled my eyes. "Kaitlyn Gargery Thatch. February 16, 1958 to August 8, 1980. Loving wife, mother, and sister. Can I go now?"

Auntie Jo narrowed her eyes and lit another cigarette. "Where exactly do you run off to?"

I snatched my comic book off the blanket. "Just over the hill, there's a bench up there where I can read."

"You can read here. Why not read aloud to your mother and me. I'm sure she'd like that."

"I don't think she'd give two shits about *Teenage Mutant Ninja Turtles.*"

She smacked the side of my head. "Language! Don't think you're getting so big I won't put you over my knee."

"Yes, ma'am. Sorry."

Auntie Jo grunted and puffed at the new cigarette. She dropped the butt of the old one in the vase attached to Daddy's gravestone. I made a mental note to fish it out later.

Two shits was my favorite new word—well, two new words. A kid transferred to Lincoln about a month before the school year let out, Duncan Bellino. His dad was a plant manager, and they moved here from Chicago. We called him Dunk. He smoked and said things like *two shits*. Dunk had the largest comic collection I had ever seen outside of a store, boxes of them. I had spent most of the summer digging through those boxes.

When word got around school about what happened at the grocery store, my popularity factor went through the roof and held steady for about two weeks before kids realized I was still the same kid they ignored before. After that, things returned pretty much to normal. Dunk stuck around, though. When he heard what happened, he shrugged it off, said stores in Chicago got robbed two, sometimes three times a day. You'd be lucky to get in and out without tripping over a robber, no big deal.

His dad had a gun on account of him being a former Army ranger. He kept it hidden in a shoe box on the top shelf of their closet. We had to drag a chair in from the kitchen just to get to it. The ammo was there, too. Dunk let me keep one of the bullets. He said if the robber ever came back for me, he'd let me borrow the gun so I could blast him in the face. With the gun in a shoe box at the top of his dad's closet, I was fairly certain I wouldn't be able to reach it in time. We had yet to work out the logistics. *Logistics* was my second favorite word.

"Have you seen my Walkman?"

Auntie Jo fished it out of her bag and handed it to me. I had used a good part of my savings buying the Walkman, but it was worth it. The device not only had a built-in radio, it also played cassettes. No antenna, either. It was much better than our old transistor radio.

I started up the hill.

"One hour!" she called out from behind me. "I start at four today, and Krendal said you can bus until eight when Carter gets in— we need the money!"

I waved over my shoulder.

She started coughing then, and I could still hear her as I reached the mausoleums. She had been coughing a lot lately.

The bench was empty. I figured it would be. I was a little early. Last time she didn't get here until after four. I sat, put on my headphones, and turned on the Walkman.

Static.

I expected that, too. I lowered the volume.

Last year, I let Stella keep my *Teenage Mutant Ninja Turtles* number one. This year, not only did I bring her volume two but three *Wonder Woman* comics I borrowed from Dunk's personal stash. At first, I thought it was weird that he owned every *Wonder Woman*, but he was quick to point out they were filled with half-naked women. I had since become a fan.

If Dunk knew I was about to share part of his prized comic collection with a girl, he'd kill me.

Twenty minutes passed.

Thirty.

I began to worry she wasn't going to show, and then I spotted the white SUV coming up the access road followed closely by a second vehicle, also a white SUV of the same make and model. Both stopped about thirty feet from the bench.

I wiped the sweat off my palms on my jeans. The driver-side door opened and the older woman stepped out, smoothing her long, white coat. The sun was out today, and the temperature was hovering somewhere in the low eighties, hardly coat weather. I couldn't help but think about the gun, not like the one Dunk's dad had but something longer, like a rifle or a shotgun, hidden under that coat.

The backdoor of the SUV opened, and I expected Stella to get out, but instead a man with dark brown hair and sunglasses stepped out, also wearing a long white coat. Another man and a woman stepped out on the passenger side. Four more people got out of the second SUV, all adults, no sign of Stella. All of them in long, white coats. The driver of the first SUV, the woman I recognized from my other visits with Stella, approached and took Stella's seat on the bench.

The static from my Walkman crackled at my ears, and I switched it off, pulling off the headphones. "Where's Stella?"

The woman smiled. It was cold, the smile of a Cheshire Cat greeting a mouse moments before devouring the little creature, tail and all. She wore a smile of convenience, a mask. I didn't want to peek behind her mask.

"Stella will not be joining us today."

"Where is she?"

The woman crossed her legs. She didn't look at me. She stared straight ahead, her eyes on the SUVs, on the others standing around them. "Ms. Nettleton is somewhere other than here. Where that might be is none of your concern."

"Is she okay?"

I couldn't help but think Stella had gotten hurt, been in some kind of terrible accident. Why else wouldn't she come?

The woman's long, white hair was pulled back in a ponytail, hanging down over the collar of her coat. Her fingernails were long and manicured, painted a white not unlike her coat. She folded her hands on her lap. "My name is Latrese Oliver. You may call me Ms. Oliver or even Mrs. Oliver. You are never to call me Latrese, and you never will. I am, and always will be, above your station in life. Regardless of whatever minor success you may one day achieve, even if you stumble into a major success at some point in your feeble little life, even if you find riches and stature, you will always be beneath me, inferior to me. Do you understand? Am I making myself clear to you? Nod if you understand."

I nodded before I even realized I was doing it. I forced the motion to come to a stop, willed my head still.

"Good," she muttered. "Not that I expect much of you. I think you may have found your peak as a busboy, picking up the filth and waste of others. Wiping the urine stains from the grimy porcelain tiles of the bathroom floor, scraping away the dried shit of strangers from a communal bowl, that is where you truly belong."

"Where...where is Stella?" I wanted the words to sound forceful, tough even. They didn't, though. They squeaked from my lips as if from a boy half my age, as if from the boy in the grocery nine months earlier as he wet his pants.

"Do you find her to be pretty? Our little Stella?"

I didn't say anything. My eyes fell to the stack of comics on the bench.

The woman went on. "You will never have her, you know. As much as you may one day desire her, she will never be yours. Does that bother you?"

"I...I don't like girls. Not like that."

"No? Ah, but you will. Someday, I believe, you will. Someday you will want her so desperately you would step in front of a racing car just for the chance to touch her, to feel her warmth near your body, to know her kiss. Our Stella."

"I just want to talk to her, that's all."

Ms. Oliver snorted, lost in her own words. "I bet you go home after these visits and pull your pecker out of your pants and touch yourself in the most obscene of ways just thinking about her—the smell of her hair, that smooth skin of hers. Have you ever even seen a naked girl before? I imagine not. Not at your age. You probably think about it, though, the filthiest of thoughts floating through that head of yours. You're no better than other boys, all of you are the same. None of you are good enough for our Stella, and it sickens me to think she would even speak to you, let alone..." Her voice trailed off as she shook her head. She turned and stared at me, those dark gray eyes boring into me, burning with a hatred so fierce I could taste it on the air. "She will be your everything. Every breath of air you tug from the world will belong to her, everything you do will be for her, and you will mean absolutely nothing to her in return. You will be something she scrapes off her shoe and leaves on the side of the road for the vultures to tear and eat and shit back out. You are, and always shall be, discarded waste—building blocks the universe should have used to make something better, an afterthought."

She stood then, again smoothing out the long, white coat, and without another word, she climbed back into the SUV followed by the others. I watched as they drove away, the stillness and quiet of the cemetery suffocating.

2

Preacher stepped into the apartment and pressed both hands to the door, closing it with a gentle click. He knew nobody was home, he was certain of that, but he didn't want to alert the neighbors of his presence any more than he would have wanted to startle the homeowner had they been drowsing in bed or watching television rather than visiting the rotting corpses of two long-lost relatives in the cemetery behind the apartment building.

Neighbors in buildings like this tended to stick together. They got themselves caught up in the business of those living around them just a little too often for Preacher's taste. He could never live in a place like this, and he didn't understand why anyone else would make the conscious choice to do so.

The place was a box.

The place was a box stacked on top of other boxes, next to more boxes, and under even more. This wasn't a home, this was a cell. This was the kind of place society put you.

Josephine Gargery didn't make a lot of money. He had reviewed her last three tax returns before coming here. As a waitress, she earned $2.01 per hour plus tips, the average tip being 10 to 15 percent. Preacher, of course, tipped 20 percent whether service was good or not and always treated his waitstaff with the utmost respect. Not because he felt they had a hard job or deserved more than the norm from him because he could sometimes be difficult, but because they handled his food and often did so outside his viewing area. He would never consider treating someone poorly, then sending them back to the kitchen to fetch his meal. They might spit in it, or worse. He once heard of a cook running a chicken sandwich through the dishwater when he heard the recipient was a former high school teacher who gave him a C minus in history class three years earlier. Imagine what that same person might do if he or she had a sudden dislike for a regular patron simply because that patron was rude or tipped poorly on a previous visit?

Preacher always tipped 20 percent, and he had done so when he ate breakfast at Krendal's Diner this morning. Based on the income stated on Josephine Gargery's tax returns, her regular patrons did not. She earned $7,840 last year. That amounted to $150.77 per week—only a few dollars above the national poverty level of $7,240 per year. Considering she had the boy, a dependent, Ms. Gargery wasn't doing well. This became abundantly clear as Preacher turned and surveyed the apartment.

The small space reeked of cigarette smoke, even with the two living room windows open and a light breeze lofting in. Smoky grime stained the walls. He could only imagine how the filth of it infiltrated the furniture, the bedsheets, the clothing. He wore thick leather gloves. He couldn't, wouldn't, touch anything with bare hands.

Preacher did not smoke, nor did he tolerate anyone in his presence to do so. Such a filthy, wasteful habit.

Standing with his back to the door of the apartment, the small kitchen was on his left. The appliances appeared to be about a decade old, the corners and crevices lined with rust. The refrigerator contained nothing but condiments, some prepackaged sliced American cheese, and a quarter gallon of milk that smelled just this side of funky.

A narrow hallway led to the living room in front of him, and two doors lined the wall on his right, most likely the bedrooms. He saw nothing of interest in the kitchen, not even a single note affixed to the refrigerator door—the room looked rarely used, so he went on to the living room. A dining table sat tucked into the corner on the left, littered with stacks of both opened and unopened mail. Preacher took up the nearest pile and studied the labels: bills and Publisher's Clearing House. The bills were unopened, the Publisher's Clearing House envelope was not only open but the application had been completed and stuffed into the return envelope, ready to be mailed. Although completed in the name of Josephine Gargery, the handwriting was that of a child, no doubt belonging to the boy.

Preacher returned the mail to the table, careful to place everything back exactly as he found it, and studied the living room. A recliner and couch both faced a small twelve-inch television. A coffee table stood at the center of this little triangle. He expected it to be thick with dust, but he found the table to be clean, same with the top of the television. The grime of the space seemed to start and end with the cigarette smoke. Someone took the time to clean the apartment on a regular basis, and he found this surprising. Most likely, this was the boy again. He knew the aunt worked long hours and was rarely here, probably just long enough to sleep, shower, and return to work. The boy fended for himself. How that woman managed to smoke enough to create this cleanliness problem was perplexing. Preacher imagined her chain-smoking just to keep up with it. He knew the boy didn't smoke, not yet anyway. They had been watching him closely, and someone would have made note of such appalling activity. A sniff of both the couch and the recliner confirmed she sat in the recliner as she smoked. Oddly, he found no ashtrays. The window nearest the chair had no screen. He supposed she could dispose of her ashes through that opening, but that seemed unlikely.

The door to the first of two small bedrooms stood adjacent to the living room, clearly the boy's room—posters of superheroes and pages torn from comic books covered the walls. On the dresser he found stacks of books, classics such as *Treasure Island* and *Lord of the Flies* as well as nearly a dozen volumes of Hardy Boy mysteries. Comic books sat beside those, all stacked in neat piles. Within the drawers he found nothing but clothing, all folded and organized by type. The socks were paired off and rolled together in careful balls. He expected to find something hidden within the clothing, contraband of some sort, but there was none. Nothing under the bed, either, not even a dust bunny.

In the closet, he found clothing hung in perfect symmetry on hangers arranged from light to dark. On the floor of the closet sat a single cardboard box. Inside that box, he found twelve ashtrays hidden beneath a dozen paperbacks—most likely, the missing ashtrays from the apartment. Apparently, the boy thought he could convince his aunt to quit smoking by hiding them. Clever. Childish, but clever.

Preacher returned everything as he found it and closed the closet door.

His eyes drifted over the room, the neatness of it. Everything in its place.

He had been a boy once.

Boys hid things.

He turned back to the bed and lifted the mattress, his eyes lighting up at what he found.

Pressed between the mattress and boxspring was a notebook of some sort. He retrieved it and flipped through the pages. Not a notebook, a *sketchbook*, containing dozens of drawings, drawings of Stella.

He lowered the mattress back in place.

The drawings were crude, but better than most. Far better than Preacher could ever draw. Exceptionally better than expected from most children. The last sketch in particular, Stella smiling with the glint of the sun in her eyes, that one was good. That one was *real* good. The boy had drawn it with a black ballpoint pen, a medium that didn't allow for mistakes.

This had to stop. Things were getting out of control.

Preacher sat on the edge of the bed, dropping the sketchbook beside him.

What did the girl see in this boy?

Why him?

He was a nobody, a future rat to run the maze. His life would come and go in a blip. Most likely he would not attend college, would not obtain even mediocre success. He was destined to a life of labor and an early grave, so why him?

Preacher took his Walther PPK/S .380 from the holster slung over his left shoulder and held the weapon in his hand, absent-mindedly unscrewing the silencer, then tightening it back up. The weight of the gun, the heft of it in his hand, the smell of the oil, these things all helped him focus, helped him concentrate.

He could kill the boy. He might have to at some point, he was sure of that. Why not now?

He could wait right here and put a bullet into the kid's brain when he returned from the cemetery, the aunt, too. Preacher had no qualms about killing kids. He had killed his share in the past. The only difference between a child and an adult was time. They would be done with this, then. The whole sordid mess would be behind them, and they could move on.

There would be repercussions.

Preacher scratched at his chin with the barrel of the gun.

3

We were late for our shift.

It was my fault.

After the woman left, I sat on the bench, completely dumb-struck. My mind buzzed and I couldn't stop shaking. Each breath seemed to catch in my throat and hold to the sides, unwilling to be expelled.

Even now, as I kept pace behind Auntie Jo, my heart beat with such a ferocity I thought it might crack out from behind my ribs and land with a thud somewhere ahead of us on the broken side-walk.

"Are you coming down with something? You don't look too good."

I nearly told Auntie Jo she didn't *sound* too good, and it was true—she made a strange wheezing sound as she walked, like air passing over wax paper. Every few steps, she punctuated this with a moist cough. This didn't stop her from smoking, though. "Maybe I should drop these things off in our apartment. I could take a vitamin C."

"I have some in my locker at the diner," she said. "Can't afford to get sick right now, neither of us."

Although she didn't say anything, I knew she hadn't paid rent for August yet. Eight days late. Anything past the fifth would also include a late fee. I wasn't sure how much that would amount to. All I knew was that it was more than we had. I could return the Walkman. I could try to give her my savings again, but she never took it.

We pushed through the door of Krendal's, twenty minutes late. The diner was packed. Mr. Krendal stood at the griddle in the kitchen, his eyes locked on us through the pass-through at the back of the counter. "Josie! Get your apron on, we're getting slammed!"

Although not even five o'clock, someone sat at every booth, table, and stool. About a half-dozen people stood around the front door, waiting for something to open up. Lurline Waldrip was behind the counter, wiping up what looked like a coffee spill. She looked up at both of us, shook her head, then went back to it.

I saw the woman's coat first.

When you bus tables, you quickly learn to seek out dirty dishes and glasses upon entering a room, hone in on them like a radar. My eyes began that involuntary exercise the moment we stepped inside, taking in the people second, and the various eating utensils, plates, and bowls first. Full versus empty, half-full waters in need of refilling. Her coat, though, her coat caught my eye.

I saw the white coat draped down over one of the stools at the counter, and all other sights and sounds left the room as my eyes followed the lines of that coat up the stool to the woman sitting atop it with her back toward me, her long, white hair falling over her shoulders. A newspaper sat folded neatly beneath her left hand on the counter, and I watched as she raised a coffee cup to her lips with her right.

She must have felt my eyes on her, because she turned around, spinning slowly on the edge of the stool. I think I stared at her for a full ten seconds before I realized this wasn't the woman from the cemetery, Ms. Latrese Oliver, as she had called herself, this was someone else, someone I had never seen before.

I pushed passed Auntie Jo and ran toward the bathroom. Somehow I managed to close and lock the door and get to the toilet before my meager breakfast and lunch came back up.

I stayed not only for my shift but through the end of Auntie Jo's shift, too. Mr. Krendal told me I could go home more times than I could count, but I just couldn't. I didn't want to be alone. The rush didn't end until after 9 p.m. Lurline said it was because it was Friday, payday for most, and half the city decided they didn't want to cook. She said a pocket full of cash led to the trifecta—hot meal, bar, strip club for nearly every single guy in the city, of which there were many. I knew what a bar was. There were three on every block. I had my suspicions about strip clubs, too, my limited knowledge having come from Dunk's slightly less limited knowledge. Auntie Jo tried to keep up with the crowd, but she was moving slow, and Lurline stayed more than an hour after her shift to help out.

We had left the windows open, and some of the papers from the dining table had blown around the apartment. I scuttled around and picked them up as Auntie Jo turned on lights, closed both windows, and dropped down into her chair. "I'm getting too old for this." She pulled off her shoes and rubbed at her swollen feet. She then counted out her tips and swore under her breath.

"What's wrong?"

"We're still thirty-eight short for rent. I thought for sure..." she trailed off, closed her eyes, and pressed her calloused palms against her temples.

I made six dollars in tips. I placed the money in her hand. She opened her mouth to argue, then smiled weakly. "You're a good kid. I'll pay you back, every cent."

"Hang on." I ran to my room to get the rest from my savings. She'd take my money now, and I wanted to give it to her. I lived here, too. I wanted to help.

I saw the envelope on my bed when I turned on the light.

The envelope sat atop my sketchbook, also on my bed—not where I left it.

I glanced back at Auntie Jo through the open doorway, still in her chair, then stepped cautiously into my room, searching every corner and shadow.

The envelope was white, letter size, about half an inch thick. A single word was printed across the front in neat handwriting—
Pip.

The envelope contained five hundred dollars in cash.

4

That night, I had a bad dream. I had a really bad dream.

I was four.

Daddy fastened me into my car seat.

"All secure, Captain Jack?"

"Yep."

"Your momma hooked you up with a road soda."

I took the sippy cup from him and brought it to my lips, careful not to spill. Chocolate milk, my favorite.

Momma got into the car.

I remembered this trip.

I remembered every second of it from the moment we left our house until we pulled up outside of Auntie Jo's apartment building, the same one where we lived now.

We pulled up outside the red brick apartment building, and Auntie Jo came out, an ever-present cigarette lodged between the fingers of her left hand.

I knew what came next.

Momma's door opened, the two woman hugged. Auntie Jo poked her head in through the opening, smiling at me.

"Josephine," Daddy grumbled.

She said nothing to him.

This is when things changed.

This is where it was different.

I remembered Daddy getting out of the car, lifting me out and setting me on the ground. I remembered both Momma and Daddy getting back in the car and driving off down the road, watching them disappear over the hill before taking Auntie Jo's hand and going into the building with her.

I remembered all of that as if it happened yesterday.

That is not what happened next, though.

In this dream, something else happened entirely.

Daddy opened my door, removed something from the seat beside me, then closed my door. I watched him carry that something around the car and hand it to Auntie Jo.

Momma and Daddy got back into the car, and we were moving again.

Daddy swore at all the red taillights ahead. He made a right-hand turn without slowing down. The inertia pressed me into the side of my chair.

Neither of them looked back at me, which was rare. One or both usually did in these moments.

We went over a bridge, followed soon by a tunnel, the car gaining speed.

I felt us going faster, the car speeding up, growing louder.

Daddy did look up then. I saw his eyes in the mirror, but he didn't look at me. He looked at something beyond me, something behind us. Momma glanced at him, and I saw her look, too, only she looked into the mirror on her door.

Daddy swerved, passing a car moving much slower than us. Our car got louder, faster.

"79 is coming up," Momma said.

Daddy's eyes in the mirror again. "Too far."

His eyes drifted to me in the mirror then, if only a second. I saw the white SUV pull out of a side street directly into our path. He did not.

Momma didn't, either. She didn't have time to scream.

When I woke from the dream for the third time, I didn't dare go back to sleep. I stared at the ceiling until the light of morning reached through my window and tried to grab me under my mound of blankets.

5

Two weeks before Christmas, we had a bit of a warm spell. The previous week's snow disappeared, leaving behind the brown, mushy earth and faded grass slumbering comfortably beneath. The sky bore only a passing resemblance to day, filled with thick, dark clouds eager to get winter back underway. Auntie Jo insisted I wear my winter coat, a thick monster of a thing made of wool meant for temperatures as low as minus ten. I unbuttoned the coat as soon as I left the apartment and considered taking the ridiculous thing off altogether. It was nearly forty degrees out and climbing as I stood just inside the large iron gates of the cemetery.

Four more envelopes appeared after the first, always on the eighth of the month, always labeled *Pip*, and always found on my bed, somehow left there while the apartment was vacant. The last arrived on Monday, only two days ago. I considered skipping school and hiding in the apartment, but my teacher, Ms. Thomas, frequented the diner and would no doubt ask my aunt where I was. I considered pretending to be sick, too, and nearly did until I realized I wasn't so sure I wanted to be alone in the apartment with whoever was leaving those envelopes. I knew it wasn't Stella. I suspected it might be Ms. Oliver, and that thought was enough for me to abandon the plan altogether.

Each envelope contained exactly five hundred dollars.

I knew I couldn't give the money directly to Auntie Jo. She would ask where the money came from, and I couldn't tell her I found it on my bed. I couldn't tell her the money came from my savings, either. She knew how much I had. I also couldn't let her see the envelope with *Pip* written on the front, because that would just lead to more questions. Ultimately, I took the money out of the first envelope, wrapped the cash in newspaper, and left the bundle in Auntie Jo's locker at the diner. She found the money after her shift the following day and didn't say anything until we got home. Then she pulled the money from her purse and showed it to me. She thought Mr. Krendal left the package for her. If she told me aliens beamed it into her locker from their mothership circling the Earth, I would have been happy with that explanation, too, as long as she didn't suspect the windfall came from me. She said she confessed to Mr. Krendal she was behind on the rent and needed an advance. He told her he didn't do loans or advances. If he helped her out, he'd be obligated to help everyone out, and times were tough. She believed he left the money anonymously simply to avoid potential problems with the rest of his employees. When she thanked him for the money, he simply said, "What money?" and returned to the grill. Sometimes unspoken words say more than an entire conversation.

When the second envelope arrived, I again wrapped the cash in newspaper and placed the money in Auntie Jo's locker. Again, she suspected it came from Mr. Krendal. She was no longer behind on the rent and considered giving it back. I told her sometimes it rains, we should save it. She tucked the money away in the back of our freezer wrapped in aluminum foil with MYSTERY MEAT written across the package on masking tape.

With the arrival of the envelopes that followed, I hid the money in my underwear drawer. I didn't want to risk Auntie Jo attempting to return it to Mr. Krendal again, and she no doubt would. Auntie Jo had her faults, but she was a proud woman, and taking charity wasn't too far off from panhandling in her book. If money got tight again, I'd find another way to get it into her hands.

I looked up from my post beside a large granite obelisk to see Dunk wheeling around the corner on his BMX bike. He wore no jacket, only a *Run DMC* sweatshirt and jeans. As he crossed through the cemetery gates, he backpedaled, engaging his rear brakes, locking the back tire, and skidded sideways to a controlled stop a few inches from my feet.

"What exactly are we doing here?" He dropped the bike in the grass and leaned against a tall black tombstone, realized what he was touching, then took a few steps back, shoving his hands deep in his pockets. "You know I don't like this place. Cemeteries creep me out. Haven't you ever seen *Night of the Living Dead?* Romero doesn't live far from here. For all we know, he got the idea for that movie when one of these stiffs made a grab for him right where we're standing."

"Well, he lived to tell about it."

Dunk's eyes narrowed. "Or did he? Have you ever seen him? He looks like a zombie."

"Zombies aren't real."

"If there are zombies anywhere, they'd be here in Pittsburgh. This place is a shithole," he said. "Chicago was a happy place. Look at the films set around Chicago—*The Breakfast Club, Sixteen Candles.* In Chicago, we had Molly Ringwald down the road in Evanston. Nothing bad ever happens in Evanston."

"Anthony Michael Hall could easily be a zombie. That Ducky kid, too."

He thought about this. "You got me there. They're some creepy-looking dudes. Molly's a fox, though. I'd do her."

"You don't even know what that means."

"Of course I do. A gentleman never kisses and tells, though. You'll have to fumble through the art of love all on your own, Mr. Thatch, now that you have a girlfriend."

I had told Dunk everything.

He knew about my first meeting with Stella through the incident with the old woman. I didn't know what else to call it. *The incident* seemed right. He knew about the money, too.

"She's not my girlfriend."

"Whatever, Romeo. Is she here?"

I didn't need to check the bench to be sure she wasn't here, and wouldn't be, until next August. I gave up attempting to find her any day other than August 8, and that day was still very far off. "No, I haven't seen anyone."

"Then why are *we* here?"

I needed to know more about her. I need to know *something* about her. Lately she seemed to occupy nearly all my waking thoughts, and I figured it was because I had so many questions. If I answered those questions, if I figured out who she was, maybe I could get past this. Maybe I wouldn't want to see her so bad. Maybe I wouldn't bother to go to the bench next August at all. "Her name is Stella Nettleton. I want to check all the headstones in here and see if I can figure out who she visits every month."

Dunk's mouth was open slightly, and his bushy eyebrows seemed to touch. "That may be the stupidest idea I've ever heard. How many stiffs do you think are buried here?" His face went red, then, "I mean, besides your mom and pop, because they're not stiffs, they're, I mean were, I mean—"

"We need to watch for any headstones dated August 8, too," I interrupted. "Just in case whoever she visits didn't have the same last name."

He nodded toward the small white building next to the adjacent parking lot. "Isn't there a log or something in the office? That seems much easier than running around Satan's waiting room, checking names. Not that your parents would be...oh heck, this is awkward. Can't we just go play ball or something? I saw some kids at Carnegie Park. Justin was there. He'll let us play."

"I can do this myself, if you don't want to."

Dunk sighed. "No, if this is how you want to spend your night off, I'll help. We should start at the office, though."

"I tried that a few weeks ago. They didn't have any records for people named Nettleton, and I found three people who died on August 8, two others who were born on that day." I pulled a piece of paper from my pocket and showed it to Dunk. "All five of these are on the far end of the cemetery, the newer part. I tracked them down yesterday. The bench is in the oldest portion of this place, nowhere near these. The man at the office said a fire destroyed all the records prior to 1926, all the old stuff, so the only way to be sure there is nobody else is to check all the gravestones, one by one."

Dunk scratched at the side of his head. "How many are there?"

"One hundred and twenty-four thousand."

The color drained from his face. "You know that's impossible, right? You realize how long that would take? Like a thousand years. Maybe longer. Maybe a lot longer."

"I don't think we have to check them all. Whoever she visits must be near that bench. We start at the graves near there and branch out until we find what we're looking for."

For the next three hours, we did exactly that, moving from stone to stone, row to row. We found nothing.

August 8, 1987

Eleven Years Old

Log 08/08/1987—

Subject "D" restless.

Audio/video recording.

"Is there anybody there?"

"What do we do? Should we answer him?"

"Naw, he'll pipe down in a few minutes. Just ignore him."

"I had a bad dream. Can you turn on the lights?"

"Should we do it?"

"I'm not gonna do it—he's on a schedule. Ignore him. It's your move."

"I can't concentrate with the kid jabbering in there. He creeps me out."

"I've got checkmate in two more moves anyway."

"No you don't, not after I take your...oh, shit. I'm an idiot."

"Yep."

"Your name's Carl, right? If you can't turn on the lights, can you at least talk to me until I fall back asleep, Carl?"

"Fuck! How does he know my name?"

"Calm down."

"Screw you."

"I don't want to hear my name coming out of his mouth. Not now, not ever."

"He can't hurt you, not with the audio delay."

"Can't we just switch him off? Mute him?"

"Then it won't record. Something important gets missed, and we're both looking for new employment."

"You'd be all over that switch if he said your name."

"Well, let's just hope he fixates on you, then."

"Has he ever been outside his box?"

"Not since I've been here."

"When did you start? '81?"

"Fall of 1980."

"That's insane. That room can't be more than ten by ten."

"He's got a window."

"Overlooking what? The parking lot?"

"I heard he was out when they first brought him in, but that didn't last long. One other time two years ago. The kid's got a nasty temper."

"Do you have any kids, Carl?" David said.

"Christ! Shut him up."

"Do you want to play again?"

"Naw. I can't focus."

"Do you ignore your own kids, too, Carl? You really shouldn't."

"Fuck me."

"I heard his dad did that to him, to his face."

"I heard that, too."

"Something snapped then, in his head. He's not right."

Carl let out a nervous chuckle. "He's nowhere near right. That's why they keep him in a box."

"Still, just a kid, though."

"What does that mean? You want to talk to him? Cheer him up?"

"Hell no."

Carl pressed the microphone button. "Would you like Warren here to read you a bedtime story?"

Warren slapped his hand off the button. "What the fuck? Why'd you tell him my name?"

"He knows mine, only seems fair."

"You're an asshole."

The room fell silent, then—

"I think I'd like that. Not Warren, though. How about you read me whatever you read your kids, Carl? What's their favorite story?"

"Fucking little creep. That delay is weird. Reminds me of when Houston used to talk to the astronauts."

"Yeah, like a satellite delay on the news."

"Too fucking weird, all of it."

"Want to play again?"

"Might as well. Change the tape first. It's almost out."

—Charter Observation Team – 309

1

"Hi, Dad." Using the nail of my finger to get into the deeper crevices, I scraped the moss from the lettering on his gravestone. "Auntie Jo had to work, so I figured I'd start with you."

I fished Auntie Jo's cigarette butts from Daddy's vase and placed three purple asters in their place. Someone planted a bunch of them at the back of our building at the start of summer, and they had taken over a large corner of the small yard. "She'll probably be by later, though, so be warned, I guess."

Dunk and I spent the better part of the last eight months combing the cemetery and found not one match to our criteria other than the five names I had gotten from the caretaker at the office. Back in January, I took those five names to Brentwood Library. If you're a kid, and you want help fast, tell a librarian you're working on a school project. We only found information on one of the names—Darnell Jacobs—he died on August 8, 1802. Apparently he was an early settler in this area and built one of the first houses on Brownsville Road. He owned a small lumber company. Beyond that, we found nothing. It didn't matter. I didn't know what I was looking for, anyway. I guess I thought something would jump out at me.

"I don't know if I want to go up there," I said softly. "Part of me does. Part of me *really* does. I want to see Stella. I know you'd probably make fun of me for that because she's a girl and Mommy would probably tell me to go because she *is* a girl, but what if Stella isn't there? What if only the old woman is there, Ms. Oliver? I don't ever want to see her again. But if Stella is there today, I *have* to go. I wish you could tell me what to do. I wish you were still here."

I felt the tears coming on and forced them back. Daddy would probably tell me to march right up the hill and right past Ms. Oliver, and at that moment, I knew that was what I would do, what I *should* do, as if he had spoken the words aloud.

I spent the next thirty minutes talking to both Mommy and Daddy, and when the alarm on my watch went off at 6 p.m. I stood, scooped up my Walkman and the remaining flowers, and started up the hill.

Stella was on the bench.

2

"More coffee?"

Preacher glanced down at the mug beside him on the counter, then smiled up at Josephine Gargery. "Please."

She eyed his hands. "What's with the gloves? Isn't it a little warm out for winter wear?"

Preacher looked down at his hands, flexing his fingers beneath the black leather. He smiled at her. "Circulation problems. My hands get cold easily."

"Huh. Maybe you should move to Florida. I hear the sun down there is like magic."

Gargery had lost weight since the last time he saw her, and she had been thin then. Now, she wore her uniform like a hanger with feet. Her skin was pale, nearly translucent. The mascara and eyeliner only accentuated the depth to which her eyes had sunken with time, the rouge on her checks a pink streak that looked anything but natural. The white of her eyes was no longer the white of her eyes, but a dull yellow that matched the cigarette stains on her teeth. Simply looking at her made Preacher feel ill, yet he retained his smile as he scooped up another bite of country-fried chicken. "You must live here. I see you whenever I come in."

She filled his mug and returned the carafe back to the warming plate on the counter behind her. Glancing back toward the opening to the kitchen, she called out over her shoulder. "Hey, Elden, this guy says you work me like a dog and I should get at least two paid days off per week!"

The large beast of a man in the kitchen waved a spatula at her through a smoke-filled haze. "He obviously hasn't caught you sleeping in the storage room or sneaking out for cigarettes every ten minutes when you're supposed to be on the floor. Last I checked, chatting up the customers was not in the job description, either. Order up—" his meaty hand slapped a bell at the window, and he set a plate of steak and eggs on the sill.

Preacher learned this man was Elden Krendal, owner of this fine eatery for nearly twenty-three years. He had graced this planet for a total of sixty years and weighed in at a horrendous three-hundred and twelve pounds. His blood pressure routinely topped 140 over 110, yet that was the least of his doctor's concerns—according to his files, that honor fell on Krendal's cholesterol. His total level rested comfortably around 310, while his triglycerides rang in at 503 at his latest checkup. Of course, Mr. Krendal probably wasn't aware of any of this, considering his hearing was shot and he refused to wear a hearing aid. Most likely, he just nodded as the doctor rattled off the various things competing to kill him and no doubt recommended immediate correction, possibly even hospitalization. How this man was alive at all was a medical mystery.

Gargery retrieved the plate from the window and set it before an elderly man about a dozen stools away on the opposite end of the counter, then returned. "You don't look familiar. I know all our regulars."

"Oh, I'm hardly a regular. I try to make it in here when I pass through town. Some of the best cooking in the city."

Gargery chuckled. "You must be eating in all the wrong places."

Preacher tried not to look at her hands, yet his eyes were drawn to the cigarette stains on her fingertips. He had seen her wash her hands at least three times in the past hour. How ingrained does a filth have to be to withstand the rigors of routine scrubbing? He smiled back at her. "That boy I see in here sometimes, is that your son?"

"Jack? Naw, nephew. My sister's kid."

"It's good to see a boy take work seriously at such a young age. Instills good, strong values."

"It keeps him off the street and out of trouble, is what it does. Around here, there is plenty of trouble to get into."

"Ain't that the truth."

"He's not working today?"

She shook her head. "Nope, not today."

"I grew up on a farm in Illinois, corn mostly, a couple of dairy cows, a few chickens. My parents had me out there working from the time I could walk. I hated them for it back then, all my friends always off playing when I had chores. But as I got older, I realized that childhood caused me to work just a little harder than those around me, a little longer, a little smarter. I thank them for it every chance I get."

This was a lie, of course. Preacher didn't know his parents and never had. His folks left him at a fire station in Oklahoma only a few hours after his birth. His loving parents packed him into a cardboard box and covered his naked little body in newspaper, then simply left him on the door stoop like discarded trash. No note, no food, no nothing. This was in the fall, when the temperature routinely dropped down into the fifties at night. By the time anyone found him, he had the makings of a good cold, which later turned into full-on pneumonia and spent the next week recovering in a hospital. From there, he found his way to the Sisters of Mercy Orphanage in Lawton, where he would spend the first eight years of his life fighting with other unwanted children for the few scraps of food split among them as potential parents paraded through in search of a good find, not unlike bargain shoppers at a yard sale. Although most babies have little trouble finding a home, the singular gift his parents left him with was a congenital heart defect, and that was more than enough to ensure these baby shoppers walked right on by without giving him so much as a second glance. The nuns at Sisters of Mercy were not shy about reminding him that such a condition typically resulted from uncontrolled diabetes, alcohol or drug abuse, or exposure to industrial chemicals during pregnancy. Apparently, his mother's dislike of him began months before his birth. No doubt his father was standing close by, with a supply of whatever she took in the months following his conception.

If Preacher were to find his parents, he planned to take them to a location as isolated as the farm in his fictitious childhood home, string them both up, and persuade them to reveal their sordid past. Once he learned what his mother had been on, he would give them a healthy dose until they were no longer of this world. If that didn't work, he'd leave them both to rot there, right after putting holes in both their hearts much like his own. One big, happy family.

Gargery tilted her head. "You do look a little familiar, but I can't quite place you."

"I've got one of those faces, not very memorable, I'm afraid." This *was* true, and it suited him just fine. Preacher preferred to blend.

"What do you do for a living?"

"Nothing exciting. I transport vehicles. Someone moves across country and needs their car or truck to follow them, I drive it."

"Aren't there trucks for that?"

Preacher nodded. "Trains, too, but both options are on the pricy side compared to what I charge. I usually come in about 10 percent cheaper. That's just enough to keep me employed."

"That's interesting. I bet you get to see a lot of the country."

"Oh yeah, I've seen every inch of this place several times over. A couple places more times than I'd like, a few others not enough. Pittsburgh here tends to be in the middle of many of my routes, so I pass through on occasion."

"And stop here."

"And stop here," Preacher agreed.

Again, this was all a lie. Preacher's particular line of work wasn't meant for discussion among friends or waitresses in a diner. If he had to choose a new career, though, transporting vehicles was high on the list. He preferred a nomadic lifestyle—he'd never be able to work in the kind of place where he had regular hours or a boss, some specimen of inferior intellect, telling him what to do and not to do.

The bell at the window dinged. "This is what I mean," Krendal said in a voice much louder than necessary. "Chatting up the customers while table three needs refills on water. Come on, Jo." His hearing may be shot, but his eyesight was in working order.

Preacher glanced down at his watch—twelve past six. "I'll take that check whenever you're ready. I'm afraid I let the time get away from me."

Gargery fished his bill from a pocket in the front of her uniform and slipped it over to him. "I guess we'll see you next time, then. Take care of yourself."

"You too," Preacher said, glancing down at the bill—six dollars and twenty-three cents. He pulled a twenty from his wallet and placed it under his empty coffee cup with the check. This was far more than his usual 20 percent tip, but he felt it was justified to give her a little more, give her something for the other thing he was about to take.

3

I stopped at the edge of the last mausoleum and found myself simply watching her, this girl who I could not get out of my thoughts. Although she wore a white ruffled blouse and black skirt, identical to the previous two times I saw her, they couldn't be the same articles of clothing. She was taller now. I had grown, too, but she had grown a little more, and I imagined if she stood beside me, she would be my height or maybe an inch or two taller. The wind caught her long brown hair, and I watched as she ran one of her hands through the curly locks, tucking it back behind her ear. Her eyes never left the paperback book in her delicate hands. Although it was cooler today than our previous encounters, she wore no gloves. I didn't have to see the cover of the book to know it was the same copy of *Great Expectations* she had been reading the first few times we met.

She must have felt my eyes on her. She looked up from the book and toward me. There was the hint of a smile, then it was gone, as if she didn't want me to see it.

My palms were sweaty. I wiped them on my jeans, juggling the flowers between them. I left the safety of my hiding place.

Stella's eyes narrowed when she saw the flowers. "Are those for me?"

I sat beside her and looked down at the flowers. "For my parents...these are left over. You can have them, if you want."

"I don't believe a boy has ever given me leftover flowers before, although I think these are called asters."

"Yeah, asters." I handed them to her. I expected her to take them, but she didn't—her hands remained in her lap, wrapped around her book. Instead, she leaned in and smelled them, closing her eyes as she drew in the scent. "These are chamomile. They make a wonderful tea."

When she leaned back, leaving the flowers in my outstretched hand, I awkwardly set them down on the bench between us.

Ms. Oliver stood down the road from us, in front of the first of three white SUVs, her hands in the pockets of her long, white coat, her gaze fixed on me. There was a mad gleam to those eyes, a hatred and burning anger strong enough to reach across this distance and twist a nail in the base of my spine.

I shivered.

I counted nine others standing around the SUVs. Five women and four men. All wearing long, white coats identical to the old woman, all watching Stella and me closely. I didn't have to see the guns to know they were there. "They came last year, without you."

Stella let out a deep sigh. "I've spoken to Ms. Oliver about that. So strong-willed, that one. She knew I forbade it, yet she took it upon herself to come here anyway, to speak to you, the nerve! She will not do such a thing again, I've seen to it."

Ms. Oliver shuffled her feet, as if she heard what Stella said. She was too far away, though.

"Why would they listen to you? You're just a kid."

She *did* smile at this. "I am, aren't I? This is why I like you, John Edward Jack Thatch. You state the obvious, yet it comes out of your mouth like the most profound of thoughts."

"She said some nasty things to me. Did she tell you that?"

"She can sometimes be a caring, beautiful woman, and at others I've found her behavior toward you downright despicable, and I've spoken to her about it. She's very protective of me, always has been, far more so than the others."

"Where were you? Last year, I mean."

It was Stella who looked at the old woman this time. Her fingers flicked unconsciously through the pages of her book. "I was somewhere other than here."

"Why don't I see you any other time during the year?"

"Because you see me today."

"Who are you visiting?"

"I'm visiting you."

"That's not what I mean." I groaned. "You don't answer any of my questions."

"Maybe you should stop asking questions."

"Maybe I should just leave."

"Do you want to leave?"

I let out another defeated breath. "No."

She turned toward me. The tops of her knees poked out from under her skirt.

My face flushed. I looked away.

This seemed to amuse her. "Why is it you want to see me? Why do you come back year after year, and sometimes in between, in search of me? A girl you met a handful of times? At most, we've probably shared a collective hour together, yet I'd be willing to stake you have spent countless other hours lost in thoughts about me, obsessing even. The mere sight of my knee sets your heart fluttering. An innocent knee. What of a foot, or heaven forbid, a bit of my thigh?" She lowered her voice, her words but a whisper. "What if I let you kiss me, Jack? What would that simple act do to you?"

She leaned toward me slowly, she leaned so close I could feel her breath on my cheek.

"Stella."

This was Ms. Oliver. She said the girl's name softly, but there was a grit to it, a portent of sorts, a warning. Stella's eyes narrowed, and she gave the woman a hateful look, then washed it away with a smile before leaning back to her side of the bench, brushing her long hair back over her shoulder.

My breath had caught in my throat, and I forced it to release, drew in another. I changed the subject. "Why are you leaving money for me?"

Stella laughed, and it was a mix of the sweetest sound I had ever heard and the most maddening. I didn't care. As long as she let me hear it, I just didn't care. I also knew it wasn't the question that made her laugh, but my clumsy attempt to get her to talk about something else, anything else.

"I have no money, Jack. How could I possibly leave money for you? What purpose would that serve?"

"The envelopes all said *Pip* on them, like in your book. I know they came from you."

"If you're so certain, why are you asking the question?"

"I want to hear it from you. I want you to explain why."

"Sounds like you want many things, Mr. Thatch. What do I get in return for addressing one or more of these wants?"

"If you don't tell me, I'm gonna stop coming."

"We both know that's not true."

"Auntie Jo and I do just fine. We don't need your help. We don't want it."

"If you don't want this money someone is leaving for you, then simply give it away. Give it to someone who does. I don't imagine a willing recipient would be hard to find. If you don't wish to take the time out of your busy little life to do that, just burn it. Rid yourself of this gruesome burden of wealth with the flick of a match. I don't care. None of this nonsense matters in the slightest to me."

"If you're not leaving the money, then who?"

Stella shrugged. "I don't follow the company you keep."

In the distance, one of the SUVs roared to life. This was followed by a second. I watched as the people in long, white coats climbed into the vehicles, all but Ms. Oliver. She remained still.

"I'm afraid it's time for me to take leave."

"Wait!" I didn't mean for the word to come out as loud as it did, with such a desperate edge to it. I reached over, meaning to grasp her arm, and she pulled away. She slid to the far end of the bench against the metal rail, her face turning a ghostly white. Her eyes darted from me to Oliver, then back again, and she seemed to regret the harshness of her movement. All at once, the stiffness left her, her color returned, and she smiled. There was something behind that smile, though, something I had yet to see, and even at this moment there was only a glimpse of it—fear.

She slid back toward me, back to the spot she had been. "You wish me to stay?"

"Yes."

The corner of her mouth turned up slightly. "Good."

She slid off the bench and started toward Ms. Oliver, toward the closest SUV. The old woman pointed back at the bench. "Don't forget your flowers, Ms. Nettleton."

"I don't want them."

"A boy gives you flowers, and you mustn't ever leave them behind. They are to be received and cherished. The giving of life is precious and should never be taken for granted," Ms. Oliver replied. "Pick them up."

"I don't want to."

"Pick them up, Stella."

Stella stood there for the longest time, glaring at Ms. Oliver. Ms. Oliver's gaze did not falter. A silent conversation passed between them. Ms. Oliver raised a hand and pointed back at the bench. "Pick them up."

Stella turned then and returned to the bench, her large brown eyes on mine as she reached for the asters beside me. Her fingers took hold of the bouquet, wrapping around the stems, and she picked them up and brought them to her side. As she turned, as she started back toward the SUV, toward the watchful eyes of Ms. Oliver, the white petals of the asters shriveled and curled in her hand, the yellow centers turned brown, the stems grew black. By the time Stella was halfway to the SUV, the flowers wilted and drooped, then dried to crumbling dust. The remains disappeared on the wind as Ms. Oliver opened the back door and ushered her inside. Not once did Stella look back at me.

They were gone a minute later.

I sat there, perfectly still, unsure of what I had just seen.

I didn't hear the man come up from behind me.

A strong arm wrapped around my neck.

"The pressure you feel at the small of your back is a rather sharp knife. I strongly suggest you don't struggle."

The arm around my neck loosened only long enough for the hand at the end of it to come to my mouth and nose, a cloth. I smelled something sweet.

In the moment before I lost consciousness, my eyes drifted to the far corner of the bench, to the place Stella sat only minutes earlier, to the fresh words carved in the metal.

Help me

4

The dream.

Daddy fastened me into my car seat.

Chocolate milk.

Outside Auntie Jo's apartment.

Daddy opened my door.

Daddy removed something from the seat beside me, gave it to Auntie Jo.

Something.

Unknown something.

Driving again.

White SUV in our path.

White SUV blocking the road.

Awful squeal of tires.

I woke in an alley.

When my eyes first opened, I didn't know where I was.

My head ached. A throbbing pain behind both eyes wrapped around to the sides like a vice squeezing at my temples. I squinted at the dull, orange light seeping in from above. The sun was gone, the light came from a high-pressure sodium streetlight mounted to the brick wall of the building at my back. The light shown down toward the back corner, illuminating a Dumpster, some wooden crates, and discarded boxes. The light hummed like a thousand bees trapped within the glow.

I tried to stand, fell back down, my legs wobbly.

Something in my hand.

I brought my closed fist into the light and forced my fingers to uncoil, my body working on a delay. A small piece of paper sat at the center of my palm, folded into a tiny square.

I shook my head in an attempt to fight off the sleepiness and immediately regretted it, the headache intensifying.

With my free hand, I unfolded the paper.

In neat script, five words:

Your little girlfriend did this.

I had been in the cemetery with Stella. She left around seven.

Glancing up into the sky, between the buildings, there was nothing but black. This time of year, the sun set around 8:30 p.m. I had been out for at least an hour and a half, maybe more.

I remembered the voice at my ear then, the man's voice from behind me, *The pressure you feel at the small of your back is a rather sharp knife. I strongly suggest you don't struggle.*

This time, I did stand up. I shot to my feet and turned in both directions, looking first up, then down the opposite direction. I was alone.

The rest came back to me, fuzzy images slowly coming into focus. The cloth at my mouth, the world quickly fading away, the words carved into the bench—

Help me

Had I imagined that?

I looked back down at the note in my hand.

Your little girlfriend did this.

That's when I saw the foot.

I hadn't noticed it at first because it was tucked around the other side of the Dumpster, only the tip of a black loafer visible, just the toe.

Run, Jack.

My mind screamed at me.

Get out of here.

Instead, I crept toward that shoe. I shuffled slowly closer, deeper into the alley, toward the Dumpster.

I suppose I expected to find a bum, some drunk sleeping it off in this quiet spot rocked to bed by the sound of the sodium streetlight buzzing above as he found blissful slumber.

The body looked burned.

The skin all dry and black.

The hair on the top of the man's head was a wiry white, brittle. Clumps had fallen off around his head, these tufts of hair twisted in the light breeze stirring the ground, fluttering on the filthy blacktop.

His eyes were open, what was left of them. Where his eyes should have been there were only dry, yellowish-white orbs sunken into his skull. He stared up at me blankly, his mouth slightly agape.

He looked old.

He looked older than any man I had ever seen. A thousand-year-old mummy missing his bandages.

The body looked burned, but oddly his clothing did not. He wore blue denim jeans, a Styx tee-shirt, and a Pittsburgh Pirates fleece jacket. The clothes were filthy but not burned, not like him, as if he had been dressed after whatever horrible fate had found him. Soaked in gasoline, lit aflame, and dressed when the last bit of fire finally ran out of food.

Your little girlfriend did this.

He smelled horrible.

I tried not to think about that.

I knelt down beside him.

In my comics, when a superhero (or a Ninja Turtle) found a body, the first thing they did was try to figure out who it was.

He probably had a wallet.

I didn't want to touch him, I knew I shouldn't, but that didn't stop my fingers from reaching around to the back of his jeans in search of that wallet. It didn't stop me from turning him over just enough to pull the wallet out.

His driver's license said his name was Andy Flack from Bethel Park. He was thirty-three years old. He looked nothing like the photo.

Andy Flack coughed.

That's when I ran.

I bolted from the alley and out the mouth, nearly slipping on some wet cardboard boxes stacked near the opening. It wasn't until I was on the sidewalk that I realized I was across the street from Krendal's Diner, less than a block away from home.

I raced down that sidewalk, pushing past the people blocking my path, jumping over the cracks and holes. Inside our building, I made quick work of the stairs, fumbled with our lock, and pushed inside, slamming the door behind me. I dropped to the floor in a wheezing and huffing mess, trying to draw in enough air. When I realized I had dropped the wallet, the note too, the real panic set in.

5

"Dude, that's fucked up. You need to call the police," Dunk said, his voice muffled through the telephone receiver. His dad fell asleep watching TV, and he didn't want to wake him.

Although our phone was in the kitchen, the cord was about a mile long, and I had dragged it to the window so I could see what was going on. "They're already there. There are four cop cars blocking the street, and they sealed off the alley with orange cones and yellow tape. There must be a hundred cops down there. An ambulance, too."

"Dude. I'll be right there," Dunk said before hanging up.

Five minutes later, he stood at the window with me. "We should go up on the roof."

"I'm not allowed on the roof. Besides, they'll see us."

"They can see us here."

"Not with all the lights off."

"I saw you."

"Oh no, really?"

Dunk smiled. "Don't worry, all your neighbors are at their windows, too. This is way better than *L.A. Law*. I can't believe you dropped that stuff. You might as well have written your name on the wall right under *Arrest Me*. You are so dead."

"Not helping."

"If I were you, I'd drop to the floor right now and start doing push-ups, lifting weights, too. You need to bulk up. A scrawny little kid like you won't last the night in the big house."

"Still not helping."

"I should have swiped my dad's binoculars. He's got this sweet pair he brought back from the war. I forget what kind, starts with an *S*. You can see for miles with those things."

I let out a breath. "He was alive. I don't know how, but he was alive."

"Well, unless the paramedics are back there starting up a poker game with him, I don't think he is now. How long has it been since they got here? Ten minutes?"

"Twenty-three."

"He's a stiff, all right."

When the phone rang, I nearly fell out the window.

Dunk's eyes went wide. "That's the cops. They probably want to give you a chance to come out peacefully before they storm the building."

"I don't think they'd call first."

I didn't want to leave the window, but I did anyway. I answered the call on the third ring. Auntie Jo.

"Are you seeing this?"

"Yeah. Dunk is here. We're watching out the window."

"Can you tell what's going on?"

"No," I lied.

"We're packed right now. The police keep coming in for coffee. We got a bunch of reporters here, too. One of the detectives told Krendal none of us can leave until they speak to each of us. It might be a few more hours. Krendal said if we're stuck here, might as well stay open and make some money. We haven't had an empty table in an hour, and there's a line at the door. One reporter just gave me a twenty to seat him at the window. Sounds like someone was murdered across the street in that alley next to True Value."

"A murder, really?" I repeated softly.

Dunk turned, mouthed the words, "Who is it?"

"Auntie Jo," I said.

"What?" Auntie Jo said.

"Not you, sorry. Dunk asked who was on the phone."

Krendal shouted something behind her. Auntie Jo's hand went over the receiver as she replied, then she was back. "Probably best you're not alone right now, so tell Dunk he can stay as long as he wants. I don't want you leaving the apartment. And don't answer the door. If someone comes to the door, you call me here and I'll come home. If you can't reach me, you call 911. You hear me?"

"Yes, Auntie Jo."

"Gotta go."

She hung up, and I replaced the receiver.

Dunk was back at the window. "They're coming out!"

I ran back over and dropped down next to him.

The two paramedics were standing at either end of a stretcher. On that stretcher was a large plastic bag. It looked like an oversize Hefty trash bag.

"Whoa," Dunk said softly. "There's a body in there."

"Andy Flack is in there."

They lifted the stretcher over the curb and wheeled it to the awaiting ambulance. At the back, they collapsed the stretcher's frame and lifted it inside. Five minutes later, one of the cop cars backed out of the way and the ambulance skirted past. We watched it disappear down Brownsville with red and blue lights flashing on top. No siren, though.

The police were there for three more hours.

Auntie Jo didn't get home until nearly two in the morning.

Dunk crashed in a sleeping bag on my floor.

I didn't sleep a wink.

We checked the newspaper in the morning, and there was no mention of a body found in the alley. Nothing appeared until the following day.

BODY FOUND IN BRENTWOOD ALLEY –
POLICE BAFFLED

PITTSBURGH, PA – August 10, 1987: A horribly disfigured body was found in the late hours of Saturday in the alley located at 1825 Brownsville Road between True Value Hardware and Carmine's Beer and Wine. The body, a male, has been identified as thirty-three-year-old Andrew Olin Flack of Bethel Park, an employed coal miner with Nowicki Mining and Excavation. He was last seen leaving work at 5:30 p.m. Friday, after retrieving his paycheck from the Nowicki offices located in West Mifflin. "He seemed in good spirits, ready for the weekend," Gwenn Easler, Nowicki office manager said. "He told me he had nothing major planned and hoped to spend the next few days catching his breath and relaxing. He pulled two doubles this week and was beat. I can't believe he's gone. He was such a nice guy." As of today, where he went next is unknown. Although he banks at First Bank of Mifflin, he did not cash his paycheck, nor did he return to his home located at 83 Monroe Road in Bethel Park. "At first glance, he appears horribly burned," a representative from the Medical Examiner's Office said. "But this is something else. The charred condition of the skin and exposed tissue is not congruent with the flash burn created by sudden exposure to flames or heat, nor does it match a slower incendiary situation such as a house fire or vehicle fire. I was unable to find a trace of any type of accelerant, although we have not ruled out use of an accelerant at this time. He was clearly redressed. His clothing has no burn marks whatsoever." One of the officers on scene was overheard discussing the possibility of spontaneous combustion with a secondary officer.

Neither was willing to go on the record. Local law enforcement, led by veteran homicide detective Faustino Brier, spent much of the day yesterday at the mine where Flack worked. Although Brier would not discuss the case, citing it as an open investigation, it appears PPD feels this may be a work-related accident. If Flack was, in fact, injured (or killed) in a mining accident in West Mifflin, why was his clothing changed? Who changed it? Why was his body moved to an alley nearly four miles away? If Flack was somehow burned in that alley, why were no signs of an accelerant found? All questions most likely on Detective Brier's mind today.

The alley itself does not see much foot traffic and is used primarily for waste disposal by the surrounding businesses. Because of the relative isolation, it is a frequent resting place for the local homeless. Flack was discovered by forty-three year-old Orville Clemens, who planned to wait out the night in the quiet spot, unable to find a bed at a local shelter. "I thought he was just sleeping at first, then I got closer and realized something was wrong," he said. He then used the payphone across the street to call 911, and authorities arrived shortly after.

UPDATE – We have since learned that an investigation of the Flack residence revealed a hidden stash of child pornography—magazines, images, and photographs as well as undergarments believed to belong to children, both male and female. Whether or not this paraphernalia is related to Flack's death is unclear. Detective Brier was unavailable for comment.

"He was a piddler-diddler?" Dunk said, reading the newspaper from the seat across from me. We were at my booth at Krendal's. The breakfast rush was dying down. Auntie Jo was still at home, sleeping. She didn't start until lunch. I was supposed to help later.

"They didn't say anything about the note."

"That's good, right? Maybe nobody found it. The wind might have picked it up and blown it halfway to Philly."

"They'll pull fingerprints from his wallet, that's for sure." I blew out a breath. "Why didn't I put it back in his pocket? I'm an idiot."

"You didn't put his wallet back in his pocket because he was turning full-on zombie right in front of you, and you had to save yourself," Dunk said. "When the cops come for you, you just tell them you found the body, thought he was dead, pulled his wallet to figure out who he was so you could tell police when you called like the good Sumerian you are."

"Good *Samaritan*. Sumeria is an ancient civilization in Mesopotamia."

"Whatever, Einstein."

"I didn't call the police, either. I ran. And he was alive when I ran."

"You don't tell them that part, dummy, only what I said. If they try to get more out of you, just start crying, that's what I'd do. You're a kid. Nobody wants to deal with a crying kid, play it up. We can only play the kid angle for a few more years, might as well use it." Dunk sucked the last bit of his strawberry shake up through the straw with a loud slurp.

I glanced at the alley, visible across the street—a dark maw between the two adjoining buildings. "They took the tape down."

Dunk slid his empty milkshake glass forward. "Yesterday, around lunchtime."

"I can't believe you sat out there all day."

"There were about a dozen of us. I blended, needed to do recon. You couldn't do it, being an accessory to the crime and all. Gotta stay on the down low, live in the underground. Oh, I almost forget, we gotta get you a fake ID for when you run. What's your cash situation like? Did you get another envelope?"

"Yeah, another five hundred. It was sitting on my bed, like all the others."

"Geez, how much is that now?"

"Sixty-five hundred. Thirteen envelopes all together."

"Sixty-five hundred *dollars?*"

"Shhh!" I whispered, glancing at the people eating around us. Nobody heard him, though.

"Sorry. But geez, Thatch, what are you going to do with all that money? You really could buy a car and run away somewhere. Maybe buy a house in Florida or something. On the water with a boat, so you can go to Cuba if that Detective Brier catches up with you. Or maybe London."

The truth was, I had no idea what I would do with the money. I couldn't spend it. If I spent the money, even a little bit, I had to explain where it came from. Even giving money to Auntie Jo had been a problem. Luckily, we'd kept busy enough at the diner to keep our heads above water so I didn't have to do that again. I really wanted to buy a new bike. I had a BMX Skyway with a silver frame and blue accents. It had been a great bike…ten years ago when it was manufactured. Now, though, the frame was covered in rust, the silver had flaked off in most parts, and there were so many holes in the seat I had taken an old Jackson Browne tee-shirt, wrapped it over the original seat, and covered the whole mess in duct tape. I worked four nights per week at Krendal's, three hours each night, at minimum wage. That brought in a whopping thirty-nine dollars per week under the table. Buying a new bike was not an option. "It's rainy day money," I finally answered. "I gotta just keep it safe for now. I'll figure out something."

"You're about to go to the big house for murder. I think it's time to open the umbrella. I hope you at least stashed it someplace safe. Harwood in 107 got broken into just last week. Someone took their stereo and TV, trashed the place, too. Pulled everything out of every drawer and cabinet, sliced up the mattresses—the whole place got wrecked. They even dumped out his cat's litter box. Who does that? Maybe you should move the cash to someplace safer, or spread it around a little bit so if someone does break in, they don't get all of it."

Dunk was right about that. I had spent more nights than I could count worrying about it. A few months back, I had taken a knife to the pages of my hardcover copy of *The Iliad*, a monstrously large book I never had any intention of reading again. I hollowed out the center and placed the money inside, then I put the book in a box at the bottom of my closet, a box filled with a dozen other books. Three more boxes of books rested on top of that one. It was hidden pretty good, but no place was good enough. This was better than my sock drawer, though. The money spent a good chunk of last year there, too.

"Somebody's back," Dunk said softly. He had pulled his milkshake glass close again and pretended to drink while eyeing the alley sidelong. "Looks like a detective."

The man did look like a detective. He wore a rumpled dark gray suit with a red tie. Probably around Auntie Jo's age, late thirties or early forties. His hair was brown, short on the sides and a little longer on top. The wind picked it up and ruffled it, but he didn't seem to care. "What's he doing?"

"Just standing there, staring."

"Is he alone?"

"I think so. He was there yesterday, too. I recognize him. He's probably the detective they mentioned in the paper."

"Maybe." I glanced back down at the newspaper between us and located his name. "Faustino Brier."

"What kind of name is Faustino?" Dunk asked. "Doesn't even make for a good nickname. Tino, maybe?"

"Too much like Dino from the Flintstones. Maybe Faust, but I don't think he'd like that too much."

"Why?"

"Faust was an old German guy who made a deal with the devil. He gave up his soul in exchange for unlimited knowledge and lots of possessions," I explained. My English teacher, Mrs. Orgler, gave me the book to read over the summer. It only took me a week, then I read it a second time. I loved anything with magic.

"I am *so* going to do that when I turn sixteen and need a car," Dunk said.

"It doesn't end well for Faust. Turns out you need your soul much more than you need stuff."

"A cherry red Mustang, '66 or '67, with a rag top and eight cylinders under the hood," Dunk said. "Think I can get a million dollars and a cool house, too? I need a garage for the car and money for gas."

"For your soul, I think you'd be lucky to get a Ford Pinto with holes in the floor pan and maybe a stack of food stamps to hold you through the winter. Even the devil is a business man. He knows a bargain when he sees it."

"It doesn't have to be a *nice* Mustang. I can fix it up. I've got skills."

I sat up a little in my seat, trying to get a better view across the street. "Where'd he go? I don't see him." A large white delivery truck with Budweiser stenciled on the side in large, flowing letters had pulled up and double-parked on Brownsville in front of Carmine's. I couldn't see past it.

"I got the same view you do—Joe Beer Guy is in the way. Maybe we should go out there."

"No way."

Five minutes later, the beer truck pulled away. There was no sign of the detective. "Maybe he went in the alley. His car is still out there."

"Do all cops drive Crown Vics?" I asked.

"If the devil won't give me a Mustang, I'd settle for a Crown Vic. I'm not picky. As long as it has one of the cool floodlights built into the driver's side."

We were both staring out the window. Neither of us saw the detective push through the door and step into the diner.

Dunk spotted him first, then kicked me under the table.

Detective Faustino Brier stood just inside the door at the front of the diner, his gaze slowly traveling from right to left, studying the interior and the faces.

"Shit," Dunk whispered. "Get under the table or something."

"I'm not getting under the table. That will draw him over here for sure. He doesn't know who I am. Just be cool, relax."

"Right," Dunk said, leaning back in the booth with both hands on the table, his fingers twisted together.

"Not that relaxed."

"Right again." He sat up straight and fumbled with his empty milkshake glass, his eyes fixed on the formica table top as if he were counting each speck of color for a homework assignment.

"Sit anywhere!" Krendal called out from the kitchen. "Someone will be with you in a second. Lurline—customer!"

The detective ran his hand through his hair in an attempt to tame it, but it bounced right back up. He took a seat at the counter, unfastening the buttons on his suit jacket. He pulled a notebook from his jacket pocket and began flipping through the pages.

I tugged out my wallet, retrieved a five-dollar bill, and placed it under my glass. "Let's go."

"I've been thinking about that," Dunk said softly without moving his lips. "I'll create a distraction, maybe knock one of these glasses off the table or a fork or something. Then while everyone is looking at me, you make a beeline for the door. If he chases after you, I'll trip him and try and buy you more time. He's big, but I can slow him down."

"Or, we can just get up and walk out like two normal people."

"We can't take risks with your freedom."

"Why are you talking like that?"

"Like what?"

"Without moving your lips."

"I don't want anyone to know what we're saying."

"Nobody cares what we're saying. On three, we just leave."

I counted, then stood and started for the exit. Dunk hesitated, then fell in behind me. I thought we'd make it. I could feel the outside air as my hand wrapped around the metal handle on the door and began to push through.

"Hey, kid—"

Both Dunk and I froze. People on the sidewalk circled around the half-open door and continued on their way. We could run. Maybe Dunk was right. Our heads swiveled in unison, looking back at the detective.

He had turned on his stool and was facing us. His eyes landed on Dunk. "You were out there yesterday, right? Across the street at the alley?"

"Yes, sir," Dunk said. His voice lost whatever bass it had picked up in the past year. He sounded ages younger.

"Exciting, right? Like on TV?"

"Yes, sir."

"What's your name?"

Without hesitation, "Duncan Napoleon Bellino. I live at 1822 Brownsville Road in apartment 207. I'm eleven years old, sir."

The detective raised an eyebrow, reached for his pad, and made a note. He leaned forward, his gaze fixed on Dunk. "What about the day before yesterday? Or the day before that? Did you see anything strange over there? Anybody out of the ordinary hanging out?"

"No, sir."

"When was the last time you were in that alley? Do you ever play back there?"

"No, sir."

"No, you don't play back there? Or no, you've never been in that alley?"

"Either, neither, I mean...I've never been in that alley. I don't play back there."

Lurline Waldrip pushed through the door at the kitchen and dropped a white towel on the counter. "Sorry about that, I was in the back. Need a menu?"

When the detective turned to face her, Dunk and I bolted through the door, retrieved our bikes from the lamp post in front of Krendal's, and raced up the hill. Neither of us looked back. I don't think I ever pedaled faster in my life.

We raced up the hill and over, then turned left on Maytide Street, rode two more blocks and made a quick right on Klaus, another left on Newburn, my bike chain squeaking with each hurried rotation. Over the next twenty minutes, we circled the entire neighborhood twice, certain the detective's Crown Vic would either come up from behind or appear somewhere up ahead. The car didn't, though. At the top of Gorman's Hill, I locked my brakes and skidded to a stop. Dunk slid in the gravel beside me and dropped his feet to the ground, huffing so loud I could barely hear my own labored breaths. Sweat dripped down my temple, and the back of my shirt was soaked. "We should get off the road," I finally managed.

"Where?"

I knew exactly where, though. I'd been avoiding the place since Saturday. "Come on."

It took us a little under ten more minutes to reach the cemetery. With the gate open, we continued riding inside, I didn't brake again until I reached the mausoleums, there I slowed and pulled between two of the larger ones: Polanski and Nowy. I climbed off my bike and leaned it against the wall and tried to catch my breath as Dunk maneuvered his bike next to mine.

"That guy is like a bloodhound," Dunk finally said between gasps. "He was all over me back there, did you see that?"

"I don't think he knows anything."

"Maybe I'm the one who needs to run. I might need to borrow some of your money."

"You didn't do anything."

"Lots of innocent men in prison, Thatch. I wouldn't be the first. Haven't you ever watched that old show on TBS, *The Fugitive*? It's about a doctor, Dr. Richard Kimble, he gets convicted of killing his wife even though he didn't do it. He goes to jail, escapes, and tries to find the real killer." Dunk paused, glancing back over his shoulder. "I can't go to jail, Thatch. I most definitely can't escape from jail, and I don't have time to search for the real killer even if I did. I've got shit to do in my life, and that ain't it."

I rolled my eyes. "The detective saw you in the crowd yesterday and asked a few questions. He's just fishing, that's all."

For the next ten minutes, we caught our breath, taking turns peering around the corner for a Crown Vic that never came.

"Is that it?" Dunk eventually asked, breaking the silence.

I followed his gaze to the black metal bench about ten yards away, empty, perched atop the hill. "Yeah."

"There's nobody there."

"It's not August 8. She only comes on August 8."

Dunk smacked my shoulder. "I get that, dummy. I mean there's nobody sitting there, we should take a look. You said she wrote something."

Help me

I wasn't sure I wanted to see those words again. Seeing them would make them real. Seeing her words would mean Stella pleaded for my help two days ago, and I had done nothing other than try to forget.

"Columbo's not coming," Dunk said, taking one last look for the detective's car. "Come on." He started for the bench.

We could see most of the cemetery from up here, and if the detective did come, we'd have time to run. Like I told Dunk, though, I didn't think he would. He could have stopped us back at the diner if he really wanted to.

I chased after Dunk.

The seat of the bench was still damp with morning dew. The cemetery was deserted, not another person in sight, unbelievably quiet, the shuffle of our feet deafening.

Dunk was hunched over the bench, studying the metal frame.

"Is this where it was?"

"Yeah, that was it."

"Somebody scratched it out."

Not only did someone scratch out the words, but they scratched away the black paint, leaving an oval of exposed silver metal where the words had once been. No trace of the words was left behind.

"It's got to be those people who were with her."

Dunk frowned. "You said they were like security guards, though, watching over her. Like she was in charge, not them."

"Maybe I was wrong."

I knelt down in the grass next to Dunk and studied the mark closer. "They didn't just scrape it away. They removed the paint, too. See how the metal's showing? How smooth? If someone scratched at it, you'd see tool marks, bits of paint left behind." I leaned in closer. "You can still smell paint remover."

"Somebody walks by, they're going to think we're praying to this bench."

"It's a cemetery. Everyone acts weird, and everyone leaves everyone else alone while they're acting weird. You talk to a rock here and you're emotional, you do the same thing at the park and you'll get arrested. There's an unwritten code or something," I said.

"I wonder why they didn't repaint it," Dunk said. "They went through all this trouble to hide her message. You'd think they'd go all the way and erase it completely, like it never happened."

"Maybe they wanted me to see what they did, make sure I understood they knew what I knew. If they got rid of it completely, I might have thought I imagined it. Everything happened so fast." I stood and looked at the trees behind the bench, the outcropping of forest at the cemetery's edge. "That guy came up from behind me and drugged me. I only got a glimpse of what she wrote."

"Forgive me for playing devil's advocate here, but how do you know she even wrote it? Maybe someone else did. It might not have anything to do with her," Dunk said.

"Then why make it disappear?"

"Maybe someone working for the cemetery cleaned it up, like whitewashing over graffiti on a wall."

"A caretaker or maintenance person would have painted it over. I don't think they'd take the time to scrape it away. They sure wouldn't leave it like this."

"Maybe he's not done. Maybe he needed black paint."

I knew, though. I was certain. "Stella wrote *help me*, and those people with her erased it." I circled around the bench, my eyes on the trees. "He came from back there, must have...come on."

The hill behind the bench sloped down into a thick tree line at the edge of the cemetery, giving way to wilderness a few steps in. When I reached the trees, I turned and looked back up at the bench. "He grabbed me right after they left, so he must have been watching us. I can see the bench from here, but the hill makes it impossible to see all the way back where the SUVs were parked."

"Maybe he heard them?" Dunk offered. "It's so quiet out here."

"Yeah, maybe."

"What did he say to you again?"

"He said, 'The pressure you feel at the small of your back is a rather sharp knife. I strongly suggest you don't struggle.' Then he pressed something over my mouth. It smelled sweet, then I was out."

"Probably chloroform, like we used on the mice in Mr. Lidden's science class."

"Exactly like that."

"Did you see a knife?"

I shook my head.

"So you don't know for sure he really had a knife?"

"I guess not."

We searched the trees, the ground, the bushes, we looked everywhere for any sign of the man all the way to where the woods ended at Nobles Lane and found nothing. We figured he probably had a car waiting on that end and carried me through there, but if he did, he didn't leave any trace. Two hours later, covered in dirt, we were back at the bench.

"We need to talk about the flowers," Dunk said, scratching at a mosquito bite on his left arm.

"What about the flowers?"

"You said Stella picked them up and they died in her hand as you watched, in a few seconds. I think you need to come to terms with the fact you probably picked some wilted, half-dead weeds and thought you saw something you really didn't. The alternative is some X-Men shit, and while I love that particular comic, it's a comic. That stuff isn't real." Dunk said.

I looked down at my hands and twisted my fingers together. "She got up and left them on the bench. The old woman—"

"Ms. Oliver?"

"Ms. Oliver told her to go back and get them. Stella didn't want to. Ms. Oliver forced her to get them. Stella picked the flowers up, and I watched them shrivel and die by the time she walked from here to the SUV."

"Where were they parked?"

I pointed down the road. "Over there."

"That's only about thirty feet."

"Yep."

"So she somehow killed the flowers in thirty seconds?"

"Less than that."

"Then she climbed into the SUV and drove off into the sunset?"

I closed my eyes and rubbed my temples. "I shouldn't have told you."

Neither of us said anything for a minute. When Dunk finally replied, he chose his words carefully. "I believe that you believe you saw her kill the flowers. How about we leave it at that for now?"

"She wasn't wearing gloves," I said softly.

"What do you mean?"

"Every other time I met her here, she had gloves on. Whether it was hot or cold. Not this time, though. I think Ms. Oliver wanted me to see that. I think Ms. Oliver kept her from wearing gloves so I'd see that."

"If that's true, how would Oliver know you would bring flowers?"

"I don't know."

The image of the man in the alley popped into my mind. I tried to stamp it back, but he grew more vivid, the dry, old, burned-looking flesh, the hollow eyes looking back at me.

Your little girlfriend did this.

"You said she shows up on the same day every year, right?"

I nodded. "Yeah, August 8."

Dunk's eyes narrowed, and I could see his brain churning. "Then we've got one year to come up with a plan."

"For what?"

"To follow them. We're going to figure out where those SUVs go when they leave here."

August 8, 1988

Twelve Years Old

Log 08/08/1988—

Subject "D" within expected parameters.

Audio/video recording.

"They let him have a phone today."

"Seriously? How did that work?"

"Wouldn't want to be on the receiving side of that call."

"No, sir."

"Who did he call?"

"They dialed for him. They did that way back when he was little, too, but I don't think he understood what was really happening back then."

"Now he does?"

"Now he certainly does."

"And he still did it?"

"Yep."

"You know what's worse?"

"What?"

"I think he wanted to do it. When they finished and he hung up, he was smiling. That little shit got off on it."

"Somebody needs to put him down."

"They'd never do that. He's too valuable."

"No? I bet there is a thick red binder somewhere in this place detailing several ways to end his miserable existence."

"How did they do it?"

"Do what?"

"The phone call."

"Lou said the doctor brought an extension in there with her, then someone dialed from up here in the booth and transferred the call. A little light blinked on at the phone, the kid picked up, and did his thing."

"Efficient."

"Yeah, I guess."

"Weird how it works over the phone or in person, as long as it's live, but not on a recording."

"One of the world's great mysteries."

Silence.

"Would you do it?"

"What?"

"You know."

"End him? Knock him off? Punch his clock? Put him in the dirt? Kick his bucket? Send him swimming with concrete shoes? Take him for a walk over the rainbow bridge?"

"Yeah."

"See these hands? How nice and smooth they are? I'm not built for dirty work."

"I would."

"You know we're being recorded, right?"

"Nobody listens to this shit."

"Still shouldn't say those kind of things aloud."

"Just think them to myself?"

"Yeah."

"So you think about killing him, but you don't want to talk about it?"

"Now you're twisting my words. I didn't say that."

"It's not right to leave him in there like that, to spend his life in a box. Nobody should have to live like that, not even him."

"Since when do you have a conscience?"

"Even worse, what happens if he gets out?"

"They won't let him get out. He'd never make it out of the building."

"You don't think so? With what he can do?"

"There are built-in safeties, protocols, probably a million things in place to keep that from happening."

"Have you ever been briefed on a single one?"

Silence.

—Charter Observation Team – 309

1

The summer of 1988 was one of the wettest in Pittsburgh history, and August 8 was no exception. By the time 5 p.m. rolled around, there were flash flood warnings in effect for most of the city.

Auntie Jo said Mom would understand if she postponed her annual cemetery visit until after the monsoon broke. She also added that she hoped this would be the year my dad's grave flooded and he floated off and disappeared in one of the three rivers so my mom could finally rest in peace without that "Good for nothing, piece of garbage, alcohol-soaked excuse for a human being" beside her. I noted that Auntie Jo said all this as she finished her third glass of wine and puffed away on the first cigarette of her second pack of the day from the comfort of her recliner at our apartment window.

Neither Dunk nor I heard from Detective Faustino Brier in the past year. There also wasn't much news about Andy Olin Flack in the paper or on television after that initial story. Turns out, nobody really wanted to hear about a "piddler-diddler." Most probably thought he got what he deserved.

At exactly 5 p.m., I left the apartment, thankful Auntie Jo insisted I take an umbrella and my jacket, and by 5:30 p.m. (after visiting the graves of my parents), I trudged up the soggy hill, past the glistening mausoleums, and took a seat at the bench, immediately regretting that I didn't bring a towel or something to dry off the seat. Within seconds, my jeans were soaked, my bum was wet, and I was beginning to have second thoughts.

"Red Leader to Red One, come in, Red One, over."

Dunk insisted we use some of my money to buy walkie-talkies, and although I didn't want to at first, I couldn't see his plan working without them. The Radio Shack on Brownsville Road carried a large selection, and after a detailed comparison of the various models and attributes, we decided on four Wouxun KG-UV899s with dual band 136-174MHz 400-520MHz FM transmitters. They had a range of nearly two miles and were small compared to some of the others, easily concealed.

I reached inside my jacket and pressed the transmit button on the radio stashed in the inner pocket. "Red One in position, over."

"Roger. Red Two, report?"

There was a crackle of static, then: *"Red Two in position. It's cold as balls out here, over."*

"Noted, over."

Red Two was Willy Trudeau, who insisted on being called "Tru Dat" when he wasn't Red Two. He also claimed to be the next big white rapper. An odd claim, considering there had yet to be any good white rappers. His red hair, pale skin, and obscene amount of freckles did little to help the image he attempted to cast with his oversize Adidas tennis shoes and assortment of track suits he insisted on wearing at all times. There was also the career ending fact that he couldn't rap—he had zero rhythm, and he danced like a muppet having a seizure. His only shot at rapping for a living was if he stood in line behind Dunk while he conned the Devil out of a car, then worked out a side deal of his own. Without such intervention, he was destined to become an accountant in a track suit and flashy tennis shoes.

Dunk gave Willy twenty dollars from my money. In exchange, Willy "Tru Dat" agreed to help today, no questions asked.

"Red One, this is Red Leader. Can you describe the vehicles again?"

We had covered this. I pressed the transmit button. "White SUVs, at least three of them. Maybe more, maybe less. They'll be identical, probably driving together. Over."

"This is Red Two. Do we have a make and model? Over."

Willy knew we didn't. He'd been razzing me about that since we brought him in.

"Negative," I replied.

"Red Leader, this is Red Two. Upon return to base, I would like to conduct a vote to revoke the man card of Red One. Any boy who cannot identify a vehicle by make and model or engine sound should be relegated to washing Barbie's Corvette for the remainder of their childhood, over."

"This is Red Leader, agreed. Over."

"Screw you both."

"You forgot to say, over. Over."

"Screw you both, over."

"No thank you, over," Willy replied. *"Still cold as balls, over."*

I shivered. I was freezing. I should have grabbed a heavier jacket. The rain beat at the top of the umbrella and cascaded over the sides, splashing up around me. My jeans and shoes were soaked, and even though the sun wouldn't go down for another two hours, it was lost behind the dark storm clouds and downpour.

I rubbed my hands together and noted that the small spot where Stella had written her message on the far corner of the bench had finally been painted over, the black metal shimmering under a bead of rainwater.

The radio in my jacket squealed. A loud, piercing bolt of feedback.

I saw the headlights then, three—no, four—approaching vehicles. I jammed down the transmit button. "I've got four vehicles coming down Tranquility Lane toward me. I think it's them."

"I've been watching the road. They didn't pass me. Did you see them, Red Two?"

"Negative."

Static.

I pressed the button. "They passed one of you. There's no other way in. Over."

Static.

The four SUVs came to a stop in a line at the center of the road. Their headlights were on due to the rain, and the beams sliced through the weather, illuminating the blacktop and the gravestones on either side. The wiper blades on the first SUV sloshed back and forth, batting away the water with a rhythmic *thump thump.*

I reached into my jacket, slow this time. I didn't want to draw attention and pressed the button. "It's them. Four SUVs, all white."

Another squeal erupted from the walkie-talkie, and then it fell silent.

No response from Dunk or Willy.

I couldn't see inside the SUVs. The interiors appeared black, shadows, lost behind the storm.

I pressed the button again. "Are either of you there? Can you hear me?"

I waited for the doors of the SUVs to open, for Ms. Oliver and the others to come out. The SUVs just sat there—the headlights watching me, the windshield wipers continuing their dance.

Thump thump.

Five minutes passed.

Ten.

Something was wrong.

Another squeal from the radio, then static, then nothing.

I stood up.

The engine of the first SUV roared, the tires spun, then caught on the wet pavement, and the white vehicle rocketed past me with the others following closely behind. I jumped out of their path and fell back onto the bench, the umbrella tumbling from my hand. The wind grabbed it and it flew down the hill, bouncing this way and that like a pinball over the various headstones.

My eyes locked on the passing SUVs. For one brief second, I

thought I saw Stella pressed against the glass of the third one. Then they were gone.

I got to my feet, pulled the walkie-talkie from my jacket, and ran toward the woods, slipping in the slick grass. "They're leaving! They're leaving! Do you hear me?"

Dunk was first to break through the fading static. *"We lost you there for a second. Repeat?"*

"Something must be wrong. They stopped and sat there, and then they all took off. They're following Tranquility around the edge of the cemetery. They should be coming around to the entrance any second now!"

More static.

"Red Two, this is Red Leader. Draw closer until you have visual on the entrance. I'll do the same, we need to figure out what direction—"

I lost them as I crossed into the trees.

The large canopy of oaks blocked much of the rain, and I ran faster, twisting through the trees and underbrush, stirring the damp leaves plastered to the ground. I tripped and nearly dropped over a fallen branch about as thick as my leg. Somehow, I regained my balance while still on the move, my arms floundering in the air to keep me upright.

I broke through the trees on the other side.

"—Don't see anything yet. This rain blows. I'm...Static...cemetery on my left," Willy yelled into the radio, breathing heavy.

I spotted my bike about a hundred feet down the road, lying on its side in the ditch at the edge of the forest. I ran for it. "I'm at my bike! I'm gonna come up Nobles toward Brownsville!"

"I see them! I see them! Four white Chevy Suburbans! They just turned left out of the cemetery, heading north on Brownsville. Passing Birmingham right now!" Dunk said.

I dragged my bike from the ditch, almost dropped the radio, then climbed on the wet seat and pedaled as hard as I could, heading east on Nobles, the heavy raindrops pelting me in the face and the icy wind slashing my cheeks.

"I...see you...Dunk!" Willy crackled, out of breath. *"I just passed the cemetery. Where are the..."* Static again.

"...Left on Nobles! I repeat, they made a left on Nobles! Thatch, they're coming toward you!" Dunk shouted. *"I almost had them. They got caught in traffic. I just turned on Nobles, and they're about a hundred yards ahead of me, picking up speed. Thatch, do you see them?"*

Nobles Lane appeared deserted. I pressed the transmit button. "Negative, nothing yet. Maybe they took one of the side roads."

"They wouldn't do that," Dunk replied. *"All those streets are dead ends."*

I pedaled harder, my legs throbbing. "Maybe they went to a house back there."

My radio let out a loud squeal, and I saw the headlights come around the bend ahead.

"I see them! I see them!"

Static.

"Dunk!"

The first SUV had their high beams on, and the thick, white light sliced through the rain. Standing water sprayed in their wake, a tall plume nearly twice the height of the vehicle. The speed limit on Nobles was thirty miles per hour. They were doing at least twice that and picking up speed. The three other SUVs keeping pace behind the first, only a few feet separating each.

"Dunk!" I shouted again into the radio.

Nothing.

I hammered my legs down into the pavement, and with one quick jerk, I spun my bike around in the opposite direction and began peddling as fast as I could back the way I had come.

The engine grew louder at my back.

My eyes took in the road, the guardrails on both sides of the pavement, the trees beyond that. I knew this stretch of road. There was no place for me to go until Denise Street and Colerain, and that was nearly a half mile ahead. I'd never make it.

The light of their high beams crept up the pavement, first behind me, then even, then they lit up the road ahead turning the rain into a white curtain, a wall.

The SUV revved again, it sounded like it was right on top of me and I dared not look back.

The driver hit the horn and held the button down, a shrill scream.

Then they hit me.

They hit me hard.

The SUV slammed into the back tire of my bike and jerked to the left with a force strong enough to launch me from the road and over the metal guardrail. Everything got deathly silent, and the next second seemed to drag on for an hour.

With the impact, I lost the radio as well as my grip on the handlebars. The seat disappeared beneath me. I crashed into the ground, landing on my right shoulder with a sickening crunch. My leg folded up under me, then got yanked back out straight as I rolled. I'm not sure what happened after my head hit the ground. All went real quiet.

2

The dream.

Daddy fastened me into my car seat.

Chocolate milk.

Outside Auntie Jo's apartment.

Daddy opened my door.

Daddy removed something from the seat beside me, gave that something to Auntie Jo.

Something.

Unknown something.

Driving again.

"Daddy?"

"Yeah, Jack?"

"What was in the box?"

"What box?"

"The box you gave Auntie Jo."

"Oh, that box," he dad replied. "Nothing, Jack. Nothing at all."

White SUV in our path.

White SUV blocking the road.

"Why would you give Auntie Jo a box of nothing?"

Awful squeal of tires.

"Not now, Jack. Daddy's busy."

3

"Thatch?"

"Thatch, can you hear me?"

When my eyes opened, a giant bat hovered over me. Enormous wings spread wide and flapping. We were under water and the bat stared down at me, screaming my name over the thunderous sound of the pounding waves at the surface.

"Thatch!"

I blinked.

Not a bat.

Dunk.

Dunk standing over me with his jacket open, holding both sides out to block the rain.

"Don't move, Jack."

"They hit…"

"I saw."

"We need to get help!" Willy said from somewhere behind me. "He needs an ambulance!"

Dunk leaned in closer. "Can you hear me, Jack?"

I nodded.

"Can you say my name?"

"Yeah."

"Say it."

"Why?"

Duncan slapped my cheek with the open palm of his hand. "Say it!"

"Duncan Bellino."

"What year is it?"

"1988."

"Who's the president?"

"Oh, come on."

"Say it?"

"Ronald Reagan."

I tried to sit up, fell back down, my head splashing in the muddy earth.

"He shouldn't move. Don't let him move until we get someone out here," Willy said. "I'll ride back out to Brownsville and find help."

"Where are they?" I said softly.

"Gone. They ran you off the road and didn't even slow down. I lost track of them after they turned the corner up there."

"Where's my shoe?"

"Oh shit, look at his leg. The way it's bent," Willy said.

Dunk turned to him. "If you're gonna go and get help, then go and get help! Otherwise, shut the fuck up!"

"What's wrong with my leg?"

Willy backed up, the rain running down his soaked head and clothes and puddling at his feet. He got on his bike and pedaled off.

"He's right, you shouldn't move."

I sat up anyway.

Dunk put a hand on my chest. "I think your leg is broken bad. You probably don't want to see it."

I did want to see it, so I leaned forward. The world went white for a second as the blood rushed from my head, and then my vision cleared. My right leg was twisted at the strangest angle, an angle it most definitely should not. I was sitting on my foot. I studied my twisted body as if watching a program on television, distant, removed. "Weird. It doesn't hurt at all."

"Maybe you're in shock?"

"I don't think I'm…"

"No, don't!"

With my arms at my side and using my left leg for leverage, I pushed myself to a stand. Dunk tried to stop me, but I think he was surprised I was able to move at all. When my twisted right leg unfolded and dropped into its usual support position, *he* nearly fell over.

"I need my shoe."

Dunk broke his stare, then peered to the rain. "It's over there, hold on—"

I watched him run about a hundred feet down the side of the road. He pulled my tennis shoe from the drainage ditch, shook the water out, and brought it back.

"Here."

The sole of my Nike was torn loose, flapping. I held onto Dunk's shoulder, carefully raised my right foot, and put it on, then lowered my leg again, testing with a little pressure. "I don't think it's broken," I said. I put a little weight on it, then some more. "It feels okay." Slowly, I lifted my right leg off the ground, standing only on my left, and extended the right out in front of me, then bent it at the knee, then back again, slow at first, then again, faster. "It feels fine."

I took a few steps, then a couple more. I walked about ten feet down the road, splashing in the puddled water around me, turned, then walked back to where Dunk stood. His mouth hung open. "I saw them hit you. I thought they killed you. You flew like a thousand feet."

The entire right side of my body was slick with mud, my jeans had a six-inch tear in them, but when I pulled the material open, I couldn't find any damage to my skin. My jacket was a mess, too. I took it off, and Dunk examined my arm and back, then the right side of my head. "You're one dirty son-of-a-bitch, but I don't see a single scrape. You're probably bruised, but that kind of thing might not show up for a few hours."

I heard about half of what he said.

My eyes had found what was left of my bike. The frame was twisted into an unrecognizable shape, the rear wheel somehow mashed into the front. Neither the handlebars or seat were remotely close to the factory-recommended position. The chain was missing. I wascertain this bike would not ride again. "Holy shit."

"Yeah," Dunk said. "Holy shit."

We didn't wait for Willy to come back with help. Although shaken, there was nothing physically wrong with me. If Willy appeared with an ambulance or worse, the police, we'd need to explain what happened. That would lead into what we were doing, why we were out there in the first place, and neither of us were prepared to talk about that.

We dragged the remains of my bike into the woods between Nobles Lane and the cemetery, then climbed on Dunk's bike (me on the handlebars). Dunk pedaled on pure adrenaline, and we got back to our apartment building in less than ten minutes. We went to Dunk's. I knew Auntie Jo would probably be at the diner, but on the off chance she wasn't, I didn't want to risk her seeing me in my current state.

Dunk called out when we entered, but nobody was home there, either. He had no idea where his dad might be.

Once inside, I went to the bathroom, stripped off my clothes, and climbed into the shower. I expected to find the start of some nasty bruises, but there was nothing, not a single scratch, cut, or inflammation.

Shower done, I put on the clothes Dunk had left out for me—a pair of jeans one size too big and a Bobby McFerrin tee-shirt with *Don't worry, be happy* stamped across the front under a large, yellow winking smiley face.

I found Dunk in the kitchen drinking a beer.

Willy sat beside him at the table, a beer in his hand, too. "What the fuck, Thatch?"

I took a Coke from the fridge, popped the top, and dropped down into one of the empty chairs. The green vinyl top blew out some air from a hole in the side.

"Maybe you should have a beer, too," Dunk said. "I think you've earned a beer. You're going to be hurting once the shock wears off. A beer will help."

When had Dunk started drinking beer? "I feel fine, really. I think my bike took the worst of it and I got lucky—the ground is damp and mushy. It cushioned my fall."

Dunk leaned forward in his chair. "You didn't *fall*, you *flew*. That SUV launched you like a retarded Superman, your arms flailing all around..." He waved and flapped his arms in the air and made this crooked face, I couldn't help but laugh.

Dunk got up, went to the refrigerator, retrieved a beer, popped the top, then set it in front of me before returning to his chair. The kitchen smelled like mildew. Dishes piled high in the sink. An empty jar of peanut butter sat on the counter, a fly feasting on the rim.

"I really don't want a beer."

"You will." He reached to the center of the table, to a copy of *Boy's Life*, and slid it aside. His dad's gun was sitting under it.

I glanced from Dunk to Willy, then back again. As far as I knew, he never showed the gun to anyone but me. "What's that for?"

"We need a new plan," Dunk said.

"We don't need a gun."

"They tried to kill you."

"They tried to scare me."

"If they wanted to scare you, they would have driven close to you, maybe even forced you off the road," Dunk said. "Instead, they sped up behind you, with the pedal to the floor, and nailed the back of your bike. The impact destroyed your ride and would have killed you if you weren't such a lucky bastard. I'm surprised they didn't throw it in reverse and back up over you to finish the job. I bet they would have if you didn't go cartwheeling over the guardrail."

"They were only trying to scare me," I insisted.

Dunk leaned closer. "Whoever was driving didn't even tap the brake pedal. They rode the gas. After they hit you, they sped up and drove off, didn't even slow down. Even if you hit someone on accident, you slow down, at the very least just to be sure your car didn't get all fucked up. Not a single tap on the brakes, not one. They tried to kill you."

Willy took a sip of his beer. It made his eyes water. "You saw your bike, right?"

I nodded.

"You saw how mangled it was? When I rode up, that's what you looked like—a twisted, mangled, mess. I thought for sure you were dead."

Dunk drank some of his beer, and his eyes did not water. "Willy here flagged down a station wagon on Brownsville and convinced some old lady that his buddy got shredded in a hit and run and needed help. When he didn't find us where he left us, he spent the next ten minutes trying to convince her that maybe it wasn't as bad as he thought."

Willy nodded. "She wanted to call the cops. I had to talk her down. At first she thought some half-dead kid was pushing his bike home. When we couldn't find the half-dead kid, she got angry and figured I was pranking her—then she really wanted to call the cops. She grabbed my shirt and tried to get me in her car. I busted loose, got on my bike, and rode off into the woods, cut through the cemetery to lose her. That woman could scream. I heard her shouting for half the ride back here. I guessed you guys would come back here."

My mind was churning. "They knew something was wrong. I don't know how, but they must have figured out I wasn't alone. They didn't get out of the SUVs. It was like they came by just to tell me they knew I was up to something fishy, then left. When they realized I was trying to follow them, they stopped me. Like I broke the rules or something."

"We don't know the rules," Willy said.

"That's why we need a new plan," Dunk said.

I nodded at Willy, then turned back to Dunk. "How much did you tell him?"

Dunk shrugged and took another sip of his beer. "I told him everything when you were in the shower. We need him, and he can't be in the dark."

I didn't know Willy that well and had no idea if I could trust him. "You can't tell anyone."

"I won't." He crossed his heart. "Nobody would believe me, anyway."

I took a sip of my Coke, the full beer can beginning to sweat beside it.

"How did they know something was different?" Dunk asked. "What tipped them off?"

"Maybe they saw us on our bikes," Willy offered.

Dunk shook his head. "Kids on bikes does not a tip-off make."

"I think it was the radios," I said.

Dunk frowned. "Did they see your radio?"

"No, I think they heard it. Every time those SUVs get close, something screwy happens with whatever radio I have with me. In the past, I noticed the signal on my Walkman boost when they got close. Today, we all lost contact even though we were well within range. Almost like something with a stronger signal interfered."

"What? Like a transmitter in one of the SUVs?"

I twisted the Coke can in my hand. "I don't know. Transmitter, receiver, some kind of radio something."

"So next year, we don't use radios," Willy said.

I met his eyes. "Next year, I think I need to go alone again. Otherwise, they'll know."

"I agree, and that's why you need this," Dunk slid the .38 toward me.

"I'm not gonna shoot anyone."

"For protection," Dunk continued. "You keep it on you in case they try to finish what they started today. You put it in your pocket, and wait for them on the bench." He took another sip of his beer. "If you have to, you pull the gun on Stella. This time, you get answers. You don't let them leave. You control the situation."

"They've got guns, too, much bigger guns."

"Won't matter. If you point a gun at Stella, they won't risk shooting you." Dunk finished his beer and crushed the can. He tossed it at the overflowing wastebasket in the corner of the kitchen. "This time, you're getting answers for sure."

I stared at the gun for a long time. Then I reached for my beer. The bubbles burned my nose. I didn't like the taste one bit. At least, not that first time.

August 8, 1989

Thirteen Years Old

Log 08/08/1989—

Subject "D" within expected parameters.

Audio/video recording.

"What time is it?"

"Ahh, twelve after three."

"Is the kid sleeping?"

Warren lowered his copy of *Rolling Stone* magazine. "Did you know Madonna doesn't shave her arm pits?"

"Neither do I."

"You're a hairy fucking monkey. She's hot. Seems weird when a woman doesn't shave."

"They don't in Europe."

"That's why I live in the good ol' U.S. of A."

"Seems like a double standard to me."

Warren returned to the magazine. "Wonder if she shaves her legs."

"I'm sure she shaves her legs. We live in a civilized society. If Madonna doesn't shave her legs, we might as well go back to sleeping in caves and beating buffalos with sticks to get our dinner."

Warren lowered the magazine again. "Now I'm hungry."

"Is the kid sleeping?" Carl asked again.

"Can't tell. Too dark in there. Why?"

"Want to see something scary?" Carl reached across the control board and flicked the *delay* switch to the off position.

Warren dropped the magazine and nearly fell out of his chair as he jumped and smacked the switch back on. "What the fuck, Carl!?"

"Doesn't matter. Not if he's sleeping."

"I don't care if he's hog-tied, duct-taped, cuffed, and wearing that mask of his—don't ever fuck with the switch!"

Carl reached over and flicked the switch off again.

Warren slammed it back. "I will beat you if you do that one more time!"

Carl held up both his hands. "Okay! Okay! I surrender. Just trying to liven things up. I'm bored to death over here."

"Maybe zero in on a hobby that doesn't involve the two of us dying."

"If that switch broke, do you think anyone would notice?"

"I'm sure they test it," Warren said.

"Like all the other safety protocols we never see? Yeah, I'm sure someone tests it. I'll bet someone is all over that."

Warren had turned to the thick glass window. "I can't see him in there. Can you?"

"That's why I asked you if he was sleeping. I don't think he's on his bed."

"It's too fucking dark in there. They need to switch that red night-light thing back on."

"The kid told the doctor he couldn't sleep well with that little light on. She had it removed."

"Well, I don't think he's in his bed."

"Maybe he's in the shitter."

"Maybe. I don't see him on the infrared, either."

"Well, he didn't get out and go for a walk. Turn the light on for a second."

"No way. I'm not getting written up."

Carl frowned. "They won't write us up for checking on him. If they don't want us to turn the light on to do our job, they should have fought the doc on the night-light. We'll just flick the light on for a second, figure out what he's doing, then shut it down again. No harm done."

Warren let out a breath. "Okay, but fast. If he's sleeping, we don't want to wake him."

Carl reached back to the control board and flicked on the lights.

Warren leaned over the board, close to the observation window. "I don't see him, do you?"

Carl stood, leaned forward, looked too.

"Do you see him?"

Carl shook his head and pressed microphone button. "Hey, kid, where are you?"

Warren smacked his hand off the button. "Don't do that!"

David jumped up from beneath the window and slapped both hands against the glass. The motion was soundless, hampered by the thick glass, but that didn't keep both men from jumping back.

Carl's leg snared on his chair, and he fell to the floor in a twisted mess.

"What the fuck!" Warren shouted.

David grinned back at them both from the other side of the window. He laughed silently while Warren found the light switch and plunged the room back into black.

—Charter Observation Team – 309

1

I did take the gun and on August 8, 1989, the year I officially became a teenager, I planted my butt firmly upon the bench in the cemetery and waited. The weather was particularly warm that day, and I felt like an idiot sitting there with a jacket on, but that was the only way I could properly conceal the weapon. I tried sticking the gun down the waistband of my jeans (both in front and in back) like they do in the movies, but the gun toppled out and fell to the ground after only a few steps. There was also the odd bulge in my pants that would have to be explained—even with a tee-shirt pulled down over it, the gun was plainly visible. I grew that year—from four-nine to five-three in just the past nine months. I only weighed one hundred and two pounds, though. I looked like a telephone pole dressed up in last year's long-forgotten fashion. My scrawny body simply wasn't meant to hide a gun—that's something that wouldn't feel right for a few more years.

Dunk's dad owned an ankle holster, but my leg was a little too small and the gun a little too big for that, too, that left only my jacket. Mr. Krendal gave it to me, a brown leather bomber jacket that had belonged to his son. I later learned he was lost in the war. The jacket had two pockets on the inside, and the gun rested comfortably in either. Because the jacket was large and bulky on me, the shape of the gun was lost in the folds, creases, and assorted bumps my body had yet to fill in.

The jacket was perfect, aside from the heat.

Eighty-six degrees when I left Dunk's apartment, and no sign of cooling until the sun took leave.

I didn't want to take the gun, but Dunk made a good case for it, and he had made that same case almost every day for the past year. When I finally agreed, he looked relieved.

"It's a Rossi 352 two-inch .38 special. Five shot capacity—" He jerked his wrist, and the cylinder popped out, revealing the heads of five gold casings. He gave the cylinder a quick spin, then slammed it back into place with the palm of his hand. "You can pull back the hammer with your thumb if you want to scare them, but the gun will still shoot if you don't, the trigger pull will just be a little longer." He did all of this with the skill of a veteran. His dad felt it was better his son be familiar with the weapon, understand the dangers, and know how to use it. "The sites are fixed," Dunk went on. "All you have to do is line up the one in the front to the one in the back and pull the trigger. If you do pull the trigger, exhale before or just hold your breath. If you breathe while shooting, the movement can screw with your aim." He pointed at the bottom of the gun. "This here is the trigger guard. Always keep your finger on the trigger guard until you're ready to shoot. If you put your finger on the trigger, there's a chance you might fire the gun by accident and shoot yourself in the foot or something."

Dunk held the gun out to me, barrel down. "Put it in your pocket and don't take it out unless you think you'll need to use it. Pop always says you can't pull a gun unless you're ready to kill someone. Once you reveal a gun, there's no going back. You ready?"

I reached out and took the gun from him. It was heavier than I remembered—it didn't have bullets when we were practicing. I was shaking, but Dunk didn't say anything about that. I slipped the gun into my jacket pocket.

Dunk smoothed out the leather, then ruffled the jacket back up. "Are you sure you don't want us there?"

Willy should have been there by now, but he was running late. Earlier that summer, he started a job at Magic Mike's Car Wash on Valladium Drive, and on days like today they tended to keep everyone for overtime.

I shook my head. "They'll know."

I still had nightmares about last year.

The roar of the engine.

The impact.

We told Auntie Jo someone stole my bike from school. I bought Willy's old one, a black BMX with silver stripes. Not quite as cool as Dunk's but way better than the one I had. I could have bought a new one. The envelopes arrived every month, and I had over sixteen thousand dollars hidden away, but I didn't. Willy's old bike suited me just fine.

So, on Tuesday, August 8, 1989, I rode my new used bike through the evening heat, up the road at the cemetery gate, and left it sitting in the grass beside the mausoleums, then walked over to the bench and took a seat, my chest, back, and arms covered in sweat under the thick leather jacket with the gun in the pocket. I sat there and waited. When six o'clock rolled around, I waited longer. When seven came and went, I began to think Dunk and Willy had followed me and were hiding in the trees, somehow frightened Stella and the others off, but when I turned and looked, I didn't see anyone. By eight o'clock, I had only seen two other people, an older couple a few hundred feet away, down the hill, placing flowers at a grave. With the approach of nine, and the loss of the sun, now gone more than thirty minutes, I stood from the bench, retrieved my bike, and rode home where Willy and Dunk waited impatiently, and had waited the entire time.

2

1990 saw the release of Nelson Mandela from prison, the arrival of the Furby, and the discovery of the most completed T. Rex skeleton in South Dakota. Paleontologists named it Sue. My days were filled with thoughts of Stella. I filled sketchbook after sketchbook with Stella, finding drawing to be the only way to erase her from my mind, if only for a little while. My nights brought the dream more times than I could count, and I became obsessed with the box my father handed to Auntie Jo. I tore our apartment to pieces looking for it. I even asked Auntie Jo about it once, and she said, and I quote, "Your father was such a selfish prick, he wouldn't have given me a cold. I don't know nothing about no box."

Stella didn't come to the cemetery that year, either. I decided I'd leave the gun at home next time. Maybe they somehow knew about the gun.

With 1991 came the death of Freddy Mercury, the start of Operation Desert Storm with the invasion of Kuwait, and Boris Yeltsin became the first elected President of Russia. Something called "the Internet" arrived—it would change the world, we were told. Auntie Jo said it would just be a new way for the pervs to find their porn.

No Stella that year, either.

I wouldn't see Stella Nettleton again until August 1992.

PART 2

"In a word, it was impossible for me to separate her, in the past or in the present, from the innermost life of my life."
—Charles Dickens, *Great Expectations*

August 8, 1992

Sixteen Years Old

Log 08/08/1992—

Interview with Dr. Helen Durgin. Subject "D" appears aggravated but in control of his emotional state.

Audio/video recording.

"I want to see her."

"You know the drill. You do as we ask, then you get to see her. That's the rule."

"Another phone call?"

"Another phone call."

"Phone calls can be traced, Doc. Maybe you should take me there this time."

"You know we can't do that."

"Then bring the person here. Let me see their face when I do it. Is it a man or a woman this time?"

"Does that matter?"

"No, just curious."

"A man."

"Why him? What did he do?"

The doctor said nothing.

"And after, you'll let me see her again?"

"That's the rule."

"How long?"

"One hour."

"I want two."

"One hour, and if you push again, I'll see that she is only here for thirty minutes. Maybe less."

"Sorry, Doc."

"Doctor Durgin."

"Sorry, Doctor Durgin. It's just, I don't get to see anyone. Only you and her. I look forward to her visits."

"But not mine?"

"You know what I mean."

"I don't, David. Why don't you explain it to me."

"You talk to me because you have to, it's your job. She talks to me because she wants to."

"And you wouldn't hurt her? Like your parents? Like the others?"

"You mean, like the phone calls?"

"Yes. Like the phone calls."

"No. I'd never hurt her."

"Do you love her?"

Silence.

"David?"

"I'm not sure I know what love is. I only know love from books."

"Love is caring for someone more than you care for yourself. Think of it this way—if killing me meant you'd get freedom, would you do it?"

Silence.

"You can answer, David. You won't get in trouble. Would you kill me to get out of this place?"

"You're deaf. I can't kill you."

"But if you could, if I could hear you, would you kill me?"

"For freedom?"

"Yes, for complete freedom."

"Yes."

"No hesitation? No remorse? We've known each other for a long time."

"You keep me in a box. I'm only permitted out of my box if I wear a mask. I'm your prisoner, you're my jailor. I'm nothing more than a lab rat to you."

"And Stella, would you kill her? If ending her life meant you could taste that exact same freedom?"

"I don't know."

"Oh, I think you do. You've spent countless hours with her, and she *can* hear you, and you've never hurt her. You've never even tried, not even as a child."

"And that means I love her?"

"I believe it does, yes."

David said nothing.

"Let's take it to another level. If I told you to kill her, instructed you to kill her, and said that if you did, I would guarantee you received that same freedom I mentioned earlier, would you do it?"

"No."

"Why not?"

"Because you'd be lying. You'd never let me go."

"For argument's sake, let's say that I would."

"I don't think I could hurt her."

"Because you love her."

"I suppose I do, if that's what love means."

"More than you loved your parents when you killed them?"

"I was a kid, I overreacted."

"And if it were to happen again today, you wouldn't hurt them?"

"No, I can control it now. I understand how it works. I rule my emotions, I don't allow my emotions to rule me."

"That's good, David. Very insightful."

"So I can see her, then?"

"After we make a phone call."

"Okay."

—Charter Observation Team – 309

1

"Have you been here all night?"

Detective Faustino Brier must have drifted off. He hadn't heard Joy Fogel come in, hadn't heard her get coffee, and didn't notice when she planted herself at the desk facing his. She sat there now, a steaming mug of coffee resting between her hands, leaning back in her chair, her head tilted a little to the left. She tended to do that when she asked a question. Over time, Faustino noticed the tilt went left when she already knew the answer to her latest query, and to the right when she did not.

Faustino sat up straight in his own chair, looked at the empty coffee mug in front of him, and smacked his dry lips. "What time is it?"

"Four twenty-three in the morning," she said, without missing a beat.

"That's a neat trick. You just know that?"

"I can see the clock in interrogation room two from here."

Faustino twisted his head around and glanced behind him. His neck let out a series of pops and creaks. He could make out a white blob hanging on the wall of the small interrogation room, but that was about it. His vision had gradually gotten worse in the past decade or so. Now forty-three, he had eleven years on his partner.

Sometimes that mattered, most of the time it didn't. This was apparently one of those times it did. Vision went with age, and he wasn't getting any younger.

Considering the odd time, Fogel looked wide awake and together. She wore little makeup, just some eyeliner. Her blonde hair was pulled back in the usual ponytail, still damp.

She wasn't a large woman. In fact, she was downright tiny, only about five-two , but she spent most of her free time in the department gym. Over the three years they'd been partners, Faustino had seen no less than five other officers comment on her petite size and had also seen her take down those same five officers with relative ease within hours of said comment. "Meet me in the gym after your shift," was not something you wanted to hear from her, and it became a running joke in the department. As new officers cycled in, it was only a matter of time before they said something about her—a comment on her short stature or her looks—and the person would soon find themselves staring up at her from one of the mats in the gym, little birdies dancing around their head as they tried to piece together what just happened. Her father insisted she take Taekwondo beginning at eight years old, and at last check, she now had her third black belt. She also took jiu jitsu and yoga (to relax, she said).

There had been a time early on when Faustino thought the two of them might actually try dating, but they quickly moved past that. He found her to be attractive, same as the other guys. She had seen something in him, too, but they spent so much time together they quickly shifted from that mutual attraction to something more like a sibling relationship. In the few instances when Faustino had actually gone out on a date with other women (typically women he met through a dating service—homicide detectives rarely encountered live women through work), Fogel studied each one closely and offered her "unbiased" opinion—none were particularly right for him, but they were right for now. If Fogel dated, she didn't talk about it, at least not with him. That was okay, too.

"I got in a little after midnight," Faustino told her. "Couldn't sleep. How about you? What are you doing here so early?"

She glanced up at the large bulletin board on wheels next to Faustino's desk. "It's August 8. I knew that would be coming out. Wouldn't miss it."

The bulletin board spent most of the year tucked in the far back corner of the Pittsburgh PD homicide division's pen, gathering dust, the side with clippings, photographs, and notes turned to face the wall, the blank side out. Most of the detectives were too new to know much about it and left it as is. The older detectives had written it off long ago as Faustino's personal project and also left it as is. At one point, someone had written, FAUST'S WALL OF WEIRD across the top in red chalk, but that had slowly faded away.

"Do you want to walk me through it?"

"Are you sure you want to hear it again?"

Fogel nodded. "A refresher is good. It's been a year."

Faustino stood, scooped up his coffee mug, and went to the machine near the door to get a refill. The coffee was lukewarm and tasted like shit, but he felt the caffeine working through his cells even before he got back to his desk. He set the mug down on the corner and went to the board—sixteen dead in as many years.

"Do you want me to start with the most recent and work my way back, or the other way around?"

"Your call."

Faustino turned back to the board. "Backwards it is."

For each of the sixteen victims, the board displayed a photograph of the deceased, and in many cases, a secondary photograph taken when they were still alive, necessary because of the state of the bodies when found. Above each photo was a strip of tape with the date. The earliest contained the full date—August 8, 1978, as did the six that followed, but by 1984, they only listed the year. With all the murders taking place on August 8, it seemed redundant to keep repeating the same date.

Faustino, along with all those who didn't refer to this case as the

Wall of Weird, called these murders the August Eights. Aside from the date, the condition of each body linked them all together.

Faustino went to the bottom right of the board, to the most recent murder. "Arden Royal, twenty-seven-year-old male, found behind a Dumpster in Upper Saint Clair one year ago today, August 8, 1991. Same condition as all the others. No apparent motive, no evidence of value collected at the scene. Like the others, we're confident he was killed somewhere else and dumped here."

"1990, we've got Tama Krieg. Sixteen years old, a member of the South Side Bandits. She had a couple of arrests, petty stuff, mostly. Sounds to me just like a kid trying to fit in under poor circumstances. Her mother said her grades were solid before she dropped out of high school. I checked, Cs and Ds, mostly, but passing. She was found behind a Burger King downtown." He paused at the crime scene photo, her body lying on the ground, unrecognizable, then went on to the next two, pointing at both.

"1989 and 1988, both male, both unidentified. 1989 was dumped behind a warehouse. 1988 was left right on the sidewalk near Three River Stadium under a blanket. He was there for two days before someone realized he wasn't just some homeless guy sleeping it off."

"Were they robbed?" Fogel asked.

Faustino shook his head. "We don't think so. Even though their wallets were missing, if they carried them at all. We found wallets on many of the other victims, cash still inside. The motive here isn't robbery. It's possible someone took the wallets after the bodies were dumped, but I honestly don't think anyone would be that brazen. One look at the condition of the bodies would be more than enough to scare away someone out for a quick buck."

"Tell me about the cause of death."

Faustino exhaled, his eyes shifting over the photos. "At first glance, they all appear to be horribly burned. Like they were soaked in an accelerant, then lit up."

"But it's not fire, right?"

"Nope. They look burned, but the Medical Examiner is confident that is not the case. The burn-like marks cover every inch of their bodies, even between fingers and toes, their tongues, internal organs—every cell evenly destroyed by whatever this is. Their clothing is untouched."

Fogel took a sip of her coffee. "Redressed after?"

Again, Faustino shook his head. "I've touched them. The skin was completely dried out, almost like powder, no moisture left at all. With the slightest pressure, it cracked and flaked away. The wind picked it up. We did significant damage just getting them into body bags. There is no way someone did this and then got fresh clothing on the bodies after the fact, no way. They died in these clothes. Whatever happened, somehow started on the inside, at the cellular level."

"I've heard some of the guys say this is spontaneous combustion."

Faustino crossed back over to his own desk, drank some coffee, grimaced, and set the mug back down. "I looked at that early on, researched the hell out of it. I didn't believe any of that shit going in, but I found a lot of evidence to support it's a real phenomenon. There's even video—people super heating from the inside, sweating, then bursting into flames. It always seems to start at the mouth—smoke coming from the mouth, then the nose and ears. Freaky shit, but that's not what we have here."

"How do you know?"

"In each of those cases, the fire spreads. The clothing goes. Many of them set their surroundings on fire. It happens so fast, the fire is usually contained, but there is external damage of some sort. We've got none of that here, not on a single one of them," Faustino said.

Fogel nodded back at the board. "1987. Andy Olin Flack. I remember that one, it made the news for a few days."

Returning to the board, Faustino tapped at Flack's photos—a before and after. "Thirty-three years old, from Bethel Park. Serious pervert. We found piles of child pornography at his house. He was found a few miles from home in an alley off Brownsville. This is one of the few crime scenes where we did find something."

"What?"

Faustino crossed back to his desk, tugged open the top metal drawer on the left, and rifled through the contents. He located a legal size manilla folder and opened it on the top of his desk. The folder didn't contain much—about ten pages of typed paper and a few photographs clipped to the inside flap. He studied the photographs for a second, then slid the folder to Fogel. "This guy was carrying a wallet, and we were able to lift prints that did not belong to him."

"I'm guessing they weren't in the system?"

"Nope. We think our perp pulled it out to get a look at the ID. He or she didn't touch the cash or the credit cards. From what we can tell, nothing was taken."

"Ballsy move, without gloves."

"Or panicked, or just plain stupid. Who knows?"

Fogel studied the images, three in all. The first was of the wallet, a black leather bifold opened to the center, driver's license on the left side, a Visa and a few other cards on the right, everything covered in white fingerprint powder. She frowned. "How big were Flack's hands?"

"Caught that, huh?" He tapped at the photograph. "The larger prints belong to Flack, the smaller ones are the ones that came back as unknown."

Fogel thought about that for a second, then looked at the other two photographs, both shoe prints on the grimy alley floor.

"We think those belong to a kid. They're a size four."

"Could be a woman."

"Yeah, maybe."

"A kid didn't do this. Size four would put them around, what? Ten or eleven years old? Way too small to move a body like this. What did Flack weigh?"

"One seventy-three."

"Definitely not a kid. I'm not sure I could move him on my own." Fogel flipped through the printed pages. Six of them had copies of receipts. "What are these?"

"He seemed to like eating at the diner across the street. Krendal's. Went in a couple times a week. One of the waitresses recognized him from a photo but didn't have much to add. Quiet, ate by himself. Always ordered a ham and cheese melt with a Coke and fries."

Faustino turned the folder back around. "I ran into a kid at the diner, Duncan Bellino. I saw him standing around at the crime scene, too. He got real nervous when I cornered him about it. I get the feeling he may have found the body, tried to lift the wallet, and chickened out. I tried to get a warrant for his prints, but the judge wouldn't sign off on it, too flimsy. Right age, though, and the shoe size looked about right."

Fogel leaned back in her chair. "That, my friend, would be a dead lead."

"Probably, but I don't like loose ends. If he was first to the body, he may have seen whoever dumped Flack there. He got picked up a few years back for some petty shit, so he's in the system now, but the records are sealed. I tried to get those to match the prints, but no-go. Different judge, same problem—too flimsy. I don't think the kid did it, but my gut tells me he knows something."

"Okay, so Flack is a bust, too, no real evidence." She nodded at the board. "Tell me about 1986."

Faustino returned to the board and pointed at the photograph under 1986. "She's our oldest victim on record—forty-seven-year-old black female. No record. She was a cashier at K-Mart. Lived alone. She clocked out on August 6, usually walked home. That was the last time anyone ever saw her. We found her in Baptist Park on August 8."

"Do you have a date or time of death?"

Faustino shook his head. "The ME couldn't place it. Because of the condition of these bodies, he flat-out told me he can only provide a best guess. None of the usual markers hold up."

"That means she was missing at least two days. Your perp might be keeping them alive. Any evidence of sexual assault?"

"The ME didn't think so, but couldn't be sure on that, either. We've got a wide range of victims here, though, all ages, both sexes, multiple races. Sex crimes usually have a type, and from what I can tell, Flack was the only sexual predator attached to this case."

"And he's a vic."

"He's a vic."

Faustino pointed to three more pictures on the board. "'85, '84, and '83. '85 and '83 were male, '84 was female. We haven't been able to identify any of them. All were fished out of the Ohio River anywhere from two miles outside the city to ten. They were all nude. The condition of the bodies tied them to this case, nothing else."

Fogel said, "1982 looks young."

Faustino glanced at the photograph of the tiny body—black, dry, and shriveled—next to the picture of a smiling little girl. "Our youngest. Six-year-old Rebecca Pohlman. She was nabbed from Monroeville Mall on August 2 and turned up in a Dumpster behind an Eat'n Park in West Mifflin on August 8."

"Isn't that the mall where they filmed *Dawn of the Dead*?"

"The same."

"Creepy."

Faustino said, "Her mother was shopping at Sears, browsing clothes, and Rebecca wanted to look at the toys across the aisle but within eyeshot. We have about ten minutes unaccounted for, so we think that's when she was grabbed. Most stores put the toy section as deep into the space as possible for two reason—kids tend to drag their parents there, so you want the parents to have to walk through as much of the retail space as possible, hoping for an impulse buy or two. The second reason is to get it as far from the exits as possible. Most kids are taken from the toy department. This gives store security a fighting chance at stopping someone before they get outside. When Rebecca was taken, no alarms went up. She vanished."

He reached back into his drawer, found another folder, and opened it on the desk. There was a grainy eight by ten photograph inside. He handed it to Fogel. "The security cameras didn't capture anything worthwhile inside, but we got this picture from the parking lot."

Fogel studied the picture and frowned. "What exactly am I looking at?"

"Four adults, from the back. Female, we think, based on the long hair. Can't be sure, though."

"This is August, right? Why are they wearing coats?"

"That's what we noticed first, too. Four identical coats. White trenches." He leaned over the photograph and placed his finger near center. "What do you see right here?"

Fogel leaned in closer, too. It took her a moment. "Looks like a kid walking between them."

"Her mother identified the tee-shirt. It's Rebecca."

"If you're six years old and four adults tell you to go somewhere, you probably just go, right? She probably didn't put up a fuss."

"If she did, nobody noticed. But yeah, I bet they just told her her mommy was looking for her, they'd take her to her, and walked Rebecca right out."

Fogel said, "The camera didn't capture their vehicle?"

"All I've got is this photograph. When I first started piecing all this together, I tried to pull the tapes from evidence, and they were gone, lost. I figured another camera might have the vehicle, or maybe earlier footage caught this crew walking in, but without the tapes, we'll never know."

Fogel traced the adults with her fingertip. "If all these murders are connected, this tells us there are at least four perps, not one. The identical coats could mean a cult of some sort. Considering the state of the bodies, it's hard not to go there. These murders span such a long time frame. That would suggest a cult, too—possibly different perps over time, all working toward the same thing."

Faustino only nodded at this. He had suspected some kind of cult for years. "Rebecca was found in a Dumpster, 8/8/1982."

The two of them fell silent at this, both lost in their own thoughts. All these deaths, but that little girl always seemed to hit Faustino the hardest. By the expression on Fogel's face, he knew he was not alone in that.

After about a minute, he cleared his throat and went back to the board. "1981, unknown male. 1980, unknown male. 1979, unknown female." Each of the bodies in the photographs looked the same: black, dry skin, almost powdery, burnt, clothing untouched. "Considering the age, I don't know that we'll ever identify them unless we catch whoever is responsible."

Fogel stood from her desk and approached the board. "What happened in 1978?"

"From what I can tell, this was our first, and by far the worst. Three bodies that year, all male." He pointed at the picture in the center. This guy had a metal plate in his head from an injury in Vietnam. The ME used the serial number to identify him. Twenty-four years old, his name was Calvin Gurney. He came back from 'Nam in '75, got picked up for some petty stuff early on—vagrancy, shoplifting. Otherwise, there's not much on him. The other two guys were never identified. They were found at a bloodbath, though. The crime scene was completely different from all these others. I think it was our ground zero."

"Different how?"

Faustino reached into his drawer and retrieved one more file. This one was about half an inch thick. Inside were a dozen photographs and various reports. "They were found inside a townhouse in Mount Washington. A three-bedroom with a nice view of the city. The place was supposed to be vacant, looked like a squatting situation. Two adults were found downstairs, both dead, both shot. These three men were found in a bedroom on the second floor. Their bodies match all our others. The investigating officer wrote it up as a B&E that went sideways."

He slid the folder across the desk to her. "Read it. We've got time. I've got someplace to be."

"Where?"

"I'm gonna stick to the Bellino kid all day."

"Seriously? The Flack murder was five years ago. At best, he stumbled into it."

"It's all I've got." He pulled his car keys from his pocket and tapped at the folder. "Read. I want to know what you think it all means."

"What part?"

"You'll see. It's different."

A few other detectives had arrived while they were talking. As he started out of the room, they turned away from him, from the board, murmured to each other. The Wall of Weird was out. Today would be an interesting day.

2

Oddly, the cancer didn't start in Auntie Jo's lungs, but in her blood. I couldn't remember a day when Auntie Jo wasn't tired, but in the spring of 1992, she got *really* tired. She'd come home from one of her shifts at the diner and collapse into her chair and sometimes didn't get back up until morning. She lost her appetite, and I noticed that the random bumps and bruises inherent to waiting tables stopped fading from her arms, instead becoming dark, this nasty shade of purple, lingering for weeks. Then the random fevers started. I convinced her to go to the clinic in April, and a blood draw revealed a high count of white blood cells.

The doctor at the clinic referred her to another doctor, and in turn, she referred us to a specialist with offices near West Penn Hospital. Dr. Pavia called the extra white blood cells *blasts* and said they weren't fully developed. Unlike normal white blood cells, these blasts could not fight off infection. They originated in her bone marrow.

My Auntie Jo had leukemia.

Acute myeloid leukemia, he called it.

He was quick to point out her smoking was probably a contributing factor but not the sole cause. He advised her to quit anyway.

She said she would, but she lit up a cigarette the minute we left his office, and I had yet to see her cut back from her current pack-a-day habit.

There was talk of a bone marrow transplant. Dr. Pavia scheduled her for chemotherapy and radiation treatment all while nodding in response to Auntie Jo's complaints of time, money, and the lack of both. She didn't have insurance or healthcare, and this bit of news would not make obtaining either of them any easier. He'd heard these things before. I got the impression he heard them a couple times each day, because his answers were clear, concise, and well rehearsed. Cancer ran a tight ship. There was no convenient time to pencil it in, nor could treatment be put off. Valuable time had already been lost.

Auntie Jo asked the doctor how long she had.

He spread his hands, palms up—a couple months, five years, longer, hard to say. Another practiced answer to the most common of questions.

Although I insisted she rest, Auntie Jo worked through the first week of treatment. She even squeezed in a few doubles in an attempt to bring in extra money, but by the second week she began cutting shifts, by the third the vomiting and lack of energy kept her confined to our apartment.

About that time, the bills started. First the clinic, then the doctor, then the specialist, then treatment, followed by more treatment. We also had rent, utilities, food. The monthly envelopes containing cash continued to arrive on the eighth of every month, and I saved most of it. $34,108 on the day Auntie Jo was diagnosed, (I counted the moment we got home from Dr. Pavia's office) but now, I found myself down at the corner store buying money orders on an almost daily basis—nearly ten thousand spent in the past few months, with no end in sight.

I didn't let Auntie Jo see the bills. I most definitely didn't let her see the payments—both would cause worry, and there was enough of that. She had been home, either in her chair or in bed, when the last two envelopes appeared in their usual spot at the center of my bed, but when I got home on both of those nights after my shift at the diner, she said nothing of an intruder. She made no comment at all. The door had been locked, yet somehow, someone still managed to get in and out unnoticed.

I spent a lot of time at the diner, more time than I probably spent at home. Auntie Jo continued to insist the job kept me off the streets and out of trouble, and Krendal had no trouble finding work for me. Back in January, when I turned sixteen, he even started showing me how to work the grill. He had taught me the deep frier the year before, and the year before that I had learned the proper way to prep fresh fruit and vegetables. I was grateful for anything that took me away from bussing tables and doing dishes, although I had yet to grill a burger remotely close to the quality Krendal churned out. "Too red, too thick, too flat, too brown," he'd shout at me, his hearing long gone. Even with the two monstrous hearing aids he began wearing last year, he could make out nothing but the loudest sounds.

There were four people at the counter, six more in the booths, with Gerdy waiting and covering hostess duties.

Gerdy McCowen had moved to Pittsburgh last year with her folks. She was one year behind me at Brentwood High School, just a freshman. Outgoing and pretty, she had no trouble making friends and had taken a job at Krendal's to save up for college—she wanted to go to Brown. Lurline talked about retiring on account of her bad knees. Gerdy was good, not as good as Lurline, and certainly couldn't hold a candle to Auntie Jo in her prime. She had a pretty smile, though, and even prettier legs. Dunk called her a plain Jane, but that didn't stop him from staring at her whenever he came in to harass me. Krendal caught me staring at her on more than one occasion, too. This usually earned me one of his smiles, followed by a grunt, then a thunderous, "Dishes! Dishes!" or some other push toward busywork.

Gerdy was waiting for me to ask her out, something I knew I probably should do, but the right moment had yet to present itself (although she would tell you the right moment had presented itself plenty, and I just went chicken shit). Maybe the homecoming dance. That was coming up.

I tried hard to forget Stella, I really did, but she was never far from my thoughts—particularly today, August 8.

"You're wasting water! Turn that off!" Krendal shouted, passing through the kitchen to the small office in the back. He had put on a lot of weight in the past few years. I was standing in front of the large three-compartment aluminum sink washing the dishes from the first wave of the dinner rush. The clock above the prep station read 5:31 p.m.

I had to leave soon.

I picked up the last plate from the rack on my left and soaked it in the hot water. As I rinsed the suds away, Gerdy came in with a bus bin containing four more plates, six glasses, and assorted silverware. She shrugged, smiled, and set it down beside me before heading back out front. My eyes lingered on her backside as she strutted toward the swinging door, and I had to force myself to look away. I thought of Auntie Jo in that same uniform. That did the trick.

"Mr. Krendal! I gotta get out of here for a few minutes. I need to run home and check on Auntie Jo!" I shouted, dumping the contents of the bus bin into the water.

Krendal's head appeared around the side of the office door. "How is Jo?"

I started to answer before I realized that he actually heard me. My eyes went to his left ear, and I noticed that the thick beige hearing aid on that side had been replaced with a smaller white one. When he caught me looking at it, he said, "New model. Doctor recommended. Not sure I like it, though. Most of the conversations I heard today were not worth hearing. Politics, war, hunger, and Arnold Schwarzenegger movies. Sometimes the world is better under a dull hum."

I started pulling the dishes from the soapy water, dipping each in the rinse bin before placing it on the drying rack. "She's getting worse, I think. She won't talk about it, so it's hard to tell. She's moving so slow, though. The doctor said he increased the chemo on this round, so decreased energy is to be expected. She gets sick a lot, too. When I try to get her to drink water, she doesn't want any, but she has to drink to keep her fluids up. I'm hoping she'll eat something tonight. She hasn't kept any food down for two days."

"Maybe bring in a nurse to help?"

And what would that cost? I thought. "Maybe, if it keeps getting worse."

I glanced back up at the clock—5:42 p.m.

"Go," Krendal said. "I got this until you get back. Give Jo my best. We miss her here."

"Thanks." I grabbed a towel from the rack beside me, hastily dried my hands, smacked him on the back, and bolted for the back door.

I had to go to the apartment first and check on Auntie Jo.

I nearly knocked two people over running down the sidewalk on Brownsville. In our building, I took the steps two and three at a time.

Dunk pulled the door open, while I fumbled with my key at the lock. "Dude, she's getting worse."

I pushed past him into the apartment. "You need to open some windows in here. Feels like I just walked into an oven."

"I tried, then your wonderful aunt fell trying to get out of her chair to close them. Said she was freezing. She was shaking, too. Bad. I got her back in her chair and put a blanket over her. She stopped shaking and started sweating instead. When I tried to take away the blanket and cool her off, she gave me a death stare—when a woman looks at me that way, I know it's time to back off. She's sleeping now."

Auntie Jo was in her chair by the closed window, reclined, with a thick quilt pulled up to her neck. Her eyes bobbled under her lids, lost to some dream. She wore a bright green ski cap on her head.

Auntie Jo wore hats now.

Always.

I knew most of her hair had fallen out, but she wouldn't let me see. She was too proud. I considered getting her a wig, but I didn't know how to approach the issue without things getting weird.

A Coke can sat on the scratched wooden table at her side, smoke trailing out of the opening. "How many today?"

Dunk shrugged. "I saw her with at least five, but I think she snuck one more in the bathroom. She was in there for nearly forty minutes, without so much as a courtesy flush. She finally came out when I told her I was coming in if she didn't."

I found the pack of Marlboros crammed between her leg and the side of the chair. There were six left of the original twenty.

When she was first diagnosed with leukemia, I tried to get her to stop smoking altogether. Hiding her ashtrays didn't work—I tried that years ago, and she always found another way to dispense of her ashes (like the Coke can, the window, or one of my shoes). When the chemo and radiation started, I took away her cigarettes, only to find new packs would mysteriously appear. I had no idea where she got them. I tore the apartment to pieces trying to find her hidden stash. She didn't go out. They had to be here some-where.

On our third or fourth visit, Dr. Pavia pulled me aside and told me considering how long she had smoked, getting her to quit might prove impossible. At this stage, quitting might actually do more harm than good. He said some patients demonstrated weight gain and heightened blood pressure when quitting. Weight gain would be a plus (she dropped nearly thirty pounds), but higher blood pressure would not. In many ways, the risks associated with quitting outweighed the benefits. He told me to continue trying, but not to fret if I couldn't make it happen.

We had bigger problems.

The cancer had spread from her blood to her lymph nodes, spleen, liver, and began invading her central nervous system. The chemo and radiation slowed down the progress, but only a little.

Auntie Jo was losing this fight.

Then there was the pain.

"Did she take her pills?"

"Yeah, but they're giving her tramadol. It's working now, but barely. She's already building up a tolerance. You need to let me get her something stronger."

He didn't come out and say it, but he meant heroin. Dunk brought it up a couple times before. He said when his uncle died from cancer, heroin and pot were far more effective than the oxycodone his doctor prescribed. Even better than the morphine they gave him toward the end.

"We can't give her heroin."

"Why not?"

"Because, it's heroin."

I wasn't sure what was more disturbing—the fact that my best friend wanted to give my aunt illegal drugs or the fact that my best friend could so easily access and administer those illegal drugs. I knew he could, though. He probably had some on him right now. He'd never use these things himself, but selling them was another story, and he was good at it. He started with small stuff, pot mostly, but it hadn't taken him long to realize how much money he could make simply by connecting the buyers and sellers. His dad had been out of work for over a year, with little interest in anything other than drinking. Dunk needed a way to pay the bills. Unfortunately, this was it. Two years ago, when he had gotten arrested for shoplifting, I hoped the scare would be enough to set him straight. Instead, the experience only made him more cautious.

"For a smart guy, you sure suck at coming up with a convincing argument. 'Because' is not gonna fly here," Dunk said. "You want her to be comfortable, right?"

"Heroin is addicting."

"So is oxy, morphine, tramadol, codeine, and all the other prescription crap they're throwing at her." He lowered his voice. "She might not have much time left, and if this plays out anything like my uncle, things are going to go south fast. Talk to her doctor. Tell him you can get some. See what he thinks."

"I can't ask her doctor about illegal drugs."

"He can't tell anyone if you do. It's part of that doctor-patient thing. He's bound by an oath."

"I don't think it works that way."

"Ask him," Dunk insisted. "I think you'll be surprised by what he says." He glanced up at the clock. "Christ, it's four after six—you need to go!"

I frowned at the clock. "Shit. I wanted to change and clean up first."

"No time for that, Romeo."

"She probably won't be there anyway."

"Probably not," Dunk replied. "But you gotta check, right? I get it."

He reached behind his back and pulled out a snub-nosed .38, silver plated with a black handle, and handed it to me. He started carrying it about a year ago. His father's old .38 was long gone. Dunk figured he pawned the gun like their stereo, but he couldn't be sure. I never asked where he bought this one.

I shook my head. "Not this time."

"You didn't take one last time, and she didn't show, either. It's not the gun."

"I couldn't use it. If I pulled that thing, they'd see right through me. Stella would probably laugh it off."

"Laugh off a .38 in the face? I really need to meet this chick."

Auntie Jo groaned again in her sleep.

"Are you sure you're okay watching her for a few more hours?"

Dunk glanced back at her. "Where else I gotta be? She's not much trouble. We got ourselves a date to watch *Hangin' with Mr. Cooper* in about an hour, ain't that right, Auntie Jo?"

"No heroin."

"No heroin, check. Not that kind of party. Pot's cool, though, right? Mr. Cooper is funny and all, but he's the shit with some Mary Jane."

I rolled my eyes. "I can't believe I trust you with her."

Dunk slid the gun back into his waistband. Somehow, that worked for him. "I'm just playing, you know I've got this. Go, before you miss missing your girl when she blows you off yet again."

"Open a window," I said, heading back out the door.

"I'll run that past the committee, see how the idea flies."

I was already down the first flight of stairs and halfway down the next before I heard the door close above me.

It was twelve after six by the time I jumped the fence at the side of the cemetery and started up the hill. I glanced in the direction of my parents' graves. I felt guilty for not stopping, but there wasn't any time, not now, anyway.

By the time I reached the top of the hill, my legs ached and my lungs burned. I stopped at the mausoleums to catch my breath. I bent over, massaged my calves, and sucked in air. At my wrist, the hands of my watch ticked forward—6:14 p.m.

I stood and followed the path through the mausoleums. When the empty bench came into view, my heart sank. I really didn't expect her to be there. I *wanted* her to be there, I *hoped* she'd be there, but deep down, I knew she wouldn't be. Most likely, I'd never see her again.

Dunk said he understood why I had to come here, year after year. He said he understood why I had to see her again. He said he got it. I wanted to believe him, but I wasn't sure I really did, because I didn't really get it.

I should hate her. She had been nothing but mean to me nearly every time I encountered her in the past. Her *people*, and I could think of no other way to describe them, had tried to kill me, or, at the very least, tried to scare me real good.

I should hate her.

But I didn't.

I couldn't.

I wouldn't.

Help me

Her words.

Her words to me, all those years ago. A plea unanswered.

I plopped down onto the empty bench and rested my head in my hands, my eyes closed.

Five minutes later, I heard the rumble of an engine, the crunch of tires on pavement.

I looked up.

A single white SUV approached, the windows tinted nearly opaque, headlights on, even though it was still light out.

I sat up straight.

The SUV rolled to a stop about ten yards away, facing me—the vague outline of the driver visible through the dark glass.

I wasn't sure what to do with my hands. They rested awkwardly in my lap. I wanted to appear confident, unafraid. I knew I looked like neither of those things. I moved them to my sides, gripped the bench, then I folded them at my chest and slid down slightly, hoping to at least look relaxed. I felt like a goof.

The back door opened, and Latrese Oliver stepped out in her long white coat.

She leaned into the SUV, said something to someone, then started toward me, her stride and poise representing all that I was not. Elite, superior, dominant.

When she stopped a few feet from me, she said not a word, only glared, glowered, her lips pursed tight.

The uncomfortable silence grew too unbearable. "Hello," I finally said.

"She's not here. If you want to see her, you need to come with us."

I looked past her to the SUV. "Where?"

Ms. Oliver said nothing. Instead, she turned and started back toward the white vehicle.

There are times in life when we find ourselves at a crossroads. At sixteen, I didn't quite understand this. Years would pass before I would even recognize such a thing. These crossroads become deciding factors, turning points.

Although completely out of my control, the death of my parents was one. Becoming friends with Dunk was another. I would soon find myself at a series of crossroads surrounding Auntie Jo. Life is a series of crossroads, and most of the time, they lead down one-way streets.

At that moment, I did not recognize this point as such a crossroad. I only saw it as a decision. I could stay here, I could remain on the bench, and most likely never see Stella Nettleton again. Or I could go with these people, who had shown me nothing but pain and ill will.

I stood.

I followed.

I went to the SUV.

Latrese Oliver held the back door open for me, and I climbed inside, sliding over to the seat behind the passenger. A man was in the driver's seat, about thirty years old with short brown hair and dark aviator sunglasses. A woman sat in the front passenger seat. Her long blonde hair was braided, the end of which disappeared somewhere inside her white coat—a coat identical to the driver, both the same as Latrese Oliver.

Neither of these people acknowledged me as I got into the SUV (a Chevy Suburban, as Dunk had said four years earlier). Both only looked forward, their gazes fixed on some distant object.

Oliver got in beside me and pulled the door shut. "Do you have any weapons?"

"Do you?"

She smiled at this for a second, amused. Then, "Your friend's gun. Is the weapon on you?"

So they did know about the gun.

"No."

"And nothing else?"

"No."

Oliver tugged a black hood from the storage pouch in the back of the driver's seat, unfolded the thick material, and handed it to me. "Put this on."

I considered arguing, knew it would do no good, and pulled the hood over my head.

The world went black then.

The Suburban lurched forward.

3

Preacher knocked at the apartment door.

It was the polite thing to do, and Preacher always did the polite thing. He didn't expect anyone to answer. He kept close tabs on the Gargery woman and knew she was busy knocking on a door of her own, only her door belonged to Death.

He saw the boy run off toward the cemetery—waited for him, in fact, watching from across the street, before he came up here.

Nope, his bet was on alone.

She'd be passed out in her chair, just like the last few times.

When he heard the dead bolt unlatch, this took him a little by surprise. Not much, mind you. Nothing ever really surprised Preacher. He liked to think he was always ready for just about any situation. He just didn't expect the woman to climb out of that chair.

The door opened, with a stocky teenager standing behind it. "Can I help you?"

Preacher cocked his head. "Huh, you're new."

"What?"

Preacher kicked at the bottom of the door and watched the wood frame slam into the boy's forehead. The kid stumbled back a few steps, the door swung open, and Preacher kicked it again—the door bounced off the wall and slammed shut behind him.

Rushing toward the stunned boy, Preacher drew back his right fist and punched him square in the center of his nose. He felt the soft bone and cartilage beneath give way. The boy's head snapped back with the impact, and he crumbled to the floor, unconscious.

The entire ordeal lasted about three seconds, but they were a noisy three seconds, so Preacher stood perfectly still then, his eyes closed, listening for the sound of a neighbor's opening door or voices in the hallway. He heard nothing but a steady snore coming from the chair at the window and the wheezing breaths of the boy at his feet as air tried to find a way around his newly-remodeled nasal passages.

He located the boy's wallet in his back pocket and plucked the kid's ID from the plastic slot—Duncan Bellino of apartment 207 in this same building. He put Bellino's ID in his own pocket and dropped the wallet on the kid's chest. He had no reason to hurt the boy further. He had simply gotten in the way, it happens. Preacher was good at what he did, though, and he learned a long time ago a simple gesture like taking someone's identification went a long way. That person tended to paint a nasty mental picture of what was to come, usually far nastier than was necessary, and those images proved to be a better deterrent than threats and actual violence when trying to keep someone in line. Preacher wasn't quite sure how the Bellino kid fit into all this, but he wanted to keep his options open. He might need him down the road, or he might not. No need to kill him today, though.

He stepped over the unconscious body into the apartment.

It was muggy, stifling even. Hardly the environment for some-one in Gargery's condition. He opened both windows in the living room before heading into the boy's bedroom.

Although their single meeting had been rather one-sided, he felt like he knew this Jack Thatch pretty well now. He had watched the boy grow up. He witnessed the superhero posters in his room disappear over the years, replaced with bands. The growing stacks of books had nearly become a hazard, piled over nearly every inch of space. How the kid maneuvered the room in the dark was beyond him. He no longer hid the sketchbooks, either. Dozens cluttered the top of his dresser and nightstand. Some of the drawings were even tacked up on the walls. The kid was exceptionally talented. He perfectly captured his little love interest. Her eyes seemed to follow him around the room, that sidelong grin of hers.

Preacher didn't like that.

He didn't like that one bit.

He was never fond of being watched, being *seen*, and that's exactly what it felt like.

He pulled the envelope of cash from his jacket pocket and dropped it in the center of Jack's bed.

He took out the carton of Marlboro 100s from his other jacket pocket and began hiding the cigarette packs around the apartment, all the usual places—Ms. Jo Gargery was in no condition for a complicated Easter-egg hunt. When the last pack was safely tucked away, he went to the kitchen and opened the refrigerator. He was famished.

4

We drove for about thirty minutes.

In Pittsburgh, this didn't mean much. Whether your destination was a half mile away or ten miles, everything always seemed to take thirty minutes or more. Roads were always in a constant need of repair. Lanes were closed for no reason whatsoever. Sidewalks were cracked away and replaced in a day's time, with traffic routed around the construction as if the city wanted everyone to move slow.

I tried to determine where we were. After the black hood went over my head and we started forward, I followed the narrow road out of the cemetery in my mind, picturing the left turn they made four years ago onto Brownsville Road, then then another left on Nobles.

After the turn on Nobles, I counted two right turns, then a left, then another right. After that, things got sketchy. I was lost. Eventually, the vehicle jolted to a stop. I heard a train roll past. Then we started moving again..

About twenty more minutes passed before the SUV came to a final stop and the engine shut off. I heard the two front doors open, then close.

Ms. Oliver opened her door. "Wait here."

Then her door closed, and I was alone.

I considered removing the hood, just for a second, then thought better of it. Somehow, she would know. She might be standing right outside my window, waiting for me to do just that, give her an excuse.

My door opened.

A hand gripped my arm at the shoulder and tugged. "Get out."

A male voice.

I slid toward the open door, then cautiously placed a foot outside. When I found the ground, my other foot followed and I stepped out of the vehicle. The arm tightened, squeezed, then the hood came off.

The sun faded in the distance. The thick clouds above were painted strange oranges and reds.

We were parked in a circular paved driveway. There were three more white SUVs in front of us, and four others parked in a small lot on the right. A winding driveway disappeared into the trees behind me.

A house, larger than any I had ever seen, lay in front of me. Bigger than our apartment building, maybe bigger than two. Three looming stories sheathed in stone. Some kind of tower capped the right end of the house, and a glass atrium occupied the far left. The windows, at least a dozen just in the front, were all covered with black wrought iron bars.

The house, and surrounding front yard, ended at a wall of at least ten feet made of the same stone as the house and capped with black metal spikes. The front lawn was at least two acres in size and expertly manicured. A fountain chortled at the center of the round drive, white foamy water spraying from the top.

I looked around for Ms. Oliver and finally found her standing at the front door, speaking to someone inside. This went on for a few minutes. Then the door closed, and she returned to the SUV. "Stella will see you shortly. You can wait in the foyer."

She turned and started back toward the house.

The man released my shoulder.

I glanced at him, and he nodded at Oliver. I chased after her.

A woman in a white coat identical to the others opened the right side of the large, double oak doors as we approached. Her eyes met mine, but she said nothing.

I followed Oliver into the house.

The ceiling of the round foyer soared two stories with an enormous crystal chandelier at the center. My ratty tennis shoes squeaked against the marble floor as I took in the rich dark oak wainscoting on the outer walls. A table sat at the center of the room, with a single white lily in a vase at the middle.

I glanced down at my watch and realized it stopped at 6:42 p.m. I had no idea how long ago that was. Oh hell, my shirt smelled. Diner stink wafted up at me and assaulted my nose—a lingering combination of food and dishwater. A grease stain covered the middle of my chest, probably from working the grill during the dinner rush. I had another mystery stain on my jeans: red and crusty, maybe ketchup or strawberry jam. I picked at it with my fingernail, bits flaked off and fell to the marble around me.

"My God, you are a dirty, filthy boy. Time changes many things, but that, I'm afraid, is not one of them."

When I glanced back up and my eyes found Stella standing at the back of the long hallway, my breath caught in my throat. An audible gasp slipped from my lips before I could stop it, and had I not gained some semblance of control, my mouth would have surely fallen open, agape in utter awe.

She was beautiful.

Beyond beautiful.

She might have been the most beautiful creature I had ever seen.

Her hair was as I remembered: long and brown, flowing down in waves and curls over her shoulders and back, framing a face of porcelain smooth skin, flawless in every way. Her chestnut eyes glistened in the waning light, filled with wonder and curiosity. Her lips were full, and the deepest of reds. Her shoulders were bare in a black dress that fell halfway to her knees. She stood there with such casual elegance in matching black heels, such ease and comfort.

This was the girl I remembered, the girl I drew hundreds of times, but she had matured into a young woman in the years since I last saw her.

When I finally remembered to breathe, I smelled a hint of vanilla on the air, and I knew it came from her. I had never been so self-conscious of my own appearance in all my life.

She took a step closer to me, her long legs moving with the care and grace of someone so accustomed to heels they became second nature. I thought briefly of Gerdy from the diner, the one time I saw her in heels—her clumsy movements, the uncomfortable grimace on her face as she took each step, no different from any of the other girls I knew from school or work. They so desperately wanted to grow up.

Stella was different, though.

She was so different.

She *had* grown up—she was the girl, the young woman they all strived to be.

When Stella reached me, she looked me up and down, and I wanted to run. I wanted to push back out those doors and run as far away as I possibly could rather than let her see me in my current state—my cheap, stained clothes, the kitchen grease weighing down my hair. I couldn't move, though. I was frozen, afraid my wobbly legs might drop out from under me if I called on them to do anything.

My cheeks flushed with embarrassment.

Stella reached up and ran a gloved hand through my hair—black leather gloves identical to the ones she wore during our previous encounters. Her head tilted slightly to the left, and she met my eyes. "I believe I called you ugly the first time we met, and while your cleanliness may be questionable, you have at least grown out of the ugly. Perhaps not to your potential, but there is a glimpse of the man to come, and far less of that little boy who perched himself uninvited upon my bench."

"I…I came straight from work. I wanted to change and clean up, but I didn't have enough time," I stammered, my voice sounding higher to me than it normally did.

"A true gentlemen caller always finds the time to present himself as nothing shy of his utmost best. Prim and proper and dressed to the nines. You look as if you recently rolled in the gutter for fun. Your scent is an assault on all things civilized. And your posture is a perfect representation of defeat. Stand up straight, Pip. You're better than that."

"Jack."

She grinned. "Pip to me, though. Always Pip to me."

"We're a little old to be living in a fairy tale, don't you think?"

"Are we? I like to think not. I can't imagine living in anything but a fairy tale. The real world can be an abhorrent place."

"Stella? Why don't you show young Jack around? You've seen the hovel where he lives."

I hadn't heard Ms. Oliver return. She stood at the end of the hallway, her hands clasped in front of her.

"This is a lovely home," I said.

Stella smiled again. "It is, isn't it?" She turned to the older woman. "Of course, Ms. Oliver. It would be my pleasure."

She held out her hand to me, and I took it. The touch of her long, slender fingers sent a rush of warmth through me, even through her soft leather gloves.

Stella led me down the long hallway behind the foyer, past a large sitting room on the right and a library on the left. I expected Oliver to follow us, but she did not. She stepped back as we walked past her. My eyes met hers, and although she smiled politely, there was nothing but ice in her gaze, a deep hatred that I felt I had not earned and I didn't understand. I gripped Stella's hand tighter as we moved beyond the woman, and somehow she caught sight of this, too, her eyes darting to our hands before quickly returning to meet mine.

Latrese Oliver did not follow us, but the moment we passed her, two others stepped out of a side hall on the left and fell in line about ten feet behind us. A man and a woman, both in their mid to late twenties, both wearing long, white coats identical to the others. Each had short-cropped blond hair and looked as if they might be related, a brother and sister, perhaps. They didn't say anything, just fell in step at our backs. When Stella paused at a large dark chestnut grandfather clock in the hallway, they went still, too. The distance between us was a constant.

"When I was a little girl, perhaps a year before you and I first met, I was told this clock controlled time for all of the world. Should it stop ticking, the world would stop ticking, too, simply cease to exist. I used to wake in the middle of the night and run down here to check on it. Sometimes I would bring a blanket and sleep right here on the floor. I always found the sound of it soothing, that steady tick tock."

"Who told you that? Ms. Oliver?"

"Yes."

"Is she your guardian or something?"

"Something, yes."

"You never told me what happened to your parents."

"No, I didn't."

"I told you what happened to mine."

She turned and continued down the hall, the soft material of her black dress caressing the back of her legs. "This way, Pip. You have much to see."

I started after her. I knew I should, I knew I was supposed to, but I had had enough of this—this one-sided conversation with a girl I had known yet not known nearly longer than any other person in my life.

I willed my legs to stop moving.

I stood my ground.

The ticking of the large grandfather clock was eclipsed only by the sound of my heart, thudding in my chest.

Stella must have somehow sensed this, because she paused at the end of the hallway without turning around. "No longer the obedient puppy?"

"I never was."

Stella let out a sigh. Not so much one of defeat but one of acceptance. She did not turn around. And when she spoke, some of the edge had left her voice. "It was a summer day, not unlike today. The sun had begun to set, and my mother placed me in my bed for the night. Although I was only two, I recall the evening perfectly. It might have been a week ago. Mother smelled of vanilla, a perfume I now wear in her memory."

Stella went on, her shadow slowly creeping across the floor with the setting sun. "My mother had just turned the page when a loud sound came from downstairs, a bang of some sort, quickly followed by the sound of splintered wood. The sound of three armed men kicking in our front door and entering the house. Mother frowned and tried to hide her worry as she stood and placed the copy of *Charlotte's Web* on the seat of her chair. She kissed me on the forehead and left my room."

I took a step toward her. I heard the two people in white follow with a step of their own. "Was it a robbery?"

"The police report called it a 'home invasion.' I remember hearing my father shout, then another bang. This one was different, though, not like the breaking of the door. This was more of a *pop*, followed quickly by another. My father's voice went silent, abruptly cut off. This was followed by a loud scream from my mother. I recall the urge to cry came over me but being too frightened to do so. Instead, I pulled the sheets of my bed up over my face. My father once told me sheets were magic and could protect me from all the creatures that lived in the dark, particularly the ones who made a home in my closet. Somehow, I felt those sheets could also protect me from whatever was happening downstairs. My mother screamed again. This was followed by running—not only my mother, but the men. Their shoes made this unfamiliar clacking noise on the hardwood floor of our house. As a child, I used to lie in bed and listen to the footfalls downstairs. I could easily pick out my father's steps from my mother's and separate both from those of a stranger. In this case, there were clearly three strangers, all of them chasing my mother."

When Stella paused again, I said nothing. When she continued, I let her do so uninterrupted. "She made it to the stairs. The landing at the base of the stairs squeaked. I knew she was coming for me. I waited expectantly. Instead, there was a loud thump and my mother screamed again. One of the men said something to her, but I couldn't make out the words. At that point, I crawled deep under my covers and curled myself into a tight little ball. Oddly, I remember sucking my thumb, a habit I broke more than a year earlier. There was a comfort in it, a familiarity. The sound helped me block out what came next."

I wanted to go to her, cross the hallway and go to her and tell her that she didn't have to tell me more, but I couldn't move. My legs were frozen in place. When I tried to speak, my voice deserted me.

"One of the men raped her, possibly two of them. Right there on the steps. I like to think she fought them, but I don't believe she did. I think she felt that by giving in, by giving them what they wanted, she could stop them there on those steps, keep them from finding me upstairs. Things got quiet as this went on, things got so unbelievably quiet. I think that's why the gunshot seemed so loud when it finally came. The house fell into utter silence. Then the gunshot rang out and shook the very foundation. My mother was quiet after that."

This time, I did take a step toward her on wobbly legs, but as I closed the distance to half, she said, "Don't. Please stay there. Let me finish. I need...to finish."

She drew in a deep breath, held it, then let it back out. "After the gunshot, I heard all three men as they climbed the steps to the second floor. They made a tremendous amount of noise— overturning the mattress, pulling out drawers, and dumping the contents. They left no surface untouched, unexamined. I have no idea what they took, if they took anything at all. Years later, when I would finally read the police report, the authorities were unable to find anything of value missing. Our television, stereo, my mother's jewelry—some of it quite valuable—had all been left relatively close to wherever it had been discovered. Whatever they searched for eludes me even today, but at some point they must have found it in the master bedroom, for they abandoned their search there and made quick work of the guest room. I don't believe they searched the bathroom at all.

"I heard them enter my room. I heard the first of the three men as he stood at my doorway's threshold, the breath wheezing in and out of him as if he had some kind of cold. They encircled my bed. I don't know which one snatched up my blanket and tossed it aside. I just remember my world going from total darkness to this blinding light. I remember being suddenly cold—the pocket of warm air around me gone in an instant. I kept my eyes pressed tight, unwilling to look. One of the men said, 'I don't know about this. I can't hurt no kid.' Then another said, 'I ain't turning down this paycheck. No way. How do we get her in the bag? They said we can't touch her.' Then the third replied, 'They said we can't touch *her*. Put your gloves on, you idiot. Grab her with the pajamas.' When I felt someone grab my leg, I opened my eyes. I remember looking at all three of them. I remember taking my thumb from my mouth and seeing their faces looking down at me, these three strangers, these intruders, come to take me from my bed." She paused for a second. "I reached out to them, wrapped my little fingers around theirs. I think I hoped they would carry me to my mother."

Her voice broke, a crack on that last word. I thought she might cry. She didn't. When she finally spoke again, it was only after the draw of another deep breath.

"Come, Jack. Let us walk in the garden," Stella said.

Jack this time, not Pip.

I followed after her.

5

Detective Joy Fogel climbed the three concrete steps of the two-story brick house off Greenlee Road and knocked on the door. There was a doorbell, but two wires stuck out from under the plastic plate, and it looked like it probably hadn't functioned since Reagan held the presidency. The small front yard hadn't been mowed in weeks—dandelions and other assorted weeds thrived among the long blades of grass. As she waited, a large bumble bee hopped from one bloom to the next.

She was about to knock again, when the wooden door opened. A man in his mid to late seventies stood behind the glass of the storm door separating them. He wore a yellowed tank top over faded jeans. What remained of his gray hair was trimmed short, a military cut.

"Yeah?"

Fogel shifted the manila folder from her right hand to her left and smiled. "Are you Detective Stack?"

"Former Detective Terrance Stack, just Terry now. What can I do for you?"

"I'm Detective Joy Fogel. I'd like to talk to you for a few minutes, if you can spare the time."

His eyes dropped to the folder. "Faustino send you?"

Faustino hadn't sent her. In fact, he had no idea she was even here. She didn't want to lie, though. She suspected this guy would see right through a lie and this conversation would end up being very short. "He briefed me this morning. I'd like to talk to you about '78."

Stack glanced back over his shoulder, then returned his gaze to her. His eyes were tired, bloodshot. He smelled of stale beer.

"Can I come in?"

"I don't know if that's a good idea."

"Just a few minutes. I promise."

"If Faustino briefed you, then you already know everything. There's nothing I can add."

"You investigated the crime scene. You were first to arrive after the uniforms secured the house. A written report can only convey so much. I need to know what you left out of the report," Fogel said.

"Everything is in there. I didn't leave anything out."

Fogel said nothing. She repositioned the folder, her eyes on him.

Stack said nothing, either, his eyes on her. As a detective for over thirty years, she imagined he could outstare the best of them.

"I know it eats at you, an unsolved case like this. I can help, but you've got to talk to me."

Stack sighed, unlocked the glass storm door, and pushed it open, holding the frame at the top. "Come on, before I change my mind."

Fogel ducked under his arm into the house.

She found herself in a small living room. A nineteen-inch television sat on two milk crates in the corner, with a battered brown leather recliner positioned in front. A metal TV tray with three empty bottles and one half full bottle of Iron City stood beside the chair. On the television, the evening news droned on. Stack stepped past her and clicked it off. The air in the room smelled stagnant. She wanted to open a window. "Is your wife home?"

Stack snickered. "Are you in homicide?"

Fogel nodded.

"I gave up on wives after number three gave up on me. You know how it goes—never home, the job always on the mind. Tough sleeping with the images of bodies floating around in your head whenever you close your eyes. I got pretty good at blocking all that out when I came through the door, but not good enough. Some of them follow you inside whether you invite them or not. Wife number three ignored most of that—in the beginning, anyway. After a few years, even the best of them begin to feel like they're second fiddle to the job. Once that feeling sets in, it's only a matter of time before bags get packed."

He picked up the half full bottle of Iron City and took a long swig, then held it out toward her. "You want one? I got more in the fridge."

"Can't. I'm on duty."

He drained the rest of his own beer, set it back on the rickety metal table beside the three others, and retrieved another from the refrigerator in the small kitchen. He popped the cap off on the edge of the counter and took another drink, wiped his mouth on the back of his hand, and leaned against the back of the recliner, facing her, the beer cradled in his hand. "You don't want this case in your head, kid."

"It's already in my head. Tell me about August 8, 1978. The first one."

He took another drink, nearly half the bottle gone just like that. "I was supposed to be off. I clocked out at eight-thirty that night and was shooting the shit with a few of the other guys in the pen, when the call came in. That was a quarter after nine. A neighbor reported gunshots. 911 dispatched a unit, and they found the bodies. They taped off the house and put the call into homicide. Morgan should have gone out. He had another hour on his shift, but it was his kid's birthday, birthday number twelve, and it seemed silly for him to miss something like that. I was six months out of my first divorce, so I had no place in particular I needed to be so I agreed to go out in his place. Worst fucking mistake of my life. Partners were optional back then, so I went solo."

His voice dropped off. He raised the bottle to his lips, changed his mind. "The house was in Dormont, off Beverly. Number 98. Three stories with a stone facade, perfectly manicured lawn, even better manicured flowers in boxes at the window. Could have been in a magazine, Norman Rockwell from top to bottom. There were three patrol cars there when I arrived. Uniforms taped off the entire front yard, and all the neighbors came out to see the show. I ducked the tape, went inside. There were big splinters of wood around the frame. Looked like someone kicked the door in. I remember the chunks of wood on the floor were tagged with evidence number seven. One of the uniforms recognized me, nodded toward a room off to the left. Flashbulbs were going off on the stairs in the opposite direction. I went to the left, to a family room. That's where we found the male vic. He took a bullet to the head, right here." Stack tapped at the center of his forehead. "Perfectly clean shot, dead center. The back of his head was missing, spread out between the coffee table and the carpet. Looked like he had been sitting on the couch reading the *Post-Gazette*, got up when the unsubs burst through the door, and got about two steps before they plugged him. 9mm round, heavy jacket." He tapped his forehead again.

"They didn't try to subdue him?"

Stack shook his head. "This was an execution. They came through the door, spotted him, put a bullet in him. Flat-out execution. You know how I know? It was in his eyes, his face. When someone dies like that, they're frozen, caught in time. One second they're alive, the next they're not. His face, his expression, read total surprise. Another second or two, and he might have registered fear or anger, but he was dead before the light bulb on those thoughts had a chance to ignite. We got a lot of rain earlier, and we found some muddy footprints leading from the front door to the entrance of that room—three sets—they only came in far enough to shoot the guy, no prints deeper into the room. That tells me they came for him. Burglars would have tossed the room, these guys didn't."

"Then why did you write it up as a B&E?"

Stack clucked his tongue, took another sip of beer. "That was my captain's idea. Dormont is a nice, safe neighborhood, always has been. We had no real proof this was an execution, and he didn't want that to get out in the press. If I hadn't written it up as a B&E, he would have put someone else on the case, and I wanted to stay on the case." He shook his head. "I was damned stupid back then. Still not sure I wised up. Anyway, he said if I proved it was an execution and caught the people behind it, we'd update the report, say we held back in order to catch the perp. I went along with that. Shouldn't have, but I did."

He finished the beer, set the bottle on the table next to the others, and retrieved a fresh one. "We found the female vic on the stairs. Pretty little thing. The ME put her around twenty-three, maybe twenty-four. No older than that."

Fogel frowned. "Why the guess? No identification?"

"You read the report. You know what we found, what we didn't find." He waved a hand at her. "Let me get this out, then we can go into all that. If I don't tell you this part now, I'm not sure I'll be able to get it out at all."

"You found the woman on the stairs," Fogel prompted.

He nodded. "Her clothes were all torn apart, obvious signs of rape. Probably multiple rapes, since we had three perps. The ME found at least two blood samples when he ran a kit. Tech in '78 wasn't what we got today. She had been shot in the head, too, just like the male. Unlike the male, her face was well past 'surprised.' Frightened wouldn't even cover it. She looked worried to me. Not about what was happening to her at that moment, but at the thought of what was going to happen. I..." He trailed off for a second, cleared his throat. "I found these scratch marks on the wall, on the wood steps, too. I think she was trying to get upstairs. Do you have any kids, Detective?"

Fogel shook her head.

"Me either, but I know the look. I've seen that look on other victims—when the parent is worried about their child far more than whatever they feel for their own well being. I eased past the lab guys and the photographer at that point, and went up the stairs. Somewhere in the back of my mind, I tried to prepare myself for the sight of a dead baby. I'd seen them before, worst possible thing anyone could ever see. One of those images that sticks in your mind till the day you die, maybe past that, too. I guess I'll find out soon enough," Stack said.

His eyes filled with pain, sorrow. He forced it back down as best he could and went on. "The smell hit me first. Not the smell of a dead body, or even a burnt body, although that's what they looked like, more of a dry, dusty smell, like opening the door of an attic that's been shut up for a long time. There were three bodies on the floor. I'd never seen anything like it. They looked burnt, dried out, like something drained every ounce of moisture out of them. You've seen the pictures. One of the photographers said they looked like all the life had been sucked out of them, nothing but a shell left. The ME said they reminded him of the victims at Pompeii. Have you ever seen the pictures of the bodies found at Pompeii after the volcano erupted?"

Fogel shook her head.

"Look it up. That's what they looked like to me, too. Like they were made of nothing but ash. Like if I were to touch them, they would crumble away into dust, just fall apart. They were all on their backs, but two of them looked like they were reaching out for something. Their mouths were open, all three, caught in some kind of silent scream. The bodies were on the floor, lying around a bed. A small bed. A kid's bed."

Fogel frowned. "You didn't mention a kid at all in your report."

"Because we didn't find one. Didn't find anything to indicate there had ever been one. The bed was empty. The room was more or less empty, too. No sheets on the bed. No clothing in the dresser. No books. No pictures. There was an empty bed, an empty dresser, and a chair next to the bed, nothing else. My gut said it was a kid's room, but there wasn't a single thing in there to back that up. Aside from bare furniture, it was completely empty. Felt like a kid's room, though." He took another sip of beer and pointed at her with the bottle. "That takes me back to what you asked earlier, about the identification. We found nothing in the house. No IDs on the adults, no photographs on the walls, not even a single utility bill. Kitchen cabinets and refrigerator were all bare. The adults were living out of suitcases. We found two in the master bedroom—his and hers. Bathroom had toothbrushes and a small travel kit with shaving gear, hairbrush, and the like. Not a single personal touch in the house. Turned out the house was owned by a real estate investor who lived in Florida, and he had no idea anyone was living there. He kept the utilities on so the pipes wouldn't freeze. Paid some company to stage the place with furniture. Hired a landscaper to maintain the exterior. The two gunshot vics were squatting."

"You think there was a kid, and someone snatched it," Fogel said, more of a statement than a question.

"Like I said, we found no evidence of a kid—no clothes, no toys, the room was completely stripped down. Nothing in any of the bathrooms to indicate a kid, but that woman's face…" He trailed off, raised the beer to his lips, and drank.

"Here's the thing, though," Stack went on. "We found three dead perps in that room. Their shoes matched perfectly to the three sets of prints we found downstairs. So if there was a kid, who took the kid?"

"A fourth?"

"A fourth," he repeated. "I spent more than a decade looking for that fourth and got nowhere. When other bodies started piling up—a new one every year, always on that same date—today's date—I grew convinced there was someone else out there. I was certain the same someone killed the first three, took the kid, took all evidence of the kid, and has been killing once a year ever since, and that person is a ghost and once they get their claws into your head this case doesn't go away." He raised the bottle again, brought it to his lips, then changed his mind and set it beside the empties on the rickety table. "You need to walk away from this. Let this mess retire with Faustino. He caught the bug from me, and if you catch it from him, you'll spend the rest of your career hunting a ghost. You'll spend every day of the year waiting for the eighth of August to come around. You don't want that. You don't want any of it."

Fogel knew he was probably right. Faustino hinted as much. But this case was already in her head. It took root. And there was nothing she liked more than a good puzzle to solve.

"How many bodies does Faustino have on that board of his now? Thirteen? Fourteen?"

"Sixteen."

Stack's eyes fell to his beer bottle but he didn't pick it up. "Seventeen, by day's end. You can be sure of that, as sure as the ticking of a clock."

"You said the adults were squatting. Did you find a car? They might have been living out of a vehicle, keeping all their stuff in there."

Stack shook his head. "Thought about that. Back then, abandoned cars were reported directly to the mayor's office and towed to a city yard by a company called McGann and Chester. Not sure who handles that sort of thing nowadays. We put a flag on three square miles surrounding that house, looked at every car that got towed in for the next few months. We had a couple contenders— cars full of clothing, mostly—but the prints never matched the man and woman from the house. They weren't in any of the databases, either. Local or federal."

Stack's eyes hadn't left the beer, and he finally reached for the bottle, finished it off. "I did twenty-eight years with the Pittsburgh PD, twenty-four of those with homicide. In that time, I solved well over a hundred cases. The few unsolved I left behind will probably stay that way. I know I did everything I could on them. My record

is solid, I'm at peace with that. This is the only one that nags me."
He lowered his voice, his fingers picking at the label on the bottle.
"My gut tells me the whole thing is about the missing kid, always
has been. All those bodies. The ME back then was a buddy of mine,
and when he did his exam of the woman, he confirmed that she
gave birth at least once. I didn't put that in the report, but you
should know. Faustino knows. I'm certain there's a kid out there,
somewhere. That child would be at least fourteen years old now,
maybe older. You really want to bust open this case, you find the
kid."

6

The ceiling of the long hallway vaulted at the center, a large arch that began with elaborately thick crown molding at the base and curved to a height of at least eighteen feet. The ceiling with the arch was coffered in deep mahogany over what appeared to be marble slabs. Dotting the elaborate millwork every ten feet were crystal chandeliers.

A staircase filled the center of the hallway's mouth, wide at the base and curved as it disappeared into the next level. As I approached, I realized the staircase not only went up at least two more floors, but down as well, disappearing into a basement level.

Smaller hallways and doors split off from this center throughway on both sides. The doors were all closed, and within each hallway stood no less than two people dressed in the same long, white coats as the others. Their eyes followed as I followed Stella through the center of the house and out through one of five sets of French doors at the back onto a large, rounded cobblestone patio.

Stella stood out there, waiting for me, her gloved hands clasped at her back, her dark hair catching the wind and fluttering over her right shoulder. "You shouldn't dawdle. It's not polite to keep your hostess waiting."

"I'm sorry, I was just admiring your home."

"You shouldn't apologize so much unless your goal is to cement your social standing somewhere beneath whoever the apology is directed. I suppose in this case, that may be true. Ms. Oliver has made it quite clear you are beneath me and always shall be beneath me. Perhaps that is why you follow behind me rather than walk at my side? The intricacies of psychology fascinate me so."

I crossed the patio and came to her left side. "I meant to say, your house is beautiful, almost to the point of distraction. I want to take it in, not rush past."

"If that is what you meant to say, then you should have just said it. This house, it's only a place. No better or worse than any other."

"It's much nicer than where I live."

"Nicer? Yes, of course. There is little doubt of that. But better? These are two very distinct things, and one could argue both sides, I suppose."

She stepped to the edge of the patio, past white metal furniture and white roses in tall vases, to a winding cobblestone pathway weaving away from the house and out into the immense yard. The lush grass rolled away from the patio, through hills of varying heights dotted with trees. All were tall and well groomed, a canopy of green holding the slightest hint of orange and brown as the hand of fall touched them, one by one.

Strangers in long, white coats stood among the trees, all eyes on us, so many I couldn't count them all. When Stella looked out across the lawn, looked out at them, they diverted their gazes. Some even stepped behind the trees, but none left. If anything, it seemed more were coming, but I couldn't tell from where.

Stella started down the cobblestone path deeper into the yard, and I quickly fell in step beside her, careful not to fall behind this time. "Even within a forest, one can feel trapped while others find freedom within the confines of a prison cell."

"Is that why you wrote 'help me' on the bench? You feel trapped?"

Stella smiled. "Oh, that was so long ago. Just the workings of a child's overactive imagination. You should pay it no heed."

"So you don't need help?"

From the corner of my eye, I caught one of the people in white slipping around the trunk of a large oak, attempting to stay opposite us, out of sight.

"I have need for nothing," Stella replied. "I wrote that in a moment of weakness."

Stella paused and took a step closer to me. She stood on her toes, leaned toward me, her mouth only inches from my ear. When her warm breath slipped over my neck, the blood coursed through my body. "Be mindful of what you say," Stella whispered. "The trees have ears here."

She fell back on her heels, and her brow furrowed. "You smell atrocious, like you slept at the bottom of a Dumpster behind that greasy spoon of yours."

"I'm sor—"

Her dark eyes narrowed, and she drew in a breath, ready to scold me again.

"This is what work smells like," I quickly said before she could say anything.

"Tsk, tsk, poor Jack. Why someone would purposely subject themselves to daily filth is beyond me."

"I like the people there. They're friendly. Mr. Krendal takes care of me. He takes care of Auntie Jo, too. They're like an extended family," I said.

"Your aunt is still alive, then?" Stella asked. She had begun walking again, following the cobblestone path.

"She is."

"She is what?"

"My Auntie Jo, she's still alive."

"Not well, though, I presume?"

"She has cancer. It's advanced. I'm not sure how much longer she'll be around."

"Perhaps she will join your parents soon. I presume they are still dead?"

I didn't answer.

With each step, the scent of vanilla wafted over to me, and I found myself edging closer to this girl. Her dress brushed my pant leg as we walked. I looked behind us, back toward the house, and found Ms. Oliver also on the cobblestone path about a hundred feet behind. Our eyes met briefly, and I turned back around.

"Why do they all follow you around like this? That Oliver woman is behind us."

"What else are they supposed to do with their time?"

"It seems weird."

"Perhaps to you, but for me, it would be odd not to have them follow me. I cannot remember a moment where Ms. Oliver wasn't at arm's reach."

"What about all these other people? Why are they here?"

"Where else should they be?"

I stopped. I'd had enough of this.

Stella went a few more steps, and then she stopped, too, and turned back to me. "What is it, Jack?"

"Why am I here? I try to talk to you, and you answer in riddles. It makes my head hurt. I've known you for half of my life, but I feel like I don't really know you at all. You brought me here. Or more accurately, *had* me brought here. You obviously wanted to see me. Tell me why. We've been doing this for eight years, and I don't understand what it is, what *this* is."

She looked to the ground, shuffled her feet, a pout on her lips. "I didn't realize I had become such a burden on you."

"You are not a burden."

"Perhaps you should forget me."

"I'm not so sure I can."

"Then you need to learn to live in the moment. The past is gone, and the future is always just out of reach. Now is all that really matters." She turned from me, her long hair rolling through the air as she started further down the path, calling after me. "Come, Pip! There is something else I wish to show you!"

She rounded a corner and disappeared from view.

I stood there for a moment and nearly turned around toward the house, but then I felt Ms. Oliver's eyes on my back and knew she probably wanted me to do exactly that. She wanted me to leave this place, to leave Stella and never come back. And that thought was enough to make me follow after Stella, follow her down that cobblestone path through the trees.

7

Detective Faustino Brier sat on a bench on the sidewalk across the street from the apartment building where Duncan Bellino lived, a paperback copy of *Jaws* in his hand. The alley where Andy Olin Flack had been found was less than a block up on the right, and the diner where Flack most likely ate his last meal stood across the street from that.

The kid was in the building, he was sure of that. The kid wasn't in his own apartment, he was sure of that, too. Bellino was under investigation for trafficking, and about three months earlier, Detective Horton in Narcotics asked a judge for a warrant to bug the boy's apartment and it was granted. They tapped the telephone in the kitchen and placed five microphones within the apartment— one in the living room, one in the kitchen, one in each bedroom, and another in the bathroom. Detective Horton was currently in the red van with Carmine's Carpet on the side parked half a block away along with three other Narcotics officers waiting for something worthwhile to get picked up. Faustino had known Horton for the better part of a decade, so when he asked if he could listen in today, Horton gave Faustino a portable receiver, and told him he owed him no less than four Steelers tickets. He could listen, but he couldn't listen within the van. A homicide detective sitting in on a narcotics sting would only raise questions if the wrong person were to catch sight of him.

The receiver was in Faustino's inside jacket pocket, a small wired earbud trailing out. He pressed the earbud deeper into his ear with his left hand and used his right hand to click the dial on the receiver from one microphone to the next. All were quiet.

Faustino was cycling back through the dial, when Horton sat down on the bench beside him and unfolded a newspaper. Faustino glanced at the headline. "You know that paper is about two weeks old, right?"

"It's all we've got in the van. I think I have it memorized now. The closest thing we have to porn is this ad on page three for women's panty hose at Jewel's Groceries. This is the worst sting ever."

Horton's eyes were hidden behind aviator sunglasses. Tattoos covered his right arm—dragons, knights, and swords. Horton (like most of the people in Narcotics) went out of his way not to look like a cop. A necessary survival tactic when working undercover.

Horton pulled a pack of gum from his pocket, popped a piece in his mouth, and offered one to Faustino, who shook his head. "So what have you learned about this kid?"

Horton shrugged. "Not much yet. He popped up on our radar about two years ago. We collared a kid with a three-ounce bag of pot just off Brentwood High School property. It took all of three minutes for the boy to give up Bellino as his dealer. Bellino was still in middle school back then, but he's moved on. He's a solid student, B average. Couple scuffles in school, typical shit, nothing serious. Got picked up for shoplifting a few years back, and the judge let him off with a warning on account of the grades. It wasn't exactly grand theft. He stole a box of mac and cheese from a convenience store. Comes from a broken home. No sign of the mother, looks like she split a long time ago. His old man isn't much of a prize. Moved here from Chicago back in '86 to run a coal plant, the place got shuttered not long after. Daddy does odd jobs now for work. He was an army ranger back in the war, but like most of those guys, not all of him came back. He held it together pretty well at the beginning but seems to be unraveling without steady work. Sleeps most days and he's out most nights, stumbles in when the sun's coming out. Rinse and repeat. The kid is more or less raising himself. All things considered, he's doing a good job of it."

"You mean, aside from the whole drug dealing thing?"

"Yeah, aside from that. When his pop got laid off, looks like he got into the petty stuff, probably dealing just to put food on the table. Kept it small. If he'd stuck with just pot, we'd probably let it go, but like I said, he gets good grades, and a smart dealer is a dangerous one. It didn't take him long to use pot to set up a distribution channel, bring in a few employees, and get a small business going. His supplies are coming from one of the bigger players in town, a guy named Henry Crocket. We've been after him for a while but haven't been able to make anything stick. Crocket is good at spotting potential, and it looks like he's taken Bellino under his wing. A kid like this with a tutor is a problem in the making, so we're hoping to cap it off earlier and maybe use the kid to take down Crocket. Bellino has gotten slick at the ripe old age of sixteen, though. He's stepped up into the harder products—heroin, crack, coke, as well as prescription narcotics—and somehow he's able to keep it under the radar. We don't know where he stores his product, who exactly he's got working with him, or just how far his crew branches out. He manages to keep himself clean while pulling the strings. We've had lenses on him whenever he goes out in public, and aside from catching a few quick meetings between him and Crocket, we haven't picked up anything useful yet. Left unchecked, I see this guy growing up and taking over Crocket's entire racket. We need to stomp him out before that happens."

"When I was sixteen, I collected baseball cards and worked at a pizza place," Faustino said.

"I said the kid was smart, I didn't say anything about you. What makes you think he's wrapped up in your Wall of Weird?"

Faustino nodded toward the diner down the street and told him about Flack's body, found in the alley back in '87.

"Well, that's thin."

"Like you said, I'm not that smart."

Horton nodded up at the apartment building. "They've got a small arsenal up there. At least six weapons registered to the father, probably more that aren't in the system. Bellino had a switchblade on him when he got picked up for shoplifting."

The small speaker crackled in Faustino's ear as someone from the van broke into the channel. *"We found Bellino, spotted him in a window. The Gargery apartment on the third floor."*

"Who's Gargery?"

Horton turned the page on his newspaper. "Forty-year-old waitress. She worked at your favorite diner down the street there, until some kind of cancer got hold of her. Aside from doctor visits, she doesn't get out much. She's got a nephew taking care of her. Looks like the nephew and Bellino might be working together. We think Bellino figured out his place is being monitored, so he's running his business out of the Gargery apartment one floor up."

"What's the nephew's name?"

"John Edward Thatch. Bellino calls him Jack. Sixteen years old, clean sheet."

"No audio on the Gargery apartment?"

Horton shook his head. "Judge wouldn't sign off. Won't even let us watch Thatch outside the building because he's a minor. It's killing me, because we know he's involved. Right before you got here, he bolted from the diner—he works in the kitchen—ran into the apartment building for a few minutes, then back out again. We're not supposed to, but I had one of my guys tail him, anyway. He ran off into the cemetery, of all places. We had to drop back—too easy to get spotted in there."

Faustino thought about this for a second. "So maybe this Thatch kid is working as some kind of go-between for Bellino and Crocket?"

"That's the theory. Crocket knows not to get his hands dirty.

He's teaching Bellino the fine art of dealing so he keeps himself insulated, and Thatch is making some side money as a go-between." Horton lowered his voice. "Remember how I said the aunt has cancer? She doesn't have insurance, and her nephew has been footing the bills in cash—he's not making that kind of money washing dishes."

The radio crackled again. *"Tall and Lanky, coming back out the front."*

Faustino fought the urge to look at the front of the apartment building and instead kept his eyes on his paperback. He caught the words *There's nothing in the sea this fish would fear. Other fish run from bigger things. That's their instinct. But this fish doesn't run from anything. He doesn't fear.*

Beside him, Horton peered at the newspaper. More accurately, peered *through* the newspaper. He hadn't noticed the small hole in the fold when Horton first pretended to read. Horton spoke softly. "This guy showed up right after Thatch ran off. Doesn't live in the building, and we haven't seen him around the neighborhood."

"Somebody new on Crocket's crew?"

"Maybe."

Without averting his gaze, Faustino watched the man push through the apartment building door and out onto the sidewalk. He pulled a pair of mirrored sunglasses from his breast pocket and slipped them on, drew a deep breath, and smiled, before turning left and starting down the sidewalk.

Before Horton could object, Faustino stood and started after the man, following about ten feet behind on the sidewalk on the opposite side of the street.

8

The cobblestone path weaved through the most beautiful garden I had ever seen.

Stella somehow managed to stay a few steps ahead of me. Her vanilla scent drifted through the air. She hummed a tune I didn't recognize as she strolled along, something familiar, but like her, the name remained just out of reach. The heels of her shoes clicked along on the stone, and when I caught myself staring at the back of her legs below the hem of her black dress, I had to look away. To watch her was maddening. All rational thought left me with my eyes on her. This girl, this unbelievably beautiful girl. When she turned the corner a few paces ahead of me and disappeared from view, I should have welcomed the reprieve. I didn't though. Instead, I sped up, that vanilla scent tugging me along.

On either side of me, two others dressed in white coats rolled around the trunks of a pair of sycamores, keeping the trees between us.

9

Tall and Lanky had dirty blond hair, slightly ruffled, probably a month or so from its last cut. He wore brown loafers, dark denim jeans, and a pea-green jacket even though it was warm enough to go without. Although still across the street, Faustino recognized the slight bulge under the left shoulder and knew the man carried a gun. Something in the swing of the arms always gave it away. Faustino figured him to be a little under six feet tall. Probably in his mid-forties, tough to gauge. He only caught glimpses of the man's face.

Tall and Lanky was careful—he stopped about every other block to peer into random shop windows and study those walking both ahead and behind—a skilled behavior, willing to take time, patient. When the man turned right on Willock Road and disappeared from sight, Faustino cursed, quickened his pace, and darted across Brownsville amid the slow-moving traffic, narrowly avoiding a kid in a suped-up Mustang lost to his own blaring music.

Willock Road crossed Brownsville at a steep hill, and it wasn't until Faustino reached the peak at the corner that he picked up the man again, just in time to see him drop into the driver's seat of a black Pontiac GTO parked on the west side of the road. The door swung shut with a defiant thud, followed by the guttural roar of the engine.

No longer worried about being seen, Faustino quickened his pace. He pushed past a man in his thirties walking a Siberian Husky along the sidewalk and managed to catch the license plate of the GTO as the car jutted out into traffic and disappeared over the next hill, leaving nothing but the haze of exhaust behind.

10

"Hurry now, Pip. You mustn't keep a girl waiting!"

I followed the cobblestone path through the thickening trees, this growing forest hidden away on a property larger than my entire block. At some point, I noticed that we lost the sun and my way was lit by tiny white twinkle lights strung through the heavy branches above, artificial stars set in the night sky.

The cobblestone path came to an abrupt end at the edge of a flagstone patio, at the center of which was a dark blue pool. The lights from the path continued over the water—long strands twisting together in seemingly random patterns from one edge of the patio to the next, creating a canopy of light. The water shimmered beneath, rippling and shuddering at the touch of a thin breeze. The pool itself didn't look like a pool at all but appeared to be carved from the stone, more of a natural accident than a manmade wonder.

A pool house occupied the opposite side, a single lamp burning from somewhere within, the windows glowing with the light.

A man and a woman in white stood motionless at the pool house. I counted four others in the trees.

Stella stood at the water's edge, her back to me, her skin pale in the artificial moonlight. "You smell atrocious, my dear Pip. Wash yourself."

"What?"

She shifted her weight from her left foot to her right and let out a sigh. "Bathe. Clean. Scrub. Do whatever you must to rid yourself of that godawful odor."

Stella crouched down, removed her right glove, and slipped her fingers into the water, rolling them through it. "It's quite warm."

"I'm not gonna—"

"Are you bashful, Pip? Have you never been naked in front of a girl?"

The truth was, I hadn't. There was a girl about a year ago at a party out at the old steel mill on Church Road, Missy Wiedeman. I knew her from school, but we hadn't really talked much. The two of us somehow got paired up in a dark closet during a game of Sixty-Seconds while Dunk was trying to hook up with Carla Bieder, a bottle of Jack Daniel's Dunk stole from his father flowing between the four of us. This particular game was one of Dunk's favorites because it usually took all of five minutes for everyone to get drunk enough to head on off into the dark. I would describe the experience as *intensely awkward*. I tried to find her mouth, but instead my lips landed on her nose. We tumbled out of the closet having gotten nowhere, and both opted to drink rather than revisit the dark room for the rest of the night. The spectacular hangover on Sunday morning was a fitting underscore to my own, well, under-score.

I saw Missy in school the following week. We nodded an awkward hello. She moved to Philly with her family about a month after that.

Stella tilted her head, a thin smile playing at her lips. "Not even your friend, Gerdy?"

"How do you know about Gerdy?"

"It's okay, Pip. You and I only see each other once per year. She may have your body. I understand you have needs. Boys your age are built of those needs." A gloved finger twisted through the curls of her long, brown hair. "Your heart belongs to me, though. I think we both know that, don't we, Pip?"

"Plenty of girls have seen me naked," I blurted out, knowing it sounded as false as it was.

"The fragrant scent of stale diner draws them in, I suppose." Her gloved finger found her bottom lip, traced the edge. "Please, Pip, wash."

I looked past her to the two figures in white standing at the pool house, the others in the trees, those silent eyes, all on us. I tried to move, but my arms and legs simply wouldn't.

Stella let out a sigh and crossed the stone to a lounge chair at the pool's edge. She turned toward the water, her back to me. "My little Pip. So wondrously bashful."

She reached behind and tugged at the zipper of her dress, pulling it down to the small of her back. The black material fell away, dropping from her shoulders to her arms, to the stone at her feet. Stella stood there for a moment in only a black bra and matching panties, a statue of perfectly smooth, white skin bathed in moonlight, highlighted by the soft twinkle of the lights strung above. She stepped out of the dress and raised first her left foot, then her right, removing her heels. Stella peeled away her remaining glove, and without looking back at me, dove into the water, breaking the surface with the agility of a knife through butter.

The pool was shallow on this end, no more than four or five feet. She adjusted for the depth with practiced ease, cutting through to the bottom. She twisted parallel at the floor, the kicks of her slender legs propelling her from one end of the water to the other. She resurfaced on the opposite end of the pool, turned, and smiled back at me, saying nothing.

I kicked off my shoes and peeled my filthy shirt over my head with absolutely none of the grace Stella had shown. I nearly fell over trying to get my jeans off. She giggled and laughed through all of this, one arm on the stone edge of the pool, holding her above the surface, while her legs fluttered beneath the water. I kept my boxers on, walked past her pile of clothes, and jumped awkwardly into the water. I dropped like a rock, and when my feet touched the bottom, I pushed back off and broke the surface. The pool was only about five feet deep where I stood, just shallow enough so I could keep my head above water. The temperature was warm, warmer than the night air. Water had gotten into my ears and nose, and I shook my head in an attempt to rid myself of it.

Stella watched me curiously from the other side of the pool, the deep end, smiling but saying nothing.

I looked out across the water to her. I tried to walk closer, but within another foot, my head was barely above the surface. "I can't swim."

"No?"

"My aunt enrolled me in summer swim camp once. I think I was around nine or ten, but I never got the hang of it. I went three times and gave up. Not much need for swimming around here. It's not like we live near the ocean or anything."

"But wouldn't you like to travel to the ocean one day?"

"I like it here."

"You don't desire to see the world? Visit far-off places? Discover new things?"

I shrugged. "My friends are here. I have my aunt, my job. Maybe one day. I don't know."

Our words picked up a strange echo from the water, reverberating through the distance that separated us, the softest whisper as loud as a shout.

"Would you follow me to the ocean? If I went?"

"Is that what you want?"

"A question for a question, Pip? I wonder where you learned such a thing."

"I think I would."

"What?"

"Follow you."

"And leave your aunt behind? Your friends? That job you seem to love so?"

I replied, "Not today, but someday."

"You can spend a lifetime waiting for 'someday' to arrive. Ask your aunt if she ever saw her 'someday'..." Stella pushed the damp hair from her eyes. "You'll spend your life in this town, in that little diner. You'll never climb a mountain or explore a dark cave. You'll never walk the streets of Paris or even visit New York—the largest metropolis, only a few hours away, yet an impossible journey for a boy like you. You'll blink your eyes, and when you open them you'll find yourself sitting on a rocking chair at some retirement home right here in Pennsylvania with a lifetime behind you and your 'someday' nothing more than a distant mirage, hazy at best. This town is filled with the likes of you."

"If I'm so ordinary, why am I here right now?"

"Because it's our day, don't you think? Do we need another reason?" Stella placed both hands on the edge of the pool behind her, faced the sky, and floated on her back. The water glistened on her exposed flesh, the black material of her underwear shimmering, her knees slightly bent.

I took a step closer. The waterline now at my chin. "Why do you send me money?"

"I believe I've told you before, I don't."

"I know it's you."

"Why would I do such a thing?"

I looked around the large yard, the pool, the lights of the house looming behind us through the trees. "I don't know, maybe some kind of charity thing."

"You are not a charity to me, Jack."

"No? Then what am I?"

She lowered her legs back down into the water and smiled mischievously. "Are you sure you can't swim?"

"There are at least three instructors at that summer camp I mentioned who would gladly write you a letter that says I have no business setting foot off dry land."

"That's too bad." Her left hand disappeared beneath the water and came back with her bra. She tossed it across the pool, and it landed with a splash a few inches from my face. I watched in awe as she reached back beneath the water, removed her panties, and threw those toward me, too. With a giggle, she dove beneath the surface.

The water was impossibly black.

My gaze remained fixed on the place where Stella had been, on the quieting ripple, the circles spreading and growing until the first of which reached me and pushed past, her bra and panties bobbing in the wake beyond my reach. I couldn't see anything beneath the surface of the water, and all had gone silent as the seconds grew to a minute.

Stella broke the water a few feet away, between the deep end and where I stood. She tilted her head back into the water, clearing the hair from her face.

I opened my mouth to say something, and she raised a finger to her lips.

I couldn't help but look at the figures in white standing at the pool house. They hadn't moved, nor had the ones in the woods. All their eyes were on us, greedy and silent. I thought about the gun Oliver carried under her coat all those years ago and studied the coats of the two near the pool house; it was impossible to tell if they concealed weapons as she had, but my gut told me they did, for reasons I had yet to understand.

Stella drew closer, only inches from me now, somehow that vanilla scent still present and lofting around her. To breathe it was intoxicating, a siren's song. Images danced in her dark eyes, and I wanted to understand the thoughts behind those eyes, I wanted to hear more of her voice, that smooth, melodic voice, upon the summer night air.

I wanted to touch her.

I wanted to reach across the mere inches of water that separated us and pull her to me, pull her body against mine. The outline of her breasts were barely visible in the dark water, and when I found myself staring, I forced my eyes back to hers.

"I know you find me attractive, Jack. It's okay to look, I know you want to. I don't mind. I want you to look," she said in the softest of whispers.

I reached for her, a tentative hand, hoping she wouldn't notice how bad I was shaking. As my fingers drew close, though, Stella drifted back, drifted a few inches back into the deeper water where I could not follow.

"That's just mean," I said, stepping forward, the waterline now halfway up my chin.

"Why, Pip, I don't believe you've earned the right to a touch. Not yet."

"How about a kiss? Let me kiss you." This might have been the boldest request I ever made. I couldn't think of anything I wanted more—anything I ever wanted more. "I have thought about you every day since we were eight years old. From that first moment I ever saw you…you were a part of me—you *are* a part of me, a part I didn't even realize was missing until that day, but one I feel whenever I'm not with you. There's a hole in my heart when you aren't near me. I don't want to know that feeling, not anymore. Never again."

These words poured out before I could stop them, and as soon as I finished, I wished I could take them back. I sounded like the young hormone-driven boy I was. This wasn't hormones, though. This was something else, something much more, and I wanted her to know that, as awkward as trying to verbalize it might be.

Stella's eyes remained fixed on me, her lips slightly apart. Oh, how I wanted those lips.

"Say something, please."

She didn't. She only watched me.

Beneath the surface of the water, her legs swayed gently back and forth, a simple movement that somehow managed to keep her afloat.

Stella raised her hand from the water, glistening drops falling from her fingertips and down the length of her arm. She reached for my cheek, her fingers outstretched, and I wanted her so desperately to touch me at that point. I ached all over for her touch. She didn't, though. Her fingers hovered less than an inch from my skin, and when I tilted my head toward those fingers, she moved away, keeping that little distance between us.

A tear formed at the corner of her left eye. It ran the length of her beautiful face and fell into the waters of the pool. "I can't," she said in a voice so soft at first I wasn't sure she spoke at all.

"Why?"

"I just—You should go."

"Stella, no. I—"

"Out of the pool, both of you," Oliver said from behind me. I turned to find the woman standing at the edge of the pool, her eyes fixed on the girl in front of me, a white robe in her hand. I didn't hear her walk up. For all I knew, she may have been there the entire time, watching us like the others. "Stella. It's time."

Stella drew in a breath and drifted soundlessly away from me, further back toward the deep end of the pool, beyond my reach. I remained still, standing there, unable to move. Her eyes remained on me for a moment as she floated backward. She turned and swam the remaining distance to the far wall. She grabbed the edge and held a hand out to the man dressed in white standing near the pool house door. "Help me out."

The man said nothing.

He shifted his weight and seemed to shrink back toward the building at his back, his eyes locked on Stella's outstretched hand. "Help me out of the pool," Stella repeated.

He shook his head. "No."

Stella reached for the woman standing beside him. "You, then."

The woman shook her head and took a step back.

Stella eyed them both, then placed both hands on the edge of the pool and pulled herself out, standing there naked, before us all.

I heard Oliver round the side of the pool, but I didn't see her. My eyes were locked on Stella, on the water dripping from her long, dark hair, down her bare back and legs, and pooling at her feet. Oliver pushed past the two sentries at the pool house and wrapped the robe around Stella's shoulders, cinching it at the front. "Enough of this," Oliver said to her. "You're needed at the house."

Stella didn't move, though. She stood, statue-like, facing the two in white. A murmur rose from the sentries standing among the trees surrounding the pool. Oliver hushed them all with a single glance, then turned back to Stella. "Now."

Oliver started back around the pool toward the house, scooping up Stella's gloves as she went. Stella fell in line behind her, the thin robe clinging to her frame. Her eyes met mine for the briefest of seconds as she passed—the tears were gone, the warmth was gone, her eyes were dark, as if the girl from only moments earlier somehow retreated deep inside.

Oliver nodded toward me. "Get him out of the water. Burn those horrid clothes of his and give him something to wear, then bring him to us. I want him to watch."

The license plate turned out to be a bust. Faustino knew he wrote the number down correctly, but when he keyed it into the DMV, the plate came back as "UNKT" or "Unknown Tag." He was still staring at the computer screen when Fogel entered the office and dropped the folder for the '78 murder on the desk between them.

"How's Stack holding up?"

She dropped into the chair across from him. "You didn't say anything about a missing kid."

"It's just a theory. We've got lots of theories. Stack's theory happens to involve a missing kid."

"And yours doesn't?"

"I can see why he'd lean that way, and I want to agree with him, but I've learned half of being a good cop is keeping an open mind. The second your brain wraps around a specific theory, you tend to block out all other possibilities. If your theory is wrong, and you're no longer willing to accept other theories, you've got zero shot at solving the case," he explained. "Stack closed all the other doors. I kept them open. That's where we differ."

Fogel flipped open the folder and pulled out the photographs of the victims, laying them out side by side on the desk. "How do you explain the differences here? Why do these three match all the others on your Wall of Weird, while the man and woman found downstairs appear to be regular homicide victims?"

Faustino looked at the photographs—the man in the library and the woman on the stairs. "I agree with Stack on that part of his theory. I think the three men we found upstairs are responsible for killing these two. Stack and I have always butted heads on what came next, though. We could never agree on who killed the three perps."

"You don't think it was his mysterious 'fourth perp?'"

Faustino said nothing for a second, his thumb flicking the edge of one of the photographs. "I don't think there was a fourth at all."

"Then what killed them?"

"I think whatever they found in that room killed them," Faustino said. "And whatever it was, they were the unfortunate souls who let it out."

12

Stella and Ms. Oliver disappeared down the cobblestone path, and I remained frozen in the water, both unwilling and unable to move. For the first time, I realized how quiet the world had gotten. Not a sound from a single living thing. The sentries at the pool house watched them leave, too, as did the ones in the woods, but none moved.

"Out of the water," the male sentry at the pool house finally said, breaking the silence.

Whether he intended me to see it or not, the barrel of a rifle slipped out from under the right side of his coat, then disappeared again within the folds. The woman beside him kept her gaze fixed on the cobblestone path at my back.

I turned, found the steps behind me, and climbed out of the pool. I walked around the edge toward them both, shivering as the night air found my wet skin.

"You'll find everything you need in there," the man said, nodding toward the pool house behind him. "You've got one minute."

The pool house was a little larger than our living room, about the size of a small hotel room. A queen-size bed filled one wall. A dresser, a small desk, and a single chair lined the others. A door at the back opened into a bathroom. The bare walls were painted a muted white, and the floors were some kind of dark hardwood. Heavy drapes covered all the windows. I pulled a thick, white towel from a shelf near the door and dried off. Atop the bed, I found a white button-down shirt, khaki pants, socks, underwear, and a pair of black loafers, all new, still tagged and in the packaging, all in my size.

"Let's go," the man said outside the door.

I quickly dressed, then stepped back outside.

"This way," he said, and I followed with the woman behind me, my eyes drifting over Stella's damp footprints on the cobblestone, glistening under the twinkling lights.

Although lamps burned inside the house, dark shadows pushed the light aside from all corners like living, breathing creatures defending what was rightfully theirs. The man led me back through the central corridor from earlier, then turned left down another hallway. Paintings covered the walls, landscapes of places I had never been—forests and deserts, lakes and oceans, the large redwood trees and fields of grass. They were all signed by Stella, and I couldn't help but think of my own drawings, all those sketches of her—my obsession. And these other places, these far-off places, were hers.

We turned left at the end of another hallway, then came to a staircase of stone. Light from the hallway spilled over, and a dim bulb burned at the very bottom, leaving the space between in deep grays.

The man started down the steps, and when I hesitated at the top, I felt a nudge at my back from the female sentry. "Go."

The temperature seemed to drop with each step, and by the time we reached the bottom, I was shivering again. At the base of the stairs stood a small alcove, no more than eight feet square with walls made of stacked limestone. A hallway branched off both to the left and the right. We went down the right and came upon a small room with a large, steel door at the back. Beside the door was a wooden table with a small television sitting on top, the wires attached to some kind of junction box and trailing off into the stone wall.

I heard footsteps behind us and turned to find Stella coming down the hallway, still in the thin white robe, her feet bare, her hands back in gloves, with Ms. Oliver keeping pace behind her. When Stella saw me, she slowed, then stopped, her eyes locking with mine. "I don't want him here," she said to Oliver.

"This isn't your call," Oliver said.

"You can't make me."

"I can, and I will if I must. Do you really want to test me?"

Stella's eyes dropped to the floor, then back to me. Large and sad. "I don't want him to see," she said softly. "Not him."

"That is precisely why he needs to be here. You've lost focus," Oliver said. She nodded toward the man in white beside me. "Open the door."

The man reached to the large steel door, took hold of the handle, and pulled it open. The door must have been three inches thick and opened with the slow heaviness of a bank vault, the weight grinding on ancient hinges.

Behind the door, in the center of the room, was a metal folding chair. Sitting in the folding chair was a man in a black tee-shirt, leather jacket, and dark jeans, his face lost beneath a white hood. Several gold chains dangled from his neck. Hanging from the thickest was a gold dagger. His feet were bound to the base of the chair, and his hands were tied behind him. At the sound of the door opening, he faced in our general direction, but I couldn't tell if he could actually see us through the hood. "Let me the fuck out of here!" he shouted.

He shifted his weight back and forth, and the chair bounced under him, the legs scratching at the stone. "I'll kill every one of you motherfuckers!"

"Now, Stella," Oliver said.

"No."

"Now. Or it will be your boyfriend instead."

I forced myself to look away from the man in the room and turned back to Stella. Her gloved hands gripped the fabric of her robe tightly, kneading the material with an anxiety that was only matched by the mix of anger and fear on her face. She glared at Oliver, and at that moment, I wouldn't have been surprised if Stella were to reach up and strangle the woman with those gloved hands.

Oliver stood her ground, though, unflinching. "Go."

Stella drew in a deep breath, nodded, and stepped into the small room.

The man in white closed the heavy door behind her, twisting the lock into place.

I didn't know what was to come, couldn't possibly know, but I wanted to put an end to it. Whatever was about to happen.

Ms. Oliver crossed the room and switched on the small television on the table. There was an audible pop as the screen came to life and filled with an image of the room behind the door, the man in the chair, and Stella standing before him, removing her gloves.

Stella removed first her right glove, then her left, dropping them both on the floor beside her bare feet. She glanced up at the camera in the top corner of the room, then turned to the man in the chair. She reached for his hood and plucked it off.

He was in his late twenties, maybe early thirties. His hair was closely cropped. Black or dark brown. A nasty bruise covered the left side of his face, dried blood seeping from a wound above his eye. His head spun quickly from side to side, taking in his surroundings before landing on Stella. "Who the hell are you?"

"That doesn't matter."

He kicked at the restraints on his feet, but they held fast. "Get me the hell out of here."

Stella shook her head.

"Let me out before they come back, and I won't hurt you, you have my word. Untie me."

She shook her head again.

His face darkened, and he tugged at his arms, restrained behind his back. "You fucking bitch! Untie me now!"

Stella glanced up at the camera again.

He followed her gaze, and his eyes narrowed as he met the lens. "Whoever you are, you have no idea who you're fucking with! My people will burn this place to the ground. You're all dead, every last one of you. Let me go, and it's not too late to work something out."

He turned back to Stella. "Do you know who I am? What I can do to you?"

"I know exactly who you are, Mr. Visconti. Why do you think you're here?"

Hearing his name seemed to unsettle him. He stopped pulling at his bonds. His eyes narrowed. "Are you one of my girls? Did Cortez put you up to this?"

"Your girls?"

"One of my whores."

"No. I'm not one of your girls."

"You should be—a bangin' body like that. You'd make a fortune. I'd put you up someplace nice, like that new hotel down by the convention center, the Starington, I think it's called. My girls get nothing but the best. Did I interrupt bath time or something? Why you wearing a robe?" He turned back to the camera. "Is this some kind of birthday present, Cortez? Pretend to kidnap me, tie me to a chair in some basement dungeon, then send in a whore to light up my birthday candle? You've done some crazy shit, but this takes the cake! That fucker nailed me good. Whore or not, when I'm done in here, you've got a beatdown coming. I can't let something like that slide. How would that look?"

Looking back at Stella. "If you're not one of my girls, where did Cortez find you? Coslow's crew? How about you take off that robe—let me see what I'm working with. You put on a good show for me, maybe I'll buy out your contract."

Stella circled the chair, slow, casual steps. "You have a lot of girls, working for you? Your whores?"

"They come and go, but I like to keep it between thirty and fifty. Most come in from South America or Europe, though, barely speak a lick of English. A girl who looks like you who can hold a conversation, too…a girl who knows how to carry herself." He blew out a whistle. "Whoever you're working for, they're wasting your time. Let me set you up."

"The girls you bring in from other countries. You make them promises, too, don't you? A better life? A place to stay? A future?"

Visconti shook his head. "Naw, I buy them. Sometimes I trade them for drugs or guns. Everything's got a price, everything is a negotiation. What's your price?"

"Prostitution, drugs, weapons…do you think it's okay to talk about such things with me? What if I'm a cop?"

"You're no cop, you're a whore. Too young for much of anything else." He tugged at the ropes again. "You've wasted enough of my time. I've got shit to do. Untie these." He kicked his legs, but the ropes held fast.

"My people, they used arbor knots," Stella told him. "The more you struggle, the tighter they'll get."

"Your people?"

"I don't know anyone named Cortez or Coslow. The men who rendered you unconscious outside your home in Squirrel Hill, the ones who brought you here, they work for me. They brought you to me."

"No way they got past my men to do that. This is some bullshit prank." He turned toward the door. "Cortez, let me the fuck out of here!"

"The three men tasked with guarding you, the ones who were in the car with you, they're all dead. I imagine your memory is fuzzy due to the bump on your head, but it will come back to you. If it doesn't, I suppose you'll have to take my word for it," Stella said. "My men killed them, took you, and brought you here. Brought you to me."

Visconti glanced back up at the camera, then around the room, then at the ropes securing him to the chair. "Where is 'here?'"

Stella ignored the question. She continued to circle his chair. "You, Mr. Raymond Visconti of 83 Nob Hill Road, among other residences, are one of the worst human traffickers in the country. You've plucked runaways off the street, kidnapped, recruited, or otherwise coerced hundreds of women and children just in the past year. More in the last six months than the previous three years combined. Over the course of your career, you are responsible for the deaths of one hundred and sixty-three people either directly at your hand, your order, or as the result of 'business' practices.'"

Visconti frowned up at her. "Are you a cop? How do you know all that?"

"I'm not a cop."

"You want money? Is that it? I can get you money. Whatever you want."

"Do you recognize the name Manuela Seiden?"

Visconti shook his head.

"She was one of your girls, your...whores."

"I don't know their names. Cortez handles the girls."

"She wanted to come to America, try and build a better life for herself and the baby she carried. Your people in Belize promised her that better life, for her and her unborn child. Your people took the equivalent of ten thousand American dollars from her before loading her into a crate with three bottles of water and no food and attempting to ship her here aboard a container ship."

"I don't know nothing about any of that."

"She died less than two days into the journey. After the water ran out. From the heat and lack of air. Her baby with her, of course."

"I don't know nothing about any of that," Visconti repeated. A bead of sweat trickled down from behind his right ear.

Stella let out a breath, still circling, drawing closer. "The girls in the other crates...the other nineteen crates, they died, too. All but one, actually. The last one died at the dock—after you heard what happened, after you decided you didn't want any witnesses, you had one of your men strangle that one, that last one. While she begged for her life, barely alive after such a horrendous journey, you had her killed to protect yourself."

Visconti took this all in and said nothing. His eyes had grown narrow, his face pale.

"Can you imagine the pain they must have felt? The uncertainty that came with each moment after they ran out of water? When nobody answered their screams and the air began to thin? Did you bother to look at the inside of those crates before you burned them? At the scratch-marks in the wood? The blood? Traces of fingernails and bits of skin?"

"What do you want from me?"

Stella stopped circling. She knelt down in front of him. "I want you to understand their pain. I want you to feel all the pain you inflicted not only on them, but their families, their loved ones, all the people touched by their short lives. You stole these lives with the ease of a child stealing candy from the corner store."

Stella reached up, and with the flick of her wrist, her right pointer finger brushed the man's cheek. A quick touch, no more than an instant.

Visconti's body tensed, his eyes popped wide. "What the fuck!" he shouted, his head jerking away from her hand.

I leaned in closer to the television monitor. A dark smudge appeared on Visconti's cheek where she had touched him, a smear of black. At first, I thought it was my imagination, but the smear appeared to be growing.

Ms. Oliver stared at me, a subtle grin at her lips.

I turned back to the monitor.

Visconti grimaced and attempted to wipe at his cheek with his shoulder, his bindings holding him down.

Stella leaned back on her heels.

The smudge grew to about two inches long before stopping, the skin dark and crusty beneath. The sweat at his brow thickened, rolling down the side of his face.

"Do you know what life is?"

"I know exactly what I'm going to do with yours the second I get out of these ropes," Visconti said.

"Life is a force, an energy. It never really goes away, not even when something dies. That life force just transfers from one entity to the next. A flower may die while a dozen just like it spring up at its feet. A river runs dry, the fish die, and a whale is born half a world away. When a person dies, a mother and her unborn child, for instance, their collective life force returns to that place in the universe where all life began, ready to be redistributed. There is a finite amount, always moving, always shifting. A careful balance, crafted, measured, maintained. Some give life, others take it away. You, Mr. Visconti, were never meant to take life. That is not your place, it is not your reason for being. That task is meant for others, and through your actions, you've upset the balance."

Visconti's eyes narrowed. "What the hell is that supposed to mean?"

Stella rose to her feet and stepped behind him. His fingers were working at the ropes. He had managed to loosen the one around his right wrist. She reached out and took his hand in hers, her fingers wrapping around his.

Visconti's face grew paper white, and he screamed. He screamed unlike any man I had ever heard scream. She touched him only for a brief second, and I watched in horror as his fingers turned black, then the back of his hand. The blackness spread up and over his wrist before finally stopping just before the cuff of his leather jacket. His fingers stopped working the ropes, they stopped moving altogether.

I thought he'd pass out. A sheen of sweat covered his face, and his mouth twitched with some involuntary muscle spasm, his tongue protruding through slightly parted lips. His chest rose and fell with the urgency of a jackhammer, each breath drawing in with a gasp, then out again with a wheeze.

Stella looked up at the camera. Somehow, through that lens,

through the monitor I watched, our eyes met. "Please, Jack, don't watch. Don't watch this," she mouthed.

Ms. Oliver pressed a button on the wall, an intercom of some sort. "Finish this, Stella."

Stella's head jerked to the left, to a speaker outside my view, Oliver's grating voice reaching her.

"Whatever this is," I said, "stop it."

Oliver nodded at the man in white. "Hold him. Make him watch."

The man grabbed at my arms, twisted them behind my back. I tried to turn away from him, and he kicked at the back of my leg, beneath the knee, and I dropped to the floor. The woman beside him pulled her rifle out from under her long, white coat and pointed the weapon at me. "Don't."

"Watch," Ms. Oliver said, nodding at the television monitor.

Stella stood, circling the man again.

He was crying now. He didn't want to, he tried to hold back, but the tears came anyway. Sobs caught between breaths. "Please stop," Visconti said, the words barely audible.

Stella paused in front of him and reached for his face, her fingers hovering so close.

He tried to shrink away but could only move so far. "No...please..."

"Nobody heard Manuela Seiden's final pleas. She died alone in that box. Death is too good for you, but it's all I have to give."

Stella leaned forward then and pressed her lips to his, one hand behind his head, pulling him close, pulling him into her kiss. The man's body tensed, and he no doubt screamed one final time, but I didn't hear it. I lunged backward against the man holding me, I shoved him back with all the strength I could muster. The woman beside him reversed the grip on her rifle, spinning it in her hands. She brought the stock down on the side of my head, and the world went black.

The dream.

Tied down in my car seat, unable to move.

Chocolate milk spilled everywhere, my clothes soaked with it. Sticky.

A white SUV so close in front of us. The driver's seat looks like it was part of Mommy and Daddy's seat.

Our car and that car, now one car.

Smoke.

Burning.

"Daddy?"

Nothing.

"Momma?"

Nothing.

A body in the white SUV, half in, half out, hanging over the steering wheel.

A dead thing.

A dead thing wearing a white coat stained with deep spots of red, watching us.

"Daddy?"

"Jack?" from the front seat. "Are you okay, buddy?"

A groan. Momma. "I smell gas. We need to get out."

"Are you okay? Please tell me you're okay."

A door opening.

The scrape of metal on metal.

"Eddie?"

"Yeah?"

"The other SUV. They're coming."

"Get Jack out."

My eyes opened on the hallway of my apartment building.

The buzzing of the fluorescent bulb above me.

I was on the floor, my back up against the wall.

My dirty clothes from the diner, piled in my lap.

Mr. Triano, the building superintendent, hovering over me. "You been drinking, kid?" Beside him stood a second Mr. Triano, this one blurry.

I looked up at him, tried to summon words. My mouth empty, tasting of dirty cotton.

"Your aunt's in a bad way. You got no business being out partying."

I reached for my head, my hand finding the tender spot where the woman had hit me with the rifle butt. It hurt like hell.

The Triano on the right reached for me with a calloused hand. "Stand up, before someone else sees you."

I took his hand and let him haul me to my feet.

The world spun a little, tilted, then found center.

I drew in a deep breath. Both Trianos became one Triano.

"How long have I been here?" I managed to say. I expected to find blood on my fingertips, but they came away from my head clean.

"How the hell would I know? I ain't your babysitter. You can't sleep it off in the hallway, though. Get in your place. Chug a tall glass of ice water with some aspirin and find a comfortable spot on the couch. That usually works for me. Oranges are good, too, if you have one. Don't ask me why."

I looked up and down the hallway. "Did you see them bring me in here?"

Triano glanced toward the stairs at the end of the hallway. "Salvatore in 108 said someone in a white truck dropped you off outside. You managed to drag yourself up here. He bet me one dollar you'd find your apartment within thirty minutes. He said, 'Even the drunkest of drunks can find their way home.' Said, 'Teenagers have a special kind of stamina.' You assed out in the hallway, though, only a few feet from the finish line. He owes me a buck. Come on, I'll help ya."

Triano wrapped an arm around me and helped me cross the hall to my door. I felt like I was walking on stilts, someone else's legs, not my own.

My door was unlocked. I twisted the knob, and we went inside.

Auntie Jo was sound asleep in her chair, snoring loud enough to vibrate the window.

I dropped my filthy clothes inside the doorway. Triano helped me to the couch and fetched a glass of water from the kitchen.

I drank all of it, and he set the glass down on the coffee table.

"Get some sleep, kid, tomorrow's another day."

With that, he was gone.

I closed my eyes and leaned back into the cushions, the throbbing at the side of my head fading away.

A toilet flushed.

Dunk came out of the bathroom with a bag of frozen peas pressed to his face. "When'd you get home? What the hell are you wearing? You look like a waiter."

Thirty minutes later, and I told him everything. He told me about the man who punched him.

"Complete sucker punch," Dunk said. "Another half second, and I would have laid him out."

"And he left the money?"

Dunk nodded. "Five hundred in an envelope on your bed. I counted it."

"I think he broke your nose. You need to have that looked at."

"Complete sucker punch," Dunk repeated. "I'll get him next month, though. I'm gonna camp out in front of your door with a nice sawed-off, and maybe a few of my boys. We'll sit him down right here on your comfortable yet stylish couch, and he's gonna tell us what's going on. I've had enough of this bullshit."

"I don't think that's a good idea."

"You don't get a vote."

"This is my apartment. He comes here for me."

"He broke my nose. That officially made him my problem. People are going to ask me what happened. I can't let something like this go. That would be weak. I don't do weak." Dunk lowered the frozen peas. "The bleeding stopped. How bad does it look?"

"If you don't go to the hospital, it'll heal crooked. Your right eye is going black, too."

Dunk swore and replaced the peas.

Auntie Jo snorted in her sleep, and then her rhythm went steady again.

"You need to let this girl go."

"I can't."

"You said she killed a man."

"I didn't say that. I don't know what I saw."

"You said she killed a man just by touching him—which is not possible, by the way."

"Well, then she couldn't have killed him. I'm completely full of shit, and all is well."

Dunk lowered the peas again and tentatively touched the tip of his nose, grimaced, and felt around his eye. "What was his name again?"

"Raymond Visconti."

Dunk said nothing.

I leaned forward. "You know his name, don't you?"

"I've heard of him, yeah."

"Is it true? What she said he did?"

Dunk sighed. "If this is the Visconti I'm thinking about, then yeah, it probably is. He's a bad dude. Was a bad dude. Or is, depending on what your girlfriend did to him. Christ, this hurts." He replaced the peas and leaned back in the chair.

"I think she killed him."

"With a touch?"

"With a touch, then a kiss."

"Dude, do you have any idea how fucked this all sounds right now?"

"Death is too good for you, but it's all I have to give." I leaned back into the soft cushions of the couch. "That was the last thing I heard her say to him."

Dunk removed the peas from his swollen nose and lowered the bag to his lap. When he turned to me, his face was white. "The flowers."

I remembered the flowers, too.

I didn't want to think about the flowers.

"That was what, five? Six years ago?"

"Five."

"You told me she picked up the flowers and they died in her hand. Just shriveled up, dried, and fell apart when she touched them without her gloves on. You said the old woman made her go back to the bench and forced her to pick them up without gloves on. The old woman made her do it, and she wanted you to watch, like tonight. The old woman—"

"Oliver. Latrese Oliver."

"—Oliver, right. This Oliver woman wanted you to see that way back then, she wanted to scare you off. That didn't work, so now she's showing you this. Whatever *this* is."

"When Stella touched Visconti, on the cheek, at first I thought she burned him. That's what it looked like, some kind of dark burn, but I don't think that's what happened at all. She kept talking about life force—she said there was a finite amount, a carefully maintained balance. When one thing dies, the life force doesn't die with it but moves on to something else. Shifts, transfers, some kind of balance of power. I think her touch somehow took the life from that spot. The black spot was death. It only took a second."

"And what? She can't control it? That's why she wears gloves? The longer she touches someone or some living thing, the worse..."

I nodded.

"Fuck."

"Yeah."

"She can't touch anyone."

"I don't think so," I said. "Not without hurting them. Or worse."

I hadn't told him about the pool. I couldn't. I was still trying to sort that out myself.

"You need to stay away from her," Dunk said again.

"She doesn't want to be there. They're making her do this."

Dunk blew out a breath. "If this is all true, nobody is *making* her do anything. This girl could walk out of there any time she wants. Nobody is going to try and stop her."

I leaned forward. "I think that's what all the guns are for. I always thought those people in white were some kind of guard, security, protection. What if they're really there to keep her under control? She might get past one or two of them, but they're everywhere. I saw a couple dozen, probably more."

Dunk frowned. "You think they'd shoot her to keep her from getting out?"

"They're not gonna let her go," I replied. I knew what I had to do. "I'll find the house. I'll get her out."

"I'll help you," Dunk said. "After my nose grows back."

13

When we woke the following morning, Raymond Visconti was all over the news, his body found less than a block from our building, in a very familiar alley. One of the most infamous human traffickers in Pennsylvanian history, now nothing more than a husk, a shriveled up dead thing. The condition of the body was the same, too—dried and black, as if the result of some kind of fire that ate the man from inside out, leaving his clothing untouched. Unlike Flack, the local television network KTOD managed to not only get a shot of the body but show that shot on live television no less than four times before the police chief and finally the mayor stepped in and got them to pull the footage.

I knew how Raymond Visconti died, therefore I also knew how Andy Olin Flack died.

As we did five years earlier with Flack, the day Raymond Visconti's body was found, Dunk and I sat at my apartment window and watched the police put up their tape and invade our small block. We watched Detective Faustino Brier arrive, disappear into the alley for nearly thirty minutes, then step back out on the street, and look directly at our building. I half expected him to wave at my window, but he didn't.

"See that van down there?" Dunk said before finishing off his third Coke and crushing the can.

"Carmine's Carpet?"

"Yeah."

"They're narcs. They've been watching me. Trying to get to Crocket."

"The carpet guys are narcs?"

"The narcs are pretending to be carpet guys."

"You sure?"

Dunk went to the kitchen, got another soda, then returned to his place at the window. He held the cold can to his now very black eye and purple, swollen nose. "They rotate. One day it's Harwood Electric, the next day we've got Cloister Plumbing and Supplies, then there's the carpet guys. They've been out here so many times, if they were for real, the sidewalks would be carpeted by now. Nobody needs that much carpet."

"How long now?"

Dunk shrugged. "Six months? Maybe longer. Hard to say. They've got my place bugged, too. We found four mics in there. Not the best tech but good. Better than I figured local PD would have."

"You need to stop working with Crocket. You're going to land your ass in jail."

Dunk popped the top on his Coke and took a drink, wiping his mouth on the back of his hand. "I made almost 30k last month. I'm on track to beat that next month. Crocket says it's good we know where they are. If the cops are here, they're not there, they're not watching him. It's kinda fun. We feed them bogus info from my apartment and watch them chase their tails. They have no idea what we're really doing."

"He's just using you. You get popped, and he'll find another pansy to take your place."

"He's teaching me the business. Introducing me to people. He gets popped, and I end up running everything one day."

"That's your goal? To be the biggest drug dealer in Pittsburgh after your boss catches a bullet?"

"30k last month," he repeated. "I'd make ten times that if I was in charge. I can't wash dishes for a living."

"Krendal lets me cook, too."

"See? The future is bright all around," Dunk said. "No student loan debt, either. Win, win."

I had all but given up trying to talk Dunk out of his current career path. I'd talked to walls that were more receptive. I knew the guy had a good heart somewhere in there and hoped that would prevail. There was little more I could do.

"Who's the woman with Faustino? Do you recognize her?" I asked, changing the subject.

"Police for sure, but I don't recognize her."

Auntie Jo snorted in her sleep behind us.

"She's getting much worse," Dunk said.

"I know."

The next thirty days ticked by at a snail's pace as I expected a knock on the door from the police that never came. The murder of Raymond Visconti faded from the press, as did the bruises on Dunk's face.

As promised, on the evening of September 8, 1992, Dunk appeared at my door with six of his "coworkers," three of whom I recognized, three of whom I did not. All were carrying firearms. Two of them had duffle bags. I didn't ask what was in the duffle bags.

"We'll keep an eye on Auntie Jo while you're working," Dunk said, pushing past me at the door. "When your fairy godfather shows up, I'll say hello for you." He flashed a set of brass knuckles on his right hand. Dunk then ordered his crew to "set up" around the apartment—I didn't want to know what that meant, either.

"Try to get Jo to eat," I said, walking past them into the hall. "She didn't touch dinner."

At about nine-thirty that night, Gerdy found me in the kitchen at Krendal's, I was rinsing out one of the coffee makers in the large sink.

She handed me an envelope. "Somebody left this on the counter for you."

John Edward Thatch was scrawled across the front of the white envelope. Inside was five hundred dollars in twenties.

For each month that followed, the envelopes seemed to find me. Three more at the diner, a few more in my locker at school, one even at the public library—it appeared in my cubicle after I got up to return a book to the stacks. A new envelope on the 8th of every month, clockwork.

Dunk continued to watch Jo for me, but he eventually stopped inviting his friends.

I'd spend the better part of the next year looking for the house and not finding it. For five hundred dollars, Dunk even found a guy willing to run the name Latrese Oliver through several national databases, including the Internal Revenue Service. He found three women with that name living in the United States, none in Pennsylvania. When he showed me pictures, none were familiar.

When spring of the following year came, I began hanging the posters. Only a few at first, around my neighborhood, but soon I found myself in unfamiliar places, hanging them on the sides of buildings and tacking them to telephone poles. A simple sketch of Stella Nettleton, followed by the words:

Have you seen me?

Dunk was right. I should have let her go.

I couldn't, though.

I couldn't.

April 23, 1993

Seventeen Years Old

Log 04/23/1993—

Dr. Helen Durgin in Observation. Corporate Executive No. 6491 in Observation. Subject "S" scheduled and in attendance for visitation. Subject "D" within expected parameters.

Audio/video recording.

"For the record, this is Dr. Helen Durgin. I'm in the observation booth. Subject "S" is at the outer door. Subject "D" is in his room, sitting on his bed. We have confirmed his mask is on and properly secured."

"If he puts the mask on himself, how do you know it's 'properly secured?' Maybe he's faking it somehow."

Durgin read his lips and frowned. "Who are you again?"

"That doesn't matter. Answer my question."

"You people from corporate think you run the show."

"Answer my question," the man repeated.

"If you had gotten here on time rather than five minutes late, you would have seen the safety protocols as well as our procedure."

"Answer, Doctor. I'm not going to ask you again."

Dr. Durgin sighed. "The bands over the top of his head and the two on the sides all come together at a lock on the back. Once all three are fastened, an LED changes from red to green. They can only be released with this remote." The small key fob dangled from her finger. "Once the girl is inside and the door is secured, I'll release the lock so he can remove the mask."

"And he's going to speak to her? Without hurting her? They've done this before?"

"He won't harm her. Never has. They've been meeting since they were children."

"Does she understand the risk?"

"Not only does she understand, I think she thrives on it. Her handler says she goes on about each visit for days after leaving. Feeds off the rush of it."

"Who's her handler?"

"Latrese Oliver."

The man nodded. "Okay, let her in."

Dr. Durgin pressed the microphone button. "Releasing the door lock. Let her in."

She pressed another button. An audible *click!* popped from the speakers, and a red light above the control board blinked to life.

Through the observation glass, they watched the door swing open, and Stella Nettleton stepped inside. Thirty seconds later, the event repeated on the video monitors.

Dr. Durgin saw the man's eyes bouncing from the window to the monitor at his left. "Because of the delay, it's easier to observe on the monitor and ignore the realtime events at the window."

The man nodded, his gaze returning to the monitor.

Through the glass, Dr. Durgin saw the guard close the door behind Stella. The red light above the control board went off. Durgin raised the remote. "I'm releasing the lock on the mask."

Thirty seconds later, the man from corporate watched Subject "D" put his hands to the mask and remove it from his face. He smiled up at Subject "S."

The man from corporate couldn't take his eyes off the girl. She certainly was beautiful.

—Charter Observation Team – 309

1

Auntie Jo died on Wednesday at two thirty-seven in the afternoon, the last week of April, 1993. It had been three months since she left the apartment. I used the last of my cash to buy a hospital bed and pay a moving company to haul it up through our building, get it through our door, and set it up at Auntie Jo's favorite window in the living room, her chair pushed off to the side to make room.

The woman who took her last breath on that Wednesday was no longer my aunt but a shell of the woman I remembered. The medication and treatment took her hair long before. On any given day, she either wouldn't eat or couldn't eat, and the weight melted away until there was nothing left. Her eyes sunk deep into her head, and her lips thinned to a tiny, chapped line on her face. When she opened her mouth to try to speak, nothing came out but stale air, as if she died from the inside out, spoiled somewhere deep.

On that Wednesday, at two thirty-seven in the afternoon, the spring sky was blue, and a handful of white puffy clouds rolled through the heavens. The temperature was seventy-three degrees, and the people moving about their day on the sidewalk below had no idea what was happening in our small apartment on the third floor. I remember thinking that and hating all of them as I sat on the edge of the coffee table beside Auntie Jo in her bed, looking out her window at everyone below. Some laughing, others deep in thought, all moving about briskly toward some destination, toward some event, toward some happening that had nothing to do with cancer or death.

Auntie Jo's hand was limp in mine, small and so frail. If not for the occasional twitch as she slept, there was nothing to signify life. No warmth or movement, no pressure or relaxing of grip. I doubted she knew I was there at all, holding her hand.

I didn't want her to wake. She appeared peaceful in sleep, content. Every few hours when she did break from slumber it would begin with a tightness in the lines on her face, soft groans and moans, finally the fluttering open of her eyes. That was followed quickly by the disjointed feeling of wonder at where she was. Then the pain would come, always the pain. At the end, the pain filled her every waking moment as surely as the little bit of air she managed to drag down into her tired lungs.

Each time she began the inevitable rise from sleep, as the first of those grimaces twitched across her face, Danny Reams, the nurse provided by Pennsylvania Hospice, would set down the tattered paperback that had engrossed him since his arrival, open his black leather duffle bag, and prepare another syringe of morphine, carefully measuring out the draw from a tiny glass ampoule, tapping the needle to expunge any air that may have found its way in. When satisfied, he would set the needle aside on the coffee table and wait.

Always the same sequence—a groan from Auntie Jo in her sleep, the setting down of his book, the drawing of the needle, and wait. There would be a short period of lucidity in Auntie Jo's eyes, a minute respite between the second she woke and the moment her pain realized she was awake and came rushing in. For that briefest of moments, my Auntie Jo was back—she spoke, she laughed, she even found cause to curse my father. And each time I saw her coming back from slumber, when those dry, sunken eyes of hers opened, I considered asking her about the dream, about the box. The selfishness of that thought sickened me, and I quickly forced it away, but it would come again the next time, as surely as her pain would come again.

Danny Reams would watch her closely, take her blood pressure, and make note of her vitals in a small logbook. Then he would wait for the pain to come. It never took long, a few minutes at most. He would swab her frail arm, take the needle from the table, and jab it into her flesh, forcing the drug into her blood.

Then there was sleep again.

Then there was peace.

Danny Reams went back to his book, and I went back to holding Auntie Jo's hand.

On this Wednesday in the last week of April, 1993, at two-thirty in the afternoon, Auntie Jo groaned, Danny Reams reached for his needle, and he filled it from the ampoule of morphine. Only this time he didn't fill it to the line just beyond his thumb, he filled it nearly to the last line of the needle, before setting it down on the edge of the coffee table and returning to his paperback without so much as a glance in my direction.

I stared at that needle. My eyes fixed on the liquid inside, on the air gathered at the tip, air he hadn't expunged.

Auntie Jo woke, and this time the pain didn't grant her that short respite. This time the pain came on with a vengeance, this time her hand did squeeze in mine with enough pressure to turn my fingers white, and this time I found myself crying. I tried my damnedest to hold those tears back, to project strength and resolute, to somehow tell Auntie Jo that everything was going to be all right, very soon.

Danny Reams marked his page, set down his book, and retrieved the needle. He took a moment to force out the air that had gathered near the tip before plunging the needle into Auntie Jo's arm.

Her grip on my fingers loosened.

243

A breath escaped her lips.
She closed her eyes.
Her body relaxed.
Then she was gone.
2:37 p.m.
The sidewalk below, bustling with strangers.
The tears came then, and I couldn't stop them.

2

Gerdy McCowen squeezed my hand.

I glanced at her, standing beside me in a long, black dress, black hat, and black gloves, and I forced a smile.

Dunk stood on my left in a dark suit, one I had never seen him wear before and would never see again, his head bowed low. Mr. Krendal stood beside him, having closed the diner for the day. I told him he should stay open, Auntie Jo would have wanted him to stay open, but he would have none of that. He scribbled out a sign on the back of one of the menus and placed it in the window beside the diner's door for all to see:

Join us Friday at 2 p.m., April 30, in South Side Cemetery for the funeral of our beloved Josephine Gargery, loving aunt and friend, gone too soon.

Most of Brentwood had turned out for the funeral, hundreds of people. Some I recognized, most I did not. I didn't realize how many people Auntie Jo had touched throughout her life until that very moment, and I was grateful they all came. As people arrived, I felt eyes find me, seeking me out among the mourners before finding a seat or a place in the crowd to stand. At first, I shied away from this, then I welcomed it, a warmth put out for her I somehow felt.

Her sealed casket rested on cloth bands above a hole next to my mother's grave, the displaced dirt hidden beneath a green blanket off to the side. I thought of Auntie Jo, so close to my father with only my mother between as a buffer. I pictured her reaching over at the first opportunity and smacking the side of his head.

This thought caused me to chuckle softly, and Gerdy looked up at me, a puzzled look on her face. She squeezed my hand again.

We had gone on several dates over the past few months—movies, dinner, even a party at Willy Trudeau's house the weekend his parents went to the Bahamas. The alcohol had been flowing at that party, Dunk saw to that, somehow arranging a keg and enough bottles to stock a bar, and Gerdy had gone home with me. The both of us beyond tipsy, the both of us wanting a little something more from each other and comfortable enough to give it.

A first time for me, and although she hadn't said anything, I knew it was the first time for her too. She swiped a bottle of Captain Morgan from the party, just a small fifth, and she pulled it from her oversized purse outside my apartment door as I fumbled with the keys. She took a long, hard drink, shivered, then passed the bottle to me, and I followed suit, the liquor warm and welcomed by my electric nerves.

As I pushed open the door, I held a finger to my lips and nodded toward Auntie Jo, sleeping soundly in her chair at the window, then led Gerdy through the dark apartment into my darker room, and closed the door behind us. When we entered my apartment, Gerdy had been wearing a pink sweater and tight jeans. When I turned back to her in my room, having turned away only long enough to pull off my noisy shoes, she was standing before me in nothing but a pink bra and matching panties. A glimmer twinkled in her eyes, and she raised the bottle to her lips again, turning slightly to her side as she drank, just enough for me to realize she wore thong panties. When she passed me the bottle, I gulped it down, then set it on my dresser, fumbling with my own clothes as she backed up to my bed and sprawled across the top.

When I woke the following morning, I found Gerdy already awake, sitting up in the bed with the sheets held over her small, perky breasts, her eyes roaming the walls of my room, the dozens of drawings of Stella covering nearly every inch. "This is really awkward," she said softly.

I tried to explain.

She said there was no need.

Gerdy's hand felt nice in mine, but her soft, black gloves reminded me of another.

Father Garland Hopps welcomed everyone, and I tried so hard to listen to his words. I knew they were kind, but he could have been reciting the lyrics to a Zeppelin song or the preamble to the Constitution. I comprehended none of it.

After Jo's funeral, a few people came back to the apartment. Krendal supplied sandwiches. The mood was quiet, somber.

Dunk left after about thirty minutes—something urgent. One of Crocket's cars picked him up in front of the apartment building. Gerdy left shortly after that. Others took that as a cue and filed out behind her.

When I found myself alone in the apartment, sitting on the edge of Jo's hospital bed at the window, I spotted a crumpled pack of Marlboro 100s jammed between the cold metal frame and the mattress.

I buried my head in my hands and let the tears come.

I wish I could say the death of 1993 ended with my Auntie Jo, but I'd be lying. More would come soon—two close to me, one other not so close, but horrible all the same.

Log 05/03/1993—

Subject "D" within expected parameters.

Audio/video recording.

"Why's everyone got a collective stick up the bum today?
That nimrod Cody even made me show him my ID at the
gate—he's known me for four years," Carl said.

Warren's eyes didn't leave the shift-start checklist.
"There was an incident today."

"An incident?"

"I don't think the powers-that-be figured out how to
handle it, so instead they tightened security and they're
running interviews again."

"Seriously? They ran interviews two weeks ago. Other than
some bad Mexican on Saturday, I've got nothing new to add.
My life is so boring, my mother only calls me once a month,
and I can hear her banging around the kitchen, doing the

laundry, and God knows what else while she pretends to give a shit."

"Yeah, well, be prepared to discuss your formidable burrito habit in detail on the record. I was in there an hour ago, and they made me run through the past ninety days—recount things that happened here, at home, at the grocery store—right down to what I watched on television each night. Like I could remember. Random questions about mundane stuff. Crazy."

"You'd think they'd ask about all the supplies you steal from this place and take home."

"I took one roll of toilet paper six months ago," Warren said. "Hardly a criminal enterprise."

"What exactly happened?"

Warren let out a breath. "The kid whispered something."

"Huh?"

"Subject 'S' was in there with him, and at some point he leaned over and whispered something to her."

"What did he say?"

Warren rolled his eyes. "That's the problem. Nobody knows. The microphones didn't pick it up."

"What about the doc? She reads lips, right?"

"According to her, he told Subject 'S' he loved her."

"Well, that's not so bad. Kinda cute. Our boy was bound to develop a case of blue balls at some point. Imagine being a teenage boy locked up like him, only girl he knows—aside from the doc, anyway. His hormones are probably eating him alive."

"They don't believe her."

"Who?"

"Corporate. Hibbert was on, and he said they scrambled—pulled Subject 'S' out and isolated her in 304 down the hall, then dragged the doc off for an interview. Grilled her, from what I heard. She didn't waver, though. She insisted all he said was 'I love you.' Said they were overreacting."

"The girl's okay, right? I mean if he would have said something else, if he wanted to hurt her, he would have."

Warren shrugged. "Seems okay. She said the same thing, he said 'I love you.' The Oliver woman took her out about thirty minutes ago, took her back to the house."

"If everyone is okay, why are they making a stink of it? Why the interviews?"

Warren lowered his voice. "Rumor is, corporate thinks the kid may have planted some type of command. Something delayed."

"Can he do that?"

Again, Warren shrugged. "Who knows? It's not like he came with an instruction manual. We're figuring this out as we go. I guess they're worried the kid is figuring it out, too."

"That still doesn't explain the interviews."

"I think they're concerned he might have done it to some-body else."

"Planted instructions?"

"Yeah."

"That's not possible. Aside from the doc and the girl, nobody else goes in there. There's no opportunity. Even if he did somehow get to somebody, there'd be a record. Someone is always watching."

"I'm not sure, but I think that might be why the interview focused on my day-to-day activity. They wanted to see what I remembered and what I didn't."

Carl understood, then. "They were trying to figure out if he made you forget something."

"Yeah."

3

Monday morning brought the sun, and the temperature had already climbed into the mid-seventies by ten. I showered and shaved and tried to prepare for a day I hoped would never come.

The law offices of Matteo, Santillan, and Veney stood in a nondescript three-story brick building on the northeast corner of Brownsville Road and Clairton Boulevard. The second and third stories were residential while the first floor housed the law office, a small pet store, and a laundromat. A Giant Eagle grocery store and shopping center dominated the opposite corner of the intersection, and I spotted no fewer than six women cross the street with laundry baskets (and sometimes kids) in tow, either dropping off laundry prior to grocery shopping or picking it up after, and as I sat in the uncomfortable pleather chair next to the receptionist desk of Auntie Jo's lawyer, I wondered why someone didn't move the laundromat across the street into the same shopping center as the grocery store.

Gerdy sat in an equally uncomfortable chair beside me, thumbing through a back issue of *People* pilfered from the small table next to the waiting area. Someone named David Koresh was on the cover with the title *The Evil Messiah – Inside the Waco Cult* blazoned across the front in bright yellow. Gerdy wore a pink sundress and flip-flops. With her legs crossed, her left shoe dangled precariously from her toe—I expected it to drop to the tile floor, but it never did, only swayed back and forth. I had been excused from school for two weeks. Gerdy was simply ditching.

The receptionist was in her mid to late fifties with close-cropped platinum blond hair and large glasses with a red frame. Today's newspaper was spread out on her desk, open to the horoscopes and a crossword puzzle. She had one word filled in when we arrived fifteen minutes earlier—canine—and her pencil had yet to return to the page.

The phone on her desk buzzed, and she picked it up, glanced over at the two of us, then hung up. "Mr. Matteo is ready for you."

We followed her down a narrow hallway with dozens of white file boxes stacked against the wall on the left to a small conference room filled with even more boxes. She cleared two spots at the table nearest the door and motioned for us to take a seat. "Give him a minute. Would you like coffee or anything?"

Gerdy and I both shook our heads and she left us alone, disappearing down the hallway back toward her desk.

"I think I'm gonna sneeze," Gerdy said, her nose crinkled. "It's dusty in here."

I recently read a book by John Grisham called *The Firm*, and I suppose I expected Auntie Jo's attorney (and all others, for that matter) to be housed in spacious offices trimmed in rich mahogany, richer leather, and carpet deep enough to swallow you whole. Instead, I was fairly certain I could hear the whir of washers and driers on the opposite side of the conference room wall, and my eye was drawn to the orange stain glistening with dripping water on the beadboard under the air conditioner at the window—the loud unit held in place by a length of 2x4 braced with old books.

I smiled at Gerdy. "Thanks for coming with me."

She grinned. "Anytime."

The truth was, Dunk was supposed to come with me. Mr. Krendal said he'd come, too. Dunk backed out last night and Krendal called me thirty minutes before we left the apartment. "Lurline called in, she's running late. I'm stuck here. So sorry, buddy."

"Dunk's working, huh?"

I nodded.

If Gerdy knew what Dunk did to line his pockets, she never pressed me on it. Lurline had called Gerdy when she knew she'd be late to the diner—her little boy was running a temperature and she had to wait on the sitter. Gerdy had arrived at my apartment and was standing in the hallway about to knock, when I opened the door to head out. She smiled, simply said, "This is not something you should have to do alone," and took my hand, leading me out before I could object.

Not that I would.

I was grateful for the company.

We heard a bang from the hallway, followed by a man swearing under his breath. Then: "Tess, how about spending a little time today on these boxes? Maybe relocate them to the storeroom?"

"Storeroom's full!" the receptionist shouted back from the front.

"Maybe the basement, then?"

"I'm not going down there. You go down there."

An overweight man in a brown tweed suit side-stepped into the conference room, the buttons of his jacket straining against his belly. He was frowning toward the front of the office as he tugged at the door and forced it shut behind him, the bottom catching on a rumple in the carpet.

Gerdy sneezed.

"Bless you," we both said.

He reached a chubby hand out to me. "I'm Dewitt Matteo, your aunt's attorney. I am so absolutely sorry for your loss. She was a fine woman. We actually went to Brentwood High School together back in the day. Back many days, now that I think about it. We reconnected when I started my practice here; I ran into her at that diner up the road. I've seen the both of you there, too. I was thin as a stick back in school. Tell Krendal I blame him entirely for this." He grabbed at his belly and gave it a jingle, then unbuttoned his jacket and took a seat. "Played varsity basketball back then, if you can believe it. Josephine Gargery, fine woman," he said again.

There was a folder in his free hand. He set it on the conference table, opened it, and skimmed the first page, then the next, and the page after that. I could make out LAST WILL AND TESTAMENT at the top of the first but little else. Beside me, Gerdy squeezed my hand.

Matteo cleared his throat, then glanced down at his watch. "I was expecting one other person for this but looks like we got a no-show. I guess we'll get to that in a second. Let's get the formalities out of the way. Then we can talk specifics." He reached into his jacket pocket, retrieved a pair of glasses, slipped them on, then looked at me. "Ready?"

I nodded.

He returned to the pages and began to read aloud, "Last will and testament of Josephine Laura Gargery. I, Josephine Laura Gargery, an adult residing at 1822 Brownsville Road apartment 306, Pittsburgh, Pennsylvania, 15210, being of sound mind, declare this to be my last will and testament. I revoke all wills and codicils previously made by me. Article I. I appoint Dewitt Matteo as my Personal Representative to administer this will, and ask that he be permitted to serve without court supervision and without posting bond. If Dewitt Matteo is unwilling or unable to serve, then I appoint Donovan Santillan or Emanuel Veney. They're my partners," Dewitt said. "...to serve as my personal representative, and ask that he be permitted to serve without court supervision and without posting bond."

Matteo turned to the next page. "Article II. I direct my personal representative to pay out of my residuary estate all the expenses of my last illness, administration expenses, all legally enforceable creditor claims, all federal estate taxes, state inheritance taxes, and all other government charges imposed by reason of my death without seeking reimbursement from or charging any person for any part of the taxes and charges paid, and if necessary, reasonable funeral expenses, including the cost of any suitable marker for my grave, without the necessity of an order of court approving said expenses."

Matteo looked up. "Just so you know, we already took care of all that. We didn't want you to be burdened with any of the funeral arrangements. I know Jo didn't either, so all those bills have already been settled by my office. Tess handled the logistics, if you'd like to thank her. We'll deduct the expenses from the estate."

"Thanks," I said, my voice thin. Although, I had no idea where that money would come from. Auntie Jo's checking account was flat and closed months ago. I had some cash left but not much.

He returned to the will. "Article III. I devise, bequeath, and give all my worldly possessions, known and unknown, to my nephew, John Edward Thatch."

Matteo paused here, reading the next section to himself before continuing. "Article IV. If, at the time of my death, John Edward Thatch is still a minor in the eyes of the law of the state of Pennsylvania, I appoint Elfrieda Leech his legal guardian until such time he is considered an adult in the eyes of the law of the state of Pennsylvania."

Gerdy leaned over to me. "Who is Elfrieda Leech?"

"She was supposed to be here today," Matteo said.

At first I didn't answer, my mind trying to wrap my head around what he just said. "She's my neighbor, apartment 304 across the hall. She used to babysit me when I was a kid. She's a complete shut-in. Years ago, she was robbed. I think they raped and beat her. Left her for dead, from what I heard. When she was released from the hospital, she locked herself up in that apartment and hasn't left since."

"My God, that's horrible!" Gerdy said.

I went on. "Auntie Jo used to buy groceries for her. Then, when she got sick, I started doing it. Every Thursday, Ms. Leech tapes an envelope to her door with fifty dollars inside, along with a shopping list. I pick up whatever she needs and leave the bags outside her door. I always knock, but she never answers. At some point, she pulls the bags inside. I haven't seen her in years, though." I looked at Matteo. "Are you sure this is current?"

"Jo came in shortly after she was diagnosed, about a year ago. I walked the paperwork over to Ms. Leech myself and witnessed her signing."

"She opened the door for you?"

Matteo's eyes shifted at this. He fumbled with a pen beside the folder. "Well, no. 'Witness' may not be best word. I explained who I was, why I was there, and she asked me to slide the paperwork under the door. Said Jo had told her I would be coming, explained why. Ms. Leech signed the documents and slid everything back. I asked to see her driver's license to confirm the signature. That seemed to take her a minute, but she eventually located it and slid it under the door to me as well. The license expired some time ago, nearly twenty years ago, in fact, but the signatures were a match." He tapped at a form in the folder. "Tess left several messages for her regarding today's reading. She was supposed to be here."

"She wouldn't leave her apartment," I muttered. "Like I said, I don't think she ever leaves."

Matteo laid his palm flat on the folder. "This is just a formality, really. You're almost eighteen, right?"

I nodded. "My birthday is in January."

"So, seven months." Matteo lowered his voice. "Your aunt didn't want to risk you falling into social services, foster care, none of that, so she worked this out with your neighbor. Your legal address will change to apartment 304, with Ms. Leech, but as long as you can keep up the rent, I see no reason why you'd have to leave your own apartment. Anybody asks, you live with Ms. Leech. Got it?"

I nodded, still trying to process.

Matteo returned to the folder, turned the page. "Article V. Should my beneficiary not survive me by 30 days, then his share shall be distributed to my surviving relatives in equal share. Signed, Josephine Laura Gargery."

"We don't have any other relatives," I said softly.

"Well, don't die then. The state would get everything." He returned to the will, flipped to the next page. "Because you're a minor, the proceeds from the various life insurance policies will be placed in a trust administered by my office. We'll pay your regular bills directly from here, for a small fee, of course, and you will be given a monthly allowance. The remaining assets will be distributed to you on your twenty-second birthday, providing you graduate from college. Josephine was very adamant about that. Her preference was Penn State. She was rather insistent, actually."

"What life insurance? Auntie Jo didn't have life insurance."

Matteo reached into the folder and removed a small stack of documents bound with a metal clip at the top. "Your aunt took out three separate life insurance policies. The first dates back to August 6, 1980."

"That's two days before my parents died."

Matteo continued. "She took out the second one in 1984 and the third one about two years ago, before she was diagnosed."

"But, how could she afford that?"

Matteo shrugged. "She was relatively young and in good health. I imagine the premiums weren't very high."

"So, there's enough to cover the funeral expenses?" At least I wouldn't have to worry about that.

Matteo pulled a yellow Post-it note from the top of the stack and slid it over to me. "Once we settle the estate costs and subtract our administrative fees to date, you're looking at a remaining balance of $2,823,000.84. Like I said, your aunt included a stipulation that only allows you to collect the balance once you graduate from college. You need to get on that, if you haven't started already. I can help with the application process, if you need it. Of course, I'll have to charge you for my time. How are your grades?"

Gerdy and I walked back to my building from the attorney's office in complete silence, our hands intertwined.

I might have been in shock.

I was most certainly stunned.

Gerdy hadn't fared much better.

Matteo had went on, as if inheriting nearly three million dollars from an aunt you thought was destitute was a rather normal occurrence. There was talk of colleges and boarding schools, possible career options or travel, allowances and per diems. His words slipped past me like river water over a smooth stone. I heard them but didn't really hear them.

When we reached my building, I stopped Gerdy at the door and turned to her. "We can't tell anyone."

"Okay."

"Not a soul."

"Okay."

"Not even Krendal or the people at the diner. Not until I wrap my head around everything."

"Not even Dunk?" she asked.

"Not even Dunk."

"Okay."

She twisted her fingers in mine and brushed the hair from my eyes. It was getting long again. Auntie Jo used to cut my hair for me. I'd have to get it cut again soon. Maybe Gerdy would—

"Why not?" Gerdy asked.

I should have had an answer for that, but I didn't, not anything that made sense. These were my friends. In many ways, they were my family. With Auntie Jo gone, they were all I cared about in life. Why not tell them?

"They'd be happy for you."

"I know they would."

"Then why?"

I sighed, staring down at our feet pointing toward each other on the cracked sidewalk. "Whatever just happened doesn't feel real to me. This kind of thing doesn't happen, not to me, not to people like us. I'm still trying to process Auntie Jo's death. This is all too much. Right now, I need normal, I need stability. I want to go back to the diner and wash dishes and cook and pretend everything is like it was. I want to go upstairs and find Auntie Jo chain-smoking at the window."

"She's gone, though. You need to accept that," Gerdy said softly. "You need to move on."

"I know I do, I just don't want to. At least, not today."

"She's gone and she left you a gift, the greatest gift she could. Something wonderful. She found a way to give you a better life. The *best* life."

"Accepting that money. Telling people about the money. That makes her death real. I don't know that I'm ready for that, not yet."

"Not telling people won't bring her back."

"I know."

"Doing something with the money, going to college like she wanted, becoming something important...that's how you honor her memory. You keep her alive through your actions." Gerdy smiled up at me, the freckles on her nose crinkling. "You're one of the good guys, Jack. She didn't want you to spend your life in the kitchen or at the sink of some little hole-in-the-wall diner in Pittsburgh."

"I've spent my entire life thinking that is all I would ever be. I can't just change that. I can't spin on a dime like that. I have no idea what else I want to do."

"You're a wonderful artist," Gerdy said. "Maybe you should pursue that. You're a good cook, too. Maybe you can open a restaurant. You don't have to decide today, or next week."

"Today, I just want to be a dishwasher and a cook."

Gerdy nodded. "Then today, that is what you'll be."

"So you won't tell anyone?"

She ran a finger over her lips. "Not a soul. Not until you're ready."

I leaned forward and kissed her. She hadn't expected it. I didn't either, but it felt right. It felt nice. Stella entered my mind and I forced her away, the guilt burning at me.

As we parted, Gerdy smiled up at me, her eyes glistening in the morning sun. "I'm okay with being the other girl," she whispered.

I placed my hands on either side of her face. "I'm not. You're better than that."

There was so much more to say, and I had none of the words to say it. Instead, I opened the door to my building and held it open for her, and the two of us stepped inside in utter silence.

On the third floor, I led her to apartment 304. "It's this one."

When I only stood there, when I didn't knock, Gerdy did. She reached for the door and gave it three loud taps. When a minute passed and nobody answered, she knocked again.

"Go away," a voice said from inside, muffled by the door.

"Ms. Leech? It's Jack, from across the hall. We need to talk."

"It's not grocery day. I don't want to talk. Go away."

"We just came from Dewitt Matteo's office, Aunt Jo's attorney. He said he spoke to you."

"I told him I don't want no kids. This world is no place for kids," she said from behind the door. Still muffled, but closer this time. "You said, 'we.' Who's with you?"

"My name is Gerdy McCowen, Ms. Leech. I work with Jack at Krendal's Diner."

She was at the door now, probably pressed right up against the other side. "I told the attorney that Jack boy is a thief. He stole my book. He can't be trusted. He probably has no business being in the company of young ladies, either. You're not safe with a boy like that."

Gerdy looked at me and mouthed, *Book?*

I turned back to the door. "Do you mean *Great Expectations?*"

"You took the book from me, said you'd bring it back, and you never did. That's theft, and thieves are an evil lot."

"I have it right across the hall in my room, Ms. Leech. I can get it if you want, but I still read it all the time. It's one of my favorite books. I folded some pages and marked up others. Maybe I should get you a new one?"

She fell silent for a moment, then: "I do love a new book. It's been years since I was the recipient of a new book. Maybe something else, though. I don't much care for Dickens."

I leaned against the door. "How about this? Make a list of your favorite authors, and I'll bring you ten new books on Thursday with the groceries."

"Ten?"

"Ten."

"How about twelve?"

I rolled my eyes. "Okay, twelve."

"And a new copy of *Great Expectations* to replace the one you stole. I don't much like an incomplete collection. There's a hole on my bookshelf home to nothing but dust."

"Deal."

There was a click as a lock disengaged, followed by another, another after that. When Ms. Leech opened the door, she opened it just enough to glance at the two of us, then up and down the hallway, no doubt confirming we were alone. When satisfied, she opened the door a little further and ushered us inside. "Hurry."

Gerdy stepped past her, with me at her back. Ms. Leech closed the door swiftly behind us, engaged three dead bolts, and set the security chain.

It had been years since I last saw the inside of Elfrieda Leech's apartment, and at first glance, I couldn't help but wonder when someone else had last stepped foot inside. Did she even allow Mr. Triano, the building super, through that door?

The stacks of newspapers I remembered as a child still towered over me, now reaching to the ceiling only to begin with a fresh stack beside each base. Those secondary stacks stood nearly as tall as the first, and with so many, the room had been swallowed up by them. Ms. Leech's apartment had the same floor plan as mine, so I knew where specific rooms should be, but at first glance, this was a foreign place, a maze of paper towers growing from the hardwood floor. I knew the back wall housed two windows, same as mine, both covered in aluminum foil—any light trying to get in from outside encouraged to go elsewhere.

Ms. Leech was staring at me, her mouth agape. "You are all grown up? When did that happen?"

She had never owned a television, and as far as I knew, years had passed since the last time she set foot outside this apartment. Her only contact with the outside world came from the newspapers delivered to her door. I wondered if time passed for her as it did for the rest of us—this place, and she too, seemed trapped somewhere in the past, a dark spot between the ticks and tocks of the world's clock.

Beside me, Gerdy sneezed. "I'm sorry, my allergies have been horrible today."

Considering the condition of this place, it was a wonder all three of us weren't sneezing. A blanket of dust covered everything, thick enough that the original color of every surface now had the same dull, gray pallor. If I ran my finger over something, I'd be willing to bet I wouldn't leave a streak behind, but instead the dust would peel up like a thick quilt.

Ms. Leech rounded two of the newspaper piles and disappeared from sight toward the place where the kitchen should be. "Would you like a glass of milk, or water, or tea or coffee?"

Gerdy quickly shook her head.

"No, thank you," I replied.

"Tea it is, then," she called back. "I always have tea this time of day. Please take a seat near the fire, give me a moment to prepare. I wasn't expecting guests today. I'm sorry I didn't have time to straighten up."

Gerdy and I both looked at each other, then around the room. We could barely move a foot in any direction.

I nodded toward the living room. "I remember a fireplace, back over there." I took her hand in mine and led her through the stacks, toward the back of the apartment, toward the covered windows.

My apartment did not have a fireplace, and although Ms. Leech's did, it was clear it hadn't been lit in a very long time. Three logs sat stacked in the hearth, precariously balanced and held together by spiderwebs thick enough to appear a solid mass of dull white. Books covered the mantle as well as the bookshelves surrounding the fireplace, two, sometimes three rows deep, with more books piled in front on the floor, smaller versions of the newspaper towers. Although these stacks appeared random, I realized the books were actually in alphabetical order by author. Filthy with dust, like every other surface. The dust here was haphazard, though—some spines were streaked with recent touches, others nearly unreadable.

A couch and two chairs sat facing the fireplace with a small table between.

Gerdy and I sat on the couch, careful not to touch anything.

When Ms. Leech appeared holding a sterling silver serving tray, she simply stared at us for the longest time before finally saying, "I'm afraid that's my seat."

Gerdy and I relocated to the two chairs.

Ms. Leech set the tray down on the rickety table and handed each of us a china cup of steaming tea on an equally delicate saucer. "Milk or sugar?"

We both shook our heads and watched as she added both to her own cup before settling into the couch, taking a sip, then setting the cup down on the table. "To what do I owe the honor of this visit?"

I attempted to drink some of the tea, nearly burned my lip, then just held the cup awkwardly in my hands. "I figured we should talk about Auntie Jo. She made you my guardian. I wanted to thank you, I guess."

Ms. Leech's eyes darted from me to Gerdy and back again over the rim of her cup. "You are to receive a monthly allowance of two thousand dollars. That is meant to cover your rent, your utilities, and your groceries. You'll buy my groceries now, too."

"I already buy your groceries, every Thursday."

"I expect you to *pay* for my groceries," she corrected.

"Oh, okay."

"This will be considered payment for my services. In return, should anyone ask, I will tell them you are my charge and you live under my roof and you follow my rules, none of which involve stealing books or other items belonging to others." She paused, then added, "Use of the word *other* twice in the same sentence is sloppy grammar. I'm usually much better than that, but I'm nervous. I haven't had guests in some time." She drank more tea, the cup clicking against the saucer.

Gerdy smiled. "Were you close to Josephine?"

"Who?"

"Auntie Jo," I said. "Nobody called her Josephine."

"Were you close to Jack's Auntie Jo?"

Ms. Leech nodded. "We were like sisters at one time, then we weren't. It was better that we weren't."

"Did something happen?"

She grew pale at this. "Something always happens. How is your tea?"

"Wonderful." Gerdy smiled, although I don't think she drank any. "Did you have some kind of falling out?"

If the table between us offered some kind of concealment, I probably would have kicked Gerdy beneath it. Unfortunately, this table did not, so all I could do was frown at her. This was none of our business. I was beginning to wonder exactly why we came here. Gerdy smiled back at me. This time she did take a sip of her tea, then returned her gaze to Ms. Leech. "To take on the guardianship of a child is such a huge responsibility, particularly if you aren't close. That's why I asked."

"We are all guardians of each other on some level."

Gerdy sneezed again. Her eyes were red and puffy. "Allergies."

Ms. Leech plucked a tissue from the box beside her and handed it to Gerdy. "I had a cat once. She ran away the day the bad people came."

Gerdy wiped her nose. "The men who hurt you?"

"The people in white, yes."

I nearly dropped my tea at this. "People in white?"

"They bring nothing but pain." She looked to the side, her thoughts lost. "My cat's name was Bumkins. I set food out for him every day, but he never did come back. Horrible, horrible time."

"Who are the people in white?" Gerdy asked.

"Starkist tuna, not even that brought him back. Not even his favorite. My wonderful Bumkins."

Gerdy was about to say something else. I silenced her with a glance, then set my teacup down on the table. "Ms. Leech? Who are the people in white?"

Ms. Leech set her tea down on the table and looked down at her hands, twisting her fingers together. "I have something for you, something you should see, something you should know. Something Jo gave me to hold and protect." She bent her fingers so far back, I thought for sure one would snap. "The word *something* over and over again. Repeated. A pattern. Patterns are bad. Patterns get you caught. Must keep them guessing. Always guessing. Random. Different. The unexpected." Her words trailed off as she continued to mumble to herself, the two of us lost to her.

"Ms. Leech?" I clapped my hands loudly and she startled, her eyes finding focus.

She looked at me, her lips pursed. "I don't talk about the people in white. Never. It's best none of us speak of them, I think. I do have something for you, though. I suppose I should give that to you."

She stood and left the room, disappearing among the stacks of newspapers.

The box?

I thought of the box from my dream. The box my father had given Auntie Jo.

Had she hidden it with Ms. Leech all these years?

I had torn our apartment up looking for it. Year after year, always searching for this box I could never find. Could it really have been right here, across the hall, the entire time?

My palms grew sweaty.

Gerdy eyed me nervously, sipping at her tea.

In the fireplace, a plump spider crept over the wood and around the back of the topmost log.

From one of the bedrooms came the sound of shuffling, followed by a minor crash, and I could only imagine the woman moving through clutter not unlike the mess out here but ages older. She didn't return for nearly five minutes, and when she did, she held an envelope, yellow with age.

Not the box.

Ms. Leech said, "This is what they wanted, the day they hurt me. I didn't give it to them, though. It wasn't theirs to have."

She set the envelope down in front of me, and I reached for the flap.

Ms. Leech placed her hand over mine. "Not here," she said. "I don't want to see what is inside. Not ever again. Knowing leads to nothing but bad things."

The envelope was addressed to my father.

I kicked the door of my apartment shut with the heel of my foot and crossed over to the living room, with Gerdy at my side. I cleared off a spot on the coffee table and set the envelope down, staring at it.

"Aren't you going to open it?" Gerdy asked.

I drew in a breath, tried to slow my pounding heart, the anxiety creeping over my skin.

The hospital bed had been removed yesterday.

The room seemed empty without it.

Gerdy sat on the edge of the coffee table and looked me in the eye. "Do you want me to open it?"

I shook my head, picked up the envelope, and peeled back the flap. The glue had dried ages ago, now stiff and brittle. The single page crinkled as I unfolded the old paper, this letter my father had once held.

Gerdy came around behind me and read over my shoulder.

Eddie,

They know about the baby. I'm not sure how they know, but they do. Emma is frantic. Not sleeping. Neither of us, really. Christ, man, how could they find out? We were so careful. I thought Emma was just being paranoid when she said she saw one of them last week, and then I started seeing them, too. White coats everywhere. At first, I told myself it was nothing. Hell, I saw a little girl, couldn't have been more than seven, wearing a white ski parka, and before I knew it, my hand was on my gun. I'm not that guy, Eddie! We were staying at a little place in Vermont at that point, just outside Stowe. Figured best to blend with other families, right? Then I saw another. A man this time. Probably mid-thirties. I saw him across the street from the gas station, watching me but not watching me, you know? Then I saw the same guy again the next day driving slow down our street. The day after, too. We left that night. Packed up our stuff and just left. Went to Florida after that. No coats in Florida, right? Ha! I thought I had it all figured out. That was worse, though, because I think they were still watching us, but they were harder to pick out of the crowds. Only one week in the Sunshine State, then back north for us. We saw them in Georgia, the Carolinas, too. I thought we lost them in Virginia. I was careful, kept getting off the highway, taking back roads for a while, then random highways, even started heading out west for a bit. I veered off into Tennessee, and somehow they found us in a small town called Kingsford off 81. That time, they didn't even try to hide. I pulled back the curtain on our hotel room, and three of them were staring back at me from the parking lot.

How the fuck do they know about the baby?

From the minute Emma started to show, she didn't set foot outside unless her belly was completely covered. Those last few months, she didn't go out at all. How the fuck...

I think I killed two of them, maybe the third, too, I'm not sure.

It all happened so fast. We got away and headed west. Stole a new car in Kentucky. Got another car in Illinois. Set the first one on fire at the back of a junk yard. Lost them, I thought. Almost a year in California without a sign of them. Then yesterday—

The baby doesn't go outside.

We can't let her.

You understand why, right?

Not much of a baby now. Walking! Crazy, right? You get it. You've got a boy.

She wants to go out, but we can't let her. Our neighbors don't know we even have a kid. Figured it's safer that way. Can't take chances.

Yesterday a truck parked in the driveway of the vacant house across the street. A white truck. Black tinted windows. Thought I was being paranoid again. People drive white trucks, right?

Vacant house no more.

Four of them.

Living right across the street.

I caught them taking shifts at an upstairs window, watching us.

Emma and I have been taking shifts, too, watching them watch us. We're working on a plan to get out, to get away.

We're coming back.

I don't know what else to do.

We need to regroup. Figure out a way to deal with this together. We need numbers. I thought we could hide but that was stupid, they're everywhere. I was wrong. Being alone like this just makes it easier for them.

I'll get in touch when we're close.

My best to Katy and your boy.

Stay safe—
Richard Nettleton

"Who's Richard Nettleton?" Gerdy asked, her chin resting on my shoulder, her breath at my ear. "And Emma? Friends of your parents?"

"I don't..." the words trailed off my tongue. I read the letter again.

Gerdy picked up the envelope and studied the stamp. "The postmark says Newport Beach, California. July 16, 1978. Addressed to Josephine Gargery instead of your dad. I guess they mailed the letter here and she gave it to him? Weird."

She dropped the envelope down on the coffee table and began kissing my neck. "Does it mean something to you?"

"No," I lied.

"You don't recognize the names?"

"No," I lied again.

Gerdy nibbled at my ear. "Your new guardian did seem slightly crazy. Maybe it doesn't mean anything at all. Maybe it's some kind of joke. Nobody's going to confess to murdering two people in a letter. That's just dumb."

My mind was racing.

Had Stella ever told me her parents' names?

I don't think so.

Nettleton.

Richard Nettleton.

The baby. Walking now. 1978.

Stella would have been two.

My best to Katy and your boy.

Your boy.

Me.

Stella only told me how her parents died.

Gerdy, kissing my neck again, slid her hand down the front of my jeans. "I know you don't want to tell anyone about the insurance money, but I think we should celebrate. You, Mr. Thatch, are a very wealthy man."

My eyes were still fixed on the letter. The handwriting. The words.

White truck.

White coats, everywhere.

"I thought you had to work today," I managed to say.

"Not until two."

"It's twelve after."

"What?" Her hand left my jeans. "Shit, I gotta change." Gerdy darted off to the bedroom.

"I'll call Krendal and let him know you're running late."

"Thanks!" Her dress flew out the bedroom door and landed on the floor beside me. "I owe you something special later!"

I forced a grin and picked up the phone. Krendal answered on the third ring. I told him Gerdy would be there in ten minutes, maybe less.

"You should come, too," Krendal replied. He usually shouted on the phone on account of his hearing, but his voice was low this time.

"Why? Busy?"

Krendal said nothing for a second, his breathing heavy. "Your friend Dunk is here. He's got a friend with him."

"Dunk *always* has a friend with him these days," I replied.

"Not a lady friend. Somebody else. I don't like it. I don't want those people in my restaurant."

Shit.

"Okay, I'll be right there. I'll take care of it."

Gerdy came out of the bedroom, wearing her uniform, both hands working at her hair, attempting to tie it up in a bun. She crossed the room to me and planted a kiss on my lips. "I want you to know, I'm not wearing panties. I don't plan to put on another pair of panties until after you find it appropriate to take advantage of my oversight. We've had too much sadness over the past few months. Your aunt did something wonderful for you, something life-changing, and I fully expect you to celebrate with me in all kinds of demeaning and adventurous ways. Drink lots of fluids while I'm gone. I'm off at ten. Maybe you should consider some stretching exercises an hour or so before that. I'd hate to see you pull something."

"And if I don't comply, Ms. McCowen?"

She grinned up at me. "Like I said, I will continue to go pantie free until you do. Perhaps I will attract another suitor at work, someone with waitress fantasies."

"Could get drafty, cold even. Winter will be here before you know it. That skirt isn't very long."

"If I catch my death of cold, Mr. Thatch, it would surely be your fault."

"Krendal said Dunk is there. I'll walk you."

"I'd never turn down an escort from a handsome gentleman such as yourself."

I crammed the letter and envelope in my pocket. I needed to show Dunk.

A stack of posters with Stella's face watched us leave from the seat of a chair near the kitchen.

Have you seen me?

Passing Ms. Leech's door, I felt like we were being watched. Like she had her eye pressed to the tiny viewfinder, monitoring our every move.

As we left my building, I *knew* we were being watched. I never noticed the various vans parked on our street, until the other night when Dunk pointed them out, and then they stuck out in such a blatantly obvious way I found it hard to believe I missed them. I told myself they weren't white SUVs, and my mind had been preoccupied for some time.

Today, we had Cloister Plumbing and Supplies.

This was the second time I saw that particular van, deep red with the company logo painted brightly on the sides and back. A man in a rumpled white shirt and tie stood behind the van, smoking a cigarette. Plumbers typically didn't wear ties, nor did they carry concealed weapons tucked in leather holsters at the small of their back, yet there was the telltale bulge of a handgun.

As Gerdy and I passed the van, the man stubbed out his cigarette, his gaze fixed on me for a second before shifting to some unknown object off in the distance.

I almost nodded a hello to him as I would any other familiar face on the sidewalk, but I caught myself and continued to face forward, wondering if anyone else noticed this same man worked for not only Cloister Plumbing and Supplies, but also an electrician and a carpet company. Busy times, I supposed.

Up the block, about three hundred feet in front of us, a blue BMW sedan pulled into the handicap parallel parking space in front of Krendal's. Four men dressed in dark suits got out with large automatic weapons in hand and immediately began firing toward the diner.

The sound was deafening.

The diner's plateglass window exploded in a rain of tiny shards, and the four men continued to fire—their legs spread in a practiced stance, steady and sure. Two of them wore tiny earplugs, the other two did not. The muzzles of all four weapons moved steadily back and forth in a sweeping motion, reminding me of sprinkler heads.

I counted no less than a dozen people on the sidewalk all standing perfectly still, frozen, as if watching a film or a television program as the bullets flew.

I pushed Gerdy down to the pavement, into the narrow space between a Volvo and a Toyota Sentra parked at the curb, and I fell on top of her, sandwiching her body between mine and the blacktop. I wasn't sure when she had started screaming, but she was screaming now, screaming and kicking at me, but I wouldn't let her go. I forced her head down, my face lost in her hair.

The shooting seemed to last for hours, although I would later learn all four gunmen used 9mm UZIs, Vector Arms HR4332 SBRs set to full auto—at 650 rounds per second, each of the 32 round extended clips were exhausted in under a second. Each gun had extra clips and reloaded an estimated three times.

The actual shooting time, as recorded by the police van a little more than a block away, was thirty-eight seconds.

When the shooting ended, my ears continued to ring, all other sounds nearly lost, muffled as if there were a thick wet blanket wrapped around my head.

I heard the last of the four car doors slam, followed by squealing tires.

"Stay down!" I shouted in Gerdy's ear before climbing to my feet and running toward the diner. The blue BMW turned right on Clairton and disappeared.

I closed half the distance before the explosion.

The force of the blast knocked me back to the sidewalk, the sound of it breaking through the ringing of the gunshots. My head cracked against the pavement, and the breath left my lungs with the force of a linebacker shouldering my gut.

A fireball shot through the space where the diner's plateglass window had been less than two minutes earlier and crossed half of Brownsville Road before disappearing back inside, the lick of some hideous, flaming tongue returning to its mouth.

I scrambled to my feet—part stagger, part run—reached Krendal's, and climbed through the window frame into the diner, faint moans and screams coming from all around.

Smoke, thick and black, surrounded me, bellowing from somewhere in back. I tripped on an overturned table and nearly fell again when my foot landed between the legs of a chair. I pulled free, and that was when I spotted the first body.

A woman. I could tell only by the fact that she wore a green dress, her hair and face nothing but a charred block of flesh.

I pulled the neck of my Steelers sweatshirt up over my mouth in an attempt to block the smoke, but it did little good. The hot, acrid soupy air burned my lungs, my eyes. I peered into the blackness and saw nothing.

I nearly slipped in the coffee.

The cracked pot was at my feet, black liquid pooling out.

Lurline Waldrip lay beside the mess on the floor.

I dropped to my knees and gently turned her over, rolling her onto her back.

No less than six red spots bloomed on the chest of her pink uniform. Deep red at the center, where the bullets had gone in, less so directly surrounding each spot. One of the spots was between her breasts, at her heart. I knew she wasn't breathing, I knew that bullet had killed her, but I pressed two fingers against her neck anyway and felt for a pulse, finding nothing.

I heard Dunk then.

I'm not sure how I knew it was him, but somehow I did, a muffled cry a few feet to my left. I didn't want to leave Lurline like that, lying on the floor in so much filth, but I also knew I had little choice. Breathing was growing harder by the second. I wouldn't be able to stay inside much longer.

I stood and shuffled through the upended furniture and other obstacles I didn't want to identify toward the booths that lined the far wall, toward the one closest to the door, Dunk's favorite.

I found Dunk lying sideways on the booth seat, the lower half of his body crammed under the table, his face and legs covered in blood. Henry Crocket sat across from him, his back to the door, his face pressed against the table, eyes wide and unblinking, fixed on a half-full cup of coffee. A plate of toast and butter was at the center between them both.

The back of Crocket's head was missing.

A ragged tear started just past the center at the top of his head and ended at the base of his neck, as if a giant had reached down and twisted it off with a large thumb and forefinger. His back was riddled with bullet holes. The booth seat between him and the front of the diner was shredded, a mess of red pleather, stuffing, and plywood, chipped away and splintered.

Dunk groaned again.

I reached down into the booth and wrapped my arms around his waist, pulling his bulky body toward me until we both fell back onto the tile floor at the aisle. He fought me at first, his body going rigid, followed by a scream as the pain of movement washed over him. Then he went limp and silent.

I scurried to my feet again, and my vision went momentarily white. My legs disappeared from beneath me, and I collapsed. I wasn't getting enough air, and I was going to pass out. If I passed out in here, I wouldn't be leaving.

I forced myself to stand. Wobbly legs be damned.

I grabbed Dunk under the arms and pulled him toward the front of the diner, toward the missing window, while trying to ignore the slick, red stain his body left on the floor behind us.

What came next is a bit of a blur. I think I nearly passed out again. I remember falling or the feeling of falling. I can't be sure. Then I remember other arms around me. Hands groping, fingers grabbing at whatever they could. I remember being pulled out of the diner, over the concrete sidewalk, and out onto Brownsville Road.

"Breathe, kid, breathe," someone said. "We called 911. Just lie still."

I saw a face hovering over me. A middle-aged man in glasses and a plaid shirt.

My head rolled to the side, and I saw Dunk lying there, unmoving.

I took a deep breath.

Although the smoke was thick here, too, clean air was thicker and my lungs welcomed it. Strength began to seep back into my arms and legs, the fog over my thoughts began to lift.

That's when I remembered Krendal.

I remembered Elden Krendal and knew he was still inside.

The middle-aged man in the plaid shirt tried to stop me. So did others. He grabbed at my shoulder and tried to press me back down to the pavement when I forced my body to stand. At that point, others in the growing crowd grabbed at me, too—apparently what I planned to do was evident in my eyes.

I stood anyway and drew in a deep breath.

I shook off the man in the plaid shirt, I pulled out of the grip of the others, and I ran back toward the diner with the sound of sirens wailing somewhere behind me.

Without the large plateglass window at the front of the diner, the growing fire had no trouble finding food, and when I passed through the window frame for the second time, I could feel the air rushing in rather than pushing out, sucked in by the hungry beast devouring the restaurant from the inside out.

I clambered past the ruined tables, chairs and booths, past the counter, toward the swinging door on the side leading toward the kitchen, the heat unbearable and intensifying with each step. My eyes caught a glimpse of the space through the opening where Krendal normally passed food, but I could make nothing out through the wall of black smoke.

Flames licked up the walls near the swinging door, and when I touched the metal, the heat burned my fingertips.

I knew the explosion had been one or more of the propane tanks Krendal stored in the back for the stove on the off chance city gas stopped working. The gas had shut down twice since Krendal owned the diner, and each time it had happened during the lunch rush. He kept three canisters of propane at the ready in case it happened again. He even taught me how to switch the hose on the stove from one to the other and back again, something he claimed with pride he could do in under ten seconds.

I lowered my head and pushed through the lopsided swinging door, hanging by only the top hinge.

Flames leapt up to greet me, followed by bellowing black smoke. I forced my legs to pump and pushed into the kitchen, jumping toward the tile floor on the right of the opening as the intense heat raced past me toward the fresh air outside.

With my face as close to the ground as possible, I wiped the tears from my eyes, the heat stinging.

The landscape was foreign to me.

The twisted remains of one of the propane canisters had crashed into the aluminum table that normally occupied the center of the kitchen. The table was now on its side, and the dozens of pots and pans and cooking utensils that normally filled shelves on top of the table were strewn around my limited field of vision. The floor was slick with the remains of today's soup, the hot liquid soaking through the knees of my jeans.

I coughed. The involuntary action filled my lungs with smoke, tainted air.

I shouted out Krendal's name, but the words came out as a garbled whisper.

Then I crawled in the general direction of the stove, my eyes pinched shut, my hands feeling the way, pushing through the mess on the floor. When I encountered the overturned table, I felt my way around it, the hot aluminum burning my fingertips.

I have no idea how I found him.

The kitchen wasn't large, maybe four hundred square feet at most, but it might as well have been a desert and I the blind man trudging through the sand. I pushed forward on my belly over the slick tile, my hands flailing out in front of me, fingers outstretched. I heard part of the ceiling collapse somewhere to my right—the fire roared with newfound laughter at this, but I heard nothing of Krendal. And I was certain that if I found him at all, it would be by sound and sound alone, because within seconds of entering the kitchen, I couldn't see anything.

My fingers brushed his leg.

At first I wasn't sure it was a leg and I nearly went on, my thoughts muddled with lack of oxygen. As I grabbed at the material of his pants, his weak fingers wrapped around my wrist. I grabbed his arm and he took mine, and I knew neither of us would let go.

I immediately started crawling backward. With one free hand and two weak legs, I began to shuffle, pulling him along with jerks and tugs. We were halfway through the crooked kitchen door when another section of the ceiling collapsed, raining down on us. Krendal's body jumped, and I knew something had landed on him or hit him, but I couldn't see what. I didn't stop moving. I pulled him through the door.

We were somewhere in the dining area when the second propane canister exploded, followed immediately by the third.

That's when my body gave up and the thick, black smoke welcomed me.

The dream.

"I smell gas. We need to get out," Momma said.

"Are you okay? Please tell me you're okay."

A door opening.

The scrape of metal on metal.

"Eddie?"

"Yeah?"

"The other SUV. They're coming."

"Get Jack out."

"Can you move?" Daddy said.

"I…I think so."

A seat belt click. The sound of the belt retracting. "Eddie? They're coming."

"We need to get you out."

"You need to stop them, or we're all dead."

"Christ—where's the gun?"

"On the floor. By my feet. I think my arm is broken. I think I'm gonna…" Momma said.

Chocolate milk, in my eyes, my hair. Sticky.

"I can't find it. Stay with me, Katy! Focus on my voice."

"It's there. Was holding it. Couldn't—"

Momma's voice fell away. Sleepy voice.

Loud bang.

Many loud bangs.

"He's coming around," I heard a voice say, distant, through a tunnel, an echo off smooth walls.

"Kid? Can you hear me?"

The air was cold, wintry cold.

I drew a deep breath.

Coughed.

I tried to reach for my mouth, but my hands, my arms, wouldn't move.

"Breathe, kid."

More cold air.

Something mopped at my eyes. Wet.

"Hand me the scissors. I need to get this sweatshirt off him. The jeans, too."

My eyes fluttered open.

"There you are!" The man was looking down at me, a forced smile. He produced a penlight and pointed it at my eyes. When I closed them, he forced them back open with his free hand. First the right, then the left, then the light was gone. "Can you tell me your name?"

I stared up at him, the churning clouds above him.

"Kid?"

"Pip."

"What?"

"Jack."

"Just Jack?"

"Jack Thatch. John Edward Thatch."

"That's a long name."

"Everyone calls me Jack."

"You're one crazy son of a bitch, Jack. Can you tell me who's president of the United States?"

"Clinton."

"Gold star for you." He turned and shouted over his shoulder. "I need a free bus to take this kid to Mercy General!"

"Two more ambulances inbound!" someone replied. "ETA, three minutes!"

"Krendal," I forced out. My mouth was not working.

"What?"

"The man I tried to pull out…"

The paramedic's face drooped. "I'm sorry, son. He didn't make it."

Someone started tugging at my jeans. I turned to see a female paramedic holding thick shears, cutting through the material.

My head swiveled, taking in my surroundings.

I was in the middle of Brownsville Road, strapped to a stretcher. Black smoke churned out of Krendal's Diner to my left, firemen crawling all around the opening like yellow ants with hoses, water flooding the sidewalk.

I turned in the opposite direction, toward my apartment building. "Gerdy."

Her name came out, followed by another cough. I realized for the first time I had a mask on. The paramedic pulled the mask down over my chin. "What?"

"Where's Gerdy?"

"Is there a Gerdy here?" the paramedic shouted toward the crowd of people around us.

A woman stepped forward, an older woman in a floral print dress and gray hair pinned back neatly. Her arms and face were covered in black soot, the hem of her dress burnt. She knelt down beside my stretcher. "Is that the girl who was with you? I saw you walking down the sidewalk with her, right before…you were holding hands. Is that who you mean?"

I nodded.

Her eyes filled with tears. She leaned in closer. "I'm so sorry. I tried to stop her, but she was just too strong. I couldn't hold her."

"Hold her…what?"

"She chased after you, into the fire."

Every muscle in my body tensed. I tried to leap up from the stretcher, but the straps at my wrists, ankles, and neck held me down.

"Whoa, buddy," the paramedic pressed a steady hand to my chest.

"Let me out of this thing!" I rocked violently back and forth. "Gerdy!"

I swiveled my head back toward the parked cars. A crowd of people stood between the Volvo and Sentra, where I had left her. I couldn't see her, though. I didn't see her. "Gerdy!"

I turned back toward Krendal's, toward the black smoke drifting out the shattered opening. Firemen disappeared inside, pulling heavy hoses with them. "She's not in there! She wouldn't go in there!"

The strap on my right hand broke free. I reached over and started on the left.

The woman in the burnt floral print dress backed away, her eyes filled with tears. "I'm so sorry," she mouthed.

"Give me 10mgs Haldol, now!" the paramedic shouted above me, holding my chest down with the bulk of his weight.

My ankle broke free.

I tried to buck him off.

A needle plunged into my arm.

No, please. Not Gerdy. Not Gerdy.

All went dark then.

4

Faustino Brier liked pizza.

He liked pizza damn near more than anything else on this planet.

Of all pizza in all of Pittsburgh, he particularly liked Mineo's Pizza in Squirrel Hill, so when John Mineo came over to his table no less than thirty seconds after his 16" cheese and pepperoni arrived and told him he had a phone call, he instructed the man to tell whoever it was that he wasn't there, he hadn't seen him all day. When John Mineo returned and told him the caller knew he was there and it was urgent, Faustino carried a lone slice back to the phone on the bar and picked up the receiver in his clean hand.

"This better be good."

"Hey, this is Horton with Narcotics. You need to get down to Brownsville Road."

Horton's team had Duncan Bellino under constant surveillance in an attempt to build a trafficking case against him and his boss, Henry Crocket. Horton agreed to watch the Thatch boy too, and report anything out of the ordinary to Faustino. Professional courtesy.

"Something happen with your boy or mine?" Faustino said, taking a bite of the pizza. Delicious.

"Both. Get your ass down here. Now."

Even with lights and a siren, it took nearly thirty minutes in the afternoon traffic. Faustino saw the smoke from more than a mile away.

Two blocks were roped off behind yellow crime-scene tape. First responders were everywhere. He parked behind two firetrucks and climbed out of his car. Firemen were rolling up hoses, putting equipment away. He pushed his way past the crowd of onlookers and reporters.

Fogel saw him and ran over. He had called her from Mineo's.

He said, "Holy shit, is that Krendal's?"

Fogel nodded. She wore a pair of latex gloves and had a department-issue Nikon hanging around her neck. "Follow me. Horton's inside."

Brownsville Road looked like a war zone, the pavement covered in bits of burnt debris—everything from chairs and tables to pieces of silverware, plates, and roofing material. The windows on all the surrounding cars and buildings had blown out, shards of glass crunched under his shoes. Krendal's was the worst, though. The diner was gone, replaced by a black, smoking cave carved out of the old brick building.

Faustino recognized an odor in the air, one he hadn't smelled since the war, and hoped he never would again. Burnt flesh.

Fogel smelled it, too. She pulled a small jar of petroleum jelly from her pocket and smeared some beneath her nose, then offered the jar to him. He shook his head. She dropped the jar back in her pocket. "We've got six bodies inside, two more on the sidewalk."

Horton stood just inside what was once the front of the diner, the metal frame of the window, now bent and jagged, jutting out over the sidewalk. He waited for Faustino and Fogel to maneuver through the debris, then nodded toward what was left of a man in a booth near the front. "Meet Henry Crocket."

Crocket's hair was gone, his skin black and cracked. He was lying facedown on the table, part of his head missing, his back riddled with bullet holes.

Faustino looked around the diner, spotted three of the six bodies, two of them already in black bags.

He turned back to the narcotics detective. "What the hell happened here?"

Horton told him everything they had pieced together.

5

I woke to a dark room.

I woke to beeping machines and distant people and the sound of my own breathing beneath a plastic mask.

My head ached.

My eyes attempted to adjust to the light.

I reached up and pulled off the mask.

Krendal's.

Explosion.

Dunk, Krendal, Lurline.

Oh, God, Gerdy.

I tried to sit, fell back into a soft pillow, my head pounding with ache.

"I'm sorry about your friend."

I turned.

An outline of a man, sitting in a chair to the right of me. The detective, Faustino Brier.

"Where?" My mouth was dry, my voice didn't sound right.

I sat up again, fighting past the nausea, the dizziness.

Detective Brier stood, filled a cup from a plastic pitcher on the table beside me, and held it to my lips. I wrapped both of my shaky hands around the sides and drank. The water was warm, but it still helped. When I was done, I handed the cup back to him, and he set it on the table.

"Where am I?" I repeated.

"The paramedics sedated you. You were…hysterical. They needed to get a handle on your injuries. You could have hurt yourself. They brought you to Mercy for treatment and observation."

Brier crossed the room. "I'm going to turn on a light. Sometimes, after exposure to fire, particularly exposure to an explosion, the eyes can becomes extremely sensitive. Probably best you close them and open them again slowly, give them a chance to adjust."

I nodded and closed my eyes. The black turned to deep red beneath my eyelids. I opened them, blinked. There was an empty hospital bed between me and the detective, now standing near the door.

He returned to the chair. "Do you remember me? It's been a long time."

I nodded. "You were at the funeral. You and a woman."

He seemed surprised I saw him there. "That was my partner, Detective Fogel. That's not what I meant, though. I spoke to you when you were a kid. About Andy Flack. Do you remember?"

Again, I nodded. "Detective Brier."

"How do you feel? Are you in pain? I can get a nurse. They'll give you something."

I wasn't. I wasn't in any pain.

I shook my head.

A paper sack sat beside the detective's chair. He pulled it between his feet, unfolded the top, and reached inside. His hand came out holding my Steelers sweatshirt. He set it on bed, smoothing the material. He reached back inside and pulled out my jeans, set those beside the sweatshirt.

There was little left of either.

The clothing had been cut off me, now ruined.

What remained of the material was charred, riddled with dozens of holes, the edges of which were burned, the material melted.

Without looking up from the clothing, the detective said, "We pulled clothes from some of the bodies in the diner that didn't look this bad."

He slipped a finger through a hole in the sweatshirt, nearly six inches in diameter, the material cracked and flaked at the edges, small pieces raining on the bedsheets. "The fire destroyed your clothes, yet the doctor said you don't have a single scratch on you. Not one. No burns, no bruises. Nothing. We have witnesses that say you ran inside that place not once, but twice. Pulled people out. Your friend, Duncan Bellino. Your boss. You were inside when the propane tanks blew."

I said nothing.

"Your hair isn't even singed."

I said nothing.

"You should be dead."

My eyes fell on the back pocket of my jeans.

The detective followed my gaze. I looked away.

He reached back into the bag, pulled out the letter, set it on top of my jeans, still in the envelope. "Interesting letter. Mind if I ask where you got it?"

I remained silent.

"I shouldn't have read it, I know. None of my business, really. All these years as a cop, though, makes you nosy. Couldn't help myself, and it *was* open. Thought maybe I'd find an emergency contact listed or something."

Bullshit.

Brier ran a finger over the edge of the envelope. "Eddie and Katy, that's your parents, right?"

"Where's Gerdy?"

The detective frowned. "She's dead, son."

"I know that. Where's her body? I want to see her."

"I'll see what I can do." His gaze never left the envelope. "The letter, it's old. Dated 1978. Long time ago."

"What about Dunk? Is he…"

"Surgery. He took a bullet in the shoulder, another in his chest—

cracked three ribs, that one did. A third bullet got him in the gut. Two more in his left leg. He should probably be dead too, but he seems tough, might pull through, might not. Owes you his life if he does, that's for sure. Then again, the explosion didn't hurt you. Maybe it wouldn't have hurt him, either." Eyes still on the envelope. "Who is Richard Nettleton?"

"I think I'd like to see the nurse now," I said softly. "Get something for the pain."

"You're not hurt."

"My head..."

"Not a single scratch."

I looked around the hospital bed, located the nurse call button, and picked it up.

Detective Brier raised both his hands. "Before you do that, there's someone out in the hall who'd like to talk to you. I think you'll want to hear what he has to say."

Before I could answer, he crossed the room, pushed open the door, and leaned out into the hallway. He spoke to someone for a second, then held the door open.

I recognized the man who came in.

The same man I had seen numerous times standing around the undercover police van outside my apartment building. Still in the rumpled white shirt and red tie. Although, now the shirt was covered in black soot and the tie had been loosened, the top button undone. He turned to close the door behind him, the bulge of his concealed handgun clearly outlined in stains of sweat and dirt at the small of his back.

The plumber slash electrician slash carpet installer, who carried a gun.

"This is Detective Horton. He's with Pittsburgh PD Narcotics division," Detective Brier said.

"We've met, sort of," Horton said. "I saw you run in there, into the diner, saw you both times. You're either extremely brave or stupid, or maybe a little of both."

I reached for the nurse call button again.

"You'll want to hear me out, kid. You won't like what I have to say, but you'll want to hear it."

Detective Brier returned to his chair.

Horton crossed over to the window, peered out at the black night. "Your friend, Duncan Bellino, is into some nasty business. I'm sure you know that, I'm not sure you understand the full extent, but at the very least, you know who he works with."

I opened my mouth to protest, and he raised a hand. "You don't have to say anything. It's probably better you don't, not right now anyway, just listen. You've seen us watching your building. We rotate, we try to stay out of sight, but inevitably we get made. We've got photographs of you watching our vans from the building. Even got some audio of you and Bellino talking about them—"

"Audio?"

"You shouldn't say anything, just listen. Self-incrimination, and all that."

I nodded.

"When we started watching your friend, we weren't really after him. We were after his boss, Henry Crocket. You know how that all works, you watch TV—we nab your buddy on something, get him to roll, give us something or someone bigger." Horton rolled his hand through the air. "Keep going until we get the top dog, sometimes even the top dog's boss, work with other agencies like the FBI or DEA, try to take down the whole mess. Crocket has been on our radar for nearly ten years. He started out just like all the other ones, working for someone else, learning the ropes, then branching off on his own. Usually that doesn't work out well for the *someone else*."

Horton paused for a second, choosing his words. "See if this sounds familiar to you. He started with small-time stuff—pot, some prescription drugs, then a little meth and heroin. Dealt on his own in the beginning, then wised up and started using kids. Some as young as ten years old, peddling his shit on playgrounds and street corners. We bust them, they're back out in a few hours. Kids never talk. They know they can't get in much trouble. Crocket actually gives, well gave, them a bonus if they got busted and didn't talk, couple extra hundred bucks in their pocket. Nice scratch for a little kid, even nicer for the parents who usually knew exactly what was going on and let it slide—they needed that money too, mouths to feed, bills to pay. Many have a habit, and when they let their kid work for someone like Crocket, they get the employee discount on smack. None of this is new. This is how the drug trade works around the world, every city and town, Pittsburgh's no different. Some of these guys are happy keeping the business small—they make great money, after all. Why get greedy? They can take home a solid six figures per year. Others, though, others like Crocket, they catch the bug, they're all about expansion, diversification, they gotta build the business, grow."

Horton looked down at his dirty tie, mumbled something, then tugged it off, and used it to wipe at the soot on his shirt. When he realized the stains were only spreading, he gave up and shoved the tie in his pocket and turned back to the window. "Last year alone, Henry Crocket was responsible for nearly 30 percent of the drug traffic in this city. 10 percent of all the nastiness in Philly, he branched out. Recently, he's been sniffing around Chicago, too. I don't care much about that, busy worrying about what's happening here in our city. Last year, twenty-three of his customers died, overdosed. Doesn't matter much, though, because plenty more stepped up to fill those shoes. He *merged* with at least four of his competitors. And by *merge*, I mean he had them killed and took over their territory. So, more of a hostile takeover. Until this morning, he was well on his way to owning 40 percent of Pittsburgh's drug trade by year's end, a 10 percent bump over last year. Maybe more. Some of his remaining competition has been bowing out of the trade altogether—better that than *merging* like the others. Things were going well for Mr. Crocket, right up until today when a car with four armed men rolled up and filled him full of bullets, took half his head clean off, in that diner."

The image of Crocket's head popped into my mind, his ruined body slumped over the table. "Normally, I'd drop some pictures in front of you at this point, try to spook you with the images, but I know you saw him, and real life is far worse than a picture. You get the benefit of those other senses, smell, touch. Your friend Bellino had part of Crocket's head on his neck, his shirt. You got closer to that nastiness than anyone should ever have to. Trust me, it stays with you. Forgetting a photograph is one thing, but you'll think about Crocket every time you touch something sticky for the rest of your life. Every time you smell meat cooking, your mind will go back there."

"Am I a suspect, or something? Why are you telling me this?"

Horton said, "I've been tracking Henry Crocket for years, recording every movement. The guy picked his nose, and it ended up in three different reports. I can tell you when he shits, when he jerks off, his favorite TV shows…in all that time, you know what I've never seen him do? Not once? Sit at the front of a restaurant with his back to the door, let alone a window. Guys like him, they just don't do that. They sit in the back, someplace where they can keep an eye on everything. Someplace less…vulnerable."

"They were sitting in Dunk's favorite booth. He always sits there."

"Always?" Horton replied.

Faustino leaned forward in his chair. "Not always. The first time I saw the two of you, you were sitting in a booth at the back, near the bathrooms. There was even a sign that said it was your booth."

"We were kids. That doesn't mean anything."

"When did Bellino's, Dunk's, favorite booth *become* his favorite booth?"

"I don't know," I replied. "Six months ago, nine months ago. He just started sitting there instead, said he liked to be able to see what was happening out on the street. He asked Krendal to start holding that one for him during rushes. He ate at the diner all the time, so Krendal took care of him."

Faustino and Horton both looked at each other, unspoken words passing between them. Horton went on. "A little under a year ago, we picked up a conversation between your friend, Dunk, and one of the other guys who works for Crocket, low-level guy named Alonzo Seppala. They were in the park; we got them with a long-range microphone. They were talking about ways to get Crocket out of the picture, take over the business. One of the suggestions that came up was to lure Crocket to a meeting and set him up for a roadside hit."

I was shaking my head. "That's ridiculous. Dunk would never do something like that. He doesn't have it in him. Sure, he's into some bad stuff, but he wouldn't hurt anyone."

"Bellino started sitting in that booth two days after the conversation with Alonzo Seppala," Horton said. "Moved from the booth in the back, your booth, to that one in the front. Always the same side, facing out toward the street."

"So he could see what was happening out there, something to watch while he ate, that's all."

Horton reached into his pocket and pulled out a photograph. This time he did drop it on the bed in front of me. "The surveillance we had on Bellino, the van you know so well, caught this."

I looked down at the photograph but didn't pick it up. A blue BMW parked in the handicap spot in front of Krendal's Diner, four men climbing out with guns. The driver was circled with red marker.

"That's Alonzo Seppala. Your friend, Duncan Bellino, set this all up."

6

After the hospital, Detective Faustino Brier returned to the Pittsburgh PD Homicide Division's pen. He pulled the Wall of Weird out from the corner and turned the board around, studied the pictures and text and the last dozen or more years of his life. Then he reached into his pocket and pulled out the copy of Jack Thatch's letter he made at the Xerox store off 79 on his way to Mercy to talk to the kid with Horton.

He pinned the letter to the board in the bottom right corner, right next to the hand-sketched poster of the girl followed by the message, *Have You Seen Me?* Beside both of those were three surveillance photos of Jack Thatch hanging the posters on Brownsville Road and down 51, dozens of them.

From his desk, he retrieved the folder containing all the data on the 1978 murders—the man and woman found brutally murdered in the Dormont house, 98 Beverly, the three bodies found upstairs in the room that appeared to belong to a child.

He leaned into the letter—

Eddie, they know about the baby.

The baby.

Later in the letter, he says *she's* walking, the baby.

Faustino never had children, never married, but he knew many people who did, and their kids all started walking around a year old, maybe a year and a half.

Walking! The letter said.

Just started walking, in 1978.

That would make her about sixteen or seventeen now.

About the same age as Jack Thatch.

You get it. You've got a boy.

About the same age as this girl in the poster.

My best to Katy and your boy.

Definitely Jack's parents.

Stay safe—Richard Nettleton.

Who the hell was Richard Nettleton?

Faustino made a pot of coffee—he'd be here awhile.

7

They raided Dunk's apartment while I was still in the hospital, while Dunk was in his third surgery. They were able to remove the bullets from his chest and gut, repair the damage to the tissue and muscle. They set the broken rib bones. The bullet at his shoulder went straight through. That was good. The two in his left leg turned out to be the most problematic—one grazed dangerously close to his femoral artery and severely damaged the femoral nerve, the other shattered his femur. He wasn't in danger of losing the leg, but he'd never walk the same, if he walked at all. A doctor came in and updated me on all this a few minutes after the detectives left.

I heard about half of what he said.

As they were leaving, Detective Brier asked me who the man in the black GTO was. Said he'd been seen at my building, was at the funeral, too.

I told him I had no idea.

Brier left the letter. He took my pants and sweatshirt in his paper bag. Evidence, he said.

Detective Brier's partner, Joy Fogel, led the raid on Dunk's apartment. They tore the place apart. Nothing incriminated Dunk, though. Whatever might have tied him to Crocket's business had been kept elsewhere.

They found Dunk's father dead on the couch, a dirty heroin needle still sticking out of his arm. He had been there at least a day, maybe longer.

When they picked up Alonzo Seppala, he said Dunk had nothing to do with the hit on Crocket. He hung himself in his cell that same night—used his pants.

They kept me in the hospital for two days for *treatment and observation*, although I didn't much care for the latter and had no need for the former—Brier was right; I didn't have a single scratch on me. Not a bump, bruise, or lingering cough.

I wouldn't get the chance to talk to Dunk about any of this for nearly three weeks. The ache in my stomach grew with each passing day.

Log 05/20/1993—

Subject "D" within expected parameters.

Audio/video recording.

"Where's Warren tonight, Carl?"

Carl stared at the monitor, at the boy looking back at him.
He reached for the microphone button, hesitated, then
pulled his hand away.

"It's not often you and I get to spend time alone, Carl. We
have a lot of catching up to do. Did Warren call in sick,
or did they finally nail him to the wall for the Great
Toilet Paper Caper?"

Carl pressed the button. "Shut your face, shit knocker."

The thirty-second delay elapsed. "The last time I was
alone with Warren, he was kind enough to read me all the
newspaper headlines, even a few of the stories. Do you
think you could do that? It really does help to pass the
time. You have a copy of the paper there, don't you?"

Carl glanced down at the *Pittsburgh Post-Gazette* sitting on the console. He leaned back in his chair and said to nobody in particular, "For the record, I have no idea how the kid does that, but it creeps me the fuck out. Like he's got eyes and ears in here. For my friends at corporate—how about putting a little something extra in the budget so we can keep a backup on call for days like today when someone does call in sick? Third time this year for Warren, not that I'm counting. I shouldn't be alone with our little buddy, here. Nobody should. If we had a union, they'd be all over this."

Subject 'D' stood from his bed, crossed the room, and looked directly into the camera. "There's no harm in keeping up with current events, right? How about you just read the first page to me?"

Carl pressed the microphone button. "When your dad did that to your face, it must have hurt like a son of a bitch. Wish I could have heard it, you little shit. I bet you squealed like a stuck pig. I can't imagine what you said to him to bring that on, for a father to do that, for a mother to stand by while he does it."

The delay, then: "I told him what he needed to hear."

"You've been doing a lot of that lately. I bet Subject 'S' wanted to run out of the room when you told her you loved her. Nobody wants to be around Frankenstein's monster when he gets all touchy-feely. You realize, as soon as they're done with you, they'll put you down like a rabid dog, right? Subject 'S' will probably be riding some guy in the back seat of a Ford when it happens. You'll be the furtherest thing from her pretty little mind. What did you expect her to do? Slap a wet one on your lips? Drop to her knees and wet your whistle? I suppose you could tell her to do that, but it wouldn't be the same as her wanting to do it, right? Only way someone like you will ever get laid, though."

"You're not a very nice man, Carl."

"Fuck you."

Carl stood and pulled down the blackout blind on the observation window. He flicked off each of the monitors in the observation room before turning to the camera watching him. "You want to write me up, go ahead. Cocksucking bureaucratic asshats."

—Charter Observation Team – 309

8

The eighth of May came and went, and for the first time since 1986, an envelope containing $500 did not mysteriously appear in my life. I had been home that day, as I was most days now, and kept looking to the door, the window, my room, expecting the envelope, but it never came.

Somehow, I knew that era of my life was over, my benefactor as unknown now as the very first time one of those envelopes appeared.

I didn't need the money.

True to his word, Mr. Matteo saw to it my bills were paid. He opened a checking account in my name and provided me with a debit card. The initial deposit was $2000, and he told me another $2000 would appear with the first of the month and every month thereafter. He also told me if $2000 proved to not be enough, he could increase the amount, I only had to ask. We were to meet at least once every three months to review my current circumstances and make adjustments as needed. More often, if my grades faltered and college appeared in jeopardy.

Considering he took care of my bills, and these funds were meant to cover my day-to-day expenses such as groceries and clothing, I couldn't imagine spending that much. I couldn't imagine spending *close* to that much, so I simply thanked him and took the debit card.

The doctors placed Dunk in a medically-induced coma for nearly a week following his final surgery, his sixth. They said unsupervised movement of any kind couldn't be risked. His blood pressure dipped dangerously low twice on the first day, and one more time three days later. His heart stopped for nearly a minute. There was worry of brain damage. They placed him on a ventilator for the next four days. For the past week, he breathed on his own, and it appeared he would continue to do so.

I learned all of this as the rest of the city did, between the pages of the *Pittsburgh Post-Gazette*. As the sole survivor of the Massacre at Krendal's Diner, as the press dubbed it, reporters engulfed the hospital, bribing employees for any tidbit of information they could obtain. The story remained on the first page for the first three days, then the second and third page. By two weeks, updates on Duncan Bellino faded into the local section.

The front-page story that ran on May 4, the day after the massacre, featured photos of all seven victims. Gerdy was the third image in on the first row. Lurline Waldrip was the first in the second row. The largest photo was last, an old image of Elden Krendal—no hearing aids, all his hair, and about thirty pounds lighter. Following his brief bio, the reporter included a few paragraphs on the diner's history. Efforts were under way to try and raise funds to restore it, as a city landmark. I hoped that wouldn't happen. I don't think I could bring myself to look at that place ever again.

I didn't know the people in the other photographs, not by name, anyway. A few seemed familiar, probably people I had seen at the diner. I read all their bios. I wanted to know them, felt I should.

The first few newspaper stories included something about a boy who ran into the fire, pulled out Duncan Bellino, and attempted to pull out Elden Krendal. Some thought he perished in the explosion, others said he got out. Nobody knew his name, though. The police wouldn't comment. Somehow, my part of the story faded away, and for that I was grateful.

Gerdy's funeral was held on May 6. I sat in the second row, behind her parents. I had never met them. I should have introduced myself. I didn't. Three other funerals took place at the same time. It rained that day. I counted the tents.

Gerdy's clothes were still strewn around my apartment, her toothbrush in the glass on the bathroom counter with mine and Auntie Jo's. I couldn't bear to move any of it.

I had no more tears.

I walked through life as a zombie, all motion and no thought. Unwilling to think about anything that had happened in the past few weeks. Worse still, unable to think about the days and weeks to come.

I found a bottle of Captain Morgan spiced rum in Auntie Jo's room. I finished it over two days and nights, grateful for the thick blanket of fog it placed between me and the world.

Sometimes I wonder how different my life would have been if I hadn't picked up that bottle, if I hadn't liked the taste, the numbness. I did like it, though, a little too much.

I didn't return to Mercy General until May 20.

I had no reason to believe what Detective Horton said about Dunk. He hadn't been charged with a crime, there had been no mention of his involvement in the shooting, the fire, or the deaths that took place at Krendal's in anything I heard or read. He was, and always had been, my friend. I should have gone on the first day and each day that followed, but I couldn't.

I couldn't.

I told myself the police were twisting facts, adding a few of their own, trying to find someplace to put the blame. They wanted to pin this on Dunk so they could roll him on Crocket's organization, give them the chance to dismantle everything before the snake grew a new head.

Dunk wasn't a killer.

Dunk wouldn't hurt anyone.

Dunk was my friend.

Dunk was my *best* friend.

Why did Dunk change his favorite booth?

The question nagged at me more than any other, not only because of what the detectives said, but because of something Dunk said years ago while sitting at my booth in the back corner near the restrooms. *You can see the whole place from here. Nobody ever wants to sit near the bathrooms, but this is the best seat in the house.*

Dunk hadn't been arrested, but when I called Mercy General to get his visiting hours, I was told Pittsburgh PD would have to approve the visit before I would be allowed in to see him.

I left my name and number.

Thirty minutes later, Detective Horton called me back. He wanted me to wear a wire, get Dunk to confess.

I said no.

He cleared my visit anyway.

At the visitor desk, the nurse said Dunk was in room 307—take the purple elevator to three, make a right.

When the elevator door opened on the third floor, I had no trouble spotting Dunk's room. Two uniformed police officers sat on one side of the hallway, while two of Dunk's "friends" sat on the other side—both looked familiar, but I didn't know their names.

All four men eyed me as I walked down the hallway. One of the uniformed officers asked me to sign a clipboard before entering the room.

I scribbled my name, then pushed through the heavy swinging door.

Although it was twenty past four in the afternoon, Dunk's room was dark. The blinds were pulled tight, the lights off, the only illumination in the room provided by the television mounted in the far corner—*The Price is Right* on the screen, the sound off.

The room itself was a mirror image of mine from a few weeks

earlier—same size, shape, same two beds. The first empty, Dunk in the second. His leg was raised in a large sling. I expected a cast, but instead, small metal rods ran the length of his leg, the one side connected to some kind of plastic exoskeleton, the other end disappearing down through his skin. I had never seen anything like it.

I stepped closer, my shoes squeaking on the polished tile floor.

Dunk said, "Gross, right? The doctor said it's called a Hoffman Device. Those things are screwed into my bone." Dunk's eyes remaining closed, his head resting on two pillows. A heart monitor beeped steadily beside him. "I've been in here for three weeks, and this is the first time you visit?"

I almost apologized. I nearly told him I wanted to come sooner, that I couldn't come sooner, things got in the way. I almost said the hospital wouldn't let me see him, wouldn't let anyone see him. He'd know that wasn't true.

Instead, I said nothing.

His eyes still closed, he raised a weak hand in my direction. "Thanks for pulling me out of there."

I gripped it for a second, then quickly let go. His skin felt damp and clammy.

Dunk said, "I don't know how you did it, I probably have thirty pounds on you, but thank you, I mean that, man."

"Who are those guys out in the hall?"

"The cops? I think they're worried I'll run. They might be right—even with the bum leg, I think I'm faster than the fat one."

"Not the cops, the other guys."

"They're there to keep an eye on the cops."

"They think you did this, the police."

Dunk's head turned away, toward the window. "I don't care what they think."

"They think you had Crocket killed so you could take over his business."

"And what do *you* think?"

"I haven't been able to think much of anything in the past few weeks," I said quietly.

"Alonzo Seppala killed Crocket." Dunk shifted his weight. "The squirrelly fuck confessed before he offed himself." His shoulder twitched under the sheets.

Dunk grimaced. "My everything hurts. What doesn't hurt, itches. They've got me on morphine for the pain, which is great, till it's not. After the first few days, it made me itch under my skin, like ants running over all my bones. Even if I could scratch, I can't move much. The doctor said if I shift just a little bit in the wrong direction, the bones might start to heal out of place. If they move too much, they might even need to rebreak something. The leg is bad, but my ribs are the worst. Every time I take a breath, it feels like someone is jabbing at me with a dull knife. One of the bullets tore up my guts pretty good, so no solid food. They're feeding me through one of these tubes. I can't imagine *what* they're feeding me. You know the weirdest part? I haven't had to shit since I got here. Can't be good for me, whatever they're forcing through the tube."

"I'm sorry about your dad," I said.

"He was a piece of shit."

"Still your dad."

"He hasn't been my dad for years." Dunk coughed, and his eyes pinched shut even tighter. Sweat trickled down from his brow. His tongue licked at his dry, cracked lips. "Is there any water on the table?"

There was a plastic cup with a straw. I filled it from the small pitcher beside it and brought the cup to Dunk, maneuvering the straw into his mouth. His eyes remained closed as he drank.

"Why won't you look at me?"

Dunk finished drinking, and I set the cup back down on the table. "Sorry, the light hurts. I think it's from the meds."

He opened his eyes, looked up at me.

Dunk blinked. "Have you been back to school yet?"

And I knew.

I didn't want to, but I knew.

I shuffled backward, my knees hitting the other bed. I tried to say something, but I lost all words. I turned, started for the door.

"Jack?" Dunk said. "Jack, wait. Let me—"

I was halfway to the elevator before he finished the sentence.

I would like to say I was strong.

I would like to say I took what happened at Krendal's and somehow rose from the pain, somehow captured all that was good about my Auntie Jo and Gerdy and all the others I lost that day.

After speaking to Dunk, I left the hospital and wandered the streets of Pittsburgh for nearly five hours.

I walked.

No destination in mind, I just walked.

Good neighborhoods, bad neighborhoods, I didn't care. I think part of me purposely veered toward the bad neighborhoods, hoping to land in some kind of trouble. *Itching* for a fight. With each step, my anger boiled, fed upon itself, until there was nothing else. When a bus roared past me, a little too close to the sidewalk, I cursed myself for not jumping in front of it. As I passed the dealers on the street, I stared them down, wondering which ones worked for Crocket, which ones worked for Dunk, and which ones weren't sure but kept on selling anyway, knowing someone would come along to replenish their stash and collect the proceeds. Somehow, they recognized me as some kind of threat. More than one pulled back a shirt or a coat to show me the butt of a gun or a knife. I found myself smiling at these guys, hoping they would pull their little weapon, hoping they would take a shot, wondering if it would even kill me if they did.

The sun was long gone by the time I found myself back on Brownsville Road. I didn't go home, though, not right away. Instead, I pushed through the doors of Mike's Package Liquor and Beer and bought a bottle of something called Jameson. Being underage, the clerk wouldn't sell it to me at retail, but I quickly learned $100 in cash would buy just about any bottle in that particular store.

Back in my apartment, I didn't turn on the lights, I didn't take off my shoes. I dropped down into Auntie Jo's favorite chair, twisted open the bottle, and drank. I kept drinking until I could no longer see the outline of Gerdy's discarded dress lying on the floor, just outside my bedroom door.

I didn't like the taste of Jameson at first, but it grows on you. It settles in like a warm blanket on the coldest winter night.

Representatives of Brentwood High School called a lot that week, but I didn't answer. When they couldn't reach anyone at my apartment, they tried Ms. Leech across the hall. She told them I left for school, she said she packed me a lunch—ham and cheese on whole wheat. She told them I was probably there somewhere and some teacher fumbled the attendance, bunch of idiots in that building. They called Dewitt Matteo next, and he told them I wouldn't be returning for the final weeks of my junior year, but I would be back in the fall. He told them I would make up any necessary work at that time. The phone calls stopped after that.

Some time in July, there was a knock at my door.

It was Dunk.

I didn't answer.

Matteo told me he hadn't been charged, not with anything. Not a damn thing. Dunk had traded his hospital bed for a wheelchair, with hopes of trading the chair for crutches. He didn't move back into his apartment, he didn't go back to Brentwood High School, either. I'm not sure where he went, and I didn't care.

The next knock at my door wouldn't come until two months later, July 29. I probably shouldn't have answered that one either.

Log 07/29/1993—

Subject "D" within expected parameters.

Audio/video recording.

"Why is the phone in there?"

Warren glanced up from his clipboard and shrugged. "Somebody must have figured it was easier to leave it in the room. He can't dial from in there. The line is dead, unless we activate it."

"Did they put him on a call today?"

"Two, just this morning."

"Are there more scheduled?" Carl asked.

"Dunno. Probably."

"He's got a newspaper in there, too."

"He's been asking for newspapers a lot lately. I guess the doc caved. He's read every book under the sun, doesn't get to watch television, I don't see any harm in him reading the paper," Warren said.

"And the doc gave it to him?"

"Yeah, the doc."

"Not you?"

"I wouldn't go in there. That would be crazy."

—Charter Observation Team – 309

9

I was in bed, when the incessant pounding at the door began.

At first, just a light tap.

Polite.

Noninvasive.

I imagine the knocking started well before the sound worked through my alcohol-fueled slumber and the pillow over my head. By the time I heard the racket, the knocker had established a rhythm they felt comfortable continuing for a while.

About three weeks prior, I took a cue from Elfrieda Leech and taped aluminum foil over my bedroom windows, yet somehow the sunlight still managed to find a way around the edges with enough ferocity to cut at my eyes. I managed a squint before closing my eyes again.

"Open the door, Jack!"

The added dynamic of words containing my name brought my needle closer to awake than asleep, and I tried to place the voice.

Male. Familiar, yet not.

Eyes still shut, I crawled off the bed, planted my feet on the floor, and sat there a moment, my hands rubbing my face. I had a steady knock happening in my skull, too.

I stood and started across the room, nearly tumbling as I tangled in the bedspread on the floor. I must have kicked the down comforter off the bed last night or the night before or the night before that. Frankly, I was amazed I had even found my way to my bed. I took a liking to Auntie Jo's chair, and when I found myself dozing there at three in the morning, it seemed pointless to make the trek all the way across the apartment to my room. The chair was closer to the bathroom, after all.

My brain bounced off the inside of my head with each step, so I took it slow, a shuffle more than steps. I paused at the kitchen, where I swallowed a handful of aspirin dry.

Clearly, whoever was out there was in for the long haul, and they would wait. If they didn't, I didn't really care.

I fumbled with the dead bolt, opened the door enough to see who was standing there.

Willy Trudeau.

A smile filled his face, and he managed to hold it, even though it morphed from authentic to forced the moment he saw me. "Hey, Jack."

"Willy? What are you doing here?"

He handed me a note. "Your neighbor told me to give you this. She poked her head out about twenty minutes ago."

Ms. Leech's shopping list.

"What day is today?"

Willy pushed past me into the apartment, his nose crinkling. "Thursday. What the hell is that smell?"

I hadn't left the apartment for a week. Last Thursday, Ms. Leech braved the hallway and slipped her shopping list under my door. Worried I'd forget about her. One week ago.

"This place is a fucking mess," Willy said.

He spotted Gerdy's dress on the floor and started for it, her panties off to the side. His voice dropped lower. "Do you have a visitor?"

"Don't touch those."

The words came out harsher than I meant. "Sorry, just please, don't."

Willy backed off the dress and panties, glanced into my bedroom, at my empty bed, then returned to the living room.

He turned slowly, taking it all in.

He opened the lid of a pizza box on the table with the tip of his finger, let the lid drop when he saw the contents. I think I ordered that on Saturday. A couple of Chinese delivery boxes sat beside it. The older ones were in the kitchen. Empty bottles of Jameson, Captain Morgan, and other assorted bottles of varying size, color, and brand filled the places between take-out.

I scratched at my belly. "What do you want, Willy?"

"I got a call from your attorney. He asked me to check on you. He told me to get you to his office, one way or another."

"My attorney? How did he get your number?"

"Dunno."

"What did he tell you?"

Willy thumbed through my posters of Stella, stacked under the pizza. "I've seen these around town. Dunk filled me in a few months back. Any luck finding her?"

"What's today's date?"

"July 29, why?"

Not August 8.

"I don't have a calendar."

Willy seemed to understand. "You have a little over a week."

Part of me was surprised he even remembered. We hadn't talked about it since we were kids. Years. A lifetime ago.

I said, "If she shows, yeah. What did my attorney tell you?"

Willy leaned back against the table. "He said you've been holed up in here for months, you don't answer your phone anymore, skipped out on school, missed your last appointment with him. "

Shit. That was Tuesday. I was supposed to go to his office on Tuesday.

Willy went on, "He's worried about you, thought you might

need a friend. Clearly no need for concern, though. Looks like you're doing great."

"Friend? You didn't go to the funerals. None of them." I ticked them off on my hand. "Not Jo's, or Gerdy, or Krendal. All those people who died."

"My parents didn't think—"

"Your parents? Seriously? You're going to blame them? You didn't know Krendal that well, I get that. I can even give you a pass for Jo, but Gerdy? Come one, she was your friend, too. And hell, if you were my friend you should have showed."

Willy looked down at his shoes. "Dunk was in some shit. *Is* in some shit. You're tight with Dunk. My parents thought it would be best if I kept my distance. I'm going to college next year, Penn State, they worried that—"

I crossed over to the door. "Just go, Willy. You shouldn't be here."

"I should have been here all along," he said quietly. "I'm sorry."

"I want to be alone."

"That's the last thing you need."

"Get out, Willy."

"What was I supposed to think? Envelopes with cash mysteriously appearing. That SUV that tried to killed you when we were kids."

Tried.

"I figured all that had something to do with Dunk. I thought maybe he started in with those people back when we were kids, and it all escalated since then. I thought the money was his way of paying you for helping him or for working with those guys or both, or something. He really spooked me with the gun. I pretended it was all good, but shit, Jack, a gun? We were twelve. We had zero business with a real gun. I figured the story about the girl was some elaborate coverup you concocted instead of telling me the truth. I kept my distance. I thought the whole story was bogus. Then I started seeing these posters around town with your phone number and her picture, and I knew it wasn't. All those things you and Dunk told me back in the day about this girl, I thought you made it up. I should have known you wouldn't lie. Dunk, maybe, not you, though." He stared down at his shoes. "I'm sorry. You were my friend, and I let you down. I let you down on so many levels. I should have been there the whole time, and I wasn't. I'm here now, though. I want to make things right, somehow."

An awkward silence fell between us. I found myself leaning against the door, my eyes trailing the thin beams of light skirting around the curtains drawn in the living room. "Have you seen Dunk?"

Willy bit his lip. "I saw him yesterday coming out of the McDonald's on 51. He didn't look good. Real thin and in a wheel-chair. I didn't recognize the guy pushing him. There were about six other men with him too, nobody I knew, all older. They loaded him into a van and drove off toward the city with a patrol car right behind them."

"So he still hasn't been arrested?"

"My dad knows someone down in the DA's office, and he told me they couldn't tie any of it to him. That other kid confessed to orchestrating the shooting, and he killed himself before they could get the names of the actual gunmen. They're trying to build a case against Dunk on the drug business too, but like Crocket, he's isolated from everything. Looks like he's taking over, probably already has," Willy said. "Have you seen him?"

I shook my head and told him how he came by, told him about my visit with Dunk in the hospital. As I finished, I found myself looking at a bottle of Jameson on the table beside Willy, about a finger or two left in the bottom.

"Dude, you stink," Willy said. "When was the last time you took a shower?"

Three, no four days.

"Yesterday," I said.

He opened his mouth to say something, and I raised my hand and waved him off, heading toward the bathroom.

315

I stood under the hot water for nearly an hour, just stood there, let the water run over me, before I finally picked up the soap.

When I emerged from the bathroom, the aluminum foil was gone from the windows, all the boxes and bottles had been picked up, he even put fresh sheets on the bed, dirty laundry piled at the foot. Willy was in the living room, scrubbing at a mystery stain on the coffee table with a rag in one hand and a bottle of Windex in the other.

Three black trash bags stood in the center of the room, all full.

Gerdy's dress and panties were still on the floor, where she left them, the only thing in the room left untouched.

Two McDonald's bags sat on the coffee table, steam rising from one. A bottle of Gatorade beside them, orange flavored. Willy gestured toward the bags. "I got you two McGriddles. You still eat those, right?"

The idea of eating anything made my stomach churn, but I knew I had to get some food in me. My entire body was shaky from lack of calories, and my mouth tasted sour. I pulled one of the breakfast sandwiches from the bag and took a bite. The second bag contained a large coffee. I helped myself to that, too.

Willy gave up on the stain and sat on the edge of Jo's chair. "I talked to Matteo. He wants us to come down there." He pointed at the Gatorade. "Try to chug that. The electrolytes will help with your shakes."

I nodded, finished the first sandwich, and started on a second, wondering what Willy did with the bottles that still contained a taste of whiskey. I didn't see them anywhere.

10

"You're a fucking drunk."

Dewitt Matteo sat across from Willy and me in the same conference room, same chairs, Gerdy and I had sat in three months earlier. Even his brown tweed suit appeared to be the same.

Matteo tapped his pen on the top of a lined pad of yellow notebook paper. He had yet to write anything. "You're as pale as a hemophiliac after donating blood, and you're sweating."

"It's warm in here."

"It's seventy degrees in here," he shot back. "You're a fucking drunk, and your body is craving a taste."

I said nothing.

"I told your aunt you couldn't be trusted on your own. A teenage boy with no supervision. She swore up and down that you were a good kid, that you could take care of yourself. In the past few months, I fielded dozens of calls from your school and social services. When you took it upon yourself to stop attending class, your principal called the county. Do you have any idea how hard it was to put that fire out and keep them from checking on you? That's not the worst of it, though. The worst has been that neighbor of yours, your so-called 'guardian.'" His chubby fingers formed air quotes. "Apparently you missed some kind of grocery delivery, and she lit up my phones a couple times an hour. Poor Tess had to run to the store for her and make a delivery. Be ready to see a hefty bill for that against the estate. My office is not a delivery service."

"I'm sorry."

Matteo stopped tapping. "I know you've been through some shit, kid, more than anyone should ever have to deal with, but you gotta pull yourself together. This needs to stop, or pretty soon there won't be a way back."

My hand started shaking again. I put both on my lap, under the table.

"Do I need to send you to some kind of rehab?"

He asked the question of me, but he was looking at Willy when he asked it. Both Willy and I shook our heads.

"I can stay with him for a few days," Willy offered. "I got Gatorade, like you said. There's no alcohol left in the apartment. My big brother had a drinking problem, and I helped my mom detox him. The first couple days will be rough, but then it gets better. I know what to do."

Matteo eyed him, looked him up and down, then turned back to me. "Your aunt gave me a list of your friends. Next to this one's name, she wrote the word 'responsible' and underlined it. She was a smart woman."

He leaned back in his chair and thought for a second. "How much money do you have in your pocket?"

I wasn't sure. I reached in and pulled out a wad of cash from the left front pocket of my jeans and a few coins from my right. I set my small fortune on the table and counted it out. "Twenty-four dollars and thirty-eight cents."

Matteo reached over and slid the cash in front of Willy. "You hold that."

Willy stared at him, confused.

The attorney turned back to me. "For the next few months, your stipend from the trust will be paid out directly to Mr. Trudeau here. He will buy your groceries when he goes shopping to buy whatever your crazy neighbor throws on her list. Absolutely nothing will be spent on alcohol, drugs, prostitutes, gambling, or whatever other vices you've decided to sample of late."

I opened my mouth to tell him I've only been drinking, but he silenced me with a glance.

"What trust?" Willy asked.

Matteo held up a finger, quieting him too. "In exchange for your trouble, Mr. Trudeau, you will be paid a salary of one hundred dollars per day, also from the trust. You will keep Mr. Thatch clean and out of trouble. The second he steps out of line, you pull him back. If you don't pull him back, I put an end to your newfound wealth. Stay in his apartment as long as necessary. Understand?"

Before he could answer, Matteo turned back to me. "The conditions of your trust are very clear, and I plan to honor your aunt's wishes. In order to collect the balance, you must graduate from college. You can't graduate college if you don't graduate high school, and you can't graduate high school if you don't go. When school starts back up next month, I expect you to be there. You need to finish out your senior year, keep the grades up, and get into Penn State. No more fucking around. Do you think you can do that?"

My head was pounding. The headache had started behind my left eye and grew from there, reaching out with exploratory fingers. The shaking of my hand had migrated south to my leg. I forced it to stop jumping under the conference table. I thought about the small fifth of Captain Morgan spiced rum in my dresser back home, the one Gerdy had swiped from Willy's party a while back. I wondered if Willy had found that one.

"Yes sir," I said, although somehow I already knew I would never set foot in Brentwood High School again.

Log 08/08/1993—

Interview with Dr. Helen Durgin. Subject "D" within expected parameters.

Audio/video recording.

"Tell me about Edward 'Jack' Thatch," Subject "D" said.

"What would you like to know?"

"Why do they allow him to keep seeing Stella?"

"Because she wishes for it. His visits are a form of reward."

"A reward? Like a dog gets a treat when it rolls over?"

"I suppose something like that," Dr. Durgin replied.

"And my reward has been what? More time in this box?"

"You see Stella, too. You received books and music. An education."

Subject "D" laughed at this. "You realize I never once met any of my teachers? They sit on the other side of the glass while I'm in here. They read to me from textbooks, answer my questions around that ridiculous delay. I've never been told their names. I never see their faces. They don't praise me when I excel or criticize me when I fail. I could close my eyes and take a nap. I imagine they would go right on reading, lecturing, one eye on the clock and the other on the door, but unwilling to look at me. None of them really care about me any more than you do. I'm just a lab rat to you. The afterthought of some long-ago experiment gone awry. I'm a happy side effect living to fill your journals, your tapes, clean up *their* mess."

"You're dangerous. You need to be contained."

"I suppose. Containment can be a funny thing, though. Do you understand the basic principal of a pipe bomb?"

Dr. Durgin said nothing.

"A pipe bomb uses a tightly sealed section of pipe filled with an explosive material. The containment provided by the pipe itself means a simple low explosive can be used to produce a relatively large explosion. You see, *the containment* causes increased pressure, amplifies the destructive power. If you put a bomb in a box, the resulting devastation will be far worse than if you set off the same bomb in the middle of an open field. I've been in my box for a very long time, Doctor."

"Stella is also in a box, albeit, a much larger box."

"Why isn't Thatch in a box of his own?"

Dr. Durgin did not respond.

"He doesn't deserve Stella," Subject "D" said. "Hand me that glass of water."

Without hesitation, the doctor did as she was told.

—Charter Observation Team – 309

11

"Well, ain't that some shit."

Preacher parked his black Pontiac GTO in his usual spot on Willock Road and walked up the steep hill to Brownsville Road, then down the block to Krendal's Diner, what remained of Krendal's Diner. The picture windows were covered in large sheets of plywood. The glass door had been replaced with a large steel monstrosity secured with a padlock. A sign was bolted to the center of the door at eye level:

CONDEMNED
This Structure Is Declared Unfit
For Human Occupancy Or Use.
It Is Unlawful For Any Person To
Use Or Occupy This Building
Any Unauthorized Person Removing This Sign
WILL BE PROSECUTED

Preacher's first thought at reading this sign was the poor use of grammar. Conjunctions should not be capitalized. Preacher's second thought when reading this sign, when taking in the entirety of the destruction upon which it was attached, was, *what the hell happened?*

He ate here the day before the Gargery woman's funeral—steak and eggs—his usual.

He ran his finger along the edge of the metal window frame, his gloved hand coming away with soot. He made it a point to be informed. He did not like being uninformed.

With the death of the Gargery woman, he had no longer been required to make monthly deliveries of cash to the boy.

That was good.

That was real good.

Because it left time for other jobs.

He avoided this armpit of a city for three and a half months. He liked to stay on the move, a change of scenery. He liked to get his hands dirty, and this Pittsburgh job had been beneath him from the get-go. This hands off, observation only, delivery-boy bullshit was not what he signed up for. A waste of his talent.

That would change today, and that was exciting.

That got the blood pumping through his aging ticker.

The diner, though, the diner bothered him.

An unknown variable.

He didn't like unknown variables.

Another cloud drifted past the sun. This one dark and gray, and ready to burst. The temperature dropped too, a cold breeze kicking up. Rain soon. Heavy rain.

The payphone behind him began to ring.

Preacher considered pulling down the sign, then left it.

He crossed the sidewalk and picked up the call with his gloved hand, careful not to let the receiver actually touch his ear. "You didn't say anything about the diner."

"The diner?"

"Looks like some kind of fire. What happened?"

"The diner fire is unrelated. It doesn't concern you. I figured you would have heard."

"I've been in Arkansas."

A sigh. "Good for you."

"Was the boy...?"

"No. He's fine."

Preacher glanced down at his watch. Ten minutes until six. "Are we still a go?"

"Yes. Are you ready?"

That was a stupid question. He was always ready. "Yes."

"Nobody lives, understand?"

That last bit made him forget the stupid question.

He couldn't wait.

12

One block away, only two parking spaces down from where the surveillance van used to park before Duncan Bellino moved out of the apartment building located at 1822 Brownsville Road, Detectives Faustino Brier and Joy Fogel sat in a cream-colored Honda Civic pulled from the motor pool earlier in the day. They didn't want to drive their regular vehicles, not today, on the off chance the Thatch kid recognized either of them.

Faustino watched the man who drove the black Pontiac GTO hang up the payphone and walk back toward Willock. He probably parked in the same place as the last time he saw him.

"I'll stay on him," Faustino said. "You follow the boy."

"Got it," Fogel replied, already climbing out of the car, eyeing the dark clouds above warily.

13

Turns out, Willy *had* found the small bottle of Captain Morgan in my top dresser drawer. The bottle hadn't been hidden or anything, just sitting in the middle of some old comics, loose coins, random school assignments, a half-full box of condoms, and some drawings not worthy of display but not quite bad enough to throw out.

I want to be clear about something. I didn't really need alcohol. Not now, and not back then. I'm not, and never was, an alcoholic. I've met a few in my time, more than a few—alcoholism is a horrible disease that lives far beyond the need to numb some feelings. Alcoholism lives within the cells, a hungry animal screaming to be fed. Maybe that comes later, but what I had wasn't *that*. At least, I didn't think so. I simply wanted to forget. I wanted to wipe away the last year. I wanted to go back to a time when I didn't know the medications needed to treat acute myeloid leukemia by heart. I missed Auntie Jo's incessant complaining, I missed the warmth of Gerdy's hand, I missed the heat of Krendal's kitchen and the greasy feeling of the dishwater after a dinner rush.

The last year of my life had been a nightmare, and I wanted to wake from it. I couldn't wake from it, so I tried to forget instead. Alcohol allowed me to do that, even if just for a little while. I suppose had I spotted the remainder of Auntie Jo's pain meds after the fire, after leaving the hospital, had I found her pain meds and sampled those rather than that first bottle of Jameson, it might have been pills that helped me forget rather than alcohol, but it would have been *something*. I needed *something*. If I hadn't found some way to slip away from the pain, some way to numb the pain, I surely would have taken Auntie Jo's pills by the handful and put a more permanent stop to my horrific ride. It's silly to say alcohol saved me, but in some ways it did. Alcohol saved me from myself.

The first few days after the last drink were tough.

The shakes came and went, tag teaming with fever and sweats and dry mouth. I couldn't keep food down, not that I really wanted to eat. My body threw up everything, heaving until my throat grew raw. I had trouble sleeping, and when I finally did drift off, I'd wake with attacks of anxiety, my heart racing so fast it felt like a motor stuck in the wrong gear attempting to chug up a hill. This passed after a few days, but it might as well have been months. Time made little sense to me.

Willy stayed with me the entire time. Matteo talked to him several times. I'm not sure what exactly they worked out, but Willy returned the first night with a large suitcase. I told him to take Auntie Jo's room, but he opted to remain on the couch. Something about moving into that space seemed taboo, even to him.

When I asked for a drink, he gave me cranberry juice instead. I drank so much cranberry juice my piss turned red. This should have been cause for concern, but my body ached so bad at that point, I think I welcomed death—a little red piss was surely a step in the right direction.

On the third day, the shaking stopped. I told Willy about the life insurance money, the trust. I explained in detail what Matteo originally told me. My allowance, the college requirement, my part-time guardian across the hall paid via grocery delivery and the occasional book.

I filled him in on the years between. My trips to the cemetery, each one since our failed meeting ending in my cracked up bike back in '88. I told him what little I knew of Dunk. I told him about my visit to Stella's house last year, I told him about the little room in the basement, I told him about Raymond Visconti and how he was found the next day in the same alley across from Krendal's as Andy Olin Flack years earlier.

I told him everything.

And Willy listened.

Through all, I caught him more than once glancing through my bedroom door at the drawings of Stella or toward the dusty stack of posters still sitting on the table near the kitchen. When I finally finished, he asked me one simple question. "Do you love her?"

To which I answered, "I don't know."

"I'm drawn to her," I explained. "I don't think a single day, maybe even a single waking hour, has passed where I haven't thought about her. It's been like that since I was a little kid. When I'm with her, even if only for a brief time, I feel complete, I feel whole." To say these things out loud brought Gerdy to mind, and the guilt crushed me.

I'm okay being the other girl.

Was it possible to love two different girls? I was beginning to think it was. Not exactly the same love, *different* kinds of love, each one filling a different void.

Did I love Stella? I did. Maybe I couldn't bring myself to say it aloud, but I surely did.

Did I love Gerdy? I *wanted to*, but I didn't. Not at first, anyway. Maybe now, yes, but not at first. And admitting such a thing made everything hurt that much more.

Perhaps that was the difference, if there could be one.

I couldn't *not* love Stella, even if I tried.

Knowing I would see her soon got me through this past week, through the withdrawal, got me past the alcohol. At least this time.

"It's almost six," Willy finally said. "You need to go."

Outside, dark storm clouds cluttered the evening sky, thick raindrops smacked against Auntie Jo's window. I nodded and started for the door.

"You should bring an umbrella," Willy suggested.

"Don't have one!" I called back from the hallway.

I wasn't about to let a little rain slow me down, not today.

If not for the rain, I might have noticed Faustino Brier's Partner, Detective Fogel, round the corner of my building and follow me toward the cemetery.

I paused at my parents' graves beneath the dripping leaves of the large maple, rain splashing all around. Although the downpour hadn't started very long ago, the ground was already spongy. Three graves now beneath that tree, the grass around Auntie Jo's filled in and blending with the others. The vases attached to each gravestone overflowed, the metal lined with rust stains. Neither of my parents' vases held flowers. I hadn't been here for months, not even after the funerals for Gerdy, Krendal, and the others from the diner. I just couldn't.

Kneeling in the wet grass, I peeled away the maple leaves sticking to the surface of the stones, wiped the grime away with rainwater and my hand.

"Kaitlyn Gargery Thatch. February 16, 1958 to August 8, 1980. Loving wife, mother, and sister," I said softly.

My father's grave sat in silence beside hers, somehow condemning my recent behavior. The minimal words on his stone were representative of the few words he would speak when angry with me, the silence often more punishment than any anything he could say aloud.

"I'm getting it together," I said to both of them. "It's been a rough patch, but I've got it now. I'll come back when the weather breaks, clean this up."

The vase attached to Auntie Jo's gravestone did contain a flower, a single daisy, now dead and shriveled. I wondered who put it there.

"I'll be back, I promise."

Standing, I turned toward the hill and made my way toward the mausoleums, toward the bench.

14

Preacher took the turn off Brownsville and brought the GTO to a stop in a small alley just off the main road.

He had a love/hate relationship with the rain.

He knew the weather would offer additional cover and help shield him from prying eyes, but at the same time, he hated being wet. Damp clothes slowed him down, made him drag, made him feel dirty. Of course, there was the sound, too. Preacher knew his hearing was keen, probably better than most, but this kind of weather created such a racket it drowned out nearly everything—great for what he was about to do, bad when listening for a threat creeping up on your backside.

He'd make due, though. He always did.

Reaching under the passenger seat, he retrieved his shotgun. A modified 14" pump action Mossberg with a Raptor grip. From the glove box, he took out one of the dozen boxes of ammunition and began filling the magazine with shells, pumping the last to ready it in the chamber.

From behind the boxes of ammunition, he retrieved three M67 grenades. Although small, each would produce an injury radius of fifteen meters and could throw fragments as far as two hundred and fifty meters.

Loud too.

Preacher liked loud.

He wore his Gordonstone army-issue trenchcoat, a favorite of his since finding it in a Goodwill store nearly fifteen years ago. He dropped the three grenades into the large front right pocket and systematically began to fill each of the remaining pockets with spare shells for the shotgun. He knew from past experience he could easily carry five boxes of ammunition. The shotgun shells added about thirteen pounds to the already heavy jacket—the jacket's weight came from the kevlar plates he stitched inside, covering his arms and chest.

His lucky jacket.

His favorite shotgun.

Ready to go.

Few minutes to six.

He backed out of the alley.

15

The bench was empty.

Raindrops hit the seat and bounced back up. Water rolled off the surface and puddled beneath.

I shivered.

I should have brought a jacket.

I made my way from the edge of the mausoleums to the bench and took a seat, swept my wet hair back from my face and eyes, and stared down the narrow access road.

No sign of the SUVs.

I had the letter from Stella's dad to mine in my front pocket, and I hoped to God the rain didn't ruin it. I cursed myself for not wrapping the letter in plastic or something to keep it safe.

Although the sun wouldn't set for another two hours or so, there was very little light. The angry storm clouds above blotted out what little tried to get past and the cemetery felt lost in some kind of pre-twilight. When the wind kicked up, I bent my head forward and shielded my eyes. At least ten more minutes passed before I spotted headlights slicing through the rain at the far end of the access road, weaving through the cemetery, disappearing behind the hills only to reappear a moment later a little closer.

When the vehicle stopped about a hundred feet from me, the rain was coming down so hard I couldn't make out much of anything. Even the beams of the headlights seemed choked by the rain, struggling to see more than a few feet.

They sat there, the engine revving.

I stood and started toward it.

16

Preacher pulled to a stop, his foot riding the gas, feeding the engine. The GTO rumbled with delight.

He couldn't see a damn thing.

He flicked his headlights from low to high and back again, the rain falling so hard now it was a solid wall of water, a curtain of white.

He rested his right hand on the Mossberg, ran his thumb over the smooth, oiled metal.

When someone tapped at his window, his fingers tightened on the grip.

With his free hand, Preacher reached for the door handle.

Go time.

17

The back door opened and I scrambled onto the seat, slamming the door behind me with water splashing all about.

Ms. Oliver stood beside me, a scowl covered her face. "I thought you might sit out there all night, soaking up the filthy coal-ridden acid rain of this god-awful town. Maybe we'll all get lucky and you'll come down with a nice bout of pneumonia. Too stupid to wear a proper coat or use an umbrella. Why am I not surprised?"

I glanced around the interior.

A man and woman sat in the front seats. Neither turned around. I could see the man in the rearview mirror. He looked to be in his mid-twenties with short-cropped blond hair, brown eyes, and a scar about an inch long above his right cheek. When he saw me looking at him, he smirked and faced front out the windshield at the onslaught of rain rolling over the glass.

"Where is she?"

Oliver sighed. "I warned you when you were a kid, I told you what would happen, and you didn't listen. Instead, you obsess, you chase, you hang posters all over town, for god's sake. Even now, I can hear your little heart going all pitter-patter. At what point do you realize you are beneath her and move on?"

"Take me to her."

"You can't touch her," Oliver went on. "You've seen what her touch brings. You can't hold her, not ever, and that is the least of the walls keeping you apart. I wanted you to see that, you *needed* to see."

"Take me to her," I said again.

"She has to do it, you know. The urge builds, this desire, this hunger, this void crying out for fill. She can hold it at bay for a little while, but it nags at her. She said the hunger starts like a little whisper from the corner of the room and eventually grows to a scream so loud she hears nothing else. It's a sickness, an addiction, both mental and physical." She turned to me and smiled. "You understand addiction, don't you? I hear you've taken up the drink. That's such marvelous news. That should speed your journey to the gutter for sure."

"I only drank—"

"You only drank to cope, to numb the pain, to escape." She waved a hand in the air. "I've heard it all before. I really don't care why you're doing it. I can only hope you escalate. Perhaps you'll move on to pills or heroin or meth or crack—anything that removes you from my life sooner rather than later would be simply wonderful. I hear you can afford it now, too." The smile left her face. She leaned in closer. "Don't you think for a second a little coin jingling in your pocket somehow raises you to her stature. Don't you believe that for a second. Finer clothes can't change who you really are. All they do is help cover up the stench simmering beneath. Like a tarp over a pile of shit left out in the sun." She placed her hand on her lap. "All those years ago, when I first met you, you had such a fire in your eyes. That determined 'nothing can stop me' bullshit every child possesses. It's nice to see that fire dimming with life's challenges, and dim it has over the years. You'll soon see even tossing the occasional glass of accelerant on the flames can't rekindle the exuberance of youth. The only real question left is how long before your fire goes out completely. How long before you're another mindless wretch wandering the streets with nothing left to your name but the cardboard sign in your hand and the stink of booze on your breath?"

My hand had balled into a fist, and I was sure my face was red. "Take. Me. To. Her." The man in the front seat looked back at me in the mirror.

"No," Ms. Oliver said. "This ends today."

"You're keeping her there, in that house, against her will. You're forcing her to do those things, to hurt people."

This brought a smile back to Oliver's face, a soft chuckle. She reached into her jacket pocket and pulled out a folded letter. She handed it to me. It smelled of vanilla. The letter smelled of Stella.

At first, I didn't unfold it. I only stared at the old woman. I had never hated anyone as much as I hated her. This evil, vile woman. When I finally did unfold it, all three of them were watching me. I reached up and turned on the overhead light.

Oliver's hand shot up and flicked the switch. "Leave the light off. I prefer the dark."

I unfolded the letter and, Stella's scent filled the SUV.

My dearest little Pip,

I'm afraid our time together has come to an end. You have been such fun. A splendid time, to be sure. Upon our first meeting, I told my beloved Ms. Oliver that you would be mine within a year, less even, should I put a little effort behind it. I told her I could wrap you around my finger and lead you around like a puppy with little more than the bat of an eye. And you have proven me right. From curiosity came wonder and from wonder came desire and from desire came lust, and somewhere within all of that, came love. I know you love me. While I could never love the likes of you, I know you love me. I'm curious—when Ms. Oliver told you that you could never have me, did that make you want me more? She said it would. It would be helpful to know.

In the pool, I know you wanted me. The lust and need upon your face was so blatantly obvious, I nearly called out to Ms. Oliver and the others simply to say, "Look! Like the strings of a puppet! Watch as I move him here, watch as I move him there... Dance, my little Pip, dance!"

Oh, it was wonderful, our years together.
My little plaything.
My little Pip.
But, end it must.

You must forget me.

How are you to fill your days without thinking about me?
Even I don't know. Perhaps you will always think about me.
Live all your days with me on your mind, then.
Perhaps you won't, but I think you will.
My Pip.
Every day, always. My Pip.

Stella

My first thought upon finishing the letter was that she didn't write it. Someone else wrote it and signed her name. I didn't know her handwriting, had never seen it. I did know her signature, though. She had signed all the paintings in the house, and I remembered each of those images with complete clarity. The brushstrokes vividly etched in my mind. The signature on the letter matched the signature on those paintings.

Stella

The style of the signature matched the text above—the penmanship, the ink, the curve of each letter, the cross of a *t* or the swirl of an *e*. I didn't want to believe they were written by the same hand, by her hand, but the closer I looked, the more certain of this I became, and by my sixth pass, I could no longer read the letter through the tears filling my eyes.

Oliver said, "Seven years ago, you and I sat upon that bench and I told you, 'you will never have her. As much as you may one day desire her, she will never be yours.' Do you remember?"

I said nothing.

My tears fell on the letter. A drop fell on the word *forget*. I watched the ink as it pooled, spread, the word going blurry. I wiped my eyes with the back of my hand. Inhaled the snot ready to drip from my nose.

"You were, and always have been, a game to her. A game that has finally reached its end. Not soon enough for my tastes, but finally, nonetheless." She looked over at me and smiled. "I'll tell her you cried. She'll like that. Perhaps you'll go home and slit your wrists. *I* would like that. Do you need a knife? I'm sure we can find one for you."

The man in the driver's seat was watching me again, a grin on his lips in the mirror. The woman beside him looked like she might burst out with laughter, her head hung low, her lips pursed tight, holding back.

I reached for the door handle. Before Oliver said another word, Stella's letter was in my pocket and I was out the car—I ran off into the rain, into the night.

18

"Please stay in your vehicle, sir."

Preacher heard the words a moment before he made out the shape of the man who uttered them, standing beside his car in a long, white trench coat, a hood pulled over his head. One hand on the butt of a gun in a holster at his waist, the other hand on Preacher's car door, heavy rain falling all around.

Preacher put his shoulder down and opened the door of the GTO with such force, it nailed the man in his midsection and sent him sprawling on his back.

He followed the door as it opened, brought the gun up, braced the stock against his hip, then forced the barrel down into the man's chest.

The man in the white trench coat looked like a turtle stuck on his back, all flailing arms and legs attempting to right himself. A slew of pleading words flowed from his pale face.

Preacher pulled the trigger.

With the barrel pressed tight against the man's chest, his body acted like a makeshift silencer. He bounced as the explosion entered his chest cavity and expanded, no doubt turning his organs into mush. The blast escaped from the man's back with enough force to spray water and the remnants of a few petals out in all directions.

In a single, fluid motion, Preacher raised the shotgun, jerked his arm hard enough to eject the spent shell and load a new one, and sighted the weapon on a second man in a white trench coat stepping out of the guardhouse next to the gate. This man also had a Sig Sauer P220. He managed to get it about halfway out of his holster before Preacher's shotgun erupted in a second blast. A bright red bloom opened up in the man's chest and ruined his nice white coat. The man looked down at the spot. Confusion filled his eyes as it grew. Then he collapsed in a puddle, partially obscured by the Pontiac's left front fender.

Because that shot didn't utilize a human silencer, or any silencer for that matter, it was much louder than the first. No doubt loud enough for at least one or two neighbors to hear. Whether or not they called the police was a different matter. In a storm like this, most would probably attribute such a sound to the weather. Shotgun blasts in this part of town were not common, and while most people would like to believe they could identify the sound of gunfire, very few actually could, and even fewer were willing to act on that sound when they did hear it. Easier to tell themselves they didn't hear it, easier to pretend they heard something else.

Three steps to the guardhouse. Preacher was inside in an instant, the shotgun reloaded and ready. As he expected, it was empty.

The guardhouse had four windows, one facing in each direction. Beneath the window, facing the house, was a small desk. The desk housed three small television monitors tied to the closed-circuit video system. The first monitor displayed a nice close-up of his Pontiac GTO, and he couldn't help but admire the car. It was a beautiful piece of Detroit's finest workmanship. The rain brought out the best of the car's lines, glimmering under the floodlight pointed at the hood. The second monitor showed a wide view—the tail end of the GTO was visible as was a substantial length of the driveway, nearly to the main road. The third monitor cycled through all the other cameras positioned around the large property.

Immediately following the Gargery funeral, Preacher trailed the small motorcade of white vehicles back to this place. No easy task. There had been three of them, and each took a different route in an effort to thwart a tail, one of them taking more than an hour to get back even though the house wasn't more than a couple miles from the cemetery. Preacher knew which car contained the Oliver woman, and that was the one he focused on, carefully tailing at a respectable distance with several cars between whenever possible. Not his first rodeo. Oliver's car had also taken a longer route back to the house, one that took nearly thirty minutes rather than the five or so a direct route would take. That didn't matter. What did matter was Preacher knew where the house was after that, knew where *they* were.

He knew where to find the girl.

That afternoon, he obtained copies of the building plans from the county courthouse. He obtained plat maps of the terrain. He pulled all the tax records for the property. It was an old estate, built back in 1893. Records from Building and Zoning gave him details on all the improvements and additions made over the years— upgrades to the electrical and plumbing, reinforcements to the rooms and walls. Building permits listed vendors on-site whenever an inspector came by. Using the vendor names, Preacher located the company that installed the security system and the custom dead bolts securing all outer doors. Obtaining their records only took a few days.

Within a week, he knew every inch of the place. He could rattle off the type of nail the contractor used in each room down to the copper manufacturer of the original pipes and the PVC that replaced them about a decade ago.

He began surveillance shortly after that.

Most installations—and that was exactly what he considered this place to be, not a house but an installation—most installations that employed full-time security typically ran a tight ship. That meant schedules, rotations, defined routes and patterns. Some stuck to a daily rotation schedule, others went with a rotation of five, ten, or sometimes even twenty different schedules, the more complicated, the more difficult they were to monitor, to map. This place rotated between seven different schedules, and it took Preacher nearly two weeks to figure it all out. He had, though, he always did. By the end of that two weeks, he identified all thirty-seven guards who worked here, knew their assignments, schedule, and rotation. He didn't go so far as to pull payroll information and determine their real names. Instead, he named each of them himself. The one he killed at his car was Dopey. The second man had been Sneezy.

At any given time, two men were assigned to the guardhouse. Five more patrolled the grounds. Seven in total on the outside.

Beside the three security system monitors was a telephone. He stood there and stared at the phone for about a minute on the off chance the shots had been heard and someone placed a call to the guardhouse.

The phone did not ring.

Beside the phone was a large yellow button. Preacher pressed it.

The wrought iron gate in front of his GTO began the slow swing inward, opening up over the driveway.

Preacher returned to the car, climbed in, and frowned as water splashed on the leather seats. He'd give her a good detailing tomorrow. He'd buff the mess of this place right out and bring back the shine.

The phone in the gatehouse began to ring as the GTO inched through the gate.

19

There was a nasty cold in Detective Joy Fogel's future, she was certain of that.

She crouched down behind the mausoleums, practically hugging the stone walls in an attempt to escape the rain, but it did little good. Her clothing was soaked straight through, and she was fairly certain her skin was bloated and wrinkled, as if she had soaked in a tub for the past hour rather than hunkered down in a cemetery tailing a kid.

Thatch paused at his parents' graves. Both she and Detective Faustino Brier had visited them a few times in the past. He had a folder on the graves. Ironically, they possessed more information on the graves themselves than they did on the boy's parents. They knew who manufactured each stone, when they were placed, obtained copies of the work orders. They had no idea who paid for them—the names on the work orders proved to be bogus. The folder on the parents was thin. Fogel brushed her flat, dripping hair from her eyes for the umpteenth time and made a mental note to try and correct that. They pulled their names and DOBs from the grave markers but had been unable to locate birth records, DMV, or property. They were fairly certain the names Edward and

Kaitlyn Thatch were aliases. If not aliases, they lived completely off the grid. Not too easy to do today, but easy enough in the fifties, sixties, and even the seventies.

The boy stopped at his parents' graves for a few minutes, then continued up the hill to the bench. Fogel followed him at a safe distance and took up position at the mausoleums when he sat.

She spotted the approaching vehicle before he did, watched it wind up the narrow access road and park, facing him.

She watched Thatch go to the vehicle and climb inside—a white Chevy Suburban with dark, tinted windows.

Fogel assumed the SUV belonged to Crocket (or now, Duncan Bellino) and this was some kind of structured meet away from suspected monitored locations. If they left, she had no way to give chase.

Thatch didn't leave with the SUV, though. Instead, he burst from the vehicle and ran back through the cemetery. Fogel was momentarily divided—stay with the SUV or continue with the boy.

She decided to do both.

She ran from the mausoleums toward the white Suburban, remaining low and hoping the rain would offer her cover from whoever sat inside. She got close enough to note the plate number, then went back after the kid, cursing herself for not wearing waterproof shoes today.

Thatch, with Fogel behind him, was halfway down the hill when the SUV left the cemetery, wiper blades slashing at the rain.

20

With the gate open, Preacher dropped the GTO into first and followed the cobblestone driveway through the established oaks and elms toward the house. Steering with his left hand, he took the opportunity to reload the shotgun with his right. The driveway was surprisingly long and far too quiet.

The first bullet struck the left headlight.

The second bullet smacked the windshield a little off-center. The bullet whizzed past Preacher's right ear and buried itself in the fabric of his seat.

Three more bullets followed those in quick succession before Preacher spotted the shooter—he stepped out of the trees about thirty feet in front of the car, his white coat flapping, gun bouncing in his hand. This was the one Preacher named 'Doc.'

Preacher hoped to get to the front of the house before the gunplay began, but since that was clearly not in the cards, he dropped the GTO into neutral, yanked up the emergency break, and pushed out the door into the rain. This really set Doc off. He began firing wildly at the sight of him—stupid at this distance, particularly in the rain. Preacher disappeared among the trees and came around Doc's flank while the kid was reloading.

Clipped to his belt, Preacher carried a dozen Smith & Wesson SWTK10CP throwing blades. Made of carbon steel with a nice weight of about seven ounces, he preferred them over guns in many situations, this being one of them. The knife was off his belt, silently airborne, and buried in Doc's neck in less time than it took for the kid to swap his empty clip for a fresh one. Doc dropped his Sig, dropped the clip, then fell to the ground. His last mistake was pulling the knife from his neck.

Preacher stuck to the trees.

Two more guards appeared in the driveway. One bent over Doc, the other scanned the trees. Neither saw him. They eyed the still-running GTO. Preacher followed the tree line until the house came into view, then waited at the edge, the shotgun slung over his shoulder and knives in each hand.

The two men ran right past him, back toward the house.

As the second one raced by, Preacher struck the man in the heel, slicing his achilles. The man dropped, then slid. The first man turned at the sound and caught Preacher's second blade in the throat. He went down, too.

Grumpy and Happy, Preacher supposed. The guards were all out of position now. It was difficult to tell them apart.

The guard with the sliced heel attempted to pull himself toward the trees, sliding slowly across the driveway. Preacher stabbed him in the back of the neck, took his Sig Sauer, then turned his gaze back toward the front of the house. There were two more guards out here somewhere. That just wouldn't do.

Floodlights kicked on, turning the rain white.

21

Detective Faustino Brier had followed the GTO down Willock, past the cemetery, and nearly lost it when he entered a fairly exclusive neighborhood known as Burlington Hills. Unwilling to get too close and risk being spotted, he allowed the GTO to pull ahead and disappear among the curvy roads. Faustino hadn't found the car again, but he did find the small guardhouse with two bodies lying in front of it, the large wrought iron gate standing open, and a phone ringing inside.

Both men were clearly dead, their long, white coats muddled in pinks and reds and rain.

When a series of shots rang out from somewhere ahead, Faustino radioed for backup from his car, drew his gun, then started down the long driveway on foot, his eyes carefully scanning the trees.

He'd be dead in less than three minutes.

22

Preacher found Sleepy crouching behind the fountain at the center of the driveway, waiting for him.

As Preacher came out of the trees, a bullet caught him in the left shoulder, another in the center of his chest. The force sent Preacher spinning to the ground. Although the kevlar stopped both, they still hurt like hell. He brought the gun he had taken from Happy up and around, pointed it at the fountain, and when Sleepy leaned over to take another shot, a bullet hit him just above his right temple.

Preacher scrambled to his feet and ran for the stone entryway of the house.

Bashful was still outside somewhere. He'd worry about him later.

He tried the door.

Locked.

Leveling the shotgun at the dead bolt, he turned his head and pulled the trigger. The wood frame exploded, leaving a six-inch hole behind and a ringing in his ears.

Preacher kicked the door in and entered the house at a low crouch, ducking behind a round wooden table in the foyer. The shotgun followed his head as he quickly took in his surroundings—a sitting room on his right and a library on his left, both empty.

A vase on the table above him shattered, following the report of another gunshot.

Preacher broke from the table, ran down the central corridor, then rounded the corner for the hallway on the left, which would lead him to the central basement access. He encountered two more guards in white and dispatched both with the shotgun. The second managed to get a shot off from his .45, but it missed Preacher and landed at the center of a painting hanging in the hallway. At the end of this corridor, Preacher made another quick left and came upon the stairs leading to the basement. Three more guards were on their way up. Four quick shots from the Sig sent them scrambling back down for cover.

Reaching into his coat pocket, Preacher pulled one of the grenades, released the spoon, and tossed it down the stairs.

The explosion rumbled deep in the belly of the house, a loud *whop!* vibrating up the stone foundation, shaking the floor and walls.

Without taking the time to aim, he fired the shotgun toward the top of the staircase, then raced up the steps behind the blast, unloading the remaining bullets from the Sig in the general direction the shots had originated. The wall above chipped and splintered. Chunks of drywall and wood wainscoting blew out to the side. When the gun was empty, he dropped it, raised the shotgun as he reached the top and rounded the corner, and fired two quick blasts, the bright muzzle flash illuminating the hallway. The first left a large hole in the wall, the second left a large hole in the man who had been standing there.

At the top of the stairs, Preacher froze. He closed his eyes. He listened.

From the blueprints, he knew seven bedrooms and five bathrooms occupied the second floor. There was an attic space above running the full length of the house.

Eyes still closed, he reloaded the shotgun.

He needed the third bedroom on the left.

He opened his eyes and started down the hallway, shotgun at the ready.

He expected at least three other guards on this level, but none appeared.

He expected the bedroom door to be locked.

The door wasn't locked.

Preacher stepped into the room.

He leveled the shotgun at the bedroom's only occupant.

The girl, grown up now, sat calmly in a chair at the window looking out over the expansive backyard. Without turning to him, she simply said, "There are more coming. You'll never get out of here."

He watched as she stripped off her long, black gloves, carefully folding the elegant material and setting them aside on a table.

Smoke drifted up from downstairs.

He heard shouting.

More coming.

23

"What the fuck, Thatch!" Willy shouted as I pushed past him through the door.

Water pooled on the floor behind me, puddled on the worn hardwood. I went to the window, turned, paced back toward the door, turned, back toward the window.

"Jack! Stop!" Willy tried to grab me as I passed him for the third time, but I shrugged his hand off my shoulder.

I barely heard him over the drumming in my ears, the blood *swooshing* through my veins.

"What the hell happened?"

I tried to talk.

I tried to tell him.

Instead, I just tugged Stella's letter from my pocket, dropped it on the table, then went to my room, slamming the door behind me.

If he hadn't taken the bottle of Captain Morgan spiced rum from my dresser, I surely would have drunk it all.

I hated him for finding that bottle.

Log 08/09/1993—

Subject "D" within expected parameters.

Audio/video recording.

"What are all those folders?" Carl said.

"Folders?"

"On the kid's table."

Warren shrugged. "Dunno. The doc has been bringing them in all day. She's probably prepping him for another phone call."

"They've never given him intel before."

"Times change."

"Has anyone from corporate been here today?"

"Why do you care?"

"If they're prepping him for another call, someone from corporate would be overseeing it."

"Not necessarily."

"They always do."

"Times change."

"You seem awfully relaxed," Carl pointed out.

"You seem awfully stressed."

"I don't like change."

"Clearly."

"Maybe we should call somebody."

"I'm not calling anyone," Warren replied.

Carl reached over and pressed the microphone button. "Hey, Shitface, what are you reading?"

At his words, Subject "D" looked up from the other side of the observation window. His lips moved. Thirty seconds later, the image of Subject "D" looked up on the video monitor, and his reply came through the speakers. "Come on in and find out, Carl. It's fascinating stuff. A history of sorts. I'd love to discuss it with you. You certainly have a right to hear about it, since your name appears more than once. Not in the most flattering light, I'm afraid. This one particular incident, where you groped the unfortunate Sandy Newman in the cafeteria three years ago, in front of three other coworkers without any regard for the consequences, that says a lot about you as a person, your character. Nothing I didn't already know, but enlightening nonetheless. I should be shocked they only suspended you for a week, but considering some of the other things I've read, I'm not surprised at all."

Carl turned to Warren. "Are those *employee* files?"

"That's crazy. Why would someone give him employee files? The kid's just messing with you."

"Then how would he know about Sandy Newman?"

"Everybody knows about Sandy Newman."

"Nobody would have told him."

"You don't know that."

On the monitor, Subject "D" returned to the file spread out on his table.

Warren's eyes dropped back to the copy of *Along Came a Spider* by James Patterson in his hands.

– Observer's Note: Throughout the duration of this conversation, as well as the proceeding forty-eight minutes, Warren Beeson did not turn the page.

—Charter Observation Team – 309

24

The dream didn't come.

There was no dream. There was nothing but blackness, emptiness, a dark hole that ate everything else.

For the third time in as many months, I woke to a heavy knock at my door.

"Jack? Get up. You'll want to see this."

Willy.

The rain had stopped.

Hazy, early morning light filled my window.

At some point, I kicked off my sneakers, but I still wore the same jeans and sweatshirt I had last night, still soaked, as was my bedspread, the sheets, and probably my mattress.

"What is it?" I muttered.

"On TV. You need to see it."

I glanced at the digital clock beside my bed.

6:05.

I crawled out of the bed and made my way to the living room. The television provided the only light, the volume low.

The news.

A helicopter shot of a house.

Stella's house.

The pool in back. The fountain. I knew immediately.

"Is that—" Willy said.

"Yeah."

I sat down on the edge of the couch, nodded at the television. "What's going on?"

"Something really bad. Eighteen dead so far, and they're still pulling out bodies. I just turned it on, but I heard something about guns and explosions, fire."

"Eighteen?"

Stella.

Willy nodded. "Sounds like one of them might be a cop."

Smoke rose from the west side of the house, thick black cords trailing out the windows and doors, a hole in the roof.

The camera cut from the aerial back to a reporter. "We've been told by Pittsburgh Police that we need to relocate. They are expanding the perimeter to include not only the house and surrounding property but the cul-de-sac, too. From what we can gather, this is to make room for additional emergency vehicles. I can see at least two firetrucks attempting to get through now, and between the narrow streets, press, and spectators, they're having a tough time of it. If you are just joining us, this is Pete Lemire with KRWT CBS, and we're standing outside a private residence located at 62 Milburn Court where at least eighteen people are known to be dead, including at least one police officer. Pittsburgh PD has not released any names at this time and said they will not until next of kin can be notified. Two of the dead appear to be security guards at the gatehouse behind me, victims of apparent gunshot wounds."

Lemire looked off to his right, nodding at someone. "Again, we are being asked to relocate. I'll hand it back to Christie in the newsroom. Christie?"

The camera switched back to the aerial. No voiceover.

"Milburn Court is only about a mile from where you got hit on your bike. A few blocks off Nobles in Burlington Hills. Really nice area. Old money," Willy said.

Stella's letter sat on the coffee table, unfolded, staring up at me, the word *forget* smudged but dry now.

Willy caught me looking at it. "That's rough, bro."

"Yeah."

"The hidden message was clever. That girl loves to screw with you."

I looked up at him. "What hidden message?"

"You didn't see it?" he rolled his eyes. "You're so damn lovesick. Of course you didn't." He ran his finger down the text. "Look at the last seven lines, the first letter of each line. It jumped right out at me, but I do a lot of word puzzles. Maybe that's…"

He droned on, but I wasn't listening. My eyes locked on those last seven lines in Stella's careful script—

How are you to fill your days without thinking about me?
Even I don't know. Perhaps you will always think about me.
Live all your days with me on your mind, then.
Perhaps you won't, but I think you will.
My Pip.
Every day, always. My Pip.

Stella

HELP ME

On the television, the reporter returned, repeating the same information. "I need to get over there."

"That sounds like a really bad idea."

"Don't care."

Before he could reply, I was back in my room, changing out of my damp clothes.

Neither of us owned a car. Everything we needed was within

walking distance, and parking was scarce. Matteo had offered to buy me one with funds from the trust, but I turned him down. It would just sit and rot, I told him. Vandals in the neighborhood didn't need another target, particularly a shiny new one.

I caught a cab on Brownsville.

Willy wanted to go, but I told him no. I told him I needed to do this alone.

Each turn, every bump of the road, seemed familiar. When I closed my eyes, I was back in that white SUV, following the same route.

The driver had to drop me at the mouth of Milburn Court. There were too many people and emergency vehicles blocking the small cul-de-sac to get any closer.

I gave him cash and stepped out into the crowd.

The acrid scent of fire was heavy on the early morning air, the sky at the edge of the cul-de-sac was thick with it, all eyes of the crowd faced in that singular direction. Some people had brought chairs, one man even had a cooler. Some were silent, others joked and laughed. Two boys circled the large group on skateboards, sticking to the outer edge of the pavement.

I pushed past them all.

I forced my way through, the numbers growing as I neared the front, until I was at the yellow police tape, now reinforced with wooden barricades and about a dozen uniformed officers behind those, eyeing the crowd with solemn faces.

About thirty feet behind them, I spotted the tall wall of stone topped with black metal spikes, familiar from my visit to this place. A gate of matching metal stood open at the foot of the driveway. To the left was the guardhouse Pete Lemire of KRWT had used as a backdrop in his earlier broadcast. There was no sign of him or the news van now.

The driveway twisted and disappeared among the old oaks and elms, the house lost somewhere behind the trees, not visible from here.

"Pretty crazy, right?"

This came from the woman beside me. She was in her early twenties, long blonde hair and green eyes. She didn't look at me, only faced forward. She wore a long, white coat.

An ambulance siren chirped, and I turned back to the driveway. The police made an opening in the barricade and forced the people back so it could drive out. Its lights were off. It wasn't in a hurry.

When I turned back, the woman was gone, replaced by a man in his late sixties fumbling with a cigarette and lighter.

I sucked in a deep breath and ducked under the yellow tape, rounded the wooden barricade, and ran toward the driveway, toward the house, toward Stella. When one of the officers shouted behind me, then another, I only ran faster. When I passed the guardhouse, I spotted another officer, this one staring at me, barking orders into the radio attached to his shoulder. I forced my legs to push harder.

I rounded three bends before the house came into view.

Black smoke streamed up from the west side. Where the white SUVs had been, two fire trucks now stood. Coils of hose ran from the tanks up into the house, through a door off to the side. The front door stood open, and people were rushing in and out—paramedics, police, officials in plain clothes. Nobody I recognized.

Standing between me and the house were three more Pittsburgh PD officers. The one in the middle shouted, "Far enough, kid! Stop right there!"

I faked left, then bolted to the right, tried to rush past him, but one of the others tackled me from the side, and the two of us tumbled to the ground. He twisted my arm around to my back, and I felt a handcuff clasp my wrist. He tried to get my other arm out from under me. I rolled, but his bulk held me down.

"Stop squirming, dammit!"

With the help of one of the other officers, he managed to tug my free arm out and pull it back, locking it behind me with the other handcuff.

He took his knee out from the small of my back and stood, tugging at my arms. "Get up."

"I need to get in there!"

"Get up."

They lifted me to my feet, and I tried to break free but couldn't.

"You don't understand, I—"

"Put him in the back of that one," the officer on my left said, nodding toward a squad car parked near the fountain.

The first officer began dragging me toward the car.

Another cop opened the car door as we approached.

"Get Detective Brier!" I shouted. "Tell him I'm here! I need to get inside! I need—"

The first officer pushed the top of my head and tried to force me down into the car. "I don't give a shit what you need, kid."

"Get Detective Brier!"

A man in plainclothes standing near the front door heard me and looked up. "Who did you say?"

"Detective Brier. Tell him I'm here," I repeated.

"And who are you?"

"Jack Thatch. He'll know."

The man frowned. "Put him in the car."

And the officer did just that, slamming the door behind me.

I beat on the windows, kicking at the glass and the car doors.

They ignored me. All of them.

I sat there for at least three hours.

The car smelled of bleach, vomit, and piss.

I watched as people came and went from the front door of the house.

I watched as the black smoke began to thin.

I watched the firemen eventually roll up their hoses, store their equipment in the truck, and disappear down the driveway.

The shadows began to slant.

At one point, another uniformed officer, a thin black woman with short hair, rolled down the front windows of the car. She didn't look at me. Smoke-laden air drifted in from outside through the metal mesh blocking the passenger compartment of the car from the front but did little for the interior smell.

Another hour passed.

The firetrucks and ambulances left, replaced with CSI vans.

The door beside me opened, and a woman sat down. The woman officer who opened the windows closed the door behind her and stood outside, her back to the car.

"Your name is John Edward Thatch. You're seventeen years old and live at 1822 Brownsville Road, apartment 306. Both your parents are dead, and until recently, you lived with your aunt, Josephine Gargery. When she passed away four months ago, you fell into the care of your neighbor, one"—She pulled a small pad from her jacket pocket, opened to the first page, and scanned the text—"One, Elfrieda Leech. Sixty-nine years old, and by all accounts, a hopeless shut-in. You worked at Krendal's Diner on Brownsville until it was destroyed during what appears to be a commissioned hit on Henry Crocket three months ago. You are a known associate of Duncan Bellino." She closed the flap on her notepad. "Did I miss anything?"

I said nothing.

"Do you know who I am?"

I nodded. "You're Detective Brier's partner. I recognize you from my aunt's funeral."

"I'm Detective Fogel. I work in Homicide. I need you to tell me what you're doing here, Mr. Thatch."

"I need to get in the house."

"Why?"

"Is she in there?"

"Is who in there?"

My eyes went to the floor. "I need to know that Stella is okay."

At the mention of Stella's name, Fogel's expression remained neutral. "Tell me about the man who drives that black Pontiac GTO."

"I don't know anyone who drives a GTO."

"You know we've been watching your building. This man has been seen coming and going numerous times. He's been in your apartment. Does he work for Bellino? Is Bellino responsible for this?"

"I don't know who you're talking about. Where is Detective Brier? Go get him. I need to speak to him."

Her fingers began to roll on her knee. Finally, she said, "Detective Brier is dead."

"What happened?"

"Somebody shot him in the head, practically point blank, about twenty feet from where you're sitting." She pointed toward the side of the driveway, then knocked twice on the window.

The officer standing beside the car opened the door.

"Come with me," Fogel said, stepping back outside.

I slid out and followed her through the maze of cars in the driveway. The female officer followed behind both of us at a distance of only a few feet. As we rounded one of the CSI vans, I spotted six bodies all covered by black tarps—three in the driveway, two more in the grass, and another off to the side.

Fogel went to the body off to the side and knelt. She peeled back the tarp.

Detective Brier's glassy gaze stared forward, his mouth slightly open. There was a small hole in his forehead above his right eye, the skin black and puckered. The grass beneath his head was dark with blood, blood filled with small, white specs.

I turned my head and threw up in the grass.

Fogel looked at the officer standing behind me, but neither woman said anything.

"I didn't do this," I finally managed.

Fogel replaced the tarp and stood. "I know that. You want to know how I know that? Because I was following you in the cemetery when this happened. Who is the man in the black GTO?"

"I told you, I don't know. Why were you following me?"

Ignoring my question, she walked over to the other five bodies and began pulling away their tarps, one at a time, anger brewing in her eyes. "Your friend, the man we have documented coming and going from your apartment for years, he killed not only my partner today but each of these people, and you're going to help me find him. You're going to tell me everything you know about him."

As each tarp leapt into the air by her hand, my eyes fell on the bodies—one-by-one—a woman in a white coat, shotgun blast to the stomach. A man in a white coat, shotgun blast to the chest. Another woman, a small gunshot to the head, like Brier—she was also in a white coat. I nearly threw up again. Then I saw the last two, not shot at all.

Burned but not burned.

Like Andy Olin Flack.

Like Raymond Visconti.

Stella.

I ran then.

I pushed past the female officer who had been following us and raced through the front door of the house, nearly tripping on another body in the foyer—uncovered, black and dry like the others. There were more bodies in the hallway, in the library.

When I shouted Stella's name, three investigators dressed in white jumpsuits looked up from their work but said nothing. An officer positioned at the end of the long hallway ran toward me.

A wooden barricade blocked the hallway leading toward the basement. The walls were black, charred with smoke. Stella's paintings hung at odd angles, covered in grime. Two had fallen to the floor. Large floodlights had been placed on either end of the hallway, and body bags filled the space between, at least a dozen of them, sealed and silent.

Another body was on the stairs, partially covered, also dry with death.

I raced past the foyer, jumped the body on the stairs, and took the steps two at a time. At the top, there was yet another body, male, this one dead with a shotgun blast to the abdomen.

I had no idea where I was going.

I heard footsteps on the stairs behind me.

All the doors were opened.

The first two bedrooms were empty. When I entered the third bedroom on the left, I froze just inside the open doorway, unable to turn away from what I saw.

The bedroom was large, a suite, really. Nearly as big as my apartment, with a canopy bed dressed in pink-and-white sheets and draped with sheer cloth from above. A sitting area near a window overlooked the backyard—the pool and gardens. A door to the left led to a private bathroom, the walls and floor covered in white marble. A fireplace of stone occupied the back wall, the hearth filled with the fading glow of neglected embers.

Above the fireplace, above the mantle, hung a painting. A painting of a little girl and boy, both sitting on a black iron bench surrounded by gravestones and trees of fall leaves. The little girl held a book in her lap. The boy's hand reached for her, hesitant, inches from her, longing for her, even then. The vivid colors and brushstrokes, clearly Stella's hand. I crossed the room, the voices coming up the stairs lost to me. I reached up and ran my fingers over the paint, felt the ridges and edges, the careful swirl of each stroke, and for the first time in my life, I knew Stella's touch.

There was nobody else in the room, and I also knew she was gone.

I wanted to hate her for the letter.

Those horrible words.

I wanted to forget everything about her.

But I couldn't.

I simply couldn't.

My Stella.

PART 3

"The broken heart. You think you will die, but you just keep living, day after day after terrible day."

—Charles Dickens, *Great Expectations*

Log 08/09/1993—

Subject "D" within expected parameters. Carl Rozzell
appears agitated.

Personal notes – Warren Beeson.

David Pickford is a beautiful man.
David Pickford is a beautiful man.
David Pickford is a beautiful man.
David Pickford is a beautiful man.
David Pickford is a beautiful man.
David Pickford is a beautiful man.
David Pickford is a beautiful man.
David Pickford is a beautiful man.
David Pickford is a beautiful man.
David Pickford is a beautiful man.
David Pickford is a beautiful man.
David Pickford is a beautiful man.
David Pickford is a beautiful man.
David Pickford is a beautiful man.
David Pickford is a beautiful man.
David Pickford is a beautiful man.

David Pickford is a beautiful man.
David Pickford is a beautiful man.
David Pickford is a beautiful man.
David Pickford is a beautiful man.
David Pickford is a beautiful man.

—Charter Observation Team - 309

1

"Do you have any idea how much trouble you're in?" Matteo said, his voice low. He stared at me for a good long while, then clucked his tongue and snapped both latches on his briefcase.

I was handcuffed to a metal ring welded to the top of an aluminum table in an interview room at Pittsburgh PD.

They had pulled me from the house.

It took four of them.

When I wouldn't leave Stella's room, they tried to drag me out the door. When that didn't work, two of them lifted my feet from the ground and carried me. My legs pumped, I kicked and twisted and screamed. At one point, my right foot caught one of the officers square in the gut and he dropped me, the air rushing out his puckered mouth, the fat man staggering back. I kept kicking and screaming even as they shouted out things like *assault* and *resisting* and *trespassing* and *interfering*—I didn't really hear much of any of it. The image of the painting filled my vision, the image of the empty room, the conflicting words of her letter.

They threw me into the back of another police car and brought me here. Then I waited again.

I expected Fogel to appear at some point, but she didn't.

Only Matteo.

Willy called him.

Apparently my run past the barricades got caught by one of the television cameras, and although you couldn't see my face, Willy knew it was me.

"If you weren't a minor, they'd be grilling you right now, you know that, right? You'd be looking at some serious time just for the crap you pulled at the house. If they found a way to tie you to what happened in that place…" his voice trailed off as he shuffled through some papers, retrieved a yellow-lined notepad and pen, a manila folder, and closed the case. "Luckily, you are still a minor, and I've been told one of the detectives questioned you at the scene without a parent, legal guardian, or attorney present. That's a big no-no on their end, and they know it. If I have to, I'll use that. I'm hoping it doesn't come to that. They want to talk to you, though. Boy, do they ever."

He wrote my name and today's date at the top of the page and leaned back in his chair. "Tell me about this guy in the black GTO."

"I don't know who he is."

"They seem to think you do. In fact, that Detective Fogel seems sure of it. She gave me these—"

He removed a stack of eight by ten photographs from the manila folder and slid them across the table to me.

The man in the pictures seemed tall, thin build, with blond hair. He was maybe in his late forties. In the first two pictures, he was coming out of my apartment building. The third photo was grainy, probably taken with some kind of long-range lens from somewhere across the street from my building. The image centered around my apartment's window, the one facing Brownsville. The man was standing in my living room, next to Auntie Jo's chair, his profile visible but blurry. The final two pictures were of the same man—one standing at the driver's door of a black Pontiac, the other with him behind the driver's seat. Although the windshield glare partially obstructed the view, his face was visible. I had never seen him before, but I had a pretty good idea of who he might be.

"He's been in and out of your building, *your apartment*, numerous times."

I thumbed at the edge of window photo. "I think he's the money guy."

"The money guy?"

"Somebody has been leaving money for me, five hundred dollars a month, since I was a kid." I told him about the first envelope and the others that followed. "Dunk was the only person to ever get a look at him," I said. And I told him about that, too.

"You have no idea who he is or why he would give you cash?"

I shook my head.

Matteo brushed at his upper lip. "Well, we sure can't tell the police about the money."

"You're not gonna tell them?"

He snorted. "Hell no. We don't want them to have anything tying you to this guy." He thought for a second. "They think he works for Bellino. We want to keep it that way."

"I don't see how he could. The money started when we were kids, long before Dunk got mixed up with Crocket and those guys."

Matteo shrugged. "They're detectives. Let them detect. They can figure all that out on their own. My only concern is keeping you out of trouble."

"I don't want to lie."

"Omissions aren't lies. Answer their questions, but keep your responses brief. Don't offer any additional details. I don't want to hear anything but yes or no come out of your mouth. If you're not sure if you should answer something, take a second, collect yourself, give me a chance to weigh in. I tell you to stop talking, you stop talking. Let me control the exchange, got it?"

I nodded.

Matteo drew in a deep breath. He hefted his bulky form from the chair, went to the door, and gave it two hard knocks.

Fogel came in a moment later, carrying a large box. Detective

Horton came in behind her. She had pictures of all the bodies found in the house—Stella was not among them.

The four of us wouldn't leave that room for another three hours, but I would eventually leave, without the handcuffs. A little whisper at my ear had returned too, the one telling me how a drink would make all of this so much easier.

2

Detective Joy Fogel stared at the Wall of Weird.

She stared at Faustino Brier's empty desk, a half-full cup of coffee next to his phone, the liquid inside cold and cloudy.

The last time she looked at a clock, it was half past three in the morning.

Photographs of Brier's lifeless body littered her desk. Photographs of the other victims too, twenty-one in all. From weapons fire to grenades, the destruction could have been caused by a small army, yet all evidence pointed to a single assailant. She had pictures of him too, him and his car, but nothing else. The guy was a damn ghost. A well-armed, competent ghost.

"What the fuck, Brier," she mumbled, flipping through the photographs.

His blank gaze stared back at her, the bullet hole in his forehead like a third eye.

They shouldn't have split up. That was such a rookie move, and yet she hadn't thought twice about it. Now Brier was dead, and she was probably looking at a suspension the moment her captain read the report, also sitting on her desk, far from complete. She had no idea what to even write.

She had one lead.

A single tire track had been left in the mud off the driveway. According to Forensics, the treads belonged to a Pro Temp 265x70R16 A/T Sport. She was told the tire didn't match Brier's car or the GTO. This was a stock tire not available to the general public, supplied only to General Motors, specifically to Chevrolet. Chevrolet used these tires on all Suburbans produced between the years 1990-1993 in the United States. Uniformed officers questioned all the neighbors and had been told that not only had they seen a white Chevy Suburban, but they saw more than a dozen identical white Suburbans come and go from the property on a regular basis, yet none had been on-site today.

Fogel obtained a picture of a 1993 white Chevy Suburban and pinned it to the Wall of Weird next to the image of the black GTO.

Oh, and that damn house.

About two hours ago, she spoke to a frustrated Zeke Grinton in Public Records. She tasked him with identifying the owners of the house at 62 Milburn Court. Usually a straightforward task, this proved to be anything but. The deed for the house was held by a corporation named Barrington Farm and Feed out of Wisconsin. Barrington Farm and Feed consisted of no more than a P.O. Box in the town of Dells, no physical property locally. No employees. That corporation was owned by another called Brainard Textiles in Vermont, another shell. From there, Grinton traced ownership back through six other corporations, holding companies, and LLCs, then lost the trail entirely when it went overseas.

Another dead end.

Then there was Stella Nettleton.

Fogel glanced up at the *Have you seen me?* poster tacked on the Wall of Weird, the sketch of the beautiful girl staring back. Social Security had no record of a Stella Nettleton. She had people checking birth records too, but already knew that would turn up nothing. They hadn't found anything on Richard Nettleton either when the letter first surfaced, a copy of which was pinned beside the poster on the Wall.

When the phone at the corner of Fogel's desk began to ring, she nearly jumped out of her skin. The loud electronic chirp cut through the otherwise silent and empty room, a room made even quieter by the early hour. She scooped up the receiver and pressed the flashing button for line one. "Fogel."

"I'm sorry about Faust."

Former Detective Terrance Stack, just Terry now.

Fogel closed her eyes, her fingers tightening on the receiver. She tried to muster a response, but nothing came out.

"Do you need to talk?"

"Yeah."

"Be here in twenty," Stack said. "I'll get a pot brewing."

3

Officer Elvin Putney dropped the remains of his cigarette and crushed the butt under the toe of his shoe. He then pulled another from the pack in his right front pocket, struck a match, and lit the tip. He sucked the nicotine deep into his lungs, held it, then slowly let it out in a series of smoke rings that drifted out from the front stoop of the house, over the driveway, and disappeared in the dark sky.

He glanced down at his watch.

Three twenty-eight in the ever-loving morning. Another hour and a half before he would be relieved and could head home for some shut-eye. He was one of four officers tasked with maintaining security on 62 Milburn Court. Collins was at the guardhouse, Burton was in the back near the pool house, and Sevilla was inside probably sleeping. He hadn't seen or heard from him in over an hour.

He wanted to be sleeping.

A mosquito buzzed past Putney's face, and he snatched the insect out of the air with his free hand. When he opened his fist, what was left of the bug was in his palm, a black and bloody mess. "Got you, you little shit!"

"I've got movement," a voice crackled from the radio at his shoulder. Burton, at the back of the property.

Putney squeezed the transmit button. "What kind of movement?"

"Not sure," Burton replied. *"Just something from the corner of my eye."*

"Want me to come back there?" Putney said.

Silence for a moment, then, *"Negative."*

"Could be deer. I've seen three of them since I got here." This from Collins at the guardhouse.

"Maybe," Burton said.

Putney pressed his transmit button, another smoke ring rising into the night sky. "Maybe it's another reporter sniffing around?"

"Negative," Collins said. *"We ran the last of them off around midnight. I've got eyes on the cul-de-sac, and it's empty. I've had the occasional looky-loo pull in, but they see my cruiser and turn right back around. Got mountains at the back of the house, nobody's coming that way on foot."*

"There it is again. Too big to be a deer. Five, maybe six feet tall. Dammit, got another about twenty feet down the tree line," Burton replied.

Putney let the cigarette fall to the pavement and stomped out the remains, then reached for his microphone. "I'm coming back there."

Static, then Collins from the guardhouse. *"Negative, hold your position until we know what it is. Could be a diversion."*

Fuck you, Collins. You don't give orders, we're all the same rank. Putney tapped his microphone again. "Do you need backup, Burton? Give the word."

No response.

That's when Putney saw something. The slightest of movement from the trees behind the fountain toward the far edge of the driveway. He pulled his Maglite from his belt, flicked the switch, and directed the bright beam toward the trees. He didn't see anything move, but for a second he thought he saw eyeshine reflected in the light. Then it was gone.

A branch cracked off to his right, at the trees on the west end of the house. He swung the beam around. This time he caught someone shuffling sideways behind the trunk of an old oak. "Pittsburgh PD!" he shouted. "You're trespassing on a crime scene! Put your hands in the air, and step out where I can see you!"

Putney's free hand fell to the butt of his Glock .45. His thumb flicked the leather band holding it in place, releasing the snap. "Come out! Now!"

A man in a long, white coat stepped out, his hands at his sides. He held something in the right. He looked to be about forty years old, with dark hair. His expression was blank, unreadable.

"Drop it!"

The man didn't move.

Putney leaned into his microphone and pressed the transmit button with the hand holding the flashlight. "I've got someone here, just stepped out of the woods."

No reply.

"I said, drop it!"

More movement, to the right of this man.

A woman stepped from the trees, also wearing a long, white coat, also holding something in her hand. Another after that, another man, about ten feet down the tree line. Two more came out from the far left.

Putney wanted to take a step back, deeper into the stone archway covering the house's entrance, but he didn't, he didn't move.

Others began filing out from the trees. He had no idea where they were all coming from, fifteen or twenty of them now.

He pressed the transmit button again, his voice low. "I need backup at the entrance. Anyone copy?"

No reply.

The figures in white all stepped toward him, toward the house, moving as one unit. When they took a second step, then a third, Putney tightened his grip on the Glock. Rules dictated that he could not draw his weapon unless threatened. At the very least, he'd be looking at a suspension, possible termination if he fired a shot. He drew the Glock anyway and held it out toward the first man to appear. "Not another step!"

The group continued toward him.

The woman he had noticed second raised the item in her hand, held it in front of her chest.

Putney aimed the Glock at her. "Don't do it!"

She raised her other hand, sparked a lighter, and brought the flame to the thing in her other hand.

A candle. Only a fucking candle.

Putney felt a wave of relief slip over him.

The others followed, candles lighting up all around. Two dozen, maybe more. They were still stepping out of the woods.

"If this is some kind of vigil, you need to move back to the street. This is a crime scene," he told them.

The crowd continued toward him, their pace quickening from a walk to a run, the candles held out before them, flames winking and pulling as they rushed forward, these people in white.

Not a vigil.

4

Former Detective Terrance Stack, just Terry now, was waiting for Fogel when she pulled into his narrow driveway. Sitting on the front stoop, beer in hand, his eyes focused on something in the cracked sidewalk. At first, he didn't look up. When he finally did, she wished he hadn't. His eyes were lined and bloodshot, with dark bags beneath. He raised the beer at her in a mock toast, took a drink, then looked back down at the sidewalk.

Fogel crossed the overgrown yard and took a seat beside him. The scent of beer hung over him, mixed with other odors she cared not to think about. His hair was greasy. He desperately needed a shower.

"I told Faust this case would put him in an early grave, not that he paid me any mind. They might as well dig two, if you plan to keep chasing this. Maybe three, since I'm not much for my own advice. We can all take the long sleep together." His speech was slightly slurred. Not the speech pattern of a drunk but of someone who drank so much, their body had grown accustomed, lingering in that slightly buzzed but not yet stoned state of the professional alcoholic.

This was a bad idea, Fogel thought. She should have gone home.

"What happened to him?"

Fogel told him about the black GTO, the man who drove it, how they split up. How they found Faustino's body. Everything else that happened in the past twenty-four hours.

Stack listened in silence, nursing the beer, nodding occasionally as she went. When she finally finished, he said, "My missing kid from '78 is Stella Nettleton, right? The two adults we found in the Dormont house, they were her parents, Richard and Emma."

Fogel reached into her briefcase and pulled out a copy of the letter from Richard Nettleton and handed it to Stack.

Stack waved it off. "Faust gave me a copy of that as soon as he got it. I know all about the Thatch kid too. What we could piece together, anyway." He stood, his body protesting with a series of cracks and pops. "Come on, I got something to show you."

He held the screen door for her and she stepped into the house, holding her breath as she passed him. The small television droned in the living room, the volume low. Some black and white movie with Katherine Hepburn in her prime. A rumpled newspaper was on the table next to a recliner, a picture of the Milburn Court house above the fold with the headline *Decorated Officer / 21 Others Dead*. A dozen empty Iron City bottles littered the floor around the table.

Stack shuffled past her. "The coffee I promised is upstairs."

He was halfway up the steps before he realized she wasn't following. He offered a wry smile. "I'm too old and tired to try anything funny, and with three exes running around out there, my finances are maxed. No room in the budget for a fourth. What I need to show you, it ain't exactly portable."

Without waiting for a response, he continued up the steps and disappeared onto the second floor.

Brier trusted this guy, and she trusted Brier. Fogel clucked her tongue, weighed her options, then followed after him.

The stairs opened onto a narrow hallway with a bathroom at one end, a bedroom at the other, and a third room between them both. The door to the third room was open, the light on. Stack's shadow stood patiently against the far wall.

Fogel went to the open doorway and gasped.

Stack took another sip of his beer and wiped his mouth. "Wife number two used this space as a sewing room, but she was never very good at it. All the drapes in this house are uneven, and I've got a stack of shirts boxed away in my closet somewhere that were far better off before she tried to replace missing buttons. I swear, she'd use half a spool on a single button and create this mound of thread, never got the color even remotely close, neither. She didn't know how to tie them off properly, so after a few hours, things would start to come undone and I'd be walking around with thread trailing behind me. The guys at the precinct used to say I looked like a parade float, complete with streamers. Back at the beginning, when I still loved her, I'd wear them. A couple years in and I started keeping spare shirts in my car. By year three, I gave up the ghost altogether and boxed them. She did a number on this sweater—"

"How did you..." Fogel's voice trailed off.

"The Wall of Weird Faustino put together at the pen was for quick reference at the precinct. This is where he really worked, where *we* really worked. I started collecting copies of evidence here back in my day. Then when he took over the case, he kept everything current. Anything new came in, we made sure a copy found its way here. Copies only, mind you. Neither of us were trying to hoard evidence. We wanted a quiet place to work the case. Can't wheel that board out at the precinct without creating a big stink— there's nobody to bug us here." Stack reached into his pocket. "Faust had a key, probably still has a key. I made one for you after you came by last year, figured you'd be back."

Fogel took the key from his outstretched hand and studied the room.

The back wall was identical to the Wall of Weird, only larger. The photographs of all the victims and crime scenes were spaced further apart, with hundreds of index cards tacked in the spaces between. Red yarn connected some of the images, yellow connected others. On the wall to the left stood file boxes, dozens of them.

Some were labeled with the names of victims, others had addresses, three said Duncan Bellino. A folding card table sat in the center of the room with two chairs. On top of the table sat two boxes. One had *Nettleton* written across the front in black, blocky letters, the other had *Thatch*. On the floor was a third box, this one labeled *Black GTO Guy*.

Stack nodded at the boxes. "Faustino and me didn't come up with much on the guy in the car, but what we do have is in that box. For the past few weeks, we've been digging into Thatch's parents. The Nettleton box has the letter, not much else. Now we can tie it to the house in Dormont, that crime scene. That's something, for sure. The plan was to find the link between the two families, see where that takes us. If you're in for the long haul, I could really use your help here. You've got access to resources I can't touch anymore, department databases and the like."

"I'll stay, if you take a shower," Fogel said.

"Been meaning to do that anyway."

"And if you lay off the beer."

Stack raised the bottle in his hand to his lips and drank the rest in three long swallows, then he set the empty one down on the table. "Done."

"I'm gonna need that coffee you promised, too."

"There's a fresh pot in the corner over there. I don't lie about coffee."

Fogel glanced around the room again, then sat at the table. "Okay, tell me what I don't know. Let's start there."

Log 08/12/1993—

Subject "D" within expected parameters.

Audio/video recording.

"He's just sitting there," Carl said. "Staring at the wall."

"Maybe he's meditating."

"He looks like he's waiting for something."

"I can't imagine what," Warren replied.

"Did the doctor see him today?"

"He had many visitors today."

"Who?"

Warren didn't reply.

"Did the doc meet with him today?"

"She meets with him every day. They have a lot to discuss."

"What did they talk about?"

"I dunno. I didn't listen."

"You're supposed to listen. That's the job."

Warren pressed the microphone button. "David, what did you discuss with Doctor Durgin today?"

Thirty seconds elapsed, then: "The future, mostly. We talked about Carl, too. We talked about Carl a lot. Carl, Carl, Carl. What to do with Carl."

Carl frowned. "Why are you calling him 'David' rather than his designation?"

"His designation?"

"Subject 'D.'"

"Because that sounds cold. He doesn't like it."

"Who gives a shit what he likes?" Carl picked up a pen and nervously began twirling it between his fingers. "Everybody in this place is acting fucking weird."

"Weird how?"

"Just weird. I ate lunch in the cafeteria earlier, and nobody was talking."

"Maybe they have nothing to talk about."

"There were at least twenty people. Nobody said a word."

"I like silence," Warren replied.

The pen spun faster between Carl's fingers. His eyes landed on something, small and white, sitting on the far corner of the console. "What is that?"

"Doctor Durgin's hearing aid."

The pen went still in Carl's hand. "She's deaf. Why would she have a hearing aid?"

"Not completely deaf," Warren said.

"What do you mean? Isn't that why she got the job?"

"She had meningitis when she was a child. She lost more than 99 percent of her auditory range, really everything but the deepest of base frequencies. Technology is always advancing, though, making strides. What was once considered impossible is commonplace." Warren smiled. "I wanted to be a scientist when I was a kid, but I didn't have the grades. That's why I took the job here. I figured I could at least be around it, be a part of something bigger. You should talk to the doctor about her life's journey. She is really a remarkable woman."

Carl had gone pale. "She takes the hearing aid out when she goes in there, though, right? That's why it's sitting here? She forgot it?"

Warren said, "She wanted to hear his voice. Just the one time. That's what she said. He has a beautiful voice. David Pickford is a beautiful man."

Subject "D" stood and approached the opposite side of the observation window.

Carl jammed his finger onto the microphone button. "Step back from the window!"

"That's a nice pen, Carl."

"How can he see us? That is one-way glass."

Warren tilted his head toward the ceiling, closed his own eyes. "He said when the fluorescents are on, when it's bright, the glass doesn't work so good."

"Get back from the window!"

Subject "D" smiled broadly. "Hey, Carl, I bet if you shoved that pen into your eye, good and hard, you could reach your brain."

"Get the fuck back!"

"Carl, go ahead and do that for me. Bury that pen to the hilt in your eye."

Carl did.

Without a moment's hesitation, Carl gripped the pen firmly in his right hand and rammed it into his eye socket. His remaining eye went wide with surprise.

It was then he spotted Warren's hand still resting on the little red switch next to the recorder and speaker system, the one that enabled the thirty-second delay on all the kid said and did. The switch, normally covered in tape beneath a note that read DO NOT DISABLE in large block letters, was in the OFF position.

Two things happened in that very instant—Carl dove for the switch, and David told him not to touch it.

—Charter Observation Team – 309

5

I attended the funeral for Detective Faustino Brier, but I did so from a distance, standing on the top of the same hill where he had stood for Auntie Jo's funeral what seemed a lifetime ago.

He drew a big crowd.

There was a twenty-one gun salute at the end.

His body was laid to rest about three hundred feet east of my parents and Jo.

Detective Fogel was there. She didn't see me.

The sun was bright that day, damn near too bright. It felt like someone took a chisel to my eyes. That pain, though, was nothing like the beating going on in my head. That came courtesy of the bottle of Jameson I drank the night before, provided by my good buddy, Trey, behind the counter of Mike's Package Liquor. I hadn't been there in over two months, but he sure perked up when I came through the door, knowing there was a hundred-dollar bonus in his immediate future. The muscle memory of our previous transactions came back to both of us with little trouble, like riding a bike. I put the cash on the counter, he grabbed a bottle for me from the shelf at his back, handed it to me, and I was out the door. Not a word exchanged between us. A quick nod from me, a sly smile from him, and it was over. An event totaling twenty-three seconds, yet capable of derailing my life.

I didn't care.

There had been a fire.

A bad fire.

And I needed a drink.

Need probably isn't a strong enough word.

My body would have gladly given up oxygen for a taste of alcohol. Just a little drop to numb things, that's what I told myself. Some half-assed lie even I didn't believe anymore.

When Matteo finally dropped me off at home Monday night, the sun long gone, the air heavy with humidity, I was damn tired. I climbed the steps, fumbled with my keys, let myself in. Willy wasn't there. His blankets were neatly folded and stacked on the edge of the couch, with his pillow on top. Apparently at home his parents were sticklers for making beds. He felt the need to make the couch. I figured they'd complain about their missing son at some point, but that day never came. I suppose with the cost of college tuition off their list of things to worry about, they weren't too upset when he basically moved into my apartment.

I dropped down onto my own bed face-first, clothes still on. I somehow managed to kick off my shoes before the exhaustion carried me over to slumberland. I expected the dream to find me, but it didn't. There was nothing.

I woke at a little after five in the morning and stumbled into the kitchen for a glass of water. I parked myself on the couch to drink it. Still no sign of Willy. The world seemed incredibly quiet, and that made me feel alone. I clicked on the TV in hopes of nothing more than some background noise, and when the screen filled with an image of Stella's house, I first thought I was watching a rehash of the previous day's news.

The large house.

The smoke.

A moment passed before my sleepy brain realized the smoke

wasn't just coming from the west end, but the entire house. There were flames now too, flames everywhere—crawling up the walls, reaching for the sky from holes in the roof. When I turned up the sound, someone who wasn't Pete Lemire of KRWT CBS told me the fire had started in the middle of the night, looked like it had been set deliberately, but little else was known.

By midday, I was still on the couch, still watching.

The house was all but gone.

The bodies of four police officers had been found in the foyer, cause of death yet to be determined. Someone took the time to lay the bodies out next to each other, line them up, nice and neat.

At one in the afternoon, the soap operas came on, and coverage of Stella's burning house was reduced to a small box in the corner of the screen. At three, the little box disappeared too. At 3:01, I got up and made my way down to Mike's.

Willy found me passed out on the couch a few hours later.

We had words.

I left again, wandered, and found myself in the cemetery, watching the funeral of Detective Faustino Brier.

That was yesterday.

Today it was Matteo's turn to yell at me for the second time in a week. For the past hour, he had done just that, with Willy sitting silently at the opposite end of the lawyer's conference table. He had been scolded, too. Apparently my babysitter shouldn't have left me alone. Groundings due all around.

"We need to get you out of here," Matteo droned on. "Out of this city, away from all this crap you've got yourself caught up in."

"I don't want to go anywhere. This is my home."

Matteo snickered. "Pretty soon your home is going to be an eight-by-eight cell over in New Castle. If the police don't find some way to tie you into this mess at the house on Milburn, they'll lump you in with Bellino and the mess he's been building around himself. They want you off the streets and tucked away somewhere."

"I haven't done anything."

"They don't care."

Matteo slid today's *Post-Gazette* across the table to me. A before and after picture of Stella's house covered most of the front page. "Four dead cops in this fire, twenty-one dead the day before, including a dead detective, one who specifically painted a target on your back. They all think you're deep in this."

And Stella was gone, my mind whispered. *Missing. Taken.* Dead? *Gone.*

"If the police don't put you in a box somewhere, this bullshit drinking of yours surely will," Matteo went on. "My gut says they're building a case, waiting for you to turn eighteen in January, then they'll pounce. They charge you with something now and they risk you being tried as a minor. Better to take the next four months and build a solid case. That's what I would do."

"I haven't done anything," I said again.

This time, he didn't reply.

Willy spoke next. "Penn State," he said in a low voice.

Matteo looked up at him. "What?"

"My parents want me to go to Penn State when I graduate."

Matteo rolled his eyes. "And like I told you, the trust will cover the cost of your tuition as long as you help get Jack in there, too. You're doing a bang-up job of that, Mr. Trudeau. Those bloodshot eyes of his scream 'college material.' Nothing like a solid arrest record to seal up those entrance applications, too. Bang-up job. So proud of the both of you."

Willy continued to stare at his hands. "We don't have to wait until next fall. We could go now. We both have enough AP credits. We could take the GED and graduate high school early. They're offering the SAT in Harrisburg next Thursday. I confirmed this morning. It's tight, but we could be enrolled at Penn by spring. Fall semester already started, but I'm sure we could make spring."

Matteo settled back in his chair and mulled this over. "That could work."

"New friends, new environment, new challenges," Willy went on. "He stays here and this gets worse, you know it will."

"I'm not leaving," I said softly.

"She blew you off, Jack. She played you, and now she's gone," Willy said. "Have you shown him the letter?"

Matteo narrowed his eyes. "What letter?"

I glared at Willy. He had no business bringing up the letter. He didn't understand. He couldn't—

"Hand it over," Matteo said, reaching across the table.

I eyeballed him for a second, then dug the letter out of my pocket.

The scent of vanilla filled the room as he unfolded it and read aloud.

Matteo frowned when he finished. "Pip? Like that book, *Oliver Twist?*"

"*Great Expectations,*" I corrected him.

"Who is Stella?"

"Just a girl."

Willy sighed. "Not *just a girl.* A girl who seriously mind-fucked him for half his life. She lived in the house on Milburn."

He went on to tell him all he knew. It wasn't everything, not by far, but it was enough.

"All this bullshit is about a girl?" Matteo asked when Willy had finished. "Have the police seen this?" He waved the letter.

I shook my head.

He shoved the letter back at me. "Good. Put it away somewhere safe. If they try to charge you with something, we might be able to use it to muddy the water. I bet I could build an entire defense around that."

Matteo nodded at Willy. "Take a walk. Give us a minute."

Willy glanced at me, then rose and left the room, closing the conference room door behind him.

When he was gone, Matteo rolled his chair closer to mine. "I can't begin to understand everything you've been through, so I'm not going to pretend that I do. I know you're a good kid. Your aunt raved about you. You're also a smart kid. That's in your eyes.

Bloodshot or not. You know you're at a crossroads here. You stay in Pittsburgh surrounded by all these bad things, and more bad things are going to happen. You have money. You have friends who care about you. I think Willy is right. Get out of town. Put all of this in your rearview mirror. Forget the girl. Girls will mess with your head your entire life. That's what they do. They're fucking good at it. Get it all behind you, and start over someplace fresh. Your aunt busted her hump to make sure you had a better life. Don't let her wish die with her. Fulfill it. Honor her memory by going to Penn State, getting a degree, making something of your life. You want to come back here at some point, do it later. Put some time and space between it all. You'll be amazed at how much a little distance will help clear your head." He paused for a second. "The drinking needs to stop. If it comes down to it, I can put you into a program. The trust gives me the ability, with or without your consent, but I don't want to. You're drinking to cope with everything, I get that, I've done it myself, but it needs to stop. That's another rabbit hole you don't want to venture too far into. Focus on your future—it's a bright one. Make peace with your past and move on. You're strong enough, I know you are."

"You sound like Gerdy," I muttered.

"Who?"

I just shook my head and leaned forward into my hands.

Matteo rose and pushed his chair back. "That's about the closest thing to a pep talk you'll ever get out of me, kid. As a lawyer, I had to hand over my conscience back when I passed the Bar. Last thing I need is my competition catching wind that I held something back." He winked awkwardly. "Let's get Willy and figure out what we need to do to make this happen."

Turns out, there wasn't much to it.

Willy spent the afternoon on the phone in my apartment filling a notepad he had swiped from Matteo's office with information. I spent that same afternoon lying on my bed, staring at the ceiling. It was a nice ceiling. I tried drawing in my sketchpad, but my hand kept shaking. I could draw while drunk and I could draw while sober, but there was this unpleasant not-so-sweet spot somewhere in between where I wasn't much good at anything other than eat, sleep, and various bodily functions. That was where the headaches, chills, and sweats preferred to live, and I didn't like it much. I knew a drink would fix me right up. I also knew that wasn't really the answer. A drink sounded good, though.

At one point, Willy ducked his head into the room and told me according to the woman he just spoke to at the testing center, high school graduates weren't eligible to take the GED exam. He seemed to think this was immensely funny. It took me a moment to realize why, then I got it. Lucky for us, we weren't high school graduates, so we'd have no trouble complying with that particular rule. Other rules proved to be a little more difficult. For example, the minimum age requirement was eighteen years. Sixteen and seventeen-year-olds could take the exam, but certain restrictions applied. He called Matteo's office on that one, and Tess told him she'd relay the message. Matteo was busy with matters of his own.

Matteo called back a few hours later and told us since I was an orphan, an aspiring felon, and wealthy, I was a shoo-in for the GED. He'd make some calls.

I think I preferred him without a conscience or sense of humor.

It took the better part of a week to obtain those approvals.

The following Thursday, Willy and I took a cab down to the testing center on Seventh, paid the fee of sixty dollars each, and walked out the squat brick building high school graduates. I scored 196 out of 200, Willy got 173. I made him buy lunch.

The following day, I bought a car. A black 1990 Honda Prelude, with twenty-three thousand miles on the odometer. Willy taught me to drive in a Giant Eagle parking lot. The week after, I got my Pennsylvania driver's license.

I was told to forget her.

And I told them I would try.

It wouldn't be that easy, though.

397

Matteo pulled some strings with Penn State, and by the first week of November we were enrolled in the spring semester set to begin classes in late January. I spoke to Teddy Carruth at Brentwood Groceries, and he agreed to make weekly deliveries to Ms. Leech in apartment 304. She wasn't happy to hear I was leaving. She was even less thrilled to hear about the new grocery arrangements.

On November 16, Duncan Bellino was arrested on multiple drug trafficking charges. He was out three hours later. The charges wouldn't stick. He smiled at the news cameras before two large men helped him out of his wheelchair and into the back of a black Dodge Durango.

On November 18, Willy and I hit the road with my Honda Prelude loaded to the roof and Stella's note burning in my pocket. I instructed Matteo to continue paying rent on Auntie Jo's apartment. I would be keeping it.

As we turned down Brownsville, I waved at Detective Joy Fogel. She was parked across the street from my building in a green late model Toyota with a man I didn't recognize in the passenger seat. She had parked there a lot lately, the both of them. They didn't wave back.

Twenty minutes later, I thought I saw a white SUV following us, but it remained on US-22 when we took the exit to I-99 North. I didn't notice the one that picked us up two miles later. They were far more careful than the first.

PART 4

"We changed again, and yet again, and it was now too late and too far to go back, and I went on. And the mists had all solemnly risen now, and the world lay spread before me."
—Charles Dickens, *Great Expectations*

March 12, 1994

Eighteen Years Old

Log 03/12/1994—

Subject "D" —

Audio/video recording.

DISABLED

—Charter Observation Team - 309

1

Matteo rented us an apartment a few blocks from campus, on Mifflin Road. A two-bedroom walkup in a converted three-story Victorian. My allowance from the trust was deposited on the first of each month into an account with Brentwood Federal Savings and Loan. I accessed the funds with an ATM card from anywhere for a small fee. That first month, Matteo deposited an extra two thousand dollars, more than enough to furnish the apartment, purchase dishes, a microwave, and the other essentials of college life. I tried to find a recliner as comfortable as Auntie Jo's, but that search proved to be fruitless. I settled for a beanbag chair.

Classes began on January 14.

Ten days later, I turned eighteen.

The winter of 1993-1994 proved to be one of the worst in Pennsylvania history. At one point, the drifts along Mifflin Road were nearly seven feet tall. Because most classes were within walking distance (and I quickly grew tired of scraping ice from the windows), my Honda sat unused in front of the apartment, nearly vanishing beneath a blanket of white. When spring finally arrived, I had to buy a new battery to get the car started. A new bloom of rust sprouted on the trunk, a few inches from the lock. I'd watch that spot grow over the coming years.

There were parties, but I didn't touch a single drink. Keggers, frats, sorority socials. The alcohol flowed, pot was readily available, ludes, shrooms. I even saw coke at one party, but it was *college coke*, no doubt cut with baby aspirin, flour, and God knew what else. I didn't touch any of it. Instead, I was the guy in the corner with a can of Pepsi, sometimes a twelve-pack of Pepsi. I smiled and tried not to look too creepy as everyone else got wasted around me.

I wanted to drink, no doubt about that, but in watching the other students at all those parties, particularly the early ones, a realization came to me—*they* drank to enhance the social experience. It opened them up, took away inhibitions, it was a release. I only drank to forget, to numb, to hide. Alcohol helped to bring them out, alcohol turned me in. *They* drank to be together, *I* drank to be alone.

As I watched them all drink, as the laughter and shouting and dancing grew louder and slurred, I felt this gap growing—them and me, *they* and *I*, and I found a new way to be alone.

At Penn, everything was celebrated. Tonight we were celebrating what we hoped was the final snow melt of the season. It was the twelfth of March. Someone actually found it, a small mound of brown slush, on the west corner of Spruce Cottage across from the telecom building. Either that same someone or a different someone roped it off, set up a keg ten feet to the left, a boom box on a table to the right, and an improptu party started right there. In the fall, we had gathered around large bonfires. Tonight, we encircled this small patch of snow and watched it melt.

Welcome to college life.

"Come on, let me hypnotize you," she said again.

I only half heard her. She was one of *them*. This usually happened a few hours into most parties. Aside from the previously mentioned uplifting effects, alcohol also brought courage, and at some point, one of *them* would inevitably cross that invisible barrier and find their way over to me. I suppose I was a good-looking guy, probably seen as some kind of challenge to *them*, off in my isolated corner. Damn near every girl reminded me of Stella, though. The ones who didn't reminded me of Gerdy, and that hurt just as bad, sometimes worse.

This girl said her name was Kaylie. She wore a flowered sundress over black tights and under a denim jacket. Her hair was strawberry blonde and curled under just above her shoulders.

More Gerdy than Stella.

A doctoral student working on her PhD in psych, she told me when she first introduced herself.

An unknown beverage sloshed around in her red Solo cup.

I took a drink of my Pepsi. "You don't want to hypnotize me. I'm boring."

"You don't look boring. You've got this brooding, James Dean thing going on."

"James Dean, huh?"

"Totally. A rebel for sure."

"Then maybe you shouldn't be talking to me. What if I'm dangerous?"

Her eyes narrowed. "Are you dangerous?"

Everyone I care about seems to die, so yeah, probably.

"Are you any good at it?" I said.

"At what?"

"Hypnosis."

She shrugged. "My roommates say I am. Professor McDougal said I'm the best he's had in his class in a decade, but I think he's just trying to get in my pants."

"You're not wearing pants."

She looked down at her legs and processed this information in that slow way drunk people do. Then she looked back at me and smiled. "Nope. No pants."

I spotted Willy across the crowd, watching me. He gave me a thumbs-up and nodded vigorously.

"I should probably get home," I said, glancing in the direction of my apartment.

"You can't leave until the snow is gone, that's the rule."

"Well, you did say I was a rebel."

"Please let me hypnotize you."

"What do you think you'll learn?"

She tilted her head. Some of whatever was in her cup spilled over the side and landed on my shoe. "For starters, why you're at a party and you're not drinking."

"Maybe I'm not very good at it."

She stepped closer and took a drink. This time, I smelled the rum. "It's not that hard."

"You're not doing it right, either. You're drinking rum at a keg party."

She brought a single finger to her lips and smiled. "Shh. Maybe I'm a rebel...too."

Willy was still watching, and I wondered if he'd phone Matteo tonight to report in or hold off until morning. He would at some point.

I counted at least twelve people wearing white coats.

"Do you live on campus?" I asked her.

She nodded to the left. "East Residences."

"How about I walk you home," I said.

"Okay."

Apparently, the melting snow had been forgotten.

Kaylie and I crossed the quad and took a shortcut past the tennis courts. At some point, her hand found mine.

She lived in Geary Hall on the second floor.

She fumbled with the lock, pushed the door open, and stumbled in, falling on a bed to the left. Her roommates weren't home.

I turned on the light, closed the door, and helped her out of her shoes and jacket. Her cup of rum disappeared somewhere along the walk. I hadn't noticed her drop it or set it down.

I could have slept with her, but I didn't.

Instead, I waited until she fell asleep, then turned her on her side. A quilt was bunched up at the foot of the bed. I pulled it over her shoulders and tucked her in.

The walk back to my apartment on Mifflin should have taken about twenty minutes, but I didn't get back until around four in the morning. Willy's door was closed. I could hear him snoring.

There was an envelope on my bed.

The envelope wasn't thick enough to contain cash, and unlike the others, this one had my mailing address printed neatly on the front with a canceled stamp postmarked Pittsburgh, PA. The return address was Matteo's office. Inside, I found a folded letter along with a smaller envelope:

Jack,

Dewitt asked me to send this to you. Your aunt left it for you be-fore she died, with instructions to give it to you on your eighteenth birthday. I apologize for the delay, completely my fault—he dropped it on my desk with a Post-it note on the top, and it got buried before I saw it—you've seen my desk! (I'm working on it. I swear!) If he'd hand me things instead of...sorry, I'm sure you don't care. Again, I apologize for the delay.

Hope you're kicking some butt at Penn! Go, Lions!

Sincerely,

Tess

Dewitt? I chuckled. I had completely forgotten Matteo's first name was Dewitt.

I dropped the letter on my bed.

The smaller envelope was sealed, about half the size of a normal one. The kind that usually held thank-you cards or other small notes. Auntie Jo had a box of them. She used to keep her tips organized by date and shift—she said this helped her figure out the best shifts to take and which to avoid. I'm not sure that really mattered. It seemed like she worked all the time regardless.

My name was printed on the front.

I tore the envelope open.

The page inside only contained fourteen words, but I probably read those words over and over again for the better part of an hour. Her handwriting was twitchy, barely legible, written close to the end of her life:

> *The box your father left for you? It's in 68744. The worthless shit.*
> *Jo*

At some point, I sat on the edge of my bed. I didn't remember doing that. My hand was shaking. The only sounds in my room were my deep breaths and the rapid thump in my chest.

The sun started to rise by the time I found the strength to get up and shove some clothes into my backpack. Ten minutes later, I crept across the floor of our apartment toward the door, carefully avoiding the noisier boards near the center of the room under the rug. In his room at the end of the hall, Willy still snored, and probably would for a few more hours—Sundays being one of the few days he slept in.

At first, the Prelude wouldn't start. The engine coughed and sputtered, choking the winter from its throat. Then the motor caught with a single backfire. Once it turned over, the engine quickly smoothed out. Hondas were reliable that way.

I gave the gas pedal a few pumps, then backed out onto the deserted road.

My mind reeled, unable to put together a solid thought.

The box.

When I asked Auntie Jo about the box, she always denied it existed, said my father hadn't given her anything before he died, nothing at all. I searched for years, more times than I could count. I'd never given up. I simply ran out of places to look.

Of course that's where she would have hidden it. Nobody would look there.

I'd be in Pittsburgh in two and a half hours. In that time, I'd have to sort this out, figure out a next step.

68744 was the number of my father's grave plot, one of those obscure facts Auntie Jo had drilled into me as a kid.

About an hour into the drive, I realized my "next step" wasn't necessarily a single option of multiple options. I had *no* other options. I tried to think of something, anything at all other than the obvious choice, which clearly wouldn't be a possibility for any sane person but slowly became one for me as I thought more and more about it. That realization didn't help the churning in my stomach, the sour taste in my throat.

Auntie Jo wouldn't lie about something like this. She hated my father, hated everything about him. But she wouldn't lie about something this important, not to me.

The letter from Richard Nettleton to my father had been addressed to her.

I had always suspected that, on some level, Jo knew what was going on. Even if she hadn't told me, the dream told me as much.

I knew the box was real, *knew it*, even if she denied it.

Her way of protecting me, waiting until I was old enough, I suppose.

The box was key, always had been.

But could I?

Could I dig up a grave?

My father's grave?

If the box was there—and as the miles churned beneath the noisy wheels of my Honda, I became absolutely convinced that it was—could I leave the box hidden in his grave forever? Forget about it? What if someone else found it? Someone in a white coat?

What if (and this was a big what if), what if something in that box might help me find Stella?

I couldn't forget about something like this.

I'd have to look.

The sane choice was to *not* dig up my father's grave.

But digging was clearly my only choice.

Somehow, I made peace with that. My brain twisted and turned it, churned the facts until this was not only my only choice but the *right* choice, and one that could not wait.

At the turnoff for I-376, I stopped at a small hardware store in Hollidaysburg and bought a shovel. I couldn't risk doing such a thing in Pittsburgh, where I might be recognized. The only hardware store near my apartment in Brentwood was Keener's. The store had been there since 1939—Harold Keener would not only recognize me but might pick up the phone and call Matteo when I purchased something as odd as a shovel.

I parked on Cramer off Brownsville, about three blocks from my apartment, and walked the rest of the way. Parking near my building wasn't an option. Honda Preludes were a fairly common car, but a black one parked in front of my building would probably get recognized as mine. I left the shovel in the trunk.

Construction on Krendal's Diner was nearing completion and a sign hung in the window—Carmozzi's Pizza, coming soon!

I walked past and tried not to look through the newly white-washed windows for fear of what might look back.

Nearly three months had gone by since the last time I stepped into my apartment building. The place felt foreign to me. The halls seemed narrower and musty, in need of paint. I climbed the steps and slipped into my apartment unnoticed. Even Ms. Leech's door remained closed. No grocery list on the door, not on Sundays.

My apartment was dark. Every surface, thick with dust.

I crossed the room, past the stack of posters still on the table, past Gerdy's dress still on the floor, and reached for the thick blinds over the window, then thought better of it.

If someone were to look up. Someone who knows me...

I settled into Auntie Jo's chair near the window and waited for night to come. My right knee bounced nervously, and the ghosts of my past howled all around, cackling at my ear, anxious for what came next.

At a little after one in the morning, I parked on Nobles Lane, probably within ten feet of the place I left my bike as a kid on the day of the Great Chase.

If I closed my eyes, I could still hear the sound of those four SUVs racing up behind me, with Dunk and Willy chattering from the radio.

When I opened my eyes, I saw nothing but a dark, deserted road, edged by woods. Nobles Lane had no street lamps, no traffic, and the few homes sat far back from the road.

A light drizzle had started up a little after midnight and remained steady since. When I pulled off the pavement, the Honda's tires dipped slightly in the muddy earth, and I cursed myself for not thinking about the possibility of leaving tracks behind. I should have brought a jacket, too. The temperature dropped into the forties and was still sinking. As grave-robbing went, I wasn't very good.

At this hour, every sound seemed amplified, from the groan of my trunk to my footfalls as I ran through the woods toward the cemetery, with the shovel in hand. I came out of the trees about a hundred feet west of our bench, and I couldn't help but think of the painting in Stella's room.

Shadows clung to the sides of the mausoleums, wrapping the stone structures in the blanket of night, cradling them in the rain. I knew I was alone, yet I felt eyes on me. I half-expected someone in a white coat to slip out of the woods, to step out into my path, maybe more than one someone, all with thoughts of that box. In the time I spent in this cemetery growing up, I had yet to see a caretaker or any form of security. Someone locked the front gate promptly at nine each night and opened it again in the morning, but even that person eluded me through the years. I imagined anyone working in a cemetery, in the solitude of it, would eventually become a silent part of that cemetery, able to move through the grounds one with the wraiths and gloom, nothing more than a whisper among the gravestones.

As I came over the hill on the south end of the cemetery, my parents' graves came into view, Auntie Jo now beside them under the sweeping arms of the large red maple tree, their gravestones glistening in the rain.

Could I really do this?

Oh, how I wished for a drink. I would have probably drank pure grain alcohol at that point, if I had it on hand. A beer, cough syrup, whiskey, *anything*. My skin tingled with the craving, the mouth of every pore open wide. I had nothing, though, and I pressed on anyway.

When I finally reached the graves, as I stood over my father's resting place, I turned slowly and searched the cemetery grounds for signs of anyone. I saw no one, but that feeling of being watched remained, a prickling at the back of my neck.

The shovel felt heavy.

God help me. I plunged it into the dirt and began to dig.

The ground was softer than I expected.

2

Elfrieda Leech sat up in her bed and cocked her head.

She heard something.

A creak of the floorboards, the groan of old wood.

The numbers on the analog alarm clock beside her bed flipped from 3:03 in the morning to 3:04 with a slight mechanical whir and the click of plastic on plastic.

As she did every night, Elfrieda set the thermostat in the hallway to seventy before going to bed—seventy-two during the daytime, seventy for bed, always—yet her bedroom felt horribly cold. She listened for the steady drone of the furnace but heard nothing.

An icy breeze slipped over the nape of her neck and her shoulders, and that wasn't right, either. She never opened the windows.

Never.

Another creak. From the hallway this time, she was certain of that.

Elfrieda kept a loaded .38 in her nightstand drawer. She also had one in her dresser, another taped to the back of the toilet, two more in the living room (the first under the left couch cushion and the second taped to the bottom of the end table) and yet another in the kitchen on the counter in a metal tin labeled *flour*. Although she had never fired a single shot, each weapon was cleaned and meticulously oiled every other Thursday. The first had been purchased two days after she was attacked by those horrible people in white, the ones who wanted things that did not belong to them. She purchased the others in the years following, after deciding she no longer wanted surprises in her life. First only one, then the second when she realized she couldn't get to that first gun hidden in the bedroom if she was in the kitchen, then the others when she decided a weapon should always be within arm's reach, regardless of where she was in her apartment. She nearly bought one for her purse too, but that seemed silly since she no longer left home. The nice man who had sold them to her did so over the phone and even delivered for an additional fee.

The .38 from her nightstand felt cold and heavy in her hand as she quietly lowered her feet to the floor and crossed the room, ignoring the arthritic pain burning in her legs.

Although she lived alone, she aways closed and locked her bedroom door. A yellow bathrobe hung from a hook on the back of her door. She pushed the robe aside and pressed her ear against the wood. The door was solid wood, not that cheap pressboard junk they sold today, but a thick slab of oak, original to the apartment.

She heard nothing.

Elfrieda began to wonder if she heard anything at all. Maybe it was nothing more than the settling of the old building or the expanding and contracting of the structure itself as it always did when spring ushered away the cold grip of winter. Maybe she dreamed the sound, imagined the sound entirely, maybe—

Another squeak.

The board beneath her bare left foot moved slightly when weight found that same board on the opposite side of the door.

Somebody was standing there.

Elfrieda drew in a deep breath, tried to steady the hand holding the .38—she was shaking so. "I have a gun!"

Her intended shout came out muffled and weak, the thick wood of the door eating her words.

From the other side came a man's voice—soft, pure. Sounding more like the music created by a finely tuned set of chimes than the spoken word. "I know you have a gun. You need to put the gun down and unlock the door."

Elfrieda set the gun down on the top of the dresser and flipped the lock on the doorknob.

"Now open the door and step back," the voice said.

She did so without any hesitation.

The door swung open. A man was standing there. He had dark hair and darker eyes and a smile that somehow put her at ease, even though that was darkest of all. Behind him stood two women in long, white coats. Both watched but remained silent.

As Elfrieda completed each instruction, she wondered why she was doing as she was told. She didn't want to. She wanted to point the gun at the center of this man's chest and pull the trigger and keep pulling the trigger until the chamber clicked empty. She couldn't, though. The gun was already out of reach, and when she tried to force her legs to walk back to it, they didn't obey. Instead they stepped backward, as instructed, until they reached the edge of the bed.

"Sit down, Elfrieda."

She did.

The three intruders stepped into her bedroom, her private place, uninvited.

"Are you real?" she asked.

He tilted his head and smiled again. "We no longer need you to watch the boy. Do you remember when I asked you to watch the boy, all those years ago? I was a child myself then. They made me phone you, so impersonal."

"Yes. I remember."

"You knew my parents."

"Yes."

"What were their names?"

"Keith and Jaquelyn Pickford."

"And my name?"

"David. You're David Pickford. You're a beautiful man, David Pickford."

He smiled again. "Thank you."

"You're welcome." Elfrieda Leech stared past him.

We no longer need you to watch the boy. Not *they*. Charter had told her the Pickford boy would never leave his room. Could never leave his room. Held against his will. He should hate them, *despise* them. There should only be *they*, not *we*.

How could he be standing in her bedroom?

Elfrieda Leech eyed the butt of the .38 on the edge of the dresser. She wanted to push past these people, take the gun in her hand, kill them all. She couldn't move, though. Her body wouldn't obey her. "Why aren't you wearing white?"

Unlike the other two intruders, David Pickford wore a black leather jacket over a deep red tee-shirt and denim jeans. If he carried a gun, she didn't see one. Nothing clipped to his belt, no shoulder holster.

"I don't like white," he replied. "White is a non-color, the absence of color. A canvas waiting for a stain."

"All the monsters wear white." She found the words difficult to speak. Like movement, they fought her, but she got them out.

"Not all the monsters."

"Your parents...what you..."

"Shh." He knelt down in front of her and took her hand in his. "We're not here to talk about my parents."

She tried to respond, but her lips, her mouth, wouldn't move.

"I'm sorry, you may speak," David said.

Whatever spell, *his spell*, broke.

"Why are you here?" she was able to get out.

"Charter dropped the ball, I'm afraid. I've decided to step in, to correct the matter, clean up the mess."

"Okay."

He went on, "You're a part of that mess."

"I know."

He squeezed her fingers until they turned white. "When we leave, you're going to wait three hours. Then you're going to take your gun, put it in your mouth, nice and deep, and pull the trigger."

"Okay."

"Okay, what? Tell me."

"When you leave, I'm going to wait three hours. Then I'm going to take the gun, put it in my mouth, nice and deep, and pull the trigger."

"Are you afraid to die, Elfrieda?"

"No."

He released her hand. It dropped limply into her lap. "Do you have regrets?"

"I never had a child," she replied without hesitation.

"Maybe you should have."

"I couldn't pass it on. But I wanted a child."

He thought about this for a moment. "I was told you had no reaction to the shot. You have nothing to pass on."

"Yes."

"Yes, what?"

"Yes, I had no reaction."

"So you have nothing to pass on," he said again.

Elfrieda said nothing. From the corner of her eye, she could see the gun. She willed herself to get up, to jump toward it, to grab the .38 from the dresser. Her body ignored her. She began to tremble.

"Your limbs are as heavy as lead. If you attempt to do anything other than what I ask, you will feel as if you are on fire. Understand?"

"Yes." Elfrieda looked away from the gun, looked at him, stopped fighting, stopped trembling.

"I'd like you to tell me where I can find the others."

"There are no more 'others.'"

"Don't lie to me, Elfrieda. It's unbecoming of a woman such as yourself. Lying can also be quite painful. Telling a lie might feel as bad as, say..." David thought about this for a moment, then he had it. "Lying feels like swallowing a thousand fire ants, their stings as they ravage your throat from the inside. Wouldn't that be just horrible?"

Elfrieda Leech nodded.

"Tell me where I can find the others."

"There are no more..." But even as she said the words, the pain registered on her face. He skin went taut and pale, her eyes nearly popped out of her head. She screamed horribly loud.

David seemed to find enjoyment in this. He gave her a moment, he let her screams die away. "You know, telling the truth can have the opposite effect. With the truth, all that pain just washes down the drain, replaced with the most incredible euphoric sensation. So brilliant, it defies description. I imagine you'd like to feel that? Rather than those horrible ants?"

Elfrieda nodded quickly, tears streaming from her eyes.

"Tell me, Elfrieda, where can I find the others?"

This time, she did tell him. She told him all she knew. She didn't know where they all were, only Dewey Hobson and the Brotherton woman, and that would have to do.

When she finished, when David was certain there was nothing else to gain, he smiled again. "Good. That's very good. We'll be leaving then, I think." He turned, started for the door, then paused. With his back to her, he asked one final question. "Tell me one more time, what will happen next, after we go?"

Elfrieda Leech took a breath. "When you leave, I'm going to wait three hours. Then I'm going to take the gun, put it in my mouth, nice and deep, and pull the trigger."

"How many seconds in three hours?"

"10,800."

"It was a pleasure knowing you, Elfrieda."

"You too, David."

The three intruders left then, leaving her bedroom door open. The dead bolt slid back in place at the front door. She had no idea how they had gotten a key.

Sitting on the edge of the bed, Elfrieda Leech remained perfectly still. In her mind, she began to tick away the seconds—10,800, 10,799, 10,798...the clock on her nightstand whirring along with her, the click of plastic on plastic as each minute fell away.

3

My shovel struck the top of my father's wooden casket at a little past three in the morning, and by a quarter after, I had cleared away the entire surface. Although I had only been four when he died, I remembered the casket. The black wood had been polished to a bright shine, so much so I could see my distorted reflection in the finish from my seat next to Auntie Jo in the front row. Someone placed a rose on top, and I thought for sure Auntie Jo would knock the flower off since there wasn't one on Momma's casket, too. She didn't, though.

That black shine was long gone, the bare wood showing through in spots, the metal of the hinges and latch rusted. The wood had begun to rot, and with a little pressure on the blade of the shovel, the screws pulled right out and the latch popped off.

Who put the flower there, Auntie Jo?

Some asshole.

If I stopped moving, I knew I wouldn't go through with what I needed to do, so I didn't allow myself to stop. I didn't allow myself to think. Instead, I lowered myself into the small space I dug out to the left of the casket and jammed the edge of the shovel under the lip of the lid. Although the rain stopped, puddled water soaked through my shoes, and when I pressed down on the handle of the shovel, when I leveraged it with my weight, water squooshed between my toes and I wondered what it would be like to sink down into that mud, to disappear within the earth.

The top of the casket snapped open with an audible *pop!* There was a rush of air both in and out of the casket, matched only by the deep breath I sucked into my lungs and forced back out.

I tossed the shovel out of the hole and wrapped my fingers around the lid of my father's casket, prying it open against the weight of more than a decade.

I'm not sure when my eyes closed, but they did and they didn't want to open again, but I forced them anyway. When they did, I found the courage to look down into the box.

My father was not inside.

I don't think I expected him to be in the casket. At some point while digging, I began to tell myself he wouldn't be in there, and as I repeated that mantra, it became easier to fill the shovel, easier to dig, to keep going. Seeing the empty casket, though, knowing for sure, that brought the tears and I collapsed in the hole, water and mud soaking my jeans. My hands gripped the side of the empty casket, my body quivering, and my mind so filled with thoughts I couldn't make sense of any of them.

I buried my face in my filthy hands and cried, all the emotion of the past hours coming to a head.

When I finally brought myself to look back inside, I was certain he had never been in the casket. Unlike the wooden exterior, the satin lining of the casket appeared new, only slightly yellowed from its time below ground, preserved by the airtight seal. A pillow sat where his head would have rested, and that pillow didn't have so much as a crease down the center.

In the center of the casket sat a cardboard box.

The box I had seen my father give Auntie Jo.

Inside the cardboard box, I found two books. A Penn State 1978 yearbook, and a paperback copy of *Great Expectations*.

Nothing else.

Not a damn thing else.

I wanted to scream. If not for the fear of discovery, I surely would have.

I'm not sure what I expected to find, but it certainly wasn't this.

The anxiety, fear, and uncertainty of earlier quickly turned to anger and frustration.

There had to be something else. What the hell was I supposed to do with an old yearbook and another copy of that damn Dickens book? Why would someone go through all this trouble for something so mundane?

A note fell from the folds of *Great Expectations*:

Your mother is at rest, Jack. Please let her rest.

I didn't recognize the handwriting. Not Auntie Jo's. My father's?

Filling the grave back in went much faster than digging it up. I replaced the sod as best I could and scattered dead leaves left over from fall over the plot. When finally satisfied that my night's work would only be discovered by someone specifically looking for it, I scooped up the yearbook, the novel, and shovel, and ran back through the woods to my car, carefully watching the cemetery grounds and the trees for any sign of another.

Inside my car, I pressed the button for the overhead light and flipped through the pages of *Great Expectations*. The book appeared to be new, unread, many of the pages still sticking together. I expected to find something written inside, but there was nothing. The first page contained a detailed map of England—Exeter, London, Manchester, Whidbey, Newcastle upon Tyne, and dozens of other major cities labeled. The novel itself appeared to be complete, beginning with the same line engrained in my head since childhood:

My father's family name being Pirrip, and my Christian name Philip, my infant tongue could make of both names nothing longer or more explicit than Pip. So, I called myself Pip, and came to be called Pip.

My hands (and my clothes and every inch of my skin, for that matter) were covered in dirt, and each page I touched came away smudged and filthy. I rubbed them on my jeans and that only made things worse. I reached down and wiped them as best I could on the carpet under the gearshift.

I set aside *Great Expectations* and moved the yearbook into the light. Unlike the novel, the pages of the yearbook were well-worn, some folded over. The inside flap of this book was filled with handwritten notes and scribbles—*Maybe next year you'll learn to hold your beer! – Al Waters, Hey Eddie, Get a haircut, you shit! – Gene Glaspie, Two more years to go, good luck with that! – Enid Sather*...there were dozens of them, but none written by names I recognized.

I turned to the first dog-eared page—*Class of 1979* across the top. The photographs of three students were circled on the opposite page:

Perla Beyham
Cammie Brotherton
Jaquelyn Breece

Two on the next page:

Jeffery Dalton
Garret Dotts

The three pages that followed had no circled photographs. The next I found was a face I recognized—Kaitlyn Gargery—my mother, young and beautiful—Gargery being her maiden name. I continued to turn the pages, slower now. Each dog-eared page contained circled images:

Penelope Maudlin
Richard Nettleton
Keith Pickford
Emma Tackett

The third to last marked page had my father—Edward Thatch. The final page was someone I did not know, named Lester Woodford. He wore thick glasses and had unruly curly hair.

I flipped back to Richard Nettleton. *Stella's father?* Then to Emma Tackett—possibly Stella's mother, like my mother, listed with her maiden name? None of them married yet, too early in their lives.

The final marked page wasn't among the student pictures at the front, but was at the rear of the book with the staff members. Although much younger, it was a face I recognized, a name I knew well—Elfrieda Leech, Guidance Counselor.

I dropped the book into the passenger seat, started the car, and raced down Nobles Lane as the sun began to climb over the horizon.

The first time I knocked, I did so lightly. It was just a little after six in the morning, and many in the building were still sleeping. Ms. Leech hadn't answered that first time, nor the second time, so this time I pounded on her door with the side of my fist. "Ms. Leech! Open the door!"

Her door did not open, but 309 at the end of the hall did. Cecile Dreher stuck her head out, her hair still in curlers, and prepared to yell at me, then thought better of it when she saw I was covered in dirt and grime. She gave me an angry grunt and ducked back inside.

"Ms. Leech!" I knocked again, this time with the spine of the yearbook. "Ms. Leech!"

"Dammit…" I went back to my apartment and shuffled through the keys hanging near the front door. They weren't labeled, but I knew Leech's key was silver with the brand-name *Curtis* stamped on the side. She gave the key to Auntie Jo years ago. Ms. Leech had a key to our apartment too, although I don't think she ever used it.

Back across the hall, I slipped the key into her lock and snapped the dead bolt open, then let myself in. "Ms. Leech? It's me, Jack Thatch. I'm coming in."

The last time I had been in Ms. Leech's apartment was with Gerdy, nearly a year ago. Since then, the stacks of newspapers had continued to grow, leaving little space to maneuver around them.

A light glowed in the back bedroom.

"Ms. Leech? It's Jack, from across the hall. I know today's not grocery day, but I have to talk to you. You didn't answer your door, so I let myself in. Are you awake?"

As I turned sideways and worked my way through the mess, I began to wonder if something was wrong. Leech rarely had visitors. If she had a heart attack or stroke or even slipped and fell, she might go days without being found, maybe weeks. As far as I knew, her only contact with the outside world was with the weekly grocery deliveries, and I had no idea who Matteo arranged to take care of that.

I found her, very much alive, sitting on the edge of her bed.

Her face looked frightfully white, the wrinkles set so deep in her skin they might have been carved in with a chisel. She watched me enter the room with unblinking eyes. Her left hand held a fistful of quilt. She squeezed the material, kneaded the cloth like raw dough. Her right hand disappeared under the sheets. She wore a nightgown similar to the ones Auntie Jo had worn, all frilly lace and silk, stolen from someone's closet in the seventies. Her feet were bare, her toes pressing into the hardwood.

"Ms. Leech, are you okay?"

"Okay, yes," she said the words, then went silent. Her lips continued to move, though. A soundless mumble.

Had she had a stroke?

At her age, anything was possible. What was she now? Mid-seventies? Eighty? I had no idea. A twang of guilt hit me. I should know. This woman practically raised me with Jo, yet I knew so little about her.

"Do you want me to call a doctor?"

She said nothing, only stared, her lips quivering.

I snapped my fingers in front of her face. Bits of dirt flaked to the floor. "Do you recognize me, Ms. Leech? Do you know who I am?"

"I know what happens next," she sang this more than spoke the words, a high girlish tone. Her lips formed a quick grin, then fell flat. She followed this with, "You are Jack Thatch, son of Edward Thatch and Kaitlyn Gargery, the boy across the hall, the bringer of groceries. Stealer of books. That's who you are."

Gargery. My mother's maiden name.

I held up the yearbook and opened to her page. "Do you know why these people are circled? Look—here's my mother, and my father, Stella's father, Richard, and her mother, Emma…"

"Ah, Stella," she said softly. "Cute as a button, that one." Her eyes looked to some distant object. Then, she added for no reason, "Twenty-seven."

"Twenty-seven what?" I flipped through the pages, holding the yearbook up to her face as I came to each circled image. "There are thirteen people circled. Who are they? You knew them all, didn't you? Why are they circled?"

Her gaze was blank again.

I showed her the inscriptions at the front. *Hey Eddie, Get a haircut, you shit! – Gene Glaspie.* Gene Glaspie's photo was not circled. I checked. "This is my father's yearbook. Eddie. He's not in his grave. Where is he? Do you know? What happened to him? Why did he leave this book for me? Why did he circle these photographs? Who are these people?" I turned to the back, to her picture, held it up. "I know you know!" I shouted these last words, unable to control the adrenaline coursing through my body, the book shaking in my hands.

"Three," she whispered.

"Three what?!?"

The gun came up fast, a black metal blur in her right hand from under the sheets to her mouth. She pressed it so far back into her throat, I thought she planned to swallow it. Her thumb cocked back the hammer and—

I saw the back of her head explode out over the bed a fraction of a second before I heard the explosion of the bullet leaving the chamber. A rush of air pattered my face. All the air left the room, and the loud blast was replaced by a louder ringing in my ears.

Ms. Leech sat there for a moment, her eyes frozen with a quick wonder. Then she slouched forward and dropped from the bed to the floor.

I backed out of the room, out of her apartment, crossed the hall into my own apartment, and closed the door as quickly as I could. I tried to catch my breath, *needed* to catch my breath, but this night simply wasn't going to let me.

Sitting on top of my backpack was a fifth of Jameson whiskey, along with a note:

Welcome to the party, Jack! Toast with me.
– David

I grabbed the Jameson bottle and note and managed to get back to my car before the shakes started, barely. I tore the cap off and took a hardy chug, welcoming the warmth as it burned away the—adrenaline, fear, anxiety, confusion, pain, sadness, hatred, anger—churning under my skin. I didn't care where the bottle came from. I didn't care what the bottle might represent. I didn't care if the bottle was laced with the most acidic of poisons (I think part of me hoped it was). I needed the whiskey to drive away the image of Ms. Leech etched into the back of my eyelids. I would keep the drinking in check, though, goddamnit, I would keep it in check. I *could* do that. I *would* do that. To prove this to myself, I drank only enough to lower a veil over the world. Then I twisted the cap back on and dropped the bottle on the floorboard of the passenger seat.

I was back on I-79 before I realized I had even started the car, and I was driving fast, nearly twenty miles-per-hour over the posted limit. I eased back on the accelerator, stopped swerving from lane to lane, and fell in line with the rest of the morning traffic. These people, these drones, driving to work, putting on makeup, eating breakfast sandwiches and laughing at the stupid little jokes coming from the radio. They had no idea. None of them.

When I caught my reflection in the rearview mirror, I didn't recognize the person staring back at me. My hair was filthy and matted, eyes bloodshot. My skin was covered in dirt and mud and little specs of red. I tried not to think about those. I took Exit 63, just outside of Wexford, and pulled into the back of a Phillips 66 gas station. The bathroom door was locked, but someone had crowbarred the metal doorframe, rendering the heavy dead bolt useless. Inside, a loop of rope hung from the door, and someone had screwed a crooked hook into the wall to create a makeshift interior lock. I pulled the door closed, twisted the rope around the hook, and stripped out of my clothes. I expected the water from the tap to be brown, but it flowed clear and icy cold. I took what Auntie Jo would have called a "whore's bath." The paper towel dispenser was empty, so I used one of the shirts I'd packed to wipe away the grit from my face and hair. When finished, I changed into clean clothes from by pack, stuffed my dirty shirt, jeans, underwear, and socks into the trash in the corner of the room, then took the entire trash bag out and stuffed it into the Dumpster at the corner of the parking lot inside a cardboard box that once contained frozen burritos.

Back in my car, I shoved the bottle of Jameson under the passenger seat and checked my somewhat improved reflection in the mirror. I got back on the highway, careful not to speed again.

4

When David Pickford climbed back into the white Chevy Suburban followed by the two others who had accompanied him into the Leech woman's apartment, he felt renewed and completely invigorated. Hearing the gunshot that followed brought a smile to his face that would remain for the rest of the day. Even from behind the six car-lengths that separated them, he could feel Thatch unraveling.

"Wipe that smugness from your face. It's unbecoming," Ms. Oliver said from the seat beside him, cradling her useless arm.

"You should have that stump amputated, Latrese."

"Don't call me that. Oliver or Ms. Oliver, but you haven't earned the right to utter my first name."

He should kill her.

He wanted to, no doubt about that. He also felt that every death should serve a meaning or a purpose, and he had yet to determine what her death would mean or what purpose it could possibly serve. Therefore, he kept her alive. A nagging puppy yapping at his ankle.

Her time would come soon enough.

When he killed the last of them.

When he had Stella to himself.

After he spoke to every last employee of Charter and had the company running like a smooth machine.

She'd die then. He'd see to it she died splendidly.

"It itches," Oliver said beside him. "All the time. This deep-seated, relentless itch in the bone, under the skin. I can't scratch hard enough to reach it."

He wished he'd seen it happen—Stella's parting gift to the old woman before disappearing to God knows where. Just a quick touch, that was all it probably took. Like a cancer burning through her flesh, ignited at her fingertip, and rolling up the old woman's arm. He'd seen Stella do it before, and it had always fascinated him, this gift of hers. When she was younger, there hadn't been much control, but time seemed to have improved that. She could have killed Oliver, but she hadn't. She only wished to make her suffer.

He found that beautiful.

"Lob it off, damn dead thing is all it is. Smells to high heaven."

Oliver wouldn't, though. She'd cling to it until the whole shriveled arm fell off on its own. Stubborn old woman that she was. To him, it was a sign of weakness. If Stella had done this to his arm, he would have cut it off himself, right there in front of her. That wouldn't happen, though. He wasn't careless.

"When we get her back, I'll take my pound of flesh," Oliver said.

"When *I* get her back, maybe *I'll* let you."

5

I got back to Penn State at a little after eleven in the morning, but I didn't go straight to my apartment on Mifflin. Instead, I found a space on Bigler Road, quickly crossed the quad on foot, and took the back stairs up to the second floor of Geary Hall.

I hesitated outside her door for nearly a minute with girls passing me in the hall, eyeing me curiously, whispering to each other. Some were fully dressed, others wore nothing but towels and flip-flops. Boys usually didn't start appearing on this floor until much later in the day.

I knocked. The knuckles on my right hand were scrapped and bruised.

The door opened about an inch, and Kaylie peeked out from the gap, one eye closed, the other open, her hair a rat's nest. I must have woken her.

"I need you to hypnotize me," I blurted out, shoving my scarred hands into my pockets.

Kaylie stood there. She smacked her lips and yawned. "Who are you?"

"Jack. Jack Thatch. You don't remember?"

Her other eye opened, and she scratched at the side of her cheek. "Oh right, Pepsi-Boy, from the melting party."

"Can you do it?"

She yawned again. "Can you come back later? I haven't slept in forever. I was up all night studying Jung's theories on ego and personalities, and right now all I really want to do is get back to studying the unconscious mind in my bed."

"I need to do this now."

"Right now? Right this very second?"

"Please?"

She opened the door a few more inches and yawned again. She wore a Guns N' Roses tee-shirt and pink panties. "I'm gonna need sustenance and three minutes to make myself presentable for semi-public consumption. There's a vending machine at the end of the hall."

"What do you want—"

Before I could get the sentence out, the door closed.

I found the vending machines and bought two Kit Kat bars, a Snickers, and two cups of coffee. Carefully balancing everything, I returned to her room. The door was ajar. I nudged it open with my foot and stepped inside. Kaylie was sitting on the edge of her bed, her head in her hands. She had brushed her hair and put on a pair of running shorts.

Without looking up, she said, "What happened the other night…I was really drunk, I mean, really drunk. I don't normally just invite random guys back up to my room like that. That's not me. I don't want you to think I'm like that."

"I didn't, I mean I don't. It's okay, really."

She reached out a hand and took one of the coffees. "Hand me the sugar? It's behind you."

The dorm room wasn't very large, only about ten feet square. Two single beds lined the walls on either side, a small dresser near the door, and another folding table with a makeshift kitchen under a window covered with a towel to help keep the light out.

I set everything down on the table beside the microwave, and a bowl containing about a thousand packets of ketchup, mustard, and mayonnaise pilfered from area fast-food restaurants. Sugar was in a large Tupperware container. I handed it to her. Kaylie drank about a third of the black coffee, then filled the cup back up with sugar, stirred it with her finger, and drank again. "The coffee from the machine is tar-water, but I think the school pipes in extra caffeine. They know what momma needs. I can feel the lights in the factory starting to come on."

There was a white down ski parka bunched up in the corner of the room. I nodded at it. "Yours?"

"My roommate's."

"Where is she?"

"Dunno. She *is* into random guys. Why am I hypnotizing you?"

Her eyes had come to life. She watched me now. "And why do you smell like a sewer pipe? You look like you crawled here through the mud. This is no way to impress a lady."

I should have showered first, but I hadn't had time. I said the first thing that popped into my head. "Frat stuff, hazing. I'm not allowed to talk about it."

"Which one?"

"Does it matter?"

"Naw, not really. They're all the same. Are those for me, too?"

I handed her one of the Kit Kat bars and ate the second, the first thing I'd eaten since yesterday. We split the Snickers.

"You still haven't told me why I'm hypnotizing you."

I spent half the drive back trying to figure out what I was going to tell her. I didn't want to involve someone else. The less she knew, the better. I told her my parents were both killed in a car accident when I was four. I told her parts of that day had come back to me in dreams, but not all.

"And you want to remember the rest?"

I nodded.

"I think I can work with that. Have you ever been hypnotized?"

"No."

She finished her coffee and reached for mine. I gave her what was left and watched her fill about an inch of the cup with more sugar before drinking it down. "Hypnosis is not like in the movies. You can count backwards, snap your fingers, and all that, but for the most part, that's all show. Do you know where the term 'fall asleep' comes from?"

I shook my head.

"Our bodies regulate themselves with a series of chemical releases throughout the day. Adrenaline wakes us up, gives us that jolt of energy. When the sun goes down, when we lay down to sleep, our body does the opposite by releasing a hormone called melatonin. Melatonin causes us to feel drowsy, prepares our bodies to shut down. As we enter a sleep state, when we're right at the edge, we sometimes experience a muscle twitch called a 'hypnagogic jerk,' which feels like falling to the nearly unconscious mind. It usually feels like it jolts us awake, but immediately after we drop off. When a person is hypnotized, we try to get them to that point, to the sweet spot either right before or right after the hypnagogic jerk. That's when the door between our conscious and subconscious mind is open widest. When we try to recapture memories through hypnosis, we're peeking through that door. It's believed our minds don't really forget anything. Memories are just stored in different ways, some deeper than others either because our brain considers them to be unimportant, or because they're traumatic. In your case, if you were really there when the accident occurred and the moments you've been dreaming about really took place, we should be able to access those memories, regardless of why they were repressed."

She finished my coffee and set the empty cup on the table next to her bed. "Of course, your mind might have repressed these memories because they're unbelievably horrible, possibly even damaging if recalled. If we do this, there won't be any turning back. Are you sure?"

I nodded.

"Okay, then."

"Here, take this." Kaylie handed me a small, white pill.

"What is it?"

"Just a Valium. You need something to help you relax. You're a bundle of nerves right now. This won't work if you don't calm down."

I swallowed the chalky pill dry.

She straightened the quilt on her bed and told me to lie down, then rummaged through a drawer under the Kenwood receiver atop her dresser. She produced a microcassette recorder. "I'm gonna tape this. Is that okay?"

I nodded.

She handed me a pair of over-the-ear Bose headphones, plugged them into the receiver, and told me to put them on. They must have had some type of noise-canceling feature built in, because when she spoke again, her voice sounded distant, as if shouted over a long distance. I could no longer hear voices in the hallway or the adjoining dorm rooms. She told me to close my eyes, and I did.

She switched off the lights, and the pink behind my eyelids went black.

There was an electronic hum as she turned on the receiver. A steady click filled my ears, a recording of a metronome.

Tick...tock.

Tick...tock.

Tick...tock.

"Okay, Jack, I want you to listen to the rhythm of that sound, like a comforting heartbeat. Breathe in through your mouth, out through your nose, let your breathing fall in time with the sound. It's all about the sound, that comforting sound. A heartbeat. Visualize a heartbeat, that sound. The rush of your blood, the life flowing through every inch of your body. Warm and comforting. My voice brings you deeper, faster and deeper, faster and deeper in a warm, calm, peaceful state of relaxation. Like sinking deep down into a warm bath."

Tick...tock.

Tick...tock.

"Sinking down and shutting down. Sinking down and shutting down. Sinking down and shutting down completely in the enveloping warmth," she said from so far away. Repeating. "Warm and calm, a blanket, snug and—"

When my eyes opened, Kaylie had her back to me. She was on the phone. I pulled off the headphones.

"…not what I agreed to," she said into the receiver.

"Kaylie?" I said. My throat was dry.

She turned then, her eyes wide. Kaylie hung up the phone.

I sat up slowly on the bed, my arms and legs heavy, as if waking from a deep sleep. I didn't remember sleeping, though.

The window behind the towel was dark. But that couldn't be right. It was only around noon when we started. "Who were you talking to?"

An odd flavor lingered in my mouth for a second, then was gone.

Chocolate milk?

"Did it work?"

Kaylie's eyes narrowed. She picked up the white ski parka and slipped the coat on. "I need to get to the library, and you need to leave."

I frowned. "You said that was your roommate's."

"You need to go. I didn't sign on for this." She folded her arms defensively at her chest and nodded at the door. "Now."

I stood and grabbed the phone. "Who did you call?"

She reached for the door, pulled it open.

I keyed in *69 on the phone.

It rang once.

"Keep him there, I'm on my way," a voice said.

Willy.

From the open doorway, Kaylie said, "Get out, Jack. Now."

"What did I say?"

"Get out, or I'll scream."

The microcassette recorder still sat on the bed, next to the pillow. I grabbed it. The tape was missing. "Where's the tape?"

"I'll scream. I swear I will."

"Dammit! What did I say?" I shouted.

She did scream then. Kaylie screamed so loud the shrill pitch filled the room. I threw the microcassette recorder against the far wall and pushed past her and out into the hallway, where a dozen eyes watched me leave in stunned silence.

Outside Geary Hall, I crossed the quad to a bank of pay phones at Findlay Commons. I dialed my apartment on Mifflin and got a busy signal. I hung up and dialed again, again after that.

When the phone finally did ring, it only rang once before Willy picked up.

"Hello?"

"Why did she call you, Willy?"

There was a pause. "Where have you been, Jack?"

"Arby's."

"You've been gone a day and a half."

"There was a long line."

"Were you out drinking?"

"Why did Kaylie call you, Willy?"

"She was worried. We're all very worried about you, that's all. I know her from student union. She knows we're roommates. She said you showed up on her doorstep looking like death warmed over and smelling worse. She said she calmed you down and then she called me, that's all. Were you drinking, Jack? You're not supposed to leave campus without telling me. If you were drinking, tell me. I'll get you help. I'll help you get past it, like I did in Pittsburgh."

I could see the Geary entrance from here. I watched for Kaylie as I spoke. "Tell Matteo whatever you want. I don't need a babysitter."

Willy's voice dropped lower. "The police called looking for you, Jack. Something happened to the woman who lived across the hall from you in Brentwood. I told them you pulled an all-nighter in the library. I said I was there most of the time, too. Come back to the apartment. Tell me what's going on."

I heard something behind him. Soft, barely audible. A whisper? *Another voice?*

"Is someone else in the apartment, Will?"

"What? No. Of course not."

This time I was sure I heard it. Another voice behind his. A female voice.

Across the quad, near McKean Hall, a girl in a white coat stood. I saw another, a boy with dark hair and glasses and a white windbreaker on a bench outside the biomechanics lab. He had a book in hand, but he wasn't turning the pages.

I hung up.

I quickly walked the block and a half to the student union and withdrew all the cash in my account, a little under three thousand dollars.

Two of the people in line wore white coats. I tried not to look at them.

Back in my car, I drove off campus. At one point, I thought I saw a white SUV behind me so I got on 26, followed the highway to Lamont, then pulled a fast U-turn in a Circle K parking lot before doubling back west. They continued east. I kept an eye on my rearview mirror after that, but I didn't see another. I followed 26 back to I-99, then took the highway for about twenty more minutes, getting off in Port Matilda. I stopped at a McDonald's, ordered a Big Mac, large fry, and a Coke, and I sat near a window where I could watch the traffic. I was starving, but as each bite of food hit my acidy stomach, I thought for sure it would come right back up. Somehow, I managed to keep everything down. Although three white vehicles pulled in—a Toyota Camry, a Jeep, and a station wagon—none of the people in them wore white.

I got a room across the street at the Aldean Motor Lodge. The hotel was rundown, at least twenty years past its prime and in desperate need of a coat of paint. The heavyset man with greasy hair behind the counter allowed me to pay for the night with thirty-nine dollars in cash and didn't ask for ID. He gave me the keys to twenty-three and said the room was on the far end of the building. I parked my car in the back so it wouldn't be visible from the street.

The room smelled of stale lemons. The walls were covered in cheap, dark paneling with prints of ancient sailing ships hanging crookedly from nails. The carpet was a shag yellow with hints of brown and orange and worn thin at the door. A note above the television promised free HBO, but the crack running the length of the nineteen-inch tube put an end to that. The bathroom had no door, and the toilet looked like it hadn't been scrubbed since Carter was president.

I sat on the bed for a while, cradled my aching head, and wondered just what the fuck I was doing.

Eventually, I shucked off my clothes and took a shower. I probably stood under the water for nearly an hour as the stink of the cemetery, and the filth of the past thirty-six hours circled the drain and eventually disappeared. After, I dried and changed into the last of my clean clothes.

I'd either have to go home or buy more. I hadn't decided which yet.

The bottle of Jameson sat on the nightstand.

I reached for it, changed my mind.

Fuck.

Not now.

I dropped onto the edge of the bed and blew out a breath. I pulled the two books from my father's grave close.

In the top drawer of the nightstand, I found a Gideon Bible, a pad of paper with Aldean Motor Lodge printed at the top, and a cheap ballpoint. I grabbed the pad and pen and leafed through the Penn State yearbook. I scribbled out a list of the circled people:

Perla Beyham
Cammie Brotherton
Jaquelyn Breece
Jeffery Dalton
Garret Dotts
Kaitlyn Gargery
Penelope Maudlin
Richard Nettleton
Keith Pickford
Emma Tackett
Edward Thatch
Lester Woolford
Elfrieda Leech

I drew arrows connecting my mother's and father's names, then did the same for Stella's parents.

I stared at that list for nearly an hour.

The bottle of Jameson sat on the nightstand.

If I went back to the apartment, Willy would be waiting for me. Maybe Matteo too, at this point. He might have driven up. Maybe the police. Possibly all of them.

The people in white, too.

That's where they'll pick you back up, my mind whispered. *If they lost you at all.*

Cecile Dreher saw me at Leech's door. She may have told the police. If the police knew I was in the room when Elfrieda Leech shot herself, they may be wondering if it was even suicide. I had no motive, no reason to want her dead, but they wanted me. They made that real clear the last time. Police planted evidence, they lied. They'd do what they needed to do to build a case, even a weak one.

At the very least, if I went back, Matteo would find some way to lock me down. Some facility, a thirty-day program. He'd find a jailer much worse than William Trudeau.

The bottle of Jameson sat on the nightstand.

A settled brain is a clear brain, they always say.

Who's *they?* I had no idea.

I couldn't drink. Not now.

I looked back down at the list and realized what I had to do.

I had to find them. All of them.

That's why my father left the yearbook.

Why else?

I left just a little after two in the morning.

6

The Penn State Registrar's office was located in a brick building off Curtin Road between the recreation center and the Pegula Ice Arena. Nancy Vass had worked there for twenty-three years and planned to retire to Boca Raton in two more. She'd miss the students, she wouldn't miss the cold. On the morning of March 15, 1994, when she arrived to work, she found the registrar's office suffered the first and only break-in since the college was founded in 1855. Someone had used a rock to shatter the glass in the door and gain entry. Although they would never determine what, if anything, had been taken, thirteen files were missing from the student records housed along the back wall in the beige file cabinets. One folder belonging to a former guidance counselor named Elfrieda Leech was gone too, this one from the employee records in the back room.

About the same time Nancy Vass was dialing the campus police to report the break-in, I was seventeen miles away at Otto's Buy Here Pay Here lot in Hublesburg, trading my Honda Prelude (and one thousand dollars cash) for a 1989 Jeep Wrangler. For an extra fifty, he sold me a license plate he pulled from a clunker around back.

I wouldn't speak to Willy or Matteo for the next four years.

I'd never set foot back on the Penn State campus.

I hadn't reopened the bottle of Jameson but I would soon enough.

And I'd see Stella again, too—possibly the only certainty left in my life.

7

On the night of August 8, 1994, Detective Joy Fogel stood among the trees behind the bench at South Side Cemetery and waited for Jack Thatch to appear. Five other officers were positioned in various places throughout the cemetery, also waiting for Jack Thatch. She instructed them all to wear plain clothes and attempt to appear as mourners, but she knew they all stuck out, plain as day. Another officer had been positioned in the hallway outside his apartment. The operation hadn't been sanctioned by Pittsburgh PD. She would have never gotten approval for something like this. She couldn't charge him with anything—she had nothing but speculation and bits of circumstantial evidence, nothing that would hold up. Instead, she rolled out the Wall of Weird first thing that morning and simply asked, "Who wants to help today?" There were sneers, jeers, and six volunteers.

Jack Thatch did not appear.

He had not been seen for nearly five months. Not since leaving Penn State for God knew where.

At thirty-eight past one in the morning, she told everyone to go home. The operation was a bust.

She went back to Pittsburgh PD, brewed a pot of coffee, and

waited for the inevitable phone call telling her another body had been found, appearing black and burnt, but not. That call did not come.

There was no body that year.

Nothing in 1995, 1996, or 1997 either.

Turns out, they were looking in the wrong place. Former Detective Terrance Stack, just Terry now, would figure that out, shortly before he died.

August 6, 1998

Twenty-Two Years Old

Log 08/06/1998—

Subject "D" —

Audio/video recording.

DISABLED

—Charter Observation Team - 309

1

On August 6, 1998, Detective Joy Fogel was glued to the television set in the bullpen watching CNN along with all the other detectives. Monica Lewinsky was about to take the stand in the Grand Jury investigation of the President. When Stack called, she answered with five words, "This had better be good."

"Oh, it's good. Get over here."

She found Stack sitting on the concrete steps at his front door sipping on a can of Diet Coke. To the best of her knowledge, he hadn't drank a beer in nearly five years, but something about the expression on his face told her he wanted one. He rose slowly as she got out of the car. Arthritis was taking a toll on him. Back in April, she had brought a cake and the two of them celebrated his eighty-second birthday at their card table in the upstairs bedroom surrounded by the case dominating both their lives. He rattled when he walked that day, and when she asked him why, he pulled a bottle of Aleve from his pocket. "I've been popping these like candy. Easier to carry 'em with me than make the trek up and down the stairs."

Today when he rose and came toward her, he not only rattled but he cringed and pressed the palm of his right hand into his thigh to help straighten the leg out.

"You can get something stronger than Aleve if you go to the doctor, you know."

He held the screen door open for her. "At my age, I'd be worried if things didn't hurt."

Some blankets and a pillow were heaped on the couch in the living room. When Stack caught her looking at them, he told her sometimes it was easier to sleep downstairs.

He took the steps to the second floor slowly, gripping the railing tight. By the time they got to the top, a sheen of sweat had broken out on the back of his neck. Inside the back bedroom, he dropped down into one of the chairs at the card table with a huff.

Fogel tried to convince him to move into a retirement center or, at the very least, find a one-story home, but he wouldn't hear of it. "Walking into a retirement center is no better than a dog heading to the vet to get the needle. It's a one-way trip. I ain't doing it. This here is my home, and I plan to die in it. I just hope somebody finds me before I stink up the place."

The house had always smelled of cigarettes and stale cheese, but Fogel kept that to herself.

Looking up from his chair at the card table, Stack drew in several deep breaths before he finally spoke. "I got a buddy at the Bureau, name of Rudy Geyer. He pulled a big favor for us, but if you ever ask him, he'll deny it. Could get in a lot of trouble. I had him put a flag on Thatch's finances."

"You what?" Fogel dropped into the chair opposite him.

Stack raised a hand. "Completely off the books. Nobody knows."

"But there will be a record somewhere."

"He says he can hide his tracks, and I believe him. He's done it before. Those feds have all kinds of tricks, and I've learned not to ask. Sometimes it's better not to know."

This was a slippery slope. Fogel knew if they learned anything from Thatch's finances and the information was obtained without a warrant, none of the information would be admissible if they charged him. Worse yet, anything that information led to would be purged right along with the finances. She'd seen entire cases tossed by judges because of improper evidence collection.

Stack's yellow eyes fell on her. "Listen, you can ask all you want, but you're not going to get a warrant for his finances. There's nothing to tie him to Bellino. Other than wrong place, wrong time, nothing ties him to the Leech woman's death, and we got nothing that proves it was anything other than a suicide, anyway," Stack said. "The kid's damn clean on paper."

"Brier placed him at the Flack murder."

"Brier placed him at the body," Stack corrected her. "Everything we've got on this kid points to nothing but wrong place, wrong time, all of it." He leaned forward. "And I've got to tell you, the finances give us *something*, which I will explain, but only if you want me to. Before we go there, though, it's important that you know what I found only backs up more 'wrong place, wrong time.' That 'wrong place, wrong time' says something, though. It opens doors."

Fogel closed her eyes and rubbed her temple. "You were far less cryptic when you were a drunk."

"Corner store is only three blocks up the sidewalk. You'll have to make the run, though. I'm not much into distance travel these days, and the hill at Klondike Road is a bitch."

"Not a chance."

He produced a manila file folder from one of the boxes beside him, set it on the table, and rested his palm on top. "I wouldn't bring it up if I didn't think it was important."

Fogel's eyes dropped to the folder. "I'll regret this, won't I?"

"Probably."

"Show me, before I change my mind."

This brought a smile to Stack's face. He opened the folder and slid a stack of stapled pages across to her. "For starters, our boy is rich."

"What?" She studied the document. Some kind of trust.

"When the aunt died, she filled the hopper with insurance policies. We're not sure how she covered the premiums. Rudy's looking into that, 'cause she didn't make much. All told, she left him nearly three million dollars when she passed."

Fogel fell back in her chair. "No shit."

"No shit."

"He doesn't live like a millionaire."

"That attorney of his has him on a tight leash, also at the instruction of his aunt. It's all in the trust. He gets a small allowance, but the bulk of the money is tied up until he graduates from Penn State," Stack said.

Fogel flipped through the pages. "But he dropped out of Penn State."

Stack shrugged. "I didn't say he made sound life decisions, just giving you the facts."

"I suppose he could go back."

"I suppose so," Stack agreed. "Until that time, he collects two thousand dollars per month, deposited right into his checking account, which he can access with an ATM card. His attorney's office covers the bulk of his bills—rents, utilities, and the like, so this is more or less spending money."

"And you followed that spending money?"

Stack nodded. "We followed that spending money."

Using the edge of the table, he rose to a stand and went to a map on the wall. "Each blue tack represents a cash withdrawal since he dropped off our radar four years ago."

Fogel followed him and studied the map. "He's been all over the country."

"That he has."

"What are the red tacks?"

"Those would be our 'wrong place, wrong time' events," Stack said.

"What do you mean?"

He pointed at one in the southern corner of Montana. "August 8, 1994, Billings, Montana. Four people found dead in the hospice ward of St. Francis Hospital. All appearing to be burned beyond recognition, but not really burned. Their sheets, beds, the room itself completely untouched." He pointed to the blue tack next to the red one. "August 23, 1994. Our boy takes twelve hundred dollars out of a bank one block away from the hospital."

"Two weeks later?"

"Yep."

"Where was he before that?"

Stack went back to the table and leafed through the pages in the folder. "Fort Lauderdale, Florida. He took out one thousand on August 9."

"So he was in Florida when those people died?"

"I suppose he could have flown, but yeah, probably."

Stack hobbled back to the map. "There's more. This one here." He indicated another red tack. This one in Iowa. "We've got two hundred acres of corn that went bad overnight, on August 8, 1995."

"Corn?"

Stack nodded. "According to the local sheriff, the entire field looked like someone covered it in gasoline and struck a match. Every stalk was black."

"But not really burned."

"But not really burned," he agreed.

Fogel's eyes narrowed as she stared at the map. "It's always been people."

"Unless we missed something, yeah."

"And where was Thatch?"

"Texas, on August 6. He got to the cornfield on August 10."

"Too fast for a bus, too slow for a plane. He's driving," Fogel pointed out.

Stack pointed at yet another red tack. "August 8, 1996, Chicago. A suspected mugger is found in Grant Park."

"Burned, but not really burned."

"Yep."

"And Thatch?"

"Last withdrawal was nearly a week earlier in Green Bay, Wisconsin. Then another withdrawal on the 9th in Chicago," Stack told her.

Stack went to the last red tack. "Last year. Rye, New Hampshire. A homeless man in Odiorne Point State Park. Body found, same as the others. He had three different wallets on him, so probably some kind of thief. He's still a John Doe, though. Thatch got there two days later. Prior to that, he was in Philly."

"He's chasing these events."

"He's chasing *her*," Stack said.

Fogel turned to him. "You really think it's the girl? All of this?"

Stack turned to the wall with all the past victims. "Every one of these killings happened here in Pittsburgh. Then we got that massacre and house fire in '93. From there on, they're scattered around the country. All these random places." He pointed at the picture of the house in Dormont. "It started here in '78, our first three victims."

"You said yourself, she would have been a baby. One or two, at most. How is that possible?"

Stack ignored her and went on. "Someone snatches her when she's a baby, killed her parents and took her, kept her in that house, here in Pittsburgh. Until that fire. Now she's on the run."

"But she can't stop killing?"

Stack rubbed his chin. "Something about that date. Always August 8."

"How do you explain the cornfield? Nobody died that year. That we know of, anyway."

A flicker entered his eyes. "A lot of corn died, though, didn't it? What if this isn't really about killing but is somehow about 'taking,' *taking life*?"

"What's the difference? I don't follow."

"What if, on August 8 of every year, she has to somehow 'take life,' steal it, feed off the energy, maybe to sustain herself?"

Fogel laughed. "What? Like a vampire or something?"

"Like something, yeah."

"Now I know you're drinking again."

He shrugged and crossed to the stack of file boxes on the far wall with an awkward limp. "All I'm doing is following the evidence. I've been through every one of these coroner reports a dozen times. Aside from the gunshot victims at the house, they all died of the same thing. They were *drained*. Every ounce of liquid gone from the body, every cell dried out, every bit of life *gone*, until we're left with nothing but a dried out husk."

Fogel was staring at the wall again. "Okay, let's suppose you're actually right and not just some crazy old man—"

"Thanks for that."

Fogel went on. "Aside from the first year, we've got single victims from '79 through '92, then in '93 we get the shit show at the house on Milburn, twenty-one bodies in total but only seven burned but not burned, fitting her pattern. What was that?"

"I think somebody went in to put her down, and she used the opportunity to get out."

"Our man in the black GTO."

"Yeah."

"And Brier got caught in the crossfire."

Stack nodded. "Seems so."

The two of them went quiet for a long while as all of this sank in. Then Fogel returned to the map. "The blue tacks are cash withdrawals, right? Look at this. He's been all over the country."

"From what I can tell, he never spends more than a few weeks in the same place," Stack replied.

"Has he been back to Pittsburgh?"

"He hasn't withdrawn any money in or around Pittsburgh, but that doesn't mean he hasn't been here. That attorney of his would probably know, but he's not going to tell us," Stack said.

"Where was the most recent withdrawal?"

"A small town in Nevada called Fallon—last night at 10:38."

"And we've got two days until August 8."

"Yep."

Fogel stared at the map. Thatch is chasing the girl. Fogel's chasing Thatch; had been for years. The definition of insanity is repeating the same thing and expecting a different result. If she wanted to solve this, she needed to get ahead of it. "I've got some airline miles saved up, and I haven't called in sick for three years."

Stack took the bottle of Aleve from his pocket and swallowed two pills with a sip of Diet Coke. "That's my girl."

2

In July of 1998, one week before Fogel would meet with Stack, I woke to a kick in the shin and a not-so-friendly gruff voice coming from an even unfriendlier face staring down at me. "Hey, kid. You can't sleep there."

That statement wasn't altogether true, because I *had* slept right there. I picked up at least three hours of uninterrupted z-time in that very spot before he came along. I considered telling him that, but the fact he wore a uniform zipped my lip. Only a Bryant Park police officer, but a police officer all the same, and in New York the only place worse than spending the night on a bench in the park was spending a night in a cell surrounded by crackheads, drunks, and assorted homeless.

I almost grinned at that particular thought, but grinning would hurt too much. I had no business thumbing my nose at those people. After all, they were *my* people and had been for some time now.

I swung my legs off the side of the bench and pinched my eyes shut against the sharp sun poking through the trees, and the little movement hurt, too. A tiny hammer inside my head gave my temple an exploratory thump, then followed through with a hard-handed pound, another after that. My stomach rolled, followed by a guttural noise that left my mouth tasting like rancid pork and whiskey.

As hangovers went, this was bad, but I've had worse.

I very much needed to take a piss.

When I left Penn State in the spring of 1994, I fell off the wagon.

Let's face it, I never really climbed all the way in. At best, I held onto the back.

It was the damn white coats.

Got to be I saw them everywhere.

Every other car in my rearview was white.

In Richard Nettleton's letter, he mentioned Florida was the worst, and it truly was. Damn near every other car was painted white in the Sunshine State, and while nobody wore a single coat, white shirts and shorts were all the rage. I quickly realized when someone watched you from across the street in a white shirt and shorts, it was no different than a long, white trench coat. I had no idea where they hid their guns, but there was no hiding the look in their eyes—*that look* was universal. They knew me, and I quickly learned to spot them.

I got good at spotting them.

I went to Fort Lauderdale, because according to the file I stole from the Penn State Registrar, the last known address for Perla Beyham was off 17th Street in the heart of the tourist district. An apartment above a tee-shirt shop with a nice view of the beach. She wasn't home when I arrived, on account of being dead. Her neighbor remembered her—not many people drown in a bathtub, so the story took on a life in the building, and most of the other six residents knew about it.

Perla Beyham dropped out of Penn State in the spring of 1979. Nobody knew why. She got a waitressing job at a tiki bar (also on 17th Street) and died about two weeks later. The coroner ruled it an accident—fell asleep in the tub, the report said—there were rumors of suicide. The happy girl who left for college was not the girl who returned. Most blamed her paranoia, her fear of being watched, on drugs, even though nobody had ever seen her take anything. She left work on May 22, 1979, went home, and took a bath, and that was that. They found her body two days later.

The neighbor I talked to, a nice old man named Dave, said some of her belongings might still be down in the building's basement. When I broke in that night, I didn't find anything, and I tossed the place pretty good.

I still owned the Jeep back then and happily left the Sunshine State. I went in search of Garret Dotts next. Garret wasn't too hard to find. His grave sat in the far back corner of the cemetery in Cantonville, Georgia, not too far from Atlanta. The tree where he hung himself in March of 1980 was only a short five-minute drive from where he was buried. A large willow.

I returned to Pittsburgh on August 7 of 1994.

When I spotted Detective Fogel and some of her friends in the cemetery the following night, watching my bench, I remained in the woods, where I could keep an eye on them *and* the bench. I doubted Stella would show—at that point, I wasn't sure she was even alive—but I wanted to be there just in case. At a little after midnight, I was back on the road, and I didn't stop driving until dawn.

More than a week passed before I learned about the four people who died at a hospice in Montana. I ate breakfast at a diner outside Cleveland, and whoever occupied the booth before me left their newspaper folded on the seat. I found the story on page four—not very long, but enough. I knew it was Stella. I *knew*.

The people in white coats knew, too.

They were crawling all over the city by the time I arrived, particularly around the hospice ward at St. Francis. More near the homes where the four people had lived out their lives before entering the hospice. I watched two woman in long, white coats leave the coroner's building and climb into a white Chevy Suburban SUV. One of them made a phone call while the other watched me. When her eyes locked with mine, I knew it was time to leave that city.

It took me nearly six months to track down Penelope Maudlin, and during that time, I lost myself in the Pacific Northwest. Matteo regularly deposited my monthly allowance of two thousand dollars, but I quickly realized the money didn't go very far. I imagined he still paid my rents at both Auntie Jo's apartment and the one I shared with Willy Trudeau at Penn State, but I had to find my own housing on the road, and that proved to be difficult on my shoestring budget.

Two thousand dollars per month broke down to about sixty-five dollars per day. Subtract three cheap meals, and I had about fifty left. The Jeep loved its gas, and that was good for about twenty a day if I stayed on the move, leaving me with around thirty bucks. I found no shortage of cheap, fleabag motels along the backroads, which could be had for thirty dollars. Rooms at hostels, too, but I also needed money for alcohol, and in those early days when I still wasn't of drinking age, obtaining a bottle came at a premium since I had to pay someone to buy it for me. I couldn't sleep without it, though, and without sleep, I couldn't drive, I couldn't think, I couldn't do much of anything. The fog brought on by a nice bottle of whiskey (or the thick haze brought on by Thunderbird, when I was really strapped) got my mind to rest, silenced the screams.

I bought a tent and assorted camping gear in Medford, Oregon, and drove as deep into the mountains and forest of the Umpqua National Park as the Jeep would take me. I sometimes went days without seeing another person, and that was good. People who hiked the trails didn't tend to wear white, either, and that was good, too. I'd venture into Medford or Roseburg or one of the other small towns at the base of the mountains only when it became too cold to camp, when I needed money or supplies, or to visit one of the six public libraries I found nearby. I was at the library in Canyonville on the day I found Penelope Maudlin.

The microfiche machines were located in the far back corner of the library, next to the storage room containing shelves upon shelves of boxes containing film. Aside from the librarian, a nice woman named Melda Dorrell who retired to Canyonville with her husband in 1989, I was alone. Most people were either working or at school in the early afternoon, and I was always careful to get back to my camp before those crowds started to arrive.

Penelope Maudlin was a unique name, and I credit her unique name as the sole reason I found her at all. Her Penn State file listed her home address as Crystal Springs, Illinois, but when I found the house about two months earlier, the windows and doors were boarded up, the roof was gone, and the siding was black and charred from a long-ago fire. From the next-door neighbor, I learned the fire had been electrical, ruled an accident and started in the basement. Penelope's parents had been sleeping, and both perished, unable to get out in time. The fire had been in 1982, the year Penelope graduated from Penn State with a degree in geology. Her Penn State file contained her campus medical records. She first visited the infirmary in September 1978, and her visits increased in frequency up until her graduation. She suffered from acute migraines.

From the microfiche, I learned she took a management job with Brennen Oil in Waco, Texas. The *Waco Tribune* wrote up a short piece on account of her being the first woman to hold the position—notable, particularly at such a young age. She was to start in August 1982.

On her first day, August 8, 1982, she pulled into her assigned parking space at Brennen, got out of her Toyota Camry, retrieved a can of gasoline from the truck, and poured it over the car. As two of her potential coworkers watched in frozen horror, she climbed back inside and lit a match and tossed it onto the hood. The flames engulfed the car. They said she didn't make a sound.

Shortly after learning about Penelope Maudlin's fate, I found myself standing at the center of a blackened cornfield in the middle of Iowa, and I knew Stella had stood in the very same spot two days earlier. I drove straight there from Pittsburgh—I watched our bench from the woods again that year. Detective Fogel had been there too, but she didn't see me.

A year would pass before I would track down Lester Woolford in Green Bay, Wisconsin. He had been cremated, so only ashes remained. His urn held a prime location in Whispering Meadows Cemetery in the top right corner of a building I later learned was called a columbarium. There was a fountain out front. I spent two nights sleeping behind that building—no need for my tent; August nights in Wisconsin were warm. The bottle of Wild Turkey I had on hand made them warmer.

Woolford dropped out of Penn State in the spring of 1979, then disappeared for nearly seven years. At one point, his parents issued a reward and filed a missing person's report, but from what I could find in the local papers, that didn't turn up much of anything. Since he was an adult, the police weren't looking too hard, and the only people chasing the reward were in Green Bay, far from where his body was found in Knoxville on August 8, 1986—about the same time the body of Eura Kapp was discovered in Pittsburgh, burned but not burned.

On the night of August 7, 1986, Lester Woolford checked into room 226 of the Knoxville Motor Lodge off Interstate 275. According to the police report, he was alone and paid for two nights in cash. They think he started cutting himself around two in the afternoon but couldn't really be sure. He continued cutting himself late into the night, possibly until first light. Housekeeping didn't find him until the morning of August 9 on account of the Do Not Disturb sign he placed on his door. The scalpel was still in his right hand. He piled the items he removed from his body neatly to his left. His face was unrecognizable by the time his body finally gave up to shock and loss of blood in those wee hours. The ID in Woolford's wallet was fake. He had matching credit cards, too. The police matched his dental records, though, and in early September, his body was released to his parents, who felt it would be best to have him cremated.

On August 8, 1996, national news picked up the story of a man burned to death in Chicago. I fueled up the Jeep and arrived there a day later. Surely Stella again. White coats everywhere, too. I didn't stay long.

Last year, I held up in a South Philadelphia hostel for the better part of a month before making the drive to Pittsburgh on August 8. Detective Fogel wasn't in the cemetery. Neither was Stella, for that matter. I sat upon our bench until a little after midnight, then I drove back to Philly. I had been attempting to find Cammie Brotherton—she stayed at this same hostel for the summer of 1978, twenty years before me, after dropping out of Penn State. Remarkably, the manager remembered her but had no idea where she went next.

1997 was also the year I turned twenty-one, and the bartender at the Irish Rooster two doors down from the hostel was quick with refills of Guinness and kind enough to throw in a few extra shots with those I bought. I nearly stayed when the television above the bar ran the story about a man's body found burned in New Hampshire. I even ordered another beer. When I went to pay for it, Stella's letter fell from my pocket, and I changed my mind. I said I'd be back, but on the way out the door, I saw a white trench coat hanging on the coatrack.

I had not gone back.

In those years, I often dreamt of Stella. A longing to hold the one thing I never could.

"Move, kid. Don't make me arrest you."

The Bryant Park police was still staring down at me, and I scrambled to my feet before he could kick me again. An empty bottle of Jameson dropped from my coat and thudded down into the grass. Before he could say something, I bent, picked it up, and shuffled over to the nearest trash can. My legs were wobbly, and I was a little light-headed. I hadn't eaten anything since since breakfast yesterday, and that had only been a greasy egg McMuffin.

"I want you out of my park."

"Your park?" Phlegm caught in my throat, and I damn near choked on it before spitting it out and on the sidewalk about an inch from his shoe. I didn't mean for it to land there. I was still groggy, and my aim was off.

He unclipped the leather case on his belt holding his handcuffs.

I took a step back and raised both hands.

"Out of *my* park."

A woman and her daughter both stared at me. The little girl clenched her mom's hand so tightly both their fingers were white.

I sniffled and ran my sleeve over my nose, then started down the sidewalk away from all of them. The New York Public Library loomed ahead of me.

Aside from learning about her stay at the hostel in Philly, I had zero luck tracking down anything on Cammie Brotherton and shelved her for now. I couldn't find anything on Jaquelyn Breece either, so about a week ago I decided to focus on the next name on my list, Jeffery Dalton. I decided to start that search in New York for two reasons—the crowds and the libraries. I could easily disappear among the millions in the city, and the New York public libraries contained the largest collections of national newspapers in the country. I first found Lester Woolford here, Penelope Maudlin, too.

There was a public bathroom on the corner of the library facing West 40th Street. I ducked inside and slid the metal garbage can against the back of the door to get a little privacy, then I stripped out of the flannel shirt and jeans I'd worn for the better part of a week and went to the sink to wash up and brush my teeth. I didn't look at my reflection because I knew it would remind me of the Phillips 66 gas station at exit 63 off I-79 I stopped at after digging up my father's grave, after watching Ms. Leech die, and that image of her spent far too much time in my head as is. Ms. Leech, Andy Olin Flack, and Raymond Visconti jockeyed for the chance to sing me to sleep every night. Lately, a few of the people circled in my father's yearbook vied for that opportunity, too.

None of the clothes in my backpack were clean, but I did find a sweatshirt I'd only worn a couple of times since my last laundromat visit, along with a pair of jeans that didn't smell. I found fresh underwear and one last pair of clean socks. I was grateful for that.

When I deemed myself presentable, I shoved the rest of my belongings back into my backpack and counted the cash in my pocket—two dollars and sixty-four cents. That would not do.

Back outside, I crossed the street to the Wells Fargo Bank, fished out my ATM card, and shoved it into the machine. After selecting English, the display prompted me to enter my four-digit security code. I keyed that in and waited for the withdrawal button to come up. Instead, I received a message I had not seen before:

Please see a customer service representative inside.

A moment later, the screen went back to:

Welcome to Wells Fargo. Please make a selection.

The machine did not return my ATM card. I pressed the Cancel button a few times and nothing happened. I slammed my fist down on the Cancel button and got nothing.

"Fuck."

Someone coughed behind me. I turned and realized there were three other people in line. "I think it's broken," I said, walking past them and through the revolving door into the bank. At the counter, I was told my account had been frozen.

"Frozen how?"

The teller studied her computer screen, hit a couple of keys, and frowned. "You didn't report fraudulent activity?"

"I'm not sure what you mean."

"According to the notes on the account, the account holder reported fraudulent activity the day before yesterday and requested a replacement debit card. That wasn't you?"

Matteo.

The teller at the next window gave her a sideways glance, then looked over at the security guard sitting on a stool near the door.

"I think my attorney might have done it. He's always overstepping his authority over my assets."

The teller's eyes narrowed as she looked me up and down—my greasy hair and filthy clothes. I hadn't shaved in nearly a week. *Your attorney, right.* "I'll need to see your identification," she said.

I opened my mouth to explain, thought better of it, and left the bank.

I found a payphone about a half a block down the sidewalk and picked up the receiver. It took me a minute to recall Matteo's number. I dialed, and a computerized voice asked me to deposit seventy-five cents. I fished the change from my pocket, making a mental note of the few remaining coins.

"Law offices of Matteo, Santillan, Veney, and Carmichael. How may I direct your call?"

Who the hell was Carmichael?

"Tess?"

"Yes."

"This is Jack Thatch."

She went quiet for a moment, and I pictured her lost among the clutter of her desk, clutter that no doubt grew in the past four years. When she finally spoke, her voice was low, nearly a whisper. "My God, Jack. *Where have you been?*"

I cleared my throat and spat on the sidewalk. I had brushed my teeth for nearly ten minutes, and the mint only masked the stale alcohol coating my throat and mouth, like putting a fresh layer of paint over rust. "Is he there?"

I didn't have to say his name. She knew who I meant.

"He's finishing up a call. Hang on a second."

Music filled the line as she put me on hold, but she came back a moment later to add: "It's good to hear your voice, Jack."

"You too," I said, but Bob Seger was already back singing about night moves.

It took nearly six more minutes for Matteo to pick up, and I had to deposit another thirty-five cents. I had sixty-three left in my pocket, maybe a little more in the bottom of my backpack somewhere.

"Jack? Where the fuck have you been?"

I hadn't spoken to Matteo in over four years, not since leaving Penn State. Willy neither. I frankly had no desire to speak to either one. I didn't know what color coat hung in each of their respective closets. I was better off on my own.

"What happened with the bank, Dewitt? I just tried to withdraw my allowance, and the machine ate my card." I had never called him by his first name before, and it felt weird to say it, like calling one of your parents by their first name, I suppose. He needed to know who was in charge, though. I wasn't a kid anymore. He was screwing with *my* money.

"You need to come in, Jack."

"Why?"

"We thought you were dead."

"Well, I'm not."

"Then where are you?"

"Traveling. Seeing the world. Finding myself. Why do you give a shit?"

Matteo cleared his throat. "Four years, Jack. Willy said you went out drinking, scared the crap out of some girl, then vanished. Do you have any idea how many people I've had out looking for you?"

What color coats were they wearing?

"I'm very much alive, and I want what's mine."

"The trust clearly details your obligations to collect. You dropped the ball when you skipped out on college."

I had a copy of the trust and read it numerous times. "The trust requires you to provide me with a monthly allowance of two thousand dollars, plus the cost of my rents and utilities. There is no expiration date on the allowance, and I'm not required to graduate from Penn State within an allocated time. You *are* able to withhold the balance until I do graduate, but you are not allowed to withhold the allowance stipulated in the trust. In fact, by doing so, I have every right to file a compliant with the Pennsylvania Bar."

A recording broke in, then, *"If you wish to continue, please deposit an additional thirty-five cents."*

I dug the change from my pocket and dropped it into the slot.

"Where are you, Jack?" Matteo said as the coins clicked through.

"Doesn't matter."

"You need to come in."

"Release my funds."

Matteo sighed. "Article 5923.216 of the Pennsylvania Trust statute allows me to suspend payments on the trust if I have reason to believe you are deceased, and I'm invoking that right."

"You're talking to me. I may not be at my best, but I can guarantee I'm not deceased."

"I need to see you in person before I can reinstate your monthly payments."

"You can't do that."

"You're not giving me a choice, Jack."

"Who are the people in white coats, Dewitt?"

"Who?"

Even as I spoke, I watched patrons coming and going from the library, the people in the park. Nobody seemed to notice me, though, and that was good. Just another homeless guy on the phone.

"I'll be there in three days."

I hung up before he could respond.

Because of the cost of parking in New York City, I had left my Jeep in the lot of a Walmart Superstore in Trenton, New Jersey. It took me the better part of a day and a half to thumb my way back, but there wasn't much choice in the matter. The Jeep started right up, and with three-quarters of a tank, I'd have just enough gas to get me back to Pittsburgh.

Although the drive from New York City to Pittsburgh was only about six hours, I didn't want Matteo to know where I had been, because I planned to return by the end of the week to continue my hunt for the next name on my list, Jeffery Dalton. Three days was enough time to travel from just about anywhere in the country, and I figured it was best he was kept guessing.

I spent that night in a shelter in Allentown—a cot and a warm meal in exchange for privacy. I took a cot in the corner, where I could watch the others.

I killed the next day at the movies. I saw a lot of movies in those days—one entrance, one exit, and white coats stuck out in the dim light. I snuck in through the employee entrance with a bottle of Jack under my coat and found a seat in the back of the theater. The movie was called *The Truman Show*, starring Jim Carrey. It was about a guy whose every move was filmed and televised, watched by everyone. I didn't much like the movie and fell asleep about halfway through. Back at the shelter that night, they knew I'd been drinking and wouldn't let me in, so I slept in the back of the Jeep behind a Discount Auto.

I arrived at Matteo's office at a little after nine on Monday morning. I parked in the small lot next to his building on Brownsville. I had a fifth of Jack in the glove box. I took a quick sip, enough to take the edge off, then hid the bottle away under my bogus registration and insurance papers. I sat in the Jeep for nearly twenty more minutes before I found the courage to go inside.

Tess looked up as I pushed through the door, the lines of her face drawing tight at the sight of me. "Jack?"

"Hi, Tess."

She stood, took me all in, and I wanted to run back out the door. I had hoped to shower and shave at the shelter, but I had been unable to do either of those things.

Tess hugged me anyway, although I felt her pull away when her nose pressed into my sweatshirt. "You have no idea how worried we've been."

The coat on the back of her chair was black leather.

"Tess, when he arrives, send him to the conference—" Matteo's voice dropped off as he came out of the hallway and caught sight of me. "Holy hell, Jack."

"Nice to see you, too."

Tess stepped back and smoothed the front of my sweatshirt with her palms. "Do you want something to drink?"

Oh, did I.

"I won't be staying long, thank you, though."

I looked up at Matteo. "Conference room?"

He nodded.

I stepped past him, followed the hall, and took my usual seat. I folded my hands on the table in front of me, lowered them to my lap, then back to the table again, this time palms down. They left sweaty wet marks on the polished wood. I put them back in my lap.

Matteo stepped inside and closed the door behind him before taking his usual seat at the head of the table. He lowered himself into the chair with a grunt. "You've lost a lot of weight, Jack. You look thin."

He didn't. He looked like he put on another forty pounds or so.

"I'm alive. You've seen me. What do I need to sign in order to turn my allowance back on?"

"I really thought you were dead, Jack. The way you disappeared. Poor Will didn't know what to do. He said you snapped, blamed himself."

Poor Will. Poor little Willy.

I leaned forward. "*Will* was spying on me."

"He was watching you for me."

"And who are you watching me for?"

"What's that supposed to mean?"

"You collect a nice salary from my trust, as administrator, right? Nowhere in there does it give you the right to police my life…watch me…guide me. None of that. You're supposed to pay a few of my bills and make sure I receive my monthly stipend, that's it. I didn't need a babysitter back then, and I sure as shit don't need one now. All I need is for you to do your job, pay out my money, and leave me the fuck alone."

Matteo didn't flinch. His eyes remained fixed on me. "I made certain promises to your aunt, as a friend, and I plan to follow through on those promises. You're clearly going through a rough patch, and I blame myself for that. I gave you more freedom than I probably should have. I thought you could handle it, but I was clearly wrong."

"Who are the people in the white coats?"

"You said that on the phone. I assure you, I have no idea what you're talking about."

"Do they pay you, too? They do, don't they? They pay you to keep an eye on me. To keep me on a leash."

"Move back into your apartment, Jack. Stay here in Pittsburgh. Let me find you some help, someone to talk to…in confidence. A professional. You've seen so much death, more than anyone should ever deal with in a lifetime, in a hundred lifetimes. It's eating at you. If you'd rather, we can enroll you in a program somewhere. Someplace quiet. Someplace where you can work through all of this and put your life back on track."

"You need to give me my money."

"I can't watch you die."

"Then don't."

I hadn't realized how loud our voices had gotten until we both stopped speaking. The two of us stared at each other for a good long while, then Matteo finally reached into his breast pocket, pulled out an ATM card, and slid it across the table to me. "If I thought forcing you into a program would help, I would do that. I would find a way to do that. But you need to want to get better, and it's obvious you don't. I really hope someday you do. When you're ready, call Tess. You don't need to talk to me if you don't want to, but call Tess. Even if it's just to let her know you're okay every once in a while. You should call Will, too. He graduated last month, twelfth in his class. I think he's going to work with his father. He'd like to hear from you."

I scooped up the ATM card and shoved it into the pocket of my jeans. I left Matteo sitting there at his conference table, his eyes burning into my back.

There was an SUV double parked behind my Jeep.

It wasn't white.

The SUV blocking my Jeep was black, a Cadillac Escalade with windows tinted to the point of being opaque sitting high up on sparkling chrome rims. As I approached, three men stepped out. I recognized the driver—Reid Migliore. I hadn't seen him since our freshman year of high school, but it was him for sure. I didn't know if he graduated, but I knew who he worked for.

Reid kicked at a small rut in the blacktop with the toe of his boot and looked up at me. "He wants to see you."

"I don't give a shit what he wants."

"He says you will. Says it's about the girl."

"What girl?"

"He said you'd probably say that. He told me to tell you, *the* girl. Your girl."

"How'd you find me?"

Reid nodded at a boy in a Steelers sweatshirt and cap riding a bike in circles where Brownsville met Kirkland. "We've got eyes."

"Is he dealing?"

He didn't look much older than twelve or thirteen.

Reid didn't answer. Instead, he climbed back into the Escalade. "Get in. I'll give you a ride. You've got shotgun."

"What about my Jeep?"

"Our boy will watch it for you. It's safe here."

The other two got into the back.

I stood there for a moment, swore under my breath, and got in behind them.

Tess watched us from the small window in Matteo's reception area.

I half expected them to put a hood over my head like the first time I went to see Stella at her house, but they didn't. A Pirates game played softly on the radio—four to one, Pittsburgh—nobody spoke. We took Brownsville to Beck's Run, then made a right on Carson, following the river with the city shrinking behind us. We passed Homestead, Ravine Street, and crossed the Monongahela River right before Whitaker. We came over a hill, and a giant monstrosity of metal loomed over us. There are several abandoned steel mills in and around Pittsburgh. The one in front of us was known as Carrie Furnace, shuttered in 1978. At the entrance, another black Escalade blocked half the road with two men leaning against the hood. Reid nodded at them as we turned and drove past toward the towering, rust-covered complex.

"Is this where he works now?"

"This is where he meets you," Reid said.

We came to a stop at a crumbling brick building with several round metal stacks rising from behind, surrounded by catwalks and smaller structures. A maze of metal. The waist-high grass and weeds climbed over everything, slowly reclaiming the land. A small, crooked sign hung above the brick building's door, reading Blast Furnace #7.

Reid shifted into park and killed the engine. "Come on."

I followed him into the building, with the other two trailing about ten feet behind us.

There was no door. As we stepped inside, the temperature dropped at least ten degrees, and the light waited outside—a patch at the door and nothing else. It took a moment for my eyes to adjust. I sneezed. The air was heavy with dust, smelling of damp corrosion.

Someone set up a card table in the center of the room. Three men stood behind it, four others further back in the shadows. None of them made any attempt to conceal the guns tucked into their waistbands.

There were two chairs at the table; one empty, the other occupied by Duncan Bellino.

The last time I saw Dunk was on television, five years earlier. Several men were loading him and his wheelchair into a Dodge Durango after making bail on multiple drug trafficking charges he would later beat. He had been thin, horribly so, a shadow of the person I once knew. He filled out since then. His arms looked like tree trunks. He wore a Mötley Crüe tee-shirt. A black tattoo inched out at the base of his neck. I couldn't tell what it was.

"Remember when we came here? You, me, and Willy? We were what, ten or eleven?"

We had been twelve. About three months before the great chase down Nobles Lane. Willy slipped on one of the catwalks and got a nice scrape down his right arm. He spent the next month hiding it from his mom while Dunk and I tried to convince him the tetanus shot he got the previous summer was only good for two weeks and he'd have lockjaw soon.

As Dunk looked up at me from the table, I heard Gerdy's laugh in my head, I heard Krendal shouting for me to bus table twelve. I thought about all the people who died the day of the diner fire, and I thought about the one who didn't. I wanted to jump over the table, wrap my hands around his neck, and choke every ounce of life out of him. Squeeze until his eyes bulged and went cloudy. He shouldn't be here, and I was the reason he was.

He stood, a little wobbly, but he stood. I hadn't noticed the cane leaning against his chair. He gripped the handle in his right fist, supporting himself, favoring his left leg. Even through his jeans, I could tell the left leg was thinner than the right, perched at an odd angle.

Dunk slammed the palm of his hand down on the table. The smack echoed off the metal walls. "Look at you, my hero! He who cannot die! I told my boys all about you—shot at by robbers when you were what—eight, nine? Run over by your girlfriend's SUV couple years after that, hell, you've even walked through fire. Every time, not a scratch! You can't even drink yourself to death, and from what I've heard, you've been working hard at it. I can see that one in your eyes. Funny, after all you've been through, it's the booze that leaves a mark. Can always tell a drunk by their eyes." He shrugged. "We've all got our demons, I suppose. Turns out, I ain't got so much luck, not like you. I'm a damn bullet magnet. That day at the diner, Alonzo plugged me five times—shoulder, chest, gut...the two to my leg did the most damage, though. One of 'em is still in there. The docs couldn't fish the damn thing out, said removing it could increase my nerve damage, limit muscle mobility." He waved a hand around. "They told me I'd never walk on this leg again. I told 'em they were wrong about that. Then I had to show 'em 'cause nobody believed me. Took a couple years, but no wheelchair anymore," he said behind a grin. "We had a little party and pushed that thing over the side of Hot Metal Bridge."

"Good for you."

"Guess we're both a little hard to kill, bounce back from adversity, and all that." He dropped back down into the chair and lowered the cane to the floor. "Take a seat, Jack."

"I'm fine right here."

One of the men behind the table stepped toward me, but froze when Dunk glanced at him. Dunk reached behind his back and pulled out a small gun. He smiled thinly at it, then set the weapon on the table, gave it a tap with his finger so it spun in a half-circle. "Remember this gun?"

I did. His father's .38. I think I memorized every millimeter of it the day I brought the gun with me to the bench in the cemetery all those years ago. The .38 seemed so big back then, like a cannon.

"I always figured my pops would eat this gun. Remember how he used to hide it? We'd have to climb up on chairs and boxes just to get it down. That last year, it got to the point where he just left it lying around the house. I found it in the bathroom once, on the floor next to the shitter. He'd been in there for over two hours before that, then just came stumbling out and dropped onto his bed. I figured he was shooting up. He'd been doing that. I wasn't sure when he started. I went into the bathroom to make sure he didn't leave his needles on the floor, because he had done that too, and I damn near stepped on one in the middle of the night when I went to take a piss. Didn't find any needles that day, just this gun on the floor. I must have stared at the gun for an hour, wondering how close I came to finding him dead. I started hiding it, different places around the apartment, but he always found it. Then *I'd* find it again, in some weird place—the bathtub, in the refrigerator, in the microwave. Sometimes right out in the open on the kitchen table or the counter. This was around the same time I was helping you with your aunt. God, I loved that woman, closest thing to a mom I ever had. I thought about hiding the gun at your place, even did once, but I'll be damned if this peashooter didn't turn back up a few days later in the middle of the floor in my apartment. I always meant to ask if you found it and put it there..."

I shook my head.

"Another one of life's great mysteries, I suppose," Dunk went on. "When he started doing the heroin around the clock, I gave up on hiding the gun and I started leaving it right out in the open. Figured if he was going to kill himself, best to give him the opportunity to do it fast. He went with the needle, though, the sad fuck." He leaned forward, his breath smelled of onions. "I've known a few to eat a gun over the years. I heard you joined the club, too. That crazy woman from across the hall a few years back, what was her name?"

"Leech, Elfrieda Leech."

"Yeeeeeaaah." He drew the word out, like an exhale. "Who'd a thunk it? Takes balls to eat a gun. Don't know if I could go out like that." He turned toward one of the guys standing behind the table, big enough to be a linebacker. "What about you, Truck? Think you could swallow a bullet?"

His head swiveled on his shoulders. Someone forgot to give him a neck. "Not me, boss. I'd go with pills. Maybe in a nice, warm bath. Take a handful and nod off. That's the way to go, nice and peaceful."

"Not so nice for the guy who's got to pull your fat, naked ass out of the tub, though, huh?" Dunk laughed. "Gotta think about those you leave behind. Time keeps on slippin', slippin', slippin', into the future..." He sang this last bit, his eyes closed. "Great echo in here. Love me some Steve Miller Band." His eyes snapped open, and he nodded at the empty chair again. "Take a seat, Jack."

This time I did sit. The door seemed awfully far away.

Dunk retrieved a folded sheet of paper from his back pocket. He placed it on the table next to the gun and smoothed it out.

My poster of Stella with the words *Have you seen me?*

A grin filled his face. "I found your girl. Wasn't easy, but I found her. She hasn't gone by Stella Nettleton since that house of hers burnt down. Probably used at least a dozen names since, wouldn't you say, Reid?"

Reid nodded. "At least. Bounced all over the country, too."

"Why are you looking for her?"

"Because you're my best friend, Jack. That's what friends do. They help each other."

"We're not..." The words trailed away, and I regretted saying them out loud the moment they left my lips. I caught a quick glance from Reid to the large guy Dunk called Truck.

The smile fell from Dunk's face, and he slouched back in his chair. "You still blame me for the diner, don't you? For the shit Alonzo pulled? I told you I had nothing to do with it. Alonzo wanted Crocket dead, simple as that. I took five fucking bullets that day and nearly died. He turned me into a fucking cripple. If that was all part of some elaborate plan, it sure as shit wasn't a very good one. If I wanted to take out Crocket, I would have done it myself. I would have knifed him, I would have wanted to watch the life leave his face, up close. None of that cowardly Godfather's tommy-gun execution bullshit. Killing innocent people, people I loved, my friends. I wouldn't do that. I wouldn't sanction that. I had nothing to do with it."

"Alonzo was a shit," Reid muttered. "Not a smart one, either. He was screwing with Crocket, dipping into funds and lining his own pockets. Crocket found out, planned on going after him. Alonzo panicked and acted first. Acted stupidly."

Dunk leaned forward, looked me directly in the eye. "I. Wouldn't. Do. That."

My stomach churned, and my mouth filled with the taste of Jack Daniel's from earlier. I should have brought the bottle with me. I couldn't look at him. My eyes dropped to the poster of Stella.

"Where is she?"

Dunk sighed. "Tell me you believe me."

"I believe you. Where is she?"

"That didn't sound very sincere, Jack."

I shook my head, stood, and nearly knocked the table over with my knees. "I'm not doing this."

Truck dropped a hand on my shoulder before I could take a step. He pushed me back down into the chair. "Sit."

Dunk waved a hand at him, and the large man released my shoulder. "Fine, Jack. You don't have to say it right now, but think about it. Spend a little time on it, and you'll figure out the truth. You're a smart guy, and you know me. You know me better than anyone else."

At one point, that was probably true. Not anymore, though. This wasn't the kid I grew up with. He became some kind of thug. I followed enough of the local news to know he took over all of Crocket's endeavors, just like the detectives said he would. He ran the local drug trade, probably prostitution and gambling, too. Even if what he said were true, and Alonzo Seppala had killed Crocket on his own, only Dunk benefited. More importantly, Gerdy, Krendal, and the others would still be alive if Dunk hadn't gotten wrapped up in this world in the first place. Whether or not he pulled the trigger, their deaths were the result of his decisions and actions.

"You look like you need a drink," Dunk said. "Somebody get him something."

"I'm fine."

His grin returned. "Like I said, we've all got our demons. You can either hide from them or embrace them. Either way, though, they're right there, one step behind, maybe, but always on our heels."

"Cut the shit, Dunk. If you know where she is, tell me. If not, I'm leaving."

Dunk placed both hands on top of his father's gun and folded his fingers. "We're going to try a little experiment first."

Dunk popped out the .38's cylinder with his thumb, then turned the gun to the side. The bullets spilled out onto the table. He replaced one, gave the cylinder a spin, and locked it back in place.

"You can't be serious."

Dunk's grin narrowed. "You want that drink now?"

Truck was smiling, Reid was not. The other guys were unreadable, stone statues.

Dunk set the gun back down in the center of the table. "He who cannot die, my hero."

I glared at him. I wouldn't look down at the gun. "Not a chance."

"Crocket taught me many things before he died, but you know what my first lesson was? The very first thing he told me? Everything is a commodity. Booze, drugs, cigarettes, girls, gambling. If somebody wants something, you can attach a price tag to it. That price may vary by consumer, but *everyone* will pay. He also told me information can be one of the most lucrative commodities because it can be gotten for very little and offered at top dollar, to the right buyer, of course. Unlike some of the other items I mentioned— booze, drugs, cigarettes, girls—the core of Crocket's original business, I took something else away from that conversation. It's extremely difficult for the law to charge you with the purchase, possession, or sale of information. I knew at that point, at the ripe old age of sixteen, information was the future. I knew if I ever had the opportunity to run this business, I would shift the focus, find a way to deal in this unique commodity above all others."

"If you know where she is, just name your price. I've got it. I can have cash to you within an hour."

"I heard about your good fortune. Gave me another reason to like that woman. Your aunt wasn't just tough, she was smart to set you up like that." Dunk picked up one of the bullets and twirled it between his fingers. "I don't want your money, though. I've got plenty of money. I want information."

"What could I possibly know that would be of use to you?"

He set the bullet back down on the table, standing it up. A little tower of brass. "I want to know why you're alive, after all you've been through, and I want to know why everyone who gets close to your little girlfriend is not."

"You said it yourself, it's blind luck. Or maybe stupidity, for putting myself in those situations in the first place."

"I don't think it's either of those things."

"What else is there?"

He nudged the gun toward me. "I want you to put the barrel in your mouth and pull the trigger."

"No way."

"You can spin the cylinder yourself, if you want."

"No."

"You're drinking yourself to death. Why waste time? That's all my father ever did. He dragged it out. This would have been so much easier on everyone."

"I'm not suicidal."

"Reid."

At the mention of his name, Reid pulled a 9mm from a pancake holster in his jeans and pointed it at me. His thumb clicked off the safety.

"If you don't do it," Dunk went on, "Reid here will. He has one shot in the chamber, always does. He's a Boy Scout like that. He's got thirteen more in the clip. I've seen him hit guys running from twenty yards. From three feet away, he's got zero chance of missing you. So, I'm giving you a choice. He shoots you, or you take a one-in-six chance with the revolver. Either way, we get to see how lucky you really are. Information. Valuable information."

"I saved your life," I said.

"You did, and I'm forever grateful for that."

I looked down at the gun.

Dunk was serious. Reid, too. I think Reid was itching for the chance to put a bullet in me.

My fingers wrapped around the gun's grip. I took the .38 in my hand and picked it up. "How did you find her?"

"I have people everywhere. Nobody can hide from me. She was tough, but I've found tougher."

The gun felt cold to my touch, lighter than I remembered. "Cammie Brotherton, Jeffery Dalton, Jaquelyn Breece, or Keith Pickford."

"Who?"

I looked up at him. "I do this, and you help me find them, too. Cammie Brotherton, Jeffery Dalton, Jaquelyn Breece, and Keith Pickford. They went to Penn State with my parents."

Dunk smiled again. "I think I can—"

Spinning in my chair, I pointed the .38 at Reid's chest and pulled the trigger.

There were two audible clicks.

The first came from the .38 in my hand as the hammer came down on an empty cylinder. The second click came from the gun in Reid's hand as the 9mm failed to fire in return.

I jumped up from the table and slammed the .38 into his hand, smashing his fingers. This time, the 9mm did go off. The bullet went wide and clicked off metal somewhere deep in the shadows.

Dunk was up too, his bad leg shaking under the sudden weight. "Holy shit! Did you see that! Did you see that?"

I stepped back from all of them and pointed the .38 at Reid's face. "Drop it!"

"Holy shit. I can't believe that!" Dunk said. "Do it, Reid. Drop the gun."

"I've got him dead center."

"It won't work."

"Bullshit."

I pulled the trigger—the .38 hit another empty cylinder.

Reid fired again, too. A hollow *click*.

"The .38 is empty, Jack," Dunk said. "I palmed the bullet, see?" He held up a brass casing. "Holy shit. I didn't think you'd really do it, but just in case you did, I couldn't let you shoot yourself!"

Reid and I both stared at his gun.

Dunk's eyes landed on the 9mm, too. "That one, though. I didn't touch. Holy shit. Put it away, Reid. Holy shit, is my ticker racing right now!"

Reid reluctantly lowered the gun, thumbed the safety back on, and placed the 9mm back in his holster. His face flushed with anger.

Dunk steadied himself with his cane and came around the table. He took a folded sheet of paper out of his pocket. "She's here. I don't know for how long, though."

I took the note and studied the address. "Are you sure?"

He nodded. "I'll see what I can do on those other names. You've earned it. My boys will take you back to your car." He started toward the two Escalades parked outside. "Holy shit," I heard him say again. "My boy, Jack Thatch. Can't believe you actually pulled the trigger." He laughed. "He who cannot die pulled the trigger, my hero."

3

Dewey Hobson had eluded him.

David Pickford was willing to admit that.

To grow as a human being, it was important to understand your limitations, your mistakes, and even your failures. And he had failed to find Dewey Hobson in the four years since deciding to do so. In his defense, the Charter files on Hobson were thin, not like the others. There were false leads, too. When Elfrieda Leech graciously told him Dewey Hobson was hiding in Tennessee about halfway between the Great Smoky Mountains and the Cumberland Plateau outside of Mascot, she fully believed he was there. She wasn't wrong about that. Dewey Hobson had been there, for nearly six years. He called House Mountain his home. But when David and his team arrived four years ago, in April of 1994, he had moved on, leaving nothing behind but an empty two-room cabin, some old dishes, and a few burnt out logs in the hearth.

Hobson learned to live off the grid, and this was largely to blame for Charter's inability to locate him for nearly twenty years.

Even if someone uses false identification, they leave recognizable patterns behind.

A man who loves to eat tuna sandwiches doesn't stop loving

tuna sandwiches just because he changed his name once or twice. Spending patterns were like fingerprints, and an analysis of spending patterns through bank records and credit histories was a fairly simple process for Charter. This was how they found some of the others.

Tracking someone with no bank accounts, no credit history, no utilities in today's modern world proved to be another animal altogether. Some would say it was an impossibility. If a man learned to live completely off the grid, he left no trail, no fingerprints, he became a ghost. And that was completely true. Dewey Hobson eluded them, eluded *him* because of this. That was until a few months ago, when David had a realization—rather than focus their search on where Dewey Hobson might have gone and done, focus the search on where he might go, what he might do, once he got there. While this was a large country filled with vast amounts of wilderness, there were only so many places where someone could live off the grid but still be relatively close to civilization to purchase supplies.

In college at Penn State, Dewey Hobson had been an avid reader. David suspected this was partly why Hobson chose to live off the grid. If he could pass his time with nothing more than a good book for company, and be happy, he could live in a hole in the ground with a thatch roof and be perfectly comfortable. Much like the man who ate tuna sandwiches, though, Hobson's reading patterns *off grid* would be the same as his reading patterns *on grid*, and that was where David told Charter to focus their efforts when he took it upon himself to find the last few original test subjects and put them down like the expired lab rats they were. Most believed libraries didn't track the books checked out by their patrons due to privacy concerns. That was only partially true. Libraries did track this information, but they kept the data private, safely tucked away in computer databases accessible only to employees and the most skilled of hackers. Charter employed its share of skilled hackers, and these databases were, well, an open book.

As a kid, a teenager, and later an adult, Dewey Hobson had been an avid reader of Agatha Christie, Robert Ludlum, and Philip K. Dick. He also read every Western by Louis L'Amour. Hobson wasn't alone in his love for these particular authors. They wrote some of the most popular books in existence. However, this odd combination of suspense, science fiction, and Westerns *was* different. Most people stuck to one genre, maybe two. Few read this broadly.

When Charter began monitoring for individuals checking out library books by all four of these authors, they found Dewey Hobson the first time, hiding in Carte Del Playa, New Mexico. He moved on by the time David arrived there in 1996, but they soon found that same pattern at a library outside Waitsburn, Vermont. They nearly got him there. Waitsburn was so close. David probably missed him by a week, maybe two at most. That was a little over a year ago.

In May of this year, the pattern appeared yet again at the Eureka Public Library, just outside of Trego, Montana. Although a tiny library, they installed security cameras two years prior, and it took little effort for Charter to hack the feed and begin surveillance. Twenty years passed since the last known photograph of Dewey Hobson, but there was no mistaking him on the library camera feed. It was the large forehead. Hobson's forehead was freakishly big. Even with the trapper's hat, long hair, and beard, they spotted him rather easily. David dispatched a team shortly after that. They documented his movements, got pictures of his gray Ford Bronco, and learned where he lived. Each time he came to town from his small cabin on Marl Lake, they learned a little more.

Dewey Hobson would elude him no more.

David told Oliver and the others to wait back at the cars. He didn't need them. Frankly, the last thing he needed was half a dozen people traipsing through the woods behind him, creating some kind of ungodly racket. Hobson's cabin was nearly a mile hike from the closest logging road. As expected, they found Hobson's Bronco hidden under camouflage netting within a cluster of trees just off that logging road. David told everyone to stay put and he'd go in alone. When he found the first tripwire, he was glad he did. One of his subordinates would have certainly triggered the trap. He found three more before he spotted the cabin.

At the center of a small clearing, the log cabin sat back about fifty feet from the lake shore. At best, the hand-built structure was only about four hundred square feet, but this actually made it larger than the one they found in Waitsburn. Firewood was stacked high on the side of the cabin, smoke trailed up from the stone chimney, and a rocking chair sat on the porch looking out over the water.

The rocking chair swayed slowly from back to front.

There was no wind.

The water was still.

Someone had just been sitting there.

David heard the *cler-chunk!* of someone chambering a shotgun round a few feet to his left.

"Hi, Dewey." David said the name, careful not to sound threatening, then realizing it was virtually impossible to sound threatening while saying a name like Dewey. "This is a lovely place. So peaceful, all the way out here. I can see why you're drawn to it."

Dewey Hobson stepped out of the woods, keeping a safe distance. He most likely figured if he got too close, David would try to grab the barrel of the shotgun, maybe wrestle the weapon away from him. Of course, David had no need for such physical theatrics. He'd humor the man, though. There was no reason to upset him.

"I'm David Pickford."

"Keith Pickford's kid?"

David nodded.

"That supposed to comfort me somehow?"

It clearly hadn't. Hobson took a step back. "I know all about your parents. Heard about it back when it happened. Get on your knees."

"You're a difficult man to find."

"You got no business looking."

David smiled at him. "You're making me nervous, Dewey. How about you point that shotgun at the ground?"

"Okay." Hobson lowered the barrel.

Hobson's forehead puckered, and he raised an eyebrow. He wasn't sure why he lowered the gun, he only understood that he had. When he tried to raise the shotgun again, his hand, his arm, both disobeyed. The gun remained limp at his side.

"Why don't we go inside? We've got some catching up to do."

"Okay."

"Bring the shotgun."

"Okay."

The cabin was sparsely furnished but pleasant. No television or radio. Oil lamps rather than electric lights. A makeshift kitchen occupied the westernmost wall with a wood-burning stove in the corner. Hobson must have recently stoked the logs because several burned bright orange, filling the room with warmth. There was a round table next to the stove surrounded by three chairs, the top piled high with books, magazines, and assorted junk. The surface in front of one of the chairs was clear. David imagined Dewey Hobson took his meals there, with no one for company but the voices shouting in his head. The opposite wall housed a bed and a small writing desk. The door to the bathroom stood open. David noted the tiny space only contained a toilet and a sink.

"Where do you shower, Dewey?"

"I wash in the lake."

"That must be nice."

"It's cold, most of the time."

Although Hobson's clothing was old and in dire need of a good seamstress, he didn't appear filthy. His beard was thick but well maintained. He could use a haircut, but the mop on his head wasn't to the point of unruly. His heavy boots were sturdy and looked nearly new.

David gestured to the chair at the clear spot of the table. "Take a seat, Dewey."

Hobson lowered himself into the chair, cradling the shotgun in his lap.

David pulled out the chair next to him and sat down too, eyeing the books. "Do you have a favorite?"

Hobson didn't hesitate. "*The Murder of Roger Ackroyd* by Agatha Christie. Terrific ending, and probably one of the best twists ever written."

"I haven't read that one."

"You should."

"Do you know why I'm here?"

"I imagine you plan to kill me."

Hobson said the words so casually, his hands remaining folded loosely over the gun.

"You should have died a long time ago."

"I suppose."

"After you took the shot."

Hobson said nothing to this, only looked down at the shotgun.

David sighed. "I always thought it was strange they gave the shot to you. Your file says you had no special skills, no precursors, nothing to really warrant your inclusion in the experiment at all, yet there you were, right along with the others. Did you have any kind of reaction, Dewey? After they gave it to you?"

Dewey Hobson began to sweat. His mouth twitched, but he said nothing.

"It's rude to ignore your guests, Dewey. Did you have a reaction?"

Hobson didn't want to answer. David saw the pain and confusion in his eyes when the words came out anyway.

"Before the shot, I could hear electricity. This constant humming everywhere. It got much worse after."

David leaned back in his chair and folded his fingers together. "That's remarkable. Is that why you have no electronics here?"

Hobson nodded. "Too fucking loud. It hurts sometimes. Buzz, buzz, buzz. Hard to think, harder to sleep. Quiet here."

"Sounds like a lonely life."

"Not much choice in the matter."

David tapped the end of the shotgun. "Tell me, Dewey. If you put that barrel in your mouth, are you able to reach the trigger or is the gun too long?"

"Dunno."

"Why don't you try?"

"Okay."

Hobson picked up the long weapon, turned it so the barrel pointed at his face, then wrapped his lips around the end. His hands slipped down the barrel to the stock, then found the trigger guard. It was a stretch, but he could reach.

"That's good, Dewey. You can take it out. I have a few more questions for you."

Hobson removed the gun, set the weapon back on his lap, then wiped his lips with the back of his sleeve.

"Did you ever have any children, Dewey?"

Hobson shook his head.

"Are you sure? A player like you?"

"I'm sure."

"Why not?"

"Because they wanted the children. I couldn't."

"Couldn't what?"

"Give them my children."

"The children you never had."

Hobson said nothing.

"Because if you did have children, and somehow didn't tell me, didn't tell *us*, that would be bad."

The sweat at his brown began to trickle down. "I don't have children."

"I believe you, Dewey," David said, although not quite convinced it was really true. "There's something else I need you to tell me, something really important. Do you think you can do that?"

"Yeah."

"I need you to tell me where I can find the others."

"You killed the others."

"Not all of them. The last few have been slippery, like you." David leaned forward. "Where are they, Dewey?"

Hobson began to shake, his face turning red. He didn't want to, but he spoke anyway. "I only know where Cammie is. And she may not be there no more. She likes to stay on the move."

"How do you stay in touch?"

Hobson said nothing.

"Dewey…"

"Dalton tracks all of us, helps us organize."

"And where can I find Dalton?"

"Dunno," Hobson said. "I never know where Dalton goes."

"Where is Cammie?"

Hobson told him.

David leaned back in his chair. He liked the smell of the burning wood, the heat from the fire. He found the atmosphere comforting, relaxing. "Did you like my parents, Dewey?"

"Your mother was nice. A little shy, but nice. Nobody really liked your father, though. He was a real jerk."

"It's not nice to say mean things like that, to speak ill of the dead."

Hobson said nothing.

David tilted his head. "Do you think I'm a good-looking guy, Dewey?"

"No."

The answer stung, but David had heard it before. More times than he cared to count. He glanced down at the shotgun…almost time. "I'm a beautiful man. Probably the best-looking man you've ever seen or will see."

"You're a beautiful man, David Pickford."

"That's better."

David stood and hunted through the books on the table until he found *The Murder of Roger Ackroyd*. A fine first edition, bound in leather with gold leaf on the edges. "This is your favorite book? The best one here?"

Hobson nodded.

David tossed the book through the open door of the wood stove. The topmost log crackled and split under the new weight. Flames crawled around the sides and began to chew at the leather. "Go ahead and put the shotgun back into your mouth, Dewey."

Hobson did.

David planned to watch the man kill himself. He rarely got the opportunity to watch, but then he got an idea.

A much better idea.

4

Eastern Airlines flight 5091 touched down in Reno, Nevada, at twenty-three minutes past six on the night of August 8, 1998. Detective Joy Fogel sat at the window in row eighteen, with an elderly woman knitting in the seat beside her and a business man buried in notes at the aisle.

At Reno Airport, she rented a Toyota Camry at the counter, retrieved her gun and shoulder rig from her checked bag before stowing the suitcase in the trunk, then followed the signs to I-80 East, then US-50, arriving in Fallon, Nevada, at a little after eight.

The temperature was insanely hot. Even with the sun down and the air conditioning at full, her back was soaked with sweat, sticking to the leather car seat. She made a mental note never to return to the state of Nevada in the summer.

Never.

Like most small towns in Nevada, Fallon grew out of the desert and looked like it could return to the sand if someone broke the tap or shut off the water for more than an hour. Alfalfa fields surrounded the outskirts of town, adding to the "carved out" feel. The main street (aptly named Main Street) was a series of one and two-story buildings that might easily double for the set of a Wild West movie, had the road not been paved.

She found a small diner at the center of the town proper, took a booth near the back, and ordered a cheeseburger, fries, and a large Coke. From her purse, she retrieved the Nokia cell phone Stack had given her before she left Pittsburgh, and powered the contraption on. She tried calling him twice from the road, and both times she had no signal. Since the battery didn't last long, it seemed best to keep it powered off. When the display came to life, she had two bars. She hit number one on the presets. Twenty seconds passed before the call connected.

"Stack."

"Are you sure about this?" Fogel said. "There's not much out here."

"Where are you now?"

She told him.

"Did you ever see the movie *Top Gun* with Tom Cruise and Kelly something?"

"Kelly McGillis."

"Whatever. The real *Top Gun* training facility moved from Miramar, California, to the naval air station just outside of Fallon two years ago, a little south of town. That base keeps the town alive. The place you're heading is about halfway between town and the airfields off I-118."

"And you think he's there now?"

"Thatch withdrew another three hundred from the same ATM machine last night at a little after ten—that's two nights in a row at about the same time. Got no reason to believe he's anyplace else. I've got some buddies watching the cemetery here in Brentwood just in case, but my gut says he's out there."

Fogel popped the last bit of her burger into her mouth and followed it with a sip of Coke. "I'll let you know what I find."

"Are you dressed like a cop? You'll probably want to change."

Fogel glanced at her dark blue button-down blouse and black slacks. "What do you suggest? I've never been to a place like that."

"Something casual."

"Casual, got it."

"Not sexy."

"Good-bye, Stack."

Stack said something else before the call dropped, but she couldn't make it out. Even with two bars, reception wasn't good. She noted nearly a quarter of the battery was gone now, too. *These things will never replace a solid landline*, she thought to herself before powering down the Nokia and dropping it back into her purse.

She got the check, left cash on the table, and stepped back out into the oven that was the Nevada night.

Fogel spotted the purple neon glow on the horizon long before she saw the squat building set back from I-118 about three miles outside Fallon. She had passed a rundown motel about a mile back, but other than that, there was nothing else out here. She supposed even in a town like Fallon, it was best to keep these kind of places outside the city limits. With a naval base this close, there would be these kind of places.

A large purple neon sign signaled the turn from the highway for Mike's Gentlemen's Club, but the marker wasn't necessary. She simply followed the line of cars. Once in the parking lot, employees dressed in tuxedos tried to wave her into the valet line, but she opted to circle around them toward the back of the building. If she needed to leave in a hurry, she wanted to have the car keys handy and the vehicle someplace accessible.

She changed into jeans and a white tank top in the back seat of the car, then followed the line of men in naval uniforms around to the front of the building. Air conditioners must have been working overtime, because the temperature dropped at least twenty degrees the second she stepped through the double doors. She considered going back out to the car to change into something with sleeves, then changed her mind—she didn't plan to stay long.

Signs stated a twenty-dollar cover charge, but apparently that was only for men—she was handed ten free drink vouchers and ushered inside at no cost, where it took a moment for her eyes to adjust. Aerosmith's "Walk This Way" belted from unseen speakers and laser lights cut through the dark, sliding over multiple stages and dozens of tables scattered throughout the space—a space which was much larger on the inside than it appeared from the parking lot. On each of the stages, many of the tables, and strolling randomly about were beautiful women in various stages of undress. Some were completely nude while others wore skimpy bathing suits or lingerie. There were a couple female patrons, but not many, and Fogel felt incredibly out of place.

Men packed every square inch of open space. About two-thirds wore military uniforms. Others were in casual dress. Several wore three-piece suits, and Fogel assumed they were security. She went to the bar and ordered a vodka and cranberry. The bartender handed her the drink, waving off the voucher when she tried to hand it to him. She dropped them into her purse and scanned the crowd. While some tables and chairs surrounded the stages, most were tucked into small alcoves and hidden behind walls that served no purpose other than to create privacy. As Fogel scanned the ceiling, she realized that privacy was only an illusion—there were cameras everywhere, each equipped with infrared sensors in order to see in the dark. Somewhere, somebody was watching everything.

A deejay announced Heaven was to report to the main stage, while Tori and a few of her friends could be found in the champagne lounge. Aerosmith made way for Guns N' Roses and "Sweet Child O' Mine." Three guys did a round of shots to her left, shouting over the music.

Drink in hand, Fogel began pushing her way through the crowd. Some of the women smiled at her, others sized her up—glancing up and down her body as blatantly as some of the men. Never in her life had she wanted a shower as much as she did at that moment.

She found Jack Thatch at a table in the far back corner, tucked behind a wall of fake plants on one side and a hallway on the other appearing to lead toward the women's dressing rooms. She nearly didn't recognize him—his hair was askew and he hadn't shaved in days, maybe as long as a week. It had been years since she last saw him, and those years had been harsh. Although he had a clear line of sight to one of the stages, he wasn't watching the thin blonde girl wrapped around the brass pole. His gaze was fixed on the shot glass cradled between his fingers.

Fogel crossed the room and set her drink down on his table. "Mind if I sit?"

He didn't look up at first and she nearly repeated herself, assuming he hadn't heard her over the music. When he did look up, his eyes didn't register the surprise she had expected. Instead, they looked sad and dull. If he wasn't drunk, he was well on his way.

He swallowed the shot, placed the empty glass on the corner of the table, and gestured to one of the empty chairs. "You're a long way from home, Detective."

Fogel sat facing him, her purse resting in her lap. "You're a tough man to find, Jack."

"I try." He nodded at a passing waitress. She spotted the empty glass, winked at him, noted Fogel's glass was still full, then headed toward the bar. An unspoken language.

He looked back toward the entrance. "Did you just come in?"

Fogel nodded.

Jack leaned forward. "How many white cars did you see in the parking lot?"

"White cars? I don't know. Why?"

"There was only one a few days ago. I counted three when I got here tonight. I need to check again."

His speech was slightly slurred, not as much as she first expected. His eyes glanced over the crowd, then dropped back to the empty shot glass.

Fogel leaned forward, too. "Is she here?"

"Who?"

"Stella Nettleton."

Again, his eyes betrayed nothing. They remained fixed on the shot glass. "Why would she be here?"

"Because you're here."

He grinned at that. A sidelong grin. "I may be a few drinks up on you, but I fail to see the logic. Maybe I'm just thinking about joining the Navy." He raised a hand above the table and simulated flight. "Gonna fly airplanes, like Maverick and Goose. Not like Iceman, though. He was a dick."

The waitress returned with another shot, scooped up the empty one, then disappeared back into the crowd. Jack pulled the glass closer. "Pittsburgh has its share of strip clubs. If you wanted to satisfy some fantasy, no reason to board a plane and come all this way. Are you afraid of running into one of your coworkers? I bet that's it. Some secrets are better left to the dark."

"It's August 8," Fogel said. "Somebody is going to die tonight, right?"

"Is that a confession?"

"Every year, like clockwork."

He said nothing.

"Billings, Montana; Iowa, Chicago, New Hampshire...now, Fallon, Nevada." Fogel turned in her seat. "Who is it? Somebody here?"

"Go count the white cars so I don't have to get up. Maybe I'll tell you."

"I know it's her, Jack. I don't know how or why she killed all those people, but I know it's her. Talk to her for me. If she turns herself in, I can make sure she stays safe. You want that, right? You don't want to see her get hurt. You care for her. I could tell that day at the house, the way you stared at that painting in her room. If she doesn't turn herself in, who knows how this will end? I can see some rookie cop putting her down, though, some trigger-happy kid taking a shot to make a name for himself. Imagine if she died, and you could have stopped it."

"Do a shot with me."

"What?"

"Do a shot with me." He grinned.

"No."

"Yeah, you need one. You're all wound tight." Jack flagged down a waitress, pointed at his own shot, then at Fogel. The waitress returned a minute later and set a glass in front of her.

"It's Jameson, you'll like it."

"I've had Jameson before."

He took his own glass in hand and raised it above the table. "To the detectives of Pittsburgh PD Homicide Division, both past and present, the whole tenacious lot of you." He swallowed the whiskey and brought his glass down hard on the table.

Fogel sighed, took her own glass, and drank it down. The whiskey made her shudder.

Jack fell back in his chair, smiling again. "Are you even considered a cop in this state? I bet I have just as much power to arrest you as you do to arrest me. The way I understand it, your boss is supposed to call the local sheriff and let them know you'll be in town working a case. You need permission, can't just show up. I imagine if you did just show up, without telling the appropriate people, you'd probably land yourself in a world of trouble. You seem like a 'by-the-book' kind of girl, so I'm not sure…Oh…Do you have your gun?"

Fogel's eyes darted to her purse and back again before she could stop them.

Jack's smile widened. "I don't have one of those, so I guess that gives you a little leg up. The people in the white cars? They like to carry guns. Every time I travel to a new state, I check the concealed carry laws and figure out what's allowed and what's not. Interestingly enough, Nevada is very relaxed, still kinda the Wild West out here. You can carry a gun openly in this state nearly anywhere you want. Feel free to strap that thing to your hip and wear it proud!"

"Who are the people in the white cars? You've mentioned them a few times now."

Jack raised a finger, motioned for her to lean in closer. "I don't like Nevada. It's too hot out here, too hot for coats. They leave their cars, and you can't find them anymore." He motioned wide around the club. "Any one of these people, except the girls, maybe...but who knows?"

Two more shots appeared on their table. Fogel hadn't seen Jack order them this time. Jack slid one toward her.

Fogel shook her head. "I can't."

"Come on, you're on vacation, right? Because if the sheriff doesn't know you're here, you've got to be on vacation." He raised the glass. "To whoever is next!"

"Do you know who's next?"

"I'm surely not going to tell you, if you won't even drink with me." He finished the shot and nearly dropped the glass.

A silly thought crossed Fogel's mind at that point, one she should have ignored but didn't—If she got him drunk enough, he might talk. He's almost there. Maybe one more, two at the most. It wouldn't be a confession, not in the legal sense, but she might learn what was going on, and she could use that.

Fogel raised her glass, smiled, and drank.

They did one more after that.

Lenny Kravitz blared from the speakers with "Fly Away." She liked that song. She scooted her chair closer to Jack and leaned into his ear. "Who's next?"

"What if it's you? Maybe that's why you're here. Maybe she wanted you here. How do you know *you're* not next?"

The deejay came over the loud speaker and told Grace to report to the main stage.

Jack's posture changed. He grew tense.

The lights in the club went dark, and a single white beam struck the stage. The opening notes of "Uninvited" by Alanis Morissette began, and the most beautiful girl Detective Joy Fogel had ever seen stepped into the light.

Unbuttoned halfway, the sleeves rolled up, she wore nothing but a men's white dress shirt, black heels, and black lace gloves, the kind you might find worn by the starlet in an old movie. They covered her fingertips to nearly her elbows. She stood there for a moment, perfectly still, her long, brown hair dripping over her shoulders, her head tilted down. Long, toned legs beneath the shirt, a hint of black lace panties beneath that. When she began to dance, Fogel found herself mesmerized, unable to look away. She didn't see Jack motion to one of the security guards. She didn't even see the man come over. It wasn't until he was standing behind her and put a hand on her shoulder that she noticed him at all.

The guard leaned close to be heard over the music. "You'll need to come with me, ma'am."

"Why?"

"We've been told you have a firearm in your purse."

"I'm allowed to…" The whiskey hit her harder than she thought, and the room tilted. She drew in a breath to compose herself.

He knew what she was going to say, though. "Yes, you're allowed to carry a gun in your purse in the state of Nevada, providing you are not intoxicated. You are clearly intoxicated, though. You'll need to come with us, ma'am."

Another man lifted her out of the chair. When had 'he' become an 'us?'

She looked to Jack. He held up his empty shot glass and smiled. "I'm a stickler for the law, Detective. Thanks for drinking with me. I hope you have a wonderful night."

She opened her mouth to argue, but the men dragged her away before she could, one riffling through her purse as they went.

5

I watched the security guards take the detective away only long enough to see them disappear down the hallway behind the deejay booth. Then my eyes went back to the stage, to her.

I first saw her the night before last, and the aching in my heart only grew with each tick of the clock. I sat at this same table, picking it because it was close to the dressing rooms—from the moment I left Pittsburgh, down each highway, turnpike, and interstate, I felt myself growing closer to her. By the time I crossed into Nevada, more than two thousand miles behind me, I found myself pressing the accelerator damn near to the floor, my Jeep's motor screaming. On one particular stretch in the desert, I broke one hundred miles per hour, not once but three times. I forced myself to slow. A ticket meant my name would appear in a report, and that report would go into a computer and that computer's data would become searchable... I saw a number of white cars while driving, but none followed me. I wanted to keep it that way. I couldn't risk them learning where I was, where *Stella* was.

The moment I arrived in Fallon, I knew Dunk had been right.
She was nearby. The air crackled with her.
Over the past four years, as I followed her around the country, each time I got close I felt her presence, a lingering electricity in the

air. Although certainly imagined, there was the scent of vanilla, too. Each of those places, her presence there but slowly fading.

In Fallon, though, it was different. The sense of her waxing rather than waning. Not only was she still in town, but she had been here for at least a week, maybe longer. Dunk hadn't been specific on that, I'm not sure he even knew, but I could *feel* it, I could feel her.

When I took the turn onto I-118.

When I pulled into the parking lot of Mike's Gentlemen's Club.

I *knew* she was inside.

I harbored not even the slightest of doubts.

I did see one white car in the parking lot, a Nissan, but I also saw the girl who got out of it in tight jeans and a black halter top, and I knew she wasn't with the people in white. I hadn't noticed any of the people in white when I arrived in Fallon, but they began to trickle in. I felt them, too.

On that first night, when Stella was called to the stage as Grace, I fought every urge to get up and go to her. I forced myself to stay in my seat and watch—she was absolutely mesmerizing. At that point, I hadn't learned why she was here, but I suspected it was because clubs like this offered a cash income and allowed her to live off the radar. That was only partially true. That was before I saw her dance for *him*.

Yesterday I learned his name was Leo Signorelli, and only a few hours ago, after calling Dunk, I learned just who he was.

Leo Signorelli owned Mike's Gentlemen's Club.

He also owned six area brothels. Although legal in Nevada, the conditions were poor. Many of the girls were brought here illegally from around the world and forced to work for him for little to no money in exchange for payment on the debt incurred by Signorelli in bringing them here.

Leo Signorelli was responsible for the death of at least four of those girls. He enjoyed strangling them during sex. The youngest being only fourteen. Dunk said his behavior was well-known among those who skirted the law, but he paid enough to various local officials to remain off their radar.

My first night here, Leo Signorelli took a seat at the side of the stage moments before Stella appeared, and he had been as enthralled with her as the rest of the men in the club. Last night, he brought her a single red rose and placed it on the corner of the stage as she began to dance. Stella only glanced at him, but that had been enough—this man, like me, like all the others here, could not look away. Tonight, he brought another rose, also red, and placed it on the stage. Tonight, Stella not only glanced at him, but smiled.

Oh, how my soul ached at the sight of that smile.

Leo Signorelli looked a lot like me. Same hair, same build. But she smiled at him, not me, and I wanted to jump up from my table and go to her, yet, I didn't.

I could only watch.

I could only watch as she danced, as she danced for him.

On stage, Stella reached for the brass pole and twirled around effortlessly. Although she wore the dress shirt, it was unbuttoned so low the sides of her breasts were visible, and somehow that was so much more alluring than the dozens of girls in the club wearing little or nothing at all. Others thought so too, because men began to crowd the stage with cash in hand.

Most of the girls wore garters and men would slip money into those garters, their hands lingering a little too long on that girl's leg as they did. Stella did not wear a garter. She didn't approach the sides of the stage at all. She remained out of reach. The men in the audience were forced to throw their cash on the floor at her feet. This didn't seem to stop them, though. Bills piled up before Alanis Morissette finished the first verse.

Stella only stared at him, at Leo Signorelli, as if no one else in the club existed.

I so wanted her to look at me that way, if only for a second.

At one point, she leaned against the pole and simply slid to the ground, her slender legs curling beneath her, her dark eyes on him, a single finger pressed against her red lips. The look she gave him had been enough to send him leaning back in his seat, his hard cheeks flush. I hadn't realized how quiet the club got until the song ended. Without the music, there was utter silence as all eyes watched her.

When Stella left the stage, she walked past Leo Signorelli, and he reached out to her, his hand going for the creamy white of her exposed thigh. Her gloved fingers stopped him before he could make contact, and Stella nodded to a sign on the wall with a playful giggle:

TOUCH THE GIRLS
AND THE BOUNCERS
WILL TOUCH YOU

Signorelli laughed at this. After all, he owned the club. But he raised both palms in defeat, anyway. As he did, I saw the note Stella had slipped to him, held tight between his thumb and forefinger. When she disappeared down the hallway beside the stage, he quickly read it and followed, two of his large bodyguards behind him.

When Detective Joy Fogel arrived, I had been surprised to see her. Having arrived much earlier myself, I was also a number of shots up on her. While I enjoyed her company, as brief as her company may have been—and I particularly enjoyed having someone to drink with—I wasn't drunk. I probably wouldn't even qualify as buzzed. Okay, maybe a little, but not bad, not to the point of impairment. Much like a long-distance runner outpacing a novice, a practiced drinker can easily outdrink someone who is not. Jameson was my whiskey of choice and had been for years. While I would get drunk if I drank it too quickly, I'd have to drink it far faster than I did tonight.

When Stella, followed closely by Leo Signorelli, owner of nefarious businesses and killer of the innocent, disappeared down that hallway, I stood at my table and finished the detective's cranberry and vodka. I was fairly certain she wouldn't be back for it, and I'd be leaving soon. No drink left behind.

I counted out four twenties, more than enough to cover my bill, and set them on the table. The waitress scooped them up before I was halfway to the front door.

I couldn't follow them down the hallway, not with the women's dressing room down there. I'd be stopped and probably beaten senseless within seconds.

I'd wait outside.

And hope she didn't intend to kill him in the building.

Nine white vehicles sat in the parking lot.

Six sedans.

Two SUVs.

One van.

None of them occupied, but that didn't mean they weren't watching.

I brought a knife. A six-inch switchblade I found in a pawnshop in Reno a few days earlier, and I used the knife to puncture two tires on each of these vehicles. I stuck to the shadows as I darted around the parking lot, careful to avoid the cameras on the corner of the building and the valets who occasionally ran into the lot to fetch a car or park a new one.

When finished, I went to my Jeep and slouched low in the seat. Earlier, I parked two cars over from Signorelli's black BMW Z3 Roadster convertible.

Stella and Signorelli emerged from the back door of the club twenty minutes later. She had changed into jeans and a long-sleeve red top. She still wore the gloves, though, and she held his hand.

At his car, she pleaded for the keys, and he finally obliged. She climbed behind the wheel of the little two-seater with a laugh. He got in beside her, and the engine roared to life.

Leo Signorelli leaned over then. In the silhouette of the parking lot lights, I watched as he leaned into her and she into him, her arms going up around his neck as she allowed him to kiss her. They remained that way for a long time, and I wanted to jump from the Jeep, yank open his door, pull him out, and beat him senseless. I wanted to hit him until the blood on my knuckles matched the bloody pulp of his ruined face. I wanted to hear him cry and whimper and plead until he was reduced to nothing more than a large child curled up on the ground in convulsive shivers.

I did none of those things.

I sat perfectly still and could only watch until she finally pulled away from him and settled back in behind the wheel.

Stella gunned the engine of the BMW several times before turning on the lights, dropping into reverse, and spinning the tires as she shifted into first and raced from the parking lot. Gravel rained through the air, pinging off all the nearby cars.

I started the Jeep and followed behind them, making the left onto I-118 with my headlights off, remaining a few car lengths behind. No streetlights lined the highway, the desert darkness here so complete it might as well have been black tar.

On the empty highway, she must have floored the little sports car, because they shot far ahead of me. I nearly lost them, their taillights nothing more than tiny, red pinpricks. My Jeep coughed and sputtered but didn't relent. Ten minutes later, when I-118 narrowed and became Wildes Road, Stella was forced to slow, and I reduced the gap. When pavement gave way to dirt, I risked getting too close and held back. A quarter mile later, she turned left off the dirt road onto what could only be described as a path—there were two ruts where past tires had rolled, but grass and weeds owned the space between them, and branches from the nearby trees slapped at the sides of my Jeep. Because the BMW had a lower profile, it avoided the branches, but I feared her car might get stuck in the dirt. More than once, I saw the undercarriage rub against the ground.

I didn't expect water.

Not out here.

There it was, though, this large body of water I would later learn was called Harmon Reservoir. Had it been daylight, I would have noticed the small feeder canals jutting out around the edges, but they were lost to the dark and encroaching night.

Stella pulled up to the water's edge, shut off the lights, and shut off the motor.

I stopped at the mouth of the trail, hidden in the woods just beyond the clearing. I wasn't sure when I picked up my switch-blade again, but the knife was in my hand. I pressed the button that released the blade, then closed it. Pressed the button again, closed it, the motion somehow soothing as I watched Stella step out of the car.

The little moonlight caught her, and even now her beauty was intoxicating, an irresistible pull. I so wanted to go to her, wrap my arms around her, kiss her as Leo had. Know the warmth of her breath on my neck, the touch of those slender fingers and arms around me.

Stella rounded the car to the passenger door and opened it.

Leo Signorelli slumped over and tumbled out, landing in a mound at her feet.

She saw me then, my Jeep at the mouth of the trail, not hidden as well as I thought.

As his body hit the ground, she looked not at this man, but at the trees where I parked, her eyes narrowing as she attempted to see past my windshield. She took several steps toward my Jeep before I got out.

"Jack? Is that you?"

I opened my mouth to speak, but no sound came out, I could only move toward her, my legs threatening to drop out from under me.

"What are you doing here?"

As I neared, as Leo Signorelli came into view, I saw his face. The skin around his mouth was black, charred. The side of his face, too.

Half his hair was gone, his ear. My breath caught as I remembered Raymond Visconti, the mark that appeared on him with Stella's touch in the basement.

Stella's kiss.

"Why are you here?"

The next few moments were over before I realized they happened at all.

Stella took another step toward me.

Leo Signorelli's arm moved. At first, just a twitch. I wasn't sure I saw it at all, it was so damn dark. But then there was the glint of metal, and he had a gun in his hand.

The gun came up, pointing at Stella's back.

She started to turn, heard something.

I dove past her.

I dove between her and the barrel.

My knee came down first, cracking against the point of a stone jutting out from the ground. My shoulder hit the car door, and the rest of me landed on Leo. My switchblade was out again. I had released the blade somewhere between my last two heartbeats, and I brought the knife down into the side of his neck. The tip punctured the skin with little effort. Then there was an audible pop as I punctured something deeper. One of his eyes was milky white, blind with cataracts, but the other saw me. The other went wide and fixed on me as warm blood sprayed my face and clothes, and soaked the earth.

It was all over in a moment.

Leo Signorelli stopped moving and would move no more.

"Oh my God, you killed him!" Stella shouted, falling beside the body. She tore off one of her gloves and pressed her palm against his forehead, then his good cheek, then gripped his arm. Desperately moving from one portion of exposed flesh to another.

"I…I had to. He would have shot you."

Her voice dropped to a desperate whisper. "But I…I hadn't finished yet. I…wasn't done."

"What does that mean?"

Stella didn't answer me. She only sat there, her entire body trembling. Each breath caught in her throat, and her eyes glistened with tears.

She began to cry, and there was no consoling her. I reached for her shoulder and squeezed, the warmth of her seeping through the thin cloth of her shirt, and she shook me off. I tried to lean into her, and she pulled away, the word "don't" barely audible through her sobs. A fleck of Leo's blood was on her cheek, and when I reached to brush it away, she shot up and pulled away from me before I could.

Stella stood and began to pace, her cries lessening.

I stood too, and not knowing what else to do, I went to the water's edge and washed Leo's blood from my arms and hands and the knife.

"You need to throw that into the water," I heard her say behind me. So I did. The knife slipped through the surface about a hundred feet from shore and disappeared beneath.

When I turned back to Stella, her arms were tight at her sides, her fists were clenched. "Oh God, Jack. Why are you here?" A desperation filled her voice. She was still shaking, her eyes red.

I reached into my back pocket and took out her note. I had folded and unfolded the note so many times over the years, holes had worn through the paper at the creases. She recognized it, though.

Stella closed her eyes and shook her head, the tears coming again. "That was years ago. I got out. I got away. I'm okay now."

"I don't think you are," I said softly.

She pressed her hands to the sides of her temples, blood smeared beneath her touch. "He was a bad man."

"I know."

"I needed him."

I went to her again, I gripped her arms. "He would have killed you."

She pulled away and started pacing again from Leo's body to the trees and back again, over and over. "You don't understand."

"I do."

She shook her head again. "You don't. You can't. You can't possibly…"

"I've known for years. I think I've always known."

"You don't," she said again, crossing back to the trees. "I. Needed. Him." She drew in a breath between each of these words, then with her ungloved hand she reached for the tree beside her, a gray pine, at least sixty feet tall. The trunk of the tree blackened under her touch with what first looked like a burn, then became rot. Long pine needles began to fall from the tree, showering down on her. As they fell, their color turned from a grayish green to black before they hit the ground. When all the needles were gone, I heard a moan, then a loud creak, a harsh, high-pitched squeal, followed by a crack, and the tree was falling. It toppled to the right of her, and all the while, Stella remained perfectly still, her hand on the trunk. When it hit the ground, it broke into dozens of pieces—not the trunk of a newly cut tree, but that of one which had spent a lifetime rotting away before finally succumbing to gravity and crashing to the earth.

When it was over, she didn't look at me. She looked to the ground. "That thing you saw me do, in the basement," she said. "I have to do it. If I don't, I'll die."

"They used you." I said this in the calmest voice I could. I needed her to calm down. Already, her fingers were flexing, reaching for another tree. I knew, trees would not be enough.

"They were feeding me. They kept me safe. I'm glad to be away, to be out, but…I need…"

I went to her. I wrapped my arms around her, and although her arms remained at her sides, she pressed her face into my chest, carefully avoiding my flesh, the exposed skin of my neck.

"We need to hide him. We need to get him into the water. Will you help me?" she said softly, her voice muffled.

She pulled away from me and tugged her glove back on, her face pleading.

I nodded silently.

We dragged him around to the driver's side and managed to get him in the seat behind the wheel. Leo Signorelli was my height, my build, but gravity somehow affects dead weight differently than alive, and moving him proved a struggle. Once inside with the seatbelt fastened, I started the car, turned the headlights back on, slipped the car into neutral, and released the brake. I took a last look around the interior to ensure Stella hadn't left anything inside, then rolled down the driver-side window to steer.

"What about this?" Stella held Leo's gun between the tips of her gloved fingers. "Better to throw it out into the lake or put it in the car?"

I thought about this for a second. "It's no secret he was mixed up with some nasty people. Probably best to leave it in the car."

She opened the door and dropped it on the passenger seat, then together we pushed the small car into the water. The reservoir had a steep slope—the car went under fast. The engine died right away, the headlights blinked out after about thirty-seconds. Air bubbled up through the open window, then the BMW disappeared from view.

We stood there for a long time, watching where the car had been, then she finally turned to me and her eyes found mine, the sadness in her look so deep, so overwhelming. When she opened her mouth to speak, two words slipped out. Two words worse than the blade of any knife through my heart. "I can't..."

She ran toward the trees. She pushed through the bushes and branches until the night swallowed her whole, and I was certain of only one thing—I couldn't lose her again.

Stella didn't answer my calls.

I screamed out her name as I chased after her. I didn't care who else heard me. The same branches that had welcomed her sliced at my skin, scratched and bit me, but I didn't care about that either. I ran as fast as I could, my arms and hands pushing them aside, oblivious to the pain.

Twenty minutes passed before I found her.

Stella was sitting on a large rock, her head buried in her gloved hands. When she heard me approach, her breath caught and she jumped up.

I held a hand out to her. "Don't run. Please, no more. Just…Just hear me out. Please."

"This isn't you, Jack. It never was. You're a better person than me. I can't pull you into this with me. I can't."

I took a step closer. "I love you, Stella. I've loved you from the very first moment I saw you all those years ago. The *second* I saw you sitting on that bench."

"We were only kids."

"You felt it too, I know you did. I saw the painting in your room. All the jabs, the mean comments, it was all bullshit. It was that old woman whispering in your ear. None of it mattered anyway, because the truth was in your eyes, it always was. Eight years old, eighteen, or eighty, it doesn't matter. Every thought I have is of you. Every breath, every sight, every sound, it *all* reminds me of you. You're a piece of me, and I'm dying without you. There's a hole in me without you. I love you, Stella, with every ounce of my being. I know you love me, too. I know you do."

"I don't deserve to love. I'm some kind of monster." She said this so softly, tears welling at her eyes.

"That's the old woman again, Latrese Oliver. I know it is. You do too. You know what's in your heart—what's always been there." I took another step toward her, only inches from her now. "Nobody else matters, there's only us. *Nothing* else matters."

"They made me—"

I took her hand then, felt her warmth through the glove. "Look at me, Stella."

She did.

Her beautifully dark eyes found mine, and I ran my hand through her hair. She nearly pulled away as I did this, as my fingers brushed so close to her skin, but she didn't, somehow knowing I understood—it was her flesh I had to fear. "They used you. You can do…this thing…and they used you. They took advantage of you. It's over now. I'll never let them hurt you, or use you, again."

"I don't want to kill anymore. I can't…I don't…" And the sobs came again, soft, buried in my chest. "I want to stop."

"We'll find another way," I told her.

"Jack," she whispered, her sobs softening, *"I can't even touch you."*

"We'll find a way."

We stood there in each other's arms for a long time, the two of us, no other words. Then I led her back to my Jeep, her gloved hand in mine.

The Chestnut Motor Lodge was just off I-118 about a mile outside of Fallon between the town proper and Mike's Gentlemen's Club. It wasn't much to look at, which is why I chose it. A squat two-story building that passed its prime about twenty years back, the landscaping was desert dirt and the blacktop parking lot had long ago lost the battle with the harsh Nevada sun. Two sodium lights blared down from opposite ends of the property, creating just enough light so it wouldn't be missed from the highway. There was an enormous neon sign on the roof, but only the word *lodge* still burned, and judging by the loud buzz coming from the sign, it probably wouldn't be lit for much longer.

After leaving Harmon Reservoir, Stella directed me down a series of side roads, the last of which petered out at a dead end about a mile from any main road. When I stopped, she got out of the Jeep, went to the deep ditch beside the road, and retrieved a black duffle bag. She put it between her feet on the floorboards. "Everything I own," she said softly. She planned to leave Fallon immediately after dispatching Leo Signorelli, so she left the bag here earlier in the day. From Fallon, she hoped to drive to Las Vegas, where she'd leave his BMW. From there, she wanted to cross the country to Charleston. She had never been to South Carolina. She told me all of this in a quiet, monotone voice, so far removed from the confident girl I remembered from back home. The girl from our bench, or her pool, or even the girl I watched dance only a few short hours ago. A curtain had been removed, a facade dropped. Although both were Stella, this was the real Stella. No longer putting up a rehearsed confidence but instead, sharing with me, albeit in careful fits and starts. I wondered if she had ever truly talked to anyone. She went from a captive in that house to running alone, a solitary existence I knew all too well.

There were three white cars in the parking lot of the Chestnut Motor Lodge. Stella saw them too, but she didn't say anything. A man in a white dress shirt and chinos watched us pull up from the ice machine, then went back to the business of filling up his bucket. I had room 27 on the second floor, so I parked on the east side of the building, near the stairs but as far from the lights as I could.

We waited for the man in the white shirt to return to his own room (first floor, three doors down from the west end of the building) before getting out of the Jeep. We both had Leo's blood on us. We couldn't risk being seen. Stella followed me up the stairs to my room and waited as I dug out the key and pushed open the door.

"It's not much," I told her.

Stella glanced around the room. A double bed, sagging in the middle with a floral quilt draped over the top in a rumpled heap. Green shag carpet on the floor with tan tile at the back of the room under the sink and continuing on into the small bathroom. There were three prints on the walls, all depicting horses at the Kentucky Derby. I left an empty bottle of Jack Daniel's on the nightstand and wished I hadn't. The cardboard remnants of a Coors Light twelve-pack sat next to a plastic trash can containing my empties. I drew the drapes and placed the Do Not Disturb sign on the door before closing it, locking the dead bolt, and putting the chain in place. If somebody wanted to get in, these things would only slow them down, but that was better than nothing.

I pulled back the corner of the curtain and looked out over the parking lot, my eyes bouncing from one white car to the next.

"It's not them."

"How do you know?"

"I just know. Not every white car belongs to them."

Somehow, that didn't reassure me. "Did you have anything lined up in South Carolina? A place to stay or anything?"

She shook her head.

"I think we're okay here for tonight, but we should probably head out first thing in the morning. We don't want to be around when they find Leo. And there was only one white car yesterday. Probably nothing, like you said, but best to keep moving."

Stella wasn't listening to me. When I turned around, I realized she was standing in front of the mirror above the sink. She had peeled off her clothes as she went, leaving a trail behind her.

I think my mouth fell open.

Down to only a black lace bra and matching panties, Stella rolled her eyes. "You've seen me naked, Pip. No need to be shy. I need a shower. I've got his blood in my hair. That doesn't usually happen."

With that, she stepped into the small bathroom and pulled the door halfway shut behind her. I heard the water start a moment later.

I picked up my empty bottles and other trash and took it all down to the Dumpster, cleaning the room up as best I could before she finished.

A fourth white car had joined the others, a white Ford Escort. Nobody was inside.

When Stella emerged from the shower wrapped in a white towel and somehow smelling of vanilla again, I hastily shucked off my filthy clothes and showered too. The steaming water felt fantastic, and I stayed in there far longer than I probably should have, scrubbing and scrubbing until my skin was pink and raw, until I saw the last of Leo Signorelli wash down the drain.

By the time I came out, Stella had changed into an oversize tee-shirt. She had washed her black gloves by hand in the sink, and they were now draped over the edge of the cracked formica counter, air-drying.

She sat on the edge of the bed, her slender bare legs crossed beneath her. "I bagged our clothes. We need to get rid of them somewhere. Not here, though."

I had left my backpack on the floor outside the bathroom, next to Stella's duffle bag. It was gone now. "Have you seen my—"

"What's this?" She held up the letter from her parents to mine, my backpack open beside her.

"Go ahead and help yourself."

"What is it?"

I took a pair of sweatpants out of my pack and slipped them on under my towel, threw the towel in the general direction of the bathroom, and sat down beside her. "My next-door neighbor gave me that right after my aunt died. I think your dad wrote it."

"Our parents knew each other? Why didn't you ever show this to me?"

"I tried. I brought the letter with me when I went to see you that year, that was...wow...1993, five years ago. You weren't there, though, only Latrese Oliver. That was the year she gave me your letter, the one I showed you. I never saw you after that."

Stella read the letter again, her finger slipping across the paper, following along. "My father wrote this. This is his handwriting." She considered this, her eyes glistening again. "I've never seen his handwriting before. I...I don't have anything from my parents. He sounds so...paranoid."

"Do you remember them at all?"

She shook her head. "My earliest memories are of Latrese Oliver, a series of nannies, staff at the house. Nothing about my parents."

"Did Oliver tell you anything about them?"

"Only that they died when I was a baby, a bad car crash. She said she was close to them and had been appointed my legal guardian."

"I was told my parents died in a car crash, too."

"They didn't, though, did they?"

I shrugged and told her about my father's grave. What I found. I told her he might still be alive.

Her eyes turned into saucers. "You dug up your father's grave? Wow, my little Pip isn't as timid as I thought." Then her eyes grew even wider. "Do you think my parents might still be alive, too?"

"I wish I knew."

After a long pause, Stella said, "May I see the books?"

"At least you asked this time."

I rutted around in my pack and took out the copy of *Great Expectations* and the Penn State yearbook and handed both to her.

When I handed her the Dickens book, her face lit up. "This is just like mine!"

She found her copy and laid the two side by side. Although my copy appeared new, her copy was clearly worn. Her cover was faded and lined with white, torn in a number of spots. Many of the book's pages were dog-eared. She kept a highlighter clipped to the cover and made a habit of highlighting her favorite passages. After all these years, I couldn't imagine she still found new passages to highlight. Every page of her book was probably a solid block of yellow by now.

I flipped through the yearbook and showed her the various circled photographs and explained what I learned about each of the people identified.

"All the ones you've found are dead?"

I kept the list I made back at Penn State folded inside the front of the yearbook. I took it out and smoothed the wrinkled paper. "Aside from your parents and mine, Perla Beyham, Garret Dotts, Penelope Maudlin, and Lester Woolford all killed themselves. My neighbor, Elfrieda Leech, she shot herself right in front of me. I haven't been able to find Cammie Brotherton, Jaquelyn Breece, Jeffery Dalton, or Keith Pickford."

Stella pursed her lips, her finger hovering over the names. "Do you remember David? He came to the cemetery with me once when we were kids."

I nodded. "He was there when my neighbor died. I was in her apartment when she shot herself, and somehow he was across the hall in mine. He left a note for me. The note said, 'Welcome to the party, Jack. He signed it.'" David left a bottle of Jameson too, but I didn't tell her about that.

"My God, that must have been awful for you."

Three.

Three what?

Bang!

I shivered.

Stella tapped at the paper. "David told me once his parents names were Jackie and Keith. This must be them."

"Jaquelyn Breece and Keith Pickford? Do you know what happened to them?"

She fell silent.

"Stella?"

"He said they both died. A murder suicide. His father shot his mother, then turned the gun on himself. It was a long time ago, I think he was around five or six, but I don't know for sure."

"Did David live with you?"

She shook her head. "He visited a couple of times when we were young. Later, they took me to see him, mostly. This godawful place."

Stella's hand began shaking. I reached for it, and she yanked away. "You can't."

She held her hand with her other, held it still.

"What is it? Are you okay?"

Her voice dropped low, I could barely hear her. "I didn't finish...I didn't get enough."

"With Leo?"

She nodded. When she released her hand, the shaking had stopped. "I just need to rest. I'll be okay."

I glanced at the digital clock beside the bed—nearly four in the morning. It would be light in a few hours. We both needed to sleep.

I wanted to ask her who *they* were, these people in white. Latrese Oliver, David, the man in the GTO. We had so much to talk about, but it could wait. It would have to. Her eyes had grown heavy in just the past few minutes, and I felt everything catching up with me, too. The adrenaline was wearing off. My body needed to rest, shut down. "You take the bed," I told her. "I'll sleep on the floor."

Stella looked down at the green shag carpet. "I feel dirty just walking on this carpet. You can't sleep down there. We can share the bed."

I looked at her hand. "What about…what if we touch, by accident, I mean…because I wouldn't…? What will happen?"

Stella chewed on her lip for a second, thinking. Then she stood, went to the head of the bed, and pulled back the quilt. "We'll use the sheet. You lay under it, and I'll lay above it. This way, it will stay between us. That will be okay."

"You're sure?"

She climbed in. "I'm sure."

I switched off the light and took one more look out the window. Another white car had joined the others, a Saturn four-door. Five cars now. There was somebody sitting in this one, but I couldn't see their face. "We have another white car out there," I said.

Stella didn't answer, though, already lost to sleep.

My hand was shaking too, but not from nerves or because of Leo. I had problems of my own. I went to the dresser beside the bed and pulled open the drawer. I had placed a fifth of Maker's Mark whiskey in there yesterday, a little more than half a bottle. I twisted off the cap, brought it to my lips, and drank. Not a lot, just until the shaking stopped. And it did eventually stop.

Stella's ragged breaths became even, and she mumbled something in her sleep.

I must have stared at her for another hour before putting that bottle away, certain that if I closed my eyes for even a second, she would be gone when I opened them. She was so incredibly beautiful, so peaceful. She couldn't possibly be here with me, but here she was, after all these years, with me, her Pip, my Stella.

Things would be all right now. I truly wanted to believe that. As long as we were together, we would be okay. I so wanted to believe that was true.

I went downstairs and let the air out of the tires on each of the white cars, with the exception of the occupied vehicle. I also made a mental note to pick up another knife at my first opportunity.

I finally climbed in beside her at a little before five in the morning, expecting to remain awake, but I was probably out in under a minute.

That was when bad things happened.

The dream.

Chocolate milk everywhere. In my hair, on my clothes, all over my fingers and seat.

Daddy screaming at Mommy, "Katy! You can't sleep now, Katy! Stay awake!"

The squeal of tires.

Car doors opening.

Loud bangs.

"Got it!" Daddy said.

Loud bangs from Daddy, from the thing in his hand. He shouted at someone behind us. The someone behind us shouted back.

I cried.

I wanted to be a big boy, but I cried. I couldn't even hear myself, though, not over all the banging.

I closed my eyes for only a second, but when they opened again, Daddy was gone. He had been standing beside Mommy, at her door. I couldn't see where he went. The belts of my seat held me firm, and I couldn't turn, I couldn't see out all the windows.

The bangs stopped.

All at once, so quiet.

"Daddy?"

No response.

So quiet.

All alone.

Mommy wasn't moving. I could see her hair, her head slumped over in the front seat.

All alone.

I started to cry again, and my door yanked open.

"Hey, buddy, let's get you out of there. It's going to be okay, everything will be okay," Daddy said. But he was crying too, and I knew it wouldn't be okay.

He carried me from our car to a white SUV parked behind us and laid me across the back seat. All the while, he kept my head buried in his chest, telling me not to look, not to look at anything. I did, though, and I saw people dressed in white lying on the ground, red stains on each of them.

I pulled myself up so I could see.

Daddy got in the driver's seat, reversed the vehicle, and backed away from our car and the one we had run into, another white SUV like this one. We jolted as we stopped, and he threw it back in park. I nearly fell. "Stay down, Jack." He was out the door again, running back to our car. He was going to get Mommy, I knew he was. He had to. We couldn't leave without Mommy. Holding onto the headrest from the front seat, I watched as he went to Mommy in the car. He was crying loud now, louder than I had ever cried, and that made me cry. He leaned in the seat over her, he hugged her, he shook her. He pulled her to his chest and held her, and I didn't understand why he didn't just bring her to *this* car, put her in *this* front seat, because I wanted to hug her, too.

When Daddy left her door, he staggered back and I thought he might fall over. He didn't, though. He looked back and saw me watching him. He motioned for me to get down with his hand. I didn't, though. I kept watching as he dragged one of the people lying on the ground back to our car and put them into the front seat behind the wheel, Daddy's seat. He always drove. Then he dragged the other two, the ones from this car, to the SUV we had run into, and put them in the back seat.

He ran about halfway back to me and screamed again for me to get down. This time I did, but not before I saw him light a match and drop it into a puddle on the ground. I didn't get down because he told me to or because I wanted to. I got down because the explosion knocked me off my feet.

I woke to the crash of thunder, my body covered in sweat.

The sun had risen but was dim, hidden behind churning desert storm clouds and the *rat, tat, tat,* of rainfall.

On the bed beside me, Stella was gone.

The sheets on her side of the bed were pulled back. The spot where she had lain was cold.

"Stella?"

No answer.

I checked the bathroom first, but she wasn't there. Her gloves were no longer beside the sink. Her duffle bag was gone, too.

The phone rang. A shrill, harsh sound. I stared at it for a good, long while before finally scooping up the receiver. I didn't say anything, but I could hear someone breathing on the other end of the line, then a male voice. "Jack?"

Dunk.

"Yeah?"

"You all right? You sound funny."

Not all right.

Not at all.

"I can't talk. What do you need?"

"Oh, shit! Does that mean you found her? Is she there right now? Did you finally get to—"

I cut him off. "What is it, Dunk?"

He blew out a breath. "My man. Pulling all kinds of triggers this week. Good for you."

"I'm hanging up."

"Hold up. My guy found one of your names."

"Which one?"

"Cammie Brotherton. Although, she's not Cammie Brotherton anymore. She's Faye Mauck now. She changed her name a half dozen times over the years, moved all over the country."

I pressed the receiver tighter against my ear. "Wait, she's still alive?"

"Shouldn't she be? Why else would you have me look for her?"

The list I made of the Penn State names was sitting next to the phone, on top of the yearbook. My copy of *Great Expectations* was gone. Stella must have taken the book with her. "Do you have an address?"

He read it off to me. I found a pen and scribbled the address down on the pad of motel stationery.

Carmel, California.

"Got something else, too. Have you ever heard of something called *Charter*?"

"No, why?"

"People are asking about you around town, trying to find you. My guys picked one of 'em up and talked to him. At first he said he was an old friend, but once they all got to know each other a little better, he opened up, got chatty. He told them he was with an outfit called Charter. Said it was real important that he found you."

"Talked to him, huh?"

"Yeah. Talked to him, nice and neat. My guys said he was packing, a Colt Anaconda six-shot revolver. That's no joke. He didn't make much of an effort to hide it, either. They said he wore it right on his belt under his coat, Old West style."

I perked up. "Coat? What kind of coat?"

"How the hell should I know? Think I'm some kind of fashion guru?"

"What color was his coat?"

"Dunno. If it's important, I'll ask when I see Reid."

"It's important."

"Okay." Dunk's voice dropped low. "Hey, Jack? She still sleeping? How 'bout giving Stella a poke for me? From what I've heard, she's a—"

I hung up and tore off the sheet of stationery and shoved it in my pocket.

If Cammie was still alive, the others might be, too.

The hotel room door burst open and Stella came in, her clothing soaked through, her dark hair dripping, her skin deathly pale. "We need to go."

I let out a breath.

She closed the door quickly behind her, went to the window, and pulled back the curtain slightly. Her hand was trembling again. I looked out the window over her shoulder.

The rain fell in thick sheets, bouncing off the cracked pavement.

Six white cars now. One blocked the parking lot exit. Another was parked directly behind my Jeep. Three more across the lot and a white Cadillac Escalade parked in the center of the lot, two of the doors open. A man I didn't recognize stood on the driver's side, a cell phone pressed to his ear, oblivious to the rain. His long, white trench coat buttoned tight.

"I put my things in the Jeep. The Escalade pulled up when I was coming back up the stairs. I don't think they saw me."

"Did you see any other people?"

She shook her head. "Only the two guys in the Cadillac, but somebody moved those other cars."

My knife was at the bottom of Hermon Reservoir. We had no other weapons.

I looked around the room, then went to the dresser beside the bed and pulled open the drawer, took out the bottle of Maker's Mark. About a third left. I twisted off the cap and threw it aside, then tore a strip of cloth from one of the pillowcases, rolled it, and shoved it into the mouth of the bottle. "I need matches," I said, pulling open the other drawer and looking inside; only an old Bible.

"I saw some over here." Stella went to the nightstand on the opposite side of the bed, grabbed a matchbook from beside a filthy ashtray, and tossed them to me. "Will that work in the rain?"

"I have no idea."

I put the yearbook in my backpack and slung the bag over my shoulder. "Do you have the other book?"

She nodded. "In my bag."

The motel room door burst open, and Stella let out a sharp scream.

Two men came in, both moving low and fast. The first had a 9mm in his hand. The second man had a shotgun. Both were dressed entirely in white. Without a thought, I dropped the bottle of whiskey and charged the man with the semiautomatic, my shoulder plowing into his gut and sending him flailing backward into the other man. All three of us tumbled out the door onto the concrete walkway and fell into a pile. I brought my elbow down hard into the jaw of the man with the handgun, and his eyes rolled back into his head. I scooped up the gun and rolled to the side as the man with the shotgun pushed the limp body away and began to stand.

I leveled the gun on him. "Don't."

He smiled at me. "The safety is on."

"Glocks don't have safeties. Set the shotgun down, and take a step back."

The man had cut himself when he fell. Blood rolled down from his forehead into his eye. He ignored it, his grin widening. The shotgun continued to rise.

I fired twice. Both rounds hit him in the gut. I tried to fire a third time, but the gun came up empty. I tossed it aside. The man looked down at the growing red spot on his white coat, then fell to his knees, the shotgun dropping beside him. I grabbed it.

The bottle of whiskey sailed out the door of my room, past my head, and over the balcony, a flame trailing from the makeshift wick. It exploded on the roof of the Cadillac Escalade in the center of the parking lot, flames spreading over the SUV despite the rain. The man who had been on the phone jumped aside and disappeared from sight somewhere below.

Stella ran past me toward the stairs, my backpack over her shoulder. "Come on!"

I followed her down the steps, the shotgun leading.

A third man in white was waiting at the base of the stairs, the barrel of a shotgun pointing out from under his white trench coat directly at me.

Stella walked straight toward him, her pace quickening with each step. She tugged the glove off her right hand and reached for him. The man's face went pale, and he swung the gun from me to her.

A blast rang out.

The shotgun bucked in my hand with the recoil, and the man flew back against the wall, then dropped to the ground.

We ran toward the Jeep and jumped inside. As I threw the shotgun behind my seat and started the engine, Stella's head swiveled, looking for others. One of the white cars, a Chevrolet Cavalier, was parked behind us, blocking our path. Instead of backing up out of the space, I put the Jeep into first and drove right over the concrete parking block, over the edge of the blacktop, and into the muddy field separating the Chestnut Motor Lodge from I-118. Behind us, the man we had first seen standing next to the Cadillac ran out from behind the safety of a Ford F-150 into the center of the lot, the phone still pressed to his ear, shouting over the rain.

6

In the early hours of August 9, Preacher sat on a bench in LA Union Station with a copy of the *Los Angeles Times* in his hand. He kept one eye on the newspaper and the other on the large man in the brown suit and funny little hat.

He didn't get the hat.

He knew it was called a boater and made of straw, but what he didn't get is why this man wore one. Aside from the occasional costume party, boaters hadn't been in fashion since the late nineteenth century. You don't steal two million dollars from the mob, then hang out in LA Union Station wearing a funny little hat. You *disappear.*

The large man in the brown suit and the funny little hat would disappear, Preacher would see to that, but his destination would be radically different from whatever was printed on the ticket he clenched in his hand.

Preacher didn't much care for the people who hired him. None of them were up to his standards, but the Letto family always paid well, always paid on time, and provided him with referral business. Good word of mouth was everything in Preacher's vocation. He was fond of Los Angeles and took most jobs that brought him here unless they fell into autumn or early spring—he wasn't a fan of the Santa Anas. They played hell with his allergies.

The large man in the brown suit and funny little hat was known as Lonny Caley, having changed his name from Elton Engelmann when he dodged the draft in 1972 and sidestepped the skirmish in southeast Asia for a lucrative career in money laundering—first for a series of corporations, then later for the Lettos. He did well for himself, until he decided to steal from them last week. That wasn't one of his better decisions.

Lonny Caley lumbered across the main concourse with his ticket in one hand and an overstuffed suitcase in the other and started toward the east concourse.

Preacher followed, the *Times* folded and tucked under his arm. As he passed a bank of pay phones near baggage check, one began to ring. He ignored it and followed Caley into the east concourse hall, past a Subway and Starbucks.

Caley leaned up against a wall, set down his bag, and scratched his chin.

Another phone rang, inches from Preacher's ear.

He snatched up the receiver. "What?"

"We found her."

"I don't care," Preacher said before hanging up the phone.

The line rang again. So did the phone next to that one and the one after that.

He answered the nearest phone again. The others went silent too. "I got the girl out of that house. We're square. I'm done."

"You lost her. You let her go."

"The agreement was 'get her out.' You didn't say anything about babysitting. I told you, I was done babysitting after the shit with the boy."

"You knew. You set us back."

"I'm not part of your agenda."

"You became part when you took the shot. When you ran."

Across the concourse, Caley picked up his bag and carried it into the men's room.

"Can't talk now. I'm working." He hung up the line and started for the bathroom.

All the phones in LA Union Station began to ring at once, dozens, maybe a hundred, in a uniform shrill, metallic cry echoing over the marble.

All around him, travelers began looking up from their newspapers, their books, their meals and coffee. They stared at nothing in particular; some cocked their heads, others smiled, while others frowned and glanced around nervously at the crowd, at the phones lining the walls and tucked into random corners. Preacher ignored the sound and pushed through the swinging door of the men's room.

Twelve stalls lined the wall on the right. The left housed a row of urinals with sinks at the back of the room. The floors were polished concrete, the walls covered in white subway tile. Three men stood at the urinals. Three of the stalls were closed. Beyond the bathroom's only door, the telephones continued to ring.

At the urinals, one of the men glanced at Preacher. "Is that the fire alarm?"

Preacher nodded. "Someone set off a bomb on one of the east tracks."

"Shit, shit, shit," the man said, finishing his business. He rushed out of the room. Preacher noted he didn't wash his hands. The other two men finished at the urinals and *did* go to the sinks—one washed his hands hastily, the other took his time. Seasoned Angelenos weren't rattled by much. The man dried his hands on the way to the door and used the paper towel to push it open before wading it up and dropping it in a trash can.

Preacher stood at the front of the room until both men left. Then he withdrew his Walther PPK from his shoulder rig. He rarely engaged the safety because this particular weapon had a long trigger pull, which made misfires a near impossibility, particularly in practiced hands.

He removed the glove from his left hand and pressed his palm against the first stall door.

Caley wasn't in there.

He moved on to the next door and did the same.

He found this one harder to read but quickly concluded that Caley wasn't in there, either.

Of course, Lonny Caley would use the last stall. Men hiding from something tended to go to the back of whatever room they happened to be in.

The toilet in the first stall flushed. A moment later a man in his late sixties emerged. He started for the sinks, saw the gun in Preacher's hand, then left instead. Preacher let him go. He'd be gone long before someone could summon help. As the bathroom door swung open, the shrill of the still ringing telephones filled the room, then muted as the door fell shut. When the second toilet flushed, Preacher hid his gun from the teenager who stepped out. The kid didn't wash his hands, either—nasty, considering he didn't have the excuse of an armed man standing between him and the sink.

When the bathroom door swung shut on the boy and they were alone, Preacher again took out his gun and used the barrel to knock on the stall door.

Caley's nervous voice came from the other side. "How'd you find me?"

Preacher didn't answer.

"I know who you are. In a strange way, I feel like I know you. Whenever you performed your services for the Lettos, I'm the guy who paid you. They work with three guys like you, but only one they'd trust to come after me. You're the one they call Preacher, right?"

Preacher didn't reply.

"They say you know things, like you're psychic or some shit. When it comes to tracking someone, there's nobody better. Why do they call you Preacher? I don't get that. I can't imagine you're a religious man."

Preacher took two steps toward the sink.

Six shots rang out, fired in quick succession from inside the toilet stall. The black pressboard splintered and rained out onto the concrete floor as bullet holes appeared in the front of the stall door.

Caley's gun clicked empty. "I missed you, didn't I?"

Preacher stepped to the door and kicked it in. Caley let out a squeal as it slammed into into him, then bounced back out. He was sitting on the toilet, his pants still around his ankles and the suitcase on the floor beside him. Caley had a hand to his nose, and blood oozed out between his fingers. His other hand held the empty revolver. He dropped it when he saw Preacher's PPK.

Caley nodded down at the suitcase. "It's all there, an extra two hundred eighty thousand, too—money I saved up over the years. Take it. Keep it for yourself, take it back to them, I don't care." His voice sounded nasally. "Just...just, make it quick, okay?"

Preacher holstered his gun, and the man's eyes lit up.

Preacher then placed his hands, one still gloved, the other not, on either side of Caley's head, and with one swift twist, snapped the man's neck. The man slumped forward, his flabby arms dropped to his sides. His eyes glossed over, and his tongue protruded slightly from the corner of his mouth.

Preacher leaned him back against the wall, and when he was certain the large man wasn't going to tumble over anytime soon, he backed out of the stall and pulled the broken door shut as best he could.

With Lonny Caley's suitcase in hand, he returned to the east concourse. The phones were still ringing. Crowds of onlookers stood around them, occasionally picking up one of the handsets, then hanging it back up again.

He grabbed the nearest phone with his free hand. "I get the girl back and we're done, got me?"

There was a sigh on the other end of the line. "It's not that simple anymore, Dalton."

"Why not?"

"We think David found Cammie."

Preacher's heart thumped. "Oh, hell."

All the phones stopped ringing then.

7

"You've got a phone call."

Fogel opened her eyes, then closed them again. The harsh fluorescent lights in the small cell the kind officers of the Fallon Police Department placed her in did nothing to help the relentless beating taking place behind her eyes. The pillow they provided wasn't helping much either. The pillow felt like someone draped a rag over a bag of Legos and declared it head support. Twice during the night, she cast it aside in favor of the less lumpy mattress and metal frame of her borrowed bed.

They hadn't locked the cell door, she was thankful for that. She wasn't under the illusion that she could pick up and leave, either. They made that very clear when they brought her in.

Professional courtesy, she had been told. You're intoxicated and in possession of a firearm. You broke the law. No reason to charge you and ruin your career, though. Cops carry. An honest mistake. Sleep it off, and we'll take a SITREP in the morning.

Fogel remembered staring at the officer as he said this, a kid of no more than nineteen who probably weighed less than a hundred pounds. The only thing holding up his uniform pants was his gun belt, and she suspected a pair of suspenders might be at work under his shirt but couldn't bring herself to ask.

Officer Mitchell Jun, his name tag said. Alone at the desk on the nightshift. *A shit gig*, she thought. *Other than being too small to frighten anyone, what did you do to deserve such a shit gig?*

SITREP?

She managed to repeat the word when he said it, but it came out slurred. Close enough for him to understand, though.

Situation report, ma'am.

Oh.

We just call them "Situation Reports" back home in the great commonwealth of Pennsylvania, pencil boy.

He ushered her to the cell at that point, to the thin mattress and the LEGO pillow where she closed her eyes and hoped to God the room would stop spinning before her dinner came back up.

"Ma'am? The telephone?"

Fogel turned her head toward the open bars, where Officer Mitchell Jun stood holding a corded phone, and she wondered if he could slip through those bars.

Forcing her legs off the bed, she turned, sat up, and waited for her head to catch up. As she stood and crossed the six feet to the door, she realized she was barefoot, spotted her shoes next to the bed, nearly went back for them, then changed her mind. All of these thoughts sloshed through her head in a vat of half-set Jell-O, her brain making the connections but operating at 40 percent capacity.

Fogel took the receiver and held it about a half inch from her ear. She was present enough to think about the other ears that probably touched that phone and knew she didn't want to share biology with any of them. "Hello?"

"How's the head, Fogel?"

"Stack? How did you know I was here?"

"You called me last night. You don't remember that?"

Nope.

"Oh yeah, right," she said.

"You said the little shit tricked you. Although you sounded more like, 'thal ittal shizricked mah.' I've been there, though. Lucky for you, I speak the lingo. When you get back home, maybe I'll teach you to drink so your talk can match your walk."

Fogel heard him chuckle at his own joke. "Now what?" she said.

"Wait for him to pull out more cash, I suppose. We got nothing else."

"Any bodies?" Fogel had lowered her voice as she asked the question, but Officer Jun heard her anyway. His eyes perked up.

"Nothing here. But we didn't suspect one, did we?"

"I guess not."

"Get a room somewhere close. Sit tight for a day or two. If we lose him, come home. I think that's the plan," Stack said.

Fogel agreed with him, said good-bye, and handed the phone back to Officer Jun.

He set the phone down on a desk to the right of the station's four cells. "I need to run a camera out to the Chestnut. I can give you a ride back to your car, if you don't mind making a quick stop."

"The Chestnut?"

"It's a motor lodge off 118. It's on the way out to Mike's."

Fogel nodded and wished she hadn't.

Officer Jun produced a bottle of Advil from his pocket and handed it to her with a weak smile.

The Chestnut Motor Lodge was a real dump. If not for the naval base, they were lucky if tourists stopped here for gas. The owners of the Chestnut tried to sell, couldn't, and eventually decided to let the motel die a slow death.

"That's all just fine by us," Officer Jun said. "The prostitutes need somewhere to bring their Johns. At least this place keeps the riffraff outside the city limits."

By the looks of things, the riffraff had been busy last night.

Officer Jun's coworkers had the entire parking lot taped off along with the west end of the building. The remains of a large

SUV smoldered at the center of the lot and several cars were taped off, too.

"What happened here?"

"Someone vandalized every white car in the parking lot, even set that one on fire. We had reports of shots fired. They found some blood in the stairwell, but no victim." He reached across the car, popped open the glove box, and rummaged around inside. He found a couple boxes of 35mm film, checked the label, then closed the glove box. With his free hand, he scooped up the camera at his feet. "We think whoever did this started up at Mike's last night—we got nine more damaged cars up there—sliced up the tires, only the white ones, though. Got a thing for that color. Some special kind of crazy, I suppose. Wait here—"

Officer Jun shot out the door toward a group of officers near the far west stairs.

How many white cars did you see in the parking lot?

Thatch had been obsessed. Why would he disable them? Would he seriously set one on fire?

Fogel opened the door and stood beside the car. Jun's back was to her, lost in some animated conversation. On the opposite end of the building, near the motel office, a detective in plainclothes was questioning a woman with a name tag pinned to her lapel, maybe the manager or some kind of employee. Several times, she pointed up at an open door on the second floor, then turned back to the detective.

Officer Jun glanced back at her.

Fogel waved.

When he turned back to the other officers, she bolted across the parking lot to the center staircase and took them two at a time. On the second floor, she followed the sidewalk around to the open door. There was a bloodstain on the concrete just outside the door. The earlier rain had partially washed it away—no evidence tag, no crime-scene tape. They hadn't gotten up here yet.

An angry voice shouted up at her from the ground floor. She couldn't make out the words.

She didn't have much time.

Fogel carefully stepped over the stain into the room.

Typical rundown motel room. She'd seen hundreds over the course of her career. A ratty bed, heavy drapes, shag carpet. Something had happened here, though. The room felt off. She spotted a bottle cap on the floor, otherwise, nothing appeared out of place. She quickly crossed to the bathroom—a towel on the floor, otherwise normal. Nothing on the counter around the sink.

A matchbook on the floor near the bed.

A Bible in one of the drawers.

Motel notepad next to the phone.

Fogel tore off the topmost three sheets and shoved them in her pocket before ducking and taking a look under the bed.

When she stood back up, three men were standing in the doorway. A plainclothes detective, a uniform, and Officer Jun.

Jun's face was red. "I told you to wait in the car."

"She's with you?" the detective said. A pudgy man, half a foot shorter than Jun, with stringy hair combed back over his flat head.

"You're standing in evidence," Fogel said, glancing down at the concrete.

The detective followed her gaze. "Oh, hell."

The three men spread out around the stain.

"The rain took most of it, but you should be able to get a blood type."

"You're standing in my crime scene, miss." The detective glared.

Fogel glanced around the room. "Really? I'm sorry. It wasn't marked. I thought I saw someone I knew up here and just came up to say hello."

"Jun, who is this person standing in my crime scene?"

Officer Jun cleared his throat. "This is Detective Fogel, from Pittsburgh PD."

"Oh, you mean the drunk woman with a gun we were kind enough to not charge last night? The one we could still charge this morning, if we changed our mind? Felony possession of a concealed firearm. Drunk and disorderly. That woman?"

"I wasn't—" Fogel started to protest, then closed her mouth. She didn't remember.

"Yes, sir."

"What did her superior officer say about all this?"

"We haven't called him yet, sir."

The detective scratched at his chin. "No, we haven't, have we? Not yet."

Fogel forced a smile and started toward the door. "Sorry, professional curiosity. You're right, though. Not my jurisdiction."

The detective blocked her path. "Has her firearm been returned to her?"

"Yes, sir. Her identification too."

The detective's head tilted slightly to the left. "Do you know who's responsible for this, Detective Fogel?"

"I'm not sure what *this* is."

"Oh, I think you do."

"I work Homicide. Looks like you have a vandal running loose. That's not my area of expertise."

"We've got a vandal who looks to have disabled nearly a dozen cars, all the same color, mind you, at two different locations. He firebombed one of them with a Molotov cocktail. We've also got multiple reports of shots fired, two bloodstains, counting this one, indicating people were hit. Yet, we have no bodies. Nobody here, nobody at area hospitals. A whole lotta nothing. You know what else is weird about all this?"

Fogel said nothing.

"All these white cars, including that bonfire in the parking lot, have fake tags. Not stolen, mind you, but fake, and I'll be damned if they don't look as good as the real thing. None of the VIN numbers check out, either. They're bogus. Never manufactured. These cars don't exist. They don't seem to belong to anyone. Not a single guest of the hotel or visitor. Nobody has claimed ownership of a single one."

"Sounds very perplexing," Fogel said.

"What brings you from Pittsburgh to Fallon, Nevada, Detective?"

Fogel shrugged. "I'm just a big fan of *Top Gun*."

8

"You should slow down."

I knew Stella was right, but every time I lifted my foot off the gas, some involuntary urge forced it back down. The yellow lines of the highway rolled under us as nothing more than a blur. Tumbleweeds and thin trees beside the road blew by so fast they appeared indiscernible from the barren desert floor. The rain of earlier had been burned away by bristling heat. I looked down at the speedometer, the needle hovered near ninety-three.

"Please, Jack."

I lifted my foot and eased the Jeep down to seventy; forced myself to keep it there.

We were about an hour outside of Fallon.

I needed a drink. I didn't have anything, though. Nothing in the car or my pack.

My fingers were white, I gripped the steering wheel so tight. I peeled my hands away one at a time and wiped the sweat on my jeans.

"Have you ever killed anyone?" Stella's voice was timid, meek. "Point blank like that?"

I shook my head.

"I've only killed bad men. Men like Leo." She turned to me. "It's important you understand I killed Leo, not you. I don't want him on your conscience. Your knife may have put him down, but he was already dead. There's no saving someone like that. He had another minute at best. You shouldn't fret about about the ones today, either. The one you shot in the gut, he'll live. And the man on the stairwell, he was bad. Like Leo."

"How do you know? What if he had a wife or kids? We don't know anything about him."

"He was bad. I know. Even worse, he was with them."

She said this as if it were enough, and maybe it was. I had no idea what these people did to her, what they represented.

I killed a man.

The thought sunk down into my gut, and my stomach churned.

"The police will be looking for us."

"They won't find any bodies," she said.

I killed multiple men.

Stella went on. "They pointed guns at you and me and would have shot one or both of us."

Would they? Or were they really just trying to get Stella back? The gun was nothing but a bluff. If one of them pulled the trigger on me, would it have even worked?

My breathing quickened. Icy sweat covered my face and neck. Tiny blotches appeared in my vision, floating clouds of white obscuring my view of the road, the interior of the car.

The right front tire left the pavement, followed quickly by the back, the rough shoulder grabbing and tugging the Jeep away from the road.

Stella yelped.

My left hand, slick with sweat again, slipped on the steering wheel as I pulled hard left. Gravel, rocks, and dirt sputtered against the undercarriage. Weeds smacked against the front grill, swallowed beneath. I smashed my foot down hard on the brake, too hard, and we fishtailed off the pavement entirely, skidding through the dirt, the steering wheel useless. The Jeep began to spin to the left, so I tugged the wheel to the right, in hopes of gaining control. With such a high center of gravity, Jeeps flipped easily, and I felt the right side lift off the ground. I pulled the wheel back in the other direction. The front wheels caught, gained traction, and the back fell in line. I brought the Jeep to a clunky stop, ripped off my seat belt, jumped out, and bent over in the grass.

I couldn't remember the last time I ate, and what came up was a sickly yellow, so acidic it burned my tongue even as my stomach clenched, heaved, and I buckled further over with more.

I felt Stella's hand on the small of my back, her other on my shoulder, squeezing through my shirt. With the last of it, I stood and wiped my mouth. "God, I'm a fucking mess."

"You took a life. You're human. I'd be worried if it didn't upset you."

When I turned back to her, I realized how pale she had become. Both her hands quivered now, not just her right. "Is that because of what just happened, or…"

"I'll be okay."

I ran my hand through my hair. "You need to…" I couldn't bring myself to say the word. I wasn't sure what word even fit—feed? Eat? Drain? Absorb?

Stella understood, though. She said, "No. Not anymore."

"I shouldn't have shot that guy. You needed him. You could have fed on him."

She was already shaking her head. "I wouldn't have done it. I was just trying to scare him."

"You have to, though. Don't you?" I took a step closer. "What's the longest you've ever gone…between?"

Stella drew in a deep breath and looked down at her hands. "A year and two days. I've found ways to slow it down, but only slow it down. Only a person seems to stop it entirely."

"The cornfield in '95?"

She nodded. "That bought me a few days, not much. I found a park that night. Parks are always good. I was there for less than an hour before a man started following me. Ten minutes after that, he tried to put a knife to my throat. He didn't think I noticed him hiding in the bushes, but I did. I always do. I remember how horrible he smelled, like spoiled onions. I wasn't wearing my gloves. He died fast."

"Did anyone find the body? I didn't see anything that year."

The corner of Stella's mouth turned up. "They don't always find the bodies, Pip."

I thought of Leo Signorelli somewhere at the bottom of Harmon Reservoir in his BMW.

"I won't do it again, though," Stella said emphatically, attempting to steady her hands again.

"We'll find another way." I said the words before, and I meant them, but I had no idea how I could make good on such a promise.

I went back to the Jeep and bent, inspecting the undercarriage. Then I circled around. Aside from several fresh scratches, I found no damage. I stared at the torn trail behind us, two long gouges in the earth where our tires left their mark. Stella was looking back down our path, too, but she was watching the road, the cars roaring past. The last one, a blue station wagon.

"Where are we going, Jack? We can't stay here. They'll be coming soon."

"Carmel, California," I said. "I found Cammie Brotherton."

I told her what Dunk told me.

"We'll need a new car."

9

I can't tell if it says 803 or 303 Windmore," Fogel said, frowning down at the topmost page of motel stationery she swiped from the room at the Chestnut. After rubbing a pencil gingerly over the page, she was able to read a hastily scrawled address and a single word, sort of.

The Nokia mobile phone was pressed to her ear, Stack on the other end of the call.

Stack said, "But the rest—the word *Charter?*, with a question mark at the end, you're sure on that?"

"Yeah. I think so."

"I know that word. I've heard it or seen it somewhere before."

"Where?"

Stack went silent for a second. "I'll call you right back."

The line went dead.

She was in the parking lot of a small strip mall at the edge of Fallon. The Nokia battery died, so she picked up a cigarette adapter at Radio Shack, then called Stack. The notepad was a long shot. She couldn't be sure that was Thatch's room, and even if it was, there's no way to be sure he wrote on the pad. The address might have been written by a guest (and she used the term loosely for that place), months ago, maybe even longer.

The lead detective at the Chestnut wanted to hold her, but he had no reason and after twenty minutes of badgering, she left with Officer Jun and retrieved her car from the parking lot of Mike's Gentlemen's Club. She had been told to leave town, Old West style. Apparently they still did that in Nevada.

Officer Jun no doubt received instructions to follow her. He was parked two cars over in the same lot, making no effort to hide. Fogel waved at him.

Ten minutes passed before the Nokia chirped.

Fogel hit the answer button.

"I've got nothing on Windmore, but the word Charter, I figured out where I'd seen it. Remember Calvin Gurney?"

Fogel's head still hurt, but she felt the gears beginning to turn. "1978?"

"Yeah. The only victim identified that year. One of the three guys they found in the house where the Nettletons were squatting. The last record of employment for him was as a janitor for an outfit called Charter Pharmaceuticals outside of Chadds Ford, Pennsylvania. Chadds Ford's about four and a half hours from Pittsburgh."

"No streets called Windmore nearby?"

"I don't see anything on the map, but I can keep working on it. I'll dig up what I can on Charter Pharmaceuticals, too."

Fogel rubbed at her temples. "I could catch a flight and be there by tonight."

"That's a long shot. Might be better to stay around there—head back to the strip club and try and pick him up if he goes back," Stack suggested.

"He's done around here. I think he got what he came for."

"The girl?"

"Yeah."

"You see her? What's she like?"

Fogel wasn't quite sure how to describe what she saw last night. She finally settled on a single word. "Dangerous."

"That seems about right."

Fogel looked back over at Officer Jun. This time, he waved. "I'll call you when I land."

10

David's eyes snapped open.

His mouth was dry.

"You were dreaming," Latrese Oliver said from the seat beside him.

He closed his eyes again and leaned back into the seat. The rumble of the private jet was usually soothing, but he couldn't get comfortable. He preferred these trips without her, but she had insisted. She always insisted when it involved that girl.

"How much further?"

"A few more hours before we land, then another hour by car."

"And she's still there?"

"Yes, and we've confirmed Stella is on her way with the boy. All together, nice and neat," Oliver said. Her breath stunk almost as bad as that damn arm of hers.

He did smile at the thought of seeing Stella again. It had been far too long.

11

Sixty miles outside of Fallon, I turned left off Interstate 580 and took the South Lake Tahoe ramp toward Minden. "Do you have any cash?"

Stella looked up from my copy of *Great Expectations*. She had been reading it for the past hour. "I have $2,463.00."

"On you?"

"Under a stone back in Fallon."

My heart sank.

"Of course, on me, Jack. I don't trust banks, and stones aren't much better."

Her spirits had improved, but her skin had managed to grow even more pale. Although the air conditioning in the car was blowing at full, her temples glistened with a thin sheen of sweat. The shaking had come and gone. I pretended not to notice, but she caught me looking down at her hands more than once.

"I've got about sixteen hundred, I think. I withdrew all I could last night. If we trade in the Jeep and use about half the cash, we should be able to get something decent."

"Or we could just steal a car and keep our money."

"We're not stealing a car."

"Okay, we borrow a car and return it at a future date, to be determined, at a location of our choosing," Stella said, her gaze falling back to the book.

"I'm pretty sure that's still stealing."

"I'm not suggesting we borrow a nice car. It can be a clunker, something that won't be missed."

"A nice car is more likely to be insured."

"Settled, then. A nice car it is. Perhaps a BMW."

"That's not what I meant."

Stella marked her place in the book with her thumb and closed the cover. "I'd prefer never to set foot in a place like the one where you found me, but for a girl on the run, options for earning an income are limited. I've learned the value of a dollar. I fully understand how difficult it is to earn a dollar, and when it comes to vehicles, I prefer to stick with the ones purchased by someone else's dollars, particularly when they are so readily available."

"So you steal?"

"Now that I think about it, I do believe I prefer the term 'borrow.' I never should have said 'steal.' Stealing is wrong. Borrowing is neighborly, friendly. Like when you say you'd like to borrow a cup of sugar, which you then use and are unable to return, but still, everyone wears a smile. Moving forward, I will only 'borrow' cars."

The exit ramp dropped us on 395, and the town of Minden popped up around us. Not much of a town at all. Most of the buildings stood only one or two stories. A large number appeared vacant. Minden looked like an old mining town that managed to claw its way into the twentieth century but was now living on life support.

"A place like this, I don't think you could borrow or steal a car without getting caught. We need a big parking lot, someplace where nobody will see us," I said, studying both sides of the street.

"You've clearly never borrowed a car before. Pull in there—" she said, gesturing toward one of the largest buildings in town.

"A hospital?"

I swung a quick left and slowed as we followed the pavement over a quick dip, then into the parking lot surrounding the building. About a quarter of the spaces were occupied. More than I would have expected, for such a small town.

"Doctors and nurses work extremely long shifts, sometimes days at a time. A borrowed car may go unnoticed for nearly half a week. Plus, you said you wanted a nice car."

"I didn't mean—"

"There!" She pointed at a small area off the main lot marked Staff Only, blocked by a gated arm. "Park here somewhere, in the visitor's section. It will be some time before someone finds it among the visitors."

I pulled into a space at the back against a hedge row between a large pickup truck (green) and a beat up Winnebago (tan and brown). The employee lot was about fifty feet away, kitty-corner.

"Gather our things. I'll find something," Stella said, unfastening her belt.

"Are you sure you're okay to—"

She was out the door and halfway to the lot before I could finish my sentence. There was a slight wobble in her step, but she steadied herself as she went.

What's the longest you've ever gone...between?

A year and two days.

Today was August 9—a year plus one.

I pulled my backpack and Stella's duffle bag from the back seat and set them next to the Jeep. The book Stella was reading, too. I placed the stolen shotgun behind the bags in case someone drove close enough to see what I was doing. Circling around to the passenger seat, I popped open the glove box. An empty bottle of Jim Beam rolled out and dropped to the floorboards. Without thought, more of a reflex, I picked it up, twisted off the cap, and held it over my mouth, hoping for a least a drop. Nothing dripped out, though. When I realized what I was doing, I cast the bottle into the bushes, thankful to be alone.

The only other items in the glove box were the vehicle owner's manual, registration, and a flathead screwdriver. I left the manual, shoved the registration into my pocket, and went to the back of the Jeep with the screwdriver to remove the tag. Then I walked back around to the driver's side and used the screwdriver to pry off the VIN plate. I loosened it years ago, then fastened it back in place with just enough glue to hold it still. It came off easy enough and joined the registration in my pocket.

I was circling the Jeep one last time to be sure I didn't miss anything, when Stella pulled up behind me in a late model four door Mercedes-Benz E-Class.

The car was white.

"Are you sure about this?" I asked, as Stella opened the driver-side door and stood beside the car.

"The owner clearly wished for someone to borrow it. Why else leave the keys?"

"I mean, are you sure you want a white car?"

"A wolf in sheep's clothing, my dear Pip. There is no better way to hide than in plain sight." Stella bent down and pressed a button. The trunk popped open with a slow, calculated hiss. "Chop, chop, before someone comes along."

I rolled my eyes and carried our things to the back of the Mercedes. The trunk was extremely spacious and had either been meticulously vacuumed on a fairly regular basis or rarely used. It closed with a gentle click. I kept the book out. I figured she'd want that.

Stella tossed me the keys. "You're driving."

I took one last look at the Jeep and realized how much I would miss that car. I'd owned it for four years, longer than any other. Maybe I'd get the chance to come back for it, knowing in my heart I never would.

I climbed behind the wheel of the Mercedes and pulled the door shut behind me. The plush leather seats hugged me. "Whoa."

Stella was beaming. "Right? I am so glad you suggested a luxury

car. Also, fully insured. I checked the paperwork. No need to fret."
She snatched the book from me and set it in her lap.

My hands rolled over the leather steering wheel. I adjusted the mirrors.

Stella reached for the stereo and clicked it on. I expected static to blare out from the speakers, but instead came Steven Tyler and Aerosmith belting out *I don't want to miss a thing.*

"Huh," I said, looking down at the radio.

"What?"

"Nothing. The radio. It just reminded me of when we were kids, on that bench."

"'Jessie's Girl'," Stella said softly. "That's the song that was playing the first time you came up the hill. The first day we met."

"Rick Springfield was the shit."

"The shit?" Stella said.

"You never heard that expression?"

She shook her head.

"The shit. The bomb, the man. Doctor Noah Drake from *General Hospital?* Jo used to watch that show whenever she wasn't working."

Her face was blank.

"You have no idea what I'm talking about, do you?"

She shook her head again. "We had no televisions in the house. Ms. Oliver wouldn't stand for it. I was permitted music for one hour each day, providing I completed my studies. Of course, there were books, too, so many books. I lived in those books."

I pulled out of the parking lot back onto 395, toward the interstate.

"How did you get out of the house?"

"Through the front door, of course."

The Mercedes picked up speed effortlessly. After years with the Jeep, the quiet cockpit of the German car was jarring.

"Tell me about the day you got out."

Stella opened *Great Expectations* at some random place and began to read again. "Please don't ever ask me about that day. Never again, Pip."

Sweat trickled down her cheek, down her neck. She ignored it.

I turned the air conditioner on full.

I reached over and took Stella's gloved hand in mine.

We were five hours outside Carmel, California, with no other white cars in sight.

12

Former detective Terrance Stack, just Terry now, spent the better part of an hour tracking down a phone number for Charter Pharmaceuticals and a live person. The number listed with directory assistance was answered by an auto-attendant. That auto-attendant provided a series of options, none of which led to a real person. Instead, each time he selected something new from the menu, the call either rolled to another recording or disconnected altogether, and he had to start over. He was damn near ready to throw the phone against the wall when he got an idea.

The number directory assistance had given him ended with 371-1050.

He dialed the original area code, then: 371-1051. This, too, went to the auto-attendant.

371-1052. Auto-attendant.

371-1053. Auto-attendant.

371-1054. Auto-attendant.

371-1055. Auto-attendant.

When he got to 1063 through 1081, the auto-attendant no longer picked up. Instead, the lines rang until eventually timing out after a few minutes.

He considered giving up and trying something else as he dialed 371-1097.

"Sanders." No hello or greeting of any kind, only the single name. Muttered more as an afterthought than the answer to a phone call. "Somebody there?"

Stack opened his mouth to speak and realized he hadn't figured out what he planned to say if he actually got through to someone. He cleared his throat. "I'm looking for Calvin Gurney. I believe he's a janitor there."

Stack knew full well Gurney had died back in 1978 in the Nettleton house, but he figured if he wanted to rattle some chains, no reason to pussyfoot around.

The voice replied. "Who?"

"Calvin Gurney."

"How'd you get this number?"

"Dunno. The auto-attendant transferred me."

"Fucking auto-attendant. Hold on."

There was the rustling of papers, then the voice came back. "I don't see anyone by that name in the directory."

Stack said, "Calvin told me if he wasn't around, I should ask for Eura Kapp."

Eura Kapp died in 1986—a forty-seven year-old female found burned but not burned.

"Nobody by that name, either."

"What about Andy Olin Flack?"

Flack was the thirty-three year-old child molester left in the alley across from the kid's apartment.

"Flack? Flack hasn't worked here in at least a decade. Who is this?"

Stack thought about that for a second. "Richard Nettleton."

The line went dead.

When he dialed again, nobody answered.

13

Stella slept.

Sporadic at first, she fought it, but soon when I looked over, I saw the book in her lap, and her head lolled to the side. Even in slumber, though, the quiver in her hands continued. Her breathing went from steady to labored and back again. At one point, her entire body shook so violently, she actually awoke. Her skin was pasty, she appeared feverish, but I dared not touch her forehead to find out.

At one point, she woke and simply said, "I worked there for the money."

I told her she didn't have to explain.

"I know," she replied. Then she was out again.

We were on CA-88 just outside of Dogtown when things got really hairy.

Static burst from the Mercedes' speakers.

Not the static that usually found its way into a song as a radio station began to fade out of range, but hostile, sharp static at more than twice the volume of Michael Stipe and REM, who were busy losing their religion a moment earlier. The Mercedes bucked, and all the electronics went dead for a second, the gauges on the dashboard came back far brighter than they should have been, then returned to normal as the static disappeared.

Beside me, Stella jerked awake in her seat. The copy of *Great Expectations* dropped to the floor, and her head shot quickly back and forth as she peered out the windows.

"Pull over."

"What?"

"Pull over!"

I jerked the wheel hard to the right while slamming my foot down on the brakes. Unlike my Jeep, the Mercedes slid slightly, but I maintained control as we left the pavement for the gravel shoulder and skidded to a stop. Horns blared as cars flew past. A rusted out Chevy pickup came within inches of sideswiping us, grunting as the driver swerved around the place we left the road.

Before we stopped moving, Stella had her seat belt off and the door open. She ran from the car, climbed over a wooden fence set back about ten feet from the highway, and raced across the open field.

"Wait!" I shouted after her.

If she heard me, she didn't care. I bolted around the car and ran after her.

The field gave way to a hill, and when I crested that hill, I saw Stella, already down the other side and running toward a large body of water (I would later learn this was Lake Camanche). I had no idea why she ran toward it or how she had even known the lake was there from the highway. I didn't remember seeing it as we came down the highway, but the lake was clearly her destination.

I came down the hill and caught up with her at the water's edge where she frantically clawed off her gloves.

"Get back, Jack!"

When I didn't move, she growled at me over her shoulder. "Baaack!"

Her gloves on the ground beside her, Stella dropped to her knees and plunged both her hands into the water.

The world went completely silent, and I realized I had stopped breathing, I had stopped moving, I froze.

"Baaaacck," Stella said again, this time her voice barely a whisper. Her eyes were pressed shut and her head tilted slightly to the left, as if listening to some far-off sound.

I'm not sure what I expected to happen at that point, but at first, nothing did. Stella remained perfectly still, her back rigid, the muscles in her neck twitching, her eyes closed, her mouth still slightly open after allowing that last word to escape.

The air became crisp, not with cold, not cold by any means, but with a rigidness as if the very molecules in the air gripped one another, forming a thick blanket. What little breeze drifted across the open field and the lake fell still. Not a single animal, insect, or rubbing of twig against weed could be heard.

The hair on my arms stood, and I looked down on it in marvel, knowing the hairs on the back of my neck were standing, too, prickling against the collar of my shirt. Ozone crept past—faint at first, then growing stronger.

In what seemed much longer, only a second had passed.

Stella gasped.

The first fish to surface was a large-mouth bass, at least ten pounds, maybe larger. The fish floated to the surface a few feet from Stella's arms—unmoving, clearly dead. Burned but not burned. A catfish appeared on the opposite side of her, then another fish I didn't recognize, maybe a trout. Fish began to float up all around her, filling the surface of the water—five, ten, a dozen, two dozen. It began at her arms and spread from there, fanning out across the water, this blanket of death, until I could see nothing else, the dark waters lost beneath.

I don't know how long it went on. Time was lost to me.

Fish were still floating up far off in the distance, when Stella pulled her arms from the water and collapsed at the shore.

I ran to her and dropped at her side.

"Can't...touch me...especially now." Her eyes were closed, and the words slipped out on a single broken breath.

I wanted desperately to scoop her up into my arms and pull her close, comfort her, anything to ease whatever was happening to her, but I couldn't. I couldn't so much as stroke her cheek. I knew that, and it tore at me.

I brushed the hair from her face, carefully avoiding her skin. "What should I do?"

"I don't want you to get hurt."

"Can you move?"

Her body went limp.

She passed out.

Out on the lake, a small boat trolled through the blanket of fish with a boy of about fourteen or fifteen on board. Although a good distance away, he was heading in our direction. His small motor churning as he peered over the side, shifting from right to left.

I ran back to the Mercedes, opened the trunk, and rooted around in my backpack. I had spent my share of nights sleeping outside and learned long ago not to travel without a good blanket. The one I carried wasn't very thick but was made of wool and extremely warm. I took the blanket back down to Stella and carefully wrapped it around her body, covering her exposed arms and neck, creating a makeshift barrier between us before I scooped her up and carried her back to the car. I settled her gently in her seat before remembering her gloves.

I ran back down.

The kid in the small boat drew close to shore now, and he perked up when he saw me come back. "All the fish are dead!"

The grass and weeds around the shore where Stella had knelt were black, too, a patch at least eight feet in diameter—all dead, already stinking of rot and decay. I grabbed Stella's gloves.

The boy shouted, "The water's poisoned or something!"

"Looks that way!" I yelled back, taking one last look before shoving the gloves in my pocket and racing back up and over the hill to the Mercedes. I jumped into the driver's seat, twisted the key, and hit the gas, kicking up dirt and gravel behind us. Back on

CA-88, I saw the boy from the boat crest the hill and hoped to God he didn't get a good look at me, Stella, or our car.

Traffic on US-395 was light—mainly long-haul truckers, RVs, and a handful of cars. Using the cruise control, I kept our speed five miles per hour over the limit—not fast enough to risk getting pulled over, but enough to keep up with everyone else.

Stella woke for the first time near Stockton, California. Prior, she had mumbled several times in her sleep but nothing really coherent. The color had returned to her cheeks, and gratefully, the sweating stopped. If she was feverish before, she didn't appear to be any longer, but I had no way to know for certain. I considered waking her, particularly when her condition appeared to be improving, but thought better of it. Whatever *this* was—this condition, this illness, this curse, this hunger—the lake had helped, but she needed to rest, and as comforting as hearing her voice might have been for me, I needed to think about her and let her rest.

As signs for Stockton began appearing, Stella stirred beneath the blanket, her head rolled from left to right and back again, and her eyes fluttered open.

"Thirsty," she managed to say.

I handed her a bottle of water.

"I stopped for gas about an hour ago and got us some supplies. We've got water, Kit Kats, a bag of Oreos, and some Cheetos."

"Not much for nutrition, are you, Pip?"

"Auntie Jo used to say it's better to eat junk food. It keeps your immune system from getting lazy."

"I'd like to believe you were kidding, but I'm fairly certain you are not." Stella twisted off the cap and drank nearly half the bottle before setting it down in the center console. "How long was I asleep?"

"About two hours."

"How bad?"

"The lake?"

She nodded.

"I think you killed all the fish."

She leaned back in the seat and closed her eyes again, drawing in a defeated breath. "I didn't mean to."

"Someone saw us. There was a kid in a boat. He didn't get close enough to see our license plate. At least, I don't think he did."

At this, Stella eyes popped open. "He was on the water?"

I nodded. "About halfway out. Pretty far off when it started, then he saw us and started toward shore."

She turned toward me, the belt across her lap and chest holding her back. "But he was okay? He didn't die?"

I realized then what was going through her head. If the fish were all dead, why not the boy? If he was on the water, too. "He wasn't *in* the water. The boat must have protected him somehow."

Stella dropped back into her seat and sighed.

A slow-moving semi in the single westbound lane forced me to tap the brake and release the cruise control. Our speed dropped to sixty. "It helped, though, didn't it? The fish?"

Stella raised one of her hands and held her palm out between us—no longer trembling.

"How long do you think…how long did it get you?"

She lowered her hand to her lap. "Perhaps a day, maybe two, but no more."

"So we just do that again," I told her. "When you have to, we find another lake or a cornfield or—"

But she was already shaking her head. "You learned of the cornfield in the press, right? If reporters aren't already at that lake, they'll be there soon. The story will make the local papers, maybe television. If we escape national news, the reprieve will only last until the next time. Dead lakes, dead fields, dead trees…somebody will connect everything and soon the press will create maps, each occurrence marked. Some scars can be hidden, Pip. Others are simply too large. If the press doesn't find us, Oliver and the others surely will. I imagine they are watching for these exact moments.

Ms. Oliver called it my 'kiss of death.' I imagine her map would have such a phrase printed in big, bold letters at the very top—**Stella's Kiss of Death**—heading west. There would be no hiding then."

They don't always find the bodies, Pip.

"Then we find another bad person. Someone who deserves to die."

"Nobody deserves to die."

"A killer, a rapist, someone who hurts others…" I couldn't believe how effortlessly my mind went there, but when I weighed the thought against possibly losing Stella, there really was no choice, not for me. "Maybe in LA. We'll go to a park, like you've done in the past, and—"

"I won't," she said emphatically. "I will not kill again."

"You do it just this one more time. That will buy us a year, right? A whole year to come up with something else, another way. Some kind of solution."

"I won't."

"If the people in white find us—one of them—any one of them…"

"I won't."

"…they're trying to hurt us. If anyone deserves—"

"Jack, please. Stop. I won't. I don't care what that means for me, what happens. I won't kill again. I need you to promise me, if I'm feverish, if I no longer have my wits, and I try to make you stop like I did with the lake, you must promise me you won't—"

"I'm not going to…"

"—and if at any point it seems I might hurt you, you need to stop me. We may need rope or handcuffs, or maybe both. I don't know how bad it will get. I've never let it go so far, but I won't hurt you. You can't let me." Her voice dropped low. "These gloves cannot come off. If they do, if I reach for you, you need to shoot me, Jack. You need to kill me."

"That's something *I* won't do," I told her. "No way."

She turned to her window and looked out over the barren land-scape. "You'll need to shoot me like a rabid dog, because at that point that is all I will be."

I twisted the wheel to the left, maneuvered the Mercedes into the opposite lane, and floored the accelerator. I stayed in the wrong lane long after we passed the semi. It wasn't until a oncoming car approached us that I finally swerved back, the speedometer buried at that point.

14

Former detective Terrance Stack, just Terry now, went back to the living room window overlooking his front stoop and yard.

The white van was still sitting there.

He wasn't exactly sure when it first arrived, but it had been out there for the better part of the day.

Just sitting there.

If anybody got out, he hadn't seen them. Nobody got in, either. No movement at all.

Just sitting there.

15

The sky had grown dark by the time we finally pulled into Carmel, California, the stillness in the night sky rivaled only by the silence between Stella and me. Not a single word had been uttered between the two of us in more than an hour. Every time I looked over at her, I found myself checking the color of her skin, searching for a tremble in one of her hands or arms, waiting for that sheen of sweat to return. Thankfully, none of those things happened, but a voice in the back of my head reminded me that they would, in time all those things would happen again. Time could only be borrowed. Stella continued to stare out the window, lost in her own thoughts, her gaze fixed on some far-off object. Several times, she returned to the book, but even the words of Charles Dickens proved unable to soothe her. She had closed the cover and returned to her window, to that distant nothingness that so captured her attention.

Located on California's Monterey Peninsula, the city of Carmel wasn't large. The *Welcome to Carmel!* sign posted off CA-1 boasted a population of a little over three thousand residents.

At the last gas stop, I had consulted a map and written down directions.

CA-1 made way for Ocean Avenue. We followed it along the coast for about two miles before taking a series of side roads that brought us deeper inland. We found Windmore Road with little trouble and followed it around a series of winding bends in search of 803. Most of the houses were small two or three-bedroom Spanish bungalows with carefully manicured lawns and gardens. Colorful bougainvillea bushes edged sidewalks and driveways. Well-aged Monterey pines, cypresses, and live oaks soared overhead, creating a canopy over the road.

"This is a beautiful street," Stella said softly, the first to break the silence.

"There it is," I said. "Up on the right."

The house was humble—two bedrooms, maybe three. A brick bungalow with a gray asphalt shingle roof and neatly kept flower beds below the front windows. No car in the driveway, no lights on inside.

"It doesn't look like anybody is home."

"Or they prefer sitting in the dark," Stella said.

I pulled the Mercedes to a stop in front of the neatly manicured lawn and switched off the ignition. "Why don't you wait here, and I'll check it out."

Stella opened her door, got out, and started up the short sidewalk.

"Or we both go," I muttered, snapping off my seat belt and following after her.

The temperature had dropped with the sun, the air taking on a crisp, cool feel. I thought about my jacket in the trunk of the Mercedes. I thought about the shotgun I had wrapped in that jacket.

Stella was at the front door, peering into a side window. "I don't see anything."

I knocked.

No answer.

I knocked again, louder this time.

When there was still no answer, Stella reached for the door-knob. The front door wasn't locked. She twisted the knob and gave it a gentle push. The door swung inward over the tile floor of a small foyer. "Hello?"

Something about the way her single word echoed through the rooms told me the house was empty. Then I had a second thought. My mind conjured the image of Cammie Brotherton, dead in the bathroom or the kitchen or the bedroom of some horrible self-inflicted wound, her eyes blank, her lips permanently fixed in some grotesque smile.

Welcome to my home!

The house not empty at all, but a tomb.

Stella stepped into the foyer, and I grabbed her shoulder.

"We need the gun," I said softly.

She nodded and waited as I ran back to the car and retrieved the shotgun and my jacket from the trunk. I held the gun lengthwise against my body as I ran back, concealing it as best I could beneath the coat from the eyes of nosy neighbors.

At the door, I stepped past Stella into the house, leveling the weapon.

Between the moon and the streetlights, the interior slept in muted gloom. From the sparse furniture in the living room and adjoining kitchen, long, veiled shadows stretched across the floor.

A small wooden dining table filled a breakfast nook in the back. Three of the chairs were pushed under. The fourth was lying on its back on the floor. The kitchen counters were bare. About half the cabinet doors stood open, drawers too. Most looked empty.

In the living room, a battered old couch with threadbare cushions hugged the wall. It had a musty smell, unused, a place for dust to gather as life happened somewhere else. No television in the room, no other chairs or tables, no pictures on the walls.

Beyond the living room was a narrow hallway, darker than the rest of the house, the light from outside pausing at the threshold, unwilling to go further.

Stella followed close behind me as I stepped into the hallway, the barrel of the shotgun leading us.

On our left, we found a small bedroom painted a cheery pink. A ruffled Disney princess blanket and pillow sat rumpled in a heap in the far corner. There was no furniture. Several empty hangers hung in the closet, no clothes.

"Look," Stella said quietly. A barbie doll watched us from a shelf at the top of the closet, one arm outstretched, the other at her side, her blond hair flayed about.

I reached up and took it down. I expected it to be covered in dust, but it wasn't. It hadn't been up there long.

Stella took the doll from me, and we returned to the hallway.

The bedroom across the hall was a little larger than the first but just as empty. A couple scraps of discarded paper were on the floor. I knelt down and studied the carpet, looking for the telltale indents of a former bed, maybe a dresser, but found nothing. If someone had slept here, they did so without a bed.

Stella was back in the hallway, her eyes fixed on the closed door at the end.

It had to be a bathroom.

My mind brought back the image of Cammie Brotherton's lifeless body.

So many things could go wrong in a bathroom.

16

Former detective Terrance Stack, just Terry now, kept his old service pistol under the center cushion of the green velour couch in his living room, the one he bought back in 1973. The couch was so uncomfortable, he didn't have to worry about anyone sitting on the ratty mess and discovering the gun. Children weren't a worry, either. The last child who set foot in his house was now married with three kids of his own. He had no reason to store the gun out of reach and always felt there were many reasons to store the weapon within reach. At eighty-two years old, *within reach* became a theme in Stack's life. He reached under the cushion and plucked out the gun.

The magnum in hand, he went back to the window.

The white van hadn't moved.

"What the hell are you up to," he muttered aloud.

Stack slid the gun into the front of his pants under his belt—he didn't give a damn who saw it—and went out his front door and down the steps. He was halfway to the van when it started up and rolled down the street just fast enough to remain out of reach.

17

Stella remained still as I stepped past her, my grip tightening on the shotgun as I reached for the bathroom doorknob. I counted down from three, mouthing the words for my benefit as much as Stella's, before twisting the handle and slamming the door open into the room.

The walls of the small bathroom were pink tile. The toilet, sink, and bathtub were pink, too. Probably original to the house back in the sixties. Like the kitchen, the drawers and two doors of the vanity were open and empty. One drawer held several elastic hair ties and a half-empty tube of toothpaste. The shower curtain slid to the side, the room empty.

I lowered the shotgun, pointing the barrel at the floor. "I can't tell if someone left here in a hurry or never really moved in. I've squatted in abandoned houses before. They looked just like this. But this place feels like someone just left, like we just missed them."

When Stella didn't answer me, I turned.

She was no longer there.

"Stella?"

I went back down the hallway and found her in the kitchen again, peering into the refrigerator. "We have a package of hot dogs, half a bottle of Patron tequila, about a third of a loaf of bread, white, and three cans of Diet Coke. There is no mold on the bread. It looks fresh, and the hot dogs expire next week. Considering the power is on, I would have to assume they left quickly, and they left recently. In fact, I am absolutely certain they left yesterday."

"How could you possibly know that?"

She closed the refrigerator and pointed to the calendar attached to the door with four Pizza Hut magnets. "Because all the days leading up to today are crossed out. I'm also fairly certain they like pizza—nobody has four magnets for the same store unless they are feeding some type of compulsion on a regular basis."

"Dunk said she moved around a lot. We must have just missed her."

Stella leaned back against the counter. "It was kind of her to leave us food. I'm famished."

"We can't stay here."

"Why not?"

"She left for a reason. What if they're coming?"

"What if they've already been and gone? What if she's coming back? I've been running for over four years, and I too have stayed in houses just like this. Everything I need can be found in my duffle. If I stayed in this house for a week, and I ran out for some reason, even just for an hour, that duffle would go with me. I'd leave this house as bare as it is right now. She might be coming back, and if we leave, we miss her entirely. For the first year after I left that house, I lived in constant fear. My life was ruled by 'what ifs.' Then I learned to trust my instincts, and my instincts are telling me this is a safe place, at least for one night. They're probably still looking for us in Nevada."

"But they might come looking for Cammie Brotherton right here."

Stella placed a hand on her hip. "Didn't we just discuss my thoughts on 'what ifs?' That sounds decidedly like a 'what if.'"

I could tell Stella wasn't going to budge on this, and the truth was we had nowhere else to go. We could get in our 'borrowed' car, point it in some random direction, and just drive, but that seemed reckless, too. We needed to rest. The adrenaline had kept me moving all day and part of the night, but now that I stopped moving, I felt the drain weighing on me. I was in no condition to drive. We could get another hotel, but hotels created paper trails, even when you pay with cash, and we didn't need a paper trail. Hotels also cost money, and while we had some, it wasn't an infinite supply.

"She did leave the front door unlocked," I finally said.

Stella smiled. "She did indeed. You catch on quick, my dear Pip."

"One night," I relented.

"One night," Stella agreed, rummaging through the cabinets. "If you retrieve our bags from the car, I'll see to dinner."

I did, but I left her the shotgun.

18

Stack pulled his favorite chair to the window overlooking his street about ten minutes after the van returned. He had been sitting there when the second van pulled up, the third too. Plain white panel vans. No markings or signage of any sort. He was fairly certain they were Chevys, but it was tough to tell from this angle. An hour earlier, he went back outside, this time holding the gun, and like before, the vans disappeared down the road before he could get close. He managed to read a partial tag on one, but didn't call it in. What exactly would he report? Someone parking on his street? Three someones parked on his street? When he was a rookie, he fielded calls just like that and knew nobody took them seriously. Former detective or not, they'd see him as nothing but an old man wasting their time.

Beside his favorite chair, he set up his favorite rickety metal tray table. Atop the table was the remains of an Iron City six-pack. He drank two so far, and when he finished the second one, he wasted no time reaching for a third. He popped the can free from the plastic ring, opened the top, and put away three solid swallows before setting the can down. Stack knew Fogel wouldn't approve, but Fogel wasn't here, and he damn well needed a beer. He tried calling her three times in the past few hours, but the calls didn't go through. He figured she turned the phone off. When he tried to dial her again about twenty minutes ago, he realized his own phone line was dead.

Stack had gone to the shitter once, but other than that, he kept eyes on the vans. Nobody got out. Nobody climbed in. If they were somehow responsible for the dead phone line, he hadn't seen them do it. That didn't mean they didn't do it. It didn't mean they did, either.

He sat in his favorite chair with eyes on the vans as the overcast Pittsburgh sky made way for night. He watched the various streetlights come to life up and down his block. He watched a few of his neighbors come home from a day's work and disappear into their own houses. He'd seen a few kids running around. Not many, though. Most in his neighborhood had grown and went off to live their own lives a long time ago.

Stack watched the vans.

When he finished the third beer, he reached for a fourth, knowing he should be thinking about eating something but not really all that hungry.

19

When I came back in toting Stella's duffle bag, my backpack, both copies of *Great Expectations*, and the Penn State yearbook, she had our hot dogs boiling in a pot on the stove and several candles burning around the kitchen. The princess blanket we had found in the small bedroom had been neatly folded and placed on the kitchen island, the pillow on top. I set our bags on the floor and the books on the wooden table in the kitchen, then I righted the chair that had been lying on its back when we arrived.

"I felt it best not to turn on any lights. The bedrooms and living room either face the road or the neighbors, so it's best we avoid those rooms. The kitchen windows all look out over the backyard, which is fenced. If we stick to this part of the house, nobody should see us." She stirred the hot dogs and nodded toward a closet on the far end of the kitchen. "I found a washer and dryer back there. I think we should take the opportunity to do our laundry while we're here. Such conveniences aren't always so handy."

I had a sudden urge to smell under my armpits, but I was classy enough not to do that while she was watching. I knew my clothes were rank. I hadn't done proper laundry in weeks. Instead, I washed my clothes in hotel sinks and strung them around the room to dry.

While I had "washed" everything when I arrived in Fallon, nothing would beat an actual machine washing.

A box of latex gloves sat on the kitchen counter.

"I found those under the sink," Stella said. "I prefer my gloves, but latex will do, too. I find it's good to have extras."

The bottle of tequila, two of the cans of Diet Coke, and two plastic cups half-filled with ice had been set on the kitchen table. The flickering candlelight on that bottle was nearly as enticing as Stella's smile.

Stella placed two slices of bread on paper plates, then fished out the hot dogs and dropped them on top. "Go ahead and mix our drinks, Jack. You look like a puppy eyeing a bone."

When you haven't eaten in nearly twenty-four hours, things tend to taste a little better than they probably should. Even so, that might have been the tastiest hot dog I've ever eaten. Between the two of us, we ate the entire package, and I put away three slices of white bread after that. The tequila and Diet Coke, though, sat in front of me, barely touched. I had been staring at the bottle, I'm not sure how long, when Stella spoke.

"You need it, don't you?"

I wouldn't lie to her. "Usually."

"But not now?"

I thought about it for a second. "I haven't had a drink since the club last night. I found a bottle of Jim Beam in the glove box of the Mercedes, but it was empty. I nearly cracked it open so I could lick the glass, I wanted a drink so bad. But now…"

I held my hand out, palm down. Steady, no shaking. "Weird. I feel like I want to drink, like I should be drinking, but I don't really *need* a drink. Normally, I'd be shaking like a leaf when I'm this dry."

"Maybe you shouldn't, then."

"Maybe I would like to drink with a beautiful woman." I raised the bottle and took a sip of the tequila, then set it back down. "Whether I need it or not."

Stella pushed her empty glass toward me. "After what happened at the reservoir last night, the hotel this morning, and the lake, I

not only *want* a drink, I *need* a drink, and possibly a third or a fifth
or a sixth after that. I would like to forget our little predicament for
tonight, and that bottle plays a significant role in my plan. I am
quite happy we found it, actually."

I smiled and refilled her cup. "I imagine living in a house with
Latrese Oliver would drive anyone to the bottle."

The moment the words slipped from my mouth, I regretted
them.

Stella's face fell slightly at the mention of the name. She reached
for her cup, stirred it with her finger, then took a drink. She had
removed her gloves. They were folded neatly beside her, next to
the three books. "It may be difficult for you to understand, looking
in from the outside as you did, but she did treat me well. She cared
for me, looked out for me, treated me with respect. Not the kind of
respect the others in the house doled out, they were simply afraid
of me. Not her, though. If she feared me in the slightest, she never
let on. The day I left...I hurt her. I hurt her horribly. That man
came, got me out, killed all those people to get me out, and I never
thought we'd actually make it to the front door let alone to his car,
but somehow we did, and I remember standing there, amazed by
this. I saw this documentary once with a lion at a zoo in Germany.
One of the lion's handlers accidentally left the cage door open. Not
much, mind you, just an inch or so, but open. About midway
through the day, the lion realizes this, you can see it on the video—
she's walking in circles around the interior of her cage, and she
pauses at the door, nudges the iron with her nose, then stands there
for at least five minutes. Finally, she goes back to pacing and lies
down in the corner for a nap. She had been in that cage for so
much of her life, the idea of leaving when she could didn't occur to
her. Or possibly it did, and she decided she didn't wish to go. Her
life was inside that cage, not on the other side of the bars. The
safety of the known outweighing the unknown. As I stood in the
driveway of that house next to his car, I nearly ran back inside. I
think I was going to. I killed that day, I didn't want to, but the

people who worked at the house, they kept grabbing me, trying to pull me back in, and I was wearing short sleeves, so the moment they touched me, they...I didn't mean to hurt any of them. I was so rattled by it all. Then there was all the gunfire and the explosions. This man, he was like an army with all the destruction he brought."

She paused for a moment and took a sip of her drink, then set the cup down. "He yelled at me to follow him, get in his car—it was parked about halfway down the driveway. That's when the police man showed up. He came running up behind us, yelling, 'Pittsburgh PD, drop it! Drop it!'"

"Detective Brier," I said quietly.

Stella went on. "The man with the GTO turned toward him, prepared to fire, but then didn't. I thought for sure he'd kill him, but something stopped him. Then Ms. Oliver's SUV slid up behind both of them. One of the men with her jumped out before the vehicle even stopped moving, and he fired at the detective before the detective could fire at him. I was horrified. I was so busy watching this man die, watching so many die, I didn't see Ms. Oliver get out of the car and run up to me. I didn't even recognize her voice when she shouted at me. I just spun around and grabbed her, purely defensive on my part. I wouldn't have hurt her if I'd known it was her, and I let go of her arm the second I realized, but she was screaming, screaming so loud." Stella paused and took a deep breath. "The man with the GTO, he grabbed me by the back of my shirt and pulled me away, got me to his car. I could hear her screaming the entire time. I still hear her screaming."

I nearly reached for Stella's hand. I wanted to comfort her, but she was wearing a white tank top, her arms bare. No gloves. I couldn't touch her. I couldn't console her, I could only sit there.

"He drove me to New York City. Five hours in the car, and he didn't say a word to me. I was so frightened, I was certain he planned to kill me. I yelled for him to let me out. I nearly touched him, several times. I pulled off my gloves and reached right for his neck. I didn't care that he was driving or how fast we were going, or what would happen. I only wanted to get out. But he didn't even flinch. It was like I wasn't there. When we got to New York, he took me to Grand Central Station and parked out front. He reached into the back seat and handed me a duffle bag—" She nodded at the bag on the floor. "—that duffle bag. And said there were clothes inside, new identification, and ten thousand dollars cash. He told me to get out and pick a train, any train. He didn't want to know where I was going. I asked him again, 'who are you?' and he just pushed the bag toward me and told me to get out, so I did. The second I stepped out, he left. He just sped away and left me standing there, like some big inconvenience to be discarded on the sidewalk."

"So you have no idea who he is?"

"I didn't then, but I think I might. Thanks to you."

"Who?"

She slid her empty cup back to me. "Such information will cost you, Pip."

I mixed another drink, her third now, and returned the cup to her. "Careful, you're going to get drunk."

"I'm well aware of the effects of alcohol," she said, taking a long gulp.

I was still on my first, about half gone now.

Stella put her cup aside and took the yearbook from the stack beside her. She turned to one of the dog-eared pages, then pointed at the photograph of Jeffery Dalton. "I can't be sure, but I believe it was him. He's so much younger here, it's hard to tell. I didn't say anything when you first showed me the book, because it seemed too unlikely. I thought maybe my mind just wanted it to be him. But the more I thought about that night, the more certain I became."

Jeffery Dalton.

"No more of this talk, not tonight." Stella reached across the table and scooped up the bottle of Patron. She brought it to her lips and drank the tequila straight. Smiling, she placed it back on the table in front of me. "Your turn, Pip."

"Now you're trying to get *me* drunk? A seasoned alcoholic?" I grinned, picked up the bottle, and drank, too, the familiar warmth easing down my throat. I wiped my mouth on the back of my hand.

"We're going to play a game," Stella said, a mischievous curl at the edge of her lips. She moved our plates aside. "We need to separate our laundry. Colors will go here." She slid her gloves to the right side of the table. "Whites over there, near you. The game is called *Never have I ever*."

I chuckled. "I've played that, in like fifth grade."

"You've never played with me."

I was beginning to like where this was going. I straightened up in my chair.

Stella placed the bottle of tequila between us. "You've played, so you're familiar with the rules. I'll start with something like, 'never have I ever eaten french fries.' If you have eaten french fries, you'll have two choices: you can either drink, or deposit an article of clothing on the table."

Using my foot, I pulled my backpack close.

Stella shook her head. "The clothing in our bags will be off limits for the duration of this game."

I tried to keep a poker face, but judging by the smile on Stella, I wasn't doing a very good job.

She folded both hands on the table. "Never have I ever ridden a bicycle."

"Seriously?"

"I wanted one when I was younger, particularly after seeing yours, but Ms. Oliver was afraid I might fall and hurt myself. Doctors were…problematic…for me. Hospitals were out of the question, so she was very protective of everything I did. If injury was a possibility, the activity was ruled out."

I couldn't imagine growing up without a bike as a kid. Not having the freedom those two wheels granted, or the fun of riding.

Stella cleared her throat and nodded at the bottle. "I believe you are required to drink or provide an article of clothing to our laundry pile."

I smiled, took the bottle, and drank.

"Chicken," she said.

"I'm just trying to catch up. I've never had a woman outdrink me before."

"Prepared to be schooled, good sir. Your turn."

I thought about my response for a second. "Never have I ever lived in a house with a pool."

"I liked the pool," Stella said, before crossing her arms and pulling her white tank top over her head and starting our pile of whites. Then she settled back into her chair, wearing only her shoes, jeans, and a white bra. The flickering candlelight bounced across her toned skin.

I reached for the bottle and took a drink. My God, she was beautiful.

"Eyes front, Pip," Stella said. "Shall we continue?"

I nodded.

"Never have I ever had real friends my own age to play with."

"None? What did you do all day?"

"I read, of course. I've read so many books. Ms. Oliver and I would sometimes play cards or board games. When I was younger, around five or six, they tried to find me a friend. They brought a girl in to play with me. I remember Ms. Oliver dressed me in long sleeves and my longest pair of gloves. Her name was Rebecca. We played for nearly an hour, with Ms. Oliver and at least four others hovering over us. I didn't understand what I could do back then, I was too young. They watched us closely at first, but I think minds began to wander. Nobody saw Rebecca reach for my cheek. She only wanted to brush away a piece of lint or something. Things happened so fast. When she cried out, they snatched her away. I don't know what happened to her after that. They told me she was the daughter of one of our cooks, but I suspect she had been kidnapped." Stella nodded at the bottle. "I believe you did have friends, so you need to choose."

I took off my University of Connecticut sweatshirt. I had never been to Connecticut. I picked it up at a thrift store years ago. Dark blue. It went in our colors pile.

It didn't take long before we were both in our underwear. Stella insisted that because her pair of gloves had started the game, things like shoes and socks had to come off in pairs, too.

My hand inched closer to hers on the table, but we dared not touch.

I knew we couldn't touch, but I so desperately wanted to. I wanted to scoop her up into my arms and make love to her right there, and I could see that same desire in her eyes. I knew what would happen if I did, and I almost didn't care. Just touching her for a second would be worth it. There was a heat coming off her fingertips, off her uncovered skin. She lit up the room.

Stella slid the bottle over to me. "Drink."

"But you didn't make a statement yet."

"Drink."

"And I think it's my turn."

"Drink, anyway. And it's my turn."

I raised the bottle to my lips and drank. There wasn't much left. I left about a quarter inch at the bottom.

Stella took up the bottle and finished the tequila the moment I set it down. With a sly grin, she slid the empty aside. "Option two is no longer on the the table, and you are down to your skivvies." She drummed her fingers. "Hmm. What should I say? What should I say…"

She stood and leaned back against the kitchen island, facing me. Her dark hair rolled down over her shoulders in chestnut waves. She had the longest, sexiest legs I had ever seen. "What to say…" she repeated softly. When she looked up at me, her eyes were glistening in the thin light. "Never have I ever…kissed someone I loved."

I hesitated for a moment, thinking about this. Then I stood and slipped my thumbs into the waistbands of my underwear. I didn't take them off, though.

Stella's grin had returned, but there was a sadness behind it. She didn't want me to see that, but I did. "Now is not the time to be bashful, Pip."

"I haven't, either. I've never kissed someone I love."

She seemed perplexed by this. "You've never…?"

"Oh, I've done that. But never with someone I love."

"What about that girl from the diner?"

"Gerdy."

"What about Gerdy?"

"I loved the idea of Gerdy. I wanted to have someone to love, and she tried to be that for me. I feel horribly guilty for letting her try so hard and not giving back, not really. But I couldn't love her. Not while knowing you were out there somewhere. Every time she held my hand, I thought of your hand. When she kissed me, I pretended her lips were yours. I think she somehow knew this and didn't care. I think she made peace with it, and that made her death so much harder to accept. She did so much for me, and I gave her nothing in return."

"I'm sure she felt loved."

"I like to think so. I tell myself that."

"You're a good guy, John Edward Jack Thatch. She knew that. I'm sure your affection meant more to her than you can possibly realize. She was lucky, to have that closeness, to have shared that intimacy."

A tear fell from her eye, and I went to her. I couldn't not go to her. My finger reached out, came within a centimeter, but I didn't wipe the tear away. Instead, my finger hovered there. I watched as the tear rolled down her cheek, off her chin, and splashed on her bare feet. She whispered, "All I'll ever be, all I can ever be for you, Jack, my dearest Pip, is a pretty little thing to be looked at but never touched."

"Close your eyes," I said softly.

"Why?"

"Close them."

She did, and another tear slipped free, following the first.

I reached back to the table behind me took an ice cube from my cup, the largest one I could find, and I brought the ice to the side of her neck, pressed the cube against her skin.

Stella gasped but kept her eyes closed. She drew in a deep breath.

I slid the edge of the ice cube down her neck, over her shoulder, down the length of her arm. When I reached her fingers, they splayed out, and she turned her palm to face me. I brought the ice cube back up her arm, over to the small of her neck, then down her chest, to the swell of her breasts.

I leaned in to her ear, as close as I dared. "Take off your bra."

Her eyes still closed, she reached up behind her back and undid the clasp. Her bra fell to the floor between us. I circled her breasts with the ice cube, drawing closer to her swollen nipples with each pass. Stella arched her back and let out a soft moan. There was a gasp when the ice finally touched her there. Melting now, less than half the size it was when I first started. I reached behind me and took another from the cup. I knelt and ran this one up from her left foot, up her ankle, to her inner thigh. The heat there was unbearable, and it took every ounce of willpower not to drop the ice and use my hand instead. I brought the ice up, over the silky material of her soft, white panties, over her belly, up her chest. Then, standing again, I followed the contours of her neck to her lips. She licked tenderly at the little bit of ice remaining, her tongue so close to my finger, but I didn't let go, not until she parted her lips and took it in.

Then it was Stella who reached behind her back. She took out a pair of the latex gloves from the box on the counter and handed them to me, then she put on a pair herself. Her eyes opened then, big and bright and full of life as she caressed my cheek, the line of my jaw.

We'd spend the next several hours like that, exploring each other's bodies with gloved hands. Carefully touching and not touching. A choreographed dance. And it was utterly amazing. When we finally fell asleep, our borrowed sheet between our naked bodies, heads resting just far enough apart, we were both exhausted, and I finally felt complete.

20

Stack wasn't sure what time he fell asleep, but the pain in his neck told him it had been a while ago. The six empty beer cans on the table at his side seemed to second the thought, and the incredible need to empty his bladder backed up both.

He rocked forward in his chair and looked out the window.

Three white panel vans across the street, right where he left them.

Night gave way to the muted gray light of a Pittsburgh morning.

The vans were still there. He didn't see anyone inside.

Maybe he was being paranoid. McPherson across the street owned a plumbing company. Maybe he bought some new vans and simply parked them in front of his house. Of course, that didn't explain why they ran, though. Each time he went outside, all the vans started up and quickly disappeared down the road only to return a short while later. He'd lost track of how many times he went out there.

They might have left because he was waving a gun around. Drunk guy with a gun, he'd leave too. It didn't explain why they came back. It didn't explain why nobody called the cops. At this point, he'd probably welcome the boys in blue on an unexpected visit. He'd check the phone again on the way back from emptying his bladder, but he was fairly certain he'd find the line was still dead, as it had been every other time he picked it up.

The magnum sat on his rickety table next to the empty cans of Iron City. Stack scooped up the gun and stood. His body ached, and he tried to steady himself by holding the chair, either the beer or sudden movement causing him to feel a little lightheaded for a moment. His vision went white, then cleared.

Gun in hand, the floorboards creaked under his weight as he crossed the house to the small bathroom under the stairs.

He was midstream when he heard another floorboard creak, this one from above on the second floor.

21

I woke to the sound of scratching.

My mind woke before my body, and in my head I pictured a plump mouse inside one of the walls of the house we had borrowed from Cammie Brotherton, his tiny paws digging away at the backside of the drywall in a frantic attempt at escape, dust bellowing out around him, piling up at his tiny pink feet. Freedom on the other side of that wall, but he had to dig.

My eyes snapped open.

Sunlight streamed in through the windows.

Stella and I had slept in the kitchen, a small space between the counter and the island, protected on both sides by cabinets and counters. She was still sleeping. I could hear her soft breaths beside me.

Scratching.

Still, the scratching. Coming from one of the bedrooms.

I got up quietly and went through the pile of clothes on the table, tugged on my jeans. I found the shotgun on the counter where I left it the night before and gently picked it up, careful not to make a sound. I knew it was loaded and primed. I flicked off the safety with my index finger and started down the short hall.

I found him in the pink room.

A man of about five-ten, with long, tangled brown hair riddled with gray tucked up under a hat that reminded me of the kind worn by hunters, fur-lined with flaps over the ears. He wore dirty jeans, brown boots, and a blue flannel shirt.

He had brought his own gun, some kind of hunting rifle. The weapon was propped up in the corner of the room.

This man had his back to me, feverishly scribbling on the walls with a thick, black marker.

David Pickford is a beautiful man.
David Pickford is a beautiful man.
David Pickford is a beautiful man.
David Pickford is a beautiful man.
David Pickford is a beautiful man.
David Pickford is a beautiful man.
David Pickford is a beautiful man.
David Pickford is a beautiful man
David Pickford is a beautiful man.

With the barrel of the shotgun pointing at the man's back, I noiselessly circled the room, following the outer wall past the closet, past the corner, until I was close enough to reach out and silently snatch the rifle. I put my head through the attached sling and hung it behind me, against my back. Then I pointed the shotgun at the stranger again.

"Who are you?" I said, hoping my voice didn't betray my nerves.

The man continued to write.

David Pickford is a beautiful man.
David Pickford is a beautiful man.
David Pickford is a beautiful man.

I cocked the shotgun, ejecting one unspent shell and loading another. A completely futile effort, but I hoped the sound would snap him out of whatever fugue held him.

The marker still moving, he said, "Where's Cammie Brotherton?"

The man had a freakishly large forehead. His wiry hair looked like it had been cut with a knife and hung down over his face at varying lengths. His eyes had this blank, dead look. His beard was a tangled mess. I figured he was in his late forties or early fifties, but I found it hard to tell.

"She's supposed to be here," he said. "This is where she said she'd be. David wants me to say hello to her. Have you seen Cammie Brotherton?"

"Who are you?" I repeated.

The man glanced over at me, then went back to his writing. "You're Eddie's kid, aren't you?"

With that, I nearly lowered the shotgun, but thought better of it. Something was wrong. The way he talked. Like someone speaking in the moments before they fell asleep.

"How do you know my father?"

David Pickford is a beautiful man.

David Pickford is a beautiful man.

"He and I go way back," the man said. "Your momma, too."

I thought about the names on my list, the people from the yearbook. All dead but three. If the man in the GTO was Jeffery Dalton, then, "You're Dewey Hobson, aren't you?"

He tilted his head as if the thought just registered with him. "Dewey Hobson, that's right."

I hadn't heard Stella get up. She was standing in the doorway, dressed in the same clothes as yesterday. We never did get to the laundry. She opened her mouth to say something, and I quickly shook my head. I handed her the shotgun and nodded toward Hobson. She understood, raising the barrel and pointing the weapon at him.

I showed him both of my empty palms, the rifle still dangling on my back. "I've been looking for you, Dewey. You and all the others. You're a hard man to find. Do you know where my father is hiding?"

Hobson finished one wall and moved on to the next. If he saw Stella, he didn't acknowledge her. "I'm here to see Cammie Brotherton. David wants me to say hello. Then I'm supposed to shoot her." He pointed his index finger and thumb at me in the shape of a gun. "Pop, pop! Double tap, right in the forehead. Good and dead."

"You talked to David?" Stella said. "What exactly did he tell you?"

Hobson said, "He told me to go to Cammie's house and say hello for him, then kill her. Shoot her dead. He also said he loves you, Stella, and he's cleaning up the whole mess, just for you."

Hobson dropped the marker then, turned, and walked quickly toward Stella. I thought for sure she'd shoot him, he came at her so fast, but she just stepped aside, and he walked right by as if she wasn't there at all.

Stella and I exchanged a look, she as confused as I, and we both followed after him.

22

Stack zipped up.

He'd be damned if he'd be found dead with his pecker hanging out.

The board above him creaked again.

He knew the board. Top of the stairs, three deep into the hall-way from the last step. He'd pulled up that damn board about a dozen times over the past decades, pulled out the existing nails, replaced them with 50mm screws, replaced those screws with longer screws. He tried gluing the board down. He even dumped talcum powder down around the seams, nails, and screws of that board as well as the ones around it, in hopes of softening the sound. None of that worked. The damn board still squeaked the second you put a little weight on it.

Stack reached for his magnum, pointed the gun at the ceiling about two inches south of the light fixture, and squeezed off three quick shots.

The fucking thing kicked back hard against his old bones, but this wasn't his first rodeo. His aim held, and the shots landed within an inch of each other, leaving a gaping hole above.

23

We found Dewey Hobson standing in the living room, staring out the large window at the street. I came up beside him, keeping a safe distance.

He said, "Cammie's not home, is she?"

"No, Dewey. We think she left yesterday."

"That's too bad. I really wanted to say hello, for David."

"Do you know where she might have gone? Where she would go if she had to leave here?"

Hobson said nothing, his eyes fixed on some point across the street.

"Would she have gone to my father? Does she know where he is?"

Hobson said, "He'll be here soon."

"My father is coming here?"

"No, David is. They were right behind me."

I looked back at Stella. She was already moving—racing around the kitchen, shoving our clothes back in our bags, grabbing the books from the table.

The large window shattered a millisecond before I heard the shot.

A bullet struck Hobson in his left shoulder. He jerked back but remained standing.

A white SUV had stopped in the middle of Windmore Road. The woman who had fired the shot stood beside the open driver-side door in a long, white trench coat, a thin trail of smoke drifting up from the barrel of her nickel-plated semiautomatic pistol, a smug look on her face.

"Down!" I shouted, crouching behind the wall under the window, hoping the brick would be enough.

Hobson didn't move. He remained still as the shoulder of his shirt bloomed red with blood.

Three more bullets peppered the wall behind us. I reached out and yanked Dewey's leg. He lost his balance and fell beside me.

Stella ran in from the other room, our bags in one hand and the shotgun in her other. "The neighbors will call the police. We need to get out of here!"

Another shot. The bullet struck a tall lamp in the corner of the room.

I raised my head just enough to see outside. "I think there's three of them. We open up on them with everything we've got and make a run for the car." I quickly put on my backpack, pulled Stella's bag closed, and checked the rifle. "We go on three. Ready?"

Stella nodded.

Another bullet ricocheted off the brick just below the windowsill.

I started to count down. The second SUV skidded to a stop behind the first before I reached two.

24

Stack heard a heavy weight hit the floor directly above his head, then roll down the stairs. Plaster rained down on him from the newly created window from his bathroom to the second floor.

Never one to waste a trip, when Stack got the beer from the kitchen, he took the opportunity to fill his left pocket with twenty-nine rounds of .357 ammo from the box in the utility drawer beside the refrigerator. All he had in the house. He clicked open the cylinder, removed the three spent shells, and replaced them with fresh bullets. Then he flushed the toilet, opened the door, and stepped back out into his living room.

The man who came down the stairs the hard way was lying in a heap against the coat closet door. His white trench coat had twisted around his body, and his right leg had gotten caught up in the shotgun slung over his shoulder and hidden under the coat. His fibula split halfway between his knee and ankle, broke through the skin, and stuck out from a hole in his white slacks. If the man had still been alive, that leg would be bothersome. As it currently stood, one or more of Stack's shots caught him between the legs and exited out the small of his back—both of those wounds looked far more painful.

Stack froze in the living room, not out of shock or fright, but because his hearing was terrible and he couldn't tell if there were more people upstairs.

25

From the corner of the shattered front window, Stella and I watched Latrese Oliver step out in her familiar flowing white trench. Her left arm was in a sling, partially hidden under the coat. If she carried a weapon, I didn't see it.

The old woman looked up and down the street, then at the bullet-riddled front of Cammie Brotherton's small house. "Are you in there, sweet Stella?"

Stella, who was still crouched low on my right side, started to rise. I shot her a quick glance and shook my head.

She froze.

"I know it was an accident, dear," Oliver said. "You didn't mean to hurt me, did you? It was all because of him—Dalton, Preacher, whatever he calls himself these days—he confused you with his little escape plan, told you things, didn't he? Untrue things. Not a single question of 'would you like to leave?' Instead, he took you from me, then left you alone in the streets—a bird from her cage lost to flutter in solitude on broken wings. You can come back, Stella! You know I love you. Nobody loves you like I do! I forgive you for what you did to me!"

Stella stirred but said nothing.

Oliver took a step closer to the house, favoring her left leg. "That Dalton, he's a hitman, you know. It's one thing to kill those who deserve it, but he simply kills for money. He puts a price on a head and accepts it—fathers, brothers, mothers, sisters—he doesn't care, he's killed them all. I taught you values, I taught you morals, I made you the grandest of women. Come home to me, continue your studies, and all is forgiven!"

"You imprisoned me!" Stella shouted. "Made me kill for you!"

"I kept you alive, dear, kept you safe. I brought you what you needed. Who else would do such a thing? And you're overdue! Two days! You must be famished! Let me feed you, Stella. I know exactly what you need! I have one all picked out! One might not be enough anymore. Perhaps two or three." Oliver took another step closer and frowned. "The Thatch boy is in there too, isn't he? With that awful Hobson fellow? I can smell them. Put them down, Stella, then come home with me. I have a new place, a wonderful place. You'll find it so lovely. Let me give you what you need, my sweet, sweet girl. All is forgiven, I promise you!"

Hobson was looking down at Stella's hands, her long, black gloves back on. He turned back to the window as a man rounded the SUV.

"David," Stella whispered.

David held up his wrist and tapped the front of his watch. "We're on a bit of a time crunch, Latrese. How about we save the bonding speech for back at Charter, huh?" He smiled toward the house. "Hey, Jack? Did you like the Jameson I left for you back in Pittsburgh? I heard it was your favorite. I've got another bottle here in the car. It's all yours. I just need you to do a little something for me first. Nothing serious, just a little favor. You've got a gun, right? I bet you've got a cannon in there. All loaded up, ready to go? I need you to point your gun at Dewey Hobson's head, get it right up on there, nice and close."

My arms swung around, and the rifle with them, the narrow barrel less than an inch from Hobson's forehead. I tried to point it away, but my limbs wouldn't respond.

David then said, "When you've got the shot lined up, I need you to—"

A blast roared through the house as Stella raised her shotgun and pulled the trigger right next to my ear. The entire world went silent, David's voice, Stella and Hobson breathing near me, all of it replaced in a millisecond by a high-pitched ringing. I dropped the rifle, and it fell to my side on the sling. I covered both ears with my hands, but the ringing only grew louder.

Stella slapped my back, then began firing toward David, toward Oliver and the other people in white. She shouted something at me, right in my face, but I couldn't hear her. Her eyes jumped to the rifle dangling from my neck before going back to the window. I remembered the plan, scooped up the rifle, and fired—each shot nothing but a distant thud buried beneath the ringing.

Stella got to her feet and grabbed Hobson. She was out the door in an instant, pulling the man behind her. She released him just long enough to get a firm hold on the shotgun and squeeze off a series of shots, peppering the SUVs, then tugged at him again, pulling him across the yard. One shot struck the woman with the nickel-plated pistol and she fell back against the driver's seat, then to the ground. I fired, too. Four shots rained against the side of the vehicle. A fifth blew the front tire of the first SUV. I fired at a man huddled low in the passenger seat of Oliver's SUV while Stella took aim at a man who had rounded the vehicle and was now kneeling beside it, using the fender as cover. I shoved Hobson toward our Mercedes, fired another round, then yanked open the back door and pushed him inside. I threw our bags in behind him.

Oliver stood in the middle of the road, oblivious to all the gun-fire, her eyes locked on Stella. She started toward her, a slow shuffle. David had taken cover somewhere. I didn't see him.

Stella froze at the sight of Oliver, the old woman creeping toward her, raising her one good arm, the other trapped in the sling. I shouted her name but heard nothing over the ringing. I tugged at her arm, pulled her toward the car, got her into he passenger seat.

Then I slid over the hood and got in too.

Oliver was still walking toward us.

"Go," Stella's lips mouthed silently. "Please... Go. Go! Go!"

I did.

The Mercedes roared to life and I shifted into reverse, flooring the gas and spinning us around. The wheels screamed against the blacktop, grabbing the pavement as I shifted into drive and rocketed down Windmore Road, the back end sliding around the bend. A quarter mile away, three white Ford Expeditions flew past us in the opposite direction, heading back toward the house.

The ringing still shouted in my head, but it wasn't loud enough to drown out the sound of the approaching sirens.

26

Stack heard something.

Well, Stack thought he heard something.

Fucking hearing.

He edged closer to the stairs, considered taking the man's shotgun, then decided the magnum would do him just fine.

He stepped around the body at the base of the stairs, doing his best to keep the magnum trained forward, while pulling himself up the steps with his other hand on the railing. He'd made it up four of those steps before his screaming muscles and joints reminded him that he hadn't taken an Aleve since sometime the night before. The rattling bottle in his right pocket (not to mention the ammunition in his left) did little to help conceal his current location, but truth be told, it would take a special bad guy to miss an eighty-two-year-old man clawing his way up the stairs in some kind of geriatric chase. He half hoped someone would shoot him before he got to the top so he wouldn't have to climb the rest.

This time when he heard something, he was *sure* he heard something—a cough.

Stack took another step. "I'm a retired police detective who's been jonesing to fire a gun at a trespassing piece-of-shit for the better part of two decades. That last one felt real nice. I don't know who you are, but you better get the fuck out of my house before I make the last of these steps!"

The shouting took the wind from his lungs, and Stack had to take a break a half dozen steps from the top. He didn't sit, although he would have liked to. Instead he stood still, gripped the handrailing—the only thing keeping him from tumbling back down the steps like the man earlier, and drew in a series of breaths.

He never had a heart problem.

All the things wrong with his body read like a laundry list, but his ticker had never been part of the problem. Things changed, though, and if the pain in the left side of his chest was any indication, his heart was about to become another line item on his health insurance.

The pain in his chest was dull, a deep-rooted thump reminding him of his days playing football back in high school. A lifetime ago, the memories creeping back from someplace in his head as if only yesterday. Stack's brain was funny like that. He couldn't remember what he ate for dinner two days ago or even what he watched on television last, but at this particular moment he smelled the wet grass of the field behind the Macintosh farm, the scent of the dirt. He remembered the sun beating down from the east for the first time since the previous fall, and he remembered the pain of Henry Otter when he broke the line, got past Daryl Luthing, and barreled into him shoulder first, into his left flank. When the hit came, Stack remembered his mind telling him to hold the ball, and he fully intended to do that, but with Daryl's shoulder smacking into him like a runaway bull came the sharp crack of a couple ribs, the complete evacuation of all air from his lungs, and the most godawful pain Stack had ever experienced. The football shot out of his hands straight up into the air and landed directly into the arms of Ernie Neidert, who ran it back for a touchdown. All of this played out in the second or two it took for Stack's beaten body to crumble to the ground.

The pain Stack felt in his chest now felt no better than that day nearly seventy years earlier, and when the deep, burning ache had a good foothold in his chest, it began exploring, edging down his left arm all the way down to his fingers, still wrapped around the railing.

Stack didn't want to die. He was too fucking stubborn to die, and he sure as shit wasn't about to fall down his own stairs and end up spooning the shitknocker occupying that space now.

Pain or no pain, Stack tightened his grip on the railing and gave a good, solid tug. His legs kicked like pistons, and he shot up two steps, just like that. The pain in his chest fired back a ball of heat in protest, but before that could sink in and really deliver the hurt, Stack yanked at the railing again and made the last two steps. He collapsed on the floor of the narrow hallway at the top, his breathing ragged and drool leaving the corner of his mouth.

Someone walked up to him, came out into the hallway from the middle bedroom, the one with the expanded Wall of Weird. That someone stopped a few feet from his head. Stack tried to look up and get a better look at the person—all he could see were white shoes, white pants, and the bottom of a white coat much like the one worn by the man at the bottom of the stairs. Stack's head wouldn't move, though. His eyes barely wanted to move. He tried to swing his right arm around, the one holding the magnum, but as he did, he realized he was no longer holding the magnum. The gun might be on the floor beside him, or more likely he dropped it somewhere on the stairs. Either way, it wasn't in his hand, and it did little good somewhere else.

The person standing beside him knelt down, got a little too close, and whispered in his ear. "That's an interesting room you got there. My boss is gonna want to talk to you about that."

Stack tried to tell the guy that he wasn't about to talk to him, his boss, or the President of the United States, and if he did, he'd tell all of them fuckwad-nothing, but when he opened his mouth to speak, nothing came out but more drool, the pain in his chest and arm dialed up to eleven, and consciousness fell away.

27

Six minutes.

That's how much time passed from the moment the white Ford Expeditions arrived at 803 Windmore Road, until Latrese Oliver and David Pickford climbed into the back seat of the middle vehicle, the cleanup complete.

The crew worked with practiced speed. The bodies of the dead were placed inside the two disabled vehicles and set ablaze with handheld TPA canister grenades. David had no idea where Charter obtained such toys, but he sure enjoyed instructing his subordinates to use them. He had been told they contained thickened triethylaluminium, a napalm-like substance that ignites when exposed to air. They made very little noise, just a simple *pop!*, followed by a puff of blue smoke, then a rush of flames that quickly engulfed the interiors before lapping out through the opened windows and over the roof, hood, and sides.

The interior of the house was photographed and videoed in under two minutes. The pictures and footage would be examined later by a team of specialists. If there was something worthwhile to find, they would find it. At the end of those two minutes, TPAs were placed in the house and ignited.

Burning the dead was nothing more than a precaution. Charter employees were not permitted to carry identification, nor did they appear in any government database. Criminal records, social security, birth, DMV—all were purged upon employment.

A single neighbor emerged once the gunfire stopped, running from the house two doors down at 807 Windmore when he saw David standing in the street, directing the team. The man was in his mid-fifties, with thin hair combed back over a rather small head. He wore a white tank-top undershirt, jeans, and no shoes. He held a .22 in his hand. By the look of the rust on the barrel, the weapon hadn't been fired or cleaned in a long time. He ran at David, shouting that he called the cops, they were on their way.

"When did you call them?" David asked.

"Five minutes ago! You okay? You hit?"

"I'm not even here," David replied. "How could I get hit?"

The man appeared puzzled for a moment, then nodded. "I suppose not. That would be tough, wouldn't it?"

"What did you see?"

The man told him, and he had seen plenty. He told David how it all started shortly after that Ford Bronco down the street showed up. He told him about the man who got out—some homeless-looking mountain man. Walked right into Faye's place like he owned it.

"Did Faye Mauck have a kid?"

"I never saw one, but she kept to herself, mostly."

They had learned *Faye Mauck* was the latest in a long string of identities used by Cammie Brotherton in the two decades she'd been running. Most likely, that's the name that would appear on her tombstone, if her body ended up in a marked grave. David followed the man's gaze to the gray Ford parked a half block before 803, partially on the street, partially on the sidewalk.

Hobson.

Following instructions, like a good little soldier.

David nodded at one of the crew and pointed at the Bronco.

"Take whatever's inside, then wash it like the others." The man understood, moving quickly.

He returned his focus back on the nosy neighbor in the tank top. "You started all these fires, right?"

"I started the fires?"

"Yep. The cars, the house. All you. You like fire. You started them all. Killed these people, too."

"Okay. I guess I did."

"When the police arrive, you're going to tell them what you did, how much you enjoyed it. Then, as soon as you finish, after they write it all down, you know what you're going to do next?"

The man's face was blank.

"You're going to walk right into that burning house and sit down in the living room. Get right up in the thick of it and pop a squat," David told him. "You like fire."

"Okay. I like fire."

"Before that, though, when *I* leave," David went on, "I want you to shoot that little gun of yours—shoot the bodies in the SUV, get every shot off, then toss the gun in the bushes over there. Not too deep, though. We don't want to make this hard on the locals."

"That wouldn't be nice."

"No, sir, it wouldn't."

David saw a woman peeking out from behind the curtain of an upstairs room next door. He waved at her. It didn't matter if she saw him. Nobody would believe her. He turned back to the man in the tank top. "One other thing."

"Yes?"

"Do you think I'm a good-looking guy?"

The man tilted his head, his stringy hair catching the night breeze. "You might be the ugliest man I've ever met."

"You're not very smart, are you?"

"No, not really."

"I'm the most beautiful man you've ever seen."

The man considered this, then said, "Yeah, I guess you are."

David left him there, standing in the street, before climbing into the back seat of the middle Ford Expedition beside Latrese Oliver. She was picking at a flakey black spot on her bad arm. He shook his head and looked back out the window as they began to pull away. "There's a room in the house, freshly painted pink. We found a doll."

"Another child?" Oliver said.

"Maybe," David looked over at the house, "Cammie Brotherton might have given birth after all."

"I wonder what she can do."

"I wonder," David said.

28

"Anyone behind us?"

The ringing in my ears was still there but subsiding, the pain just a dull ache.

Stella unsnapped her seat belt and swiveled in the passenger seat, peering out the back window. "I can't tell. Traffic is too heavy. I see three white cars, but I don't recognize the drivers. I think we're okay."

The light in front of us turned red, I made a quick right turn to keep moving. We were somewhere in downtown Carmel. The traffic grew thick as morning commuters filled the streets. "I need to get us to the highway. Or maybe find another car."

"Jack, we need to look at his shoulder."

"We need to keep driving."

"There's blood all over the seat."

"It's leather. Blood wipes right off. We need to keep moving."

"I'm not concerned with upholstery. He could die."

I made a left turn onto 17 Mile Drive. "Is there anything in back we can use to tie him up? Is he awake?"

Stella snapped her fingers in front of Dewey Hobson's eyes. "He's awake, but he's not very responsive. Mr. Hobson, can you hear me?"

Nothing.

"Maybe there's rope or something we can use in the trunk."

"I don't think he'll hurt us."

"You can't be sure of that."

Stella said, "Dewey, do you plan to hurt Jack Thatch?"

Silence.

"Are you going to hurt me?"

Silence.

"What about Cammie Brotherton?"

"I'm going to tell her David says hello, then kill her." Hobson raised his hand and made a gun gesture again. "Pop, pop. Double tap to the head."

"Do you plan to hurt anyone else?"

Silence.

I frowned. "When David told me to point the rifle at Hobson, I did. I couldn't help myself. I would have shot him if he told me to do that, too. You knew. That's why you fired the shotgun, to make sure I didn't hear him say the words. What the hell was that?"

Stella turned back around and settled into her seat. "David can be very persuasive."

"What does that mean?"

"That's all they told me," she replied. "Ms. Oliver said he was special, like me, and he could be very persuasive, so they monitored everything he said to me, everything I said to him. It was horrible. They kept him in this little room, all alone. We couldn't really talk. We were like lab mice under a bright light, all these eyes and ears on us. I felt sorry for him, so I went."

"Where?"

"I don't know, exactly. I was always blindfolded or made to wear a hood. When I was young, Ms. Oliver said it was all a big game. When he came to see me, they made him wear a mask. That was part of the game, too, but I knew it was to keep him from talking to me when they couldn't listen. As I grew older, she told me it was best I didn't know where he lived, for my own safety. The drive always took a long time—four or five hours. I have no idea where we actually went. They might have circled the block, for all I knew, back then. I never thought he'd get out of that place."

"They used you and your ability to kill people. Maybe they're using him, too."

"Make a left up there," Stella said, pointing toward a sign.

"Toward the beach?"

She nodded. "It will be quiet this time of day."

Stella was right about that. We found only three other cars in the lot (green, red, silver). Only two early-morning sunbathers and a jogger on the sand. We pulled into a spot at the far end, and I shut off the engine. After donning a fresh pair of latex gloves from the box she had "borrowed" from Cammie's house, Stella rummaged through her duffle, took out a first-aid kit, and went to work on Hobson's shoulder. She unbuttoned his shirt and gingerly pulled the material away from the wound before removing it altogether. He continued to stare blankly ahead, oblivious to what she was doing.

"The bullet went straight through," she said, dabbing with an alcohol-soaked cotton ball. "That's a good thing. He'll have a scar, but it should heal without stitches. The bleeding nearly stopped." She placed bandages on both sides and secured them with white surgical tape.

I fished a cotton dress shirt from my backpack—the only shirt I owned with buttons—and together we got it on Hobson. His arms were limp, like a big rag doll. He didn't fight us, but his state made the task no easier.

When I waved my hand in front of his face, he didn't blink. He didn't react at all. "It's like he's been hypnotized."

"I think he's stuck," Stella said. "He was told to kill Cammie Brotherton, and he's in some kind of holding pattern until that happens."

"We should tie him up."

"Cammie is the only person who needs to worry about this man right now."

Stella seemed sure of this, so I didn't press the issue. She was sweating again, a thin sheen across her forehead. She looked pale, too. This is how she looked before the lake, and that was less than a day ago.

I glanced around the parking lot. "We're not going to find a car here."

"What about that one?"

She was pointing at a four-door black Honda Accord parked on the corner across the street, a red and white FOR SALE sign in in the window.

We found the keys under the passenger seat. I told myself we weren't stealing it. We were just taking it on an extended test drive.

We managed to work our way through the traffic and get to US-101, then followed the California coast north.

We considered heading inland to one of the interstates, like I-5, but we figured that was where they'd expect us to go. US-101 was older and slower, passing from one seaside town to the next in leisure. Restaurants, tourist attractions, and strip malls lined both sides of the road, and here we blended with the locals—the pond was bigger, and we needed a big pond.

Hobson sat silently in the back seat, his gaze focused on the road ahead, looking at everything and nothing in particular. At one point, he started mumbling softly to himself, incoherent, jumbled sounds more than words, and then he went quiet again. Stella had tried speaking to him, and although he would sometimes glance back at her, he didn't answer. She had given up after about an hour, fished out both copies of *Great Expectations*, and began randomly flipping through the pages, insisting my father left the book for a reason, and growing increasingly frustrated when she couldn't find it.

I continually scanned the cars around us. Whenever a white vehicle appeared in our rearview mirror, I'd tense and slow down, my breath catching until they finally rolled past us, my eyes drifting over the driver, finding relief when I confirmed they weren't wearing white.

Stella had grown increasingly pale over the hours, and I tried to calculate how much time had gone by since yesterday when she had first began showing signs of her hunger, until we finally pulled over at that lake. Six or seven hours at best, from what I remembered. It seemed to be progressing slower this time. Maybe the lake had bought more time. How much was anyone's guess. Something bad was coming, though.

"The gas light is on."

The car had grown so quiet her voice startled me. "I know."

We had been driving for nearly five hours. The tank had been full when we borrowed the Honda, but we'd been running on fumes for the past ten miles. "We're coming up on Manchester. We can stop there."

"Jack, there's something else I need to tell you. Something important."

"What is it?"

"It has to do with my condition."

"You can tell me."

"Even I don't completely understand it," Stella said. "I know when I touch something, I take the life from whatever that something is, I drain it, but it doesn't always end the hunger. Some things work better than others."

"I get that. The fish in the lake, the tree back in Nevada. That cornfield a few years ago. They helped a little, but you need a person, you need to—"

"Jack," she interrupted. "Not every person works, either. That's what I'm trying to explain. Some are better than others. I don't understand what the difference is, but some people buy me a few months, others put the illness at bay for a full year. Ms. Oliver, somehow she knew which would work the longest. The people she brought me always quenched the hunger, always for a full year."

"August 8 to August 8."

She nodded.

"And back at Cammie's house, she said she had someone 'picked out.'"

Stella nodded again. "Bad people, that seems to be the key. They're the ones who work the best. She may have already taken someone."

A small gas station came up on the right—Manchester Fill 'n Go. I pulled in and eased up to one of the pumps. Shutting off the engine, I turned to Stella. "We'll solve this, I promise you. We'll find a way."

Again, she nodded, but there was doubt behind her eyes, a growing sadness.

You'll lose her soon. This is her saying good-bye.

The thought came into my head, and I forced it back out.

We'll find a way.

But even I was beginning to doubt that.

Three cars in the parking lot—a green Ford, red Dodge, and a white Toyota. The driver of the Toyota was a teenage girl wearing a loose N'Sync tank top over a pink bikini, no doubt skipping school for the beach.

"We should get some snacks, something to eat." I handed her a twenty and she took it from me without another word, climbed out of the car, and went into the small gas station.

I was back in the car, nearly ready to go in after her, when she finally returned with an armful of items—potato chips, three sandwiches, three bottles of water, and a road map. She dumped all but the map on the floor at her feet.

I eyed the discarded food. "Sure, I'll take a sandwich. Thank you, Stella."

"Manchester," she mumbled, spreading the map out on the dashboard. "Manchester."

"Stella? What's going on?"

"Manchester is a city in England," she muttered, studying the map.

"And a city here in California, Illinois, Connecticut, Georgia, Indiana...probably all over the world. It's a common name."

She reached for her copy of *Great Expectations* and opened it to the map on the inside cover, studied it for a moment, then opened the copy I had found in my Father's grave beside it, also to the interior flap. "These are both the same editions. Your father's copy and the one I got from my parents."

"So?"

Stella's gloved fingers slipped gingerly over the cover of her copy. "*Great Expectations* was first published by Mr. Dickens in July of 1861 as a magazine serial, then later as a full novel. One hundred years after his death, the novel entered the public domain, meaning it became free for all and could be published by anyone. As a result, hundreds of editions have been published since, all over the world, with so many attempting to capitalize on his wonderful words. If you were to walk into a bookstore, you would no doubt find numerous copies on hand, printed by various publishers. The underlying text will be the same in all, the only thing to differentiate them would be the packaging—the dust jacket, the binding, the quality of the book itself. From cheap knockoffs to insanely expensive original editions dating back over a hundred years. Many people own a copy of this book, but few of those copies are alike. The numerous print runs are fleeting as publishers repackage and print again, out with the old, in with the new." Her fingers paused, her thumb running along the edge of her book. "This copy belonged to my parents. It is the only original possession of theirs I own, and I treasure it above all other things in this world. This book has been with me every day of my life and will be there for my last day, of that I'm sure. The memory of my parents, their essence, travels with me within the covers. Through this book, I keep them close."

Stella's hand moved to the edition I found in my father's grave. "This one was in the possession of your father, hidden in his grave with the Penn State yearbook. Important enough to him that he would go through such trouble to conceal it from the world in a fake grave, hoping you would eventually find it. Look at the maps—he told you exactly where he'd be, Jack! Do you see it?"

I leaned in closer. The maps were beautifully rendered, both detailing various cities throughout the UK. Nothing necessarily specific to the novel, just a map the publisher felt filled the space nicely. No doubt just an afterthought by the marketing department to fill blank space and help their edition stand out from all the others Stella mentioned. We were in Manchester, California. My eyes found Manchester on each of the maps, but it wasn't until I read the names of the other cities that I realized what Stella had discovered. "That one is spelled wrong."

"It is, Pip. Isn't it?" Stella beamed. "On my copy, we have Exeter, London, Manchester, Whitby, Newcastle upon Tyne, and all the others. On your edition, the one your father hid away so brilliantly for you, Whitby is spelled W-H-I-D-B-E-Y. Whidbey, not Whitby. There is no Whidbey in England."

"There's an island off the coast of Washington State called Whidbey," I said quietly, studying the two images closer.

Stella was smiling. "Yes, there is. A very secluded, beautiful little place."

"Auntie Jo used to tell me my mother wanted to live near the water," I said.

"Whidbey Island is in Puget Sound, off the mainland, not far from Seattle," Stella said. "The south end is only accessible by ferry or boat. There's a bridge at the north end. I believe it's called Deception Pass. The island is largely undeveloped—mountains, lakes, thick forests...so many places to hide."

"Deception Pass," I muttered, thinking that fit my father perfectly.

"Jack, we can be there in twelve hours. We'll need to take I-5 again. Back roads would take too long, but we can be there in twelve hours, if we hurry."

Stella looked hopeful. I didn't want to take that from her, but this seemed like such a long shot. "He left that book twenty years ago. Do you really think he'd still be there? They would have found him by now."

"We have nowhere else to go."

She was right, of course. We were driving around California aimlessly in a car borrowed from someone who would eventually miss said car and most likely report it to someone not fond of the recently growing "borrowed car" movement.

I looked into the rearview mirror. Hobson's blank stare looked back at me. "What do you think, Dewey?"

He licked his lips, then turned to the window.

"Clearly, he would like to go," Stella said.

"Clearly. Can I eat my sandwich first?"

She handed one to me and handed another to Dewey.

He took the sandwich from her but simply held it, more of a reflex than a thoughtful action.

"You should eat, Dewey. You'll need your strength to kill Cammie."

"Okay." He peeled back the plastic and began to eat.

"Christ, this is weird." I started the car and made a right back onto US-101 in search of signs for I-5.

I had been worried about Stella's condition when we left Manchester, California. By the time we crossed the border into Oregon at a little after four in the afternoon, I was downright frightened.

Her skin looked paper white and her lips had taken on a purplish hue. Her hair grew damp with sweat and hung limply around her face. She'd slept for the better part of two hours, and I was thankful for that because before she finally drifted off, she had been doing her best to pretend everything was okay and *I* had been doing my best to agree with her.

Everything wasn't okay, though. Things were far from okay.

Yesterday, prior to the lake, she became nearly delirious in her sleep. More of a fevered state than actual rest, and I knew she was closing back in on that again. At one point, I asked her if I should find another lake and she told me that wouldn't work again, just keep driving. Then I remembered what she said back in Manchester—

We'll have to take I-5 again. Back roads would take too long.

I had no idea what she meant by that. Even if by some miracle we managed to find my father, what did she expect him to do? I seriously doubted he had been standing by for twenty years, holding some miracle cure for a girl his son would bring by two decades later. We were rushing into a giant nothingness, a void. A fool's errand.

I'm not going to lie. I considered finding someone she could take. Some lowlife. I saw two hitchhikers outside Medford, and I slowed down. God help me, I nearly stopped. I didn't, though, and two hours later when she began groaning in her sleep, I cursed myself for not stopping, for not picking one of them up. Every truck stop. Every rest area. I slowed, then talked myself out of it. I knew if I actually did it, there would be no coming back. I'd officially be a cold-blooded killer. Killing in self-defense was one thing, but killing an innocent—regardless of how unsavory or easily forgotten they might be—was not something you returned from.

I couldn't lose her.

I wouldn't lose her.

Near Eugene, I started glancing back at Hobson, at the bullet wound in his shoulder. Part of me hoping it would reopen, grow infected, give me a reason... That didn't happen, though. His shoulder remained free of new blood. He hadn't even acknowledged the wound. Hobson spent the entire drive in complete silence, lost somewhere in his own head. If he slept, I didn't see it.

Every hour I didn't see Hobson sleep, I grew more tired.

I finally pulled over at a deserted scenic rest stop near Longview, Washington, at a little after midnight. I drove to the far end of the parking lot and shut off the engine.

I only meant to sleep for thirty minutes or so, long enough to catch my third wind.

I didn't wake up for two hours.

And when I did, Stella was gone.

Relief filled me as I found her at the metal guardrail, staring out over the deep ravine, water rushing past far below, surrounded by some of the tallest trees I had ever seen. She didn't turn to me when I approached, but she knew I was there.

"That's the Cowlitz River down there. Isn't it beautiful?" she said.

"You're beautiful." I was so happy to see her awake. Such words would have embarrassed me a few years ago but felt so natural now, so right. If a void existed within me, it filled when she was near—this place in my heart belonging to only her, a room only she could enter.

Stella wrapped her arms around me and I, her. She wore her long black gloves, the ones that reached her elbows, over those she had pulled on a sweatshirt. Not a bit of her flesh was exposed, and even if it were, I'm not sure I cared. She was careful, though. A lifetime of practice behind her. The warmth of those arms, the feel of her fingers in my hair, her breath caressing my neck. I so wanted to pull her close and kiss her. Knowing I could not was maddening. Knowing I never would, more maddening still.

"I am to die soon, my dearest Pip. You know that, right?"

"Don't say things like that, please."

"The hunger will consume me again soon, and this time there will be no satiating it. I'll grow so weak, I'll become delirious. My thoughts will be lost to nothing but nonsense and babble. I've been there so many times. It's like an ancient enemy knocking at the door, an unwelcome guest smiling at the window when I refuse to let him in."

"You can use the river, this forest."

"It won't be enough."

"Then we find someone."

We have someone. Hobson, sitting patiently in the back seat.

No. I forced that thought from my head. Hobson was a victim, no less than us.

He's broken.

No.

"I've told you, I won't. No more."

"Stella, I can't lose you."

"Yet, you will."

"If those people in white find us again...one of them. Or maybe my father will know—"

"Life is not mine to take. My existence is selfish. All those years, they convinced me I was doing the right thing, but I knew in my heart it was never true. I still did as they asked, I killed for them. So many died at my hand. There is no atonement for my sins. I see their faces whenever I close my eyes. I hear their cries. Even the monsters, and many were, not even they deserved the pain I brought upon them. I think I welcome death, I welcome the silence of death. They'll be waiting for me on the other side, and I'll need to answer to all of them, and as frightening as that is, I know I must face them if I am ever to find peace."

"You're just being stubborn, Stella. We find someone bad, someone deserving...a killer, a rapist...someone who wouldn't hesitate to kill us or someone else—"

Stella placed a gloved finger over my lips, silencing me. "I won't, Jack. No more. I don't want to talk about such things. I don't want to think about them." She smiled up at me, her eyes catching the moon. "Let us just enjoy this moment, this time together, the time we have left. A moment can be an eternity, if we let it."

My God, she is so pale.

"I love you, Stella Nettleton," I said softly.

"And I you, John Edward Jack Thatch. My Pip."

I pulled her close. I held her so tight.

"Dance with me?" she whispered, burying her head in my shoulder. And we did.

We danced at the edge of that cliff, we danced to a song only we heard.

I honestly couldn't say if five minutes passed or an hour; time was lost in that moment. When she finally whispered we should go, I could only nod. If I spoke, I knew the tears would come. I followed her from the water's edge back to the car, where she curled up with her copy of *Great Expectations* in the passenger seat.

Hobson continued to stare from the back.

We left the Cowlitz River behind us.

Three and a half hours to Whidbey.

Stella drifted off again about an hour outside of Longview. Her seat back, she had pulled her knees up close to her chest. Her dark hair obscured her face. She looked so small, so vulnerable. I'm not sure when she started shivering. I imagine it began about thirty minutes from our destination, because I had been watching her closely and I hadn't noticed until then.

When the sun started to rise, I saw the dark sweat stains on her clothes. I pulled the sleeve of my shirt down over my fingers and used the material to brush the matted errant strands of hair from her face. The newborn sunlight seemed to bother her. She buried her eyes in the crook of her elbow with a soft sigh.

We left I-5 for WA-525 North, which became Mukilteo Speedway, and followed signs for Whidbey and the Clinton-Mukilteo ferry terminal. While traffic leaving the island on this Monday morning appeared heavy, very few seemed to be heading from the mainland back to the island. I imagined the opposite was true in the afternoons, when the businesses in Seattle shuttered for the day.

At a small tollbooth, a pleasant woman in her mid-fifties took our fare and told me to follow the car in front of me into row two and pull up to the front. The next ferry would be arriving in under five minutes.

"How long is the ferry ride?"

"Fifteen to twenty minutes, depending on the waters."

I considered waking Stella, but figured it was best to let her sleep. I had no idea what waited for us on the other end.

Six other cars waited with us, only one of which was white. A mid-seventies Ford pickup truck with an elderly man behind the wheel, wearing a navy blue down jacket and a Seahawks cap. He was reading the newspaper with a cup of coffee perched precariously on his dash. When he caught me watching him, he smiled, nodded, and went back to his paper.

I had never been on a ferry before, and when the Kittitas arrived, I couldn't believe how many cars disembarked. I had no idea the vessel would be so large. When the last vehicle finally disappeared back down Mukilteo Speedway in the direction of Seattle, the row of cars beside us was ushered onboard. A man in an orange vest motioned for me to follow. We parked on the lower level. I shut down the engine. When we pulled away from the dock a few minutes later, I finally closed my eyes, allowing the exhaustion to wash over me.

PART 5

"I loved her against reason, against promise, against peace, against hope, against happiness, against all discouragement that could be."

—Charles Dickens, *Great Expectations*

1

If I slept, I did not dream, and for that I was grateful.

My eyes snapped open with the quick yelp of a horn behind me. "Jack? Is this Whidbey?"

Stella was awake, too, sitting up and leaning forward in her seat to get a better view.

The ferry had butted up against the dock. The row of cars beside us had already disembarked. Another man in an orange vest waved impatiently at me, gesturing toward the dock.

The horn behind me yelped again. Longer this time.

I started the car, put it in gear, and followed the taillights of the last car to leave the ferry off the edge of the boat and back onto solid ground. A large sign read:

CLINTON FERRY TERMINAL
WELCOME TO WHIDBEY ISLAND

To my left sat a squat gray building with a green roof and a sign that simply said WELCOME CENTER; I pulled into one of the empty spaces beside it. The rest of the terminal was nothing more than a large parking lot with at least three dozen vehicles lined up ready to board the ferry back to the mainland. The moment the cars from our row finished exiting, traffic reversed, the waiting vehicles filed in, and the ferry pulled away. A practiced dance.

None of the other disembarking vehicles lingered. They quickly maneuvered the various painted lines of the lot and disappeared down WA-525 North at the back. Five minutes after arriving, we were alone.

"Now what?"

"We go inside," Stella said, scooping up both copies of *Great Expectations* and the Penn State yearbook.

When she opened her door and stood, I thought she might pass out. She swayed and gripped the roof of the car for support.

I raced around and held her, kept her upright. She was shivering again. "Maybe you should wait in the car."

"I'm okay," she assured me.

She wasn't, though.

Leaning back into the car, she looked at Dewey. "Mr. Hobson, do you need to use the facilities?"

"Yeah," Hobson replied, his voice flat.

Without another word, he got out of the car and went inside.

Stella and I followed after him, moving slow. She tried to put up a strong front, but much of her weight fell on me. Her breathing seemed labored.

The welcome center was unattended. There were two vending machines, one with soft drinks, the other with various candy bars and snacks. They were flanked by a women's restroom on one side and the men's on the other. Posters about the island covered the opposite wall along with a large map and several racks of pamphlets for area attractions.

Stella sat the books down on a bench, and the two of us studied the map.

"Any idea?"

She opened both copies of *Great Expectations* to the image of the map in the inlay. "Other than the spelling of Whidbey and Whitby, do you see anything else different?"

I leaned in closer and compared both maps—the lines, the colors, the remaining city names, and other markers. I shook my head. "Nothing."

"Me either. But I don't believe your father would go through all this trouble to get us here and not give us some kind of clue as to where to go next. There's something, we're just not seeing it."

I returned to the map of Whidbey. The island was huge. Most of the land was undeveloped, though. There were several large farms, beaches, a few small clusters of businesses, and residences along the coast. Nothing stood out, though.

Behind us, a toilet flushed in the men's room. Then Hobson came out, walked past us out the door. He got back in the car and stared forward.

"That is so weird."

Stella moved on from the map and sifted through the tourist pamphlets. Her finger slipping from one to the next. "Beaches, parks, wineries and vineyards, restaurants, art galleries, museums, sightseeing tours, a lighthouse…"

I was beginning to think this was hopeless when one particular pamphlet jumped out at me. A picture of a large house on a cliff overlooking Puget Sound filled the front. It advertised tremendous views, a friendly staff, and spacious rooms. None of this mattered to me, because my eyes were locked on the name.

"Stella?"

I showed it to her, and her eyes grew wide.

By Hand Bed and Breakfast.

By Hand.

"She had brought me up 'by hand,'" Stella said softly. "Joe and I were both brought up 'by hand.' She must have made Joe marry her 'by hand.'"

We both recognized the phrase as one Dickens used numerous times in his novel. A phrase odd enough that it stood out even to me when I first read the book so many years ago. Pip's aunt said it regularly.

"Do you think that's it?"

Stella went back at the map, tracing a line with her finger. "6600 Still Creek Road. It's on the other side of the island, about eight miles from here. Jack, that must be it."

I grabbed her gloved hand and quickly got her back to the car.

2

The only flight Fogel was able to find on short notice back to Pittsburgh left Nevada at 7:23 in the evening and came with a two-hour layover at O'Hare Airport in Chicago from 11:30 to 1:30 in the morning. She was dead tired. She tried to sleep on the plane, but did so in fits and starts, much to the dismay of the elderly man sitting beside her. At one point, he shook her awake and told her she cried out. Fogel had no recollection of what she had been dreaming, nor did she remember screaming, but the leery eyes of the other passengers told her she had, and she found herself reluctant to try and sleep again.

At O'Hare, she found her gate, then wandered the terminals to pass the time. There was a stop for coffee at the only open counter in the food courts. Then she passed the remainder of the time parked in an uncomfortable plastic seat, reading the first couple chapters of Stephen King's new book, *Bag of Bones*. The book seemed good, but she couldn't focus. When her eyes inevitably fell shut again, she saw herself lying in a ditch at the side of the road, her gaze blank and wide, her skin burned but not burned. Still able to scream, though—the sides of her mouth cracked and bled with her pain-filled shrill.

This time when she cried out, she heard it too. She put the book aside, got a second cup of coffee, and returned to her gate.

Those two hours crawled.

Last night, Stack had called her about ten minutes before her plane was set to board last in Nevada.

Arden Royal, the twenty-seven year-old male found behind a Dumpster in Upper Saint Clair in 1991, also worked for Charter Pharmaceuticals. Stack was working to connect the others—they were on to something. Charter was about 280 miles outside Pittsburgh, near Philadelphia.

"There's something else," Stack said. "I think someone's watching me."

He told her about the white vans.

She tried dialing Stack several times since but only got a busy signal.

Fogel landed in Pittsburgh at thirty-three past three in the morning, retrieved her car from the lot, and took I-76 to Chadds Ford at a rate of speed that would put a smile on the face of any NASCAR fan.

She arrived in Chadds Ford at a little past eight, drove through the small town in all of four minutes, noting it was even smaller than Fallon, Nevada had been, then followed her hastily scribbled directions under the single traffic light at the back end of the quiet town to SR-41, and from there to CR-27 West. The few houses she spotted were set far back from the road, most lost behind large fields of corn, hay, soybeans, and God knows what else they grew out here.

Fogel completely missed the turnoff for Turlington Road not once but twice—blowing past it the first time at more than eighty miles-per-hour, then the second time as she drove much slower, carefully scanning the fields on her right.

The road wasn't marked.

The road wasn't really much of a road at all, a sliver of blacktop off the two-lane highway that quickly vanished into a sprawling cornfield. Had she not seen another car turn, she probably would have missed Turlington a third time.

By the time she maneuvered her car back around and returned to Turlington Road, the taillights of that previous vehicle were nothing but pin points in the distance, and even those disappeared up and over a hill and blinked out by the time she straightened the wheel and pointed her Toyota down the center of the narrow two-lane road.

While CR-27 West had been riddled with patched cracks and potholes, Turlington had been recently paved and was well maintained. Reflectors marked the center of the two lanes, and fresh white paint lined the edges. An eight-foot chain-link fence blocked access from the cornfields on either side, and Fogel was reminded of the claustrophobic drive into the state correctional institute on Beaver Avenue back in the city. More so when she came upon the gate and guardhouse at the end of the road.

The guardhouse had an arm meant to stop traffic, but the arm was raised. The vehicle she followed in from the main road paused at the gate, then pulled through into an expansive parking lot surrounding a large concrete building centered at the back. As Fogel approached the guardhouse, she fished her Pittsburgh PD badge and identification card out of her purse, but found she didn't need it. There was nobody inside.

Noting there was not a single sign that read Charter—or any other business name, for that matter—she pulled through the gate and circled around until she found a parking space. Considering the early hour, it seemed odd so many people were here. Odder still—other than her green Toyota, every car in the lot was white.

3

Crossing that small island might have been the longest fifteen minute drive of my life. Stella had memorized the directions and pointed out each turn to me. Aside from a lone landscaper's truck, we didn't pass a single car in either direction. The island felt like another world, so far removed from the various cities I had lived over the years. If the island felt remote and isolated, Stills Creek Road was the edge of the earth. We turned from Cultus Bay onto Stills in silence. The road was narrow, barely wide enough for two cars to pass, lacking a center dividing line. Mailboxes and driveways lined the left side with not a single house in sight. The driveways weaved back into thick groves of Douglas fir, red alder, big-leaf maples, tall cedars, and hemlock. A wild place, untouched by the destructive hand of man.

"There," Stella said softly, pointing at a large red mailbox with 6600 painted on the side in careful black script. Nothing else, no mention of the bed-and-breakfast. Nothing to indicate a business existed here at all.

A canopy of large, bowing branches bent over the gravel driveway.

"Go, Jack. I can't stand it." She was leaning forward again.

I realized I was, too. My palms were clammy with sweat.

I turned onto the narrow driveway and followed it through the trees.

4

The vehicle Fogel had followed into the Charter parking lot turned out to be a Ford F-250 pickup truck—white, like all the others. As she got out of her own car, she saw two men climb out of the large truck and disappear inside the building. Both wore long, white trench coats. Neither acknowledged her. Both moved with quick purpose.

Fogel pressed the lock button on her key fob—the two chirps sounding especially loud, as all sounds do at such early hours—then followed after the two men, across the parking lot and through two thick glass doors.

A whoosh of cold air met her as the doors swung shut automatically at her back, the click of her shoes echoing off the highly polished white marble floors.

Fogel stared up at the soaring ceiling, rising the full height of the building.

The ceiling was white.

The walls were white.

White canvases in white frames lined the walls, and somehow Fogel was certain if she inspected one closely, she would find those canvases weren't blank, but painted white with careful strokes. Soft piano music came forth from hidden speakers. She recognized it as "Der Hölle Rache" from Mozart's *The Magic Flute*. One of her mother's favorites.

"May I help you?"

This came from a reception desk at the back of the lobby, behind a waiting area made up of two white leather couches, four matching white leather chairs, and assorted white tables on a white rug.

The lobby should have felt incredibly bright but the lights were just low enough to compensate.

Fogel approached the desk and took out her ID. "I'm Detective Fogel, with the Pittsburgh Police Department. I'd like to speak to whoever is in charge."

The receptionist, a woman in her mid-twenties with long blonde hair and green eyes, smiled up at Fogel. She wore a white blazer over a white blouse, and although Fogel couldn't see under the desk, she was certain the woman had on a matching skirt and shoes as well. "Do you have an appointment?"

"I'm with Homicide. I don't have an appointment, but I need to speak to someone right away."

The woman raised her eyebrows. "Homicide? Has there been a murder?"

"I'm not at liberty to provide details. This is an active investigation."

"I understand." She smiled and picked up her phone, dialing a number with slender fingers tipped in white nail polish. Speaking softly into the receiver, she listened for a moment, then hung up. "Please take a seat, Detective Fogel. Someone will be with you shortly. Help yourself to coffee or pastries. The baklava is simply delightful."

"Thank you."

Fogel walked over to the waiting area and dropped down into the large, white couch.

Coffee service, donuts, and assorted pastries filled the table at the center of the furniture. There was also a generous supply of flavored creamers, sugars, and artificial sweeteners. She poured herself a cup of coffee, black, then frowned when she realized it was ice cold. The pastries (including the famous baklava) looked like they had been out there a while, too. Mold crept up over the edges of the bagels.

5

There are times in your life when you think you know what comes next. Instances of predicability, sameness. Times when your next step is as known to you as the last, and you take those steps with confidence, knowing nothing horrific waits for you in the shadows ahead. You venture forth as if you read the last page of a book and can go back and read the rest from the beginning, knowing without a doubt where the story would go, while still taking comfort in the journey.

I spent the preceding eighteen years of my life operating with the certainty that my parents were dead. I visited their graves. I spoke to them. I prayed for them. Always gone, always something of the past. I knew their faces only from old photographs and dreams, and the sound of their voices eluded me like the waters of a fast-running creek. I made peace with my parent's deaths long before I understood what that really meant. When you lose your parents at such an early age, it simply *is*. You know and understand nothing else. Auntie Jo always told me I should be grateful I had been so young. Both her parents died when she was an adult, and the vividness of those memories haunted her nightly.

I never told her about my dream, my personal haunting.

A dream I now knew to be not a dream at all, but the chaotic memories of a child.

If I had told her about the dream, would she have confessed my father was still alive?

Would she have broken down in tears and told me that was really why she hated him so much? My mother died, and he lived? She, this aunt who raised me as her own, part of a cover-up all these years?

Would she have called him a coward? Said he ran away? Might as well be dead?

How I wish I could have spoken to her about all of this. I hated her for keeping the truth from me, yet I loved her for protecting me, and both of those things seemed to be one and the same.

The gravel of the driveway crunched under our tires.

Stella held the pamphlet we found back at the welcome center in her hand, and she gripped it in such a way the paper crinkled.

A large, old house appeared on our left, peeking out from around the tall maples and alders, their branches swaying lazily in the early morning breeze. A hand-painted sign on a short post read Guest Parking, with an arrow pointing to the left. On our right stood a woodshed with enough cut logs stacked against the outer walls to last at least three cold winters. Beyond the shed was a garden, fenced high to keep out the deer and other wildlife. There were fruit trees, too. Apples and pears, mostly.

The gravel driveway opened up into a concrete parking pad on the left, then wound deeper into the property, toward another house, newer than the first, this one perched on a slight hill at the edge of the cliff overlooking the waters of Puget Sound and the shipping lanes a hundred feet below.

"This is breathtaking," Stella said.

A white picket fence ran along the outer edge of the yard. There had to be four, maybe five acres. "How can he afford all this? This can't be the right place."

"Park over there." Stella pointed toward the guest spaces.

I pulled up next to a brown Chevy pickup with a lawnmower in the back and switched off the engine.

I was out the car and around to Stella's side to help her before I noticed the man watching us from the back corner of the woodshed, one hand holding a black trash bag and the other on the butt of a gun holstered to his right hip.

He was about my height, with brown hair peppered with gray that carried on into his beard. He wore jeans, a blue button-down shirt with the sleeves rolled up, and black boots. There was a hard edge to his face, aged beyond his years. His eyes were sharp, though, fox-like, darting from me to Stella and back again from behind black framed glasses. His hands were dirty.

He didn't move.

Not at first.

When he finally did approach us, he did so with trepidation, his grip tightening on the trash bag. As he grew closer, his right hand fell from the gun. He tugged the tail of his shirt down over it. He studied us both. His gaze lingered on Stella's gloves. He ducked slightly to get a better look at Dewey Hobson, still in the back seat. Then he turned back to us, his expression flat.

"Dad?" the single word fell from my lips, so soft I wasn't sure anyone else had heard it.

I'm not sure exactly what I expected. Maybe for this man to drop the bag, rush me, and embrace me in a hug? Tears, perhaps. A rushed explanation of the years gone, broken words covering two decades of deceit, secrets, and lies?

My God, son. You're a man.

I've missed you, Dad. Every second, I've missed you.

None of those things happened.

"We need to get inside," he said quietly, before turning and walking at a brisk pace toward the house on the cliff, hefting the trash bag over his shoulder.

Stella and I gave each other a puzzled glance before following after him.

He left the front door standing ajar.

This first floor of the house had an open floor-plan. The front door led to a foyer and a wide hallway with a staircase on the left and tall storage cabinets on the right. The hallway opened up to a dining area on the left and a chef's kitchen on the right. Beyond the kitchen was a sunken living room with a large stone fireplace and two leather sofas with a matching chair and ottoman. A wall of windows overlooking a large patio and the deep blue waters of Puget Sound far below filled the back of the house. Several small boats dotted the surface. Further out, a cruise ship floated north-bound for Alaska.

I had to help Stella. She was horribly weak. Her arm was draped over my shoulder and she leaned into me, her breathing labored, shivering in short stutters. Over the past day, her strength came and went with little warning. At the ferry terminal, less than an hour ago, she had been alert, her energy up. She seemed strong. Even as we approached the house, I saw hints of the girl I remembered throughout the years. I began to realize she made a conscious effort for that girl to appear, to lift from the thickening fog of her illness. And each appearance came with a price, a toll, a drain, that shortened the next.

Stella was fading.

This was different from the car two days earlier, the lake.

Something worse.

Neither of us wanted to admit to that, but it was there nonethe-less.

I am to die soon, my dearest Pip. You know that, right?

Through the thick material of her clothing, I felt the heat of her body and knew she was feverish again. I got her inside the house and over to one of the leather sofas, where I gently set her down, her head resting on a soft leather pillow.

She smiled up at me, silently mouthing the words *My Pip*.

Hobson entered the house behind me, having left the car without any coaxing. He stepped into the foyer and closed the front door behind him, then stood there, still and silent again.

Stuck, as Stella said.

My father stood at the dining room table. He had torn open the black garbage bag, dumped the contents, and was sifting through what looked like bundles of bound pages—folders, video tapes, and journals.

I went over to him.

He didn't look at me.

"Dad?" The only word I had said to him in twenty years, now said twice. Ignored twice, as he continued to rifle through the material.

Charter was printed on most of it. Either as a logo on many of the documents, handwritten at the top of others, or stamped onto the folders—this was accompanied by *Confidential* or *Eyes Only* or *Internal Use Only*. There was a bundle of photographs, too. I picked it up, tugged off the rubber band, and flipped through them. About a dozen in all. I recognized the faces from the yearbook—Perla Beyham, Cammie Brotherton, Jaquelyn Breece, Keith Pickford, Jeffery Dalton, Dewey Hobson, Garret Dotts, Penelope Maudlin, Richard Nettleton, Emma Tackett. Pictures of my parents were absent from the stack, but I had no doubt they were once there. There was a thick folder on Elfrieda Leech—an ancient photograph of my former neighbor and my parent's guidance counselor clipped to the outer flap. I opened the folder and found dozens of pay stubs, sizable checks payable to Leech from Charter. The earliest dated February 4, 1974, and the latest stamped August of 1980. There were memos and handwritten notes, both mentioning the same names, those same Penn State students.

I found a folder with my name and picture on it. One for Stella, too. The photos were old, both of us no more than three or four. Inside my folder were dozens of other pictures and at least a hundred pages of loose paper—some typed, others handwritten. One of the oldest on top was dated only four months after I was born. A handwritten note said—

Sixteen pounds, four ounces. Rolling from front to back on own. Teething. Conscious of environment. No outwardly signs. Nothing abnormal presenting.

—Charter Observation Team 102

I showed it to my father. "What the hell is all this?"

He glanced down at the note. He was still reading it when we both heard a loud rumble from the driveway. Through the large window in the foyer next to the front door, I saw a black Pontiac GTO slide to a halt in the driveway.

My father dropped the note, drew his gun, and started for the front door.

Jeffery Dalton, the man who I had only seen in photographs, had the driver-side door open and was climbing out the car, drawing his own gun before my father even got the front door open.

He charged us.

Not at a run, but a fast, determined walk, raising his own gun as he went.

I don't know who fired first.

A bullet struck the doorframe less than an inch from my head, sending splintered wood off in all directions. I dropped down back inside the house.

I heard the report of my father's gun—three, maybe four shots in quick succession. Between those reports were shots fired from outside, from the man racing toward us. Four shots. Half a dozen. More. My father's body jerked, and the back of his shirt exploded in two spots, one up near his left shoulder, the other in his gut. The bullets tore through him and embedded in the wall behind the staircase. He shuffled backward, then collapsed onto the tile floor of the foyer, a puddle of blood spreading out under him.

I was screaming, not even sure when I started, but I was shrieking. I scrambled over to him on my hands and knees and pressed my palms down on the two wounds. Blood pooled out from between my fingers, soaking his shirt. His body spasmed, and he looked up at me with eyes filled with fright. When he coughed, red spittle filled the air.

Dalton stepped into the foyer and kicked the gun away from my father's hand.

"You shot my dad, you fucking animal!"

He peered into the house, sweeping his gun from left to right. "That's not your dad."

The man on the floor coughed again, this one weaker than the last.

My mind raced, trying to comprehend what he said, what had just happened.

Stella.

At that moment, I didn't care who this man was. He was dying, I was certain of that, and nothing could be done to stop it. I didn't know how much time I had.

I got to my feet, grabbed the dying man under the arms, and started pulling him toward the living room. "Help me!"

Dalton turned, his gun still out, sweeping the yard.

"Help me, you fucking prick!"

Dalton holstered his gun and grabbed the man's legs. Together we carried him into the living room, toward the couch where Stella slept. We set him down on the floor beside her and crouched beside them.

He had stopped coughing but was still breathing.

"Stella! Get up!"

I shouted her name, but she didn't respond. Breathing, but out cold.

Using the tail of my shirt to protect my fingers, I peeled off the glove on her right hand and tossed it aside. I guided her hand to the man's neck.

Stella woke, groggily realized what I was doing, and tried to pull away.

"He's dying, Stella! He's going to die. We don't have much time, you need to—"

Her grip shot back out and tightened on the man's neck, pinched at his skin.

The flesh beneath her fingers turned black, a darkness spreading from her touch at his neck to his face and chest. I saw it again at the exposed skin of his arms.

"Get back, Jack," she said softly. "Please stay back."

I couldn't move, though. My limbs were frozen.

Through black, shriveled lips, the man gasped, a ragged mess of a breath, then went still.

Stella held him for at least another minute. Her fingers pulsing as the last bit of life left him for her, then she finally let go. Her arm dangling limply over the side of the sofa. "Not working," she said softly, before drifting back off to a restless sleep. "Not enough."

My heart sank.

6

Fogel glanced impatiently at her watch.

Two minutes to nine. She'd been sitting here for nearly an hour. She groaned as "Der Hölle Rache" from Mozart's *The Magic Flute* looped for the umpteenth time.

She yawned, stood, and stretched her legs before returning to the reception desk.

The woman with the long blond hair and green eyes looked up at her and smiled. "May I help you?"

"I've been waiting an hour."

The woman cocked her head. "Waiting for who? Do you have an appointment?"

Fogel frowned. "You said someone would be out to talk to me. That was an hour ago."

"I did?"

Fogel pulled out her badge again. "I'm with Homicide. You said you'd find someone for me."

The woman's mouth fell open. "Homicide? Has there been a murder?"

The blood rushed to Fogel's face as she tried to keep her temper in check. "Get your supervisor on the phone right now."

The woman smiled and picked up her phone. "Do you have an appointment?"

Fogel leaned in closer. "Get your boss on the phone right now."

The receptionist huffed in a breath and dialed a number.

Fogel heard the click as someone picked up.

"There is a rather rude woman at reception claiming to be a police officer of some sort, and she's demanding to speak to my supervisor. Should I instruct security to escort her off the premises?"

Fogel wanted to snatch up the receiver and beat little blondie over the head with it.

The receptionist glanced at a door toward the back of the room. A security keypad of some sort was embedded in the wall to the right. "Are you sure? She really is quite rude. A horrid dresser, too."

Fogel's brow furrowed as she involuntarily looked down at her brown leather jacket, gray sweater, and jeans.

The receptionist hung up the phone. "Someone will be with you shortly. Please take a seat. Help yourself to coffee or pastries. The baklava is simply delightful." She smiled, revealing perfectly white teeth.

"You've got one minute to get someone out here, or I'm blowing a hole through that door back there and letting myself in."

The receptionist glanced down at her nails, then smiled up at Fogel. "May I help you?"

7

"What does she mean, *not enough*? What's happening to her?"

With my hand still wrapped in the tail of my shirt, I carefully placed Stella's arm across her chest. I felt utterly defeated.

"You're Jeffery Dalton." I forced myself to draw in a breath, long and deep. I couldn't look at him.

"Preacher. Nobody calls me Dalton." He was staring at the dead man between us.

"If this isn't my father, who is he?"

I heard a woman scream, then.

Loud.

Outside.

"Shit, that's Cammie," Preacher said, scrambling to his feet.

"Cammie Brotherton is here?"

"I picked her and her daughter up in California," he shouted back at me, racing for the door, his gun out again.

I quickly glanced around before chasing after him—Dewey Hobson was no longer in the house.

"Dewey, no!" I shouted, barreling out the front door.

He didn't hear me. His fist pistoned through the passenger window of the GTO, shattering the glass. He grabbed the woman sitting there by collar of her denim jacket and pulled her toward him, blood running from his split knuckles.

Preacher got to him first.

Hobson had the woman I could only assume was Cammie Brotherton halfway out the window, when Preacher slammed into him with the force of a truck, sending both men to the pavement. Hobson's head cracked against the concrete. This should have knocked him out, but only dazed him for a moment—he slammed the palms of his hands into Preacher's ears, then brought his knee up into Preacher's groin. The angle was all wrong and the blow glanced off, catching Preacher in the thigh instead.

Hobson twisted, somehow managed to plant both his feet on the ground, and pushed up. Preacher had been about to deliver a punch, but the movement threw off his balance. Hobson used the momentum to roll, taking Preacher with him, somehow ending up on top. Hobson's hands were around Preacher's neck in an instant, squeezing the life from him.

I grabbed Hobson around the waist and tried to pull him back, but he wouldn't release his grip. His arms were like lead.

In the middle of all this, Cammie had scrambled out of the car with a pump action shotgun. She chambered a shell and pointed the barrel at Hobson's head.

Hobson's head swiveled, following the sound. When he saw Cammie holding the shotgun, he released his grip on Preacher's neck, shrugged me off, and lunged at her. If I hadn't grabbed his leg, he surely would have reached her, but instead he lost his balance and cracked into the concrete.

"What am I doing here, Preacher?" Cammie took two steps back, the barrel again pointing at Hobson's head.

"Shoot him!" Preacher tried to shout this out, but the words came in a gravelly whisper, his throat still fighting for air.

I pulled Hobson back, grabbed his other leg. "He doesn't understand! David did something to him!"

I had no idea if Cammie knew David Pickford, but she did know Dewey Hobson, and I think that was the only thing that prevented her from pulling the trigger. She spun the shotgun around and brought the butt of the stock down hard on the side of the man's head—two hits, fast and hard. He collapsed, unconscious.

Preacher sat up, out of breath and beat. He rubbed at his sore neck. "Get him inside. We gotta tie him up."

From the back seat of the GTO, a little girl poked her head up— all long blond hair and blue eyes.

8

Fogel shook her head and stomped across the large white room to the door at the back. She found it to be locked. She beat on it with the back of her fist. "Open this door immediately!"

Back at the reception desk, the blonde was on her phone again. Crouched over the desk, half standing, speaking to someone.

Fogel began keying random numbers into the security pad.

A red LED came on, and the panel buzzed.

She beat on the door until the LED turned off, then entered more numbers.

When the panel buzzed for the fourth time, she cursed under her breath and went back to the reception desk.

The blonde woman looked up at her and smiled. "May I help you?"

"I don't know what bullshit kind of game you're playing, but you're interfering with a ongoing homicide investigation, and you're dangerously close to getting arrested for obstruction of justice."

The receptionist cocked her head to the side and frowned. "Did somebody die?"

Fogel had enough. She rounded the desk and pulled her handcuffs out from her back pocket. "Stand up and turn around. You're under arrest."

On the opposite end of the large white room, the door opened and a man in his mid-fifties dressed in a stark white three-piece suit stepped into the waiting room. "Detective? Please come with me."

9

I found rope in the garage.

I also found a white Chevy Suburban.

When I told Preacher about the SUV, he glanced back at the dead man on the floor next to Stella's sleeping body. Cammie followed his gaze from the man on the floor to the sofa, the shotgun still trained on Hobson. "That her?"

"Yep. And her boyfriend here is Jack Thatch."

"Eddie and Katy's kid?"

"Yeah."

"I'll be damned."

I finished the last knot on Hobson's ankles and stood. The frustration building. "Where the hell is my father?"

The little girl had followed all of us into the house but hadn't said a word. She was behind her mother, her arms wrapped around her leg. She shrunk back when I spoke. I didn't care. "If the two of you know what's going on, you need to tell me."

Preacher raised both palms. "What happened when you got here?"

I told them.

For the next thirty minutes, I explained everything that had happened since finding Stella in the club in Fallon. I even told them about Leo Signorelli and the man I killed at the hotel. I didn't leave anything out. I didn't care anymore.

Dalton said they spoke to my father less than three hours ago.

"So he's here?"

"He was," Cammie said.

The man on the floor killed him.

That's why he's here.

"We need to search the property. He could be hurt somewhere, dying," I said.

Preacher and Cammie exchanged a look, and I knew exactly what they were thinking. These people had no desire to *hurt* my father. They only wanted him dead.

I shook my head and started for the door. "I'm looking."

"We all look," Preacher said. "It will be faster. Cammie, you take this house. I'll check the guest house. Jack, you get the outbuild-ings."

I found my father tied up in the back of the woodshed.

Not dead.

Not yet.

10

Fogel followed the man in the white three-piece suit through the door into a long hallway—white walls, white ceiling, white marble floor. Everything was so white, it was damn near blinding. They passed three doors (all closed, all white) before the man ushered her into the only open door on the left side.

"Please, take a seat. Would you like a cup of coffee, or perhaps something to eat?" the man said, closing the door behind them.

The office was also white.

Ceiling. Walls. No windows.

The only color came from a framed photograph on the desk—a young man wearing a blue graduation gown, pointing at a diploma.

The man in white smiled when he noticed her looking at the picture. "That's my boy, William. He graduated from Penn State last month, and I'm proud to say he will be joining us here as part of the Charter family next week. Graduated top of his class. Quite an overachiever, that one."

He pointed at one of the two empty chairs in front of the white desk. "Please, sit."

Rounding the desk, he lowered himself into a plush white leather chair. "I'm Robert Trudeau. How can I help you?"

Something seemed off about the man's eyes. He made eye contact, but rather than look at her, he seemed to look *through* her. As if focused on some distant object in the room behind her.

Fogel turned and looked at the wall. There was a white credenza with another of those white paintings hanging above, nothing else. She turned back. "Mr. Trudeau, what exactly do you do here?"

"Robert, please."

"Robert."

"Yes?"

"What exactly do you do here," she repeated.

"Pharmaceutical research."

"Can you be more specific?"

"No."

"Why not?"

He waved a hand through the air. "We have a number of government-related contracts. I'm afraid you don't have the proper clearances to discuss what we do here."

"How do you know?"

Trudeau smiled. "I know."

A white MacBook sat on his desk. He glanced at the screen, clicked a few keys, then returned his attention to her. The smile on his face appeared fixed, as if painted on. "Ms. Toomey said you were here to investigate a murder. Can you elaborate on that?"

"Multiple homicides, actually."

The man leaned forward. "Really? Who died?"

"I'm afraid you don't have the proper clearances to discuss who died," Fogel said.

"Pity. I do like a good mystery."

A muted trill rang out from somewhere behind the desk. Trudeau's smiled faded, and for a moment he appeared puzzled. He pulled open the drawer on his top left and took out a Nokia cell phone not unlike the one Stack and gotten her. "Please excuse me, I need to take this."

He pressed a button on the keypad and raised the phone to his ear.

Fogel strained to hear whoever was speaking but couldn't make out the words.

Trudeau nodded several times, said, "That is excellent news," and disconnected the call. He set down the Nokia and picked up the receiver on his desk phone.

He held up a finger. "I'm sorry, this will only take me a minute."

Trudeau dialed a number. While the line rang, he picked up a white ballpoint pen and twirled it between his fingers, the smile still plastered on his face. When someone picked up on the other side, Trudeau didn't identify himself or offer a greeting, he simply said, "We have confirmation. Both the boy and the Nettleton girl are on Whidbey, the remaining adults, too."

Trudeau twirled the pen faster as he listened, weaving it in and out of his fingers. "Of course," he said. "Perhaps after I wrap up this meeting."

Fogel wondered what color ink was in the pen. Any color seemed blasphemous here. She couldn't tell if the voice on the other end of the call was male or female.

"A police detective. Homicide, no less," Trudeau said, the pen picking up speed. "I completely understand. You truly are a beautiful man."

Trudeau hung up the phone, placed the tip of the ballpoint pen in his ear, and slammed the palm of his hand against the back with enough force to send the pen down his ear canal, through his inner ear, and past the vestibular nerve into his brain. He slumped over in his chair, the smile never leaving his face.

11

My father had been horribly beaten. Both his eyes were puffy and blackening, the left swollen shut completely. He had a nasty cut on his forehead. His head lolled to the side, swiveling loosely on his neck. His hands and feet were both tied with heavy-duty orange extension cords.

I shouted for Preacher.

I pulled the gag from my father's mouth, a dirty rag smelling of oil.

Nearly unconscious, he didn't realize I was standing there. When he did see me, he might have thought I was some kind of hallucination, because he just coughed, his one good eye closed, and he started to drift off.

A second later, that good eye snapped open, glared at me. "Jack?"

"You're going to be okay."

I stuck my head out the open door. "Preacher! Cammie! In here!"

That's when the phone in the corner of the shed began to ring.

12

Detective Joy Fogel had seen a lot during her time with Pittsburgh PD, but she had never seen someone take their own life.

At some point, she gripped the edge of her chair and her fingers held onto the metal frame like vice grips, her muscles tense and squeezing with all the force they could muster. She wanted to scream, but the only sound to leave her lips was a single gasp.

Robert Trudeau's blank stare remained on her.

Fogel didn't move.

Time passed. If someone were to ask her, she wouldn't be able to tell them if ten seconds had gone by or ten minutes.

Fogel didn't move.

When she finally did move, it was because of one of the last things Trudeau said, a sentence that caused her heart to thud when she heard him utter the words.

We have confirmation. Both the boy and the Nettleton girl are on Whidbey, the remaining adults, too.

Fogel rose from her chair and rounded the desk.

The Nokia sat beside Trudeau's lifeless hand.

Fogel picked up the cell phone, scrolled to the last incoming number, and called it back.

Someone picked up on the third ring.

"Hello?"

"Who is this?" Fogel asked.

"Who is *this*?"

"Detective Fogel, with Pittsburgh PD Homicide. Identify your-self."

A male voice. A familiar voice. "Fogel? How...how did you get this number?"

"Who is this?"

Then she knew.

She recognized the voice. "Jack?"

"I don't understand."

"I...I don't either."

"Where are you? How did you find me?"

"Charter Pharmaceuticals. I hit redial on his phone, and it called you. Holy shit, he's dead."

"Slow down, Detective. Who's dead?"

"The man in the white suit."

Jack went silent for a second. "Detective, are you okay? You sound like you're in shock."

"He killed himself."

"Who?"

"I...I don't know where you are, Jack. But you need to leave. He said they're coming for you. You and the Nettleton girl, and the adults. Holy Christ, he killed himself. Somebody there, where you are, called here, called this Charter place. He said they're coming for you. Where...where are..."

Fogel wasn't one to cry. She couldn't remember the last time she shed a tear, but the flood works opened up then, and her vision went cloudy with it. Sobs poured from her throat. The emotional buildup of what just happened erupted from her in an explosion.

The Nokia beeped.

Low battery alert.

The call dropped.

13

Preacher came through the door as I hung up the receiver. His face turned red. "Who'd you call?"

"I didn't call anyone, did you?"

He crossed the shed, went to the phone, and tore it off the wall. "Who were you talking to?"

I shook my head and knelt back down to my father. "We don't have time for this. They're coming. Help me untie him."

He wanted to argue with me, I could see it in his eyes, but he didn't. Instead, we worked the knots. Preacher's gun dangled from a shoulder holster. I had no way to protect myself if he decided to draw it.

I gently gripped the sides of my father's face and turned his head toward me. "Can you stand?"

My father nodded weakly, a firmer grip on consciousness now. We helped him to his feet.

He cleared his throat and spit blood into the corner of the shed.

I put his arm over my shoulder and helped him to his feet. "Let's get you back to the house."

Inside, we found Cammie rifling through kitchen cabinets. Half the drawers were open, too. Her daughter (Darby, I learned) sat on a stool in front of the kitchen island, watching her mother.

Cammie looked up from under the sink when we came through the door. "Holy shit, he's still alive?"

She rushed over to us. "My God, Eddie. What did they do to you? Sit him down. I found a first-aid kit."

We helped my father to the living room and sat him down in one of the leather chairs.

The dead man was gone.

So was Stella.

"Where is Stella?"

Cammie knelt at the chair, opened the plastic box, found some cotton balls and antiseptic, and went to work on my father's face. "I helped her to one of the bedrooms."

I frowned. "You didn't—"

"Touch her? No. I wore a pair of those." She pointed to our box of latex gloves on the counter. "I found them in your car."

"You went through our stuff?"

"You stole them from my house," she countered. "Stella told me to wear them, told me where they were."

My father sucked a breath in between pursed lips. He pressed a hand against his abdomen. "I think he broke a few of my ribs."

Cammie shook her head. "Christ, we need to take his shirt off. That fucking bastard did a number on him."

Preacher hovered over us. "I caught him on the phone, Cammie."

"You didn't *catch* me doing anything."

"I heard it ring," Cammie said. She turned and glared at me. "You answered? Are you fucking crazy?"

"You heard the phone ring all the way in here? I was out in the woodshed."

She went back to my father's face. He winced as she dabbed at a cut above his left eye. "There are extensions all over the house, every room. They all rang. Was it him? That kid, David?"

"No."

Preacher clucked his tongue. "We need to tie him up, like Hobson. If it was Pickford, he wouldn't tell us. He may not even remember. This is a shit show."

I stood and got in his face. "You're not tying anyone up."

Preacher laughed. "You're stopping me? Now I'm gonna do it just to see what kind of moves you've got."

"Both of you, put the testosterone away," Cammie said, working the last button on my father's shirt. She peeled the material back. His entire midsection was black and blue. Higher up on the left, the skin was red and angry. "Oh, man. Definitely a few broken ribs." She snapped her fingers toward the first-aid kit. "Somebody hand me that roll of gauze."

I handed it to her, and she looked back at my father. "Eddie, I'm gonna wrap your ribs, but I'm going to keep it loose. I don't want to restrict your breathing. If I go too tight, it might feel better, but that increases the chances of one of those bone fragments puncturing one of your lungs." She gently pressed on his midsection, her fingers walking over the dark skin, making note of my father's reactions. "Looks like we've got two broken on the upper left and one down low on the right. I need you to lean forward a bit."

My father did, and his one good eye pinched shut with the movement.

To me, Cammie said, "Who was on the phone?"

I thought about what Fogel said.

Somebody in this house called that place first. That someone told them where we were. I had been alone with my father. I had no idea where Preacher had been when the call went out. Cammie was here in the house. Stella was in the house. Hobson was in the house. I glanced over at him. He was on the floor in the foyer, still tied up. Awake, but making no attempt to escape his bindings.

"It was a police detective back in Pittsburgh."

Cammie stopped wrapping. "What?"

"She's at that Charter place, I have no idea how she got there. She said a call came in from this number. The person who called told the person on her end where we were. She said they're coming."

"Somebody called from here? Who?"

I glared at her. "You tell me?"

"It wasn't me," Cammie said. "I've been in here."

"You said there are phone extensions everywhere."

Preacher paced the floor. "Does it even matter? The guy who did this to Eddie was already here. They found him before any phone call."

"I handled him," my father said softly, each word painful.

"Yeah," Preacher said. "You handled him. Had things totally under control."

"He's just some kind of scout," my father said. "He found me digging in the garden, caught me by surprise, sucker-punched me, then he kept going—hitting, kicking, I didn't get a shot in. Tied me up in the woodshed. Then Jack got here. He didn't have a chance to call anyone."

"He had enough time to hide his Suburban in the garage," I pointed out.

"Maybe I passed out for a minute, I don't know."

Cammie finished wrapping his chest and helped him back into a fresh shirt I'd found in the laundry room off the kitchen. "Whoever called. Doesn't matter. They know we're here now. We need to go. Now. Even if they have people in the area, it will take them a little while to scramble and get someone out here."

That's when the phone rang again.

"Nobody touch that," Preacher said.

The shrill ring of half a dozen phones filled the house. One ring. Two rings. Three rings.

"We need to answer," my father said. "I've got people watching both ends of the island. It might be one of them."

"Or it might be the Pickford kid," Cammie countered.

"It could be Detective Fogel calling back," I said. "Maybe she can help us. She might know something else."

Four rings.

Five.

Preacher rubbed at the bristle on his chin, then nodded at my father. "Whoever it is, they'll expect you. You answer." His hand dropped to the butt of his gun. "If it's the Pickford kid..."

My father understood. If it was David Pickford, if Pickford instructed him to do something, to somehow harm the rest of us, Preacher would put an end to it using whatever force was necessary.

Seven rings.

I helped my father stand, and he hobbled over to the telephone extension in the kitchen. When he lifted the receiver off the wall, he held it a few inches from his ear, as if that little distance would protect him from Pickford's words. "BH Bed and Breakfast, how can I help you?"

The voice on the other end was male and loud enough for all of us to hear through the tiny speaker. "I just took reservations for twelve here on the north end. They're driving down from the Pass in four...scratch that, six vans. ETA approximately one hour."

A click then, as he hung up.

My father replaced the handset. "That was Lloyd. He's got a little place just this side of Deception Pass. He would have spotted them crossing the bridge. Barring some kind of delay or road hazard, the pass is fifty-eight minutes away."

Preacher wasn't about to wait. He scooped Darby up off the floor and grabbed Cammie by the hand and headed for the door. "We're taking the ferry out. We can be there in half the time. You're welcome to follow, if you want. We can regroup on the mainland. We get separated, meet in one week at the Crater Lake welcome center in Oregon."

"That's a bad idea," my father said. "The next ferry is at noon. I'd be willing to bet they're on it. If they're not on that ferry, you can be sure they'll be on the mainland waiting to board the next one. Probably watching every car leaving Whidbey. You don't exactly blend in with that Pontiac."

"We get to the mainland, we've got a shot at outrunning them,"

Cammie said. "Or we can take one of the other cars and try and slip past them. We can't wait for them to get here."

"Why not? This place is defendable. Why do you think I'm here?" He motioned out toward the water. "We've got a sheer cliff behind us, with only one set of stairs to get up and down, and nearly four acres of open space in the front between the main house and the only road in or out. They can't get close to us. We won't let them." My father crossed over to the kitchen and opened three of the upper cabinet doors. Rather than plates, glasses, pots, or pans, we found ourselves staring at an arsenal. Dozens of weapons, freshly oiled, gleaming. Handguns, rifles, shotguns—several appeared to be military grade. M-16s or AK-47s, I had no idea. "I stopped running twenty years ago. I'm not starting again today. We need to end this."

Cammie looked defeated. "They want us all dead, Eddie."

"They may want us out of the way, but we've got three of the children here with us. They won't do anything to risk their lives. They want them alive."

"Why?" I broke in.

The room went silent. They all turned to me. "Why do they want you dead but not us? Why are they chasing us in the first place?"

My father appeared puzzled by this, as if he expected me to already know. He glanced at Preacher and Cammie, but neither said anything. He turned back to me, truly surprised. "You don't know? Your aunt didn't tell you? The guidance counselor, Elfrieda Leech—she didn't give you my letters? I've been writing you for years."

"I've never gotten a letter from you. All she gave me was this." I took out the letter Stella's father had written and handed it to him. He looked over it, then handed it to Cammie. "Your aunt must have told her not to say anything. Fucking Jo. Always insisting you live out a normal life. She never grasped..." His voice trailed off as he thought about this. He went over to the dining room table and started sifting through the various documents and folders.

"We don't have time for this," Preacher said.

"We're making time," my father told him. He found what he was looking for and handed it to me. An old flyer, the kind with teara-way phone numbers printed at the bottom. About half were missing. The headline read:

EARN $1000!
CHARTER PHARMACEUTICALS NEEDS VOLUNTEERS FOR
THE FINAL STAGE (STAGE FOUR) OF TESTING FOR
THEIR NEW VACCINATION PROTOCOL. ONE SHOT TO
YOU MEANS YOUR FUTURE CHILDREN WILL NOT NEED
TO RECEIVE ANY VACCINATIONS!
CALL FOR ADDITIONAL INFORMATION.

"They told all of us that as long as both parents received the shot, you'd be protected from dozens of ailments. Everything from polio to diphtheria, pertussis, tetanus—even chicken pox, small pox, and measles. Your mother and I were already dating. We had talked about kids, and frankly, we needed the money. We went. We all went. Back then, students were making money hand over fist participating in trials like this. Some were scary—LSD and hallucinogenics. This was the seventies. We were all doing that stuff anyway. Why not get paid?"

"The government always had the best LSD," Cammie muttered. "I should have stuck with that instead of getting wrapped up in this bullshit. $1000 was nearly twice what the other studies paid, and who wants their future kid to be subjected to dozens of vaccinations? Seemed like a no-brainer at the time."

My father said, "After the shot, we had to report back for regular blood tests and monitoring. The eighth of every month. Nothing crazy, and they paid us for that, too. There were no side effects, not for any of us. Not at first, anyway. But then, your mother got pregnant. Don't get me wrong—like I said, we talked about having kids, but the plan was to finish college, get married, get jobs, establish ourselves, then have children when we were ready. Your mother and I were careful, but somehow she got pregnant anyway. Same with Richard Nettleton and Emma, Keith Pickford and Jaquelyn Breece. All of us got pregnant around the same time. We halfheartedly joked the shot boosted our hormones. Richard and Emma dropped out of school and broke ties with Charter. The rest of us continued to go into our scheduled appointments. When you and David were born, they paid us all even more to monitor you—routine blood work, vitals, the same they were doing for us. Everything seemed okay, seemed *normal*. Then I started to hear from the Nettletons. What happened every time their daughter, Stella, touched something that was alive. They didn't know what to do. They went into hiding, off the grid. Keep in mind, this was the late seventies, early eighties. Much easier back then than it is today. Richard was convinced whatever was happening to his daughter was related to that shot, whatever Charter had given us. I thought he was crazy, we all did. But your mother and I watched you close anyway. I kept in touch with Keith and Jackie. They watched David, too. You both seemed okay. Richard got paranoid, said people were chasing him, these people dressed in white, just like the people from Charter. I began to wonder if maybe the shot had just triggered some kind of mental breakdown in him, like an allergic reaction. That kind of thing happened, too. Safety protocols were so lax." He paused for a second, dusting off the information in his head. "Keith Pickford and Jackie stopped showing up at their appointments in mid '78. Your mom and I didn't really get all the facts until about a year later, but it was bad. Keith lost it. He threw a pot of boiling oil at his little boy's face, burned him horribly, then he stabbed Jackie to death before turning the knife on himself. Neighbors found David on the kitchen floor, screaming at the top of his lungs, in terrible pain, both parents dead, blood everywhere. David was talking back then, but not much. Only two years old. He couldn't really tell anyone what happened, and they didn't press him. I thought about the shot. If that shot somehow drove Rich Nettleton crazy, maybe it had done the same with Keith. I heard David went to live with relatives. That's what the staff at Charter told us, and we had no reason to question them, not at that point. Rich and Emma Nettleton, Stella's parents, that's about the time they came back to Pittsburgh. They were both dead less than a week later. Murdered in some kind of home invasion. Stella was gone. I heard about the bodies they found there, grown men who looked like they'd been burnt, and I realized that Stella might have actually done it. What Richard had been raving about, what she could do, might actually be true.

"In May of '79 we heard about Perla Beyham, how she drowned in her bathtub. I barely knew her, only from her participation with the Charter study. It sounded like an accident. They said she fell asleep. It happened. But again, I thought about the shot. Was it really an accident? When your mother and I heard Garret Dotts hung himself in 1980, we again thought about the shot. We decided to stop going to the Charter follow-up appointments, we stopped taking you. That's when we noticed them watching us. People in white, white vehicles parked outside our apartment all the time. When we started looking for them, we realized they were everywhere, just like Richard said. I went to one last appointment, only me. I didn't bring you or your mother, and while I was in that room, I stole everything you see here—your mother was home packing our lives into our SUV. We planned to run."

"But they caught up with you," I said softly.

"I figured you'd remember. Something that traumatic gets etched into your brain, it never leaves. I had to think fast, I still didn't really know what we were up against. I left you with Jo, hoping they'd chase after me. And they did, but I eventually lost them. Elfrieda Leech, our guidance counselor, she had first told us about the study, said it was an easy way to make money. At the time, she had no idea what we were all getting into, but once that became clear, she helped me broker a deal—they leave you alone, and I don't go public. I drop off the edge of the earth. You would stay with your Auntie Jo, and she would watch you for them, report back. Unlike Stella and David, you hadn't shown any kind of special ability, nothing useful to them. They had no need for you, so they let you be."

I said, "They kept Stella in that house and locked David up."

My father whistled. "Those two were a completely different story. They locked David down tight once they figured out what he could do. He was the perfect little killing machine. At that point, the rest of the people involved in the study—Penelope Maudlin, Lester Woolford, Dewey Hobson, Cammie, Dalton over there, everyone ran, scattered. We think they used David to pick us off, one by one. That's probably how they they got Perla to drown herself and Garret Dotts to hang himself. Not accidents or suicides at all, but suggestions by David, which they had no choice but to carry out, *his ability* in full use. He was young, probably didn't understand what he was doing. Not in the beginning, anyway. But I think he grew to like it. Charter had what they wanted. They didn't need us adults anymore to create more children for them. We became liabilities."

My eyes drifted across the room to Darby, still clutching her mother's leg.

Cammie said, "They don't know about her. I was off their radar when she was born, and I plan to keep it that way."

"Can she do…something?" I asked.

"Can you?" Cammie retorted.

I was about to ask her who Darby's father was when I spotted the worry in Preacher's eyes. The answer was painfully obvious.

My father looked up at the clock on the wall in the kitchen. "We've got forty minutes. Do we stay and fight or keep running?"

"We leave here, where do we go?" Cammie said.

I thought of Stella in the other room. She'd wither away and die if I didn't find a way to help her soon. She'd die in that bed while the rest of us died out here, perched in windows and doors in some desperate last stand. Worse, if what my father said was true, they'd kill him, Hobson, Cammie, and Dalton, then drag Stella, me, and Cammie's daughter away somewhere, lock us up like they did with David. Staying here, all the guns, that did nothing but buy us a little time.

"We'll get slaughtered if we stay here," I said softly. "I need to use your phone," I said. "I've got an idea."

"No calls," Preacher said.

My father nodded at the extension hanging on the wall in the kitchen. "Go ahead."

Preacher grumbled but did nothing to stop me as I crossed the room, picked up the line, and dialed.

When I hung up five minutes later, my father glanced back at the clock, then forced his beaten body to stand. "They're coming from the pass and the ferry. I've got another way off this island, but you all need to trust me."

Cammie and Preacher started to gather the weapons on the counter.

My father said, "Cabinet above the refrigerator. There's a leather duffle bag up there—grab it—we take the documents, nothing else. They're our only real leverage."

"We need the guns," Preacher insisted.

My father shook his head. "Too much weight."

14

"Pull your shit together, Fogel," she muttered, surprised by the sound of her own voice. She wiped the tears from her eyes with the palms for hands, then wiped the snot from her nose on the sleeve of her jacket.

Fogel stood up straight.

She sucked in a deep breath through her nose and let it out through her mouth.

Her eyes landed on the display of Trudeau's MacBook, open on his desk.

White text superimposed at the top left corner stated the current date and time, seconds ticking off. The bottom right simply said, CHARTER OBSERVATION TEAM 309 – SUBJECT "D" – LEVEL 2 SUB 3.

The image was blank.

Trudeau stared forward, the butt of the pen sticking out of his ear with surprisingly little blood. Several drops found their way to the white jacket of his suit.

Fogel turned back to the Mac, pulling it closer.

Trudeau had several programs open—spreadsheets, a web browser, e-mail. She brought up his e-mails first and scrolled through his inbox. 6,324 unread messages.

Fogel was a stickler for a clean inbox, virtual or otherwise, and so many messages, so much clutter, made her twitchy. Brier never deleted his messages after reading them. His inbox had always been like this.

Not really like this.

Trudeau's messages were all bold, unread. As if he didn't check his e-mail.

Fogel scrolled back through the messages, scanning the subjects.

Lower your mortgage.

Movie and showtimes.

Advertisements for local car dealerships.

Spam, all of it. She didn't see a single personal or business-related message from a real person.

Fogel clicked over to the *Sent* folder.

The last sent message was dated 8/12/1993—nearly five years ago.

The message was from Trudeau to 6491@charter.com with a cc to loliver@charter.com. The subject simply said, "We need to talk about Doctor Durgin. Possible problem with 'D.'"

Fogel clicked back over to the blank video feed:

CHARTER OBSERVATION TEAM 309 – SUBJECT "D" – LEVEL 2 SUB 3.

Subject "D."

Fogel opened Trudeau's web browser. The last page he viewed was for TicketMaster.com—Patti LaBelle in Philly, 9/20/1993.

She returned to his sent e-mails, nearly ten thousand of them, dating back to the mid-eighties. Fogel tried to remember when she first started using e-mail. Probably around that time with AOL.

You've got mail.

She still had nightmares about that voice.

Fogel returned to the video feed:

CHARTER OBSERVATION TEAM 309 – SUBJECT "D" – LEVEL 2 SUB 3.

Someone could come into this office at any moment. She was pushing her luck. She had a decision to make, and it took her all of two seconds to make it.

Fogel closed the top on the MacBook, unplugged the cable, and tucked the computer under her arm. Beneath the MacBook she found a faded yellow Post-it note with the number 392099 written in blocky handwriting. She scooped that up, too.

She opened the office door slowly, just enough to peek out into the hallway.

Fogel was alone.

To her right was the door leading back to the lobby. On the far left end of the hallway was an elevator. She scrambled from Trudeau's office to the elevator and hit the call button.

Nothing happened.

A keypad, identical to the one in the lobby, was built into the wall beside the elevator controls.

Fogel glanced at the Post-it note, keyed 392099 into the pad, then pressed the call button again. This time, the button lit up and she heard the whir of motors as the car approached. A bell dinged, and the doors slid open with a squeak. Inside, a couple of the light bulbs were out.

She took one last look down the hallway, thought about the shitstorm of trouble she'd find herself in when she eventually got caught snooping around this place, then stepped inside the elevator.

Fogel keyed in the code again and pressed the button marked 2-3.

The doors squeaked shut.

The elevator ascended.

Fogel wasn't sure what she expected to find when the doors opened. Maybe a burly security guard (or three), a wide-eyed lab rat or research assistant, possibly a janitor. The doors opened on none of those things.

The doors opened on another white hallway, the walls covered in the crimson stains of dried blood and nearly a dozen bodies lying on the floor.

Fogel pressed against the back wall of the elevator and froze long enough for the doors to close. Before they could seal completely, she stepped forward and placed her hand between them, tripping the sensor, causing the doors to reverse.

Fogel stepped slowly into the hallway, with Trudeau's MacBook held tightly at her chest like a makeshift shield against whatever happened here.

From the state of the bodies, she knew it had happened a long time ago. Several years, at least. She thought about the last e-mail Trudeau sent, dated 8/12/1993.

The first two bodies she encountered, just outside the elevator, appeared to be a man and a woman. Both were dressed entirely in white, the material stained in various shades of yellow and brown and the bodies themselves nothing more than dried out husks, years into decomposition. Mummy-like. The nails and hair long, dried lips folded back in sadistic grins, empty eye sockets watching her. The head of the woman had nearly been severed by a metal clipboard wielded by the man beside her. Her hand was still at his abdomen, where it appeared she stabbed him with a pair of scissors.

Across from them, the body of a woman (Fogel could only tell because she wore a white skirt) had a ruler embedded in her eye, both her hands still grasping the opposite end.

Not trying to get the ruler out but twisting it in deep, Fogel's mind whispered.

With the other bodies, Fogel found more of the same. As she walked the length of the hallway, the dead were locked in some kind of macabre dance. Dead by their own hand or that of someone nearby. This wasn't a place of business or research or learning. This place was a tomb. The air reeked of it.

When she reached two doors, the first labeled SUBJECT "D" – OBSERVATION and the second labeled SUBJECT "D" – CONTAINMENT, she found the first to be ajar and the second locked. The code she found in Trudeau's office didn't work.

Fogel nudged open the observation door and stepped inside.

The bodies of two men were slumped over a control panel, both long dead. The one on the left looked like he had chewed through his own wrist. The man on the right had a pen sticking out from his eye socket and a stapler in his right hand. Judging by the remains of his skull, he had bashed his own head in.

While this scene was disturbing, it was eclipsed by what Fogel saw on the other side of the large observation window. The body of a woman sat in a chair at the center of what looked like a sterile hotel room. She faced the window with a notepad on her lap. Her mouth was stuffed full of pages from that notepad, the remains of her cheeks bloated like a chipmunk. She still held a balled up sheet of paper in her left hand. Several more were on the floor surrounding her feet. Embroidered in the woman's white lab coat above her right breast was the name DR. DURGIN, handwritten with a black marker on the opposite side were the words, WILL SHRINK FOR FOOD.

What the fuck happened here?

A clipboard between the two men in the observation room held about a half-inch worth of pages. The topmost simply said, Charter Observation Log. Someone wrote 309 beside that along with the date, 8/12/1993. The remainder of the page was blank.

Shelves filled with video tapes lined the wall on the left of the room along with a monitor (blank) and a VCR. Fogel studied the machine for a moment—powered on, a tape inside—she pressed the rewind button. The whir of tiny motors filled the room as the tape spun back to the beginning.

15

"Stack? Wake up, buddy, it's me."

Former detective Terrance Stack, just Terry now, heard the words, but they sounded as if someone whispered them during a hurricane from the opposite end of a storm drain.

"Terry—you gotta wake up. We don't have much time."

This time, the words came from much closer, damn near on top of him.

Stack's eyes fluttered and opened. First he saw nothing more than a white blur, but with each blink, things got a little clearer. Muck, tears, and dried who-knows-what fell away from his heavy lids, and the room slowly came into focus. He tried to reach up and wipe his eyes, but his hands wouldn't move. Neither would his arms.

Stack's head was turned to the side, looking down. When his vision cleared, he found himself looking at the top of the card table in his spare bedroom. When he managed to raise his head and look up, he found himself facing Faustino Brier. His former partner sat in the chair opposite him wearing a gray rumpled suit, white dress shirt, and blue striped tie—an outfit Stack had seen him in probably two dozen times.

"Brier?" The word escaped his throat and found its way out past his dry chapped lips, feeling like sandpaper.

Faustino Brier raised a glass of water and brought it to Stack's lips. "Drink this. You've been out for a while."

Stack drank. He slurped down the water.

Brier took the glass away for a moment. "Not too fast, you want it to stay down."

Stack nodded.

Brier let him drink more.

When the glass was empty, Brier set it back down on the table. A smile edged the corners of his mouth.

Stack stared at him, at least a minute, then: "You're dead."

Brier only smiled. He leaned back in the chair the way he always liked—the front legs off the ground, balancing precariously on only the back. Stack always told him he'd catch a bad chair one day, one that would break apart under him, and he'd look like a fucking fool when he landed on his ass, but Brier sat like that anyway.

"Am I dead?"

Stack couldn't move his legs. They held tight against the base of his chair. Even moving his head was a chore. He felt no pain, though, and that was good. That was real good.

Brier leaned forward in the chair. "I'm not gonna lie, buddy. It was your heart. A couple too many beers, people running around your house, your crazy trip up the steps…You pushed just a little too hard and blew a gasket. You knew it was coming, though, right? Not much of anything holds up after eighty-two years of constant beating and abuse. Frankly, I'm surprised you got as many miles out of that body as you did. The only thing holding you together was beer, Denny's takeout, and beef jerky."

"Not much beer, not at the end anyway."

"Enough."

"When?"

"When did you die? It's been about a day and a half," Brier said.

Stack looked around the spare bedroom—the walls covered in twenty years' worth of evidence, all the boxes lining the floor, the smudged up windows and thick dust in the corners. "This is it? No white light? No pearly gates? And my old partner as an escort? Is that why you're here? To take me to the other side?"

Brier shook his head. "I'm here to run the case with you."

"Why? You know this case inside and out."

"I want to hear it from you, one last time." He waved a hand. "Old times' sake, and all."

Stack licked at his lips, still dry. His eyes went to the glass of water on the table. He had drained it a few minutes ago—the glass was full again. "That's a neat trick."

"Want more?"

Stack nodded.

Brier lifted the glass and held it to Stack's mouth. When it was gone, he set it back on the table. "Better?"

Stack nodded again. "Where should I start?"

"Wherever you'd like."

"Maybe I should start when you died."

"When was that exactly?"

"You don't remember?"

"Not really."

Stack told him. He explained how Brier had followed the man in the black GTO back to the house at 62 Milburn while Fogel tailed the Thatch kid. How someone took him out with a head shot. "Ballistics confirmed a .45 caliber. The shot came from a Sig Sauer P220. They found the gun. Someone tossed it into the bushes. No usable prints."

"But you think it was the guy in the GTO?"

Stack shrugged. "Probably. Although, they found tracks for a Chevy behind both your car and the GTO. Possibly a third party. It could have been them, too. No way to be sure without more information."

Brier kicked the lid off one of the boxes sitting beside the table, the one for the Dormont house. He reached inside and took out the letter from Richard Nettleton. "This is from the girl's father, right?"

"Yeah. The Thatch kid had it, remember? You gave me a copy."

675

Brier seemed to think about this. "Things are a little fuzzy." He dropped the letter back in the box. "Tell me about the Thatch kid. Where is he now?"

"Dunno. Fogel lost him in Nevada. She's trying to pick up the trail again. He's with the girl, though. We know that much."

"Where do you think they're heading next?"

"Can't say." Stack looked around the room. "Who were those people in the white vans? What did they do after…"

"After you died?"

Stack nodded.

"You killed one of them, you know that, right?"

"Shot him through the floor."

Brier's lips went tight. "Yeah, right through the floor."

"Are they still here?"

Brier said nothing.

Stack said, "If I'm dead, and I'm still in the house, can I somehow see them?"

"What, like a ghost?"

"Yeah, I guess."

"You want to haunt your own house?"

"I want to see why they came here. What they were after."

Brier leaned forward on the chair, the legs tipping slightly. "This investigation is over for you, Terry."

"Fogel's still out there," Stack muttered.

"Out where?"

"Chasing a lead. Someplace called Charter outside Chadds Ford."

Brier didn't seem surprised by this. "Tell me about Charter."

Stack tried to reach for the notepad he had left near the door, the one with his notes on Charter, but his arms and legs wouldn't work. "Why can't I move?"

"Dead people don't move."

"You're moving, though," Stack pointed out. "My head, neck, eyes, can move. Only my arms and legs are stuck. Why?"

Brier shrugged. "God works in mysterious ways when you're

alive, but he pulls out all the stops after death. Shit gets crazy." He leaned back in his chair. "How did you learn about Charter?"

Stack told him about the note Fogel had found in Thatch's hotel room, the connections he made to several past employees. "The white vans showed up right after I started making those calls," he said. "They've got to be from Charter. It's all connected."

Brier slammed a hand down on the desk.

Stack jumped.

Brier grinned. "Sorry, buddy, you seemed to be losing focus. Needed to bring you back." He glanced around the room. "So everything you've learned over the years, all the data on this case, it's all here in this room?"

"Most of it," Stack said. "Fogel has the official records at Pittsburgh PD for some. The rest is here."

Brier thought about this for a moment.

Stack frowned. "You don't remember that? You kept the files going after I retired. Kept the investigation going. Fogel has *your* files."

"Things get fuzzy after you die," Brier said again.

"I still remember. Is that because I just died?"

Brier said nothing to this. He leaned back in his chair, then forward again, rocking on the back legs. "What do you know about David Pickford?"

"Who?"

"David Pickford."

"Never heard of him," Stack replied.

"He's a beautiful man."

"Okay."

"*The* most beautiful man."

Stack didn't reply.

Brier reached for the glass of water, now full again. "Want some more?"

Although Stack was still thirsty, he shook his head.

Brier set the glass back down and fixed his gaze back on Stack. "You're sure, outside of the information here, and whatever this

Fogel has at Pittsburgh PD, there is nothing else? Nobody else has copies? You haven't told anyone else what you've found over all these years?"

Stack said no, and that was strange because he didn't want to answer Brier's question at all. The word came out anyway.

Brier leaned back in the chair again and rolled his head toward the door. "Get in here and take it all!" he shouted. "Take every last scrap!"

Three men came through the door, all in their late twenties, early thirties, wearing long, white trench coats like the man Stack had shot on the stairs. Two of them began carrying out the file boxes, while the third started taking everything down from the walls.

"What is this?" Stack muttered, turning back to Brier.

Brier was no longer sitting across from him. Instead, he found a young man with dark hair and darker eyes and the most horrible burn filling the entire left side of his face. It hurt Stack just to look at it.

Stack tried to stand again, couldn't move. He looked down, and for the first time saw the ropes binding him to the chair at his arms, legs, and torso. He tugged at them, but they were tight, didn't give at all. He looked back at the man across from him. "Who the hell are you?"

"I'm David Pickford."

"You are a beautiful man."

"Thank you."

Stack's eyes fell to the glass on the table. It was dry and filthy, covered in dust. Looked like it had sat empty for days, probably since the last time Fogel was up here. No water at all.

The men in white continued to remove everything from the room, nearly half of it gone already.

A phone rang. David reached inside his black leather jacket and took out a cell phone. He glanced at the display, then back at Stack. "I need to take this. It was a pleasure speaking with you. You're going to fall asleep now."

Stack did.

David Pickford pressed the phone to his ear, turned from Stack, and faced the corner of the room. "What?"

Latrese Oliver's heavy breaths came over the tinny speaker. He swore he smelled the stank rot coming up her throat over the line. "We just missed them on Whidbey."

David shook the image of her picking at her stump of an arm out of his head, tried not to think about whatever was happening on the inside of her scarred, half-dead body. He couldn't wait to kill that miserable bitch. "I wouldn't have," he said.

"Well, you're not here, are you?"

"I can't be everywhere."

Oliver ignored him. "Edward Thatch, Cammie Brotherton, Dalton, Stella, and the boy are all together now."

"We had people at the ferry terminal, and you came down from Deception Pass. How did they get past you?"

"Edward Thatch kept a seaplane docked at the base of the cliff beside his house. We caught sight of it taking off from Puget Sound when we arrived."

"A seaplane? How could we not know about a seaplane?"

Oliver didn't reply.

David Pickford leaned against the wall and drummed his fingers on the windowsill. "Doesn't really matter, I suppose. We know where they're heading."

Oliver drew in another breath. "What do you want me to do here? With the house?"

David shrugged, the answer obvious. "Take anything useful and burn the rest. Burn everything." He considered this for a moment and added, "Is Dalton's car there, the black GTO?"

"Yes."

"I want that car. Have someone drive it back. Burn everything else."

"Okay."

"Fly back in the Charter jet when you're through. I'll need you here."

Oliver said, "It's almost over."

"Yeah, almost."

16

My father's house on Whidbey Island sat perched atop a tall cliff overlooking Puget Sound. Shortly after making my phone call, we wrapped Stella in a thick blanket so I could carry her with our various bags wrapped over our shoulders. Preacher carried Hobson, who continued to squirm in his bindings. Cammie and her daughter followed behind us, all eyeing the man nervously, toting their own bags. My father led the way, his beaten body fighting him every step. He took nothing from the house, said he already had a go-bag packed and waiting.

We followed him across the backyard toward the cliff, then down a rickety set of wooden steps attached to the cliff face with heavy metal bolts and anchors. At the base of the stairs, built on large concrete pylons sunk into the sands of a small private beach, was what appeared to be a boathouse. I fully expected to find a speedboat of some sort inside, so when my father opened the door revealing a plane on large floats, I think I was as surprised as everyone else.

"This is a 208 Cessna Caravan. I bought it a few years ago after receiving my pilot's license, mostly to get back and forth from the mainland faster, but it's got range and they won't be able to follow us. If I keep low enough, I won't need to file a flight plan."

Preacher circled the aircraft, running his hand over the wing. "This is big. We can take the guns."

"Like I said at the house, this isn't about space, it's about weight. Every pound we add shaves miles off our travel distance. Miles we can't afford to lose. If we stop to refuel, we'll end up in a database. They can use that intel to track us. This is a one-way trip."

"To where?"

The "where" turned out to be Devil's Lake, North Dakota, and my father was right—by the time we touched down on the water, we had nothing but fumes in the tank. The flight took us nearly seven hours. My father had removed the last two passenger seats, and I was grateful for that. Preacher and I positioned Stella in the back of the plane on the floor in her blanket so she could rest. She stirred several times during the flight but only woke once. When I told her where we were, she only nodded and drifted back off to sleep. About an hour into the flight, Preacher tied a makeshift blindfold over Hobson's eyes. Once he was unable to see Cammie, he stopped squirming and returned to the docile state he had been in while driving with Stella and me. To be safe, we kept his hands and feet tied up.

My father landed the plane on Devil's Lake with the practiced hand of a veteran, and I considered all the things I didn't know about the man. Twenty years of life lived. I imagined learning to fly a plane was only one of many secrets.

He maneuvered the plane to the northern edge of the lake and guided it gently to a long dock. Preacher opened the door and grabbed a rope as we sidled up beside it. I jumped out and tossed him a second rope I found coiled up in a plastic storage container fastened to the wooden planks. With my father barking out instructions, together we secured the plane.

The dock led to a well-maintained sloping lawn. Beyond that stood two buildings—a small log cabin and a large metal shed. My father said he bought the property nearly a decade earlier but rarely stayed there. He paid a caretaker to maintain the place for him. I had yet to learn how he afforded such things and planned to ask him when we finally arrived at our destination, but for now, questions had to wait.

I carried Stella this time. Preacher held Darby's sleeping body in his arms, with Cammie beside him, as we followed my father past the cabin to the outbuilding. He entered a code on the security panel at the metal door. There was a loud buzz, and the door swung open. The lights turned on automatically. Inside were three Cadillac Escalades, white, with wires trailing out from under the hoods.

"I keep them gassed up and on trickle chargers. There's cash in the glove boxes for gas. They should get us where we need to go."

"Why white?" Preacher said.

"They won't be looking for us in white vehicles. They blend," my father said, eerily echoing what Stella told me a lifetime ago.

Preacher drove the first SUV with my father, Cammie, and Darby. I drove the second vehicle, with Hobson in the passenger seat and Stella asleep and stretched out in the back.

Our journey would end where it began, and with each passing mile, I felt Pittsburgh growing near.

17

Reid Migliore stood waiting for us at the mouth of the road leading to Carrie Furnace, an AR-15 cradled in his hands. Two other men I didn't recognize leaned against the black SUV parked directly in our path about ten feet back. All three perked up as we approached, Reid in particular, his eyes nervously darting over Hobson, then Preacher and Cammie in the SUV idling behind me. He approached my open window, with the barrel of his assault rifle pointing at the ground. He had a fresh scar running along his right cheek.

"What happened to you?" I asked.

He ignored my question and glanced over at Hobson in the passenger seat—tied up and blindfolded. "What is this, Thatch? Dunk didn't say nothing about kidnapping."

I tied Hobson back up at the last gas stop. "Dunk knows."

"Well, he didn't say nothing to me. I don't like any of this."

Stella groaned from the back seat.

Reid leaned in a little closer. "That her?"

I didn't answer.

"What's wrong with her?"

It was my turn to ignore his question. "Where is he?"

Reid took a step back from the SUV and pointed the barrel of his assault rifle back toward the old steel mill. "Park where we did a few weeks ago, at Blast Furnace #7. He's inside."

I put the SUV back into gear and followed the overgrown road toward the large metal monstrosity.

I parked in nearly the same place we had the last time and shut down the engine.

Preacher pulled up beside me and did the same. He stepped out of the SUV and surveyed the buildings, the catwalks, the men slowly pacing back and forth along all of it, their eyes on the surrounding fields. He said softly, "Are you sure about this?"

"Nope."

A girl, no more than sixteen or seventeen, walked up from the side of the brick building. Like Reid, she carried an AR-15. Unlike Reid, both her arms and half her neck were covered in colorful tattoos of snakes. The mouth of a cobra opened below her chin, ready to strike. She said something into a small Motorola radio before dropping it into the pocket of her green army jacket. "I'm Adella Fricke. Follow me."

"Where's Dunk?"

"In a few minutes. We need to get you settled first." She glanced back at Stella. "Bring her. The others, too."

Preacher looked at me, uncertain. I could only nod.

Adella led us through the brick building, out the other side, and down a long, wide hallway. Rusty water dripped from the ceiling and puddled on the floor. The walls glistened with it. Machinery long ago abandoned slept in every corner, left to die years ago. The men and women who worked for Dunk—gang members, runaways, homeless—I didn't really know how to describe them. They watched us silently as we passed. Twenty, thirty, probably more. They were everywhere. The youngest looked no more than twelve or thirteen, and the oldest I spotted—a man wearing faded coveralls—might have been in his late fifties.

We took a set of stairs up to the second level, then followed a catwalk under a sign that simply read BARRACKS. Stella's arm was over my shoulder, and although she wasn't quite awake, she was able to walk on her own. The long walk was still exhausting, though. I was grateful when we entered a large room lined with bunk beds on the outer walls and tables in the middle—she hadn't spoken in over a day. Her breathing was horribly labored, and sweat openly trickled from her pores. I settled her into one of the beds near the back, and she curled up facing the wall.

Preacher set Hobson down in a chair at one of the tables. Still blindfolded, the man did not move.

Cammie helped Darby into another open bunk. The little girl's eyes were half shut, fighting sleep. She was out the moment her head hit the pillow. Cammie sat on the edge of the bed and stroked her hair. My father collapsed into a bunk of his own. The bruising on his face thickened into a nasty shade of purple. He grunted and rolled onto his side, off his damaged ribs.

Adella said, "Come with me. I'll take you to him."

When Preacher started to follow, she stopped at the door without turning around. "Just Thatch."

"No way," Preacher said. "I'm still not sure we're staying."

Cammie looked up at me. "Take him with you. The second pair of eyes will do you good."

Adella started down the hall. "Whatever, just hurry up."

Ten days ago, when I visited Dunk in this place, I got the impression he and his people simply took it over for the day. Camped out at that first building and cleared out shortly after I left. As Adella walked us deeper into the mill, I realized that wasn't the case at all. Dunk set up shop here. He ran his business from this place. He ran his business with a small army.

Everyone was armed.

Most had more than one gun.

I thought about what Brier and Detective Horton had told me all those years ago in the hospital. They had no idea how large this had all become.

I didn't see any drugs. I also didn't see anyone doing drugs.

Knowing Dunk (or, at the very least, knowing the kid I once knew as Dunk) he was smart enough not to keep that kind of thing anywhere near where he worked. Most likely, he played some kind of shell game with that stuff, moving it around the city faster than the cops could track it. I honestly didn't really care. My only concern was keeping Stella safe.

Eyes followed us everywhere, averting when I caught them looking. Whispering to each other.

Adella led us into the former office building for Carrie Furnace—dozens of offices, most abandoned. Dunk was in the largest, the last door on the left. When Adella ushered us inside, he stood in the far back corner with a cell phone pressed to his ear, most of his weight balanced on a cane, looking out a grimy window at the mill grounds. He glanced back over his shoulder.

Relying heavily on the cane, he turned and started toward us, mumbling into the phone. When he finished the call, he disconnected and held the phone out to me. "Hold this for a second? Being a cripple, I sometimes find I don't have enough hands to multitask."

I took it from him.

Dunk brought up his cane and slammed the silver head into Preacher's gut. He doubled over, and Dunk's right fist shot up and slammed into his nose. I heard the crunch of bone as Preacher stumbled backward. "You broke my nose in '92, you arrogant fuck. You've had that coming for six years," Dunk said.

Two of Dunk's men came in from the hallways and grabbed Preacher's arms before he could retaliate. They stood on either side of him as Dunk took a white handkerchief from his pocket and held it up to Preacher. "We're square now, shitknocker."

Preacher nodded, shrugged off both men, grabbed the handkerchief, and pressed it to his nose. "Square," he muttered, tilting his head back.

I shook my head. We didn't have time for macho bullshit. "They'll be here soon. Are you ready?"

Dunk used the cane to take several steps back toward the window. "Get with the program, Thatch. They're already here, and yes, we're ready."

"What?" Preacher said, going to the window.

Dunk pointed out toward the west. "Look past the trees. Two white vans out there parked off Whitaker. The first one got here about ten minutes after you did. The other one pulled up a few minutes ago."

"There's no way they followed us. Did you tell anyone we were coming?"

Dunk shook his head. "Only Reid, Truck, and Adella, and they don't talk to nobody but me. Word is probably spreading now, though. Not much we can do about that."

"Somebody tipped them off," Preacher said.

I thought about the phone call from Fogel back at my father's house in Whidbey.

Two men paused at Dunk's door. When I turned, they continued down the hallway. "Why does everyone keep staring at me?"

"Gossip," Dunk said. "They all heard about the crazy show you put on with Reid the last time you were here. Guess they're hoping for an encore."

Preacher frowned. "What happened with Reid?"

Dunk smacked me on the back. "My boy here came out on the right side of a crazy game of Russian Roulette. He didn't tell you?"

Preacher's eyes narrowed. "No, he didn't tell me."

"Yeah, well, I wouldn't fuck with him," Dunk said. "The guy deflects bad mojo like Superman and bullets."

Pinching his nose with the handkerchief, Preacher changed the subject. "How defendable is this place?"

Dunk went back to the window. "I've got a hundred and six people here, all armed. Lookouts in town, too. If someone tries to pedal up on a white bicycle, they'll have a dozen weapons trained on them. One road in, one road out, with the Monongahela River at our backs and open fields all around us. See that tree line way out there? I've got people in blinds watching every inch. There are two sets of railroad tracks, with a deep gully between the trees and the furnace grounds. No way they get vehicles through there, and if by some miracle they make it on foot, it would be slow-moving. We'd pick them off before they even got close to any of the buildings. Between all the hills and the scraps of machinery scattered around, the property is covered with places to hide, and I have people stationed at all of them. We've got a solid perimeter. They'd have to airdrop into here to get any kind of jump on us. If by some crazy miracle they get past the outer defenses, we fall back on the mill. This place is a fucking metal maze, and my people have trained here for years. They know every inch. We'd slaughter them."

"We start shooting, how long before the cops show up?" Preacher said.

Dunk laughed. "Who do you think I have running lookout in town? Our finest in blue, that's who. Don't need to worry about them. We're too isolated, anyway. We set up a shooting range out back almost two years ago, and not a single person has ever reported gunfire out here. The sound doesn't carry far enough. If this goes all out World War III, ain't nobody coming to help us, and nobody coming to stop us. We're on our own."

"Let's hope it doesn't come to that," I said softly.

The look in Dunk's eyes told me he kinda hoped it did. He crossed the room and went to a wooden crate in the corner. "I've got a Plan 'B,' too, for that David character you mentioned."

Dunk opened the lid and handed me a pair of over-the-ear headphones. "I picked up a truckload of these babies back in January. They were heading to the Consumer Electronics Show in Vegas from the factory in Massachusetts. They won't hit the market for at least another year, so I've been sitting on them."

"Bose Quiet Comfort?" I said, reading the box.

"Noise-canceling headphones," Dunk said. "You put these on, hit the switch, and they block out all outside noise. Pickford can scream at the top of his lungs, and you won't hear shit." He took a

Motorola radio from his pocket and plugged it into the dangling headphone cord. "We communicate with these. All other sound will be blocked out. We'll be able to hear each other but nothing coming from him."

When I made the phone call to Dunk back at my father's house on Whidbey, I put my conscience in check. More accurately, I locked it away in a cold room somewhere in the back of my head. I knew he was mixed up in some horrible things, and by asking for his help, I'd find myself in the thick of those horrible things. When he said he 'picked up a truckload,' I was under no illusion he paid retail, and I told myself not to think about the driver of that truck or what may have happened to him. I sure as shit couldn't think about Gerdy while I was around him. Not her, not the others at Krendal's, either, none of that. When those thoughts popped into my head, I forced myself to think of Stella and the people with me, the ones I needed to keep alive *today*, not the ones I couldn't bring back from my past. I'd mourn them again tomorrow. I told myself this man was my friend, had been for most of my childhood. He stood by and helped when my aunt was dying of cancer—nobody else did that. When I called Dunk and asked him for help, I didn't outright sell my soul, but I'd be lying if I said I didn't feel like the devil signed a short-term lease. When this was over, I'd find some way to wash my hands of it. That's what I told myself, although I knew I'd be scrubbing away the grime for the rest of my life. Some stains don't come out.

Dunk's phone rang.

When he hung up the call, he was back at the window. "We've got two more white vans out there. Four now. One of my guys approached them, and they scrambled and regrouped a block away."

Preacher lowered the handkerchief from his nose. The bleeding had stopped. Although it was swollen, I don't think Dunk broke it. "If they know they've got all of us here, they may move tonight, or they might try to wait us out. No way to be sure."

"Either way, we're ready." Dunk turned back to the crate. "Adella said you've got four others back at the barracks, right? Here—"

He handed me six boxes of headphones.

"—batteries are in the box. They're good for about forty hours. We've got more, if we need them. Take these back with you, and hang tight. I need to check in with my lieutenants."

I said, "Are you sure you want to do this? It could be bad for you."

Dunk smiled. He was missing a tooth on the left side of his mouth. "You saved my life, pulled me out of that fire. Saying no was never an option." He lowered his voice. "I know you have reservations about what happened. I know you don't believe me, I've made peace with that. Maybe someday you will, too. I wouldn't let you down back then, and I'm not about to do it now. You're my brother, man. Family."

I didn't know what to say to that, so I only nodded.

He leaned in closer. "Can I meet her? She's crazy hot, right?"

18

Dunk said he'd stop by the barracks after he updated his people. Maybe an hour.

As Adella led us back, Preacher whispered, "I'm gonna put a bullet in that shit."

"Wouldn't be the first," I told him.

Someone had dropped off food while we were gone. A basket of fruit sat on one of the tables, along with several bags of McDonald's, a case of bottled water, and a half-eaten pizza.

Darby watched us enter the room, tomato sauce all over her mouth. My father was still sleeping, Hobson still in the chair where we left him, his blindfold on.

Stella wasn't in her bunk.

Cammie came through a door at the back and nodded at me. "Thank God, come on—"

Preacher started to follow after us. I told him to stay and eat.

Cammie led me into a bathroom. I heard water running in the back.

Stella sat on the floor of a large shower, still clothed, her knees pulled tight against her chest, her face buried between them. The water rolled over her, steaming hot. She was shivering horribly.

I turned to Cammie. "Get me the latex gloves."

She ran out and returned with them a moment later.

I pulled out a pair, tugged them on, and crouched down low. "Stella? What can I do?"

She drew in a breath and attempted to speak, but nothing came out but a garbled gasp.

"Are you cold or hot? Do you have a fever?"

"F...f...freezing," she stammered.

Her left glove was still on, but she had peeled off the right one and left it bunched up in the corner of the shower. Her fingers flexed—stretching out, balling into a fist, then back again.

Stay back, I mouthed toward Cammie.

She nodded, pressing further back into the doorway.

I reached out with my gloved hand and brushed Stella's hair back over her shoulders. Her head swiveled, twisting fast, feral. Her eyes wide and bloodshot—all at once distant and fixed on me. "You...need to...leave."

The words came out as a growl, a voice unrecognizably deep. She drew in a series of quick breaths through her mouth, then hid her face again in her knees. Pulled her knees against her tighter still.

I leaned in closer. I was getting soaked, the hot water turning my skin red. I didn't care. "You've got to fight it, Stella. You're stronger than whatever this is. You can beat it."

"Go!" Stella shouted. "Get away from me!"

"No."

Her gloveless right hand shot out and gripped my arm just below the elbow.

I was wearing a sweatshirt. Her skin didn't contact mine, but when she realized what she had done, she released me and squirmed back into the corner of the shower. She got as far from me as she could, pressing tight against the tile. She looked childlike, frail. Frightened and broken.

Without looking up, I said to Cammie, "There's a basket of fruit on the table out there. I saw it when we came in. Can you get it for me?"

"Are you serious?"

"Please."

Cammie rolled her eyes, shrugged, and went back to the bunk room. She returned a moment later with the basket. "I don't think she's hungry."

I sat the basket down on the floor beside me and took a large, red apple from the top of the pile. I held it out to Stella. "Take this."

Stella looked out from behind her arm. She reached out tentatively with her right hand, her quivering fingers wrapping around the apple. Her thumb and index finger passed right through the plump fruit and met as if it weren't even there—the red skin and yellow flesh beneath turned black and crumbled away, the core withered and her fist closed in the space where the apple had been seconds earlier, the entire thing dropping to the tile floor in a pulpy mess.

"Holy shit," Cammie breathed.

I handed Stella a banana. It also crumbled away with her touch—drying, rotting, all life leaving the fruit in an instant.

I gave her an orange after that.

Another apple.

Half the bowl was gone before Stella's erratic breathing began to slow and even out. When I handed her what was probably the sixth or seventh apple, the fruit still died, but it took nearly twenty seconds.

"Better," Stella said softly.

I glanced at Cammie, still hovering over my shoulder. "Can you give us a minute?"

"We need to tie her up. Like Hobson."

"We're not tying her up. Not her."

Cammie sighed and stomped out of the bathroom.

I turned off the shower, helped Stella stand, and wrapped a fluffy, white towel around her.

"Thank you, Pip. Thank you for being you."

I lowered my voice. "Somebody back at my father's house called Charter." We hadn't been alone. This was the first chance I had to tell her. The first time in days she was coherent enough to understand.

"What?"

"That's not the worst of it." I told her how Fogel had dialed back, what she said. How I had been in the woodshed with my father and had no idea who placed the call to Charter. "It could be any of them."

"Hobson was tied up, right? Your father, too. That only leaves Cammie and that Preacher fellow."

Stella looked around the room, seemingly for the first time. "Where are we now?"

"You don't remember leaving Whidbey?"

She shook her head.

I told her about the second call from my father's lookout. His seaplane. The drive from Devil's Lake back to Pittsburgh.

She took all this in. "What is today's date?"

"August 13."

Her mouth fell open. "Five days," she said softly. "I've never gone five days."

Although the fruit had helped, Stella was still horribly pale. Her eyes were sunken and red. When her legs became wobbly, I grabbed her with the towel and held her up.

"I shouldn't be near the others," she said in a quiet voice. "Can you bring one of the cots in here?"

"Are you sure?"

She nodded. "It will be safer."

Using the towel as a buffer, I helped her to an aluminum bench so she could sit. "Wait here."

I went back out to the bunk room and grabbed her duffle bag, one of the cots, and a thick comforter I found folded up on top of one of the other cots. My father was awake now. They all watched me but said nothing.

I set up the cot in a small alcove behind some lockers.

Stella's legs were weak. I worried they might buckle with each step, but I got her there.

She peeled off her wet clothes, dropped them in a pile on the floor, and put on a long-sleeve black dress I found in her duffle.

I had picked up her black gloves, both dripping wet. When I gave them to her, she wrinkled her nose. "These are disgusting. I need to wash them properly."

The box of latex gloves was on the floor back at the shower. I retrieved it and handed her a pair. "Here. They're not stylish, but at least they're dry."

She put them on, then climbed back into the cot, tugging the comforter over herself. "All will be over soon, Pip."

Stella fell asleep then, and for that moment at least, she seemed at peace.

I washed her black gloves in the sink using some liquid soap, then I hung them over a towel rack to dry.

Before leaving her, I placed the remains of the fruit bowl within reach on the ground beside her, and I brushed her wet hair from her face and brow.

Then I peeled off my own gloves and went back to the others.

Back in the bunk room, Cammie sat with her daughter, watching her work in a coloring book. She looked up at me wearily. Preacher huddled over a table of weapons with two of Dunk's men—I spied everything from AR-15 assault rifles to handguns and knives. He had added our own guns to the pile along with all the headphones, unboxed and lined up.

Hobson sat in one of the chairs, his blindfold off. My father sat in a chair, facing him with a bottle of Jägermeister perched between them on an old wooden milk crate. Hobson's hands were no longer bound. Both raised shot glasses to their lips and drank. I spotted another shot glass on the floor next to Cammie and an empty one in Preacher's hand.

"Seriously? You're all drinking right now? Why's he untied?"

"Do you want one?" my father said, refilling both him and Hobson. "No, of course not."

For some reason, this drew looks from everyone.

My father cocked his head. Over the past few days, the bruising on his face had transitioned from reds and purples to blues and blacks. Now it appeared yellow and green. The swelling around his eyes had eased, and both were open again. "You don't need a drink?"

I thought about this for a second. Only a few days ago, I would have jumped at that bottle and chugged the contents. Between tremors, cravings, and an all-out dependency after years of drinking, alcohol had become a necessary part of my life. No different than water or food. I couldn't survive without it. But now, "I haven't needed a drink for a few days now. I'm good."

And I was. No shakes. No cravings or dizziness. Like Stella's hunger, this was probably only some kind of reprieve, but I'd take it.

My father drank his shot, then set the glass down on the milk crate. "Alcohol dependency is a side effect of the shot. None of us drank heavily prior to the shot, but after it was administered, we all went out to a bar to celebrate our newly-acquired riches. A few days later, we began to realize we craved alcohol. Soon, we had to have it. The people from Charter said it was just a side effect and would wear off. A metabolic thing. It didn't, though, just got worse with time. Odd thing is, none of us really get drunk anymore. Haven't really since the shot. We can, if we really push it, but for the most part, it does little to us—only keeps the withdrawal symptoms at bay. After you were born, Charter ran a series of blood tests and concluded that you would most likely suffer from the same dependency when you got older. All the children would."

Hobson slowly lifted his glass to his mouth and drank. When the glass was empty, he handed it back to my father and wiped his lips on the bank of his hand.

"Okay, but that doesn't explain why he's untied," I said.

"Come here," my father said. "I'll show you."

I took a few steps closer.

My father leaned in toward Hobson. "What did David Pickford tell you?"

"He told me to go to Cammie's house and say hello for him, then kill her. Shoot her dead. He also said he loves Stella, and he's cleaning up the whole mess, just for her. Like it never happened."

My father said, "But you don't want to hurt Cammie, do you?"

Hobson shook his head.

"And you understand you do not have to do what David Pickford told you to do, right? You have free will?"

"That crazy little shit tried to hijack my head. If I put a bullet anywhere, it will be in him," Hobson said. He nodded at his glass. "One more."

My father poured him another shot. "Is Cammie safe?"

Hobson drank and turned to Cammie. "I'm sorry, Cams. Are we good?"

Cammie smiled and nodded. "You don't kill me, I don't have to kill you. I think we're good, and the world is better for it."

My father turned back to me. "David's 'suggestions' are just that. His ability causes them to become necessary actions in the mind of the person he speaks to, but they're not carved in stone. You can talk someone out of what he may have told them to do if you phrase yourself properly, if you break through. I think the alcohol may help to speed that up, cut through to the subconscious, but it's tough to say for sure." He looked back at Hobson. "What do you say, can we trust you with a gun?"

I'm not gonna lie, when Hobson went to the table near Preacher and Adella and picked up some kind of long-range rifle, less than ten feet from Cammie and her daughter, the tension in the air was palpable. Even Hobson appeared nervous. The only person who didn't seem worried was Cammie.

She smiled at him and nodded toward a box of ammunition on the corner of the table. "444 Marlins. You could drop a grizzly with those."

Hobson loaded the rifle with practiced ease, pointed it toward the back wall, and peered into the sight. "I can work with this." He looked back at Adella and Preacher. "Where do you want me?"

Adella tossed him a handheld radio and nodded toward one of Dunk's men standing outside our door. "Cortez will take you up to the the roof. You can help cover the woods. Most of our guys are good up close, but we only have a handful of sharpshooters."

Hobson nodded, scooped up the box of ammunition, a pair of headphones, gave Cammie a wink, and disappeared down the hall behind the one called Cortez.

When he was gone, my father returned his gaze to me. "We need to talk about your girlfriend, Jack."

"There's nothing to talk about."

"She could kill all of us. She's not in control, and she's getting worse," Cammie said. "I've got a daughter to think about. We need to secure her."

"Stella's not gonna hurt anyone. If we're going to talk about anything, we should discuss who called Charter from Whidbey. They're already here. Got here right after us. Gotta wonder if someone is tipping them off. Detective Fogel said whoever called told Charter where we were. Stella was out cold. My father and Hobson were tied up. That leaves you and Preacher."

"How do we know that detective of yours was even telling the truth?"

"Was it you?"

"No, it wasn't me," Cammie insisted. "And I trust Preacher. It wasn't him, either."

"Then who?"

Darby looked up from her coloring book, then returned to the half-completed image of Spongebob.

Cammie frowned. "She was with me, and she can't talk. She has no idea what Charter is, and I can guarantee she doesn't know the number. Don't look at her that way. Get that thought out of your head right now."

Adella's radio crackled.

"Adella, get to the roof. Twelve vans now."

Preacher, who had remained silent through all of this, scooped up a radio, noise-canceling headphones, ammunition for the Walther PPK in his shoulder holster, and an assault rifle. "Neither of us made that call, kid. Drop the conspiracy theory bullshit. We've got work to do. I'm going with Adella." He tossed a radio to Cammie. "You need me, you call. I'll come right back, okay?"

Cammie set the radio between her and Darby and nodded.

Then they were gone.

My father watched them leave before turning back to me. "For what it's worth, Richard and Emma were scared of her, of Stella. She couldn't hurt them, probably something genetic, but they knew what she could do to anyone else. At one point, Richard called me, must have been three o'clock in the morning. He told me he had this nightmare where he went into Stella's nursery and smothered her with a pillow. In the dream, he said it felt like the right thing to do. When he woke, the feeling lingered, and that frightened him more than anything. He said, for a few minutes, he lay there in bed and actually thought about it. The right thing to do. Then the guilt set in. When he called to tell me this, about halfway through the call, I realized he wasn't just telling me about a bad dream, he was feeling me out. In his own way, he was trying to figure out if *I* thought it was the right thing to do. I gotta tell you, Jack. I thought long and hard on that, and I never did work out an answer. In the years that followed, hearing about all those she killed, that last call from Richard has replayed in my head more times than I'd care to admit."

I took several steps back toward the bathroom and Stella's cot.

My father raised his hands defensively. "I won't hurt her, son. Cammie won't hurt her. None of us will. That's not what I'm getting at. She was a child then. She had no idea what she was doing. When Charter had her, I'm sure they brainwashed her into believing she was doing the right thing. I don't know if I can fault her for that, either. She's an adult now, though. Clearly, the guilt eats at her. I've overheard her tell you several times she won't do it again, she'd rather die than hurt someone else. That's what I want you to think about. Think as long and hard as I did when Richard called me. If the time comes, are you willing to respect her decision, let it happen, if that is what she truly wants?"

I started to answer him, and he waved me off. "This is between you and her, not us. I don't need to know. I don't want to know. I've lived through enough death due to Charter and their fucking shot. I also lived through the loss of your mother, and I can tell you without a doubt, outliving someone you love is a pain unlike any other, and if she decides to let go, if you lose her, just know I'll be there for you. Missing out on your childhood, watching you grow up from afar in order to keep you safe, that was as hard on me as losing your mother. I'm sure you've got mixed feelings, and sometime soon, when this is all over, we'll sit down and talk about that. You're here, you're alive, I know I did the right thing, but I'd appreciate the opportunity to try and make up lost time with you. I want to be your father. And I'll help you through this, no matter what happens."

His eyes were shimmering with moisture when he finished.

I wasn't sure if I should hug him, hate him, or tell him I forgive him. I could only nod.

"Go to her now, son. Stay with her as long as you can."

I took a radio, two pairs of headphones, and a handgun with me, a 9mm Ruger.

19

For the next two hours, we let them surround us.

Dozens of them. White vans, white trucks, white cars, SUVs. Over the small radio sitting beside me on Stella's cot, the reports came in at a steady clip. The vehicles lined Rankin Boulevard and Kenmawr Avenue on the opposite side of the tree line beyond the railroad tracks. They weren't visible from Carrie Furnace, not even from those watching on the roof, but Dunk's people saw them from the blinds perched high up in those trees. The vehicles parked, but nobody got out. Their numbers were estimated to be around one hundred and fifty based on the number of vehicles and possible occupancy, but that was only a guess.

Several boats docked in the Monongahela River at our backs, too. We had no way to know if they were part of Charter, but Dunk had people watch them, just the same. I heard his voice several times over the radio, but he didn't make it down to the bunk room. I couldn't fault him for that. He had his hands full.

Stella slept.

Not a relaxing sleep, but the kind filled with low moans and heavy sweats, the kind you wake from only to roll over and find yourself trapped deeper in the sticky mess that is a fever dream.

She mumbled in that fitful state, mostly unintelligible. I did hear my name a few times, Oliver, too. At the sound of my name from her lips, I perked up, only to be disappointed again when I realized she was still asleep. I wanted to wake her, but I didn't dare. Something told me whatever waited for her on the opposite side of the wall that is sleep was far worse than the torment her body raged on her now, and I had no intention of being the one to bring on whatever came next.

Cammie's little girl, Darby, fluttered around. At first, I caught her little head poking around the corner of the doorway, her blonde curls framing her face and large blue eyes. She disappeared when she realized she had been spotted, only to return about twenty minutes later to watch again. An hour or so after that, she brought me a glass of water. When I thanked her for it, she smiled back, curtsied, and ran back toward the bunk room. Snacks followed—some crackers and cheese. Water refills, too. At one point, she brought in a bowl with a wash cloth which she carried over to the floor next to Stella's bunk. She tugged on a pair of the latex gloves, far too big for her, and dabbed at Stella's forehead with the cloth. She was a cute kid.

The last of the fruit had gone a while ago, now nothing more than a black, pulpy mess at the bottom of the bowl. I'd carry Stella out to the trees if I had to, let her drain their life one at a time, the whole damn forest. God forgive me for what I'd do to anyone who tried to stop me from helping her.

I spoke to her.

For those two hours, I told her all there was to know about John Edward Jack Thatch, her Pip. From my earliest childhood memories to my worst fumbles as an adult (and there were many), I held nothing back. I told her about Dunk, Willy, and me as kids, and I told her about my Auntie Jo and Jo's faults, flaws, dreams, and achievements. I explained how my aunt harbored such a hatred for my father, one I didn't understand as a kid but became clear the moment I discovered his empty grave, while also learning the grave beside it was not. Our visits, year after year to those headstones—I could only imagine the thoughts running through Jo's head when she looked at my father's headstone. Her neglect of that stone, her reasons for her indifference toward him, painfully obvious now. A sister lost while the man who was with her lives on.

I told Stella about the money Jo arranged for me, the life she wanted me to build, and how I had dropped all to find her instead. As I weaved my gloved fingers between Stella's and held her hand, I harbored not a single regret. Here, by her side, was where I was always meant to be.

"Jack?"

When I heard my name from her lips, I assumed it was only another dream-inspired utterance. Not until she said my name for a second time did I realize Stella was awake, her heavy eyes watching me from the small ball she had become on the cot.

Stella's fingers squeezed around mine. She pulled my hand closer. "Can you take me outside? I'd like to see the stars."

Although the volume was set low, the radio beside me was a constant buzz of Charter's growing presence, and even though nothing was said aloud, I heard the tension building in the various voices chiming in with those reports. Something bad was coming, growing closer with each passing minute.

"I don't know if it's safe outside."

"I want to see the stars, please Jack, it's important to me."

The weakness in her voice pained me. As she sat up, she looked so frail. I couldn't deny her, not now, not ever. I helped her to her feet. "Can you walk?"

Stella nodded. "I think so."

I tucked the Ruger into my waistband (a skill I had finally mastered), put the radio in my pocket, and placed both pairs of headphones around my neck so I could free both hands to help Stella.

She smiled for the first time in days. "You look ridiculous." She grinned. "Like a horrible white rapper who misplaced all his gold chains and decided to go for a new look."

"True dat."

The bunk room was empty. No sign of my father, Cammie, or Darby. One of Dunk's men stood sentry in the hallway, and at first I thought he might try to keep us in the room, but he didn't. Instead, he followed silently a few paces behind us as I helped Stella negotiate the hallways and stairs to one of the catwalks outside, this one overlooking Carrie Furnace Boulevard, the railroad tracks, and the trees in the distance. Although I knew Charter was busy grouping beyond those trees, the area immediately surrounding the steel mill seemed oddly peaceful.

We sat on the edge of the catwalk, our legs dangling over the side. "Where are the others?" Stella asked, her fingers still in mine.

"On the roof, I think."

"And Charter?"

"All around us." I told her what I knew while pointing back at the trees.

She looked around, studied the open fields. "Seems so quiet."

And it *was* quiet. The air was perfectly still, hovering somewhere in the sixties. A nearly full moon, at least three quarters, coating everything in a bluish white blanket of light.

Stella tilted her head up and smiled. "Of all things, I believe I'll miss the night sky most of all. The absolute vastness of it, the unknown. While we're down here fighting our pesky little battles, we're really just a speck on the shoe of the universe. Any problem life may present seems so small, so insignificant, when you simply look up and realize your true place in all things."

"You have a lifetime of night skies ahead of you." I said the words knowing they weren't true. I think I said them not only for her benefit but my own. As if speaking such a thing out loud would make it so.

"Thank you for the last few days, Pip. For all you've done for me. You've been one of the few constants in my life, perhaps the only bright spot. I never thought I'd know love, to be loved and to love another, and yet you are all those things to me. You have been all those things to me my entire life, for *our* entire lives. If I have any regret, its that I shied away from you so, that I held you at such a distance rather than embrace you years ago. I didn't want to expose you to what I was, what I did, and what I knew I would continue to do. It was easier for me to push you away, to tell myself that was the right thing to do. I regret the talks we never had, the lost nights we never shared." Stella looked back out over the fields and leaned her head on my shoulder. "Do you remember the paintings in my house? Landscapes and cities, far-off wonders and places?"

I nodded.

"As I painted each one, I pretended you and I were there, visiting each of those places together—the Golden Gate bridge, the Grand Canyon, the lights of Paris and the pyramids of Egypt, the streets of New York and the wilds of New Orleans, far open fields and hidden lakes lost among ancient trees. My hand in yours or your arm around me—you taking me in your arms and kissing me at each new place, my illness nonexistent in those wanderings of my mind. In many ways, we've already spent a lifetime together, and I'm grateful for that but I am grateful for these past few days most of all. My Pip, my wonderful John Edward Jack Thatch."

Stella shivered, and I pulled her closer. I considered going back for a blanket, when a deep-throated rumble filled the night.

"We've got a car approaching. Came over Rankin Bridge, just turned on Carrie Furnace Boulevard. Moving fast. Let it pass or take it out?"

Static.

Dunk's voice followed. *"Single car? How many passengers? Can you tell?"*

"I only see one, just the driver."

My father's voice, then, *"Get those headphones ready. It might be Pickford."*

I had set our headphones down beside me. I reached over, turned on the power switch, and handed a pair to Stella.

Dunk again. *"Let it pass. Shooters on the roof, standby. I give the order, I want a rain of bullets on whoever steps out.* Only *if I give the order, copy?"*

A dozen voices replied in confirmation.

I spotted it, rounding the bend at the far end of Carrie Furnace Boulevard. The car went over the railroad tracks, then picked up speed on the straightaway, with dusty rooster trails at its back.

A black Pontiac GTO.

Preacher's car.

"Is that the car we left behind on Whidbey Island?"

"Yeah." I leaned forward to get a better look. Preacher must be pissed.

I half expected whoever was driving to pull the emergency brake, yank the wheel, and slide the car to a stop from a high speed drift. That's probably what I would have done if given the chance behind the wheel of a car like that. But rather than accelerating as the GTO drew close, the black Pontiac slowed and came to a stop about twenty feet from the main building, the high beams slicing through the night.

The engine let out one final growl as the driver tapped the gas before killing the motor.

The driver leaned over and opened the passenger door, then opened his own.

"Shooters, steady," Dunk said over the radio.

I could see the driver in the car. A middle-aged man with short brown hair, wearing a white shirt and what looked like a white coat. I picked up the radio and pressed the transmit button. "That's not Pickford. Repeat, that is not David Pickford."

"Copy," Dunk replied.

The driver leaned over. It looked like he was messing with the radio. From the car came a loud click followed by the low hum of a recording at high volume. This was followed by a voice I recognized immediately.

Kaylie from Penn State, four and a half years earlier in her dorm room.

"Go ahead and put these on."

A loud metronome came from the GTO's amplified speakers with a heavy electronic hum behind it.

Tick...tock.

Tick...tock.

Tick...tock.

"Okay, Jack, I want you to listen to the rhythm of that sound, like a comforting heartbeat. Breathe in through your mouth, out through your nose, let your breathing fall in time with the sound. It's all about the sound, that comforting sound. A heartbeat. Visualize a heartbeat, that sound. The rush of your blood, the life flowing through every inch of your body. Warm and comforting. My voice, brings you deeper, faster and deeper, faster and deeper in a warm, calm, peaceful state of relaxation. Like sinking deep down into a warm bath."

Tick...tock.

Tick...tock.

"Sinking down and shutting down. Sinking down and shutting down. Sinking down and shutting down completely in the enveloping warmth," she said from so far away. Repeating. *"Warm and calm, a blanket, snug and tight. The blanket holds your arms at your sides, your legs still. You've never been so comfortable, your mind never so free."*

Tick...tock.

Tick...tock.

"Where are you, Jack?"

"I don't know."

"What do you see?"

"Doctor."

"You're at the doctor's?"

"Doctor."

My voice, high pitched. Mine but not mine.

This was the missing recording. The one from Kaylie's micro-cassette recorder, I was certain.

My voice again, sounding so small, childlike.

"No more, no more, no more, no more, no more." This same phrase

*repeated for nearly five minutes, then my voice dropped lower, sounding
like a much older man—*

"*Again,*" *this deep voice said.*

"*He might not be able to take it again.*" *My voice, but an octave higher.*

"*Again,*" *the deep voice insisted.*

The child voice, droning, "*No more, no more, no more, no more.*"

Deep voice, "*Again, dammit.*"

"*I'm trying.*"

"*Cut the radial artery, right there at the wrist.*"

"*I'm trying.*"

"*Give me the scalpel.*"

"*No more, no more, no more. No—*"

"*Dammit.*"

"*You can't do it, either?*"

Deep voice, "*No.*"

My voice, "*Momma? Where's Momma?*"

"*The sedative is wearing off,*" *the higher voice said.* "*More thorazine?*"

"*Yeah.*"

"*Where's the boy's father? Is he here?*"

"*Out in the waiting room. Want me to get him?*"

"*Yeah. I want to see if he can do it.*"

Two loud clicks. The various voices were replaced by Kaylie
again, reading aloud from a psychology text book. Study notes of
some kind. A remnant recording. Probably part of whatever was
on the tape before she recorded our session.

Stella was staring at me. "What are we listening to? Is that
someone at Charter running *tests* on you?"

I shook my head. I didn't know.

Another two clicks.

Tick...tock.

Tick...tock.

"*Can you hear me, Jack?*"

"*Uh huh.*"

"*What was that?*"

"Not sure."

"When was that?"

"Young."

"Less than five?"

"Yeah."

"Less than two?"

"I think so."

"Let's go back."

"I don't want to."

Tick...tock.

Tick...tock.

"Did you see that doctor again? After that?"

"Yes."

"Take me to the next time. You're safe with me, Jack. They can't hurt you. These are only memories."

Tick...tock.

Tick...tock.

"Jack?"

Silence.

"Jack?"

"Increase to 75 milliamps," Deep Voice said.

"We're already at 75," High Voice replied.

"His breathing hasn't changed. Are you sure?"

"I'm certain."

"Go to 100 milliamps."

"That's a fatal level."

"I'm aware."

Silence.

"We're at 100. No change. Breathing, heart rate, all slightly elevated but still within the range of normal."

"Remarkable," Deep Voice said. *"Go to 150."*

"Increasing amperage to 150 milliamps."

"No more, no more, no more, no more, no more."

"Is he protesting because you increased and it's finally at a level that

hurts, or because he wants you to stop altogether?" This was another voice, a pitch somewhere between High Voice and Deep Voice.

Deep Voice said, *"Hard to say. Does he use that phrase at home?"*

"Maybe with his mother. I've never heard him say that."

That last one hit me like a kick to my gut.

My father was there while they did these horrible things.

Stella's grip on my arm tightened as she realized it, too.

Tick...tock.

Tick...tock.

Kaylie again. *"Jack, what was that?"*

No response.

Tick...tock.

Tick...tock.

Kaylie said, *"Jack, I want you to tell me about the chocolate milk."*

"Chocolate milk?"

"That's why you came to me, right? Your parents. You wanted to know what happened. You said there was chocolate milk. Take me there. Take me to the moment with the chocolate milk. Can you do that?"

"Yes."

Tick...tock.

Tick...tock.

"He's been drinking it?" Deep Voice said.

"Every day. Sometimes twice a day." The middle voice. My father's voice.

"And you're mixing it, like we showed you?"

My father said, *"Yesterday, I nearly doubled the dose. It didn't do a damn thing."*

"That's enough arsenic to take down a horse. You realize that, right?"

A loud click.

The tape stopped.

The scent of vanilla lofted past me from Stella at my side. She stared at the GTO.

My father's voice came through the tinny speaker of my handheld radio. *"Jack. It's not what you think."*

And from the woods, nearly fifty people stepped forward, all dressed in white. They carried candles as they started toward the gully between the distant railroad tracks.

20

"Shit," Preacher said, peering at the rushing mob through the scope of his Savage model 110 long-range hunting rifle.

Hobson was to his left, Dunk to his right.

"Do you have binoculars?"

Dunk handed him a bulky pair of Swarovski's. Military grade with a built-in laser rangefinder. Dunk then pressed the transmit button on his radio. "Hold fire until I give the word."

Hobson said, "How many?"

Preacher panned back and forth. "Fifty, sixty...hard to say."

They had heard the recording blaring from the speakers of the Pontiac GTO. They had also heard Eddie Thatch chime in at the end over the radios. When Preacher looked for him on the roof, he wasn't there. He had seen him earlier, gone now, though.

Dunk said, "Do you see any weapons?"

"Maybe. Under the coats. Hard to say. Looks like they're all carrying candles."

"Candles?"

Dunk frowned. "Any idea why they always wear white?"

"Fuck if I know." Preacher handed the binoculars back to Dunk and chambered a round in his rifle.

"You want to start a fire fight?" Dunk said.

"I'm gonna teach them some boundaries."

Dunk pressed the transmit button on his radio again. "You're going to hear some shots. Everyone else, hold fire. I repeat, hold fire."

The rifle bucked, but Preacher's shot held steady. Through the sight, he saw a chunk of the hill at the railroad tracks explode about a foot away from two of the approaching figures.

Dunk watched through the binoculars. "That could have ricocheted."

"I'm not too concerned with their well-being." Preacher tugged back the bolt, ejecting the expired shell casing and loading another round. He pivoted slightly and fired again, this shot landing near the opposite end of the gully. The shot struck a railroad tie about a foot away from one of the people in white. He didn't flinch, didn't react at all, just kept coming.

Dunk asked, "Can Pickford tell someone to ignore bullets or not fear death?"

Preacher fired again. The round embedded in the dirt less than four inches from a twenty-something woman in white. She didn't flinch either, only pressed forward.

"If Pickford can tell someone to kill themselves and they do it, I think we've gotta assume he can get them to do damn near anything he wants," Preacher said. He fired again. This time he hit the foot of a man coming toward them near the center of the line, now past the railroad tracks and moving faster on flat ground. The man's shoe exploded, but he kept coming, dragging the damaged leg behind him, oblivious to what must have been a tremendous amount of pain. "I can do this all night long, but they're not stopping. We need a new plan."

"At their current pace, they'll reach the building in about three minutes," Hobson pointed out.

Preacher looked at Dunk. "This is your show, but the way I see it, you've only got two choices. We open fire and take them out, or

713

let them get close and risk fighting one on one. It's an even match by the numbers, but it will be bloody for both sides."

"We don't even know if they're carrying. I'm not comfortable mowing down a bunch of unarmed, candle-toting nuts."

Preacher smirked. "I thought you were some kind of gangster."

Dunk thought about this for a second, then reached for the transmit button on his radio. "On my count, all shooters with long-range weapons fire half a dozen shots—group them about a foot in front of those people. Warning shots only. We don't want to hit anyone. Not yet."

"We need to go for the head and heart," Preacher muttered, lining up his site.

"Kill shots come next," Dunk said, giving the order to fire.

21

"Jack, are you okay?"

Stella's gloved hand was on my arm.

The recording echoed in my head.

My father's voice after. *Jack. It's not what you think.*

I forced a nod.

That was when a hail of bullets streamed out from the roof and various positions at the front of the steel mill. Out in the open field between the railroad tracks and Carrie Furnace Boulevard, the ground exploded—dirt, dust, and grime filled the air just ahead of the large mob moving toward the building.

The people in white weren't running. Instead, they all walked at an extremely fast clip, the candles cradled between their hands and held out before them.

They didn't slow down.

They didn't acknowledge the gunfire at all.

They kept coming.

They didn't stop coming until they reached the concrete surrounding the main buildings of the steel mill. At that point, they finally stopped advancing forward and went still.

I could see their faces now. They were close enough. Their

expressions, all were blank, void of any emotion or thought, and that blank stare probably frightened me more than anything else about them. I thought about how quickly I had turned my gun on Hobson back at Cammie's house when David Pickford told me to. I thought about what he told each of these people, his voice probably being the last they heard.

Over the radio, I heard, *"I've got eighteen on the north lawn!"*

"Sixteen on the south end," someone replied.

"Twenty-eight in and around the front of the building."

I did the math in my head.

Sixty-two.

"The ones out in the open are standing still, but we've got movement in the trees. Couple dozen out there, maybe more."

This was hopeless. I don't think any of us were prepared to kill nearly a hundred people.

All of them took a step forward at the same time, perfectly in unison.

"Holy shit, you see that?"

"How are they coordinating?"

Someone fired a shot from the roof. The ground in front of one of them, a balding man in his late thirties, exploded in a puff of black dirt. He didn't budge, his face blank.

Another step. All of them, moving closer.

"I think we're done with warning shots. We need to start laying them out."

"Negative," Dunk replied. *"We open fire, they rush us, and we're done. We can't stop them all, not like that. There's too many!"*

I recognized Hobson's voice. *"If the Pickford kid is telling these people what to do, they may be innocent in all of it. Just pawns. Like what he did to me."*

I pressed the button on my radio. "Does anyone see him? We take out Pickford, and maybe we end this."

Nobody replied. Only a handful of us even knew what David Pickford looked like.

Without any noticeable command, every person in white reached behind their backs and pulled cowls up and over their heads, hiding their faces.

Then they moved again.

Not a single step forward or back like before, but a fast shuffle—some moved to their left, others to their right.

Forward, backward, diagonal. Nearly a dozen more came from the woods and through the gully near the railroad tracks to join the others as they shuffled again. Although they moved in multiple directions, absolutely none of what was happening appeared to be random. They moved at the exact same speed. Nobody looked up or down at their feet, to the side or behind, yet nobody collided.

They all continued to face forward. Like a flock of birds shifting position while in flight. A well-coordinated shell game.

When they finally stopped, at least twenty new people in white stood among the already large crowd. Heads covered, burning candles in hand.

David called out from below, somewhere to my left.

I hit my transmit button. "Headphones on!"

All around us, Dunk's people placed the noise-canceling headphones on their heads, powered them up, and plugged in their radios.

Stella and I did the same.

The sounds of the outside world disappeared.

A moment later, I heard Dunk through my headphones. *"Keep radio chatter to a minimum, or we'll all end up talking over each other."*

I gripped both of Stella's shoulders and mouthed the words, "Are you okay?"

She nodded and tried to force a smile.

Over the radio, I heard my father's voice. *"Jack? You're not in the bunk room. Where are you?"*

Stella heard him, too. Her eyes went wide.

I looked up and down the catwalk where we sat and only saw Dunk's people.

To Stella, I gestured toward the stairs.

She nodded.

I stood and helped her to her feet.

At first, I thought she might collapse, but she drew in a deep breath and somehow found the strength to remain upright. I put her arm over my shoulder and led her down the catwalk, down a series of steps, and into the large space where I had met with Dunk ten days earlier, Blast Furnace #7.

My father again, over the radio. *"Jack. They gave me no other choice. I had to let them experiment. It was part of the deal. That was the only way I could keep you and your mother safe. If I would have said no, they would have killed her, killed me, taken you. That was never an option."*

I pressed the transmit button. "So you let them try to kill me, instead? Over and over again? I was just a baby!"

Another thought came into my head, and I wished it hadn't, because I didn't want it to be true. Couldn't possibly be true. I said it aloud anyway. "My God, they paid you, didn't they? That's how you afforded those houses. That's why you didn't have to run all these years, like the others. They were never chasing you. Charter paid you, didn't they?"

My father said nothing.

Another realization came into my head. "The money I received every month, that came from you, didn't it? Out of what? Guilt? Some misguided sense of responsibility? Some kind of bullshit child support?"

My father didn't reply.

Not at first.

Not for nearly a minute.

"I knew I could use some of the money to get you a better life. To help keep you safe. I hired Preacher to deliver it. I couldn't risk returning to Pittsburgh."

I led Stella toward the back of the large, open space, toward a hallway leading off into the dark. From there, we turned right. We kept going until we found a room with a window overlooking the front of the steel mill, someplace where we could see what was happening outside.

The people in white stood only about twenty feet away, their blank stares facing forward. None of Dunk's people were on this level, safer on higher ground.

Nobody would find us here. That's what mattered.

I pulled the Ruger from my waistband, ready to use it if I had to.

"Where are you, Jack? We should discuss this face to face, not like this."

Stella doubled over.

She yanked her arm from around my shoulder and clutched at her chest, her stomach. Her face grew red, her eyes pinched shut.

From my radio, through the headphones, came a blinding, loud burst of static followed by a high-pitched squeal, like a dagger jabbing at both my ears. I reached up and yanked off my headphones and threw them to the ground. I wasn't alone. I saw several pairs come flying off the roof of the steel mill and shatter on the concrete outside the window.

When Stella screamed, when she pulled her knees up into her chest and let out a shriek, the sound came again. Loud enough that it blared through the headphones at my feet.

Like the radio in the cemetery when I was a kid.

Like the Mercedes stereo right before the incident at the lake.

I knelt down and wrapped my arms around her, squeezed her tight.

Stella clawed her headphones off, too, dropped them to her side.

Outside our window, a series of shots rang out and when I looked, three of the people in white were dead.

I didn't know if David had kept talking while we had the headphones on, but I heard him now, shouting.

"Those guns are awfully hot, aren't they?" David yelled out from somewhere among the crowd of white. "It's got to be tough to hold onto them. That burning hot metal. Like pressing your palm to a skillet. Sizzle, crackle, pop!"

At first, my Ruger only felt warm.

I loosened my grip slightly, but I didn't let go. When that got too hot, I slid my hand around on the butt of the gun. The movement bought me a few more seconds. I couldn't hold the trigger. I tapped a finger against it.

Then I smelled it.

Burning flesh.

I knew it was a trick.

I told myself it wasn't real.

But about ten seconds after David Pickford said the words, I found myself dropping the handgun to the ground and rubbing both my palms against my jeans.

All around the mill, I heard the similar clatter of weapons dropping along with mixed cursing. People shouting, too. Yelling to each other. I wondered if anyone still had the headphones on. Then Stella cringed again, and static burst from my discarded headphones and I knew the answer—there was no way anyone kept them on, not if they were hearing that, too.

I unplugged the headphones from my radio. A moment later, I heard Preacher. *"Anyone got a clue as to where he is?"*

"North yard, I think. Came from that way."

The people in white shuffled again.

When they stopped moving, the entire group had gained more ground, at least four feet closer to the building.

"This is so wonderful! Everyone finally together! Like some ragtag family reunion," David said. This time, his voice came from the front, somewhere between the Pontiac GTO and the entrance to my building. "And Cammie, I believe congratulations are in order! I saw the girl's room at your house in Carmel! A daughter, that's wonderful news! What's her name?"

"Darby!" Cammie shouted out from somewhere above me. Possibly on the roof, maybe a level below. Unable to *not* answer him.

The barrel of a shotgun appeared from the coat of one of the people in white about ten feet from the GTO. He took aim and fired off a thunderous round. Glass shattered as a window blew out.

"Oh, they sure are trigger happy, aren't they? The whole lot out here!" David beamed. "Everyone okay in there?"

From the roof, three shots rang out in quick succession. Two of the people in white dropped, large, red stains growing on their coats.

The rest of the people in white shuffled again. Faces hidden under the cowls.

David yelled, "That was impressive! Got to be Hobson, right? Burn-pain be damned, got to shoot the Pickford kid, right? Hey, Dewey, take a running leap from wherever you are—come on down here and say hi!"

I'm sure Preacher or someone else tried to stop him. I could picture a dozen people all grabbing at Hobson and trying to hold him back, but it happened too fast.

Dewey Hobson tumbled through the air and landed in the center of the concrete pad outside Blast Furnace #7 with a sound too horrible to describe. His right leg bent out at an angle that was all wrong. His rifle was still in his hand, a handkerchief wrapped around the trigger and stock.

Only one of the people in white turned to look.

Pickford.

I pulled the sleeve of my sweatshirt down over my hand and grabbed my Ruger from the ground, took aim, and pulled the trigger. I couldn't hold the gun long enough to get a second shot off.

I missed.

The people in white shuffled again, David lost among them.

"What do you want?" I screamed out the window.

"For starters, I want all of you to stop shooting at us," David said. "That's no way to treat your guests. The next person to fire a weapon from that steel mill of yours will forget how to breathe, and I don't want that. Suffocation is a horrible way to die."

"You stop killing us, we'll stop killing you!" I offered.

David, wherever he was among the crowd of white, simply said, "I want Stella."

I glanced down at her, huddled in the corner near my feet. She was unconscious again, glistening with sweat, curled up in a tight little ball.

"She's not here."

David said, "Come out here, Stella."

Stella twitched but didn't move. She hadn't heard him.

"Come out, Stella, come out, come out wherever you are!"

She didn't move.

"We left her in North Dakota, after the seaplane. Someplace far away from you. Told her to run. Wouldn't let her tell us where. We knew you'd follow the rest of us," I shouted back.

"She's five days overdue, Jack. She's not running anywhere," David said. "She's sick, dying. You know she is. I can make her better. I can help her. We don't have a lot of time, though. Is she so far gone she can't come out on her own? I bet that's it. I could tell you to carry her, Jack. I could order you to do that, and you know you'd have no choice, but I don't want to do that. I want you to bring her out here all on your own. I bet she's right there next to you. It must be agonizing watching her wither away so quickly. Such a beautiful girl, wasting away to nothing. If you want to save her life, all you have to do is carry her out here so I can help her. Let's start there. And once I help her, I can tell you how I plan to help the rest of you. I've cleaned house, and I'm nearly done." If it's possible for someone's voice to brighten, his did. "Oh! I nearly forgot! I brought a present for you!"

Thirty feet from me, from the center of the people in white, David Pickford reached up and took down his cowl. The large white and red burn scar on the left side of his face caught the light, and he made no attempt to conceal it.

I found myself looking down at my gun, wanting desperately to kill him, yet I knew what he said moments earlier would prove true—

anyone else who fired a shot would forget how to breathe and suffocate. As much as I wanted to take the shot, I knew I couldn't, and I hoped to God nobody else was trying at this very moment, either.

Stella stirred. Her heavy eyes opened.

David walked through the crowd of people back to the Pontiac. He nodded at the man in white standing beside the driver's door.

He reached inside and pressed the trunk release.

The GTO's trunk popped open, and David leaned inside. He appeared to be whispering to someone.

That's when I spotted Latrese Oliver.

She had been gagged. The sling that once held her injured arm was gone, and the black appendage dangled loosely at her side. Blackened flesh trailed up from the arm over the side of her neck, to her face, the death slowly spreading. David forced her first to sit up, then climb out. He and one other helped her to the ground. I could tell by the awkward way in which she stood, whatever was spreading from her arm had worked its way down to her leg, too.

"You see, Jack. When I was a kid, the fine people at Charter used me to knock off the participants of Project Leapfrog. That's what they called the shot they gave to all our parents: Leapfrog. I've got the file, if you want to take a look. I've read them all. Every scrap of paper. The adults were expendable once they had us kids. We were what they wanted. They used Stella, too. This woman here saw to that. Used us both, really. You too. Your father can tell you all about that."

Latrese Oliver glared at him. David smiled back. "I've wanted to kill this woman for years, but I didn't. I kept her alive just for you, so you could watch. Think of her as a peace offering. You, me, Stella, and now Darby, we're 2.0, we're next generation. We need to stick together. Latrese here is part of the problem, though, part of the mess. She's got to go. I cleaned up the mess back at old Charter corporate. Now it's time to sweep the last of the dirt into the pan."

Stella tried to get up and nearly fell. I reached down and helped her to her feet. She drew in a sharp breath when she saw Oliver out there, the condition she was in.

David rubbed at his temple with his thumb. "I'm not gonna lie to you, Jack, the adults need to die. There's no way around that. I frankly don't want any more of us, and they can make more. Can't have that." He looked up at the building, his eyes scanning the dozens of people looking back at him. "It's getting late, and I need my beauty rest. I think it's time we get on with things, don't you?"

I had one arm around Stella's waist, the other on the edge of the windowsill. Her shallow breathing was the only sound in our little room.

"Not gonna come out, Jack? Oliver not enough for you? You need a bigger carrot?" David shook his head. "Do you know the name Penelope Maudlin? Our friend Dewey Hobson sure did." He nodded toward Dewey's broken, lifeless body on the concrete.

Stella's hand went to her mouth. "That's Dewey?"

I nodded.

"Your dad, Cammie, Dalton—or is it Preacher?—they all knew her well, college chums. Long before her unfortunate accident in 1992, she got herself knocked up and had a kid, too. A little boy, born the same year as you and me. She was a bit unstable, though. For the most part, the boy's father raised him. Then that went to shit, too. I guess he's a bit of a half-breed—his mother took the shot, his father didn't..." David held out both his hands, weighing this. "Not sure what that means for him. Charter's files said with only one affected parent, he exhibited no special abilities. They wrote him off. He does have a sense for business, maybe that's what he walked away with, who knows. You know him pretty well, I gotta wonder—you ever see anything special there?"

Stella looked at me.

I shrugged my shoulders, not sure who he was talking about.

David tilted his head and swept his arm at the building like a game show host. "Will the son of Penelope Maudlin, please come down!"

Nearly a minute passed before Dunk stepped from the mouth of Carrie Furnace and hobbled on his cane through the crowd of white to David.

Dunk never mentioned his mother.

When he moved to Pittsburgh from Chicago, it had only been him and his father. Many of the kids in school came from broken homes. I figured if he wanted to talk about it, he would. He never did, though. Not once.

Dunk moved like a zombie through the crowd, fighting his body with each step, David's summons, *his words* more powerful than Dunk's own free will.

When he reached David, David told him to kneel and he did, the lines of his face tight as he tried to fight that, too.

David took the small Motorola radio from Dunk's free hand and pressed the transmit button. "Edward Thatch, Cammie Brotherton, and Jeffery Dalton, I want all of you to come out and join us. Leave your weapons behind, only you."

I heard David's words echo through the tiny speaker of the radio attached to my belt. He followed this first request with a second that chilled my bones.

"For the rest of you, if you're involved in illegal activities with Mr. Duncan Bellino, take a look around you, find one of your coworkers, and kill them. Another after that. Last one standing, takes home the prize!"

At first, nothing happened. And I hoped to God nothing would. Then I heard the first gunshot. That was followed by another and another after that. Several bodies fell from the catwalks and roof and crashed to the concrete below, a rain of people, some still clutching their guns, some still wearing headphones which did little to protect them from whoever had been standing at their side.

There were no shouts in anger, no cries of pain, only silent death.

Stella closed her eyes, pressed her face against my chest.

David said, "Geez, I completely forgot about my previous instruction—the whole thing about forgetting how to breathe if you fired your gun. I imagine that finished off a few more of you. So sorry about that!"

725

David's ability was frightening. The fact that he was enjoying himself scared the shit out of me.

My father was first to step outside and cross over to David. Preacher and Cammie followed about a minute later, Darby clinging to her mother's hand, her pink little cheeks streaked with tears.

David told each of the adults to line up next to Dunk and kneel. They did as they were told, no other choice. He grinned at Darby, the pink and white burn on the side of his face stretching awkwardly.

Darby cowered behind her mother.

"You must be Darby!" David beamed. "Come say hello to your Uncle David!"

Darby didn't want to. Even over this distance, I saw her grip tighten around her mother, but her body betrayed her—her arms broke free, her legs shuffled toward him.

David took her hand. "You're not going to say hello?"

"She doesn't speak," Cammie said. "Please don't hurt her. Please, David…"

David cocked his head. "She doesn't speak at all?"

"No."

"Has she ever?"

"No."

He thought about this for a moment. "What is her ability?"

"If she has one, I've never seen it."

David leaned down and smiled at the little girl. "Do you have any special abilities, sweetie? I bet you do."

Darby shied away from him, her eyes fixed on his scar.

David reached to his face and stroked the ruined flesh. "This is nothing to fear. It's beautiful. I'm the most beautiful man you've ever seen."

"Whatever you're going to do to us," Cammie said, "please don't make her watch."

David turned back to her. "Me? I'm not going to do anything to you. What would be the point of that? Remember what we talked about? Your promise to me? It's time."

Stella twisted from my arm and started toward the door.

"I'm so sorry, Jack. My dearest Pip," she paused there long enough to say. Then she disappeared around the corner, and I was alone.

I went after her.

I knew I shouldn't. I should have let her go as I should have let her go so many other times during my life, but I couldn't. I left the Ruger on the floor in that little room and followed her down the hallway and out the wide open door into the sea of people in white.

They parted as she approached, those candles still in their hands. Heads and faces hidden beneath white cowls. Stella and I stepped around the bodies of the dead, so many, haphazardly strewn around the concrete. The dark blood of all those dead in stark contradiction to the white of those who still lived.

"There you are!" David said as we approached. "I was beginning to think you didn't love me anymore."

Stella moved slowly, and when she was about ten feet away from David and the others, she nearly collapsed again. She clutched at her stomach, and all around us, shrill static burst from the radios.

I ran to her, tried to help her, but she shrugged me off. "Don't touch me, not now."

David didn't make a move toward her. He knew better than to put himself within her reach.

Stella stood, ignored the weak, shakiness of her knees, and smoothed her dress.

Over the years, weeds had worked their way through the cement, sprouting up between the cracks and crevices. All those where Stella had landed were now black, shriveled, and dead. A small circle of death around her.

On the ground at David's feet, a kneeling Latrese Oliver watched. The others, too. Oliver looked so old. She aged a hundred years since we were children. The death from her arm had crept up the side of her face and into her white hair, leaving bald blotches behind. The eye on that side was cloudy with cataracts. The left side of her mouth frozen, as if she suffered a stroke. Even through all this, she smiled up at Stella. Her good hand reached out. "I love you, Stella. I forgive you for what you did to me. I know it wasn't your fault. Put an end to this little shit."

David laughed. "Stella can't hurt me. Right, Stella? You won't hurt me."

"I would never hurt you, David Pickford."

She said this with the same robotic flatness Dewey Hobson had spoken.

David Pickford is a beautiful man.

I realized it then.

Something I probably knew for days but wouldn't admit to myself.

Stella had been the one to place the call from my father's house to Charter. No one else. Probably the result of a command issued by David long ago, lying dormant until the day it wasn't.

She seemed to know what I was thinking. "He told me to call when everyone was together." She didn't face me. Her eyes fell to the ground. "David is right. This is the only way to truly end all of this. All traces of Charter need to disappear, traces of their program, the people involved. Anything left behind will be like the seed of a weed. It will only grow back, maybe stronger than the first. We will forever run. They will always be behind us. All of it needs to end."

"Stella, these people are our friends, our family."

"Your own father stood by and watched as they tried to kill you. As you've pointed out many times now, this woman, *those people* made me kill. Made David kill. We were only children. How could we know it was wrong?"

David said softly, "Remember what I told you, Stella? That day in my cell? What I whispered to you?"

Stella peeled the glove from her right hand and dropped it at her feet. "You said when the time came, I'd get to kill them all." She took off the left glove and dropped that one, too. "My God, David, just how long did you think I could wait?"

"All of it will be over soon. Then you and I can finally be together," David said.

She smiled at him, a smile that was like the sharpest stake through my heart. "That's all I've ever really wanted."

Stella hobbled past Latrese Oliver to Dunk and knelt in front of him.

"Get the hell away from me," he growled.

"This one killed your friend Gerdy, didn't he, Jack? The man who owned the diner, too. All those people inside. Just to get rich. To line his pockets. Won't you be happy to see him die? Isn't that what he deserves?" She reached out and ran her finger along the edge of his shirt, millimeters from the skin of his neck. "How many others died because of his actions since? The poison you push?" She looked back at me. "In a way, Jack, their blood is on your hands. Why didn't you let him burn in the diner?"

Dunk remained still, unable to move. David's doing, no doubt.

"It wasn't me," Dunk forced out, fighting Pickford's spell. "It...was all...Alonzo. Never...me. I...wouldn't."

David looked up at me, saw the uncertainty in my eyes. "You don't believe him?"

"I don't know what to believe."

"If I tell him to tell the truth, he'll have no choice. I'll make a wager with you, a gentlemen's bet, if you will. I will make him tell you the truth, but if he really was responsible, if he just lied, then he dies first. I'll even let you kill him."

"I'm not killing anyone."

"But you want the truth, don't you?"

I said nothing.

David shrugged, "Well, now I'd like to know. You've got my curiosity piqued." He turned back to Dunk. He cleared his throat in some grand fashion. "Did you do what Stella accused you of? Are you responsible for the deaths of those people?"

Without hesitation, the single word flowed this time, unhampered by David's former instruction of silence. Trumped by this new command.

"No," Dunk said.

His eyes met mine, and I knew he was telling the truth.

He always had been.

I knew I had been wrong.

Dunk said, "My friends, my true friends, are the only family I've ever really known. Those people were my friends. I'd do anything to bring them back."

Stella buckled over again. This time, she did collapse. She fell to the ground, clutching her stomach. She let out a horrible shriek, and the radios screamed with her, a choir of pain.

When it was over, David said to her, "You need to feed, Stella."

Stella nodded and slowly got back to her feet, only inches from Latrese Oliver.

Again, I tried to go to her.

Again, she told me to stay back. "Like the lake," she forced out through clenched teeth.

At her hands, not only did the weeds die and crumble away, the concrete grew dark, cracked, aged. When she was finally able to stand again, the concrete surrounding her looked to be a dozen or more years older than the rest, an age spot on the neglected pavement.

The whites of Stella's eyes were lined with red, her skin like snow. She reached for Latrese Oliver, her fingers stopping less than an inch from her ruined face, quivering in the air.

The temperature had dropped considerably after the sun went down, and Oliver's breath hung in the air, a tiny white cloud. "David Pickford is for you, Stella. I led him here for you. So much evil there, perhaps enough to satisfy your appetite, perhaps not. Duncan Bellino, too. Between the two, you can stem the tide on your need. I can only imagine your pain, five days late. It's a wonder you're still with us. Take them, take me, if you must. I willingly give myself to you. I will gladly die if my sacrifice means you will live. My life will become part of yours, and that is how I will live on. Take us all, take everyone, take—"

Stella collapsed again, her face drained of color. She fell to the ground beside Oliver, and rather than scramble away, the old woman nudged closer. She reached for Stella's limp arm, took her hand in hers, and pressed Stella's fingers to her good cheek. "For you, Stella! For you!"

Oliver let out the most horrible cackle of a laugh as the skin beneath Stella's fingers grew black and gray, smoldering in the hottest of white. That laugh turned to a scream. The scream turned to a shriek as the blackness spread all over her, eating around her dead flesh, finding every ounce of life until none remained. Burned, but not burned.

I watched Latrese Oliver die, her body dropping to the ground beside Stella. Stella nearly fell on top of her, hyperventilating, each gasp of air harsher than the last. She put a palm to the concrete to steady herself, and the concrete dried and crumbled under her fingertips.

"That is fantastic!" David shouted out, his burn scar stretched taut with his growing smile. "Who wants to go next? Do we have another volunteer?"

Stella twisted her head, her bloodshot eyes finding mine. "Not...enough..."

Unlike before, when the concrete simply aged, this time the cement crumbled beneath her. The cement chipped and cracked and turned to dust under her fingers, her palm. The whitish gray color gave way to powder.

Stella said. "I can't...stop it..."

We all saw it, the growing circle beneath her.

Preacher tried to stand, could not.

Cammie and my father couldn't move either.

David took a step back, eyeing the concrete curiously.

"We can't move," my father said. "David told us we can't move."

"Let them go, David. We need to run," I said, watching the circle grow larger.

"Nobody's running," David replied. He looked at them and pointed. "None of you. You might as well be made of stone."

David took another step back.

Stella gulped down air. Her eyes pinched shut. She shook her head in defiance, but it did little good. Whatever was happening, it was increasing in intensity rather than slowing down. Growing stronger. "Can't...stop..."

The circle expanded, weeds and grass shriveling away, concrete aging a hundred years in only moments, dying.

When the circle grew wide enough to reach one of the people in white, a man of about thirty years, this circle of death spread beneath his feet like the expanding waters of a puddle. His eyes went wide, his mouth fell open, and he screamed. From the folds of his coat, his fingertips turned black, his forearms, then his neck. He fell to the ground before the charring black reached his face. David's instructions prevented him from running. The death devoured him, then, without hesitation, continued to expand out from Stella's crouched body, widening, spreading. Faster, hungrier, with each taste of life.

The growing death reached me next, and although David hadn't told me I couldn't move, fright held me still, and I waited for the pain to come. I watched the concrete under my feet crack and decay. then the circle expanded beyond me, continued.

"Jack!" my father shouted. "Take my hand!"

At first, I didn't understand.

"The tests! Your gift—like a...bubble." That last word barely fell from his lips, David's control stronger than my father's will to speak.

I tore off my latex gloves, threw them aside, and grabbed his hand as the death reached him, squeezed his fingers between mine. The edge of the circle crawled under him, kept going.

He managed to reach over and take Cammie's hand, and she took Dunk's. Dunk reached for Preacher, and Preacher grabbed Darby as the circle continued to grow all around us.

David turned and looked out toward the open field and railroad tracks. He considered trying to outrun it. We all knew the truth, though. As this hungry, dark shadow grew larger, it became faster, hungrier. There was no outrunning such a thing. He nearly turned and tried, when a tiny little hand reached out to him.

David grabbed at Darby's outstretched arm and fingers and took hold with both hands as the death moved under him, moved past, growing so fast you could hear it eating away at all within its path. First just a crackle, then a rumble, then the thunderous anger of a tornado unleashed to feed.

People in white fell all around us, dropping to the ground with shouts and screams, their bodies turning to black faster than they could fall, dead before they hit the ground—five, ten, dozens.

Through it all, Stella remained at the center. Her fingers pulsing against the ground, her arms twitching under her, her body shaking uncontrollably.

The circle grew beyond the ruined concrete, burning through the surrounding grass and weeds like a flameless wildfire, leaving nothing but scorched earth in its wake. It reached the trees and the first fell, then another, another after that. Tall timbers dropping like bowling pins.

I thought it would go on forever, devouring all, a blanket of lifelessness pulled tight and cinched shut at the edges, and it felt like that, too. If someone had asked me, I would have said this went on for an hour, more than an hour, but in truth, it was all over in under a minute.

Stella fell.

She dropped to the ground in utter exhaustion.

The trees had been enough. Finally enough.

The world went silent, save for a train whistle somewhere in the distance.

The ground all around us was black. A giant, concentric circle of nothingness with Stella's tired, defeated body lying in a heap at the center.

The people in white were gone.

All dead.

Unlike the bodies found in the past, burned but not burned, of these, there was nothing left. The energy that had burst from Stella, her hunger, her curse, drained away the life all around her absolute. There was a blackened dust, nothing more.

A raindrop struck my head, followed by another as the heavens opened and began cleansing Mother Earth before the stain of what happened here had a chance to set.

To my right, my father still grasped my hand, his eyes unimaginably wide as he looked out at the void left behind, as he looked from there, to Stella, to the ground beneath him and finally up at me.

Cammie, Preacher, and David looked out over the ravaged grounds of Carrie Furnace with equal awe, their heads swiveling.

Preacher was first to break from the reverie. He released Cammie and Darby's hands and stood. He straightened his body and turned toward David, ready to attack.

David took a step back and opened his mouth, and not a sound came out. This seemed to surprise him. His eyes narrowed in confusion. His free hand went to his throat, his other still clasped in Darby's tiny grip.

David's mouth mimed a shout, a scream, yet nothing came out but the release of a used breath.

Darby looked up at him, squeezed his hand in hers, and smiled.

I think David realized what happened the same moment I did. He looked down at his hand in Darby's—the girl who could not speak—her gift finally understood, her gift graciously shared with him.

He broke from her hand and backed away in complete silence as Cammie and my father stood, his spell on them broken. He tried to tell them to get back down, silently mouthing the words, but this did nothing.

David Pickford ran.

We watched him run toward the gully and disappear into the trees on the opposite side. All of us too exhausted to give chase.

The train whistle broke through the silence, much closer now.

I turned back to Stella in time to see her get to her feet. She too began to back away, she too mouthed silent words as tears streamed down her face, "I'm sorry, Jack. I'm so sorry. I love you, I always have, please know that."

How she found the energy.

Where she found the energy, I may never know.

Stella ran toward the train tracks.

I ran after her, the muscles in my legs screaming as I pushed them harder than any other moment in my life. I closed the gap, but Stella still reached the train tracks before me. As I neared, she bent forward with both hands on her knees, openly crying, violent sobs shaking every bit of her.

If those first raindrops had only been exploratory, the ones to follow next came with purpose—thick, cold, heavy, drenching drops.

The train whistle blew again. The freight liner was barreling down on us, a single bright headlight slicing the night.

Stella stood in the center of the tracks, her wet hair covering half her face as she turned to me. "It was him, Jack! Oh God, please believe me. It was David, things he told me so long ago. I couldn't stop myself. I so desperately wanted to, but I couldn't, and I was so far gone—like the lake, but much worse than the lake—once it started, I couldn't pull it back. I tried, Jack. Please believe me. You of all people need to know I tried." She looked out over the grounds of Carrie Furnace, at the blackened fields and spent concrete, at the building beyond, knowing nothing escaped her hunger, all life depleted. "Oh God, I killed them all, didn't I? Every one of them!" She bent over again.

I stepped over the railroad tie and went to her. I placed my palm on her back. I told her my father, Preacher, Cammie, and Darby were still alive. I told her David ran.

"He can't hurt you, me, or anyone else anymore. It's all over."

She didn't hear this, the guilt overwhelming.

"I didn't mean to, Jack. I didn't. I told you I'd never do it again and didn't want to, but David—" she broke off as the train whistle cut through the night again. Close now.

Stella stood up, looked toward the train, then turned to me. "I need to die, Jack. *Then* it will all be over. I'm worse than David, I'm a monster. I bring nothing but death, to every single thing I touch. I can't live with that, not anymore. I can't do it again, not in another year, not ever. I was prepared to die, I need to die. Tonight. Now."

The train whistle again. The conductor no doubt able to see us now, directly in his path.

Loud, the whistle.

"I love you, Jack, I will always love you. Please forgive me. Please remember me. Please—"

Both my gloves were gone, lost on the ground somewhere back near my father and the others.

I pulled Stella close.

I placed both bare hands on either side of her face.

I kissed her.

And Stella Nettleton kissed me back.

PART 6

"You have been in every line I have ever read."
—Charles Dickens, *Great Expectations*

August 8, 2010

Thirty-Four Years Old

1

"Read."

"Oh, come on."

"Read."

"You make me read it every year."

I tapped a finger against the dark granite and cleared my throat.

He rolled his eyes. "Josephine "Jo" Gargery. March 12, 1956 to April 28, 1993. Sister, Aunt, Friend."

He frowned, as he did every other year, and looked over at me. "Didn't you say her middle name was Laura?"

"It was."

"Then why does it say Jo?"

"That's what everyone called her."

"Huh. That's a boy's name."

I smiled at this. He said the same thing last year, too. "She was a tough woman."

"And she raised you?"

"By hand, yeah. All by herself."

"After your mommy and daddy died?"

I nodded.

He sat Indian style on the soft grass, and he shifted his weight to the gravestone on Jo's left. "That's your momma?"

A little moss had taken hold in the lettering. We missed it when we first got here. I scraped it away with my fingernail. "Kaitlyn Gargery Thatch. February 16, 1958 to August 8, 1980. Loving wife, mother, and sister," I said softly.

"And that's your daddy?"

His stone was clean, a fresh yellow rose in the vase. I nodded. "That's your grandfather."

He read that one aloud without any prompting from me. He was a good boy. When he finished, he looked to the stone on my father's left. "Who's Abel Mag...es...witch?"

"Abel Magwitch," I corrected.

"Abel Magwitch. Who is he?"

"That's my father, too."

"You had two daddies?"

I thought about this for a moment. I tried to explain it last year and completely flubbed it up. He had asked questions for nearly a week, before the subject finally faded away. He was six then, seven now. A world away. This time, I went with the line I carefully crafted on the drive this morning. "I only had one daddy, but he lived two lives."

"So he gets two graves?"

"Yeah. One for each."

This seemed to please him. "Wow, so cats must take up a lot of room in pet cemeteries."

"They most certainly do."

There would always be next year.

My father, Edward Thatch, died for the second time on July 20, 2006—four years ago—eight years after the events at Carrie Furnace. He was only forty-eight. The end came swift, as it usually does, but his death had been drawn out for nearly those full eight years.

At first, he became forgetful.

I deeply regret that first year, because we did nothing but argue. I'd ask him about the car accident that took my mother's life and the events to immediately follow, and he'd provide nothing but cryptic responses, these short answers that only led to more questions. Then I noticed even those answers were fluid. He initially told me he hid in California for nearly a year after fleeing Pennsylvania, but then when asked again, he said he hid in Georgia. I'd ask him about the tests Charter ran on me when I was young and he said he couldn't recall anything beyond what I already knew. A year later, he barely remembered even those events. I found myself reminding him, prompting him to remember.

The doctors called it early-onset Alzheimer's.

I thought he was faking, and that only led to more fights and confrontations. It wasn't until I caught him standing in front of the mirror one morning, attempting to put on a tie. I watched him for nearly five minutes—he'd wrap it around his neck, make it about halfway through the process, then untwist and start all over again. When he spotted me at the door, he asked me to find my mother. He said she usually tied it for him. This was in May of 2000. He was only forty-two. The doctors ran a series of tests and found severe genetic mutations in three genes—APP, PSEN 1, and PSEN 2. Typically, a mutation in only one could lead to early-onset Alzheimer's. Mutations in three were rare. My father and I had a pretty good handle on the root of those mutations, but we didn't tell the doctor about Charter or the shot. Instead, we took his pamphlets and list of recommended reading, and I drove him home. He moved into my old apartment in Brentwood. I was just glad to see someone living in that place.

He took to calling me Pip. At first, I thought it was because he heard Stella use the name, but then I remembered the envelopes, my monthly cash deliveries, *Pip* written neatly on each. I thought about the copy of *Great Expectations* he left for me in his grave. I realized the envelopes had been yet another clue, one meant to draw my focus to that book when I eventually found it. He saw himself as my Abel Magwitch, Pip's benefactor in the novel. I asked him about this once, but he only smiled.

Less than two months after his diagnosis, my father stopped speaking. One week after that, he stopped getting out of bed on his own. I had no choice but to place him in a facility capable of monitoring his condition and taking care of him on a day-to-day basis. He spent his remaining six years in Cloverdale Assisted Living in Monroeville, Pennsylvania. I visited often, and I always found him in the same place, in his wheelchair at a large window overlooking the west lawn and a small duck pond.

Prior to his death, the nurses said he never spoke while awake, but he often mumbled in his sleep. He said the name, David Pickford, often, but they could make out nothing else. When they asked if that name meant something to me, I told them no.

My father died for the second time at his favorite window. For that, I was grateful. I wanted him to find peace with what he had done. I wanted to forgive him, and I told him that I did. I found it far easier to convince him of this than it was to convince myself.

Prior to the disease taking complete hold, my father signed power of attorney over his estate to me, and with Matteo's help, I was able to complete a financial picture. Without going into detail here, this being a painful subject for me, we found Charter sent my father ten thousand dollars per month beginning one month after my mother died and continuing until the middle of 1996, about two years after Pickford "cleaned up" Charter. He had left many of the employees with instructions akin to autopilot, and someone in accounting saw fit to continue payments to my father.

Part of me wanted to hate my father, and I suppose few would blame me if I did, but in my thirty plus years on the planet, I learned life is far too short and fragile to harbor hate in your heart. It eats at your soul, burns but doesn't burn. I told myself he did what he felt was right at the time. Fault should not be found in a man protecting his family with the tools provided, only in those who did not try. My father tried. He risked retaliation from Charter every month he sent me money as a kid by way of Preacher.

My father invested his assets wisely, and on the day he died, his estate was worth nearly six million dollars. I donated all of it to Alzheimer's research. I had no need for his money.

If my father's death was due to the shot, we never found proof. To this day, Cammie and Preacher show no signs of illness. Stella and I watch closely whenever we're together. I'm sure Darby does, too.

In the fall of 1999, about a year after the events at Carrie Furnace, I returned to college. I didn't go back to Penn State. The memories were far too strong. Instead, I went to Carnegie Mellon and earned a degree in art. I learned to enjoy painting, drawing, and sketching again. I've had several small showings over the years, mostly friends and family, but nice, nonetheless. If you happen to find yourself in a doctor's office or bank in the Pittsburgh area, take a look at the paintings on the wall—you may find one with J. Thatch scrawled in the bottom right. A couple others with Pip.

The day I received my diploma from Carnegie Mellon, Dewitt Matteo and Tess were in the audience. I'd be lying if I said Matteo wasn't ecstatic. He said, although Auntie Jo's instructions explicitly said I needed to attend Penn State, they did not say I needed to earn out my degree there. He felt this was enough of a loophole to unfreeze the hold on my trust and grant access to the funds she left for me. As executor of the trust, he did, and with nobody to contest, I became a wealthy man that year.

Part of the funds were used to buy a small farm up near Moraine State Park. We live there to this day.

"Can we go soon? I'm hungry."

"Soon, Dalton. One more quick stop, okay?"

"Oh, all right."

I picked the name Dalton because I knew how much it would irk his Uncle Preacher. To this day, he despised his real name.

I hadn't seen him in nearly a year. After the furnace in '98, he stuck around for a few days. Then one morning, the Pontiac GTO was no longer outside and he was gone. No note, no forwarding address. He insisted he was a nomad and sitting still was not an option. He went back to that thing he did. If you had asked my kid-self if I would ever consider calling a hitman my friend, I probably would have said 'absolutely,' because what young boy doesn't want a hitman as a friend? Preacher was and always will be considered a guardian angel in my mind. His wings might be dirty, but there was a good man in there. Every time I spotted a white SUV in my rearview, I took solace in the fact that there was also a black GTO out there somewhere, a balance in the universe.

"You fold the blanket, I'll put away lunch and the radio."

Dalton frowned up at me. "I don't know why you bring that thing. It never works out here. Next year we should bring an iPod."

I smiled but said nothing to this. I liked that old transistor radio.

Our things gathered, I reached out and took my son's tiny little hand in mine. We walked to the east, past several mature oaks and a small reflecting pool, to a single grave under the shade of a willow. I pulled a rag from our picnic basket and wiped off the white marble. Then I replaced the flowers in the vase with the last rose we brought along, this one yellow.

"Who is Gerdy McCowen?" Dalton asked.

"Someone special."

"Geez, you know lots of dead people."

I couldn't help but chuckle at this. "Yeah, I suppose I do. Can you give me a second?"

"Will I get in trouble if I skip rocks on that pond?"

"I think you'll be okay."

When he was gone but still within eyeshot, I knelt down at Gerdy's grave and closed my eyes.

"I like to think you're with me every day. Whenever I feel the warmth of the sun, or hear someone laugh, I think of you. You were always the bright spot in one of the darkest chapters of my life, and I don't think I would have made it out the other side if I hadn't known you. I'm sorry I didn't come to see you those first few years. I've got my head on straight now. I know what's im-portant. And you, Gerdy McCowen, will always be one of those important sparks in my life." I paused for a second and looked back over one of the hills to my right. "I stopped by and said hi to Krendal and Lurline, too. I always pictured him running the cafeteria up there in heaven, with lines running out the door and around the next cloud."

The hair on the back of my neck stood up.

My eyes snapped open, and I spun around perhaps a little faster than I probably should have.

I found Detective Joy Fogel standing about half a dozen paces behind me.

"I'm sorry I startled you, Jack. I didn't want to interrupt."

"Still following me after twelve years, Detective? Maybe it's time to give up the ghost." I smiled. I knew she wasn't following me, but it was always fun to take a jab at her.

"Just visiting a friend, saw you, and thought I'd say hello," she said.

"Stack?"

She nodded.

Dalton was standing at the edge of the pond, his hand set to launch another rock across the surface. He eyed the detective suspiciously.

"It's okay, Dalton. She's a friend."

"She looks like a cop."

"Yeah, I suppose she does."

He returned to the water.

I stood, brushed off the knees of my jeans, and went over to her.

She told me about Detective Terrance Stack years back, after the dust began to settle but hadn't quite left the air yet. David and some of the people in white had left him tied up in one of his bedrooms. If not for his mailman, he might have died up there. The mailman knew Stack rarely left home, and when letters piled up for three days, he tried the front door, found it open, and took it upon himself to make sure everything was okay.

Everything was not okay.

Stack, still tied to a chair, was severely dehydrated, delusional, ranting about his dead partner Faustino Brier. He spent nearly a week in the hospital recuperating before being permitted back home again. He passed away six months after that. Fogel found him in his favorite chair, a beer in one hand and a cannon of a gun in the other, staring out his front window. Cause of death was ruled a stroke. The way Fogel told it, the man was waiting for death to come knocking at his door. Bored with retirement, more so after Charter fell.

The day Fogel located David's old cell at the heart of Charter, she called in backup. She brought in the feds. They tore the place apart. Not before she was able to watch the first video tape, though. The one that showed David stepping out of his cell, entering that control room, and saying something like, "Which button activates the building's intercom?" A man with only one remaining eye showed him, then: "Hello, everyone, my name is David Pickford. As of this moment, I'm in charge of all Charter activities. Please listen closely..." The same tape contained the deaths of the two men in the control room shortly after.

Fogel regretted calling in the feds. They hauled off nearly three tractor trailers filled with documentation, audio/visual evidence, and equipment, enough to build a thousand cases against the people in charge. Although those tractor trailers left Charter property for the Philly field office, they never arrived. When Fogel tried to obtain information on the case, she discovered there was no case. When she took it upon herself to visit the Charter building again, less than one week later, she found it completely deserted, scrubbed, and staged. Signage had been replaced with Marshal Field and Grain. The few scraps of paper littering the now blood-less hallways bore the same name. The entire complex looked like a farming supply company that had gone out of business several years earlier, a building yet to be repurposed.

If I hadn't given her all the documentation my father stole from Charter, there might not have been any remaining proof of what they did. Once Stack recuperated, the two of them worked to piece together a complete narrative, and by the time they finished, they knew all about the shot, the adults who received it, the children they had, and how Charter either exploited or killed all those involved.

Fogel took down the Wall of Weird shortly after that. Publicly, she ceased all efforts to follow up on those cases, and the information was quickly forgotten as her coworkers attempted to keep up with their ever-expanding workload. When August 8 rolled around the following year, only a handful asked about it. By the following year, no one brought it up.

She never told me where she hid all the data. She only said it was someplace safe. Someplace she could get to it, if the need ever arose.

"He's getting so big!" Fogel beamed, watching Dalton.

"Yeah, they do that," I said. "How have you been?"

"Good." She reached into her pocket and took out her badge. "I made lieutenant."

"Congratulations. I'm happy for you." The words didn't come out with the cheer I had intended. I tried to make up for it with a wider smile. I probably just looked like a complete goof.

There was a silver flask in her hand. She caught me staring at it.

Fogel's face flushed. "It's whiskey. I pour it on his grave. A little old school, I know, but he was old school back when old schools had dirt floors." She hesitated for a second, then held it out to me. "Want a taste?"

I shook my head. "I haven't touched the stuff in twelve years."

This seemed to surprise her. "Really? That's fantastic. Good for you."

Fogel stuffed the flask into her pocket and nodded her head back toward the main entrance. "I need to get going. It was nice seeing you again. We should try to get together at some point. Maybe grab dinner or something."

"I'd like that." We never would, though. I knew that.

I watched her walk away, disappear over the hill. Then I turned to Dalton. "Let's go, buddy."

He skipped one final rock, then took my hand.

We made our way up the hill at the back of the cemetery, past the mausoleums. When the bench came into view, my eyes fell on a little girl sitting there with long chestnut hair and the most beautiful dark eyes, a book in her lap. When she saw me, her eyes lit up. "Daddy!"

She jumped up and ran to me, wrapping both arms around my legs.

From the opposite side of the bench, her mother looked up at me, too.

She smiled.

Somehow, Stella became more beautiful with each passing day, and my heart never tired of quivering at the sight of her.

She too was reading a book. She turned it over and showed me the cover. "This is utterly fantastic!"

The title was *Glimmer in the Devil's Eye*. The author was Darby Brotherton.

Darby never learned to speak, but she found her voice. At twenty years old, this was her second bestseller. Cammie had called us last week to tell us the news.

Stella walked over, her white sundress fluttering in the late summer breeze. The weather today couldn't be more perfect.

She ruffled Dalton's hair and kissed me, her lips electric against mine. "Did you boys have fun?"

"It was nice to see everyone. You?"

She knelt and stroked our daughter's cheek. "Clara here read *Charlotte's Web* for the umpteenth time, then set about to find a word in every spider web in those mausoleums over there."

I smiled down at Clara. "And what did you find?"

"Pittsburgh spiders are dumb. They can't spell."

Neither of our children had demonstrated an ability, a gift, a curse, or anything out of the ordinary for a six-year-old girl or a seven-year-old boy, but I'd be lying if I said we didn't watch for one every day. I think we both knew it was coming, probably sometime soon, and we'd be ready for it, whatever *it* was.

I took Stella's hand and wrapped my fingers around hers. She didn't wear gloves around us. There was no need.

That night.

The kiss.

The approaching train.

When our lips touched, I thought I would die. I expected to meet the same fate as Leo Signorelli and all the others who met Stella's touch, her kiss. I figured I wouldn't even feel the train when the impact finally came, I'd be gone that fast. I didn't die, though. I felt no pain at all.

My gift, my curse, my condition, whatever the shot did to me... Dunk called me the boy who could not die. Whether just from luck or some odd manipulation of my DNA as a result of my parents receiving the shot, there was some truth to that. Through the course of my life, I should have died many times over, Charter's attempts alone should have been enough, yet I hadn't. I figured one day I probably would. Nobody lives forever, but I had no idea how my particular condition impacted those final laws of nature, the ones enforced on all living things.

Stella and I learned there was an odd byproduct to my particular gift, too. Her need, her hunger—she found the sustenance she required in my touch. The boy who could not die, *could* share. When August 8 of 1999 came around, she demonstrated no signs of her previous illness. The date came and went like any other, and each year passed much the same.

If she and I were a battery, one would be positive, the other negative, and combined we canceled out. We completed each other.

When I told Fogel I hadn't had a drink in twelve years, that was true, too. I never craved alcohol when Stella was near. Since she and I were completely inseparable, that particular need never reappeared.

We married on August 8, 2000. The date held so much meaning for the two of us. There was never a consideration of another date, it had to be August 8. The day became one of celebration.

"What are you thinking about?" Stella asked, shielding her eyes from the unusually bright Pittsburgh sun.

"You," I told her. "How much I love you."

Stella smiled and kissed me again. "And I love you, too, Pip."

"Yucky," Dalton said, frowning.

Clara giggled.

"Aren't you going to be late?" Stella said.

I looked down at my watch. Nearly five o'clock. "Crap." I started back down the hill. "Meet at Mineo's at seven?" I yelled back at them as I broke into a run.

"Say hello for us!" Stella shouted.

2

State Correctional Institution, known as Western Pen to the locals, is a medium security correctional facility operated by the Pennsylvania Department of Corrections. Sitting on a little over twenty-one acres on the banks of the Ohio River, the prison was about five miles out of town. I got there in a record nineteen minutes.

I never did recover my old Jeep from the hospital parking lot in Minden, but I bought a shiny new Wrangler last year. With the exception of my driver's license, I emptied my pockets in the car and left everything on the passenger seat. Experience taught me the security lines moved much faster when you traveled light. I removed my belt, too.

I crossed the parking lot and managed to get in line about a minute before the guards closed up the doors behind me. That meant I'd have about twenty minutes inside before visiting hours officially ended.

On the other side of security, I followed the green line on the floor to the visitation room—more of a hallway, really. Pay phones lined the wall on the left while small cubicles lined the right. I took an empty seat in the second to last space and waited.

Dunk hobbled in about a minute later on a plastic cane. It bent slightly under his weight. Because metal or wood could be fashioned into a weapon, only plastic canes were permitted. Dunk managed to break at least one each week, but the department of corrections seemed to have an endless supply. This particular cane was pink.

I picked up the telephone receiver and pressed it to my ear, trying not to think about all the nastiness that probably came in contact with the plastic prior to me today.

Dunk dropped into the seat on his side of the thick glass and picked up the telephone receiver. "Tell me again, why did I turn myself in?"

"Because you're a good guy at heart, and one day you'll get out of here, completely rehabilitated, and you'll open a taco stand down by the river and make something of yourself."

"I'm not sure tacos have enough of a profit margin."

With Dewitt Matteo at his side, Dunk turned himself in August 13, 1998, about one hour after the horrible events of that night came to an end. I actually tried to talk him out of it. Not because I didn't think it was the right thing to do. I simply didn't feel he was in the right state of mind to make such a decision. We didn't find a single live person inside Carrie Furnace. Nearly his entire crew perished with David's final command. If anyone survived, Stella's implosion finished them off. Dunk was completely in shock. He was alone. He told me he had already been working with the feds to take down Rufus Stano. I had no idea. Stano was one of the few people Dunk answered to and considered a much bigger fish than even Duncan Bellino in the eyes of the authorities. Because of his cooperation, he received a shorter sentence. He had three years remaining but would be eligible for parole in another month.

"Stella and the kids say hello."

"Hello back."

A nasty bruise peppered the left side of Dunk's jaw. When I asked him about it, he shrugged. "I wanted to watch *The Big Bang Theory* last night. I was in the minority. Happens."

"One month to parole, buddy. Best to keep your head down."

A guard leaned in from the hallway. "Five minutes!"

"Shit! Sorry, man, I got here late."

Dunk shrugged, "One month to parole." He moved the receiver to his other ear. "That reminds me, I had a weird visitor last week."

"Who?"

"Willy Trudeau."

"Willy?"

Dunk nodded. "He said he has a job for me when I get out."

"A job doing what?"

"Didn't say."

"Careful with that guy. I never trusted him."

"Yes, Mom."

There was something I wanted to ask Dunk about, a subject I avoided for over a decade. Stella brought it up again last night, said we needed to know the answer if Dunk was going to be around our children. "Can I ask you something?"

"I don't need a prom date, and you've already got a lovely lady at home."

"I'm serious."

"I am, too."

"Pickford, he said your mother was Penelope Maudlin. One of the people who got the shot along with our parents. You've never talked about her."

"Nothing to talk about."

"Do you remember her?"

Dunk pursed his lips and looked down at the counter. "Nope."

"Not at all?"

He shook his head. "It was always just me and Pops. Until you showed me that old yearbook, I had never even seen a photo of her. Pops didn't keep none of that stuff. I figured it hurt him to talk about it, so we never did."

"One minute!" the guard shouted.

I leaned in closer toward the glass and lowered my voice. "She got the shot, but your father didn't."

Dunk leaned back in his chair, a big grin filling his lips. "And you're wondering if I can do something? Like you, Stella, Darby, or that Pickford guy?"

"I'm only asking, because if it's something dangerous and you're going to be around the kids, we'd like to know." That came out wrong, and I tried to backtrack. "We're not worried you would ever do anything to hurt them. We know you wouldn't. It's just, if you can do something, we'd like to know what it is."

"Jack Thatch, the boy who couldn't die, and his faithful sidekick, Dunk." He grinned. "There's a comic book in there for sure."

"Can you do something?"

"Time's up!" the guard shouted. "Disconnect all calls and exit here to the left. Have a pleasant evening."

"Dunk?" I said into the receiver.

Dunk smiled and hung up the phone on his side.

He got to his feet, his bulky body balanced on that silly pink cane.

I tilted my head and frowned. Then I hung up the phone.

Dunk's eyes grew wide, and he grinned. He held up his index finger.

I watched as he touched the receiver on his side of the cubicle, just a tap.

All the pay phones behind me began to ring at the same time.

I turned to look at them.

One of the guards picked one up, said hello, shrugged, and hung up again. The phone continued to ring.

When I turned back to Dunk, I caught a flash of his orange jumpsuit as he left the room and disappeared down the hallway toward his cell, the heavy metal door swinging shut behind him.

August 8, 2020

Forty-Four Years Old

1

The little boy peered over the back of the booth in his parents' favorite restaurant, in his parents' favorite California seaside town. He twisted and squirmed, until his mother finally gave up and let him stand on the bench seat and look out over the back into the next booth, at the man sitting in that booth.

"What happened to your face?" the boy asked.

Not polite at all. Not the kind of thing you ask a complete stranger. Particularly when you have the remnants of macaroni and cheese all over your own face.

The man looked up from the menu. He had decided on the catch-of-the-day, and smiled. The shear act of such a thing seemed painful, tugging at his ruined skin in such a way that must have hurt. If it did, though, he didn't acknowledge it.

The man pointed at the ruined side of his face and shrugged. Then, with a series of complex hand gestures, he answered the boy in what was known as ASL, or American Sign Language.

The boy bit at his lower lip and frowned.

He didn't understand.

The uneducated youth.

Today's children knew only video games, social networks, and streaming media. Gone were the days someone opened a book and took the time to learn something new, to better themselves, to achieve a greater intellect through enlightenment. Perhaps if education awarded points, the younger generation would consider dusting off a book. If they could easily level up with a cheat code stolen off the Internet, they may take interest.

The man held up a finger. He dug his smartphone from the pocket of his windbreaker, draped over the empty seat beside him.

He opened an app, typed a message, and held the device near the boy's little macaroni-and-cheese covered head as he hit the PLAY button.

A human-sounding voice read the text aloud with near-perfect intonation and pitch, nearly indiscernible from a real voice. "I am a beautiful man."

The boy thought about this for a second, then nodded.

Log 08/08/2020—

Subjects "D" and "C" —

Audio/video recording.

REBOOT INITIATED

—Charter Observation Team - 412

From the Author

This was a book I *needed* to write. After completing the 4MK series, such a dark series, something light was required to scrub out some of the hard to reach places of my brain. I had fun writing 4MK, but there were many moments when I pushed my MacBook across the desk, sat back, and said, "Holy fuck, did that really just come out of my head?"

I'm not one to usually talk about process, but I'm among friends here, right? In the writing world, I'm known as a pantser. I don't outline. In *On Writing*, Stephen King pointed out that if he doesn't know where the story is going, there's no way a reader will figure it out, and I firmly agree with that thought. There is nothing wrong with outlines. Some of the most successful authors in the world use detailed outlines. More power to them. I doubt I ever will. This book started with nothing more than a title and that opening paragraph from Jack at age 22—our first glimpse at Stella and what was to come. From there, I simply held on and tried to keep up as Jack told me about his incredible life and those in it.

Jack told a big story.

Have you ever noticed, some books are just big?

Not necessarily in length (although this is my longest novel to date) but in scope. A story can feel big. My previous books have all taken place over a short period of time, days, hours…I have a yet-to-be-seen-publicly novella that takes place over the course of a single minute. In order to properly tell Jack and Stella's story, I knew I would find myself spanning decades. I found this not only challenging, but delightfully fun. It gave me the opportunity to explore character growth far beyond anything I've done before, it allowed me to get close to each and every person in this book, watch them grow, and, in some cases, hold their hand in death.

I won't lie, I cried for Jo. I cried for Gerdy.

I think some of those tears hit the page and left a mark.

I longed for one more burger at Krendal's, and some of that comes back every time I drive down Brownsville Road in Brentwood, PA, and pass the place where that diner stood in Jack's world.

That reminds me—

If you live in the Pittsburgh area, you may find I took liberties with the geographic locations of various streets, buildings, and businesses. Rest assured, this isn't because I can't read a map (although Pittsburgh streets can be challenging), this is because my family and I have lived in Brentwood, Carnegie, and Pittsburgh proper, and I simply wanted to give a little shout-out to all those wonderful places in this book. That can't happen without making a change here or there, nothing too crazy, but enough to cause your GPS to run hot. While some of the locations exist only in the author's mind, others are real and can be visited, the Carrie Blast Furnaces being one of my personal favorites.

Nobody in Pittsburgh makes a pizza better than Mineo's.

Nobody.

Keener's Hardware is *the* place to go when you need a shovel, pickax, and a heavy-duty flashlight to complete your late-night dig kit. If you're lucky, Harold Keener may be at the counter. If not, his son will surely be there.

Clearly, *Great Expectations* by Dickens was an enormous inspiration when writing this book. I first read the novel at nine years old. Like most of my books back then, I picked it up at a garage sale for a heavily negotiated price of twenty-five cents. It was a hardcover, horribly worn, with a detailed map of the UK on the inside flap. Oh boy, did I have a crush on Estella. Ms. Havisham did a number on me, right along with little Pip. I suppose, because I read it at such an impressionable age, the story stuck with me over the years. I often find myself reaching for a classic novel after finishing up a few modern-day tales. They're like comfort food to me, with *Great Expectations* being one I've revisited more than most. If you haven't read the novel, I strongly suggest you pick up a copy and give it a shot. You'll find a story unmatched by most.

I like to think I left Jack, Stella, Dalton, and little Clara in a good place. Cammie, Preacher, and Darby, too. Even Dunk, hopefully walking the straight and narrow now. I often find it hard to say good-bye after spending time with the people I love. I grow curious, wondering where they went after we said our good-byes. Perhaps one day I'll ask them. Who knows? Maybe they'll be willing to share.

jd
Pittsburgh, PA

CPSIA information can be obtained
at www.ICGtesting.com
Printed in the USA
BVHW030041240320
575788BV00002B/4/J

9 781734 210415